The story is in the cards....

SEPULCHRE

"Undeniably gripping."
—*The London Paper*

"A sure, deft momentum...The secrets begin
to slip out thick and fast."
—*Daily Express* (UK)

"A historical thriller for the
Sex and the City generation."
—*Sunday Times* (UK)

"With her new esoteric historical thriller, Kate
Mosse has carved her own brilliant niche be-
tween Umberto Eco and Dan Brown."
—*Le Figaro Magazine* (Paris)

"Try this if you enjoyed *The Da Vinci Code* but
fancy something a bit more meaty."
—*News of the World* (UK)

"Imagine if Dan Brown could actually write decent prose. Imagine if he was able to generate fresh, lively, three-dimensional characters. Imagine if he was as good at capturing a place and a time as he is at producing pacy plots . . . Where Mosse really wins is in the writing department. She's the real role model there."   —*Daily Mirror*

"Mosse's latest novel about love and obsession smoothly alternates between historical viewpoints. . . . A charming tale. Mosse's careful descriptions of the French countryside, local cuisine, and her smatterings of French and Occitan phrases make this novel both an engaging travelogue and a romantic mystery."
                                          —*Library Journal*

"Mosse's gifts for historical fiction are considerable. . . . [She] does what good popular historical novelists do best—make the past enticingly otherworldly, while also claiming it as our own."   —*The Independent*

"Surprises in store."   —*Geelong Advertiser* (Australia)

"Will not disappoint readers . . . Mosse switches back and forth between the historical and the modern subplots with a deft grace."
                                      —*Fort Lauderdale Sun-Sentinel*

"If you enjoy attention to detail, French history, and an introduction to the tarot—set against a creepy background involving a demon (maybe), a serial killer (very likely), and a Visigoth tomb (very dank)—you'll enjoy many hours with Mosse's latest."   —*The Sacramento Bee*

"A page-turning saga of fin-de-siècle spiritualism and Visigothic treasure."
                                          —*Art & Book Review*

"Following on from the bestselling *Labyrinth*, here is another tale of spooky goings-on, ancient mysteries reaching into the present, and sinister conspiracies. It is a book to immerse oneself in . . . a good, entertaining read."
                                          —*MyShelf.com*

"Fans will enjoy this interesting horror thriller as the good vs. evil war occurs twice due to the linking tarot cards."   —*Genre Go Round Reviews*

"Mosse's page-turner takes readers on another quest for the Holy Grail. . . . [Her] fluidly written third novel may tantalize the legions of *Da Vinci Code* devotees with its promise of revelation about Christianity's truths."

—*Publishers Weekly*

"Magnificent . . . such a pleasurable read. Mosse infuses each scene with such depth of atmospheric detail that full immersion is inevitable. The author's vision is epic in scope. Mosse wields admirable control over the vast body of her material and maneuvers through it with subtlety and grace. [There is a] joyous, whooping pleasure evident in the work of Mosse . . . [whose] skills are generous and irresistible."

—*Mslexia* magazine

"A nice, long, escapist read."

—*The Hartford Courant*

"An ideal—if weighty—flight companion . . . The author has combined an ingenious adventure story with a wonderfully detailed account of the historical background of the Languedoc and, in particular, of the Cathar rebellion. The result is entirely compelling and full of incidental pleasures. One only hopes that it won't cause a stampede of 'Grail groupies' to the Midi-Pyrenees."

—*The Times* (London)

"Mosse's epic adventure weaves together the present and the past in an entertaining Grail-quest tale."

—*Booklist*

Also by Kate Mosse

NOVELS

Eskimo Kissing

Crucifix Lane

Labyrinth

NONFICTION

Becoming a Mother

*The House: Inside the Royal
Opera House, Covent Garden*

Sepulchre

Kate Mosse

BERKLEY BOOKS, NEW YORK

THE BERKLEY PUBLISHING GROUP
Published by the Penguin Group
Penguin Group (USA) Inc.
375 Hudson Street, New York, New York 10014, USA
Penguin Group (Canada), 90 Eglinton Avenue East, Suite 700, Toronto, Ontario M4P 2Y3, Canada
(a division of Pearson Penguin Canada Inc.)
Penguin Books Ltd., 80 Strand, London WC2R 0RL, England
Penguin Group Ireland, 25 St. Stephen's Green, Dublin 2, Ireland (a division of Penguin Books Ltd.)
Penguin Group (Australia), 250 Camberwell Road, Camberwell, Victoria 3124, Australia
(a division of Pearson Australia Group Pty. Ltd.)
Penguin Books India Pvt. Ltd., 11 Community Centre, Panchsheel Park, New Delhi—110 017, India
Penguin Group (NZ), 67 Apollo Drive, Rosedale, North Shore, 0632, New Zealand
(a division of Pearson New Zealand Ltd.)
Penguin Books (South Africa) (Pty.) Ltd., 24 Sturdee Avenue, Rosebank, Johannesburg 2196,
South Africa

Penguin Books Ltd., Registered Offices: 80 Strand, London WC2R 0RL, England

This is a work of fiction. Names, characters, places, and incidents either are the product of the author's
imagination or are used fictitiously, and any resemblance to actual persons, living or dead, business
establishments, events, or locales, is entirely coincidental. The publisher does not have any control over
and does not assume any responsibility for author or third-party websites or their content.

SEPULCHRE

PRINTING HISTORY
Orion Publishing Group / 2007
G. P. Putnam's Sons hardcover edition / April 2008
Berkley trade paperback edition / March 2009

Berkley trade paperback ISBN: 978-0-425-22584-4

PRINTED IN THE UNITED STATES OF AMERICA

10 9 8 7 6 5 4 3 2 1

To my dear mother, Barbara Mosse, for that first piano!

And, as ever, to my beloved Greg—for all things
present, past and yet to come

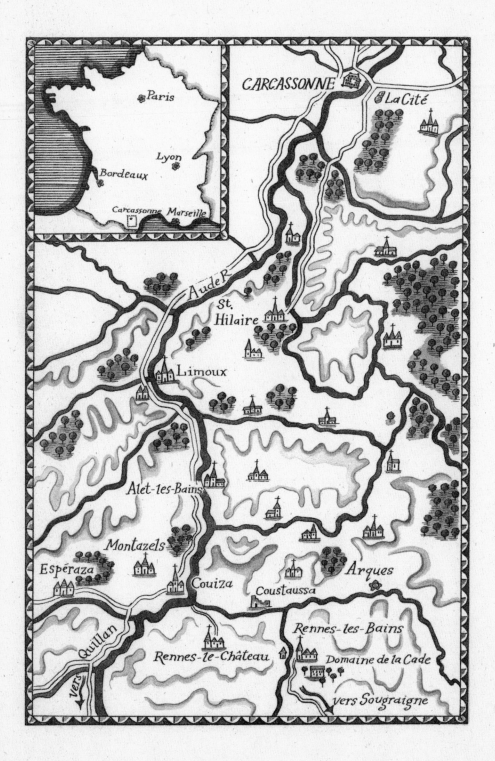

Contents

❦

Sépulture

Si par une nuit lourde et sombre
Un bon chrétien, par charité
Derrière quelque vieux décombre
Enterre votre corps vanté,

A l'heure ou les chastes étoiles
Ferment leurs yeux appesantis,
L'araignée y fera ses toiles,
Et la vipère ses petits;

Vous entendrez toute l'année
Sur votre tête condamnée
Les cris lamentables des loups

Et des sorcières faméliques,
Les ébats des vieillards lubriques
Et les complots des noirs filous.

If, one dark, oppressive night,
A Christian, moved by charity,
Should bury your lauded corpse
Behind some ancient ruin,

As the eyes of the chaste stars
Let fall their heavy lids,
The spider will spin its webs there
And the viper lay its eggs;

Season upon season
Your damned head will ring
With the baleful cries

Of wolves and raw-boned witches,
The groans of decrepit lotharios
And conspirators' dark designs.

Charles Baudelaire, 1857
Translation © Mosse Associates Ltd, 2007

L'âme d'autrui est une forêt obscure où il faut marcher avec précaution.
(The soul of another is a dark forest in which one must tread carefully.)

Letter, 1891
CLAUDE DEBUSSY

The true Tarot is symbolism; it speaks no other language and offers no other signs.

The Pictorial Key to the Tarot, 1910
ARTHUR EDWARD WAITE

Prelude

March 1891

Wednesday, March 25, 1891

This story begins in a city of bones. In the alleyways of the dead. In the silent boulevards and promenades and impasses of the cimetière de Montmartre in Paris, a place inhabited by tombs and stone angels and the loitering ghosts of those forgotten before they are even cold in their graves.

This story begins with the watchers at the gates, with the poor and the desperate of Paris, who have come to profit from another's loss. The gawping beggars and sharp-eyed *chiffonniers,* the wreath makers and peddlers of ex-voto trinkets, the girls twisting paper flowers, the carriages waiting with black hoods and smeared glass.

The story begins with the pantomime of a burial. A small paid notice in *Le Figaro* advertised the place and the date and the hour, although few have come. It is a sparse crowd, dark veils and morning coats, polished boots and extravagant umbrellas to shelter from the unseasonable March rain.

Léonie stands beside the open grave with her brother and their mother, her striking face obscured behind black lace. From the priest's lips fall platitudes, words of absolution that leave all hearts cold and all emotion untouched. Ugly in his unstarched white necktie and vulgar buckled shoes and greasy complexion, he knows nothing of the lies and threads of deceit that have led to this patch of ground in the eighteenth arrondissement, on the northern outskirts of Paris.

Léonie's eyes are dry. Like the priest, she is ignorant of the events being played out on this wet afternoon. She believes she has come to attend a funeral, the marking of a life cut short. She has come to pay her last respects to her brother's lover, a woman she never met in life. To support her brother in his grief.

Léonie's eyes are fixed upon the coffin being lowered into the damp earth where the worms and the spiders dwell. If she were to turn, quickly now, catching Anatole unawares, she would see the expression upon her beloved brother's face and puzzle at it. It is not loss that swims in his eyes, but rather relief.

And because she does not turn, she does not notice the man in gray top hat and frock coat, sheltering from the rain under the cypress trees in the farthest corner of the cemetery. He cuts a sharp figure, the sort of man to make *une belle parisienne* touch her hair and raise her eyes a little beneath her veils. His broad and strong hands, tailored in calfskin gloves, rest perfectly upon the silver head of his mahogany walking stick. They are such hands as might circle a waist, might draw a lover to him, might caress a pale cheek.

He is watching, an expression of great intensity on his face. His pupils are black pinpricks in bright blue eyes.

The heavy thud of earth on the coffin lid. The priest's dying words echo in the somber air.

"*In nomine Patri, et Filii, et Spiritus Sancti.* Amen. In the name of the Father, the Son, and the Holy Ghost."

He makes the sign of the cross, then walks away.

Amen. So be it.

Léonie lets fall her flower, picked freshly in the Parc Monceau this morning, a rose for remembrance. The bloom spirals down, down through the chill air, a flash of white slowly slipping from her black-gloved fingers.

Let the dead rest. Let the dead sleep.

The rain is falling more heavily. Beyond the high wrought-iron gates of the cemetery, the roofs, spires and domes of Paris are shrouded in a silver mist. It muffles the sounds of the rattling carriages in the Boulevard de Clichy and the distant shrieks of the trains pulling out from the Gare Saint-Lazare.

The mourning party turns to depart the graveside. Léonie touches her brother's arm. He pats her hand, lowers his head. As they walk out of the cemetery, more than anything Léonie hopes that this may be an end to it. That after the last dismal months of persecution and tragedy, they might put it all behind them.

That they might step out from the shadows and begin to live again.

. . .

BUT NOW, many hundreds of miles to the south of Paris, something is stirring.

A reaction, a connection, a consequence. In the ancient beech woods above the fashionable spa town of Rennes-les-Bains, a breath of wind lifts the leaves. Music heard but not heard.

Enfin.

The word is breathed on the wind. At last.

Compelled by the act of an innocent girl in a graveyard in Paris, something is moving within the stone sepulchre. Long forgotten in the tangled and overgrown alleyways of the Domaine de la Cade, something is waking. To the casual observer it would appear no more than a trick of the light in the fading afternoon, but for a fleeting instant, the plaster statues appear to breathe, to move, to sigh.

And the portraits on the cards that lie buried beneath the earth and stone, where the river runs dry, momentarily seem to be alive. Fleeting figures, impressions, shades, not yet more than that. A suggestion, an illusion, a promise. The refraction of light, the movement of air beneath the turn of the stone stair. The inescapable relationship between place and moment.

For in truth, this story begins not with bones in a Parisian graveyard but with a deck of cards.

The Devil's Picture Book.

Part I

Paris

September 1891

1

Wednesday, September 16, 1891

Léonie Vernier stood on the steps of the Palais Garnier, clutching her chatelaine bag and tapping her foot impatiently.

Where is he?

Dusk cloaked the Place de l'Opéra in a silky blue light.

Léonie frowned. It was quite maddening. For almost one hour she had waited for her brother at the agreed rendezvous, beneath the impassive bronze gaze of the statues that graced the roof of the opera house. She had endured impertinent looks. She had watched the fiacres come and go, private carriages with their hoods up, public conveyances open to the elements, four-wheelers, gigs, all disembarking their passengers. A sea of black silk top hats and fine evening gowns from the showrooms of Maison Léoty and Charles Worth. It was an elegant first-night audience, a sophisticated crowd come to see and be seen.

But no Anatole.

Once Léonie thought she spied him. A gentleman of her brother's bearing and proportions, tall and broad, and with the same measured step. From a distance, she even imagined his shining brown eyes and fine black moustache, and she raised her hand to wave. But then the man turned and she saw it was not him.

Léonie returned her gaze to the Avenue de l'Opéra. It stretched diagonally all the way down to the Palais du Louvre, a remnant of fragile monarchy, when a nervous French king sought a safe and direct route to his evening's entertainment. The lanterns twinkled in the dusk, and squares of warm light spilled out through the windows of the cafés and bars. The gas jets spat and spluttered.

Around her, the air was filled with the sounds of a city at dusk as day gave way to night. *Entre chien et loup.* The clink of harness and wheels on the busy streets. The song of distant birds in the trees in the Boulevard des Capucines. The raucous cries of hawkers and ostlers, the sweeter tones of the girls selling artificial flowers on the steps of the Opéra, the high-pitched shouts of the boys who, for a sou, would blacken and shine a gentleman's shoes.

Another omnibus passed between Léonie and the magnificent facade of the Palais Garnier on its way to the Boulevard Haussmann, the conductor whistling on the upper deck as he punched tickets. An old soldier with a *Tonquin* medal pinned to his breast stumbled back and forth, singing an intoxicated army song. Léonie even saw a clown with a whitened face under his black domino felt cap, in a costume covered with gold spangles.

How could he leave me waiting?

The bells began to ring out for evensong, the plangent tones echoing across the cobbles. From Saint-Gervais or another church nearby?

She gave a half-shrug. Her eyes flashed with frustration, then exhilaration.

Léonie could delay no longer. If she wished to hear Monsieur Wagner's *Lohengrin,* then she must take her courage in both hands and go in alone.

Could she?

Although without an escort, by good fortune she was in possession of her own ticket.

But dare she?

She considered. It was the Parisian premiere. Why should she be deprived of such an experience because of Anatole's poor timekeeping?

Inside the opera house, the glass chandeliers glittered magnificently. It was all light and elegance, an occasion not to be missed.

Léonie made her decision. She ran up the steps, through the glass doors, and joined the crowd.

THE WARNING BELL was ringing. Only two minutes until curtain up.

In a flash of petticoat and silk stockings, Léonie dashed across the marble expanse of the Grand Foyer, attracting approbation and admiration in equal measure. At the age of seventeen, Léonie was on the verge of becoming a great beauty, no longer a child yet retaining flashes of the girl she had been. She was fortunate to be possessed of the fashionable good features and nostalgic coloring held in high regard by Monsieur Moreau and his Pre-Raphaelite friends.

But her looks were misleading. Léonie was determined rather than obedient, bold rather than modest, a girl of contemporary passions, not a demure medieval damsel. Indeed, Anatole teased that while she appeared the very portrait of Rossetti's *La Damoiselle Élue,* she was in point of fact her mirror image. Her doppelgänger, her but not her. Of the four elements, Léonie was fire, not water, earth, not air.

Now her alabaster cheeks were flushed. Thick ringlets of copper hair had come loose from her combs and tumbled down over her bare shoulders. Her dazzling green eyes, framed by long auburn lashes, flashed with anger and boldness.

He gave his word that he would not be late.

Clutching her evening bag in one hand, as if it was a shield, the skirts of her green silk satin gown in the other, Léonie hurtled across the marble floors, paying no heed to the disapproving stares of matrons and widows. The faux pearls and silver beads on the fringe of her dress clipped against the marble treads of the steps as she rushed through the rose marble columns, the gilded statues and the friezes, and toward the sweeping Grand Escalier. Confined in her corset, her breath came ragged and her heart pumped like a metronome set too fast.

Still, Léonie did not check her pace. Ahead, she could see the flunkies moving to secure the doors into the Grande Salle. With a final spurt of energy, she propelled herself forward to the entrance.

"*Voilà,*" she said, thrusting her ticket at the usher. "*Mon frère va arriver. . . .*"

He stepped aside and permitted her to pass.

After the noisy and echoing marble caverns of the Grand Foyer, the auditorium was particularly quiet. Filled with hushed murmurings, words of salutation, inquiries after health and family, all half swallowed up by the thick carpets and row upon row of red velvet seats.

The familiar flights of woodwind and brass, scales and arpeggios and fragments of the opera, increasingly loud, issued up from the orchestra pit like trails of autumn smoke.

I did it.

Léonie composed herself and smoothed her gown. A new purchase, delivered from La Samaritaine this afternoon, it was still stiff from lack of wear. She pulled her long green gloves up above her elbows, so that no more than a sliver of bare skin could be seen, then walked down through the stalls toward the stage.

Their seats were in the front row, two of the best in the house, courtesy of Anatole's composer friend and their neighbor, Achille Debussy. To left and right, as she passed, were lines of black top hats and feathered headdresses and fluttering sequined fans. Choleric faces of red and purple, heavily powdered dowagers with set white hair. She returned each and every look with a cordial smile, a slight tilt of the head.

There is a strange intensity in the atmosphere.

Léonie's gaze sharpened. The farther she went into the Grande Salle, the clearer it became that something was amiss. There was a watchfulness in the faces, something simmering only just beneath the surface, an expectation of trouble to come.

She felt a prickling at the base of her neck. The audience was on its guard. She saw it in the darting glances and mistrustful expressions on every other face.

Don't be absurd.

Léonie had a faint memory of a newspaper article read aloud at the supper table by Anatole about protests against the presentation in Paris of works of Prussian artists. But this was the Palais Garnier, not some secluded alleyway in Clichy or Montmartre.

What could happen at the Opéra?

Léonie picked her way through the forest of knees and gowns along the row and with a sense of relief sat down in her seat. She took a moment to compose herself and then glanced at her neighbors. To her left were a heavily jeweled matron and her elderly husband, his watery eyes all but obscured beneath bushy white brows. Mottled hands rested, one on top of the other, on the head of a silver-topped cane with an inscription band around the neck. To her right, with Anatole's empty seat making a barrier between them like a country ditch, sat four scowling and bearded men of middle years with sour expressions, each set of hands resting upon undistinguished boxwood walking sticks. There was something rather unnerving about the way they sat in silence facing front, an expression of intense concentration on their faces.

It passed through Léonie's mind that it was singular that they should all be wearing leather gloves, and how uncomfortably hot they must be. Then one turned his head and stared at her. Léonie blushed and, fixing her eyes front, admired instead the magnificent trompe l'oeil curtains, which hung in folds of crimson and gold from the top of the proscenium arch to the wooden surface of the stage.

Maybe he is not late? What if some ill has befallen him?

Léonie shook her head at this new and unwelcome thought.

She pulled out her fan from her bag and flicked it open with a snap. However much she might wish to make excuses for her brother, it was more likely to be a matter of poor timekeeping.

As so often these days.

Indeed, since the dismal events in the cimetière de Montmartre, Anatole had been even less reliable. Léonie frowned at how, yet again, the memory slipped back into her mind. The day haunted her. She relived it endlessly.

In March she had hoped that it was all over and done with, but his behavior was still erratic. Often he disappeared for days on end, returning at odd hours of the night, avoiding many of his friends and acquaintances and throwing himself instead into his work.

But tonight he promised he would not be late.

The *chef d'orchestre* walked on to the rostrum, scattering Léonie's brooding thoughts. A round of applause filled the expectant auditorium, like a volley of gunfire, violent and sudden and intense. Léonie clapped with vigor and enthusiasm, all the stronger for her anxious state. The quartet of gentlemen beside her did not move. Their hands remained motionless, perched on their cheap, ugly walking sticks. She threw them a look, thinking them discourteous and boorish, and wondering why they would even bother to come if they were determined not to appreciate the music. And she wished, although it irritated her to acknowledge such nerves, that she was not sitting so very close to them.

The conductor bowed deeply, then turned to face the stage.

The applause faded. Silence fell over the Grande Salle. He tapped his baton on his wooden stand. The blue jets of gaslight in the auditorium spluttered and flickered, then dimmed. The atmosphere became charged with promise. Every eye was upon the *chef d'orchestre*. The men of the orchestra straightened their backs and lifted their bows or raised instruments to their lips.

The *chef* lifted his baton. Léonie caught her breath as the opening chords of Monsieur Wagner's *Lohengrin* filled the palatial spaces of the Palais Garnier.

The seat beside her remained empty.

2

The whistling and catcalling began almost immediately in the higher tiers. At first, the majority of the audience paid no heed to the disturbance and pretended it was not happening. But then it became more obtrusive, louder. Voices were heard in the circle and from the stalls also.

Léonie could not quite make out what the protesters were saying.

She kept her eyes fixed resolutely on the orchestra pit, and attempted to ignore each new hiss or whisper. But as the overture continued, an increasing restlessness seeped through the auditorium from top to bottom, side to side along the rows, sly and insidious. Unable to hold her tongue any longer, Léonie leaned over to her neighbor.

"Who are these people?" she whispered.

The dowager frowned at the interruption but answered all the same.

"They call themselves the *abonnés*," she replied, from behind her fan. "They oppose the performance of any but French composers. Musical patriots, they would claim. In principle, I have some sympathy, but this is not the way to go about things."

Léonie nodded her thanks and sat back straight in her seat, reassured by the woman's matter-of-fact manner even though, actually, the disturbance seemed to be growing. The closing bars of the prelude were barely dry in the air when the protest proper commenced. As the curtain rose on a scene of a chorus of tenth-century Teutonic knights standing on the banks of an ancient

river in Antwerp, a louder commotion began in the upper dress circle. A group
of at least eight or nine men leapt to their feet in a cacophony of whistling and
booing and slow hand clapping. A wave of disapproval washed along the rows
of the stalls, the upper tiers, countered by other outbursts of objection. Then
taunting from the protesters, a chant that at first Léonie could not properly
distinguish. A crescendo of noise, and it became unmistakable.

"Boche! Boche!"

The protest had reached the ears of the singers. Léonie saw darting glances
pass between the chorus and principals, alarm and indecision writ large on
each face.

"Boche! Boche! Boche!"

Whilst not wishing for the performance to be disrupted, at the same time
Léonie could not deny it was exciting. She was witnessing the sort of event
that in usual circumstances she heard about only in the pages of Anatole's
Le Figaro.

The truth was that Léonie was thoroughly bored by the restrictions of her
daily existence, the ennui of accompanying M'man to dull afternoon soirées
at the drab town houses of distant relations and former comrades of her father. Having to make painful small talk with her mother's current friend, an
old military man who treated Léonie as if she was still in short skirts.

What a story I shall have to tell Anatole.

But the mood of the protest was changing.

The cast, pale and uncertain beneath their heavy stage makeup, continued
to sing. Indeed, they did not falter until the first missile was thrown onto the
stage. A bottle, narrowly missing the bass playing the role of King Heinrich.

For an instant it seemed as if the orchestra must have stopped playing, so
deep and suspended was the silence. The audience appeared to be holding its
collective breath as the glass spun, as if in slow motion, catching the harsh
white limelight and sending out dazzling green gleams. Then it hit the canvas
scenery with a thump, fell, and rolled back into the pit.

The real world rushed back. Pandemonium broke out, onstage and off.
There was an upsurge of noise. Then a second missile soared over the heads
of the stupefied audience, bursting on contact with the stage. A woman in the
front row screamed and covered her mouth as a foul stench, of blood and
decaying vegetables and old alleyways, filtered out over the stalls.

"Boche! Boche! Boche!"

The smile faded from Léonie's face, replaced by a look of alarm. She had butterflies in her stomach. This was ugly, frightening, not an adventure at all. She started to feel nauseated.

The quartet to her right suddenly leapt to their feet as one man and began to clap, perfectly in time, slowly at first, baying like animals, imitating the sounds of pigs and cows and goats. Their faces were cruel, vicious, as they chanted their anti-Prussian leitmotif, now taken up in every corner of the auditorium.

"In God's name, sit down, man!"

A heavily bearded and bespectacled gentleman, with the sallow complexion of one who spent his time with inkwell and wax and document papers, tapped one of the protesters on the back with his program.

"This is neither the time nor the place. Be seated!"

"No, indeed," agreed his companion. "Sit down!"

The protester turned and delivered a sharp and glancing blow across the man's knuckles with his stick. Léonie gasped. Taken by surprise at the speed and ferocity of the retaliation, the man howled and let his program drop. His companion leapt to his feet as beads of blood sprang up along the line of the wound. He attempted to grab hold of the protester's weapon, seeing now that there was a metal pin deliberately lodged in the head, but rough hands pushed him back, and he fell.

The conductor attempted to keep the orchestra in time, but the players were throwing fearful glances all around and the tempo grew ragged and uneven, at once too fast and too slow. Backstage, a decision had been made. Stagehands in their blacks, their sleeves rolled to the elbows, suddenly swarmed from the wings and began to usher the singers out of the direct line of fire.

The management attempted to drop the curtain. The weights clanged and boomed dangerously as they flew up too fast. The heavy material tumbled through the air, then caught on a piece of scenery and stuck.

The shouting intensified.

The exodus began from the private boxes. In a flurry of feathers and gold and silk, the bourgeoisie made hurried exits. The desire to withdraw spread into the upper tiers, where many of the nationalist protesters were stationed, then to the circles and stalls. The rows behind Léonie also, one by one, were emptying into the aisles. From every part of the Grande Salle, she heard seats snapping shut. At the exits, the rattle of the brass rings on their rails as the heavy velvet curtains were pulled roughly open.

But the protesters had not yet achieved their goal of stopping the performance.

More missiles were hurled at the stage. Bottles, stones and bricks, rotting fruit. The orchestra evacuated the pit, snatching up precious music and bows and instrument cases, shoving through the obstacles of chairs and wooden stands, to exit under the stage.

At last, through the half-gap in the curtain, the theater manager appeared onstage to appeal for calm. He was sweating, and dabbed at his face with a gray handkerchief.

"Mesdames, messieurs, s'il vous plaît. S'il vous plaît!"

He was a substantial man, but neither his voice nor his manner commanded authority. Léonie saw how wild his eyes were as he flapped his arms and attempted to impose some sort of order on the mounting chaos.

It was too little, too late.

Another missile was thrown, this time not a bottle nor some acquired object but a piece of wood with nails embedded in it. The manager was struck above the eye. He staggered back, clutching his hand to his face. Blood spurted through his fingers from the wound, and he fell sideways, crumpling like a child's rag doll to the surface of the stage.

At this last sight, Léonie's courage finally deserted her.

I must get out.

Horrified, terrified now, she threw desperate glances around the auditorium, but she was trapped, hemmed in by the mob behind her and to the side and by the violence in front. Léonie clutched the backs of the seats, supposing she might escape by scaling the rows, but when she tried to move, she discovered the beaded hem of her dress had caught in the metal bolts beneath her seat. With increasingly desperate fingers, she bent down and tried to pull, tear herself free.

Now a new cry of protest filtered through the auditorium.

"A bas! A bas!"

She looked up. *What now?* The cry was taken up from every corner of the auditorium. *"A bas. A l'attaque!"*

Like crusaders besieging a castle, the protesters surged forward, waving sticks and cudgels. Here and there, the glint of a blade. A shudder of terror made Léonie tremble. She understood the protesters meant to storm the stage and that she was directly in their path.

Throughout the auditorium, what little remained of the mask of Parisian society cracked, then splintered, then shattered into pieces. Hysteria swept through those still trapped. Lawyers and newspapermen, painters and scholars, bankers and civil servants, courtesans and wives, all stampeding toward the doors in their desperation to escape the violence.

Sauvez qui peut. Every man for himself.

The nationalists moved on the stage. With military precision, they marched forward from every section of the auditorium, vaulting the seats and the rails, swarming over the orchestra pit and up onto the boards. Léonie pulled at her dress, harder, harder, until with a ripping of material she freed herself.

"Boche! Alsace française! Lorraine française!"

The protesters were tearing down the backcloth, kicking over the scenery. Painted trees and water and rocks and stones, the imaginary soldiers of the tenth century destroyed by a very real nineteenth-century mob. The stage became littered with splintered wood, torn canvas and dust as the world of *Lohengrin* fell in the battle.

At last, resistance was mustered. A cohort of idealistic young men and veterans of past campaigns somehow came together in the stalls and pursued the nationalists to the stage. The pass door separating the auditorium from the back of the house was breached. They charged into the wings and joined forces with the opera house stage crew, who were advancing on the anti-Prussian nationalists between the flats and the scenery dock.

Léonie watched, appalled yet transfixed by the spectacle. A handsome man, not much more than a boy, in a borrowed evening suit too big for him and with a long waxed moustache, launched himself on the ringleader of the protesters. Hurling his arms around the man's throat, he attempted to pull him down, but found himself on the ground instead. He shrieked in pain as a steel-capped boot drove into his stomach.

"Vive la France! A bas."

Bloodlust had taken hold. Léonie could see the eyes of the mob wide with excitement, with frenzy, as the violence escalated. Cheeks were flushed, feverish.

"*S'il vous plaît*," she cried in desperation, but no one could hear and there was still no way through for her.

Léonie shrank back as another stagehand was thrown from the stage. His body somersaulted over the abandoned orchestra pit and was caught on the brass rail. His arm and shoulder hung loose, twisted and crippled. His eyes remained open.

You must move back. Get back.

But now it seemed the world was drowning in blood, in splintered bone and flesh. She could see nothing else but the twisted hatred on the faces of the men all around. Not more than five feet from where she stood, frozen to the spot, a man was crawling on his hands and knees, his waistcoat and jacket trailing open. He left a smear of bloody handprints on the wooden boards of the stage.

Behind him a weapon was raised.

No!

Léonie tried to call out a warning, but shock stole her voice. Down the weapon came. Made contact. The man slipped, falling heavily on his side. He looked up at his attacker, saw the knife and threw up his hand to protect himself as the blade came down. Metal connecting with flesh. He howled as the knife was withdrawn and plunged again, deep into his chest.

The man's body jerked and twitched like a puppet in the kiosk on the Champs-Elysées, his arms and legs flailing, then was still.

Léonie was astonished to realize she was crying. Then fear rushed back, fiercer than ever.

"*S'il vous plaît*," she shouted. "Let me pass."

She attempted to push through with her shoulders, but she was too small, too light. A mass of people stood between her and the exit, and the central aisle was now blockaded with crimson cushions. Beneath the stage, the gas jets had sent sparks showering down into the sheets of music left abandoned and lying on the ground. A splutter of orange, a hiss of yellow, then a sudden billowing as the wooden underside of the stage began to glow.

"*Au feu! Au feu!*"

At this, another level of panic swept through the auditorium. The memory of the inferno that had swept through the Opéra-Comique five years ago, killing more than eighty, took hold.

"Let me through!" Léonie shouted. "I beg you."

No one heeded her. The ground beneath her feet was carpeted now with abandoned programs and feather headdresses, and lorgnettes and opera glasses, like dry bones in an ancient sepulchre, splintered underfoot.

Léonie could see nothing but elbows and the bare backs of heads, although she kept moving forward, inch by painful inch, succeeding in putting a little distance between herself and the worst of the fighting.

Then, at her side, she felt an elderly lady falter and begin to fall.

She will be trampled.

Léonie shot out her hand and caught hold of the woman's elbow. Beneath the starched fabric, she found herself gripping a thin and spindly arm.

"I wished only to hear the music." The woman was weeping. "German, French, it matters nothing to me. That we should see such sights in our times. That it should come again."

Léonie stumbled forward, taking the entire weight of the old lady, staggering toward the exit. The burden seemed to become greater with every step. The woman was slipping into unconsciousness.

"Not much further," Léonie cried. "Please try, please." Anything to keep the old woman upon her feet. "We are nearly at the doors. Nearly safe."

At last she glimpsed the familiar livery of an opera house flunky.

"*Mais aidez-moi, bon Dieu,*" she shouted. "*Par ici. Vite!*"

The usher obeyed at once. Without a word, he relieved Léonie of her charge, sweeping the old lady up into his arms and carrying her out into the Grand Foyer.

Léonie's legs buckled, exhausted, but she forced herself on. Only a few steps more.

Suddenly a hand grabbed her wrist.

"No," she cried. "No!"

She would not let herself be trapped inside with the fire and the mob and the barricades. Léonie struck out blindly but connected only with air.

"Do not touch me!" she screamed. "Let go of me!"

3

Léonie, *c'est moi.* Léonie!"
A man's voice, familiar and reassuring. And a smell of sandalwood hair oil and Turkish tobacco.

Anatole? Here?

And now strong hands were circling her waist and lifting her up out of the crowd.

Léonie opened her eyes. "Anatole!" she cried, throwing her arms around his neck. "Where have you been? How could you!" Her embrace turned to attack, as she pummeled his chest with furious fists. "I waited and waited, yet you did not come. How could you leave me to—"

"I know," he replied quickly. "And you have every right to rebuke me, but not now."

Her anger left her as quickly as it had come. Worn out suddenly, she let her head fall forward onto her big brother's chest. "I saw—"

"I know, *petite*," he said softly, running his hand over her disheveled hair, "but the soldiers are outside already. We must leave or risk being caught up in the fighting."

"Such hatred in their faces, Anatole. They destroyed everything. Did you see? Did you see?"

Léonie felt hysteria building inside her, bubbling up from her stomach to her throat, to her mouth. "With their bare hands, they—"

"You can tell me later," he said sharply, "but now we must get away from here. *Vas-y.*"

Straightaway, Léonie came back to her senses. She took a deep breath.

"Good girl," he said, seeing the determination return to her eyes. "Quick now!"

. . .

ANATOLE USED HIS HEIGHT and strength to forge a path through the mass of bodies fleeing the auditorium.

They emerged through the velvet curtains into the chaos. Hand in hand, they ran along the balconies, then down the Grand Escalier. The marble floor, littered with Champagne bottles, overturned ice buckets and programs, was like an ice rink beneath their feet. Slipping but never quite losing their footing, they reached the glass doors and were out into the Place de l'Opéra.

Instantly, behind them came the sound of glass breaking.

"Léonie, this way!"

If she had thought the scenes inside the Grande Salle impossible, on the streets outside it was worse. The nationalist protesters, the *abonnés*, had taken possession of the steps of the Palais Garnier, too. Armed with sticks and bottles and knives, they stood in lines three deep, waiting and waiting, chanting. Below, in the Place de l'Opéra itself, lines of soldiers in short red jackets and gold helmets knelt with rifles trained on the protesters, hoping for the command to fire.

"There are so many of them," she cried.

Anatole did not reply, as he pulled her through the crowds in front of the baroque facade of the Palais Garnier. He reached the corner and then turned sharply right into rue Scribe, out of the direct line of fire. They were carried along by the mass of people, their fingers laced tight so as not to be separated from each other, for almost a block of buildings, jostled and bustled and knocked like flotsam on a fast-flowing river.

But for a moment, Léonie felt herself safe. She was with Anatole.

Then the sound of a single shot from a rifle. For a moment, the tide of people halted, then, as if in one single movement, the crowd pushed on once more. Léonie could feel her slippers coming unfastened from her feet and was suddenly aware of men's boots snapping at her ankles, trampling underfoot the torn and trailing hem of her dress. She struggled to keep her balance. A volley of bullets erupted behind them. The only fixed point was Anatole's hands.

"Don't let go," she cried.

Behind them, an explosion ripped through the air. The pavement shuddered. Léonie, half twisting around, saw the dusty, dirty mushroom of smoke, gray against the city sky, rising up from the direction of the Place de l'Opéra. Then she felt a second blast reverberating up through the pavement. The air around them seemed first to solidify, then to fold in on itself.

"*Des canons! Ils tirent!*"

"*Non, non, c'est des pétards.*"

Léonie cried out and grasped Anatole's hand tighter. They surged forward, ever forward, no sense of where they would end up, no sense of time, driven only by an animal instinct that told them not to stop, not until the noise and the blood and the dust were far behind.

Léonie felt her limbs tire as fatigue took hold, but she kept running, running, until she could go no farther. Little by little the crowd thinned until at last they found themselves in a quiet street, far removed from the fighting and the explosions and the barrels of the guns. Her legs were weak with exhaustion, and her skin was flushed and damp with the night.

Coming to a halt, Léonie reached out with a hand to steady herself against a wall. Her heart was thudding feverishly. The blood was hammering in her ears, heavy and loud.

Anatole stopped, leaning back against the wall. Léonie sagged against him, her copper curls hanging all the way down her back like a skein of silk, and felt his arms circle protectively around her shoulders.

She gulped at the night air, trying to regain her breath. She pulled off her stained gloves, discolored by soot and the Parisian streets, and let them drop to the pavement.

Anatole smoothed his fingers through the thick black hair that had fallen down over his high forehead and sharp cheekbones. He too was breathing hard, despite the hours he spent training in the fencing halls.

Extraordinarily, he seemed to be smiling.

For a while, neither spoke. The only sound was the rise and fall of their breath, clouds of white in the cool September evening. At last Léonie drew herself up.

"Why were you late?" she demanded of him, as if the events of the last hour had never happened.

Anatole stared at her in disbelief; then he started to laugh, softly at first, then louder, struggling to speak, filling the air with guffaws.

"You would scold me, *petite*, even at such a moment?"

Léonie fixed him with a look but quickly felt the corners of her own mouth starting to twitch. A giggle burst out of her, then another, until her slim frame was shaking with laughter and the tears were rolling down her grimy, pretty cheeks.

Anatole removed his evening jacket and draped it across her bare shoulders.

"You are really the most extraordinary creature," he said. "Quite extraordinary!"

Léonie gave a rueful smile as she contrasted her disheveled state with his elegance. She glanced down at her tattered green gown. The hem hung loose like a train behind her, and the remaining glass beads were chipped and hanging by threads.

Despite their headlong flight through the streets of Paris, Anatole looked all but immaculate. His shirtsleeves were white and crisp, the tips of his collar still starched and upright, his blue dress waistcoat unmarked.

He stepped back and looked up to read the sign on the wall.

"Rue Caumartin," he said. "Excellent. Supper? You are hungry, I suppose?"

"Ravenous."

"I know a café not far from here. Downstairs is popular with the performers, and their admirers, from the cabaret Le Grande-Pinte, but there are respectable private rooms on the first floor. Does that sound acceptable?"

"Perfectly so."

He smiled. "That's settled then. And for once, I shall keep you out late, well past a reasonable bedtime." He grinned. "I dare not deliver you home to M'man in such a state. She would never forgive me."

4

Marguerite Vernier disembarked the fiacre at the corner of the rue Cambon and the rue Sainte-Honoré, accompanied by General Georges Du Pont.

While her escort settled the fare, she pulled her stole around her against the chill of the evening and smiled with satisfaction. It was the best restaurant in town, the famous windows curtained, as ever, with the finest Brittany lace. It was a measure of Du Pont's growing regard for her that he had brought her here.

Arm in arm, they walked inside Voisin's. They were greeted by discreet and gentle conversation. Marguerite felt Georges puff out his chest and realized he was aware that every man in the room was jealous of him. She squeezed his arm and felt him return the gesture, a reminder of how they had passed the last two hours. He turned a proprietorial look upon her. Marguerite granted him a gentle smile, then parted her lips slightly, enjoying the way he colored from beneath his collar to the tips of his ears. It was her mouth, her generous smile and her full lips, that raised her beauty to the extraordinary. It carried both promise and invitation.

His hand went to his neck and he pulled at his stiff white collar, loosening his black tie. Dignified and entirely proper, his evening jacket was skillfully cut to disguise the fact that, at sixty, he was no longer quite the physical specimen he had been in his army heyday. In his buttonhole were threads of colored ribbon signifying the medals he had gained at Sedan and Metz. Rather than a waistcoat, which might have accentuated his prominent stomach, he wore instead a dark crimson cummerbund. Gray-haired and with a full and bushy cropped moustache, Georges was a diplomat now, formal and sober, and wished the world to know it.

To please him, Marguerite had dressed modestly in a purple silk moiré dinner dress with silver trim and beads. The sleeves were full, drawing attention all the more to the slim, tapered waist and full skirts. The neck was high, allowing no more than the slightest hint of skin, although on Marguerite, this made the outfit all the more provocative. Her dark hair was twisted artfully in a chignon, with a single spray of purple feathers, showing to best advantage her slim white neck. Brown, limpid eyes were set within an exquisite complexion.

Every bored matron and upholstered wife in the restaurant stared with dislike and envy, the more so because Marguerite was in her middle forties rather than in the first flush of youth. The combination of beauty and such a figure, matched with the lack of a ring on her finger, offended their sense of fairness and propriety. Was it right that such a liaison should be flaunted in such a place as Voisin's?

The proprietor, gray-headed and as distinguished-looking as his clientele, swept forward to greet Georges, stepping out of the shadow of the two ladies sitting at the front desk, the Scylla and Charybdis without whose blessing not a soul entered the culinary institution. General Du Pont was a customer of long standing who ordered the best Champagne and tipped generously. But he had been a less-than-frequent visitor of late. Clearly the owner feared they had lost his custom to the Café Paillard or the Café Anglais.

"Monsieur, it is a great pleasure to welcome you once more. We surmised that perhaps you had received a posting abroad."

Georges looked thoroughly embarrassed. *So straitlaced,* Marguerite thought, although she did not dislike him for it. He had better manners, and was more generous and simpler in his needs, than many of the men with whom she had been associated.

"The fault is entirely mine," she said from beneath her dark lashes. "I have been keeping him to myself."

The proprietor laughed. He clicked his fingers. While the cloakroom attendant relieved Marguerite of her stole and Georges of his walking stick, the men exchanged courtesies, talking of the weather and the current situation in Algeria. There were rumors of an anti-Prussian demonstration. Marguerite allowed her thoughts to drift away. She cast her eyes over the famous show table of the finest fruit. It was too late for strawberries, of course, and in any case Georges preferred to retire early, so it was unlikely he would wish to remain for dessert.

Marguerite expertly stifled a sigh while the men concluded their business. Despite the fact that every table around them was occupied, there was a sense of peace and quiet comfort. Her son would dismiss the place as dull and old-fashioned, but she, who too often had been on the outside of such establishments looking in, found it delightful and an indication of the measure of security she had found with Du Pont's patronage.

The conversation over, the proprietor raised his hand. The maître d' stepped forward and led them through the candlelit room to a superior table in an alcove, not overlooked by any other diners and a long way from the swinging doors of the kitchen. Marguerite noticed the man was perspiring, his top lip glistening beneath his cropped moustache, and wondered again what it really was that Georges did at the embassy that meant that his good opinion was so very important.

"Monsieur, Madame, an aperitif to start?" asked the wine waiter.

Georges looked across at Marguerite. "Champagne?"

"That would be perfectly delightful, yes."

"A bottle of Cristal," he said, leaning back in his chair as if to spare Marguerite the vulgar knowledge of hearing that he had ordered the best in the house.

As soon as the maître d' had gone, Marguerite moved her feet to touch Du Pont's beneath the table and again had the pleasure of seeing him start, then shift on his chair.

"Marguerite, really," he said, although his protest carried no conviction.

She slipped her foot from her slipper and rested it lightly against him.

"They have the best cellar of red wines in Paris," he said gruffly, as if he needed to clear his throat. "Burgundies, Bordeaux, all arranged in their proper precedence, the wines from the great vineyards first, and the rest in their correct order down to the merest bourgeois tipple."

Marguerite disliked red wine, which gave her terrible headaches, and preferred Champagne, but she was resigned to drinking whatever Georges put in front of her.

"You are so very clever, Georges." She paused, then looked around. "And to find us a table."

"It's just a matter of knowing to whom to talk," he said, although she could see he was pleased with the flattery. "You have not dined here before?"

Marguerite shook her head. She, of course, like every other Parisian, knew the history of Voisin's but was prepared to pretend she did not. During the painful months of the Commune, the restaurant had witnessed some of the most violent of the altercations between the Communards and the government forces. Where now fiacres and two-wheelers waited to ferry customers from one side of Paris to the other, twenty years ago had stood the barricades: iron bedsteads, upturned wooden carts, pallets and munitions boxes. She, with her husband—her wonderful, heroic Leo—had stood on those barricades, for a brief and glorious moment united as equal partners against the ruling class.

"After Louis-Napoléon's shameful failure at the battle of Sedan," wheezed Georges, "the Prussians marched upon Paris."

"Yes," she murmured, wondering not for the first time how young he thought she was, that he should give her a history lesson of events she had witnessed firsthand.

"As the siege and bombardment deepened, of course there were food shortages. It was the only way to teach those Communards a lesson. It meant, however, that many of the better restaurants could not open. Not enough food, you see. Sparrows, cats, dogs, not a creature to be seen on the streets of Paris that was not fair game. Even the animals from the zoo were slaughtered for meat."

Marguerite smiled encouragement. "Yes, Georges."

"So what do you think Voisin's offered on their menu that night?"

"I cannot imagine," she said, wide-eyed with perfectly judged innocence. "Indeed, I hardly dare to. Snake, perhaps?"

"No," he said, with a satisfied bark of laughter. "Guess again."

"Oh, I cannot say, Georges. Crocodile?"

"Elephant," he said triumphantly. "A dish concocted from the trunks of elephants. I ask you. Wonderful, really. Quite wonderful. Shows marvelous spirit, don't you think?"

"Oh yes," Marguerite agreed, and she laughed too, although her memory of the summer of 1871 was somewhat different. Weeks of starvation. Trying to fight, to support her wild, idealistic, passionate husband, and at the same time finding enough food for her beloved Anatole. Coarse brown bread and chestnuts and berries stolen at night from the fruit bushes in the Jardin des Tuileries.

When the Commune fell, Leo only narrowly escaped the firing squad and remained at large, hidden by friends for nearly two years. In the end, he too was captured and tried. His name was published on a list posted on the wall of a municipal building: deportation to the French Pacific Colony of New Caledonia.

The amnesty for the Communards came too late for Leo. He died in the galleys crossing the ocean, without even knowing he had a daughter.

"Marguerite?" Du Pont said testily.

Realizing she had been silent for too long, Marguerite rearranged her face.

"I was just thinking how extraordinary that must have been," she said quickly, "but it says so much, does it not, for the skill and ingenuity of the chef at Voisin's that he was able to make such a dish. It is quite wonderful to sit here, where history was made." She paused, and then added, "And with you."

Georges smiled complacently. "Strength of character win out in the end," he said. "There's always a way to turn a bad situation to one's advantage, not that it's something today's generation has any knowledge about."

"Excuse me for intruding upon your dinner."

Du Pont got to his feet, courteous despite the irritation clouding his eyes. Marguerite turned to see a tall, patrician gentleman with thick, dark hair and a high forehead. He looked down at her with sharp, pinpoint pupils, black in eyes of startling blue.

"Monsieur?" said Georges, unable to keep the irritation from his voice.

The look of the man sent a memory scuttling across Marguerite's mind, although she was certain she did not know him. Perhaps about the same sort of age as she, he was dressed in the usual evening uniform of black jacket and trousers but immaculately so, flattering the strong and impressive physique that lay beneath. Broad shoulders, a man accustomed to getting his own way. Marguerite glanced at the gold signet ring on his left hand, looking for clues as to his identity. He was holding a silk top hat, together with his white evening gloves and a white cashmere scarf, suggesting he either had just arrived or was on the point of making his departure.

Marguerite felt herself blush at the way his eyes seemed to strip her bare, feeling her skin grow hot. Beads of perspiration formed between her breasts and beneath the web of tight lacing of her corset.

"Forgive me," she said, throwing an anxious glance to Du Pont, "but do I . . ."

"Sir," he said, nodding at Du Pont, by way of apology. "If I may?"

Mollified, Du Pont gave a slight bow of the head.

"I am an acquaintance of your son's, Madame Vernier," he said, pulling a calling card from his waistcoat book. "Victor Constant, Comte de Tour-maline."

Marguerite hesitated and then took the card.

"Most discourteous of me to interrupt, I know it, but I am anxious to be in contact with Vernier over a matter of some importance. I have been in the country, only arriving in town this evening, and was hoping to find your son at home. However . . ." He gave a shrug.

Marguerite had known many men. She always knew the best way to be, to speak, to flatter, to charm on a moment's acquaintance.

But this man? She could not read him.

She looked down at the card in her hand. Anatole did not confide much of his business to her, but Marguerite was certain she had never heard him mention so distinguished a name, either as a friend or as a client.

"Do you know where I might find him, Madame Vernier?"

Marguerite felt a frisson of attraction, then fear. Both were pleasurable. Both alarmed her. His eyes narrowed as if he could read her mind, his head nodding slightly.

"I am afraid, Monsieur, I do not," she replied, struggling to keep her voice steady. "Perhaps if you were to leave your card for him at his offices . . ."

Constant inclined his head. "Indeed, I will. And they are to be found . . ."

"In the rue Montorgueil. I cannot remember the precise number."

Constant continued to look hard at her. "Very well," he said in the end. "Again, my apologies for intruding. If you might be so kind, Madame Vernier, as to tell your son that I am looking for him, I would be most grateful."

Without warning, he reached down, took her hand from where it lay in her lap, and raised it to his mouth. Marguerite felt his breath and the tickle of his moustache through her glove, and felt betrayed by the way her body responded to his touch in stark opposition to her wishes.

"À bientôt, Madame Vernier. Mon Général."

Then he gave a sharp half-bow and left. The waiter came and refreshed their glasses. Du Pont exploded.

"Of all the insolent, impertinent scoundrels," he growled, leaning back in his chair. "Quite disgraceful. Who does the blackguard think he is, insulting you in such a manner."

"Insulting me? Did he, Georges?"

"Fellow couldn't keep his eyes off you."

"Really, Georges, I did not notice. He did not interest me," she said, not wishing for a scene. "Please do not concern yourself on my account."

"Do you know the fellow?" Du Pont said, suddenly suspicious.

"I said I did not," she replied calmly.

"Fellow knew my name," he persisted.

"Perhaps he recognizes you from the newspapers, Georges," she said. "You underestimate how many people know you. You forget how familiar a figure you are."

Intending to finish the matter, she took Constant's expensive card by the corner and held it to the flame of the candle set in the center of the table. It took a moment to catch, then burned brightly and furiously.

"What in the name of God do you think you're doing?"

Marguerite raised her long lashes, then dropped her eyes once more to the flame, watching until it guttered and died away.

"There," she said, brushing the gray ash from the tips of her gloves into the ashtray. "Forgotten. And if the count is someone with whom my son wishes to do business, then the proper place for such matters is between the hours of ten and five at his offices."

Georges nodded in approval. With relief, she saw the suspicion melt from his eyes.

"Do you really not know where that boy of yours is tonight?"

"Of course I do," she said, smiling at him as if letting him in on a joke, "but it always pays to be circumspect. I do dislike gossiping women."

He nodded again. It suited Marguerite for Georges to think of her as discreet and reliable.

"Quite right, quite right."

"In point of fact, Anatole has taken Léonie to the opera. The premiere of the latest work by Wagner."

"Damned Prussian propaganda," Georges grumbled. "Shouldn't be allowed."

"And I believe he was intending to take her to supper afterwards."

"To one of those ghastly bohemian places like Le Café de la Place Blanche. Crammed to the gills with artists and what have you." He drummed his fingers on the table. "What's that other place on the Boulevard Rochechouart? They should shut it down."

"Le Chat Noir," Marguerite said.

"Layabouts, the lot of them," pronounced Georges, warming to this new theme. "Daubing dots on a scrap of canvas and calling it art: What kind of occupation is that for a man? That thoroughly insolent fellow, Debussy, who lives in your building? Chaps like that. Should be horsewhipped, the lot of them."

"Achille is a composer, darling," she chided mildly.

"Parasites, the lot of them. Always scowling. Banging away on that piano day and night, I'm surprised his father doesn't take a stick to him. Might beat some sense into him."

Marguerite hid a smile. Since Achille was a contemporary of Anatole's, she thought it was a little late for such disciplinary measures. In any case, Madame Debussy had been very much too free with her hands when the children were young, and it had clearly done not the slightest bit of good.

"This Champagne is really quite delicious, Georges," she said, moving the conversation on.

She stretched across the table and took his fingers, then turned his hand over and pressed her nails into the soft flesh of his palm. "You are most thoughtful," she said, watching the wince of pain turn to pleasure in his eyes. "Now, Georges. Will you order for me? We have been sitting here for such a time that I find I have quite an appetite."

5

Léonie and Anatole were shown to a private room on the first floor of Le Bar Romain, overlooking the street.

Léonie returned Anatole's evening jacket to him, then went to wash her face and hands and repair her hair in the small adjoining closet. Her dress, although in need of the attention of her maid, she pinned at the hem, and made it almost respectable.

She stared at her reflection in the looking glass, tilting it toward her. Her skin glowed from their nighttime chase through the streets of Paris, and her emerald eyes glittered brightly from the light of the candles. Now that the danger had passed, in her mind Léonie was painting the scene in bright, bold colors, like a story. Already she had forgotten the hate on the men's faces, how terrified she had been.

Anatole ordered two glasses of Madeira, followed by red wine to accompany a simple supper of lamb chops and white creamed potatoes.

"Pear soufflé to follow, if you are still hungry," he said, dismissing the *garçon*.

As they ate, Léonie related what had happened up until the moment Anatole had found her.

"They are a curious lot, *les abonnés*," said Anatole. "Only French music should be performed on French soil. Back in 1860, they pelted *Tannhäuser* from the stage." He shrugged. "It's a commonly held belief that they do not care about the music in the slightest."

"Then why?"

"Chauvinism, pure and simple."

Anatole pushed his chair back from the table, stretched out his long, slim legs and took his cigarette case from the pocket of his waistcoat. "I do not believe Paris will ever again welcome Wagner. Not now."

Léonie thought a moment. "Why did Achille make you a gift of the opera tickets? Is he not a fervent admirer of Monsieur Wagner?"

"Was," he said, banging a cigarette on the silver lid to tighten the tobacco, "but is no longer." He leaned into his jacket pocket and pulled out a box of wax Vestas and struck a match. " 'A beautiful sunset mistaken for a wonderful dawn,' that is Achille's latest pronouncement on Wagner." He tapped his head with a mocking half-smile. "Forgive me, *Claude*-Achille, as we are now supposed to address him."

Debussy, a brilliant if mercurial pianist and composer, lived with his siblings and parents in the same apartment block as the Verniers on the rue de Berlin. He was both the enfant terrible of the Conservatoire and, reluctantly, their greatest hope. However, in their small circle of friends, Debussy's complex love life attracted more notoriety than his growing professional reputation. The current lady in favor was twenty-four-year-old Gabrielle Dupont.

"It is serious this time," Anatole confided. "Gaby understands his music must come first, and that is of course most attractive to him. She is tolerant of the way he disappears each Tuesday to the salons of Maître Mallarmé. It raises his spirits in the face of the continuing drizzle of complaint from the académie, who simply do not understand his genius. They are all too old, too stupid."

Léonie raised her eyebrows. "It is my belief that Achille brings most of his misfortunes down upon his own head. He is quick to fall out with those who might support him. He's too sharp-tongued, too ready to cause offense. Indeed, he goes quite out of his way to be churlish, rude and difficult."

Anatole smoked and did not disagree.

"And friendship aside," she continued, stirring a third spoonful of sugar into her coffee, "I confess I have some sympathy with his critics. For me, his compositions are a little vague and unstructured and . . . well, disquieting. Meandering. Too often I feel that I am waiting for the tune to reveal itself. As if one is listening underwater."

Anatole smiled. "Ah, but that is precisely the point. Debussy says that one must drown the sense of key. He is seeking to illuminate, through his music, the connections between the material and the spiritual worlds, the seen and the unseen, and such a thing cannot be presented in the traditional ways."

Léonie pulled a face. "That sounds like one of those clever things people say that mean precisely nothing!"

"He believes that evocation and suggestion and nuance are more powerful, more truthful, more illuminating than statement and description. That the value and power of distant memories surpass that of conscious, explicit thought."

Léonie grinned. She admired her brother's loyalty to his friend but was aware that he was only repeating verbatim words he'd heard previously issue from Achille's lips. For all Anatole's passionate advocacy of his friend's work, she knew very well that his tastes ran more to Offenbach and the orchestra of the Folies Bergère than to anything Debussy or Dukas or any of their Conservatoire friends might produce.

"Since we're trading confidences," he added, "I admit that I did return last week to the rue de la Chaussée d'Antin to purchase a copy of Achille's *Cinq Poèmes*."

Léonie's eyes flashed with temper. "Anatole, you gave M'man your word."

He shrugged. "I know, but I could not help myself. The price was so reasonable, and it is sure to be a good investment, seeing as how Bailly printed only a hundred and fifty copies."

"We must be more careful with our money. M'man relies on you to be prudent. We cannot afford to run up any more debts." She paused, then added, "Indeed, how much do we owe?"

Their eyes locked.

"Really, Léonie. Our household finances are not something for you to concern yourself with."

"But—"

"But nothing," he said firmly.

Sulking, she turned her back on him. "You treat me like a child!"

He laughed. "When you marry, you can drive your husband to distraction with queries about your own household budget, but until that time . . . However, I give you my word that from now on, I will not spend a sou without your permission."

"Now you're making fun of me."

"Indeed, not even a centime," he teased.

She glared a moment longer, then surrendered. "I shall hold you to it, mind." She sighed.

Anatole drew a cross on his chest with his finger. "On my honor."

For a moment they just smiled at each other, then the teasing look fell from his face. He reached across the table and covered her small, white hand with his own.

"To speak seriously for an instant, *petite*," he said, "I will find it hard to forgive myself for the fact that my poor timekeeping left you facing tonight's ordeal alone. Can you forgive me?"

Léonie smiled. "It is already forgotten."

"Your generosity is more than I deserve. And you behaved with great courage. Most girls would have lost their heads. I am proud of you." He sat back in his chair and lit another cigarette. "Although you may find that the evening comes back to you. Shock has a habit of taking hold after the event."

"I am not so timid," she said firmly. She felt completely alive, taller, bolder, more precisely herself. Not distressed in any way whatsoever.

The clock on the mantelshelf chimed the hour.

"But at the same time, Anatole, I have never known you to miss the curtain before."

Anatole took a mouthful of cognac. "Always a first time."

Léonie narrowed her eyes. "What did keep you?"

He slowly returned the broad-bellied glass to the table, then pulled at the waxed ends of his moustache.

A certain sign that he is not being entirely truthful.

"Anatole?"

"I was committed to meeting a customer from out of town. He was due at six, but he arrived rather later and remained longer than I had anticipated."

"And yet you had your dress clothes with you? Or did you return home before joining me at the Palais Garnier?"

"I had taken the precaution of bringing my evening clothes with me to the office."

Then with one swift motion Anatole got up, crossed the room and pulled the bell, stopping the conversation in its tracks. Before Léonie could quiz him further, the servants appeared to clear the table, making any more dialogue between them impossible.

"Time to get you home," he said, putting his hand on her elbow and helping her to her feet. "I will settle up once I have seen you into a carriage."

Moments later, they were standing outside on the pavement.

"You are not returning with me?"

Anatole helped her up into the cab and fastened the catch. "I think I'll pay a visit to Chez Frascati. Perhaps play a couple of hands of cards."

Léonie felt a flutter of panic.

"What shall I tell M'man?"

"She will already have retired."

"But what if she has not?" she objected, trying to delay the moment of departure.

He kissed her hand. "In which case, tell her not to wait up."

Anatole reached up to press a note into the driver's hand. "Rue de Berlin," he said, then stepped back and banged on the side of the carriage. "Sleep well, *petite*. I shall see you at breakfast."

The whip cracked. The lamps banged against the side of the gig as the horses jerked forward in a clinking of harness and iron shoes on the cobbles. Léonie pushed down the glass and leaned out of the window. Anatole stood in a pool of smoggy yellow light beneath the hissing gas lamps, a trail of white smoke twisting up from his cigarette.

Why would he not tell me why he was late?

She kept looking, reluctant to let him out of her sight, as the cab rattled up the rue Caumartin past the Hotel Saint-Petersbourg, past Anatole's alma mater, the Lycée Fontanes, heading for the junction with rue Saint-Lazare.

Léonie's last glimpse, before the carriage turned the corner, was of Anatole flicking the burning end of his cigarette into the gutter. Then he turned on his heel and walked back into Le Bar Romain.

6

The building on the rue de Berlin was quiet.

Léonie let herself into the apartment with a latchkey. An oil lamp had been left burning to light her way. Léonie dropped the key into the china bowl that stood beside the silver post salver, empty of letters or calling cards. Pushing her mother's stole off the cushion, she sank down on a hall chair. She slipped off her stained slippers and silk stockings, massaging her sore toes and thinking of Anatole's evasiveness. If there was no shame attached to his actions, then why would he not tell her why he had been late to the opera?

Léonie glanced along the passageway and saw that her mother's door was closed. For once, she was disappointed. Often she found Marguerite's company frustrating, her topics of conversation limited and predictable. But tonight she would have been grateful for a little late-night company.

She took up the lamp and walked into the drawing room. A large and generous room, it occupied the entire front of the house, overlooking the rue de Berlin itself. The three sets of windows were closed, but the curtains of yellow chintz that hung ceiling to floor had been left open.

She placed the lamp on the table, then looked down on the deserted street. She realized she was chilled to the bone. She thought of Anatole, somewhere in the city, and hoped he was safe.

At last, thoughts of what could have been started to creep up on her. The high spirits that had supported her through the long evening drained away, leaving her frightened. She felt as if every limb, every muscle, every sense was overtaken by the memory of what she had witnessed.

Blood and cracked bones and hate.

Léonie closed her eyes, but still each separate incident flooded back, distinct, as if caught in the click of the shutter of a box camera. The stench as the homemade bombs of excrement and rotting food burst. The frozen eyes of the man as the knife plunged into his chest, that single paralyzing moment between life and death.

There was a green woolen shawl hanging over the back of the chaise longue. She wrapped it around her shoulders, turned down the gas lamp and curled up in her favorite armchair, her legs tucked beneath her.

Suddenly, from the floor beneath, the sound of music began to filter up through the floorboards. Léonie smiled. Achille at his piano again. She looked to the clock on the mantelshelf.

Past midnight.

Léonie welcomed the knowledge that she was not the only one awake in the rue de Berlin. There was something soothing about Achille's presence. She burrowed deeper into the folds of the chair, recognizing the piece. *La Damoiselle Élue*, a composition Anatole often claimed Debussy had written with Léonie in mind. She knew the assertion to be untrue. Achille had told her that the libretto was a prose setting of a poem by Rossetti, which in its turn had been inspired by Monsieur Poe's "The Raven."

But untrue or not, she held the piece close to her heart, and its ethereal chords precisely suited her midnight spirits.

Without warning, another memory swooped down upon her. The morning of the funeral. Then, as now, Achille hammering endlessly on the piano, black notes and white seeping up through the floorboards until Léonie thought she would be driven mad with his playing. The single palm leaf floating in the glass bowl. The sickly aroma of ritual and death that insinuated itself into every corner of the apartment, the burning of incense and candles to mask the cloying sweetness of the corpse in the closed casket.

You are confusing what was with what is.

Then, most mornings, Anatole had disappeared from the apartment before light had given shape back to the world. Most evenings he returned home long after the household had retired. Once he had been absent for a week without explanation. When Léonie finally mustered the courage to ask him where he had been, he told her only not to concern herself. She supposed he spent his nights at the *rouge et noir* tables. She knew, too, from the gossip of the servants, that he was being subjected to vociferous and anonymous denunciations in the columns of the newspapers.

The physical toll on him was obvious. His cheeks grew hollow and his skin transparent. His brown eyes were dulled, permanently bloodshot, his lips withered and parched. Léonie would do anything to prevent such a deterioration again.

Only when the leaves were returning to the trees in the Boulevard Malesherbes, and when the paths of the Parc Monceau were filled once more with pink and white and lilac blooms, did the attacks on his good name suddenly cease. From then, his spirits improved and his health recovered. The older brother she knew and loved was restored to her. Since then, there had been no more disappearances, no more evasions, no more half-truths.

Until this evening.

Léonie realized her cheeks were wet. She wiped away the tears with cold fingers, then wrapped the shawl tighter around her.

This is September, not March.

But Léonie remained sick at heart. She knew he had lied to her. So she kept vigil at the window, allowing Achille's music below to lull her into a half-sleep, whilst all the time listening for the sound of Anatole's latchkey in the door.

7

Thursday, September 17

Leaving his lover sleeping, Anatole crept from the tiny rented room. Careful not to disturb the other lodgers in the boardinghouse, he walked slowly down the narrow and dusty wooden stairs in stockinged feet. A gas jet burned on each landing, as he descended one flight, then another and another, until he was in the passageway that gave on to the street.

It was not quite dawn, yet Paris was waking. In the distance, Anatole could hear the sounds of delivery carts. Wooden traps over the cobbles, delivering milk and freshly baked bread to the cafés and bars of the Faubourg Montmartre.

He stopped to put on his shoes. The rue Feydeau was deserted; there was no sound except the clip of his heels on the pavement. Deep in thought, Anatole walked quickly, to the junction with the rue Saint-Marc, intending to cut through the arcade of the Passage des Panoramas. He saw no one, heard no one.

His thoughts were rattling around in his head. Would their plan succeed? Could he get out of Paris unobserved and without raising suspicion? For all the fighting talk of the past hours, Anatole entertained doubts. He knew that his conduct over the coming hours, days, would determine their success or failure. Already Léonie was suspicious, and since her support would be critical to the success of the endeavor, he cursed the sequence of events that had delayed his arrival at the opera house, then the extraordinary ill fortune that had decreed that the *abonnés* should have chosen that very night to stage their most bloody and violent protest to date.

He took a deep breath, feeling the crisp September dawn seeping into his lungs, mixed with the steam and smoke and soot of the city. The guilt he had felt at having failed Léonie had been forgotten in the blessed moments when he held his lover in his arms. Now it returned, like a sharp pain in his chest.

He determined he would make it up to her.

The hand of time was on his back, pushing him homeward. He walked faster, wrapped in thought, delight at the night just past, the memory of his lover imprinted upon his mind and body, the fragrance of skin on his fingers, the texture of her hair. He was weary with the endless secrecy and obfuscation. As soon as they were away from Paris, there would be no more need for intrigue, to invent imaginary visits to the *rouge et noir* tables or opium dens or houses of ill repute to cover his true whereabouts.

That he had been under attack from the newspapers and been unable to defend his own reputation was a state of affairs that sat uneasily with him. He suspected Constant to have had a hand in it. The blackening of his name affected the situation of both his mother and his sister. All he could hope was that when the matter was out in the open, there would be time enough to repair his standing.

As he turned the corner, a spiteful gust of autumn wind blew at his heels. He pulled his jacket tight around him and regretted the lack of a neck scarf. He crossed the rue Saint-Marc, still wrapped in his thoughts—thinking of the days, the weeks to come, not the present within which he walked.

At first he did not hear the sound of footsteps behind him. Two sets of feet, walking fast, getting closer. His mind sharpened. He glanced down at his evening clothes, realizing he looked an easy target. Unarmed, unaccompanied and possibly with winnings from a night at the tables in his pockets.

Anatole walked faster. The footsteps, too, quickened.

Certain now he was being marked, he darted right into the Passage des Panoramas, thinking that if he could cut through to the Boulevard Montmartre, where the cafés would be opening their doors and there was likely to be early-morning traffic, milk deliveries, carts, he would be safe.

The few remaining gas lamps burned with cold, blue light as he passed along the narrow row of glass-fronted shops selling stamps and ex-voto trinkets, the furniture maker displaying an ancient cabinet with dilapidated gilding, the various antiques dealers and sellers of objets d'art.

The men followed.

Anatole felt a spike of fear. His hand went to his pocket, looking for something with which to defend himself but finding nothing that would serve as a weapon.

He walked faster, resisting the impulse to start running. Better to keep his head up. Pretend all was well. Trust that he would make it through to the other side before they had the chance to strike.

But behind him now, the sound of running. A flash of movement reflected in the window of Stern's, the engraver, a refracting of the light, and Anatole spun round in time to ward off a fist coming down upon his head. He took a hit above his left eye but deflected the worst of it and managed to land a punch. His attacker wore a flat woolen cap with a black handkerchief obscuring most of his face. He grunted, but at the same time Anatole felt his arms pinned from behind, leaving him exposed. The first blow, to his stomach, knocked the wind out of him, then a fist smashed into his face, left, right, like a boxer in the ring, in a volley of blows that sent his head cracking from side to side and pain ricocheting through him.

Anatole could feel blood trickling from his eyelid, but he managed to twist around slightly to avoid the worst of the hits. The man holding him was also wearing a neck scarf across his face, but his head was bare and his hard scalp was covered in angry red blisters. Anatole drew up his knee and sent his foot smashing back into the man's shin. For an instant the hold upon him was loosened, just long enough for Anatole to grab at the open collar of his shirt and, getting purchase, send him staggering against the sharp-edged pillars in the doorway.

Anatole launched himself forward, using the weight of his body to try to get past, but the first man caught him with a glancing jab to the side of his head. He half stumbled to his knees, swinging out as he fell and catching the man hard in the ribs but inflicting little damage.

Anatole felt the man's fists, clenched together, come down on the back of his neck. The force of the blow sent him staggering forward, then he stumbled and dropped to the ground. A vicious kick from steel-toed boots to the back of his legs had him sprawling forward on the ground. He threw his hands over his head and pulled his knees up to his chin, in a futile attempt to protect himself from the worst of the assault. As one blow then another rained down upon him—to his ribs, his kidneys—he realized for the first time that the beating might not stop.

"Hey!"

At the end of the passageway, in the gloom, Anatole thought he saw a light.

"Hey! You! What's going on?"

For a moment, time stood still. Anatole felt the hot breath of one of the assailants whispering in his ear.

"*Une leçon.*"

Then the sensation of hands crawling over his battered body, fingers pushing into the pocket of his waistcoat, a sharp tug, and his father's fob watch being torn from its clip.

Finally, Anatole found his voice.

"Over here! Here!"

With a final kick to his ribs, causing Anatole's body to jackknife in pain, the two attackers left, running in the opposite direction from the inconstant light of the night watchman's lamp.

"Over here," Anatole cried.

He heard the shuffling feet coming toward him, then the clink of the lamp on the ground, and the old night watchman was peering down at him.

"*Monsieur, qu'est-ce qui s'est passé ici?*"

Anatole pulled himself up into a sitting position, allowing the old man to help him.

"I'm all right," he said, trying to catch his breath. He put his hand up to his eye and brought his red fingers away.

"You've taken quite a beating."

"It's nothing," he insisted. "A cut."

"Monsieur, you were robbed?"

Anatole didn't immediately answer. He took a deep breath, then reached his hand up for the night watchman to help him to his feet. Pain shot across his back and down his legs. He took a moment to get his balance, then straightened. He examined his hands, turning them over. His knuckles were cracked and bleeding, and his palms were red with blood from the cut above his eye. He could feel a gash on his ankle where the skin was open, rubbing against the material of his trousers.

Anatole took a moment more to compose himself, then he straightened his clothes.

"Did they take much, sir?"

He patted himself down and was surprised to find his pocketbook and cigarette case still there.

"They appear to have taken only my watch," he said. His words seemed to be coming from a long way away as reality slipped into his head and took root.

It had not been a random robbery. Indeed, not a robbery at all, but a lesson, as the man had said.

Pushing the thought from his mind, Anatole pulled out a note and slipped it into the old man's tobacco-stained fingers. "In gratitude for your assistance, my friend."

The watchman looked down and smiled. "Most generous, Monsieur."

"But no need to mention this to anyone, there's a good chap. Now, if you could find me a cab?"

The old man touched his hat. "Whatever you say, sir."

8

Léonie woke with a jolt, thoroughly disoriented.

For a moment she couldn't recall why she was wrapped in a woolen blanket in the drawing room, curled up in a chair. Then she looked down at her torn evening dress and remembered. The riot at the Palais Garnier. The late supper with Anatole. Achille playing lullabies through the night. She glanced at the Sèvres clock on the mantelshelf.

A quarter past five.

Chilled to the bone and a little nauseated, she slipped into the hall, noticing that Anatole's door was also now closed. The observation was comforting.

Her bedroom was at the end. Pleasant and airy, it was the smallest of the private rooms, although nicely furnished in pink and blue. A bed, a closet, a chest of drawers, a washstand with a blue porcelain jug and basin, a dressing table and a small claw-footed stool with a tapestry cushion.

Léonie stepped out of her bedraggled evening dress, letting it fall to the ground, and untied her petticoats. The lace hem of the dress was gray, grimy, hanging torn in several places. The maid would have a task to repair it. With clumsy fingers, she unlaced her corset and undid the hooks until she could wriggle out, then threw it over the chair. She splashed a little of last evening's water, now ice-cold, on her face, then slipped on her nightdress and crawled into bed.

SHE WAS WOKEN some hours later by the sounds of the servants.

Realizing she was hungry, she rose quickly and drew her own curtains and pinned back the shutters. Daylight had brought the unremarkable world back to life. She marveled, after the excitements of last evening, at how Paris outside her window looked entirely unchanged. As she brushed her hair, she examined her reflection in the looking glass for signs of the night on her face. Disappointingly, there were none.

Ready for breakfast, Léonie put on her heavy blue brocade dressing gown over her white cotton nightdress, fastening the ties at the waist with a lavish double bow, then stepped out into the passageway.

The aroma of freshly brewed coffee rushed to meet her as she entered the drawing room, then came to a standstill. Unusually, both M'man and Anatole were already seated at the table. Most often, Léonie ate breakfast alone.

Even at this early hour, their mother's toilette was immaculate. Marguerite's dark hair was twisted artfully into her habitual chignon, and she had a dusting of powder on her cheeks and neck. She sat with her back to the window, but in the unforgiving light of morning, the faintest lines of age around her eyes and her mouth were discernible. Léonie noticed she was wearing a new negligé—pink silk with a yellow bow—and sighed. Presumably another gift from the pompous Du Pont.

The more generous he is, the longer we shall have to put up with him.

Feeling a stab of guilt at her uncharitable thoughts, Léonie walked to the table and kissed her mother on the cheek with more enthusiasm than usual.

"*Bon matin*, M'man," she said, then turned to greet her brother.

Her eyes flashed wide at the sight of him. His left eye was swollen shut, one hand was wrapped in a white bandage and there was a ring of green and purple bruising around his jaw.

"Anatole, what on earth—"

He leapt in. "I have been telling M'man how we were caught up in the protests at the Palais Garnier last evening," he said sharply, fixing her with a look. "And how I was unlucky enough to take a few blows."

Léonie looked at him in astonishment.

"It has even made the front page of *Le Figaro*," Marguerite said, tapping the newspaper with her immaculate nails. "When I think of what might have happened! You could have been killed, Anatole. Thank goodness he was there to look after you, Léonie. Several dead, it claims here."

"Don't fuss, M'man, I've already been checked by the doctor," he said. "It looks worse than it is."

Léonie opened her mouth to speak and then closed it again, catching a warning glance from Anatole.

"More than a hundred arrests," Marguerite continued. "Several dead! And explosions! At the Palais Garnier, I ask you. Paris has become intolerable. The city is quite lawless. Really, I cannot bear it."

"There is nothing whatsoever for you to bear, M'man," Léonie said impatiently. "You were not there. I am fine. And Anatole—" She broke off and fixed him with a long stare. "Anatole has told you he is fine. You are only distressing yourself."

Marguerite gave a wan smile. "You have no idea what a mother suffers."

"Nor do I wish to," Léonie muttered under her breath, taking a piece of sourdough bread and spreading it liberally with butter and apricot preserve.

For a while, breakfast continued in silence. Léonie continued to throw inquiring glances at Anatole, which he ignored.

The maid came in with the post on a tray.

"Anything for me?" said Anatole, gesturing with his butter knife.

"Nothing, *chéri*. No."

Marguerite picked up a heavy cream envelope with a look of puzzlement on her face. She examined the postmark.

Léonie saw the color slip from her mother's cheeks.

"If you will excuse me," she said, rising from the table and leaving the room before either of her children could protest.

The moment she was gone, Léonie turned on her brother.

"What on earth happened to you?" she hissed. "Tell me. Before M'man returns."

Anatole put down his coffee cup. "I regret to say that I found myself in a disagreement with the croupier at Chez Frascati. He was trying to swindle me, I knew it, and I made the mistake of taking it up with the manager."

"And?"

"And," he sighed. "The long and the short of it is that I was escorted from the premises. I had not gone more than five hundred yards when I was set upon by a pair of ruffians."

"Sent from the club?"

"I assume so, yes."

She stared, suspicious suddenly that there was more to the situation than Anatole was admitting. "Do you owe money there?"

"A little, but . . ." He shrugged, and another flicker of discomfort snaked across his face. "Coming on the heels of all that has gone before this year, it has made me consider it might be wise to make myself scarce for a week or so," he added. "Get out of Paris, just till the fuss has died down."

Léonie's face fell. "But I could not bear it if you left. Besides, where would you go?"

Anatole put his elbows on the table and dropped his voice. "I have an idea, *petite*, but I will need your assistance."

The thought of Anatole going away, even for a few days, did not bear thinking about. To be alone in the apartment with her mother and the tedious Du Pont. She poured herself a second cup of coffee, added three spoonfuls of sugar.

Anatole touched her arm. "Will you help me?"

"Of course, anything, but I—"

At that moment, their mother reappeared in the doorway. Anatole pulled back, touching his finger to his lips. Marguerite was holding both the envelope and the letter in her hand. Her pink-painted nails looked very bright against the somber cream of the writing paper.

Léonie colored.

"*Chérie*, don't blush so," Marguerite said, walking back to the table. "It is almost indecent. You look like a shopgirl."

"Sorry, M'man," replied Léonie, "but we were concerned, Anatole and I both, that you had . . . perhaps received bad news."

Marguerite said nothing, just stared intently at the letter.

"Who is the letter from?" Léonie asked in the end, when her mother still showed no signs of responding. Indeed, she gave the impression that she had almost forgotten they were there at all.

"M'man?" said Anatole. "May I fetch you something? Do you feel un-well?"

She raised her huge brown eyes. "Thank you, *chéri*, but no. I was . . . sur-prised, that is all."

Léonie sighed. "Who . . . is . . . the . . . letter . . . from?" she repeated crossly, pausing between each word as if talking to a particularly stupid child.

Marguerite finally gathered herself. "The letter comes from the Domaine de la Cade," she said quietly. "From your tante Isolde. The widow of my half-brother, Jules."

"What!" exclaimed Léonie. "The uncle who died in January?"

"Passed away, *disparu*. 'Died' is so vulgar," she corrected, although Léonie could hear that her heart was not in the rebuke. "But yes, in point of fact, the same."

"Why is she writing to you so long after the event?"

"Oh, she has written on a couple of previous occasions," Marguerite re-plied. "Once on the occasion of their marriage, then once again to inform me of Jules's death and the details of his funeral." She paused. "It is to my regret that ill health prevented me from making the journey and at such a time of the year."

Léonie knew perfectly well that her mother would never have returned to the house in which she had grown up outside Rennes-les-Bains, regard-less of the season or circumstance. Marguerite and her half-brother were es-tranged.

Léonie knew the bare bones of the story from Anatole. Marguerite's father, Guy Lascombe, had married young and in haste. When his first wife died giv-ing birth to Jules some six months later, Lascombe immediately gave his son into the care of a governess, then a series of tutors, and returned to Paris. He paid for his son's education and the upkeep of the family estate, and when Jules came of age, he settled a fair annual allowance on him but otherwise paid him no more attention than before.

Only at the end of his life had Grandpère Lascombe married again, al-though he had continued to live much the same dissolute life. He dispatched his gentle wife and tiny daughter to live at the Domaine de la Cade with Jules, visiting only when the mood took him. From the pained expression that came over Marguerite's face on the rare occasion the subject of her childhood came up, Léonie understood her mother had been less than happy.

Grandpère Lascombe and his wife had been killed one night when their carriage overturned. When the will was read, it transpired that Guy had left his entire estate to Jules, with not a sou for his daughter. Marguerite fled instantly north, to Paris, where, in the February of 1865, she had met and married Leo Vernier, a radical idealist of fiercely Republican sympathies. Since Jules was a supporter of the ancien régime, there had been no contact between the half-siblings from that point onward.

Léonie sighed. "Well, then why is she writing to you again?" she demanded.

Marguerite looked down at the letter, as if she could still not quite believe the contents of it.

"It is an invitation for you, Léonie, to pay a visit. For some six weeks indeed."

"What!" Léonie shrieked, and all but snatched the letter from her mother's fingers. "When?"

"*Chérie*, please."

Léonie paid no attention. "Does Tante Isolde give an explanation for why she is issuing such an invitation now?"

Anatole lit a cigarette. "Perhaps she wishes to make amends for her late husband's lack of familial duty."

"It is possible," Marguerite said, "although there is nothing in the letter to suggest that is the intention behind the invitation."

Anatole laughed. "It is hardly the manner of thing one would commit to paper."

Léonie folded her arms. "Well, it is quite absurd to imagine that I should accept an invitation to sojourn with an aunt to whom I have never been introduced, and for so prolonged a period. Indeed," she added belligerently, "I can think of nothing worse than being buried in the country with some elderly widow talking about the old days."

"Oh, no, Isolde is quite young," said Marguerite. "She was many years Jules's junior, little more than thirty years of age, I believe."

For a moment, silence fell over the breakfast table.

"Well, I shall certainly decline the invitation," Léonie said in the end.

Marguerite looked across the table at her son. "Anatole, what would you advise?"

"I do not wish to go," said Léonie, even more firmly.

Anatole smiled. "Come now, Léonie, a visit to the mountains? It sounds just the thing. You were telling me only last week how bored you had become of life in town and that you stood in need of a rest."

Léonie looked at him in astonishment. "I did, yes, but—"

"A change of scenery might restore your spirits. Besides, the weather in Paris is intolerable. Blustery and wet one day, and temperatures that would not shame the Algerian deserts the next."

"I own that is true, but—"

"And you were telling me how much you wished for an adventure, yet when an opportunity presents itself, you are too timid to take it."

"But Tante Isolde might be thoroughly disagreeable. And how would I occupy my time in the country? There will be nothing for me to do." Léonie threw a challenging glance at her mother. "M'man, you never talk about the Domaine de la Cade with anything other than dislike."

"It was a long time ago," Marguerite said quietly. "Perhaps things are different."

Léonie tried an alternative approach.

"But the journey will take days and days. I cannot possibly travel so far. Not without a chaperone."

Marguerite let her gaze settle on her daughter. "No, no . . . of course not. But as it happens, last evening General Du Pont suggested he and I might visit the Marne Valley for a few weeks. If I were able to accept his invitation . . ." she broke off and turned to her son. "Might I prevail upon you, Anatole, to accompany Léonie to the Midi?"

"I am certain I could be spared for a few days."

"But, M'man," Léonie objected.

Her brother talked over her. "I was just saying how I was considering a few days out of town. This way, the two things could be combined to everybody's satisfaction. And," he added, fixing his sister with a conspiratorial smile, "if you are anxious about being so far from home, *petite*, and alone in an unfamiliar environment, I am sure Tante Isolde could be prevailed upon to extend her invitation to me also."

At last, Léonie caught up with Anatole's reasoning. "Oh," she said.

"Could you be spared for a week or two, Anatole?" Marguerite pressed.

"*Pour ma petite soeur*, anything," he said. He smiled at Léonie. "If you wish to accept the invitation, then I am at your service."

She felt the first prickling of excitement. To be at liberty to walk in the open countryside and to breathe unpolluted air. To be free to read what she wished and when she wished without fear of criticism or rebuke.

To have Anatole to myself.

She weighed the matter a little longer, not wishing it to be obvious that she and Anatole were in league together. The fact that her mother had not cared for the Domaine de la Cade did not mean that she would not. She looked sideways at Anatole's battered, handsome face. She had thought the whole business behind them. Last evening had brought it home to her that it was not.

"Very well," she said, feeling a rush of blood to her head. "If Anatole will accompany me and perhaps stay until I am comfortably settled, then yes, I shall accept." She turned to Marguerite. "M'man, please would you write to thank Tante Isolde and say that I—*we*—will be delighted to accept her generous invitation."

"I shall send a wire and confirm the dates she has suggested."

Anatole grinned. He raised his coffee cup. "*A l'avenir*," he said.

Léonie returned the toast. "To the future." She laughed. "And to the Domaine de la Cade."

Part II

Paris
October 2007

9

Friday, October 26

Meredith Martin stared at her reflection in the window as the train hurtled toward the Eurostar terminal in Paris. Black hair, white face. Stripped of color, she didn't look so good.

She glanced at her watch.

A quarter of nine. Nearly there, thank God.

The gray backs of houses and small towns flashed by in the gloom, more frequent now. The compartment was pretty empty. A couple of French businesswomen in pressed white shirts and gray pantsuits. Two students asleep on their backpacks. The soft tapping of computer keys, low calls made on cell phones, the rustle of the late-edition newspapers—French, English, American. Across the aisle, a quartet of lawyers in striped shirts and chinos with razorsharp creases, heading home for the weekend. Talking loudly about a fraud case, their table covered in glass bottles and plastic cups. Beer, wine, bourbon.

Meredith's eyes drifted to the glossy hotel brochure on the table, even though she'd read it through plenty of times already.

L'HÔTEL DOMAINE DE LA CADE

RENNES-LES-BAINS

11190

Set in delightful wooded parkland above the picturesque town of Rennes-les-Bains in the beautiful Languedoc, the Hôtel Domaine de la Cade is the epitome of nineteenth-century grandeur and elegance, but with all the comfort and leisure facilities expected by the discriminating twenty-first-century visitor. The hotel is situated on the location of the original *maison de maître,* which was partially destroyed by fire in 1897. Run as a hotel since the 1950s, it reopened after a major refurbishment under new management in 2004 and is now recognized as one of the premier hotels in southwest France.

For full tariff and detailed facilities, see opposite.

The same information was repeated in French.

It sounded great. Come Monday, she'd be there. It was her treat to herself, a couple of days of five-star luxury after all the budget flights and cheap motels. She pushed the brochure back into her transparent plastic travel file with the receipt confirming her reservation and put the whole thing back in her purse. She stretched her long, slim arms above her head, then rolled her head. She couldn't remember when she'd last been so tired.

Meredith had checked out of her hotel in London at noon, had lunch at a café close by the Wigmore Hall before taking in an afternoon concert—really dull—then grabbed a sandwich at Waterloo station before boarding the train, hot and exhausted.

After all that, they'd been late leaving. When they finally got going, she spent most of the first part of the journey in a daze, staring out the window, watching the green English countryside at dusk flash by, rather than typing up her notes. Then the train plunged beneath the channel and was swallowed up in the concrete of the tunnel. The atmosphere became oppressive, but at least it killed the cell phone chatter. Thirty minutes later, they emerged on the other side to the flat, brown landscape of northern France.

Chalet-style farmhouses, the flash of small towns, and long, straight farm tracks looking as though they led to nowhere. One or two larger towns, the slag heaps grassed over by time. Then Charles de Gaulle Airport and the suburbs, *la banlieue,* the drab and depressing rent-controlled high-rises that stood mute on the outskirts of the French capital.

Meredith leaned back in her seat and let her thoughts wander. She was nearly halfway through a four-week research trip to France and the UK, writing a biography of the nineteenth-century French composer Achille-Claude Debussy and the women in his life. After a couple of years of researching and planning—but getting nowhere—she'd caught a break. Six months ago, a small start-up academic press made a modest offer for the book. The advance wasn't great but, given that she didn't have a reputation in the field of music criticism, it was pretty good. Enough to make her dream of coming to Europe a reality. She was determined to write not just another Debussy memoir but *the* book, *the* biography.

Her second piece of luck had been getting a part-time teaching post at a private college outside Raleigh-Durham, starting the spring semester. It had the advantage of being close to where her adoptive parents now lived—which saved on laundry, phone bills and groceries—and not far from her alma mater, the University of North Carolina.

After ten years of paying her way through college, Meredith had racked up a lot of debt, and money was tight. But with what she made from teaching piano, combined with the advance from the publishing company and now the promise of a regular salary, she summoned up the courage to go ahead and book the tickets to Europe.

The manuscript was due to her publisher at the end of April. Right now, she was on track. In fact, ahead of schedule. She had spent ten days in England. Now she had a bit more than two weeks in France, Paris mostly, but she'd also scheduled a quick trip down to a small town in the southwest, Rennes-les-Bains. Hence the couple of days at the Domaine de la Cade.

The official reason for the detour was that she needed to check out a lead about Debussy's first wife, Lilly, before heading back to Paris. If it had been only a matter of tracking down the first Mrs. Debussy, she wouldn't have gone to so much trouble. It was an interesting piece of research, sure, but her leads were pretty tenuous and hardly essential to the book overall. But she had another motive for going to Rennes-les-Bains, a personal one.

Meredith reached into the inside pocket of her purse and pulled out a manila envelope with DO NOT BEND printed on it in red. She slid out three old sepia photographs, the corners dog-eared and bent, and a printed sheet of piano music. She looked at the now-familiar faces, as she'd done so many times before, before turning her attention to the piece of music. Handwritten on yellow manuscript paper, it was a simple melody in common time, in the key of A minor, the title and the date hand-printed in old-fashioned italic script at the top: SEPULCHRE 1891.

She knew it by heart—every bar, every semiquaver, every harmony. The music—plus the three photos she carried with it—was the only thing Meredith had inherited from her birth mother. An heirloom, a talisman.

She was well aware the trip might turn up nothing of interest. It was a long time ago; the stories were faded. On the other hand, Meredith figured she couldn't be worse off than she was right now. Knowing virtually nothing about her family's past, needing to know something. For the price of the air ticket, it seemed worth it.

Meredith realized the train was slowing. The rail tracks had multiplied. The lights of the Gare du Nord were coming into view. The atmosphere in the carriage shifted again. A return to the real world, a sense of purpose at the end of a shared journey nearly over. Ties straightened, coats reclaimed.

She gathered up the photos and music, and her other papers, and slipped everything back into her purse. She took a green scrunchie from her wrist, twisted her black hair up into a ponytail, ran her fingers through her bangs and stepped out into the aisle.

With her sharp cheekbones, clear brown eyes and petite figure, Meredith looked more like a senior in high school than a twenty-eight-year-old academic. At home, she still carried her ID if she wanted to be sure of getting served in a bar. She reached up to the luggage rack for her jacket and tote bag, revealing a tanned, flat stomach between her green top and Banana Republic denims, aware that the four guys across the aisle were staring.

Meredith put the jacket on.

"Have a good trip, guys." She grinned, then headed for the door.

A WALL OF SOUND hit her the second she stepped down to the platform. People shouting, rushing, crowds everywhere, waving. Everybody in a hurry.

Announcements were blaring out over the loudspeakers. Information about the next departure, introduced by a kind of fanfare on a glockenspiel. It was totally crazy after the hushed silence of the train. Meredith smiled, breathing in the sights, smells, character of Paris. Already she felt like a different person.

Hoisting her bags high on each shoulder, she followed the signs across the station concourse and got in line for a taxi. The guy in front of her was shouting into his cell and waving a Gitane wedged deep between his fingers. Blue-white tendrils of vanilla-scented smoke twisted up into the night air, silhouetted against the balustrades and shutters of the buildings opposite.

She gave the address to the driver, a hotel in the fourth arrondissement, on the rue du Temple in the Marais district, which she'd picked for its central location. It was good for the regular tourist stuff if she had time—the Centre Pompidou and Musée National Picasso were nearby—but mostly for the Conservatoire, and the various concert halls, archives and private addresses she needed to visit for Debussy.

The driver put her tote bag in the trunk, then slammed her door and climbed in. Meredith was thrown back in her seat as the taxi accelerated sharply into the crazy Parisian traffic. She put her arm protectively around her purse and hugged it tight to her, watching as the cafés, the boulevards, the scooters and streetlamps zoomed past.

Meredith felt she knew Debussy's muses, mistresses, lovers, wives—Marie Vasnier; Gaby Dupont; Thérèse Roger; his first wife, Lilly Texier; his second, Emma Bardac; his beloved daughter, Chouchou. Their faces, their stories, their features were right there, at the front of her mind—the dates, the references, the music. She had a first draft of the biography, and she was pretty satisfied with how the text was shaping up. What she needed now was to bring them to life on the page, a little more color, a little nineteenth-century atmosphere.

From time to time, she worried that Debussy's life was more real to her than her own, day to day. Most times, she dismissed the thought. It was good to be focused. If she wanted to hit her deadline, she needed to keep at it for just a while longer.

The cab screamed to a halt.

"Hôtel Axial Beaubourg. *Voilà*."

Meredith settled the fare and went inside.

THE HOTEL WAS pretty contemporary. More like a boutique hotel in New York than what she expected to find in Paris.

Hardly French at all.

It was all straight lines and glass, stylish, minimalist. The lobby was filled with blocky outsize chairs covered in black-and-white dogtooth check or lime-green or brown and white pinstripes, arranged around smoked-glass tables. Art magazines, copies of *Vogue* and *Paris-Match* were stacked in brushed-chrome racks on the walls. Huge, supersize lampshades hung from the ceiling.

Trying too hard.

At the far end of the small lobby was the bar, with a line of men and women drinking. Lots of toned flesh and good tailoring. Gleaming cocktail shakers stood on the slate counter, the glass bottles reflected in the mirror beneath blue neon lights. The rattle of ice and the clink of glasses.

Meredith pulled a credit card from her wallet, different from the one she'd been using in the UK, just in case she'd hit her limit, and approached the desk. The clerk, sleek in a gray pantsuit, was friendly and efficient. Meredith was pleased her rusty French was understood. She hadn't spoken the language in awhile.

Got to be a good sign.

Turning down the offer of help with her bags, she made a note of the password for wireless computer access, then took the narrow elevator to the third floor and walked along a dark hallway until she found the number she was looking for.

The room was pretty small but clean and stylish, everything decorated in brown, cream and white. Housekeeping had switched on the lamp beside the bed. Meredith ran her hand over the sheets. Good-quality bed linen, comfortable. Lots of space in the closet, not that she needed it. She dropped her tote on the bed, took her laptop out of her purse, put it on the glass-topped desk and plugged it in to charge.

Then she went to the window, pulled back the net curtain and opened the shutters. The sound of traffic surged into the room. Down below in the street, a glamorous young crowd was out enjoying the surprisingly mild October evening. Meredith leaned out. She could see in all four directions. A department store on the corner opposite, its shutters closed. Cafés and bars, a patisserie and a deli were all open, and music filtered out onto the sidewalks. Orange streetlamps, neon, everything floodlit or silhouetted. Nighttime tones.

With her elbows resting on the black wrought-iron balustrade, Meredith just watched awhile, wishing she had enough energy to go down and join in. Then she rubbed her arms, realizing her skin was covered in goose bumps.

Ducking back inside, she unpacked, putting her few clothes in the closet, then headed for the bathroom. It was concealed behind a curious concertina-style door in the corner of the room, again aggressively minimalist in white ceramic. She took a quick shower, then, wrapped in a terrycloth robe and with thick woolen socks on her feet, poured herself a glass of red wine from the minibar and sat down to check her e-mail.

She got a connection fast enough, but there was nothing much—a couple of e-mails from friends asking how things were going; one from her mother, Mary, checking to see that she was okay; an advertising flyer for a concert. Meredith sighed. Nothing from her publisher. The first part of the advance had been due to go into her account at the end of September, but it hadn't come through by the time she left. It was now the end of October and she was getting jumpy. She'd sent a couple of reminders and had been reassured that everything was in hand. Her financial situation wasn't too bad, at least not quite yet. She had her credit cards, and she could always borrow a little from Mary, if absolutely necessary, to tide her over. But she'd be relieved to know the money was on its way.

Meredith logged off. She drained the last of the wine, brushed her teeth and then climbed into bed with a book for company.

She lasted about five minutes.

The sounds of Paris faded. Meredith drifted asleep, the light still on, her battered copy of the stories of Edgar Allan Poe abandoned on the pillow beside her.

10

Saturday, October 27

When Meredith woke the next morning, light was streaming through the window.

She leapt out of bed. She ran a brush through her black hair, tied it back in a ponytail and pulled on jeans, a green sweater and her jacket. She checked that she had all she needed in her bag—wallet, map, notebook, sunglasses, camera—then, feeling good about the day ahead, was out of the door, taking the stairs two at a time down to the lobby.

It was a perfect fall day, bright and sunny and fresh. Meredith headed for the brasserie opposite the hotel for breakfast. Rows of round tables with faux-marble tops—pretty, though—were set out on the sidewalk to catch the best of the morning sun. Inside, all was lacquered brown wood. A long zinc counter ran the length of the room, and two middle-aged waiters in black and white were moving with astonishing speed through the crowded restaurant.

Meredith got the last free table outside, next to a group of four guys in vests and tight leather pants. They were all smoking and drinking espressos and glasses of water. To her right, two thin and immaculately dressed women sipped *café noisette* from tiny white cups. She ordered the *petit-déjeuner complet*—juice, baguette with butter and jelly, pastries and café au lait—then pulled out her notebook, a replica of Hemingway's famous moleskin jotters. She was already on number three of a pack of six, bought on special offer from Barnes & Noble for this trip. She wrote everything down, however small or insignificant. Later, she transferred the notes she thought significant to her laptop.

She planned to spend the day visiting the private locations important to Debussy, as opposed to the big public spaces and concert halls. She'd take a few photos, see how far she got. If it turned out to be a waste of time, she'd think again, but it seemed a sensible way to organize her day.

Debussy had been born in Saint-Germain-en-Laye on August 22, 1862, in what was now a commuter belt. But he was a Parisian through and through, and spent pretty much all his fifty-five years in the capital, from his childhood home in the rue de Berlin to the house at 80 Avenue du Bois de Boulogne, where he'd died on March 25, 1918, four days after the German long-range bombardment of Paris had begun. The last stop on her itinerary, maybe when she came back, would be the cimetière de Passy in the sixteenth arrondissement, where Debussy was buried.

Meredith took a deep breath. She felt right at home in Paris, in Debussy's city. Everything had been so crazy leading up to her departure, she could hardly believe she was actually here. She sat still a moment, just enjoying the scene, and being right at the heart of things. Then she got out her map and spread it on the table. The corners draped and crackled over the edge like a colorful cloth.

She tucked a few strands of hair that had come loose back behind her ears and perused the map. The first address on her list was the rue de Berlin, where

Debussy had lived with his parents and siblings from the early 1860s until he was twenty-nine years old. It was just around the block from the apartment of the Symbolist poet Stéphane Mallarmé, where Debussy had attended the famous Tuesday-afternoon salons. After World War I, like many French streets with German names, it had been renamed and was now the rue de Liège.

Meredith followed the line with her finger to the rue de Londres, where Debussy had taken a furnished apartment with his lover Gaby Dupont in January 1892. Next came an apartment in the tiny rue Gustave-Doré in the seventeenth, then just around the corner to the rue Cardinet, where they lived until Gaby walked out on him on New Year's Day 1899. Debussy remained at the same address for the next five years with his first wife, Lilly, before that relationship too broke down.

In terms of distances and planning, Paris was pretty manageable. Everything was within walking distance, helped by the fact that Debussy had spent his life within a relatively small area, a starlike quartet of streets around the Place d'Europe on the boundary of the eighth and ninth arrondissements, overlooking the Gare Saint-Lazare.

Meredith ringed each of the locations on the map with black marker pen, looked at the pattern a moment, then decided she'd start at the farthest point and work her way back in the direction of the hotel.

She packed up, struggling to get the map to fold in the right places. She finished her coffee, brushed the buttery flakes of croissant from her sweater and licked her fingers one by one, resisting the temptation to order anything else. Despite her slim and lithe appearance, Meredith loved food. Pastries, bread, cookies, all the stuff that nobody was supposed to eat anymore. She left a ten-euro note to cover the check, adding a handful of small change for a tip, then set off.

It took her just short of fifteen minutes to reach the Place de la Concorde. From there she turned north, up past the Palais de la Madeleine, an extraordinary church designed like a Roman temple, then along the Boulevard Malesherbes. After about five minutes she turned left into the Avenue Velasquez toward the Parc Monceau. After the roar of traffic on the main thoroughfare, the imposing dead-end street seemed eerily silent. Plane trees with variegated bark, mottled like the back of an old man's hand, lined the sidewalk. Many of the trunks were tagged with graffiti. Meredith glanced up at the white embassy buildings, impassive and somehow disdainful, overlooking the gardens. She stopped and took a couple of photos, just in case she didn't remember the layout precisely.

A sign on the entrance into the Parc Monceau announced winter and summer opening and closing hours. Meredith walked through black wrought-iron gates into the wide, green space, immediately finding it easy to imagine Lilly or Gaby or even Debussy himself, hand in hand with his daughter, strolling along the generous pathways. Long white summer dresses swirling in the dust or ladies sitting beneath brimmed hats on one of the green metal benches set all along the edges of the lawns. Retired generals in military uniform, and the dark-eyed children of diplomats rolling wooden hoops under the watchful gaze of their governesses. Through the trees, she glimpsed the columns of a folly in the style of a Greek temple. A little farther away there was a stone pyramid icehouse, fenced off from the public, and marble statues of the Muses. Across the park, tawny ponies roped in a line carried excited children up and down the gravel.

Meredith took plenty of photographs. Apart from the clothes and the cell phones, the Parc Monceau seemed hardly changed from the photos she'd seen from a hundred years ago. Everything was so vivid, so clear.

Having spent half an hour wandering in contented circles through the park, she finally made her way out and found herself at the subway station on the north side. The sign MONCEAU LIGNE NO. 2 above the entrance, with its elaborate art nouveau design, looked like it might have been there since Debussy's day. She took a couple more shots, then crossed the busy intersection and walked into the seventeenth arrondissement. The neighborhood seemed drab after the *fin de siècle* elegance of the park. The stores looked cheap, the buildings unremarkable.

She found the rue Cardinet easily and identified the block where, more than a hundred years ago, Lilly and Debussy had lived. She felt a prick of disappointment. From the outside, it too was plain, nondescript, dull. There was no character to it. In letters, Debussy talked of the modest apartment with affection, describing the watercolors on the walls, the oil paintings.

For a moment she thought of ringing the bell and seeing if she could persuade anyone to let her in to look around. It was here, after all, that Debussy had written the work that had transformed his life, his only opera, *Pelléas et Mélisande*. It was here that Lilly Debussy had shot herself, days before their fifth wedding anniversary, when she realized Debussy was leaving her for good to set up home with the mother of one of his piano pupils, Emma Bardac. Lilly survived, but the surgeons never got the bullet out. Meredith thought the fact that she had lived the rest of her life with a physical reminder of Debussy lodged inside her was, somehow, the most poignant—although awful—part of the whole story.

She raised her hand to the silver intercom, then checked herself. Meredith believed in the spirit of place. She bought into the idea that, in certain circumstances, a kind of echo of the past might remain. But here in the city, too much time had passed. Even if the bricks and mortar were the same, in a hundred years of bustling human life there'd be too many ghosts. Too many footsteps, too many shadows.

She turned her back on the rue Cardinet. She got out the map, folded it into a neat square, and went in search of the Square Claude Debussy. When she found it, it was, if anything, a bigger letdown. Ugly, brutalist six-story buildings, with a thrift store on the corner. And there was no one about. The whole place had an air of abandonment. Thinking of the elegant statues in the Parc Monceau celebrating writers, painters and architects, Meredith felt a spurt of anger that Paris had honored one of its most famous sons so shabbily.

Meredith headed back to the busy Boulevard des Batignolles. In all the literature she'd read about Paris in the 1890s, Debussy's Paris, it sounded like a pretty dangerous place, away from the grand boulevards and avenues. There were districts—the *quartiers perdus*— to be avoided.

She continued on into the rue de Londres, where Gaby and Debussy had rented their first apartment in January 1892, wanting to feel something, some nostalgia, some sense of place, but getting nothing. She checked the numbers, coming to a halt where Debussy's home should have been. Meredith stepped back, pulled out her notebook to confirm she'd got the number right and then frowned.

Not my day.

In the past hundred years, it looked like the building had been swallowed up by the Gare Saint-Lazare. The station had grown and grown, encroaching on the surrounding streets. There wasn't anything here to link the old days with the new. There wasn't even anything worth photographing. Just an absence.

Meredith looked around and saw a small restaurant on the opposite side of the street, Le Petit Chablisien. She needed food. Most of all, she needed a glass of wine.

She crossed the street. The menu was chalked on a blackboard on an easel on the sidewalk. The large windows were modestly covered by lace half-curtains, so she couldn't see inside. She pushed down the old-fashioned handle and a shrill bell jangled and clattered. She stepped inside and was met instantly by an elderly waiter with a crisp white linen apron tied around his waist.

"Pour manger?"

Meredith nodded and was shown to a table for one in the corner. Paper tablecloths, clunky silver knives and forks, a bottle of water waiting on the table. She ordered the plat du jour and a glass of Fitou. The meat—a *bavette*—was perfect, pink in the center, with a strong black-pepper sauce. The Camembert was ripe. While she was eating, Meredith looked at the black-and-white photographs on the walls. Images of the quartier in days gone by, the staff of the restaurant standing proudly outside, the waiters with black moustaches and crisp white collars, and the *patron* and his matronly wife in the center in their starched Sunday best. A shot of one of the old trams on the rue d'Amsterdam, another modern one of the famous tower of clocks on the front concourse of the Gare Saint-Lazare.

Best of all, though, was a photograph she recognized. Meredith smiled. Above the door to the kitchens, beside a studio portrait of a woman with a younger man and a girl with a mass of tumbling hair, was a copy of one of the most famous photographs of Debussy. Taken at the Villa Medici in Rome in 1885, when he was only twenty-three years old, he glowered out of the picture with his distinctive frowning, dark expression. His black curly hair was short over his forehead, and with the beginnings of a moustache, the image was immediately recognizable. Meredith intended to use it on the back jacket of her biography.

"He lived in this very street," she said to the waiter, while she punched in her PIN. She gestured at the photo. "Claude Debussy. Right here."

The waiter shrugged, uninterested, until he saw the size of the tip. Then he grinned.

11

The rest of the afternoon went according to plan.

Meredith worked her way through the other addresses on her list, and by the time she got back to the hotel at six, she'd visited everywhere Debussy had ever lived in Paris. She showered and changed into a pair of white pants and a pale blue sweater. She loaded the photos from her digital camera onto her laptop, checked her e-mail—still no money—had a light supper in the brasserie opposite, then rounded off the evening with a green cocktail at the hotel bar that looked gross but tasted surprisingly good.

Back in her room, she felt the need to hear a familiar voice. She called home.

"Hi, Mary. It's me."

"Meredith!"

The catch in her mother's voice brought tears to Meredith's eyes. She suddenly felt a long way from home and very much on her own.

"How are things?" she asked.

They talked for a while. Meredith filled Mary in on everything she'd done since they'd last spoken, and all the places she'd visited already since arriving in Paris, although she was painfully aware of the dollars mounting up every minute they chatted.

She heard the pause long-distance. "And how's the other project?" Mary asked.

"I'm not thinking about that right now. Too much to do here in Paris. I'll get on to it when I reach Rennes-les-Bains after the weekend."

"There's nothing to worry about," Mary said, the words coming out in a rush, making it obvious how much it was on her mind. She'd always been supportive of Meredith's need to find out about her past. At the same time, Meredith knew Mary feared what might come to light. She felt the same. What if it came out that the illness, the misery that had overshadowed her birth mother's entire life, was there in the family stretching way back? What if she started to show the same signs?

"I'm not worried," she said, a little snappy, then felt immediately guilty. "I'm good. Excited more than anything. I'll let you know how I get on. Promise."

They talked a couple of minutes more, then said goodbye.

"Love you."

"Love you too," came the answer from thousands of miles away.

ON SUNDAY MORNING, Meredith headed for the Opéra de Paris at the Palais Garnier.

Since 1989, Paris had had a new, concrete opera house at the Bastille, and so the Palais Garnier was now primarily used for ballet performances. But in Debussy's time, the exuberant, over-the-top baroque building was the place to see and be seen. The site of the notorious anti-Wagner riots in September 1891, it was also the backdrop for Gaston Leroux's novel *The Phantom of the Opera*.

It took Meredith fifteen minutes to walk to the theater, weaving in and out of the tourists looking for the Louvre, then all the way up the Avenue de l'Opéra. The building itself was pure nineteenth century, but the traffic was strictly twenty-first—totally crazy, cars, scooters, trucks, buses and bikes coming at her from all angles. Taking her life in her hands, she dodged the lanes until she made it to the island on which the Palais Garnier stood. It blew her away—the imposing facade, the grand balustrades, the rose-marble columns, the gilded statues, the ornate gold-and-white roof and green copper dome glinting in the October sunshine. Meredith tried to picture the marshy wasteland on which the theater had been constructed. Tried to imagine carriages, and women in long sweeping dresses and men in top hats, instead of trucks and cars with drivers hitting their horns. She failed. It was all too noisy, too strident to let echoes of the past slip through. She was relieved to find that because there was a charity concert later, the theater was open, even though it was Sunday.

The second she stepped inside, the silence of the historic staircases and balconies wrapped her in its arms. The Grand Foyer was just as she'd imagined from the pictures, an expanse of marble stretching before her like the nave of a monumental cathedral. Ahead of her, the Grand Escalier soared up beneath the burnished-copper dome.

Meredith walked forward. Was she allowed in here? Her sneakers squeaked on the marble. The doors to the auditorium were propped open, so she slipped inside. She wanted to see for herself the famous six-ton chandelier and the Chagall ceiling.

Down at the front, a quartet was practicing. Meredith slipped into the back row. For a moment, she felt the ghost of her former self—the performer she might have been—slide in and sit beside her.

The feeling was so strong, she almost turned to look.

As strands of repeated notes soared out of the orchestra pit and into the empty aisles, Meredith thought of the countless times she had done the same. Waiting in the wings with her violin and bow in her hand. That sharp feeling of anticipation in the pit of her stomach, half adrenaline, half fear, before stepping out before the audience. Tuning, the tiniest adjustments to the strings and bow, the shower of powdery rosin catching on the black polyester of her full-length orchestra skirt.

Mary had bought Meredith her first violin when she was eight, just after she had come to live with them for good. No more going back to her "real" mother on weekends. The case had been waiting for her on the bed in the bedroom that was to be hers, a welcome gift for a little girl bewildered by the hand life had dealt her. A child who had already seen too much.

She had seized the chance offered with both hands. Music was her escape. She had an aptitude for it, was a quick learner and a hard worker. At the age of ten, she played in a city-schools prom at the Milwaukee Ballet Company Studio at Walker's Point. Pretty soon, she was started on piano, too. Before long, music dominated her life.

Her dreams of being a professional musician lasted all the way through elementary school, through the teenage years, right up to her last year of high school. Her tutors encouraged her to apply to one of the conservatories and told her she had a good chance of being accepted. So did Mary.

But at the last minute, Meredith flunked it. Talked herself into believing she wasn't good enough. That she didn't have what it took to make it. She applied to UNC instead to major in English and was accepted. She wrapped her violin in its red silk cloth and put it away in the blue-velveteen-lined case. Loosened her valuable bows, clipped them in place in the lid. Put the block of golden rosin into its special compartment. Stood the case at the back of her closet and left it behind when she left Milwaukee and went off to college.

At UNC, Meredith studied hard and graduated magna cum laude. She still played piano on the holidays and gave lessons to the children of friends of Bill and Mary, but that was all. The violin remained at the back of the closet.

Never during that time did she think she'd done the wrong thing.

But in the last couple of years, as she discovered the tiniest connections with her birth family, she'd started to question her decision. Now, sitting in the auditorium of the Palais Garnier at the age of twenty-eight, regret for what might have been tightened like a fist around her heart.

The music stopped.

Down in the orchestra pit, someone laughed, excluding her.

The present came rushing back. Meredith stood up. She sighed, pushed her hair off her face, then quietly turned and walked out. She'd come to the Opéra in search of Debussy. All she'd succeeded in doing was raising her own ghosts.

OUTSIDE, THE SUN had come out.

Trying to shake herself out of her melancholic mood, Meredith doubled back along the side of the building and headed up the rue Scribe, intending to cut up to the Boulevard Haussmann and from there to the Paris Conservatoire in the eighth.

The sidewalk was busy. All of Paris seemed to be out enjoying the golden day, and Meredith had to dodge in and out of the crowds to get through. There was a carnival atmosphere. A busker singing on the street corner; students handing out flyers for discount meals or designer-clothing sales; a juggler with a *diabolo* shooting up and down a string suspended between two sticks, flinging it impossibly high into the air and catching it in one smooth gesture; a guy selling watches and beads out of a suitcase.

Her cell rang. Meredith stopped dead and dug around in her bag. A woman following right behind drove her stroller into her ankles.

"Excusez-moi, Madame."

Meredith raised her hand in apology. *"Non, non. C'est moi. Désolée."*

By the time she found the phone, it had stopped ringing. She stepped out of the way and accessed her list of missed calls. It was a French number, one she vaguely recognized. She was about to press redial when someone pushed a flyer into her hand.

"C'est vous, n'est-ce pas?"

Surprised, Meredith jerked her head up. "Excuse me?"

A pretty girl was staring at her. Wearing a sleeveless vest and combats, with her strawberry-blond and cornbraided hair held off her face by a bandanna, she looked like one of the many New Age travelers and hippies on the streets of Paris.

The girl smiled. "I said, she looks like you," she said, this time in English. She tapped the leaflet in Meredith's hand. "The picture on the front."

Meredith looked down at the brochure. Advertising tarot readings, palmistry and psychic insights, the front was dominated by an image of a woman with a crown on her head. In her right hand she held a sword. In her left, a set of scales. Around the hem of her long skirt was a series of musical notes.

"In fact," the girl added, "she could be you."

At the top of the smudged picture, Meredith could just make out the number eleven in roman numerals. At the bottom the words La Justice. She peered closer. It was true. The woman did look kind of like her.

"I can't really see it," she said, then colored up at the lie. "I'm leaving town tomorrow, so . . ."

"Keep it anyway," the girl insisted. "We're open seven days a week, and we're only just round the corner. Five minutes' walk."

"Thanks, but it's not my kind of thing," Meredith said.

"My mother is very good."

"Mother?"

"She does the tarot readings," the girl explained. "Interprets the cards. You should come."

Meredith opened her mouth and then shut it again. No sense getting into an argument. Easier to take it and throw it in the trash later. With a tight smile, she pushed the brochure into the inside pocket of her denim jacket.

"There's no such thing as coincidence, you know," the girl added. "Everything happens for a reason."

Meredith nodded, unwilling to prolong the one-sided conversation, then moved away, still clutching her cell phone in her hand. At the corner, she stopped. The girl was still standing in the same place, watching her.

"You do look just like her," she called out. "Only five minutes from here. Seriously, you should come."

12

Meredith forgot all about the flyer tucked inside her jacket pocket. She returned the call that had come through on her cell—just the French travel agent confirming her hotel reservation—and rang the airline to check her departure time the following day.

She got back to the hotel at six, feeling tired and with sore feet from pounding the streets all afternoon. She uploaded the day's images onto the hard drive of her laptop, then started the process of transcribing the notes she'd made in the last three days. She grabbed a sandwich from the brasserie opposite at nine-thirty and ate in her room as she carried on working. At eleven, she was through. Totally up-to-date.

She climbed in to bed and switched on the TV. She channel-surfed awhile, looking for the familiar tones of CNN but finding only a fuzzy French flic movie on FR3, *Colombo* on TF1 and porn masquerading as art on Antenne 2. She gave up and read for a while instead before turning off the light.

Meredith lay in the comfortable semidark of the room, her hands above her head and her toes buried deep in the crisp, white sheets. Gazing at the ceiling, her mind wandered to the weekend when Mary had shared what little she knew about her birth family.

The Pfister hotel, Milwaukee, December 2000. The Pfister was where they went for every major family celebration—birthdays, weddings, special occasions—usually just for dinner, but this time they were booked for the whole weekend, a belated treat for Meredith's birthday and Thanksgiving, and to do a little early Christmas holiday shopping.

The hotel's elegant, understated nineteenth-century ambience, the colors, the *fin de siècle* style, the golden cornices, the pillars, the wrought-iron balustrades and elegant white net curtains on the glass doors. Meredith went down alone to the lobby café to wait for Bill and Mary. She settled herself in the corner of a deep sofa and ordered her first legal glass of wine in a bar: Sonoma-Cutrer chardonnay—$7.50 a pop but worth it. Buttery, holding the scent of the cask in its yellow tones.

How crazy, of all things, to remember that.

Outside, snow had been falling. Steady flakes, persistent in a white sky, covering the world with silence. At the counter of the bar, an old lady in a red coat and a woolen hat pulled low over her brow. She shouted at the bartender: "Speak to me! Why don't you speak to me?" Like the woman in Eliot's *The Waste Land.* Her fellow guests in the bar drinking Miller Genuine Draft, and two young guys with bottles of Sprecher Amber and Riverwest Stein. Like Meredith, they pretended not to notice the crazy.

Meredith had just split from her boyfriend, so was happy to be off campus for the weekend. He was a visiting math professor on a sabbatical to UNC. They had fallen into the affair. A lock of hair pushed back from her face in the bar. Him sitting on the edge of the piano stool while she played. A hand dropped casually on her shoulder in the darkened library stacks late at night. It was never destined to go anywhere—they wanted different things—and Meredith wasn't heartbroken. But the sex had been great, and the relationship had been fun while it lasted.

Even so, it had been good to be home.

They talked most of the cold, snowbound weekend, Meredith asking Mary all the questions about her birth mother's life and early death, all the stuff she'd always wanted to know but had been afraid to hear. The circumstances of her adoption, her mother's suicide, the painful memories like splinters of glass that she carried beneath her skin.

Meredith knew the basics. Her birth mother, Jeanette, had become pregnant at a tailgate party in high school, not even realizing it until it was too late to do anything about it. For the first few years, Jeanette's mother, Louisa, had tried to be supportive, but her swift death from cancer robbed Meredith of a reliable and stable influence in her life, and things quickly deteriorated. When things got really bad, it was Mary—a distant cousin of Jeanette's—who stepped in until finally it became clear that for her own safety Meredith could not go back. When Jeanette killed herself two years later, it made sense for the relationship to be put on a more formal basis, and Mary and her husband, Bill, adopted Meredith. Although she kept her surname and continued to call

Mary by her Christian name, as she always had, Meredith at last felt free to think of Mary as her mother.

It was in the Pfister hotel that Mary had given Meredith the photographs and the piece of piano music. The first was a shot of a young man in soldier's uniform, standing in a village square. Black, curly hair, gray eyes and a direct gaze. There was no name, but the date, 1914, the photographer and the place, Rennes-les-Bains, were printed on the back. The second was of a little girl in old-fashioned clothes. There was no name, no date, no place. The third was of a woman Meredith knew was her grandmother, Louisa Martin, taken some years later—late 1930s, early 1940s, judging by her clothes—seated at a grand piano. Mary explained that Louisa had been a concert pianist of some reputation. The piece of music in the envelope had been her signature piece. She played it for every encore.

As she looked at the photograph for the first time, Meredith wondered whether if she'd known about Louisa earlier, she would have stuck with it. Not turned her back on a music career. She didn't know. She couldn't remember her birth mother, Jeanette, playing the piano or singing. Only the shouting, the crying, and what came after.

Music had come into Meredith's life when she was eight years old, or so she'd thought. To discover that there'd been something there all along, lying undiscovered beneath the surface, changed the story. That snowbound weekend in December 2000, Meredith's world shifted. The photos, the music became an anchor, connecting her to a past that she knew she would go in search of one day.

Seven years on, she was finally doing it. Tomorrow she'd be in Rennes-les-Bains in person, a place that she'd imagined so many times. She just hoped there was something there for her to find.

She glanced at her cell. Twelve-thirty-three.

Not tomorrow, today.

WHEN MEREDITH WOKE in the morning, her nighttime nerves had evaporated. She was looking forward to getting out of town. Whatever she achieved, one way or the other, a few days of R&R in the mountains was just what she needed.

Her flight to Toulouse wasn't until mid-afternoon. She had done everything she'd intended to do in Paris and didn't really want to start something new before going off the clock, so she stayed in bed reading awhile, then got up and had brunch in the sun at her regular brasserie before setting out to see some of the regular tourist sites.

She wound her way in and out of the shadows of the familiar colonnades on the rue du Rivoli, dodging swarms of students with backpacks and parties of tourists on the *Da Vinci Code* trail. She considered the Pyramide du Louvre, but the length of the entrance line put her off.

She found a green metal chair in the Tuileries gardens, wishing she'd worn something lighter. It was hot and humid, crazy weather for late October. She loved the city, but today the air seemed thick with pollution, gas fumes from the traffic and cigarette smoke from the café terraces. She thought about heading for the river to take a ride on a Bateau Mouche. She considered paying a visit to Shakespeare & Co., the legendary bookstore on the Left Bank, almost a shrine for Americans visiting Paris. But she couldn't get the energy. Truth was, she wanted to do the tourist stuff but without having to mix with any tourists.

Plenty of the places she might have visited were closed so, falling back on Debussy, Meredith decided to return to his childhood home in the rue de Liège, called the rue de Berlin in 1890. Tying her jacket round her hips, no longer needing the map to find her way through the network of streets, she set off. She walked fast, efficiently, taking a different route this time. After five minutes she stopped and, shielding her eyes with her hand, glanced up to get a proper look at the enamel street sign.

She raised her eyebrows. Without intending it, she'd ended up in the rue de la Chaussée d'Antin. She looked up and down the street. In Debussy's day, the notorious Cabaret Grande-Pinte had stood at the top of the street, near the Place de la Trinité. A little farther down was the famous seventeenth-century Hôtel-Dieu. And at the bottom of the street, pretty much where she was standing, in fact, was Edmond Bailly's notorious esoteric bookstore. There, in the glory days of the turn of the century, poets and occultists and composers had met to talk through new ideas, of mysticism and the power of symbol, of impression rather than definition, alternative worlds. In Bailly's bookshop, the prickly young Debussy would never have had to explain himself.

Meredith checked the street numbers.

Right off, her enthusiasm collapsed in on itself. She was standing right where she needed to be—except there was nothing to see. It was the same problem she'd run up against all weekend. New buildings had replaced old, new streets had expanded, old addresses eaten up by the remorseless march of time.

No. 2 rue de la Chaussée d'Antin was now a featureless modern concrete building. There was no bookstore, no neat *fin de siècle* facade. There wasn't even a plaque on the wall.

Then Meredith noticed a narrow door set right back in the masonry, hardly visible from the street at all. On it was a colorful hand-painted sign.

SORTILÈGE. TAROT READINGS.

Beneath, in smaller letters: FRENCH AND ENGLISH SPOKEN.

Her hand flew to the pocket of her denim jacket. She could feel the folded square of paper, the flyer the girl had given her yesterday, right where she'd put it. She'd forgotten all about it. She pulled it out and stared at the picture. It was blurred and badly photocopied, but there was no denying the resemblance.

She looks like me.

Meredith glanced back to the sign. Now the door stood open. As if someone had slipped out when she wasn't looking and undone the latch. Meredith took a step closer and peered inside. There was a small lobby with purple walls, decorated with silver stars and moons and astrological symbols. Mobiles of crystals or glass, she wasn't certain which, were spiraling down from the ceiling, catching the light.

Meredith pulled herself up. Astrology, crystals, fortune-telling—she didn't buy any of it. She didn't even check her horoscope in the paper, although Mary did religiously every morning, while drinking her first cup of coffee of the day. It was like a ritual.

Meredith didn't get it. The idea that the future was somehow already there, all written out, seemed plain crazy. It was too fatalistic, too much like handing over responsibility for your own life.

She stepped back from the door, impatient with herself. Why was she still standing here? She should move on. Put the flyer out of her mind.

It's stupid. Superstition.

Yet at the same time, something kept her from walking away. She was interested, an academic rather than an emotional interest. The coincidence of the picture? The happenstance of the address? She wanted to go in.

She shuffled forward again. Leading up from the lobby was a narrow flight of stairs, the treads painted alternately red and green. At the top she could see a second door just visible through a covering of yellow wooden beads. Sky blue.

So much color.

She'd read that certain people saw music in their heads in color. Symesthesia? Synesthesia? Was that it?

It was cool inside. Air trickled from a rattling old fan above the door. Particles of dust were dancing in the sluggish October air. If she really wanted some *fin de siècle* atmosphere, what better way than to have the same kind of experience that might have been on offer, right here, a hundred years ago?

It's research really.

For a moment, everything hung in the balance, as if the building itself was holding its breath. Waiting, watching. Holding the flyer in her hand, like some kind of talisman, Meredith stepped inside. Then she put her foot on the bottom step and went up.

MANY HUNDREDS OF MILES to the south, in the beech woods above Rennes-les-Bains, a sudden breath of wind lifted the copper leaves on the branches of the ancient trees. The sound of a long-dead sigh, like fingers moving lightly over a keyboard.

Enfin.

The shifting of light upon the turn of a different stair.

13

Domaine de la Cade

O*ui, Abbé, et merci à vous pour votre gentillesse. A tout à l'heure.*"
Julian Lawrence held the phone in his hand a moment, and then replaced the receiver. Tanned and in good shape, despite his graying hair he looked younger than his fifty-some years. He pulled a package of cigarettes from his pocket, flipped open his Zippo and lit a Gauloise. The vanilla smoke wreathed up into the still air.

The arrangements for this evening's service were in place. Now, provided his nephew Hal behaved appropriately, everything should go off satisfactorily. He sympathized with the boy, but it was awkward that Hal had been asking questions around the town about his father's accident. Stirring things up. He had even approached the coroner's office to query the cause of death on the certificate. Since the officer in charge of the case in the police commissariat in Couiza was a friend of Julian's—and the only witness to the incident itself was the local drunk—the matter had been gently dealt with. Hal's questions had been seen as the understandable reaction of a grieving son rather than comments of substance.

All the same, Julian would be glad when the boy had gone. There was nothing to unearth, but Hal was digging and, sooner or later, in a small town like Rennes-les-Bains, the gossip would start. No smoke without fire. Julian was banking on the fact that once the funeral was over, Hal would leave the Domaine de la Cade and head back to England.

Julian and his brother Seymour, Hal's father, had jointly acquired the place four years before. Seymour, ten years his senior and bored after retirement from the City, was obsessed with profit forecasts and spreadsheets and how to grow the business. Julian's preoccupation was different.

From the first time he'd traveled through the region in 1997, he had been intrigued by rumors attaching to Rennes-les-Bains in general, the Domaine de la Cade in particular. The whole area was riddled with mystery and legends: allegations of buried treasure, conspiracies, cock-and-bull stories of secret societies, anything and everything, from the Templars and the Cathars back to the Visigoths, the Romans and the Celts. The one story that had caught Julian's imagination, though, was more contemporary. Written accounts, dating back to the end of the last century, of a deconsecrated sepulchre set within the grounds, a deck of tarot cards believed to have been painted as some kind of treasure map and the fire that had destroyed part of the original house.

The region around Couiza and Rennes-le-Château in the fifth century AD had been at the heart of the Visigoth empire. This was common knowledge. Historians and archaeologists had long speculated that the legendary treasure plundered by the Visigoths in the Sack of Rome had been brought to the southwest of France. There, the evidence ran out. But the more Julian discovered, the more convinced he'd become that the greatest part of the Visigoth treasure was still there for the finding. And that the cards—the originals, not printed copies—were the key.

Julian became obsessed. He applied for licenses to excavate, sinking all his money and resources into the search. His success was limited, turning up little more than a few Visigoth grave goods—swords, buckles, drinking cups, nothing special. When his permit to dig expired, he continued illegally. Like a gambler, he was hooked, convinced that it was only a matter of time.

When the hotel had come up for sale four years ago, Julian persuaded Seymour to make an offer. Ironically, despite the huge differences between them, it had turned out to be a good move. The partnership had worked well until the final few months, when Seymour had become more involved in the day-to-day running of the business. And he asked to see the books.

The sun on the lawn was strong, flooding the room through the high windows of the old study in the Domaine de la Cade. Julian glanced up at the painting on the wall above his desk. It was an old tarot symbol, similar to a figure eight lying on its side. The infinity symbol.

"Are you ready?"

Julian spun around to see his nephew, in a black suit and tie, standing in the doorway, his mop of black hair pushed back from his forehead. In his late twenties, with his broad shoulders and clear skin, Hal looked like the sportsman he had been in his university days. A rugby blue, tennis half-blue.

Julian leaned forward and ground the stub of his cigarette into the glass ashtray on the window ledge, then drained his whiskey. He was impatient for the funeral to be over and for things to get back to normal. He'd had more than enough of Hal drifting around the place.

"I'll be right with you," he said. "Two minutes."

14

Paris

M eredith reached the top of the stairs, drew back the beaded curtain and opened the bright blue door straight ahead.

The lobby inside was tiny, so confined that she could touch both walls without even stretching. To her left was a bright chart of the signs of the zodiac, a swirl of color and pattern and symbols, most of which Meredith didn't recognize. On the wall to her right hung an old-fashioned mirror with an ornate gilt frame. She checked out her reflection, then turned away and tapped on the second door straight ahead.

"Hello? Anybody here?"

There was no answer.

Meredith waited a moment, then knocked again, a little louder this time. Still nothing. She tried the handle. The door opened.

"Hi?" she said, stepping inside. "Anyone home? Hello?"

The room was small but full of life. The walls were painted in more bright colors, like a day-care center—yellow, red, green, with patterns of lines, stripes, triangles and zigzags in purple, blue, silver. A single window, right opposite the door, was covered by a curtain of transparent lilac gauze. Through it, Meredith could see the pale stone walls of the nineteenth-century building behind, with its black wrought-iron balustrade and long shuttered doors, cheered up by boxes of geraniums and tumbling purple and orange pansies.

The only pieces of furniture in the room were a small square wooden table right in the center, the legs visible beneath a black-and-white linen cloth covered with circles and more astrological symbols, and two straight-backed wooden chairs. They had woven seats, like those in the painting by van Gogh, she thought.

Meredith heard a door slam someplace else in the building, then footsteps. She could feel herself coloring. She was embarrassed to be standing there uninvited. She was about to go when a woman appeared from behind a bamboo screen on the far side of the room.

In her mid-forties, attractive, she was dressed in a fitted shirt and khaki pants, with expensively cut shoulder-length brown hair flecked with gray and an easy smile, not at all how Meredith imagined a tarot reader to look. No hoop earrings, no headscarf.

"I did knock," Meredith said awkwardly. "No one answered, so I came right on in."

The woman smiled. "That's fine."

"You're English?"

She smiled again. "Guilty as charged. I hope you haven't been waiting long?"

Meredith shook her head. "A couple of minutes."

The woman held out her hand. "I'm Laura."

They shook hands. "Meredith."

Laura pulled out a chair and gestured. "Take a seat."

Meredith hesitated.

"It's natural to feel nervous," said Laura. "Most people do their first time."

Meredith pulled the brochure from her pocket and put it down on the table.

"It's not that, it's just—a girl gave me a flyer in the street a couple of days back. Since I was passing . . ." She trailed off again. "It's kind of for research. I don't want to waste your time."

Laura took the flyer, then recognition passed across her face. "My daughter mentioned you."

Meredith's eyes sharpened. "She did?"

"The resemblance," Laura said, looking down at the figure of La Justice. "She said you were the spitting image."

She paused, as if expecting Meredith to say something. When she didn't, Laura sat down at the table. "Do you live in Paris?" she asked, gesturing to the chair opposite her.

"Just visiting."

Without quite intending to, Meredith found herself sitting down.

Laura smiled. "Was I right in thinking this is the first time you've had a reading?"

"Yes," Meredith replied, still perching on the edge of the seat.

Clear message—I'm not intending to stick around.

"Right," said Laura. "Assuming you've read the flyer, you know that a half-hour session is thirty euros; fifty for a full hour?"

"A half-hour will do fine," said Meredith.

Her mouth was suddenly dry. Laura was looking at her, *really* looking at her, as though she was trying to read every line, every nuance, every shadow of her face.

"Right you are, although I have no one after you, so if you change your mind we can always carry on. Is there some particular issue you'd like to explore, or is it just a general interest?"

"Like I said, it's research. I'm working on a biography. This street, actually right here, there was a famous bookstore that comes up a lot. The coincidence, I suppose you could say, rather appealed to me." She smiled, trying to relax herself. "Although your—your daughter, was it?"—Laura nodded—"said there was no such thing as coincidence."

Laura smiled back. "You're hoping to find some sort of echo of the past."

"That's it," Meredith said, with a sigh of relief.

Laura nodded. "Okay. Some clients have a preference for a certain type of reading. They have a particular issue they want to explore—could be work, a relationship, a major decision to make, anything, really. Others are after something more general."

"General is good."

"Right. The next decision is the deck you would like to use."

Meredith pulled an apologetic face. "I'm sorry, I really don't know anything about it. I'm happy for you to choose for me."

Laura gestured to a row of different decks of cards, all facedown, set along the side of the table. "I appreciate it's confusing to start with, but it's better if you choose. Just see if you like the feel of any in particular, okay?"

Meredith shrugged. "Sure."

Laura picked up the deck closest to her and fanned the cards across the table. They had royal blue backs with long-tailed golden stars on them.

"They're beautiful," Meredith said.

"That's the Universal Waite Tarot, a very popular deck."

The next pack had a simple white-and-red repeat pattern on the back. "This one is, in many ways, the classic deck," Laura said. "It's called the Marseille Tarot. It dates from the sixteenth century. It's a deck I occasionally use, although truthfully it's a little plain for contemporary tastes. Most querents prefer modern packs."

Meredith raised her eyebrows. "Excuse me, querent?"

"Sorry," Laura grinned. "The querent is the person having the reading, the person asking the questions."

"Right."

Meredith looked along the line and then pointed to a deck that was a little smaller than the rest. The cards had beautiful deep-green backs with filigree lines of gold and silver.

"What's this one?"

Laura smiled. "That's the Bousquet Tarot."

"Bousquet?" Meredith repeated. A memory snaked across her subconscious mind. She was sure she'd run up against that name someplace. "Is that the name of the artist?"

Laura shook her head. "It's the name of the original publisher of the deck. No one knows the artist or who commissioned the cards in the first place. Pretty much all we know is that it originates from southwest France toward the very end of the 1890s."

Meredith felt a prickling on the back of her neck.

"Where, precisely, in the southwest?"

"I can't recall exactly. Somewhere in the Carcassonne area, I think."

"I know of it," Meredith replied, picturing the map of the region in her mind. Rennes-les-Bains was right in the middle.

She suddenly became aware that Laura was looking at her with sharpened interest.

"Is there something—?"

"No, it's nothing," Meredith said quickly. "I thought the name was familiar, that's all." She smiled apologetically. "Sorry, I interrupted."

"I was just going to say that the original deck of cards—or at least some of it—is much older. We can't be sure how authentic all the images actually are, since the major arcana have characteristics that suggest they were added—or at least modified—later. The designs and the clothes of the characters on certain cards are contemporaneous with *fin de siècle* styles, whereas the minor arcana are more classical."

Meredith raised her eyebrows. "'Major arcana'? 'Minor arcana'?" She smiled. "I'm sorry, but I really know nothing about this. Can I ask a couple of questions before we go any further? Or is that not allowed?"

Laura laughed. "Of course."

"Okay, very basic to start. How many cards are there?"

"With a couple of minor contemporary exceptions, there are seventy-eight cards in a standard tarot pack, divided into the major and the minor arcana—*arcana* is the Latin word for 'secrets.' The major arcana, twenty-two cards in all, are numbered one to twenty-one—the Fool being unnumbered—and are unique to the tarot deck. Each has an allegorical picture and a set of clear narrative meanings."

Meredith glanced at the picture of La Justice on the brochure.

"Like this, for example."

"Absolutely. The remaining fifty-six cards, the minor arcana—pip cards as they're sometimes known—are divided into four suits and resemble ordinary playing cards, except that they have an extra court card. So in a standard tarot deck we have King, Queen, Knight, then the additional card—the Page—before ten. Different decks give the suits different names—pentacles or coins, cups, wands or batons, and swords. Broadly speaking, they correspond to the suits of standard playing cards: diamonds, hearts, clubs and spades."

"Right."

"Most experts agree that the earliest tarot cards, those that resemble the decks we have today, date from northern Italy in the middle of the fifteenth century. The modern tarot revival, however, began in the early years of the last century, when an English occultist, Arthur Edward Waite, produced a new deck. His key innovation was to give, for the first time, an individual and symbolic scene to each of the seventy-eight cards. Before that, the pip cards had only numbers."

"What about the Bousquet deck?"

"The court cards in each of the four suits are illustrated. The style of painting suggests they date from the late sixteenth century. Certainly pre-Waite. But the major arcana are different. The clothing of the characters is definitely eighteen-nineties European. The general consensus is that the publisher—Bousquet—didn't have a full set of cards to work from so either had the major arcana painted or else copied them in the style and character of the extant cards."

"Copied them from what?"

Laura shrugged. "From fragments of surviving cards, or possibly from illustrations of the original deck in a book. Like I said, I'm not an expert."

Meredith looked back down at the green-backed cards shot through with gold and silver. "Someone did a good job."

Laura made a fan of the suit of pentacles facing Meredith on the table, starting from the ace at the beginning to the king at the end. Then she dealt a few cards from the major arcana at the head of the deck.

"See the difference between the two styles?"

Meredith nodded. "Sure, although they're pretty similar, the colors in particular."

Laura tapped one of the cards. "Here's another unique modification in the Bousquet Tarot. As well as the names of the court cards having been changed—Maître and Maîtresse, for example, instead of King and Queen—there are personal touches in some of the major arcana too. This one, for example, card II, is usually called the High Priestess. Here, she has the title La Prêtresse. The same figure appears here in card VI too as one of the lovers—Les Amoureux. Also, if you look on card XV, Le Diable, it is the same woman again chained at the demon's feet."

"And that's unusual?"

"Many packs link cards VI and XV, but not usually II as well."

"So some person," said Meredith slowly, thinking aloud, "either independently or on instruction, went to a lot of trouble to personalize these cards."

Laura nodded. "In fact, I've sometimes wondered if the major arcana of this deck might actually be based on real people. The expressions on some of the faces seem so vivid."

Meredith glanced down at the image of La Justice on the front of the brochure.

Her face is my face.

She looked across the table at Laura, on impulse suddenly wanting to say something about the personal quest that had brought her to France. To tell her that in a matter of hours, she was heading for Rennes-les-Bains. But Laura started speaking again and the moment was lost.

"The Bousquet Tarot also respects traditional associations. For example, swords is the suit of air, representing intelligence and intellect; wands is the suit of fire, energy and conflict; cups is the suit associated with water and the emotions. Finally, pentacles"—she tapped the card of the king sitting on his throne surrounded by what looked like gold coins—"is the suit of earth, of physical reality, of treasure."

Meredith scanned the images, concentrating hard as if committing each to memory, then nodded to let Laura know she was done.

Laura cleared the table, leaving only the major arcana, which she dealt into three rows of seven cards facing Meredith, lowest number to highest. Le Mat, the unnumbered Fool, she placed alone at the top.

"You can see the major arcana in terms of a journey," Laura said. "They are the imponderables, the big issues of life that cannot be changed or fought against. Laid out like this, it's clear how these three rows represent the three different levels of development—the conscious, the unconscious and the higher consciousness."

Meredith felt her skeptical gene kick in.

This is where the facts run out.

"At the start of each row is a powerful image: Le Pagad, the Magician, at the beginning of the first row. La Force at the beginning of the second. Finally, at the head of the bottom row, we have card XV, Le Diable."

Something stirred in Meredith's mind as she looked at the image of the twisted demon. She glanced at the faces of the man and woman chained at the devil's feet with a spark of recognition. Then it faded.

"The advantage of laying the major arcana out like this is that it not only shows the journey of the fool—Le Mat—from ignorance to enlightenment, but it also makes explicit the vertical connections between the cards," Laura continued. "So, you can see how Strength is the octave of the Magician, and the Devil is the octave of Strength. Other patterns also leap out: both the

Magician and Strength have the infinity sign above their heads. Also, the Devil is raising his arm in a gesture reminiscent of the Magician."

"Like two sides of the same person."

"Could be," Laura nodded. "Tarot is all about the patterns, about the relationships between one card and another."

Meredith was only half listening. Something Laura had just said bugged her. She thought a moment, before she got it.

Octaves.

"Do you usually explain these principles in terms of music?" she asked.

"Sometimes," Laura replied. "It depends on the querent. There are lots of ways to explain how tarot can be interpreted; music is just one of them. Why do you ask?"

Meredith shrugged it off. "Because it's my area of work. I guess I was just wondering if you had somehow picked up on that." She hesitated. "I don't remember mentioning anything about it, that's all."

Laura gave a slight smile. "Does the idea bother you?"

"What, that you somehow picked it up? No," she lied. Meredith didn't like the way this was making her feel. Her heart was telling her she might learn something about herself, about who she really was. So she wanted Laura to get things right. At the same time, her head was telling her it was all irrational nonsense.

Meredith pointed to La Justice. "There are musical notes around the hem of her skirt. Weird, huh?"

"Like my daughter said, there's no such thing as coincidence. All systems of divination, like music itself, work through patterns," Laura continued. "If you're interested, there was an American cartomancer, Paul Foster Case, who came up with a whole theory linking particular cards of the major arcana to individual notes of the musical scale."

"Maybe I'll check that out," Meredith said.

Laura gathered the cards and tidied the deck. She held Meredith's gaze, and for one clear, sharp moment, Meredith was certain she was seeing right into her soul, seeing all the anxiety, the doubt—the hope, too—reflected in her eyes.

"Shall we make a start?"

Even though she knew it was coming, Meredith's heart lurched.

"Sure," she said. "Why not?"

15

Shall we stick with the Bousquet deck?" Laura said. "You clearly feel some connection with it."

Meredith looked down. The backs of the cards put her in mind of the woods around Mary's home in Chapel Hill. The colors of summer and fall all mixed up together. So different from the quiet suburbs of Milwaukee where she'd grown up.

She nodded. "Okay."

Laura removed the other three decks from the table, and the brochure too.

"As we discussed, I'll do a general reading," she said. "It's my own spread, based on a version of the Celtic cross, a ten-card reading using the whole pack, minor as well as major arcana. It will offer an excellent overview of where you are now, what has happened in your recent past and what the future might hold."

And we're back in crazy territory.

Except Meredith found she wanted to know.

"At the time the Bousquet Tarot was printed, at the end of the nineteenth century, tarot reading was still mysterious, dominated by cabals and elites." Laura smiled. "Things are different today. Modern readers seek to empower people, to give them the tools, the courage, if you like, to change themselves and their lives. A reading is more likely to be of value if the querent confronts their hidden motivations or subconscious patterns of behavior."

Meredith nodded.

"The downside with this is that there is an almost infinite variety of interpretations. Some people will tell you, for example, that a majority of major arcana cards coming up in a reading indicates that the situation is outside your control, whereas a majority of minor arcana suggests that your fate is in your own hands. All I can advise before we start is that I see a reading as a guide to what *might* happen, not what *will* happen."

"Okay."

Laura put the deck of cards down on the table between them. "Shuffle them well, Meredith. Don't hurry. And while you're doing it, think of what it is you most want to discover, what it was that brought you here today. Some people find it helps to shut their eyes."

There was a light breeze coming in through the open window, a relief after the earlier humidity. Meredith reached out and picked up the cards and began to shuffle. Slowly, the present started to recede from her conscious mind as she lost herself in the repetitive motion.

Fragments of memory, images and faces, floated into her mind in tones of sepia and gray, then melted away. Her beautiful, vulnerable, damaged mother. Her grandmother, Louisa, sitting at the piano. The serious-looking young man in military uniform.

All the family she had never known.

For a moment, Meredith felt as though she were floating, weightless. The table, the two chairs, the colors, herself, all seen from a different perspective.

"Okay. When you're ready, open your eyes." Laura's voice was very distant now, heard but not heard, like the sound of music after the note has ended.

Meredith blinked as the room rushed back to meet her, blurred at first, then somehow brighter than before.

"Now put the deck down on the table and cut it in three, using your left hand."

Meredith did so.

"Put the cards back together, the middle pile first, then the top, then the bottom." She felt Laura waiting until she was done. "Okay, the first card you're going to draw is what we call the significator. For this reading, this is the card that will represent you, the querent, the person you are now. The sex of the figure on the card isn't important, because each card carries within it archetypal masculine or feminine qualities and characteristics."

Meredith slid a card out from the middle of the deck and laid it faceup in front of her.

"La Fille d'Epées," said Laura. "The Daughter of Swords. Swords is the suit of air, remember, of intellect. In the Bousquet deck, the Daughter of Swords is a powerful figure, a thinker, someone strong. At the same time, she is someone perhaps not fully connected to others. This could be because of her youth—the card often indicates a young person—or because of decisions taken. Sometimes it can indicate someone at the beginning of a journey."

Meredith looked down at the image on the card. A slender and petite woman, wearing a knee-length red dress, with straight black hair to her shoulders. She looked like a dancer. She held the sword with both hands, neither threateningly nor as if she herself was under threat but as if she was protecting something. Behind her, a jagged mountain peak was set against a fierce blue sky dotted with white clouds.

"It is an active card," Laura said, "a positive card. One of the few unequivocally positive sword cards."

Meredith nodded. She could see that.

"Draw again," said Laura. "Put this next card beneath La Fille d'Epées to your left. This second card denotes your situation as it is now. The environment in which you are working or living at the present time, the influences working on you."

Meredith placed it in position.

"The Ten of Cups," Laura said. "Cups is the suit of water, of emotion. This is also a positive card. Ten is the number of completion. It marks the end of one cycle and the beginning of another. It suggests that you are standing upon a threshold, that you are ready to move on and to make changes from a current position, which is already one of fulfillment, of success. It's an indication of changing times to come."

"What kind of threshold?"

"It could be work, could be in your personal life, or both. Things will become clearer to you the further on in the reading we get. Draw again."

Meredith took a third card from the deck.

"Place this below and to the right of the significator," Laura instructed. "This indicates any possible obstacles in your way. Things, circumstances, people even, that might prevent you from moving on or making changes or achieving your goal."

Meredith turned the card over and placed it on the table.

"Le Pagad," said Laura. "Card I, the Magician. *Pagad* is an archaic word used in the Bousquet Tarot and not in many other decks."

Meredith looked hard at the image. "Does it represent a person?"

"Usually, yes."

"Someone to be trusted?"

"It depends. As the name suggests, the Magician may be on your side, but he—or she—may not. Often he is someone who acts as a powerful catalyst for transformation, although always with this card there is a hint of trickery, of balancing judgment with intuition. The Magician has control over all the elements—air, fire and earth—and the four suit symbols—cups, swords, wands and pentacles. Its appearance indicates perhaps someone who could use their skills, with language or knowledge, for your benefit. Equally, the person might use the same gifts to obstruct you in some way."

Meredith looked at the face on the card. Piercing blue eyes.

"Is there someone in your life you feel might have this role?"

She shook her head. "Not that I can think of."

"It could be someone from the past who, although not in your day-to-day life, still has some sort of influence over how you see yourself. Someone who, despite his or her absence, is a negative influence. Or someone you've yet to meet. Or equally, someone you do know but whose role in your life has not yet become central."

Meredith looked down at the card again, attracted by the image and the contradictions contained within it, willing it to mean something. Nothing struck her. No one came to her.

She drew another. This time her reaction was quite different. She felt a rush of emotion, of warmth. The image was of a young girl standing beside a lion. Above her head was the infinity symbol, like a crown. She was wearing a formal old-fashioned green-and-white dress with leg-of-mutton sleeves. Her copper hair tumbled in loose curls all the way down her back to a narrow waist. Exactly the way, Meredith realized, she'd always pictured Debussy's *La Damoiselle Élue*, the chosen maiden, half Rossetti, half Moreau.

Remembering what Laura had said, Meredith had no doubt that this illustration might have been based on a real person. She read the name on the card: La Force. Number VIII. The eyes were so green, so vivid.

And the longer she looked, the more sure she became that she'd seen this image—or one very similar—in a photograph or a painting or in a book. Crazy. Of course it wasn't possible. But still, the idea took root.

Meredith looked across the table at Laura.

"Tell me about this one," she said.

16

❦

"Card VIII, Strength, is associated with the star sign Leo," said Laura. "The fourth card in the reading is taken to indicate one single, overriding issue—very often unconscious, unacknowledged by the querent—that has influenced the decision to seek a reading. A powerful motivator. Something guiding the querent."

Meredith immediately protested. "But that's not—"

Laura raised her hand. "Yes, I know you told me it was chance—my daughter pressing a leaflet into your hands, you being in the area today and having time to come up—but at the same time, Meredith, there might also be something more to it. The fact that you are sitting here?" She paused. "You could have walked by. Not chosen to come in."

"Maybe. I don't know." She considered. "I guess."

"Is there a particular situation or person you might associate with this card?"

"Not that I can think of, although . . ."

"Yes?"

"The girl. Her face. There's something familiar about her, although I can't pin it down."

Meredith could almost see Laura's frown.

"What?"

Laura dropped her eyes to the four cards laid on the table. "Readings based on the Celtic Cross spread mostly have a straightforward sequential pattern." Meredith could hear the hesitation in her voice. "Even though it's early in the reading, usually by this time it's clear to me which events belong to the past, the present, and the future." She paused. "But here, for some reason, the timeline is confused. The sequence seems to be jumping backward and forward, as if there is some blurring of events. Things slipping between past and present."

Meredith leaned in. "What are you saying? That you can't interpret the cards as I'm drawing them?"

"No," she replied quickly. "No, not quite that." She hesitated again. "To be honest, Meredith, I'm not entirely sure what I'm saying." She shrugged. "Things will fall into place if we keep going."

Meredith didn't know how to react. She wanted Laura to be more explicit but couldn't think of the questions to ask to get the answers she needed, so she said nothing.

In the end, it was Laura who broke the silence.

"Draw again," she said. "The fifth card, signifying the recent past."

Meredith drew the Eight of Pentacles reversed, and pulled a face at Laura's suggestion that the card could indicate that hard work and skill might not reap the benefits they should.

The sixth card, associated with the near future, was the Eight of Wands reversed. Meredith felt the short hairs on the back of her neck stand on end. She glanced up at Laura, but she did nothing to give away that she was paying special attention to the emerging pattern.

"This is a card of motion, of clear action," Laura said. "It suggests hard work and projects coming to fruition. Things about to take off. In some ways, it is the most optimistic of the eights." She broke off and looked across at Meredith. "I assume all these references to work mean something to you?"

Meredith nodded. "I'm in the process of writing a book," she said, "so yes, it all makes sense." She paused. "Does the meaning change if the card is upside down? Like here?"

"Reversed, it indicates delay," said Laura. "A disruption of energy as a project remains suspended."

Like abandoning Paris for Rennes-les-Bains, for example, Meredith thought dryly. Like putting the personal rather than the professional center stage.

"That, unfortunately," she said with a wry smile, "also makes sense. Would you see this as a warning to not get diverted or caught up in other stuff?"

"Probably," agreed Laura, "although delay is not necessarily bad. It could be that it is the right thing for you to do at this particular time."

Meredith felt Laura waiting, watching, until she had finished with that particular card, before inviting her to draw again.

Meredith drew the seventh card and laid it down.

"This represents the environment in which current or future events are to be—or are already being—played out. Place this above card six."

The image showed a tall gray tower under a lowering sky. A single fork of lightning seemed to cut the picture in two. Meredith shivered, feeling an immediate antipathy to the card. Although she was still trying to tell herself it was all nonsense, she wished she had not drawn it.

"La Tour," she read. "Not a great card?"

"No card is either good or bad," Laura replied automatically, although her expression gave a different message. "It depends on where it comes in a reading and its relationship to the cards around it." She paused. "Having said that, the Tower is traditionally interpreted as indicating dramatic change. It can suggest destruction, chaos." She glanced up at Meredith, then back to the card. "Read positively, it's a card of liberation—when the edifice of our illusions, limitations, boundaries come crashing down, leaving us free to start afresh. A flash of inspiration, if you like. It's not necessarily negative."

"Sure, I get that," Meredith said, a little impatient. "But what about now? That's not how you're interpreting it, right?"

Laura met her gaze. "Conflict," she said. "That's how I see it."

"Between?" Meredith threw back.

"That's something only you can know. It could be what you've alluded to before—conflict between personal demands and professional ones. Equally, it could be a discrepancy between people's expectations of you and what you can give, leading to some sort of misunderstanding."

Meredith said nothing, trying to squash the thought pushing into her conscious mind from where she'd buried it.

What if I find out something about my past that changes everything?

"Is there something particular that you think this card might be referring to?" asked Laura softly.

"I . . ." Meredith started to speak, then stopped again. "No," she replied, more firmly than she felt. "Like you say, it could be so many things."

She hesitated, nervous now at what might be following, then drew again.

The next card, representing the self, was the Eight of Cups.

"You're kidding," she muttered under her breath, drawing the next card quickly. The Eight of Swords.

She heard Laura catch her breath.

Another octave.

"All the eights, what are the odds?"

Laura didn't immediately answer. "It's unusual, certainly," she said eventually.

Meredith studied the spread. It wasn't just the octaves linking the cards of the major arcana, or the repetition of the number eight. It was also the notes on the dress of La Justice, and the green eyes of the girl in La Force.

"The probability of any card being turned is, of course, the same for each," Laura said, although Meredith could see she was saying what she thought she ought to, not what she was actually thinking. "It's no more or less likely that all four of any number or picture card to turn up in a reading than for any other combination of cards."

"But have you ever had this happen before?" Meredith said, unwilling to let her off the hook. "Seriously? All of one number coming up like this?" She cast her eye over the table. "And La Tour, card XVI, too. That's a multiple of eight."

Reluctantly, Laura shook her head. "Not that I can recall."

Meredith tapped the card with her finger. "What does the Eight of Swords signify?"

"Interference. An indication of something—or someone—holding you back."

"Like Le Pagad?"

"Maybe, although . . ." Laura stopped, clearly choosing her words with care. "There are parallel stories here. On the one hand, there is the clear evidence of the imminent culmination of a major project, either work or in your personal life, or possibly both." She looked up. "Yes?"

Meredith frowned. "Go on."

"And running alongside that, there are hints of a journey or a change of circumstances."

"Okay, let's say that fits, but—"

Laura interrupted. "All the way through, I sense there's something else. It's not altogether clear, but there *is* something. This final card . . . something you are about to discover, or uncover."

Meredith's eyes narrowed. She'd been telling herself over and over how it was just a bit of harmless fun. How it didn't mean anything. So why was her heart turning somersaults?

"Remember, Meredith," said Laura urgently, "the art of divination by means of the drawing and interpretation of cards is not about saying this *will* happen or will *not* happen. It's about investigating possibilities, discovering unconscious motivations and desires that might, or might not, result in any given pattern of behavior."

"I know."

Just harmless fun.

But something about Laura's intensity, the expression of fierce concentration on her face, was making it deathly serious.

"A tarot reading should increase free will, not diminish it," Laura said, "for the simple reason that a reading tells us more about ourselves and the issues facing us. You're free to make your own decisions, better decisions. Decide which path to take."

Meredith nodded. "I understand."

"So long as you remember that."

Meredith heard the very real warning in Laura's voice. Now she had to fight the urge to get out of the chair right that second.

"This final card, card ten, will complete the reading. It goes at the top, on the right-hand side."

For a moment, Meredith's hand seemed to hover over the tarot deck. She could almost see the invisible lines connecting her skin to the green and gold and silver of the backs of the cards. Time stood still.

Then she took the card and turned it over.

A sound escaped from her lips. On the far side of the table, she was aware of Laura's hand clenched in a fist.

"Justice," Meredith said in a level voice. "Your daughter said I looked like her," she added, although she'd said it before.

Laura did not meet her eye. "The stone associated with La Justice is opal," she said. She sounds stunned, Meredith thought, as if she was reading the information from the pages of a book. "The colors associated with this card are sapphire, topaz. There is also an astrological sign linked to this card. Libra."

Meredith gave a hollow laugh.

"I'm Libra," she said. "My birthday's October eighth."

Still Laura didn't react, as if she wasn't surprised by this piece of information, either.

"La Justice in the Bousquet Tarot is a powerful card," she continued. "If you accept the idea of the major arcana being the Fool's journey from happy ignorance to enlightenment, Justice sits at the midway point."

"And it means?"

"Usually, when it comes up in a reading, it is an instruction to keep a balanced view. The querent should make sure not to be led astray but to come to a fair and appropriate understanding of the situation."

Meredith smiled. "But it's reversed," she said. She was amazed at how calm she sounded. "That changes things. Doesn't it?"

For a moment, Laura didn't answer.

"Doesn't it?" Meredith pressed.

"Reversed, the card warns of some injustice. Perhaps prejudice and bias, or a miscarriage of justice in legal terms. It also carries with it a sense of anger at being judged or judged wrongly."

"And do you think this card represents me?"

"I think it does," she said eventually. "Not only because it's come up last in the reading." She hesitated. "And not only because there is obviously the physical resemblance." She stopped again.

"Laura?" Meredith looked at her.

"Okay, I believe it represents you, but at the same time, I don't think it's indicating an injustice done to you. I'm inclined to think that it's more that you might find yourself called upon to right some wrong. You as an agent of justice." She looked up. "Maybe this was what I was sensing earlier. That there is something else—something more—lying behind the explicit stories being indicated in the spread."

Meredith cast her eyes over the ten cards lying on the table. Laura's words were spinning in her head.

It's about investigating possibilities, discovering unconscious motivations and desires.

The Magician and the Devil, both with ice-blue eyes, the former the double octave of the latter. All the eights, the number of recognition, of achievement.

Meredith reached forward and took first the fourth card from the spread and then the last. Strength and Justice.

Somehow, they seemed to belong together.

"For a moment," she said quietly, talking as much to herself as to Laura, "I thought I understood. As if, somewhere beneath the surface, it all made sense."

"And now?"

Meredith looked up. For a moment, the two women held each other's gaze.

"Now it's just pictures. Just patterns and color."

The words hung between them. Then, without warning, Laura's hands darted forward and she gathered up the cards, as if she didn't want to leave the spread intact for a moment more.

"You should take them," she said. "Work things out for yourself."

Meredith did a double take, sure she must have misheard. "Excuse me?"

Laura was holding out the cards. "This deck belongs with you."

Realizing she hadn't misunderstood, Meredith started to object.

"I couldn't possibly . . ."

But now Laura was reaching under the table. She brought out a large square of black silk and folded the cards up within it. "There," she said, pushing them across the table. "Another tarot tradition. Many people believe you should never buy a deck of cards for yourself. That you should always wait for the right deck to be given to you as a gift."

Meredith shook her head. "Laura, I can't possibly accept them. Besides, I wouldn't know what to do with them."

She stood up and put on her jacket.

Laura stood, too. "I believe you need them."

For a moment, their eyes met once more.

"But I don't want them."

If I accept them, there'll be no way back.

"The deck belongs with you." Laura paused. "And I think, deep down, you know it."

Meredith felt the room pressing in on her. The colorful walls, the patterned cloth on the table, the stars and sickle moons and suns, pulsating, growing larger, smaller, shifting shape. And there was something else, a rhythm sounding in her head, almost like music. Or the wind in the trees.

Enfin. At last.

Meredith heard the word as clearly as if she'd spoken herself. It was so sharp, so loud, that she turned around, thinking that perhaps a person had come in behind her. There was no one there.

Things shifting between past and present.

She wanted nothing to do with the cards, but in the face of Laura's determination, she felt she'd never get out of the room if she didn't accept them.

She took them. Then, without another word, she turned and ran down the stairs.

17

Meredith wandered the Parisian streets with no sense of time, holding the cards in her hands and feeling as though, at any moment, they might blow up and somehow take her with them. She didn't want them, yet she understood she wasn't going to be able to bring herself to get rid of them.

It was only when she heard the bells of the church of Saint-Gervais striking one o'clock that she realized she was on track to miss her flight to Toulouse.

Meredith pulled herself together. She flagged down a taxi and, yelling at the driver that there'd be a good tip if he could get her there quickly, they screeched out into the traffic.

They made it to rue du Temple in ten minutes flat. Meredith threw herself out of the cab and, leaving it on the meter, charged into the lobby, up the stairs and into her room. She tossed the things she'd need into her tote bag, grabbed her laptop and charger and then raced back down. She checked the stuff she wasn't taking with the concierge, confirmed she'd be back in Paris at the end of the week for a couple more nights, then jumped into the car and headed across town to Orly airport.

She made it with just fifteen minutes to spare.

The whole time, Meredith was on automatic pilot. Her efficient, organized self kicked in, but she was only going through the physical motions while her brain was elsewhere. Half-remembered phrases, ideas grasped, subtleties missed. All the things Laura had said.

How it made me feel.

Only when she was going through security did Meredith realize that in her hurry to get out of the tiny room, she'd forgotten to pay Laura for the session. A wave of embarrassment washed over her. Working out that she'd been there for at least an hour—maybe closer to two—she made a mental note to mail the money and extra besides as soon as she got to Rennes-les-Bains.

Sortilège. The art of seeing the future in the cards.

As the plane took off, Meredith pulled her notebook from her bag and started to scribble down everything she could remember. A journey. The Magician and the Devil, both with blue eyes, neither to be entirely trusted. Herself as an agent of justice. All the eights.

As the 737 swept through the blue skies of northern France, over the Massif Central, chasing the sun down to the south, Meredith listened to Debussy's *Suite Bergamasque* on her headphones and wrote until her arm ached, filling page after small, lined page with neat notes and sketches. Laura's words replayed over and over in her head, as if they were on some kind of loop, fighting with the music.

Things slipping between past and present.

And all the time, like an unwanted guest, the presence of the cards lurking in her bag in the luggage bins above her head.

The Devil's Picture Book.

Part III

Rennes-les-Bains
September 1891

18

Paris
Thursday, September 17

The decision having been made to accept Isolde Lascombe's invitation, Anatole set things in motion for immediate departure.

As soon as breakfast was finished, he went to send the wire and to purchase train tickets for the following day, leaving Marguerite to take Léonie shopping for items she might need during her month in the country. They went first to La Maison Léoty to acquire a set of expensive undergarments, which transformed her silhouette and made Léonie feel quite adult. At La Samaritaine, Marguerite bought her a new tea dress and walking suit appropriate for autumn in the country. Her mother was warm and affectionate but distant, and Léonie realized that she had something on her mind. She suspected that it was Du Pont's credit against which Marguerite made their purchases and resigned herself to the fact that they might return to Paris in November and find themselves with a new father.

Léonie was excited but also curiously out of sorts, a state of affairs she put down to the events of the previous evening. She had no chance to speak to Anatole, or to discuss with him the coincidence of timing that had led to the invitation arriving so opportunely for his needs.

After lunch, making the most of the mild and pleasant afternoon, Marguerite and Léonie went walking in the Parc Monceau, a favorite haunt of the ambassadors' children from the embassies nearby. A group of boys were playing Un, Deux, Trois Loup with great exuberance, shouting and yelling encouragement to one another. A gaggle of girls in ribbons and white petticoats, watched over by nannies and dark-skinned bodyguards, was engaged in a game of hopscotch. La Marelle had been one of Léonie's favorite childhood games, and she and Marguerite stopped to watch the girls throw the pebble into the square and jump. From the look on her mother's face, Léonie knew she too was remembering the past with affection. She took advantage of the unguarded moment.

"Why is it that you were not happy at the Domaine de la Cade?"

"It was not an environment in which I felt comfortable, *chérie*, that is all."

"But why? Was it the company? The place itself?"

Marguerite shrugged, as she always did, unwilling to be drawn.

"There must be a reason," Léonie pressed.

Marguerite sighed. "My half-brother was a strange, solitary man," she said finally. "He did not wish the company of a much younger sibling, let alone to be partly responsible for his father's second wife. We felt always like unwelcome guests."

Léonie thought a moment. "Do you think I will enjoy myself there?"

"Oh, yes, I am certain of it," Marguerite said quickly. "The estate is quite beautiful, and I imagine that in thirty years there will have been many improvements."

"And the house itself?"

Marguerite did not answer.

"M'man?"

"It was a long time ago," she said firmly. "Everything will have changed."

THE MORNING of their departure, Friday, September 18, dawned damp and blustery.

Léonie woke early, with a fluttering of nerves in her stomach. She was suddenly nostalgic for the world she was leaving behind. The sounds of the city, the rows of sparrows sitting on the rooftops of the buildings opposite, the familiar faces of neighbors and tradesmen, all seemed invested with a poignant charm. Everything brought tears to her eyes.

Something of the same seemed to have affected Anatole also, for he was ill at ease. His mouth was pinched and his eyes were wary, as he stood watchful at the drawing-room windows, casting nervous glances up and down the street.

The maid announced that the carriage had arrived.

"Inform the driver we will be down immediately," he said.

"You are traveling in those clothes?" Léonie teased, looking at his gray morning suit and frock coat. "You look as if you are going to your offices."

"That is the idea," he said grimly, walking across the drawing room toward her. "Once we are away from Paris, I will change into something less formal."

Léonie blushed, feeling stupid not to have realized. "Of course."

He picked up his top hat. "Hurry, *petite*. We do not wish to miss our train."

In the street below, their luggage was loaded into the fiacre. "Saint-Lazare," Anatole shouted, to make his voice heard over the cracking of the wind. "Gare Saint-Lazare."

Léonie embraced their mother and promised to write. Marguerite's eyes were rimmed red, which surprised her and, in turn, made her tearful, too. As a consequence, their final few minutes in the rue de Berlin were more emotional than Léonie had anticipated.

The fiacre pulled away. At the last moment, as the gig rounded the corner into the rue d'Amsterdam, Léonie pushed down the window and called back to where Marguerite stood, alone, on the pavement.

"*Au revoir*, M'man."

Then she sat back in the seat and dabbed at her glistening eyes with her handkerchief. Anatole took her hand and held it.

"I am certain she will get along fine without us," he reassured her.

Léonie sniffed.

"Du Pont will look after her."

"Did you make a mistake? Does the express not depart from the Gare Montparnasse?" she said a little later, once the urge to cry had passed.

"If anyone comes calling," he said in a conspiratorial whisper, "I wish them to believe in the fiction that we are heading for the western suburbs. Yes?"

She nodded. "I see. A bluff."

Anatole grinned and tapped the side of his nose.

On their arrival at the Gare Saint-Lazare, he had their luggage moved to a second cab. He made a great play of chatting with the driver, but Léonie noticed he was sweating, even though it was damp and cold. His cheeks were flushed and his temples slicked with beads of perspiration.

"Are you unwell?" she asked with concern.

"No," he said immediately, then added, "but this . . . subterfuge, it is a strain on my nerves. I shall be fine once we are away from Paris."

"What would you have done," Léonie said curiously, "had the invitation not arrived when it did?"

Anatole shrugged. "Made alternative arrangements."

Léonie waited for him to say more, but he remained silent.

"Does M'man know about your . . . commitments at Chez Frascati?" she asked in the end.

Anatole avoided the question. "If anyone should come asking, she is well primed to perpetrate the fiction that we have gone to Saint-Germain-en-Laye. Debussy's people are from there, so . . ." He put both hands on her shoulders and turned her to face him. "Now, *petite*, are you satisfied?"

Léonie tilted her chin. "I am."

"And no more questions?" he teased.

She gave an apologetic grin. "I will try."

On their arrival at the Gare Montparnasse, Anatole all but threw the fare at the driver and shot into the station as if he had a pack of hunting dogs at his heels. Léonie played along with pantomime, understanding that whereas he had wanted them to be noticed at Saint-Lazare, here he wished to be inconspicuous.

Inside the station, he looked for the board listing departures, then put his hand to the pocket of his waistcoat before appearing to think better of it.

"Have you mislaid your watch?"

"It was taken during the assault," he said curtly.

They walked along the platform to find their seats. Léonie read the notices on the carriages of the places in which the train was scheduled to stop: Laroche, Tonnerre, Dijon, Mâcon, Lyon-Perranche at six o'clock this evening, then Valence, Avignon and finally Marseille.

Tomorrow, they were due to take the coast train from Marseille to Carcassonne. Then on Sunday morning, they would depart Carcassonne for Couiza-Montazels, the closest railway station to Rennes-les-Bains. From there, according to their aunt's instructions, it was only a short carriage ride to the Domaine de la Cade, in the foothills of the Corbières.

Anatole purchased a newspaper and buried himself behind it. Léonie watched the people go by. Top hats and morning suits, ladies in wide sweeping skirts. A beggar with a thin face and dirty fingers lifted up the window of their first-class carriage to beg for alms until the guard chased him off.

There was a final shrill, sharp blast from the whistle, then a bellow from the engine as it spat out its first jet of steam. Sparks flew. Then the grind of metal against metal, another belch from the black funnel and, slowly, the wheels started to turn.

Enfin.

The train began to pick up speed as it pulled away from the platform. Léonie sat back in her seat watching Paris disappear in folds of white smoke.

19

Sunday, September 20

Léonie was enjoying their three-day journey through France. As soon as the express had cleared the dismal Parisian *banlieue*, Anatole had recovered his good spirits and kept her amused with stories, playing hands of cards and discussing how they would spend their time in the mountains.

At a little after six o'clock on Friday evening, they had disembarked in Marseille. The following day, they continued along the coast to Carcassonne and passed an uncomfortable night in a hotel with no hot water and a surly staff. Léonie had woken with a headache and, owing to the difficulty of finding a fiacre on a Sunday morning, they had nearly missed their connection. However, as soon as the train cleared the outskirts of the town, Léonie's mood improved. Now her guidebook lay discarded on the seat beside a volume of short stories. The living, breathing landscape of the Midi began to work its charm.

The track followed the line of the curving river south, through the silver valley of the Aude toward the Pyrenees. At first the rails ran alongside the road. The land was flat and unoccupied. But soon she saw rows of vines to left and right, and the occasional field of sunflowers still in bloom, bright and yellow, their heads bowed to the east.

She glimpsed a small village—no more than a handful of houses—perched
on a picturesque distant hill. Then another, the red-tiled houses clustered
around the dominating spire of a church. Near at hand, on the outskirts
of the railside towns, were pink hibiscus, bougainvillea, poignant syringas,
lavender bushes and wild poppies. The green prickly helmets of chestnuts
still hung on the laden branches of the trees. In the distance, gold and
polished copper silhouettes, the only hint that autumn was waiting in the
wings.

All along the line, peasants were working in the fields, their starched blue
smocks stiff and shining as if varnished, decorated with embroidered patterns
on collars and cuffs. The women wore wide, flat straw hats to keep off the
blistering sun. The men bore expressions of resignation upon their leathery
faces, turned away from the relentless wind, working so late a harvest.

The train halted for a quarter of an hour at a substantial town called Limoux. After that, the countryside became steeper, rockier, less forgiving as the
plains gave way to the *garrigue* of the Hautes Corbières. The train rattled
precariously on, perched on thin tracks above the river, until, rounding a
curve, the blue-white Pyrenees suddenly appeared in the distance, shimmering in a heat haze.

Léonie caught her breath. The mountains appeared to rise out of the very
land, like a mighty wall, connecting earth to heaven. Magnificent, unchanging.
In the face of such natural splendor, the man-made constructions of Paris
seemed as nothing. The controversies about Monsieur Eiffel's celebrated metal
tower, Baron Haussmann's grand boulevards, even Monsieur Garnier's opera
house—each paled into insignificance. This was a landscape built on an altogether different scale—earth, air, fire and water. Here the four elements were
laid out in plain view, like keys on a piano.

The train rattled and wheezed, slowing considerably, lunging forward in
jagged bursts. Léonie pushed down the glass and felt the air of the Midi upon
her cheeks. Wooded hills, green and brown, rose abruptly in the shadow of
gray granite cliffs. Lulled by the swaying motion of the train and the singing
of the wheels on the metal tracks, she found her eyelids flickering shut.

SHE WAS JOLTED AWAKE by the squeal of the brakes.

Her eyes flew open, and for an instant she forgot where she was. Then she glanced down at the guidebook on her lap, and across to Anatole, and remembered. Not Paris, but in a rattling railway carriage in the Midi.

The train was slowing.

Léonie peered drowsily out the window. It was hard to make out the lettering on the painted wooden board on the platform. Then she heard the stationmaster, in a heavy southern accent, announce:

"Couiza-Montazels. *Dix minutes d'arrêt.*"

She sat forward with a jolt and tapped her brother on the knee.

"Anatole, *nous sommes là. Lève-toi.*"

Already she could hear doors opening and falling back against the painted green side of the train with a heavy slap, like a desultory round of applause at the Concerts Lamoureux.

"Anatole," she repeated, certain he must be feigning sleep. "*C'est l'heure.* We have arrived at Couiza."

She leaned out.

Even this late in the season, and despite it being Sunday, there was a line of porters leaning on high-backed wooden trolleys. Most had their caps set back on their heads and waistcoats open, shirtsleeves rolled up to the elbow.

She raised her arm. "*Porteur, s'il vous plaît,*" she called.

One leapt forward, clearly thinking how well a couple of sous would sit in his pocket. Léonie withdrew to gather up her belongings.

Without warning, the door was pulled open. "Allow me, Mademoiselle."

A man was standing on the platform looking up into the carriage.

"No, really, we can manage . . ." she began to say, but the man cast his eyes over the compartment, taking in Anatole's sleeping figure and the luggage still on the rack, and without invitation stepped up into the carriage.

"I insist."

Léonie took an instant dislike to him. His starched high collar, double-breasted waistcoat and top hat marked him a gentleman, and yet there was something not quite comme il faut about him. His gaze was too bold, too impertinent.

"Thank you, but there is no need," she said. She identified the smell of plum brandy on his breath. "I am more than . . ."

But without waiting for permission, he was already lifting the first of their valises and boxes down from the wooden rack. Léonie noticed him glance at the initials inscribed in the leather as he placed Anatole's portmanteau on the dirty floor.

Thoroughly frustrated by her brother's inactivity, she shook him roughly by the arm.

"Anatole, *voilà Couiza*. Wake up!"

At last, to her relief, he showed signs of stirring. His eyelids flickered, and he stared lazily around him, as if surprised to find himself in a railway carriage at all. Then he caught sight of her and smiled.

"Must have dozed off," he said, smoothing his long, white fingers over his black oiled hair. *"Desolé."*

Léonie winced as the man dropped Anatole's personal trunk with a thud on the platform. Then he reached back inside for her lacquered workbox.

"Take care," she said sharply. "It is precious."

The man ran his eyes over her, then over the two gold initials on the top: L.V.

"But of course. Do not concern yourself."

Anatole stood up. In an instant, the compartment seemed very much smaller. He glanced at himself in the looking glass below the luggage rack, tipped the collars of his shirt, adjusted his waistcoat and shot his cuffs. Then he bent down and swept up his hat, gloves and cane in one easy motion.

"Shall we?" he said casually, offering Léonie his hand.

Only then did he seem to notice that their belongings had been set down from the carriage. He looked at their companion.

"My thanks, M'sieur. We are most grateful."

"Not at all. The pleasure was mine, M'sieur . . ."

"Vernier. Anatole Vernier. And this is my sister, Léonie."

"Charles Denarnaud, at your service." He tipped his hat. "Are you putting up in Couiza? If so, I would be delighted to . . ."

The piercing whistle blew once more.

"En voiture! Passengers for Quillan and Espéraza, *en voiture!"*

"We should step away," said Léonie.

"Not in Couiza itself," Anatole replied to the man, almost shouting to make himself heard over the roar of the furnace. "But close by. Rennes-les-Bains."

Denarnaud beamed. "My hometown."

"Excellent. We are staying at the Domaine de la Cade. Do you know it?"

Léonie stared at Anatole in astonishment. Having pressed upon her the need for discretion, here he was, only two days out of Paris, publishing their business to a complete stranger without a second thought.

"Domaine de la Cade," Denarnaud replied carefully. "Yes, I know of it."

The engine let out an explosion of steam and clatter. Léonie stepped nervously back and Denarnaud climbed aboard.

"Again, I must thank you for your courtesy," Anatole repeated.

Denarnaud leaned out. The two men exchanged cards, then shook hands as steam swamped the platform.

Anatole stood back from the edge. "Seemed a nice enough fellow."

Léonie's eyes flashed with temper. "You insisted we should keep our plans private," she objected, "and yet—"

Anatole cut in. "Just being friendly."

The station clock on the tower began to strike the hour.

"It seems that we are still, after all, in France," said Anatole, then glanced at her. "Is something the matter? Is it something I have done? Or not done?"

Léonie sighed. "I am cross and I am hot. It was dull having no one to talk to. And you left me quite at the mercies of that disagreeable man."

"Oh, Denarnaud wasn't so bad," he objected, squeezing her hand. "But I ask your forgiveness anyway for the heinous crime of falling asleep!"

Léonie made a face.

"Come, *petite*. You will feel more yourself when we have had something to eat and drink."

20

The full force of the sun hit them the instant they were out of the shadow of the station building. Brown clouds of grit and dust blew into their faces, agitated by the swirling wind that seemed to come from all directions at once. Léonie fumbled with the clasp of her new parasol.

As he made arrangements with the porter for their luggage, she took in their surroundings. She had never traveled this far south before. Indeed, her visits beyond the outskirts of Paris had been only as far as Chartres or child-hood picnics on the banks of the Marne. This was a different France. Léonie recognized some road signs and advertising posters for aperitifs, for wax pol-ish and cough linctus, but it was not a world she knew.

The concourse gave directly onto a small and busy street lined with spread-ing lime trees. Dark women with broad, weather-beaten faces, wagoners and railway workers, unkempt children with bare legs and dirty feet. A man in the short jacket of a workman, no waistcoat, with a loaf of bread tucked beneath his arm. Another, dressed in the black suit and with the clipped short hair of a schoolteacher. A dogcart rumbled past, stacked high with charcoal logs and kindling. She had the sensation she had stepped into a scene from Offenbach's *Tales of Hoffman*, where the old ways held sway and time all but stood still.

"Apparently there's a passable restaurant on the Avenue de Limoux," said Anatole, reappearing at her side with a copy of a local newspaper, *La Dépêche de Toulouse*, tucked under his arm. "There's also a telegraph office, a tele-phone, as well as a poste restante. In Rennes-les-Bains, too, it seems, so we're not completely cut off from civilization." He pulled a box of wax Vestas from his pocket, took a cigarette from his case and tapped it on the lid to tighten the tobacco. "But I fear there's no such luxury as a carriage." He struck a match. "Or at least not this late in the year and on a Sunday."

THE GRAND CAFÉ GUILHEM was on the far side of the bridge. A hand-ful of marble-topped tables with wrought-iron legs and wooden straight-backed chairs with wicker seats were set outside in the shade of a large awning that ran the length of the restaurant. Geraniums in terra-cotta holders and terrace trees in large wooden planters with metal hoops the size of casks of beer gave additional privacy to the diners.

"Hardly the Café Paillard," said Léonie, "but it will do."

Anatole smiled fondly. "I doubt if there will be private rooms, but the public terrace looks acceptable. Yes?"

They were shown to a pleasantly situated table. Anatole ordered for them both and fell into easy conversation with the *patron*. Léonie allowed her at-tention to wander. Lines of *platane*, Napoleon's marching trees, with their variegated bark, gave shade to the street. She was surprised to see that not only the Avenue de Limoux but also the other streets around had been surfaced rather than left as nature intended. She presumed this was because of the popularity of the nearby thermal spas and the high volume of *voitures publiques* and private carriages that went to and from in the height of the season.

Anatole shook out his napkin and laid it across his lap.

The waiter arrived promptly with a tray of drinks—a jug of water, a large glass of cold beer for Anatole and a *pichet* of the local *vin de table*. It was followed shortly afterward by the food. A luncheon of bread, hard-boiled eggs and a galatine of cured meats, salt pork, a couple of centimes' worth of local cheese and a slice of chicken pie carved and embedded in aspic, plain but satisfying.

"Not at all bad," said Anatole. "In fact, surprisingly good."

Léonie excused herself between courses. When she returned some ten minutes later, it was to find Anatole had fallen into conversation with their fellow diners at an adjacent table. An older gentleman, dressed in the formal attire of a banker or lawyer, with a high black top hat and a dark suit, starched collar and necktie despite the heat. And opposite him, a younger man with straw-colored hair and bushy moustache.

"Dr. Gabignaud, Maître Fromilhague," he said, "may I present my sister, Léonie."

Both men half rose to their feet and lifted their hats.

"Gabignaud was telling me of his work in Rennes-les-Bains," Anatole explained, as Léonie sat back down at the table. "You were saying you have been apprenticed to Dr. Courrent for three years?"

Gabignaud nodded. "Three years. Our baths in Rennes-les-Bains are not only the oldest in the region but we also are lucky enough to have several different types of water, so can treat a wider range of symptoms and pathologies than any other equivalent thermal establishment. The group of thermal waters includes the *source du Bain Fort*, at fifty-two degrees, the—"

"They don't need every detail, Gabignaud," growled Fromilhague.

The doctor reddened. "Yes, quite. Well. I have been fortunate enough to be invited to visit similar establishments elsewhere," he continued. "I have had the honor to spend some weeks studying under Dr. Privat in Lamalou-les-Bains."

"I am not familiar with Lamalou."

"You amaze me, Mademoiselle Vernier. It is a charming spa town, also

Roman in origin, just to the north of Béziers." He dropped his voice. "Although it is rather a somber place, of course. In medical circles, it is best known for its treatment of ataxics."

Maître Fromilhague brought his hand down with a bang on the table, making the coffee cups and Léonie jump. "Gabignaud, you are forgetting yourself!"

The young doctor turned scarlet. "Forgive me, Mademoiselle Vernier. I did not intend to cause any offense."

Puzzled, Léonie fixed Maître Fromilhague with a cold look. "Rest assured, Dr. Gabignaud, *I* have taken none."

She glanced at Anatole, who was attempting not to laugh. "Nevertheless, Gabignaud, it might not be an appropriate conversation for mixed company."

"Of course, of course," gabbled the doctor. "My interest as a medical man often leads me to forget that such matters are not—"

"You are visiting Rennes-les-Bains for the spa?" asked Fromilhague with ponderous courtesy.

Anatole shook his head. "We are to stay with our aunt at her estate just outside of the town. At the Domaine de la Cade."

Léonie saw surprise flare in the doctor's eyes.

Or concern?

"Your aunt?" Gabignaud said. Léonie watched him closely.

"To be precise, our late uncle's wife," Anatole replied, clearly also noticing the hesitation in Gabignaud's manner. "Jules Lascombe was our M'man's half-brother. We have not yet had the pleasure of making our aunt's acquaintance."

"Is there something the matter, Dr. Gabignaud?" inquired Léonie.

"No, no. Not in the slightest. Forgive me, I . . . I was not aware Lascombe was fortunate enough to have such close relations. He lived a quiet life and did not mention . . . To be frank, Mademoiselle Vernier, we were all taken by surprise when he took the decision to marry, and so late in life. He seemed a confirmed bachelor. And to take a wife to such a house, with such an ill reputation, well . . ."

Léonie's attention sharpened. "An ill reputation?"

But Anatole had moved to a different question. "You knew Lascombe, Gabignaud?"

"Not well, but we were acquainted. They summered here, I believe, in the first years of their marriage. Madame Lascombe, preferring life in town, was often away from the Domaine for some months at a time."

"You were not Lascombe's personal physician?"

Gabignaud shook his head. "I did not have that honor, no. He had his own man in Toulouse. He had been in poor health for many years, although his decline was more sudden than expected, brought on by the fearsome cold at the beginning of the year. When it was clear that he would not recover, your aunt returned to the Domaine de la Cade at the beginning of January. Lascombe died days afterward. Of course, there were rumors that he died as a result of—"

"Gabignaud!" interrupted Fromilhague. "Hold your tongue!"

He signaled his continuing displeasure by summoning the waiter, then insisting on relating precisely what they had eaten, to confirm the bill, making further conversation between the two tables impossible.

Anatole left a generous tip. Fromilhague threw a note onto the table and stood up. "Mademoiselle Vernier, Vernier," he said brusquely, raising his hat. "Gabignaud. We have matters to attend to."

To Léonie's astonishment, the doctor followed without a word.

"Why may Lamalou not be spoken of?" Léonie demanded, as soon as they were out of earshot. "And why does Dr. Gabignaud permit Maître Fromilhague to bully him so?"

Anatole grinned. "Lamalou is notorious as the place where the latest medical advancements in the treatment of syphilis—ataxia—are being pioneered," he replied. "As for his manner, I would imagine Gabignaud needs the Maître's sponsorship. In such a small town, it is the difference between a successful and a failing practice." He gave a brief laugh. "But Lamalou-les-Bains! I ask you!"

Léonie thought. "But whyever was Dr. Gabignaud so surprised when I told him we were to be staying at the Domaine de la Cade? And what did he mean by the house having an ill reputation?"

"Gabignaud talks too much and Fromilhague disapproves of gossip. That's all there is to it."

Léonie shook her head. "No, it was more than that," she objected. "Maître Fromilhague was determined not to permit him to speak."

Anatole shrugged. "Fromilhague has the choleric complexion of a man who is frequently aggravated. He merely dislikes Gabignaud prattling on like a woman!"

Léonie poked out her tongue at this slight. "Beast!"

Anatole wiped his moustache, dropped his napkin to the table, then pushed his chair back and stood up.

"*Alors, on y va.* We have some time to spare. Let us acquaint ourselves with the modest delights of Couiza."

21

Paris

Hundreds of miles to the north, Paris was becalmed. After the bustle of a busy morning of commerce, the afternoon air was choked with dust and the smells of rotten fruit and vegetables. The ostlers, the traders of the eighth arrondissement, had gone. The milk carts, the barrows and the beggars had moved on, leaving behind the detritus, the dregs of another day.

The apartment of the Vernier family in the rue de Berlin was silent in the blue light of the fading afternoon. The furniture was shrouded in white dust-sheets. The long windows of the drawing room that overlooked the street were closed. The curtains of yellow chintz had been drawn. The floral wallpaper, once of good quality, looked faded where the daily passage of the sun had stripped the color away. Particles of dust hung suspended above the few sticks of furniture left uncovered.

On the table, forgotten roses in a glass bowl hung their heads, almost without scent. There was another smell, barely discernible, a sour smell that did not belong. A hint of the souk, Turkish tobacco, and a stranger aroma this far inland, that of the sea, carried in upon the gray clothes of the man who stood

silently between the two windows in front of the fireplace, obscuring the porcelain face of the Sèvres clock on the mantel.

He was of strong and powerful build, with broad shoulders and a high
forehead, and the body of an adventurer rather than an aesthete. Dark clipped
eyebrows sat above sharp blue eyes with pupils as black as coal.

Marguerite was sitting upright on one of the mahogany dining chairs.
Her rose-colored negligé, tied at the neck with a yellow silk bow, lay draped
across perfect white shoulders. The material fell, exquisitely, over the yellow cushioned seat and the fabric arms of the chair, as if for an artist's still life.
It was only the alarm in her eyes that told a different story. That and the fact that
her arms were pulled awkwardly behind her, bound tightly by picture wire.

A second man, his shaved scalp covered in an angry rash of spots and blisters, stood on guard behind the chair, waiting for his master's instructions.

"So where is he?" he said in a cold voice.

Marguerite looked at him. She remembered the flush of attraction that had
come over her in his presence before and hated him for it. Of all the men she
had known, only one other—her husband, Leo Vernier—had possessed the
power to stir her emotions so instantly, and in such a way.

"You were at the restaurant," she said. "Chez Voisin."

He ignored her. "Where is Vernier?"

"I do not know," said Marguerite again. "I give you my word. He keeps his
own hours. Often he is gone for days without a word."

"Your son, yes. But your daughter does not come and go as she pleases
unchaperoned. She keeps regular hours. And yet she, too, is absent."

"She is with friends."

"Is Vernier with her?"

"I . . ."

He sent his cold eyes sweeping over the sheets and empty cupboards.

"How long is the apartment to be empty?" he said.

"Some four weeks. Indeed, I am expecting General Du Pont," she said,
struggling to keep her voice level. "At any moment he will be here to collect
me, and—"

The words were lost in her scream as the manservant grabbed her by the
hair and jerked her head back.

"No!"

The tip of the knife pressed cold against her skin.

"If you leave now," she said, struggling to keep her voice calm, "I will say nothing, I give you my word. Leave me, go."

The man stroked the side of her face with the back of his gloved hand.

"Marguerite, no one will come. The piano downstairs is silent. The neighbors upstairs are in the country for the weekend. And as for your maid and cook, I watched them leave. They, too, believe that you have already departed with Du Pont."

Fear flashed in her eyes as she realized how well informed he was.

Victor Constant pulled up a chair, so close that Marguerite could feel his breath on her face. Beneath the neat moustache, she could see full lips, red in his pale face. It was the face of a predator, a wolf. And a blemish, too. Behind his left ear, a small swelling.

"My friend . . ."

"The esteemed general is already in receipt of a note postponing your liaison until half past eight this evening." He glanced at the clock on the mantelshelf. "Some five hours and more away. So, you see, we have no need to hurry. And what he discovers when he does arrive is entirely up to you. Alive, dead. It matters little to me."

"No!"

The point of his knife was now pressing beneath her eye.

"I fear, *chère* Marguerite, that you would fare ill in the world without your looks."

"What is it you want? Money? Does Anatole owe you money? I can settle his debts."

He laughed. "If only it were that simple. Besides, your financial situation is, shall we say, perilous. And generous as I am certain your lover can be, I do not think General Du Pont would pay to keep your son from the bankruptcy courts."

With the lightest of touches, Constant pressed the tip of the blade a little harder against her pale skin, his head shaking slightly as if in regret for what he was obliged to do. "In any case, it is not a question of money. Vernier has taken something that belongs to me."

Marguerite heard the change in his voice and she began to struggle. She tried to pull her arms free but succeeded only in causing her bonds to tighten. The wire cut sharply, slicing into the skin of her bare wrists. Blood began to drip, bead by red bead, onto the blue carpet.

"I beg you," she cried, trying to keep her voice steady. "Let me speak with him. I will persuade him to give back to you whatever it was he took. I give you my word."

"Ah, but it is too late for that," he said softly, running his fingers down her cheek. "I wonder if you even presented my card to your son, *chère* Marguerite?" His black hand came to rest on her white throat. He increased the pressure. Marguerite began to choke as she flailed and struggled beneath his tightening grip, desperately stretching her neck up and away from his strong grasp. The look in his eyes, pleasure and conquest in equal measure, terrified her as much as the suffocating violence of his grip.

Without warning, suddenly he released her.

She fell back against the chair, gulping for air, gasping. Her eyes were red and her throat was bruised with ugly crimson marks.

"Start with Vernier's room," he instructed his man. "Look for his journal." He made a shape with his hands. "About so large."

The servant withdrew.

"Now," he said, as if in the midst of a perfectly normal conversation. "Where is your son?"

Marguerite met his eyes. Her heart was thudding with dread at what punishment he might inflict upon her. But she had endured ill treatment at the hands of others and survived it. She could do so again.

"I do not know," she said.

This time, he struck her. Hard, and with his fist, sending her head snapping back. Marguerite gasped as her cheek cracked. Blood welled in her mouth. She dropped her chin and spat into her lap. She flinched as she felt the tug of silk at her neck and the rasp of his leather gloves untying the yellow bow. His breath was coming faster. She could feel the heat of him.

With his other hand, she felt him pushing up the folds of material above her knees, above her thighs, higher.

"Please, no," she whispered.

"It is barely shy of three," he said, tucking a curl of hair behind her ear, in a parody of tenderness. "We have more than enough time for me to persuade you to talk. And think of Léonie, Marguerite. Such a pretty girl. A little high-spirited for my tastes, but I am sure I could learn to make an exception."

He pushed the silk from her shoulders.

Marguerite became calm, vanishing into herself as she had been forced to do many times before. She cleared her mind, wiping out the image of him. Even now, her strongest emotion was shame at the way her heart had lurched when she had first opened the door and allowed him into the apartment.

Sex and violence, the old alliance. She had seen it countless times. On the barricades in the Commune, in the backstreets, hidden beneath the respectable veneer of the society salons through which latterly she had moved. So many men driven by hate, not desire. Marguerite had made good use of it. She had exploited her looks, her charms, so that her daughter would never have to live the life she had.

"Where is Vernier?"

He untied her and dragged her from the chair to the floor.

"Where is Vernier?"

"I do not—"

Holding her down, he struck her again. Then again.

"Where is your son?" he demanded.

As Marguerite slipped from consciousness, her only thought was how to protect her children. How not to betray them to this man. She must give him something.

"Rouen," she lied through her bloodied lips. "They have gone to Rouen."

22

Rennes-les-Bains

By a quarter past four, having taken in the modest sights of Couiza, Léonie and Anatole were standing on the concourse in front of the station, waiting while the cabman loaded the luggage into the *courrier publique*.

Unlike the conveyances Léonie had noticed in Carcassonne, with black leather seats and open tops much like the landaus that drove up and down the Avenue du Bois de Boulogne, the *courrier* was an altogether more rustic form of transport. Indeed, it resembled a farmhouse cart, with two wooden bench seats running up each side facing inward, painted red. There were no cushions, and it was open on the sides, with a piece of dark canvas stretched over a thin metal frame for shade.

The horses, both grays, wore white embroidered fringes over their ears and eyes to keep the insects away.

The other passengers included an elderly husband and his much younger wife, from Toulouse. Two elderly birdlike sisters twittered to each other in low voices beneath their hats.

Léonie was pleased to see that their lunch companion from the Grand Café Guilhem, Dr. Gabignaud, was to take the same carriage. Frustratingly, Maître Fromilhague kept Gabignaud close to him. Every few minutes he drew out his watch from his waistcoat pocket by the chain and tapped the glass face as if suspicious it had stopped working, before putting it away again.

"Clearly a man with pressing matters to attend to," Anatole whispered. "He'll be driving the carriage himself soon if we don't look out!"

As soon as everyone was settled, the driver climbed up to his cab. He perched himself on top of the sundry collection of suitcases and valises, his legs spread wide, and looked up at the clock on the front of the railway station building. When it struck the half-hour, he flicked his whip and the carriage jerked away.

Within moments they were on the open road, heading east out of Couiza. The route ran along the river valley between high hills on either side. The bitter winter and wet spring that punished most of France for so much of the year had, here, created an Eden. Lush pastures, green and fertile, rather than sun-scorched earth, thickly wooded hillsides of fir and holm oak, hazel and Mediterranean chestnut and beech. High on a hill to their left, Léonie glimpsed the outline of a ruined castle. An old wooden sign at the side of the road announced it to be the village of Coustaussa.

Gabignaud was seated next to Anatole and was pointing out landmarks. Léonie caught only fragments of their conversation over the crescendo of the wheels on the road and the rattling harnesses of the horses.

"And that?" Anatole said.

Léonie followed her brother's pointing finger. High on a rocky outcrop to the right, well above the road, she could just discern a tiny hillside village shimmering in the fierce afternoon heat, no more than a collection of dwellings clinging to the precipitous side of the mountain.

"Rennes-le-Château," replied Gabignaud. "You would not believe it to look at it now but it once was the ancient Visigoth capital of the region, Rhedae."

"What caused its decline?"

"Charlemagne, the Crusade against the Albigensians, bandits from Spain, plague, the relentless and unforgiving march of history. Now it's just another forgotten mountain village. Rather in the shadow of Rennes-les-Bains." He paused. "Having said that, the curé works hard for his parishioners. An interesting man."

Anatole leaned closer to hear. "Why so?"

"He is erudite, clearly ambitious and forceful. It is a matter of much local speculation as to why he should choose to stay so close to home and bury himself away in such a poor parish."

"Perhaps he believes this is where he can be most effective?"

"Certainly the village loves him. He's done a lot of good."

"In practical matters or of merely a spiritual nature?"

"Both. As an example, the church of Sainte Marie-Madeleine was no more than a ruin when he arrived. Rain coming through, abandoned to mice and birds and mountain cats. But in the summer of 1886, the mairie voted him two thousand five hundred francs to begin restoration work, principally to replace the old altar."

Anatole raised his eyebrows. "A sizable sum!"

He nodded. "I only know what I hear indirectly. The curé is a most cultured man. It is said that many items of archaeological interest have come to light, which of course greatly interested your uncle."

"Such as?"

"A historical altarpiece, I gather. Also a pair of Visigoth pillars and an ancient tombstone—the Dalle des Chevaliers—that is rumored to be either Merovingian in its provenance or possibly also from the Visigoth era. Being so interested in that period, Lascombe was much engaged in the early stages of the renovations in Rennes-le-Château, which of course resulted in the matter being of interest in Rennes-les-Bains."

"You too seem to be something of a historian," ventured Léonie.

Gabignaud flushed with pleasure. "A hobby, Mademoiselle Vernier, nothing more."

Anatole took out his cigarette case. The doctor accepted. Shielding the flame with his arched hand, Anatole struck a match for both of them. "And what is the name of this exemplary priest?" he asked, blowing out the question with the smoke.

"Saunière. Bérenger Saunière."

They had reached a straight section of road, and the horses picked up speed. The noise grew in volume until further discussion was all but impossible. Léonie did not altogether mind the barrier to conversation. Her thoughts were racing, for somewhere in the morass of Gabignaud's conversation, she had the sense that she had learned something of some significance.

But what?

After a short while, the driver slowed and, with a clanking of harness and the clatter of the unlit lamps against the side of the carriage, left the main road to follow the river valley of the Salz.

Léonie leaned out as far as she dared, delighted by the beauty of the landscape, the extraordinary vista of sky and rock and woods. Two ruined outposts that turned out to be natural rock formations rather than the shadows of castles loomed over the valley like giant sentinels. Here, the ancient forest came almost down to the road's edge. Léonie felt as though they were entering a secret place, like an explorer in one of Monsieur Rider Haggard's entertainments venturing into lost African kingdoms.

Now the road began to curve elegantly, winding back and over itself like a snake, following the cut of the river. It was beautiful, an arcadia. Everything was fertile, lush and green—olive green, sea green, scrub the color of absinthe. The silver underside of leaves, lifted by the breeze, shimmered in the sun between the darker tones of fir and oak. Above the trees the startling outline of crests and peaks, the ancient silhouettes of menhirs, dolmens and natural sculptures. The antique history of the region was laid out plain to see, like pages in a book.

Léonie could hear the River Salz running alongside them, a constant companion, sometimes in view, a glint of sunlight on water, sometimes hidden. Like a game of *cache-cache*, the water sang its presence, rushing over stones, chasing through the entangled branches of the willows that hung low over the river, a guide drawing them ever closer to their destination.

23

The horses clattered over a low bridge and slowed to a trot.

Ahead, on the bend in the road, Léonie had her first glimpse of Rennes-les-Bains. She could see a white three-story building with a sign announcing itself to be the Hôtel de la Reine. Beside it was a cluster of rather forbidding unadorned buildings that she presumed made up the establishment of the thermal spa.

The *courrier* slowed to walking pace as they swung into the main street. To the right it was bounded by the great gray wall of the mountain itself. To the left there was a collection of homes, boarding houses and hotels. Heavy metal-framed gas lamps were set into the walls.

Her first impressions were not as she had expected. The town had an air of elegant and contemporary style and prosperity. Generous, scrubbed stone steps and thresholds abutted the roadway, which, although left as nature intended, was clean and passable. The street was lined with bay and laurel trees in wide wooden planters, which seemed to bring the woods down into the town. She saw a rotund gentleman in a buttoned frock coat, two ladies with parasols, and three nurses, each pushing a *chaise roulante*. A gaggle of ribboned girls in white frills and petticoats walked with their governess.

The driver turned off the main road and pulled up the horses.

"*La Place du Pérou. S'il vous plaît. Terminus.*"

The small square was bordered by buildings on three sides and shaded by lime trees. The golden sunlight filtered down through the canopy of leaves, casting checkerboard patterns on the ground. There was a water trough for the horses and the respectable town houses were adorned with window boxes filled with the last of the tumbling summer flowers. At a small café with striped awnings, a collection of well-dressed, well-gloved ladies and their escorts were taking refreshment. In the corner was the approach to a modest church.

"All very picturesque," muttered Anatole.

The driver jumped down from his cab and began to unload the luggage.

"*S'il vous plaît,* Mesdames et Messieurs. *La Place du Pérou. Terminus.*"

One by one, the travelers disembarked. There were awkward farewells typical of those who have shared a journey but have little else in common. Maître Fromilhague raised his hat and then disappeared. Gabignaud shook Anatole's hand and presented his card, saying how much he hoped there would be an opportunity to meet again during their stay, perhaps for a game of cards or at one of the musical soirées that took place in Limoux or Quillan. Then, tipping his hat to Léonie, he hurried away across the square.

Anatole put his arm around Léonie's shoulders.

"This does not look as unpromising as I had feared," he said.

"It is charming. Quite charming."

A young girl in the gray-and-white uniform of a parlor maid appeared, out of breath, at the top left-hand corner of the square. She was plump and pretty, with deep black eyes and a suggestive mouth. Strands of thick, dark hair were escaping from beneath a white cap.

"Ah! Our reception committee perhaps," said Anatole.

Behind her, also out of breath, arrived a young man with a broad, pleasant face. He wore an open-necked shirt with a red scarf.

"*Et voilà*," Anatole added, "unless I am much mistaken, the explanation for the girl's lack of punctuality is explained."

The maid attempted to tidy her hair, then ran toward them. She bobbed.

"Sénher Vernier? Madomaisèla. Madama sent me to fetch you to the Domaine de la Cade. She asked me to present her apologies, but there is a difficulty with the gig. It's being repaired, but Madama suggests that it might be quicker on foot. . . ." The maid glanced doubtfully down at Léonie's calfskin boots. "If you don't mind . . ."

Anatole looked the girl up and down. "And you are?"

"Marieta, Sénher."

"Very good. And how long might we have to wait for the gig to be repaired, Marieta?"

"I couldn't say. There is a broken wheel."

"Well, how far is it to Domaine de la Cade?"

"*Pas luènh.*" Not far.

Anatole peered over her shoulder at the breathless boy. "And the luggage will be brought on later?"

"*Oc*, Sénher," she said. "Pascal will bring it."

Anatole turned to Léonie. "In which case, with the lack of any promising alternative, I vote we do as our aunt suggests—and walk!"

"What?" The word burst, indignantly, from Léonie's lips before she could help herself. "But you hate to walk!" She touched her fingers to her own ribs, to remind him of the injuries he had sustained. "Besides, will it be too much for you?"

"I'll be fine." He shrugged. "I admit, it's a bore, but what can one do? I would rather press on than kick our heels."

Taking Anatole's words as assent, Marieta gave a quick curtsy, then turned and set off. Léonie stared after her, openmouthed. "Of all the . . ." she exclaimed.

Anatole threw back his head and laughed. "Welcome to Rennes-les-Bains," he said, taking Léonie's hand. "Come, *petite*. Otherwise, we will be left behind!"

. . .

MARIETA LED THEM DOWN a shadowed passageway between the houses. They emerged into bright sunlight on an old arched stone bridge. Far, far below, the water flowed over flat rocks. Léonie caught her breath, made dizzy by the sensation of light and space and height.

"Léonie, *dépêche-toi*," called Anatole.

The maid crossed the river, then turned sharply right and made for a narrow unmade path that ran steeply up into the trees of the wooded hillside. Léonie and Anatole followed in silent single file, each saving their breath for the climb.

Higher and steeper they went, along a dappled track of stones and fallen leaves, venturing ever deeper into thick forest. Before long, the path opened out into a wider country track. Léonie could see wheel ruts, cracked and pale through lack of rain, marking the route of countless wheels and hooves. Here, the trees were set farther back from the path and the sun cast its long fading shadow between each copse and cluster.

Léonie turned and looked back in the direction they had come. Now she could see, steeply below them but close still, the red and gray sloping roofs of Rennes-les-Bains. She could even identify the hotels and the central square where they had disembarked from the carriage. The water shimmered and teased, a ribbon of green and silver, even red with the reflection of autumn leaves, running as smooth as silk.

After a slight dip in the track, they reached a plateau.

Ahead stood the stone pillars and gates of a country estate. Wrought-iron railings disappeared as far as the eye could see, shielded by fir and yew. The property seemed both forbidding and aloof. Léonie shivered. For a moment, her spirit of adventure abandoned her. She recalled her mother's reluctance to discuss the Domaine and her childhood spent within it. And then the words of Dr. Gabignaud at luncheon echoing in her ears.

Such an ill reputation.

"Cade?" Anatole queried.

"It is a local name for juniper, Sénher," the maid replied.

Léonie glanced at her brother, then stepped forward with determination and put both hands on the railings, like a prisoner behind bars. She pressed her flushed cheeks to the cold iron and peered through at the gardens that lay beyond.

Everything was shrouded in a dark, filtered green, chinks of sun reflected through an ancient canopy of leaves. Elderberry trees, shrubs, formal hedges and once-elegant borders were unkempt and lacking color. The property had an air of beautiful neglect, not yet gone to ruin but no longer expecting visitors.

A large stone birdbath stood dry and empty in the center of a wide graveled path that led straight from the gates into the grounds. To Léonie's left, there was a round stone ornamental pond, a rusty metal frame stretched over it. It, too, was dry. To the right was a row of juniper bushes growing wild and untended. A little farther back were the remains of an orangery, the glass missing and the frame twisted.

If she had come upon this place by accident, Léonie would have thought it abandoned, such was the air of dereliction. She glanced to her right and saw that there was a sign of gray slate hanging on the fence, the words partly obscured by the deep scratches scored in the stone. Like claw marks.

DOMAINE DE LA CADE.

The house did not look as if it would welcome visitors.

24

There is another approach to the house, I presume?" asked Anatole.

"*Oc*, Sénher," replied Marieta. "The main entrance is on the north side of the estate. The late master had a track built, up from the Sougraigne road. But it is a good hour's walk, all the way round the town of Rennes-les-Bains, then back up the hillside. Much longer than the old forest path."

"And did your mistress instruct you to bring us this way, Marieta?"

The Toadstool Bookshop
Lorden's Plaza, Milford NH 03055
Phone (603) 673-1734
Special orders welcome, give us a call

H   74570 04/17/10 13:46

28364 1*SEPULCHRE   8.00   8.00
HERON
            Total due: 8.00
            Cash   10.00

            Your change: 2.00

Thank You!
Sign up for our email newsletter at
www.toadbooks.com and receive a coupon
for 20% off your next purchase.

The girl blushed. "She did not say *not* to bring you through the woods," she said defensively.

They stood patiently while Marieta hunted in the pocket of her apron to retrieve a large brass key. There was a heavy clunk as the lock opened, then the maid pushed open the right-hand gate. Once they were through, she shut it again behind them. It juddered and creaked, then clattered back into position.

Léonie had butterflies in her stomach, a mixture of nerves and excitement. She felt herself the heroine of her own story as she followed Anatole along narrow green pathways, clearly little used. Shortly, a tall box hedge came into view with an arch cut into it. However, rather than passing through, Marieta continued straight on until they emerged onto a generous driveway. This was graveled and well kept, no hints of moss or wild grass, and was flanked by an avenue of *châtaigniers* with fruit hanging from their branches.

At last, Léonie caught her first glimpse of the house itself.

"Oh," she gasped in admiration.

The house was magnificent. Imposing yet well proportioned, it was perfectly situated both to catch the best of the sun and to benefit from the views to the south and west afforded by its position looking out over the valley. There were three stories, a gently sloping roof and rows of shuttered windows set within elegant whitewashed walls. Each of the windows on the first floor gave on to stone balconies with curved iron balustrades. The entire edifice was covered with flaming red-and-green ivy, gleaming as if the leaves themselves had been polished.

As they drew closer, Léonie saw that a wall ran unbroken along the ledge of the entire top story of the house, behind which were visible eight round attic windows.

Perhaps M'man had once looked down from one of those very windows?

A wide sweeping semicircular stone staircase led to a substantial double front door painted raven black, with a brass knocker and trim. It sheltered beneath a curved stone portico, bordered by two substantial planters holding ornamental cherry trees.

Léonie climbed the steps, following the maid and Anatole into a large, elegant entrance hall. The floor was a checkerboard of black and red tiles and the walls were covered in a delicate cream paper decorated with yellow and green flowers, giving an impression of light and space. In the center was a mahogany table with a wide glass bowl of white roses, the highly polished wood contributing to an atmosphere of intimacy and warmth.

On the walls hung portraits of whiskered men in military uniforms and women in hooped skirts, as well as a selection of misty landscapes and classical pastoral scenes.

There was a grand staircase, Léonie noticed, and to the left of it a miniature grand piano, with a whisper of dust on the closed lid.

"Madama will receive you on the afternoon terrace," Marieta said.

She took them through a set of glazed glass doors, which gave on to a south-facing terrace, shaded by vines and honeysuckle. It ran the width of the house and was situated to overlook the formal lawns and planted beds. A distant avenue of horse-chestnut trees and evergreen firs marked the farthest boundary; a gazebo of glass and wood painted white glinted in the sun. In the foreground was the smooth surface of an ornamental lake.

"This way, Madomaisèla, Sénher."

Marieta led them to the far corner of the terrace, to a patch of shade created by a generous yellow-and-white striped awning. A table was laid for three. White linen tablecloth, white china, silver spoons and a centerpiece of meadow flowers: Parma violets, pink and white geraniums, purple Pyrenean lilies.

"I will tell the mistress you are here," she said, and disappeared back into the shadows of the house.

Léonie leaned back against the stone balustrade. Her cheeks were flushed. She unbuttoned her gloves at the wrist and untied her hat, using it as a fan.

"She has led us around full circle," she said.

"I beg your pardon?"

Léonie pointed at the high box hedge at the reaches of the lawn. "If we had come through the arch, we could have walked across the park. But the girl has led us through the grounds in a circle so as to approach from the front."

Anatole removed his straw hat and gloves and placed them on the wall.

"Well, it is a splendid building and the prospect was excellent."

"And no carriage, no housekeeper to greet us," Léonie continued. "It is all most peculiar."

"These gardens are exquisite."

"Here, yes, but at the rear, the entire property appears quite derelict. Abandoned. The orangery, the overgrown beds, the—"

He laughed. "Derelict, Léonie, you exaggerate! I admit it is more in the state that nature intended, but even so . . ."

Her eyes glinted. "It is completely overgrown," she argued. "No wonder the Domaine is viewed with suspicion locally."

"Whatever are you talking about?"

"That impertinent man Monsieur Denarnaud, at the railway station—did you see the expression upon his face when you said where we were headed? And poor Dr. Gabignaud. The manner in which that disagreeable Maître Fromilhague chastised him and forbade him to speak. It's all most mysterious."

"It is not," Anatole said with mock exasperation. "Do you imagine we have stumbled accidentally into one of those ghastly little stories of Monsieur Poe you have such a taste for." He made a grotesque face. " 'We have put her living in the tomb,' " he quoted in a trembling voice. " 'I tell you that she now stands without the door!' I can be Roderick Usher to your Madeleine."

"And the lock on the gate was rusty," she said doggedly, refusing to be teased out of it. "No one had passed that way for some time. I tell you, Anatole, it is most peculiar."

From behind them came a woman's voice, soft and clear and calm.

"I am sorry to hear you find it so. But you are most welcome all the same."

Léonie heard Anatole catch his breath.

Mortified to have been overheard, she spun round, her face aflame. The woman standing in the doorway suited her voice precisely. Elegant and assured, she was slender and tall. Her features were intelligent and perfectly proportioned, and her complexion was dazzling. Her thick blond hair was piled high on her head, not a strand out of place. Most striking of all were her eyes, a pale gray, the color of moonstone.

Léonie's hand flew to her own ungovernable curls, wayward in comparison.

"*Tante*, I . . ."

She looked down at her dusty traveling clothes. Their aunt was immaculate. She wore a fashionable high-necked cream blouse of contemporary cut with gigot sleeves, matched with a skirt, flat-paneled at the front and nipped tight at the waist, with a gathering of material at the back.

Isolde was stepping forward. "You must be Léonie," she said, extending long, slim fingers. "And Anatole?"

With a half-bow, Anatole took Isolde's hand and raised it to his lips.

"*Tante*," he said with a smile, looking up at her from beneath his dark lashes. "It is a great pleasure."

"The pleasure is mine. And, please, Isolde. *Tante* is so formal and makes me feel quite old."

"Your girl brought us through the rear gates," Anatole said. "It is that, and the heat, that have disturbed my sister." He took in the house and grounds with a sweep of his arm. "But if this is our reward, then the tribulations of our journey are already a distant memory."

Isolde inclined her head at the compliment, then turned to Léonie.

"I did ask Marieta to explain the unfortunate situation with the carriage, but she is easily flustered," she said lightly. "I am sorry that your first impressions have not been favorable. But no matter. You are here now."

Léonie found her tongue at last. "Tante Isolde, please forgive my discourtesy. It was inexcusable."

Isolde smiled. "There is nothing to forgive. Now, do sit. Tea first—à l'anglaise—then Marieta will show you to your rooms."

They took their seats. Immediately, a silver teapot and a jug of fresh lemonade were brought to the table, followed by plates of both savory and sweet dishes.

Isolde leaned forward and poured the tea, a delicate pale liquid that smelled of sandalwood and the Orient.

"What a wonderful scent," said Anatole, breathing in the aroma. "What is it?"

"It is my own blend of lapsang souchong and *verveine*. I find it so much more refreshing than those heavy English and German teas that are currently so popular."

Isolde offered Léonie a white china dish filled with large slices of bright yellow lemon. "Your mother's wire, accepting my invitation on your behalf, Léonie, was perfectly charming. I do hope I shall have the opportunity to meet her, too. Perhaps she might visit in the spring?"

Léonie thought of her mother's dislike of the Domaine and how she had never regarded it as home, but she remembered her manners and lied prettily.

"M'man would be delighted. She suffered a period of illness at the beginning of this past year, brought on by the inclement weather, otherwise she would of course have come to pay her last respects to Oncle Jules."

Isolde nodded, then turned to Anatole. "I read in the newspapers that temperatures fell well below zero in Paris. Can that be true?"

Anatole's eyes glittered bright. "It seemed the world had turned to ice. The Seine itself froze and so many were dying at night on the streets that the authorities were obliged to open shelters in gymnasiums, shooting galleries, schools and public baths; they even set up a dormitory in the Palais des Arts Libéraux in the Champs-de-Mars, in the shadow of Monsieur Eiffel's magnificent tower."

"The fencing halls, too?"

Anatole looked puzzled. "Fencing halls?"

"Forgive me," Isolde said, "the mark above your eye. I thought, perhaps, you were a swordsman."

Léonie jumped in. "Anatole was assaulted four nights ago, on the night of the Palais Garnier riots."

"Léonie, please," he protested.

"Were you hurt?" Isolde said quickly.

"A few cuts and bruises; it was nothing," he said, throwing a fierce look at Léonie.

"Did word of the riots not reach here?" asked Léonie. "The newspapers in Paris carried nothing but news of the arrests of the *abonnés*."

Isolde kept her eyes fixed on Anatole.

"Were you robbed?" she asked him.

"My watch—my father's timepiece—was taken. They were interrupted before they could take anything else."

"A street robbery, then?" Isolde repeated, as if wishing to convince herself of it.

"That's right. Nothing more. It was bad luck."

For a moment, an awkward silence fell over the table.

Then, remembering her duties, Isolde turned to Léonie. "Your mother spent some time here at the Domaine de la Cade in her childhood, did she not?"

Léonie nodded.

"It must have been rather lonely for her growing up here alone," Isolde suggested. "No other children for company."

Léonie smiled with relief that she did not have to pretend an affection for the Domaine de la Cade that her mother did not feel, and spoke without thinking.

"Do you intend to make this your home or return to Toulouse?"

She was not so happy. "Toulouse? I am afraid I don't . . ."

"Léonie," said Anatole sharply.

She blushed but met her brother's eye. "I was under the impression from something M'man said that Tante Isolde came from Toulouse."

"Really, Anatole, I am not in the least offended," Isolde said. "But, in point of fact, I grew up in Paris."

Léonie leaned closer, pointedly ignoring her brother. She was increasingly intrigued to know how her aunt and uncle had first made each other's acquaintance. From what little she knew of Oncle Jules, it seemed an unlikely marriage.

"I was wondering—" she began, but Anatole leapt in and the opportunity was lost.

"Do you have much contact with Rennes-les-Bains?"

Isolde shook her head. "My late husband was not interested in entertaining, and since his death, I regret to say I have neglected my responsibilities as a hostess."

"I am sure people are sympathetic to your situation," Anatole said.

"Many of our neighbors were most kind during the final weeks of my husband's life. Prior to that, his health had not been good for some time. After his death, there were so many matters to take care of, away from the Domaine de la Cade, and I was here less than perhaps I should have been. But . . ." She broke off and drew Léonie into the conversation with another of her calm, steady smiles. "If it would be pleasing for you, I had thought to use the excuse of your visit to hold a dinner party for one or two local guests this coming Saturday evening. Would you like that? Nothing on a grand scale, but it will be an opportunity to introduce you to them and them to you."

"That would be delightful," said Léonie immediately, and, forgetting everything else, she began to quiz her aunt.

The afternoon rolled pleasantly on. Isolde was an excellent hostess, conscientious, careful and charming, and Léonie enjoyed herself hugely. Slices of thick-crusted white bread, spread with goat cheese and sprinkled with chopped garlic, thin fingers of toast topped with anchovy paste and black pepper, a platter of cured mountain ham with purple half-moons of ripe fig. A rhubarb tart, the pastry sugared and golden, sat beside a blue china bowl filled to the brim with a compote of mulberries and blackheart cherries and a jug of cream, a long-handled silver spoon lying beside it.

"And what are these?" Léonie asked, pointing to a dish of purple bonbons coated with a white frosting. "They look delicious."

"Pearls of the Pyrenees, drops of schoenanthus scent crystalized in pieces of sugar. A favorite of yours, Anatole, I believe. And these" —Isolde gestured to another dish—"are homemade chocolate creams. Jules's cook is really quite excellent. She has served the family for almost forty years."

There was a wistfulness to her tone that made Léonie wonder if perhaps Isolde felt, as their mother had, something of an unwelcome guest rather than the rightful chatelaine of the Domaine de la Cade.

"You work in newspapers," Isolde was asking Anatole.

Anatole shook his head. "Not for some time. The life of a journalist did not suit me: domestic disputes, the Algerian conflict, the latest election crisis at the Académie des Beaux-Arts; I found it dispiriting to be forced to consider matters that did not interest me in the slightest, so I threw in my hand. Now, although I write the odd review for *La Revue Blanche* and *La Revue Contemporaine*, mostly I pursue my literary endeavors in a less commercial arena."

"Anatole is on the editorial board of a magazine for collectors and such and antique editions," Léonie said.

Isolde smiled and turned her attention back to Léonie. "I must say again how delighted I was you felt able to accept my invitation. I feared a month in the country might seem rather dull after the excitements of Paris."

"One can be just as easily bored in Paris," Léonie replied charmingly. "Too often I am obliged to spend my time at tedious soirées, listening to widows and old maids complaining of how things were so much better under the Emperor. I prefer to read!"

"Léonie is *une lectrice assidue*." Anatole smiled. "Always has her nose in a book. Although her reading matter is often rather, how shall I put it, sensationalist! Not to my taste at all. Ghost stories and Gothic horrors . . ."

"We are fortunate enough to have a splendid library here. My late husband was an avid historian and was interested in other less usual . . ." Isolde broke off, as if searching for the appropriate word. "More select matters of study, shall we say." She hesitated again. Léonie looked at her with interest, but Isolde said nothing more about what these matters might be. "There are many first editions and rare volumes," she continued, "which I am certain will be of interest to you, Anatole, as well as a good selection of novels and back editions of *Le Petit Journal* that might appeal to you, Léonie. Please, treat the collection as if it was your own."

It was now just short of seven o'clock. In the shade of the tall chestnut trees, the sun had all but gone from the terrace, and the shadows were stretching across the far edges of the lawn. Isolde rang a small silver bell that sat beside her on the table.

Marieta appeared immediately.

"Has Pascal returned with the luggage?"

"Some time ago, Madama."

"Good. Léonie, I have put you in the Yellow Room. Anatole, you have the Anjou Suite, at the front of the house. It faces north, but it is a pleasant room for all that."

"I'm certain it will be most comfortable," he said.

"Since we have eaten so well at tea, and I thought you might both wish to retire early tonight after the rigors of the journey from Paris, I have not arranged for us to dine formally this evening. Please, feel at liberty to ring for anything you need. It has become my custom to have a nightcap in the drawing room at nine o'clock. If you would care to join me, I would be delighted."

"Thank you."

"Yes, thank you," Léonie added.

They all three rose to their feet.

"I thought I might take a stroll around the gardens before dusk. Smoke a cigarette?" said Anatole.

Léonie saw some reaction flare in Isolde's still, gray eyes.

"If it is not too much of an imposition, may I suggest you save your exploration of the Domaine until the morning. It will be dark soon. I would not wish to have to send out a search party for you on your very first evening."

For a moment, nobody spoke. Then, to Léonie's astonishment, rather than object to this restriction on his freedom, Anatole smiled, as if at some private joke. He took Isolde's hand and raised it to his lips. Perfectly correct, perfectly courteous.

And yet.

"Of course, *Tante*, whatever you wish," said Anatole. "I am your servant."

25

Having taken her leave of her brother and her aunt, Léonie followed Marieta up the staircase and along the first-floor passageway that ran the length of the house. The maid paused to indicate to her the location of the water closet and, adjacent to it, a spacious bathroom, in the center of which stood a huge copper bath, before continuing to her bedroom.

"The Yellow Room, Madomaisèla," said Marieta, standing back to allow Léonie to enter. "Hot water is on the washstand. Is there anything else you need?"

"Everything looks most satisfactory."

The maid bobbed and withdrew.

Léonie looked around with pleasure at the room that was to be her home for the next four weeks. It was a well-appointed chamber, both handsome and comfortable, overlooking the lawns to the south of the property. The window was open, and from below, she could hear the quiet chink of crockery and china as the servants cleared the table.

The walls were covered in a delicate paper of pink and purple flowers, matching the curtains and linen, which gave an impression of light despite the deep hues of the mahogany furniture. The bed—quite the largest Léonie had ever seen—sat like an Egyptian barge in the center of the room, its ornate head- and footboards polished and gleaming. Beside it sat a claw-footed armoire, on which stood a candle in a brass holder, a glass and a jug of water covered with an embroidered white napkin to keep away the flies. Her workbox had also been placed there, together with her book of cartridge papers and painting accoutrements. Her traveling easel was propped against the armoire on the floor.

Léonie crossed the room to a tall wardrobe. The surround was carved in the same elaborate Egyptian style, and there were two long mirrors set into the doors, which reflected the room behind her. She opened the right-hand door, setting the hangers rattling on the rail, to look at her petticoats, after-noon dresses, evening gowns and jackets hanging arranged in neat rows. Everything had been unpacked.

In the large chest of drawers beside the closet she found her undergarments and smaller articles of clothing—camisoles, corsets, blouses, stockings—folded neatly in deep, heavy drawers that smelled of fresh lavender.

The fireplace was on the wall facing the door, and above it, a mirror with a mahogany frame. In the center of the mantelshelf was a gilt and porcelain Sèvres clock much like the one in the drawing room at home.

Léonie removed her dress, cotton lisle stockings, combinations and corset, draping garments across the carpet and armchair. In her chemise and undergarments, she poured the steaming water from the jug into the basin. She washed her face and hands, then dabbed under her arms and in the hollow between her breasts. When she had finished, she pulled her blue cashmere dressing gown from where it had been hung on a heavy brass hook on the back of the door, then sat down at the dressing table in front of the middle of the three long casement windows.

Pin by metal pin, she undid her unruly copper hair, letting it fall loose to her slender waist, then tilted the looking glass toward her and began to brush in wide, long strokes until it lay unraveled like a skein of silk down her back.

Out of the corner of her eye, a movement in the gardens below snagged her attention.

"Anatole," she muttered, fearing that perhaps her brother had decided to ignore Isolde's request that he remain inside after all.

Hoping he had done so.

Pushing the unworthy sentiment from her mind, Léonie replaced her hair-brush on the dressing table and slipped round to stand before the center window. The last vestiges of day had all but bade farewell to the sky. As her eyes became accustomed to the dusk, she noticed another movement, this time at the far boundary of the lawns by the high box hedge, beyond the ornamental lake.

Now she could clearly see a figure. He was bare-headed and had a furtive walk, every few steps turning and glancing behind him, as if he thought he was being followed.

A trick of the light?

The figure disappeared into the shadows. Léonie fancied she heard a church bell toll in the valley below, a thin and mournful single note, but when she strained to listen, the only sounds she could distinguish were those of the countryside at dusk. The whispering of the wind in the trees and the mixed twilight chorus of birdsong. Then the piercing shriek of an owl preparing for a night's hunting.

Realizing the exposed skin on her arms was covered in goose bumps, Léonie finally shut the casement and withdrew. After a moment's hesitation, she drew the curtains. The figure had almost certainly been one of the gardeners the worse for drink, or a boy on a dare taking an illicit shortcut across the lawns, but there was something distasteful about the spectacle, threatening. In truth, she was uncomfortable to have witnessed it. She felt shaken by what she had seen.

The silence of the room was disturbed, suddenly, by a sharp rap on the door.

"Who is it?" she cried.

"*C'est moi,*" Anatole called back. "Are you decent? May I come in?"

"*Attend, j'arrive.*"

Léonie fastened her robe and smoothed her hair from her face, surprised to find that her hands were shaking.

"Whatever is wrong?" he said, when she opened the door. "You sounded quite alarmed."

"I am fine," she snapped.

"Are you sure, *petite*? You're as white as a sheet."

"You were not out walking on the lawns?" she asked suddenly. "No more than a few minutes past?"

Anatole shook his head. "I did remain on the terrace for a few moments after you had withdrawn, but for no longer than the time it took to smoke a cigarette. Why?"

"I . . ." Léonie began, then reconsidered. "Never mind. It doesn't matter."

He tipped her clothes to the floor and took possession of the armchair.

"Probably just one of the stable boys." Anatole fished his cigarette case and his box of wax Vestas from his pocket and put them on the table.

"Not in here," pleaded Léonie. "Your tobacco is noxious stuff."

He shrugged, then reached into his other pocket and pulled out a small blue pamphlet.

"I have brought you something to help pass the time."

He strolled across the room, handed the monograph to her and then sat back in the chair.

"*Voilà*," he said. "*Diables et esprits maléfiques et phantômes de la montagne.*"

Léonie wasn't listening. Her eyes darted once more in the direction of the window. Wondering if whatever she had seen was still out there.

"Are you all right? You really are awfully pale."

Anatole's voice drew her back. Léonie looked down at the volume in her hand, as if wondering how it had got to be there.

"I am fine," she repeated, embarrassed. "Whatever manner of book is it?"

"Haven't a clue. Looks quite dreadful, but it seems your sort of thing! Found it gathering dust in the library. The author is someone Isolde intends to invite to supper on Saturday night, a Monsieur Audric Baillard. There are passages about the Domaine de la Cade. It appears there are all sorts of stories about devils, evil spirits and ghosts associated with this region, particularly this estate, stretching back to the religious wars of the seventeenth century." He smiled across at her.

Léonie narrowed her eyes suspiciously. "And what spurred you to this act of generosity?"

"Can a brother not, out of the goodness of his heart, undertake an act of random kindness for his sister?"

"Certain brothers, indeed, yes. But you?"

He held up his hands in surrender. "Very well, I confess I thought it might keep you out of mischief."

Anatole ducked as Léonie threw a pillow at him.

"Missed." He laughed. "Very poor shot." He swept up his cigarette case and matches from the table, sprang to his feet and within a matter of strides was at the door. "Let me know how you get on with Monsieur Baillard. I think we should accept Isolde's invitation to join her for drinks later in the drawing room. Yes?"

"Do you not think it odd that there is to be no dinner this evening?"

He raised his eyebrows. "Do you have an appetite?"

"Well, no. I do not, but even—"

Anatole put his finger to his lips. "Well, then, shush." He opened the door. "Enjoy the book, *petite*. I shall expect a full report later."

Léonie listened to his whistling and the firm tread of his boots getting fainter and fainter as he made his way along the passage to his own room.

Then the closing of another door. Peace descended upon the house once more.

Léonie fetched the pillow from where it had fallen and climbed up onto the bed. She drew up her knees, settled herself comfortably and opened the book.

The clock on the mantelpiece chimed the half-hour.

26

Paris

The fashionable streets and boulevards were smothered in a thick brown twilight. The *quartiers perdus*, the down-at-heel neighborhoods, the alleyways and labyrinthine network of apartments and slums, also gasped for breath in the polluted dusk.

The mercury plummeted. The air had grown cold.

Buildings and people, trams and landaus, seemed to loom out of the shadows, appearing and then disappearing again like phantoms. The awnings of the cafés on the rue d'Amsterdam were flapping in the blustering wind, plunging like tethered horses trying to break free. On the grands boulevards, the branches of the trees shook.

Leaves skimmed and danced along the pavements of the ninth arrondissement and the green paths of the Parc Monceau. No hopscotch, no game of grandmother's footsteps; the children were all snug inside the embassy buildings. The new telegraph wires of the post office began to vibrate and sing, and the tram rails to whistle.

At seven-thirty the fog gave way to rain. It fell as cold and gray as iron filings, slowly at first, then heavier and faster. Servants closed the shutters of apartments and houses with a clatter. In the eighth arrondissement, those still outside sought refuge from the impending tempest, ordered beer and absinthe and quarreled over the few remaining tables inside at the Café Wéber on the rue Royale. The beggars and *chiffonniers* with no homes to go to sought shelter beneath the bridges and railway arches.

In the rue de Berlin, Marguerite Vernier lay on the chaise longue in her apartment. One white arm was folded beneath her head, the other was draped over the side of the divan, her fingers trailing the carpet like a dreamy girl in a summertime boat. The lightest of touches. Only the tinge of blue on her lips, the purple bruising like a collar around her jaw, the ugly bracelet of congealed blood on her abused wrist betrayed the fact that she was not sleeping.

Like Tosca, like Emma Bovary, like Prosper Mérimée's doomed heroine, Carmen, Marguerite was beautiful in death. The knife, the blade stained red by its task, lay beside her hand as if it had dropped from her dying fingers.

Victor Constant was insensible to her presence. She had ceased to exist for him the instant he realized he had obtained as much as he would from her.

Save the ticking of the clock on the mantelpiece, all was silent.

Save the pool of light cast by the single candle, all was darkness.

Constant buttoned his trousers and lit a Turkish cigarette, then took a seat at the dining table to examine the journal his manservant had found in Vernier's nightstand.

"Get me a brandy."

With his own knife, a Nontron blade with a yellow handle, Constant cut the string, then unfolded the waxed brown paper and lifted out a royal-blue pocket notebook. The journal was a record of Vernier's day-to-day personal activities for the year: the salons he had frequented; a list of debts, recorded neatly in two columns and scored through when the obligation had been met; mention of a brief flirtation with the occultists in the cold early months of the year, as a buyer of books rather than as an acolyte; purchases made, such as an umbrella and a limited edition of *Cinq Poèmes* from Edmond Bailly's bookshop in the rue de la Chaussée d'Antin.

Constant was not interested in the tedious domestic details, and he flicked quickly through, scanning the pages, looking for dates or references that might give him information. He was looking for details of the affair between Vernier and the only woman he had loved. He still could not bring himself even to think her name, let alone speak it. On the thirty-first of October of last year she had told him their relationship must end. Before, indeed, their liaison was worthy of the word. He had taken her reluctance for modesty and had not pressed her. His shock had yielded instantly to uncontrolled rage, and he had all but killed her. Indeed, he might have done so had not her cries been overheard by neighbors in the adjoining building.

He had let her go. He had, after all, not intended to hurt her. He loved her, worshipped her, adored her. But her betrayal was too much to bear. She had driven him to it.

After that night, she disappeared from Paris. Throughout November and December, Constant thought of her endlessly. It was simple. He loved her, and in return, she had wronged him. His body and his mind would throw out relentless and spiteful reminders of their time together—her scent, her willowy grace, how still she would sit beside him, how grateful she had been for his love. How modest she had been, how obedient, how perfect. Then the humiliation of how she had abandoned him would come flooding back, together with an anger fiercer and more savage than before.

To obliterate the memory of her, Constant took refuge in the usual pastimes open to a gentleman of urbane habits and deep pockets. Gambling dens, nightclubs, laudanum to counteract the increasingly heavy doses of mercury he was obliged to take to alleviate the symptoms of his worsening condition. There was a succession of *midinettes*, whores who looked in passing like her, their soft flesh paying the price for her disloyalty. He was strikingly good-looking. He could be generous. He knew how to charm and coax, and the girls were willing enough, until the moment they realized how depraved his appetites were.

Nothing gave him respite. Nothing eased his anguish at her treachery.

For three months, Constant survived without her. At the end of January, however, everything changed. As the ice on the Seine began to melt, a rumor reached his ears that not only was she back in Paris, and a widow now, but that there was a lover. That she had given to another man what she had withheld from him.

Constant's torment was overwhelming, his rage appalling. The need to be revenged upon her—upon them—possessed him utterly. He imagined her bloody and bleeding in his hands, suffering as she had caused him to suffer. To punish the whore for her perfidy became his sole purpose in life.

It was a simple matter to discover his rival's name. The fact that Vernier and she were lovers was the first thought that came to him each dawn as the sun rose. It was the last thought that came to him as the moon arrived to greet the night.

As January yielded to February, Constant started his campaign of persecution and retribution. He began with Vernier, intending to destroy his good name. His tactic was simple. Gossip dripped into the ears of the less-reputable newspaper columnists, drop by drop. Forged letters passed palm to greasy palm. Rumors fed into the labyrinthine networks of clandestine groups of initiates and acolytes and mesmerists that swarmed beneath the respectable facade of Paris, each obligingly suspicious and in constant fear of betrayal. The rotting tidbits of news, twilight whisperings, the anonymous publication of slanders.

Lies all, but plausible lies.

But even his crusade against Vernier, well executed as it was, gave Constant no respite. Nightmares still stalked his dreams, and even his days were filled with images of the lovers entwined in each other's arms. The relentless progress of his illness, too, stole sleep from him. When Constant shut his eyes he was assaulted by nightmarish images of himself, scourged and nailed to a cross. He suffered visions of his body lying extinguished on the ground, a modern-day Sisyphus crushed by his own rock, or pinned like Prometheus while she crouched upon his chest and ripped out his liver.

In March came a resolution of sorts. She died and with that death came, for him, a release of sorts. Constant watched from the sidelines as her casket was lowered into the wet ground of the cimetière de Montmartre, feeling as if a burden had been taken from his shoulders. After that, with great satisfaction, he had watched Vernier's life crumble under the weight of his grief.

Spring gave way to the heat of July and August. For a while, Constant had been at peace. September came in. Then a chance comment overheard, a glimpse of blond hair beneath a blue hat on the Boulevard Haussmann, whisperings in Montmartre of a coffin buried six months previously without a tenant. Constant sent two men to question Vernier, on the night of the riot at the Palais Garnier, but they were interrupted before they could learn anything of value.

He flicked through the pages of the journal once more until he again reached the date of September 16. The page was empty. Nothing. Vernier had made no record of the riot at the Opéra, no reference to the attack upon him in the Passage des Panoramas. The last entry in the journal was dated two days previously. Constant turned the page and read it again. Large, confident letters—a solitary word.

FIN.

He felt cold rage flood through him. The three letters seemed to dance on the page before his eyes, mocking him. After everything he had endured, to discover that he was the victim of a hoax pulled at the chords of his bitterness with an art all its own. How lunatic to ever have thought that dishonoring Vernier would be sufficient to grant him peace. Constant knew, now, what he had to do. He would hunt them down. Then he would kill them.

The servant placed a tumbler of brandy at his elbow. "General Du Pont may soon be here. . . ." he murmured, then withdrew to the window.

Conscious, now, of the time passing, Constant picked up the sheet of greased brown paper in which the notebook had been wrapped. The presence in the apartment of the journal puzzled him. Why would Vernier have left the journal behind if he were not intending to return? Because he had left in such haste? Or perhaps because he did not propose to be absent from Paris for long.

Constant downed the brandy in one swallow and hurled the glass into the grate. It shattered into a thousand glittering, sharp pieces. The servant flinched. For a moment the air seemed to vibrate with the violence of the act.

Constant stood and replaced the dining chair precisely beneath the table. He walked to the mantelpiece and opened the glass face of the Sèvres clock. He pushed the hands forward until they showed eight. Then he struck the heavy back of the clock against the edge of the marble surround until the mechanism stopped working. Crouching, he placed the clock facedown among the glinting shards of the brandy tumbler.

"Open the Champagne and fetch two glasses."

The man did as instructed. Constant went to the couch. He took a fistful of hair in his hand and lifted Marguerite's head into his arms. The sweet metallic smell of the abattoir hung about her. The pale cushions around her were dyed crimson and a smudged pool of blood stained her chest, like the overblown bloom of a hothouse flower.

Constant tipped a little Champagne into Marguerite's mouth. He pressed the rim of a glass against her split lips until the faintest smear of lipstick was visible, then filled it halfway with Champagne and placed it on the table beside her. He poured a little into the second glass, too, and then laid the bottle on its side on the floor. Slowly the liquid began to empty, a ribbon of bubbles streaming onto the carpet.

"Our reptilian comrades of the fourth estate are aware that there might be something for them tonight?"

"Yes, Monsieur." For an instant, the servant's mask slipped. "The lady . . . Is she dead?"

Constant did not answer.

The servant crossed himself. Constant walked to the sideboard and picked up a framed photograph. Marguerite was seated in the center of the picture, with her children standing behind her. He read the name of the studio and the date. October 1890. The daughter's hair was still worn loose. A child still.

The servant coughed. "Are we to travel to Rouen, Monsieur?"

"Rouen?"

He twisted his fingers nervously, recognizing the look in his master's eyes.

"Forgive me, Monsieur, but did not Madame Vernier say her son and daughter had traveled to Rouen?"

"Ah. Yes, she showed more courage . . . initiative . . . than I expected. But Rouen, I doubt that was their destination. Perhaps she really did not know."

He thrust the photograph at his man.

"Get out and ask after the girl. Someone will talk. Somebody always does. People will remember her." He gave a cold smile. "She will lead us to Vernier and his whore."

27

Domaine de la Cade

Léonie screamed. She threw herself upright, her heart thudding against her ribs. The candle had blown itself out and the room was cloaked in darkness.

For a moment she thought she was back in the drawing room at the rue de Berlin. Then she looked down and saw Monsieur Baillard's monograph lying on the pillow beside her, and realized.

Une cauchemar.

Of demons and spirits, of phantoms and clawed creatures and the ancient ruins where the spider spins her web. The hollow eyes of ghosts.

Léonie fell back against the wooden headboard, waiting for her pulse to stop racing. Images of a stone sepulchre beneath a gray sky, withered garlands draped over a worn escutcheon. A family coat of arms, long corrupt and dishonored.

Such dark dreams.

She waited for her pulse to stop racing, but if anything, the hammering inside her head was getting louder.

"Madomaisèla Léonie? Madama has sent me to ask if there is anything you need?"

With relief, Léonie recognized Marieta's voice.

"Madomaisèla?"

Léonie composed herself and then called out, *"Viens."*

There was a rattling at the door, then: "Forgive me, Madomaisèla, but it is locked."

Léonie did not remember turning the key. Swiftly she slipped her chilled feet into her silk *savates* and ran to open the door.

Marieta gave a quick bob. "Madama Lascombe and Sénher Vernier have sent me to ask if you might join them."

"What is the time?"

"Nearly half past nine."

So late.

Léonie rubbed the nightmare from her eyes. "Of course. I can do for myself. If you could tell them I will be down presently?"

She slipped into her undergarments, then put on a plain evening dress, nothing elaborate. She arranged her hair with combs and pins, dabbed a little eau de cologne behind her ears and on her wrists, and then descended to the drawing room.

Both Anatole and Isolde stood as she entered. Isolde was dressed simply in a high-necked turquoise dress with half-sleeves decorated with French jet-glass beads. She looked exquisite.

"I am sorry to have kept you waiting," Léonie apologized, kissing first her aunt and then her brother.

"We were about to give up on you," Anatole said. "What would you like? We are drinking Champagne—no, my apologies, Isolde, not Champagne. Would you like the same? Or something else?"

"Not Champagne?"

Isolde smiled. "He is teasing you. It is a *blanquette de Limoux*, not Champagne but a local wine much like it. It is sweeter and lighter, more thirst-quenching. I confess, I have quite a taste for it now."

"Thank you," Léonie said, accepting a glass. "I began to read Monsieur Baillard's pamphlet. The next I knew, Marieta was knocking upon the door and it was past nine o'clock."

Anatole laughed. "Is it so very dull that it sent you to sleep?"

Léonie shook her head. "Quite the opposite. It was fascinating. It appears the Domaine de la Cade—or rather, the site that the house and grounds currently occupy—has long been at the heart of a great many superstitions and local legends. Ghosts, devils, spirits walking at night. Most common are stories concerning a ferocious black wild creature, half devil, half beast, stalking the countryside when times are bad, snatching children and livestock."

Anatole and Isolde caught each other's eyes.

"According to Monsieur Baillard," Léonie continued, "that is why so many of the local landmarks have names that hint at this supernatural past. He relates one tale concerning a lake in the Tabe Mountain, the Étang du Diable, which is said to communicate with Hell itself. If one throws stones into it, clouds of sulfurous gas apparently rise up out of the water, bringing ferocious storms. And another story, going back to the summer of 1840, which was particularly dry. Desperate for the rains, a miller from the village of Montsé-gur climbed up to the Tabe Mountain and threw a live cat into the lake. The animal thrashed and struggled like a demon, so vexing the devil that he made it rain upon the mountains for the two months following."

Anatole stretched back, draping his arm along the back of the settee. In the grate, a good fire crackled and spat.

"What superstitious nonsense!" he said affectionately. "I almost regret putting such a book into your hands."

Léonie pulled a face. "You may mock, but there is always some measure of truth in these stories."

"Well spoken, Léonie," said Isolde. "My late husband was much interested in the legends associated with the Domaine de la Cade. His particular passion was the Visigoth period of history, but he and Monsieur Baillard talked late into the night about all manner of subjects. The curé from our sister village of Rennes-le-Château also sometimes joined them."

A sudden image of the three men huddled together over books flashed into Léonie's mind, and she wondered if Isolde had resented being so often excluded.

"Abbé Saunière." Anatole nodded. "Gabignaud mentioned him on the journey from Couiza this afternoon."

"Having said that, it would be fair to say that Jules was always cautious in Monsieur Baillard's company."

"Cautious? How so?"

Isolde waved her slim, white hand. "Oh, perhaps *cautious* is the wrong word. Reverential, almost. I am not entirely certain what I mean. He had great respect for Monsieur Baillard's age and knowledge but was also somewhat in awe of his learning."

Anatole replenished the glasses, then rang the bell for another bottle.

"You say Baillard is a local man?"

Isolde nodded. "He has furnished lodgings in Rennes-les-Bains, although his main residence is elsewhere. Somewhere in the Sabarthès, I believe. He is an extraordinary man but a very private one. He is circumspect about his past experiences, and his interests are wide-ranging. In addition to local folklore and customs, he is also an expert on the Albigensian Heresy." She gave a light laugh. "Indeed, Jules remarked once that one might almost believe Monsieur Baillard had been a witness at some of those medieval battles, so vivid were his descriptions."

They all smiled.

"It is not the best time of year, but perhaps you would like to visit some of the ruined frontier castles," Isolde said to Léonie. "Weather permitting."

"I would like that very much."

"And I shall place you next to Monsieur Baillard at dinner on Saturday, so you may question him all you wish about devils and superstitions and the myths of the mountains."

Léonie nodded, remembering Monsieur Baillard's tales. Anatole, too, fell silent. A different mood had entered the room, slipping in among the easy conversation when no one was watching. For a while, the only sounds were the ticking of the golden hands of the long-case clock and the spitting of the flames in the hearth.

Léonie found her eyes drawn to the windows. They were shuttered against the evening, yet she was strongly aware of the darkness beyond. It seemed to have a living, breathing presence. It was only the wind whistling around the corners of the building, but it seemed to her as if the night itself was murmuring, conjuring up the ancient spirits of the woods.

She glanced at her aunt, beautiful in the soft light, and so still.

Does she feel it, too?

Isolde's expression was serene, her features impassive. It was impossible for Léonie to tell what she might be thinking. Her eyes did not flicker with the grief of her husband's absence. And there was no suggestion of anxiety or nervousness at what might lie beyond the stone walls of the house.

Léonie looked down at the *blanquette* in her glass, then drained the last of it.

The clock chimed the half-hour.

Isolde announced her intention to write the invitations for Saturday's supper party, and withdrew to the study. Anatole took the squat green bottle of Benedictine from the tray and declared he would remain a while longer and smoke a cigar.

Léonie kissed her brother good night and quitted the drawing room. She walked across the hall, a little unsteady on her feet, with memories of the day in her mind. Of those things that had given her pleasure and those that had intrigued. How clever it was of Tante Isolde to guess that Anatole's favorite bonbons were Pearls of the Pyrenees. How comfortable, for the most part, the three of them had been in one another's company. She thought of the adventures she might have, and how she would explore the house and, weather permitting, the grounds.

Her hand was already upon the banister rail when she observed that the piano lid stood temptingly open. The black and white keys were bright in the shimmering candlelight, as if they had recently been polished. The rich mahogany surround seemed to glow.

Léonie was not an accomplished pianist, but she was unable to resist the invitation of the untouched keyboard. She played a scale, an arpeggio, then a chord. The piano had a sweet voice, soft and precise, as if it was kept tuned and cared for. She let her fingers go where they wished, sounding out a mournful and antique pattern of notes in a minor key—A, E, C and D. A single strand of melody echoed briefly in the silence of the hall, then faded. Sorrowful, evocative, pleasing to the ear.

Léonie ran the backs of her fingers up the climbing octaves with a final flourish, then continued up the stairs to bed.

The hours passed. She slept. The house fell, room by room, into silence. One by one the candles were extinguished. Beyond the gray walls, the grounds, the lawns, the lake, the beech woods lay quietly beneath a white moon. All was still.

And yet.

Part IV

Rennes-les-Bains
October 2007

28

Monday, October 29

Meredith's plane touched down at Toulouse-Blagnac airport ten minutes ahead of schedule. By four-thirty she'd picked up her rental car and was negotiating her way out of the parking lot. In sneakers and blue jeans, with her big over-the-shoulder bag, she looked like a student.

The evening rush hour on the beltway was crazy, like Grand Theft Auto without the weapons. Meredith gripped the wheel tightly, nervous about the traffic coming at her from all sides. She turned on the air conditioner and fixed her eyes on the windshield.

Once she hit the autoroute, things calmed down. She started to feel confident, enough to turn on the radio. She found a station, Classique, on preset and turned the volume up high. The usual. Bach, Mozart, Puccini, even a little Debussy.

The route was pretty straightforward. She headed for Carcassonne, turning off after about thirty minutes to go cross-country, via Mirepoix and Limoux. At Couiza, she took a left toward Arques, then after ten minutes of winding road, turned down to the right. By six, feeling a mixture of anticipation and excitement, she was driving into the town she'd thought about for so long.

Her first impressions of Rennes-les-Bains were encouraging. Even though it was much smaller than she'd expected and the main street—although "main" was pushing it some—was narrow, barely wide enough for two cars to pass, there was something charming about it. The fact that it was completely deserted didn't really bother her.

She drove by an ugly stone building, then pretty gardens set down from the road with a metal sign over the entrance, JARDIN DE PAUL COURRENT, and a sign on the wall for LE PONT DE FER. Suddenly, her foot hit the floor. The car slid to a halt, just in time to avoid slamming into the back of a blue Peugeot stopped in the road ahead.

It was the last in a short line of cars. Meredith killed the radio, pressed the button to open her window and leaned out to get a better look. Ahead was a small group of workmen standing beside a yellow road sign: ROUTE BARRÉE.

The driver of the Peugeot got out and walked toward the men, shouting. Meredith waited, then when another couple of drivers got out of their cars, too, she did the same, just as the man from the Peugeot turned and strode back toward his car. In his late fifties, he was a little gray around the temples, with a little extra weight but carrying it well. Attractive, with the bearing and demeanor of someone used to getting his own way. What caught Meredith's eye was how he was dressed. Very formal, in black jacket, black pants and tie, polished shoes.

She darted a glance at his licence plate. It ended with 11. Local tag.

"*Qu'est-ce qui se passe?*" she asked, as he drew level.

"Tree's down," he replied abruptly, paying no attention.

Meredith was pissed at him for replying in English. She figured her accent wasn't so bad.

"Well, did they say how long it would be?" she snapped.

"At least half an hour," he replied, getting into his car. "Could mean anything, up to three hours Midi time. Tomorrow, even."

He was clearly impatient to be gone. Meredith stepped forward and put a hand on the door. "Is there another way round?"

This time, he at least looked at her. Steely blue eyes, very direct.

"Back to Couiza, over the hills via Rennes-le-Château," he said. "Take you forty minutes at this time of night. I'd wait. Confusing in the dark." He glanced at her hand, then back to her face. "Now, if you'll excuse me."

Meredith colored. "Thank you for your help," she said, taking a step back. She watched as he reversed up onto the sidewalk, got out, then strode off down the main street. "Not a guy to fall out with," she muttered to herself, not sure why she felt so mad.

Some of the other drivers were doing awkward three-point turns in the tight street and heading back in the direction from which they'd come. Meredith hesitated. However abrupt the guy had been, she figured his advice was probably good. No sense getting lost in the hills.

She decided to explore the town on foot. She backed her rental car on to the sidewalk and parked beside his blue Peugeot. She wasn't actually sure if Rennes-les-Bains was where her ancestors had come from, or if it was just an accident of timing that the photograph of the soldier from 1914 had been taken here rather than anyplace else. But it was one of the only leads she'd got. She might as well start investigating tonight.

She reached across the seat for her purse—the idea of having her laptop stolen didn't bear thinking about—and then checked that the trunk, with her overnight bag in it, was locked. Once the car was secure, she walked the couple of steps to the main entrance of the Station Thermale et Climatique.

There was a hand-printed notice on the door saying it was now closed for the winter: October 1 through April 30, 2008. Meredith stared at the sign in disbelief. She'd just assumed it would be open year-round. She hadn't thought to call ahead.

Hands in her pockets, she stood outside awhile. The windows were dark, the building apparently totally empty. Even though coming here to search for traces of Lilly Debussy was, in part, an excuse to get herself down here, she'd had good hopes of the spa. Old records, photographs dating back to the turn of the last century when Rennes-les-Bains was one of the most fashionable resorts in the area.

Now, looking at the shuttered doors of the Station Thermale, even if there was evidence inside of Lilly being sent here to convalesce in the summer of 1900—or else of a particular young man in military uniform—she wasn't going to find out.

It was possible she could persuade the mairie—someone—to let her in, but she wasn't hopeful. Feeling a little stupid for not thinking it through, Meredith turned away and walked back to the street.

A footpath ran down the right of the spa buildings, the Allée des Bains de la Reine. She followed it down to the riverbank, pulling her jacket tight around her against the sharp wind that had come up, past a large swimming pool drained of water. An air of neglect hung about the deserted terrace. The chipped blue tiles, the peeling pink-washed deck, the broken white plastic recliners. It was hard to believe the pool was used at all.

She moved on. The riverbank also felt abandoned, empty of human life. Like tailgate parties in high school, the morning after the night before, when the fields were muddy and skidded with tire tracks. The path was lined with metal benches, crooked and dispirited-looking. There was a rusty, rickety metal pergola in the shape of a crown with a wooden bench set beneath. It looked as if it hadn't been used for years. Meredith glanced up and saw a couple of metallic hooks, she guessed to fix some kind of awning to keep the sun off.

Out of force of habit, she dug into her bag and pulled out her camera. She adjusted the setting to deal with the poor light before taking a couple of shots, not convinced they'd come out. She tried to picture Lilly sitting on one of the benches, in a white blouse and black skirt, her face sheltered beneath a wide-brimmed hat, dreaming of Debussy and Paris. She tried to imagine her sepia soldier strolling along the riverbank, maybe with a girl on his arm, but couldn't. The place felt wrong. Everything was derelict, abandoned. The world had moved on.

Feeling somehow sad, nostalgic for an imagined past she'd never known, Meredith walked slowly along the bank. She followed the curved course of the river to a flat concrete bridge that crossed the water. She hesitated before walking over. The opposite bank was wilder, clearly less frequented. It was dumb to wander around a strange town alone, especially with a valuable laptop and camera in her purse.

And it's getting dark.

But Meredith felt something tugging at her. A spirit of exploration, she guessed, or adventure. She wanted to get under the skin of the town. The real place that had been here for hundreds of years, not just the main street with its modern cafés and cars. And if it turned out she did have some sort of personal connection with the place, she sure didn't want to feel she'd wasted her time here. Hooking the strap of her purse over her shoulder and chest, she walked across.

There was a different atmosphere on the far side of the river. Right away, Meredith had the sense of a more enduring landscape, one less influenced by people and fashions. The rough-hewn, jutting hillside seemed to rise straight out of the ground in front of her. The variegated greens and browns and coppers of the bushes and trees took on the rich hues of dusk. It should have been a landscape that appealed, but something felt wrong about it. Two-dimensional, somehow, as if the true character of the place was concealed beneath a painted exterior.

In the October evening Meredith carefully picked her way through the overgrown briars and flattened grass and trash blown by the wind. A car went by on the road bridge above, its headlights briefly throwing up a beam of light on the gray wall of rock where the mountains came right down to the town.

Then the noise of the engine died away, and all was silent again.

Meredith followed the path until she could go no farther. She found herself standing at the mouth of a black tunnel that led away beneath the road into the mountainside.

Some kind of storm drain?

Resting her hand on the cold brick wall of the surround, Meredith leaned forward and peered inside, feeling the damp air trapped beneath the stone arch whisper across her skin. The water was flowing faster here, funneled into the narrow channel. White flecks splashed up against the brick walls as the river ran over jagged rocks.

There was a narrow ledge, just wide enough for her to stand on.

Not a smart idea to go in.

Yet she found herself dipping her head and, with her right hand on the dank sides of the tunnel to keep her balance, taking a step into the gloom. Straight away, the smell of wet air, spray, moss and lichen hit her. The ledge was slippery as she edged in farther, a little farther, farther still, until the amethyst twilight was just a shimmer and she could no longer see the riverbank.

Bending her head so as not to knock it on the curved wall of the tunnel, Meredith stopped and looked down into the water. Small black fish darting, trailing tendrils of green weeds flattened by the force of the current, the lacy white crests as the ripples came into contact with the ridges of submerged stone and rock.

Lulled by the white noise and the motion of the water, Meredith crouched down. Her eyes lost focus. It was peaceful beneath the bridge, hidden, a secret place. Here, she could more easily summon the past. As she looked down into the river, she found it easy to imagine boys in knee-length britches and bare feet, girls with curled hair held back with satin ribbons, playing hide-and-seek beneath this old bridge. She could imagine the echo of the adult voices calling for their charges from the opposite bank.

What the hell?

For a fleeting second, Meredith thought she saw the outline of a face looking up at her. Her eyes narrowed. She was aware that the silence seemed to have deepened. The air was empty and cold, as if all the life had been sucked out of it. She felt her heart catch and her senses sharpen. Every nerve in her body was alert.

Just my own reflection.

Telling herself not to be so impressionable, she looked again into the choppy mirror of the water.

This time, no doubt. A face was staring up at her from beneath the surface of the river. It was not a reflection, although Meredith had the sense of her own features hidden behind the image, but a girl with long, flowing hair swaying and shifting in the current, a modern-day Ophelia. Then the eyes beneath the water seemed, slowly, to open and hold Meredith's own in their clear and direct gaze. Eyes like green glass, containing within them all the shifting colors of the water.

Meredith cried out. In shock, she sprang back up, nearly losing her balance, flinging her hands out behind her for the reassurance of the wall at her back. She forced herself to look again.

Nothing.

There was nothing there. No reflection, no ghostly face in the water, just the distorted shapes of the rocks and driftwood stirred up by the moving current. Just the water chasing over the rocks, making the weeds in the river dance and twist and sway.

Meredith was desperate to get out of the tunnel now. Slipping, sliding, she inched along the ledge until she was in the open air. Her legs were shaking. Taking her purse off her shoulder, she thumped down on a dry patch of grass and drew her knees up to her chin. Above her on the road, she saw two beams of light as another car drove out of the town.

Was it starting?

Meredith's greatest fear was that the illness that had afflicted her birth mother would one day show up in her. Ghosts, voices, haunted by stuff no one else could hear or see.

She took deep breaths, in and out, in and out.

I'm not her.

Meredith gave herself a few minutes more, then stood up. She brushed herself off, wiping the trails of slime and weed from the soles of her sneakers, picked up her heavy bag and retraced her steps back over the low footbridge to the path.

She was still shaken, but more, she was mad at herself for getting so spooked. She used the same techniques she'd taught herself way back, calling on good memories to push out the bad. Now, rather than the painful memory of Jeanette crying, she heard instead Mary's voice in her head. Regular mom stuff. All those times she'd come back home muddy and with her pants torn through at the knees, covered in scratches and bites. If Mary was here right now, she'd be worrying at Meredith for wandering off on her own, for poking her nose into places she had no business to be, just like always.

Same old same old.

A wave of homesickness washed over her. For the first time since she'd flown to Europe two weeks ago, Meredith genuinely wished she was curled up safe and sound with a book in her favorite old armchair, wrapped in that old quilt blanket Mary had made for her when she'd been off school for a whole semester in fifth grade. Back home, rather than wandering alone, on what might turn out to be a wild-goose chase, in a forgotten corner of France.

Cold and miserable, Meredith checked the time. She got no signal on her cell, but she could see the time. Only fifteen minutes since she'd left her car. Her shoulders sagged. The road was unlikely to be open yet.

Rather than go back up the Allée des Bains de la Reine, she stayed on the walkway that ran along the backs of the houses at river level. From here she could see the concrete underside of the swimming pool, overhanging the path as if propped up on stilts. The outline of the original buildings was clearer from this angle. In the shadows she saw the bright eyes of a cat as it slipped in and out of the stanchions. Trash, scraps of paper, soda bottles rolled in by the wind clung to the bricks and wires.

The river curved round to the right. On the far side Meredith saw an archway in the wall that led down to the river valley from the street high above, right to the path at the water's edge. The streetlights had come on, and she could just make out an old woman in a flowered bathing suit and bathing cap lying faceup in the water, within a ring of stones, her towel folded neatly on the walkway. Meredith shivered in sympathy before noticing that steam was rising from the surface. Nearby the woman, an old man, his lean brown body wrinkled, was drying himself on the bank.

Meredith admired their spirit, although it wasn't how she'd choose to spend a cool October evening. She tried to picture the glory days of the *fin de siècle* when Rennes-les-Bains was a thriving resort. The bathing huts on wheels, ladies and gentlemen in old-fashioned swimsuits stepping down into the hot therapeutic waters, their servants and nurses standing behind them on this same riverbank.

She failed. Like a theater after the curtain has fallen and the house manager has turned off the lights, Rennes-les-Bains seemed too desolate for such flights of imagination.

A narrow staircase with no handrail led up to a pedestrian bridge of blue-painted metal linking the left bank to the right. She remembered the sign from earlier: LE PONT DE FER. It was right where she'd left the rental car.

Meredith climbed up. Back to civilization.

29

As Meredith had suspected, the road was still shut. Her rental car was right where she'd left it, behind the blue Peugeot. A couple of other cars had joined them on the sidewalk.

She walked past the Jardin Paul Courrent and along the main street toward the lights, then turned right up a very steep road that seemed to run straight into the hillside itself. It led to a car park, which was surprisingly full given how empty the town seemed. She read the tourist information board, a rustic wooden sign advertising walks to local landmarks: L'Homme Mort, La Cabanasse, La Source de la Madeleine, and a cross-country route to a neighboring village, Rennes-le-Château.

It wasn't raining, but the air had gotten damp. Everything seemed muffled and subdued. Meredith went on, peering up alleyways that seemed to lead nowhere, glancing into the brightly lit windows of houses, then doubled back to the main street. Straight ahead was the Mairie, with the *tricolore* fluttering blue, white and red in the evening air. She turned left and found herself in the Place des Deux Rennes.

Meredith stood awhile, taking in the atmosphere. There was a charming pizzeria on the right with wooden tables outside. Only a couple of the tables were occupied, both with groups of English people. At one, the men were talking football and Steve Reich, while the women—one with stylish cropped black hair, another with blond hair cut sharp to the shoulders, the third with auburn curls—were sharing a bottle of wine and discussing the latest Ian Rankin. At the second table was a crowd of students eating pizza and drinking beer. One of the boys was wearing a blue, studded leather jacket. Another was talking about Cuba to a darker-haired friend who had an unopened bottle of pinot grigio at his feet. The last member of the group, a pretty girl with streaks of pink in her hair, was making a square with her hands as if framing the scene for a photograph. Meredith smiled as she walked by, reminded of her own students. The girl noticed and smiled back.

In the far corner of the square, Meredith noticed a *cloche-mur* with a single bell above the rooftops of the buildings and realized she'd found the church.

She walked down a cobbled approach to l'église de Saint-Celse et Saint-Nazaire. A single overhead lamp was burning in the unassuming porch, open to the elements to north and south. There were two tables, too, incongruous-looking and empty.

The sign on the parish noticeboard next to the door stated that the church was open from ten every morning through dusk, except for feast days and weddings and funerals. But when she tried the handle, it was locked even though lights were on inside.

She looked at her watch. Half past six. Maybe she'd just missed it.

Meredith turned around. On the opposite wall was a board of names, a roll call of the men of Rennes-les-Bains who'd given their lives in World War I.

A Ses Glorieux Morts.

Was death ever glorious? Meredith wondered, thinking of her sepia soldier. Of her birth mother walking into Lake Michigan with her pockets weighted down with stones. Was the sacrifice worth it?

She stepped forward and read down the alphabetical list of names right to the end, knowing that it was pointless to expect Martin to be there. It was crazy. From what little background Mary had been able to pass on, Meredith knew that Martin was Louisa's mother's surname, not her father's. In fact, on her birth certificate it said FATHER UNKNOWN. But Meredith did know her ancestors had emigrated from France to America in the years after the First

World War. And after the research she'd done, she was pretty certain the soldier in the photograph was Louisa's father.

She just needed a name.

Something caught her eye. BOUSQUET was there on the memorial. Like the tarot cards sitting in her bag in the trunk. Maybe the same family? Something else to check out. She moved on. At the bottom of the plaque, an unusual name: SAINT-LOUP.

Next to the board were a stone plaque in memory of Henri Boudet, curé of the parish from 1872 to 1915, and a black metal cross. Meredith thought about it. If her unknown soldier had come from here, Henri Boudet might have known him. It was a small town, after all, and the dates were about right.

She copied it all down: first rule of research—and the second and third—write everything down. You never knew until later what might turn out to be relevant.

Beneath the cross were inscribed the Emperor Constantine's famous words: IN HOC SIGNO VINCES. Meredith had come across the phrase plenty of times before, although this time it set some other thought racing through her head. "By this sign you shall conquer," she murmured, trying to figure out what was bugging her, but nothing came.

She walked through the porch, past the main door into the church, and out into the graveyard itself. Straight ahead there was another war memorial, the same names, with one or two additions and discrepancies of spelling, as if to mark their sacrifice only once would be too little.

Generations of men—fathers, brothers, sons—all those lives.

Meredith walked slowly in the somber twilight down the graveled path that ran alongside the church. Tombs, graves, stone angels and crosses loomed up at her as she passed. Every now and again she paused to read an inscription. Certain names repeated over, generation after generation of local families, remembered in granite and marble—Fromilhague and Saunière, Denarnaud and Gabignaud.

At the farthest boundary of the cemetery, overlooking the river gorge, Meredith found herself standing before an ornate mausoleum with the words FAMILLE LASCOMBE-BOUSQUET carved above the metal grille.

She crouched down and, in the last vestiges of daylight, read of the marriages and births that had united the Lascombe and Bousquet families in life and now in death. Guy Lascombe and his wife had been killed in October 1864. The last of the Lascombe line was Jules, who had died in January 1891. The final surviving member of the Bousquet branch of the family, Madeleine Bousquet, had passed on in 1955.

Meredith straightened, aware of the familiar prickling feeling on the back of her neck. It wasn't just the tarot deck Laura had pressed on her and the coincidence of the Bousquet name but something else. Something about the date, something she'd seen but not paid enough attention to at the time.

Then she got it. The year 1891 kept coming up, more than its fair share. She noticed that date in particular because of its personal significance. It was the date printed on the piece of music. She could see the title and the date in her mind's eye as clearly as if she were holding it in her hand.

But there was something more. She ran back everything in her mind from the second she'd walked into the churchyard, until she figured it out. It wasn't just the year so much as the fact that the same actual date had been repeated over and over.

With a burst of adrenaline, Meredith hurried back through the tombs, weaving in and out, checking the inscriptions, and found she was right. Her memory wasn't playing tricks on her. She pulled out her notebook and started to scribble, recording the same date of death for different people, three, four times over.

All had died October 31, 1891.

Behind her, the tiny bell in the *cloche-mur* began to toll.

Meredith turned round and looked at the lights inside the church, then glanced up and saw that there were now stars dotted across the sky. She could hear voices, too, a low murmuring. She heard the church door open, a rush of louder voices before it shut again with a clatter.

She retraced her steps back into the porch. The wooden trestle tables were now in use. One was covered in gifts—flowers in cellophane, bouquets, house-plants in terra-cotta pots. The second was laid with a thick red felt cloth with a large book of condolences set on it.

Meredith couldn't resist taking a look. Beneath that day's date was a name and dates of birth and death: SEYMOUR FREDERICK LAWRENCE: 15 SEPTEMBRE 1938–24 SEPTEMBRE 2007.

She realized the funeral was about to begin, even though it was late. Not wanting to get caught up, she walked quickly back into the Place des Deux

Rennes. The square was busy now. Thronging around, quiet but not silent, were people of all ages. Men in blazers, women in pressed pastels, kids in suits and smart dresses. What Mary would call "Sunday best."

Standing in the shadow of the pizzeria, not wanting to look like she was rubber-necking, Meredith watched as the mourners disappeared into the presbytery next to the church for a few minutes, then emerged and went into the porch to sign the book of condolences. It seemed the whole town had turned out.

"Do you know what's going on?" she asked the waitress.

"*Funérailles,* Madame. *Un bien-aimé.*"

A lean, thin woman with short, dark hair was leaning against the wall. She was standing perfectly still, but her eyes were darting around all over. When she lifted her hand to light her cigarette, the sleeves of her shirt slipped back and Meredith noticed thick, red scars around both wrists.

As if sensing someone was looking, the woman turned her head and looked right at her.

"*Un bien-aimé?*" Meredith said, casting round for something to say.

"Someone popular. Well respected," the woman replied in English.

Of course. Pretty obvious.

"Thanks." Meredith gave an embarrassed smile. "I wasn't thinking."

The woman kept staring a moment longer, then turned her head away. The bell began to toll more insistently, a thin and reedy sound. The crowd stood back as four men came out of the presbytery carrying a closed casket. Behind them, a young man dressed in black, late twenties maybe, with a mop of brown hair. His face was white, his jaw rigid, as if struggling to keep control.

Beside him was an older man, also dressed in black. Meredith's eyes widened. It was the driver of the blue Peugeot, looking totally in control. She felt a shot of guilt at her reaction earlier.

No surprise he was so abrupt.

Meredith watched as the coffin made its short journey from the presbytery to the church. The tourists at the café opposite got to their feet as the mourners filed past. The students stopped talking and stood in silence with their hands clasped in front of them as the slowly moving mass of people disappeared down the passageway.

The door of the church fell shut with a clatter. The bell stopped ringing, leaving only an echo in the evening air. Quickly, everything in the square returned to normal. The scrape of chair legs, people picking up glasses and napkins, lighting cigarettes.

Meredith noticed a car driving up the main street, heading south. Then several more. To her relief, the road was open again. She'd killed enough time for one day.

She stepped out of the lee of the building and, finally, took in the whole vista rather than just one detail of it. The photograph of the young soldier, her ancestor, had been taken here. Suddenly, she saw it in front of her, the precise spot framed by the buildings leading to the Pont Vieux, between a line of *platanes* and the wooded hillside glimpsed through the gap in the houses.

Meredith dug into her purse, pulled out the envelope and held the image up.

An exact match.

The café signs and the bed-and-breakfast on the east side of the square were new, but otherwise it was the same view. Right here, in 1914, a young man had stood and smiled at the camera before going off to fight. Her great-grandfather, she was certain of it.

With renewed enthusiasm for the task she'd set herself, Meredith walked back to her car. She'd been here less than an hour and already she'd found something out. Something definite.

30

Meredith fired the engine and drove her car past the Place des Deux Rennes, glancing at the place where the photograph had been taken, as if she might see the outline of her long-dead ancestor standing between the trees.

Pretty soon she had cleared the outskirts of the small town and was out onto the unlit road beyond. The trees took on strange, shifting shapes. The occasional building, a house or a shed for animals, loomed at her out of the dark. She locked her door with her elbow and heard the mechanism click reassuringly.

Taking it slow, she followed the directions on the map on the brochure. She put the radio on for company. The silence of the country seemed absolute. Beside her was a mass of forest. Above, an expanse of sky was lit with only a few stars. There was no sign of life, not even a fox or a cat.

Meredith found the road to Sougraigne marked on the brochure and turned left. She rubbed her eyes, aware that she was too beat to be driving. The bushes and telegraph poles at the verge seemed to be swaying, vibrating. A couple of times she thought there was someone walking along the side of the road, backlit by her headlamps, but when she got level, she discovered it was only a sign or a roadside shrine.

She tried to keep focused, but she could feel her tired thoughts wandering. After the craziness of the day—the tarot reading, the cab ride across Paris, the drive down here, the roller coaster of emotions—her energy had run out. She was totally gone. All she could think about now was a long, hot shower, then a glass of wine and dinner. Then a long, long sleep.

Jesus!

Meredith slammed on the brakes. There was someone standing right in the middle of the road. A woman in a long red cloak, the hood pulled up over her head. Meredith shouted, saw her own panicked face reflected white in the windshield. She jerked the steering wheel down, knowing there was no way to avoid the collision. As if in slow motion, she felt the tires lose the road. She threw up her hands to brace herself for the impact. The last thing she saw was a pair of wide green eyes staring right at her.

No! No way!

The car skidded. The rear wheels swung round ninety degrees, then back, sliding across the road, rocking to a stop inches away from a ditch. There was a roaring noise, like the sound of drums, coming from somewhere, hammering, battering her senses. It was a moment before she realized it was only the sound of her own blood in her ears.

Meredith opened her eyes.

For a few seconds she sat gripping the wheel tightly, as if afraid to let go. Then, with a rush of cold dread, she realized she had to force herself to get out. She might have hit someone. Killed someone.

She fumbled with the lock and stepped out of the car on shaking legs. Dreading what she was going to find, she walked carefully round to the front, bracing herself to see a body tangled under the wheels.

There was nothing. Not knowing what to think, Meredith cast her disbelieving eyes all around, to the left and to the right, back in the direction she had come, ahead to where the light from the headlights disappeared into a pinpoint of black.

Nothing. The forest was silent. No sign of life.

"Hello?" she called. "Is anybody there? Are you okay? Hello?"

Nothing but her own voice echoing back at her.

Bewildered, she bent down and examined the front of the car. There were no marks at all. She walked all round the vehicle, running her hand over the bodywork, but it was clean.

Meredith got back in the car. She was certain she'd seen someone staring right at her out of the darkness. She hadn't imagined it. Had she? She glanced in the mirror but saw only her own ghostly reflection looking back at her. Then, out of the shadows, the desperate face of her birth mother.

I am not going crazy.

She rubbed her eyes, then started the car. Spooked by what had happened— what *hadn't* happened—she took it pretty steady, leaving the window open to clear her head. Wake her up a little.

Meredith was relieved when she saw the sign for the hotel. She turned off the Sougraigne road and followed a winding single track, which climbed steeply up the hillside. After a couple of minutes more, she arrived at two stone pillars and a pair of ornate black wrought-iron gates. On the wall was a gray slate sign: HÔTEL DOMAINE DE LA CADE.

Triggered by a motion sensor, the gates slowly opened to let her through. There was something eerie about the silence, the click of the mechanism on the gravel, and Meredith shivered. The woods seemed almost to be alive, living and breathing, watching. Malevolent, somehow. She'd be glad to get inside.

The tires crunched as she drove slowly up a long drive lined with *châtaigniers*, sweet chestnut trees, like sentinels on duty. The lawns stretched out on either side into blackness. Finally she rounded a slight curve in the drive and, at last, caught sight of the hotel.

Even after everything that had happened tonight, the unexpected beauty of the place blew her away. The hotel was an elegant three-story building with whitewashed walls covered with flaming red-and-green ivy, gleaming in the floodlights as if the leaves had been polished. Balustrades on the first floor and a row of round windows at the very top, the old servants' quarters, a house perfectly in proportion, amazing when she considered that part of the original *maison de maître* had been destroyed by fire. It all looked totally authentic.

Meredith found a parking spot at the front of the hotel and carried her bags up the curved stone steps. She was glad to have arrived in one piece, although she couldn't quite shake the queasy feeling in the pit of her stomach from her near miss on the road. And the scene at the river.

Just tired, she told herself.

She felt better the second she stepped inside the spacious and elegant lobby. There was a black-and-red checkerboard tile floor and a delicate cream paper of yellow and green flowers on the walls. To the left of the main door, in front of the tall sash windows, was a pair of deep sofas with plumped cushions set on either side of a stone fireplace. A vast floral display stood in the grate. Everywhere mirrors reflected the light from the chandeliers, gilt frames and glass wall sconces.

Straight ahead was a sweeping central staircase, the handrails highly polished and glinting in the diffused light of the glass chandelier, with the front desk to the right, a large polished wooden claw-footed table rather than a counter. The walls were covered in black-and-white and sepia period photographs. Men in military uniform, Napoleonic rather than World War I at first glance, ladies in puffed sleeves and wide skirts, family portraits, scenes of Rennes-les-Bains in days gone by. Meredith smiled. Plenty to check out over the next few days.

She stepped up to the front desk.

"*Bienvenue,* Madame."

"Hi."

"Welcome to the Domaine de la Cade. You have a reservation?"

"Yes, it's Martin. M-A-R-T-I-N."

"It is your first time with us?"

"It is."

Meredith filled in the form and gave her credit-card details, the third she'd used that day. She was handed a map of the hotel and grounds, another of the surrounding area, and an old-fashioned brass key with a red tassel and a disc with the name of her room on it: La Chambre Jaune.

She suddenly felt a prickling on the back of her neck, as if a person had come up behind her and was standing a little too close. She was aware of the rise and fall of someone's breath. She glanced over her shoulder. There was no one.

"The Yellow Room is on the first floor, Madame Martin."

"Excuse me?" Meredith turned back to the clerk.

"I said that your room is on the first floor. The elevator is opposite the concierge," the woman continued, indicating a discreet sign. "Or, if you wish, take the stairs up and go to the right. Last orders for dinner are at nine-thirty. You wish for me to reserve a table?"

Meredith glanced at her watch. A quarter of eight. "That'd be great. Eight-thirty?"

"Very good, Madame. The terrace bar—the entrance is through the library—is open until midnight."

"Great. Thank you."

"Do you need help with your luggage?"

"No, I'm good, thanks."

With a backward glance at the empty lobby, Meredith took the stairs to the impressive first-floor landing. At the top, she looked down and noticed there was a boudoir grand tucked into the shadows beneath the staircase. Nice instrument, by the look of it, although it seemed a weird place to put a piano. The lid was closed.

As she walked along the passage, she grinned at the fact that all the rooms had names rather than numbers. The Anjou Suite, the Blue Room, Blanche de Castille, Henri IV.

The hotel reinforcing its historic credentials.

Her room was pretty much right at the end. With the shimmer of anticipation she always got when going to a new hotel for the first time, she fumbled with the heavy key, pushed the door open with the toe of her sneaker and then flicked the switch.

She gave a wide smile.

There was a huge mahogany bed in the center of the room. The dresser, closet and two nightstands all matched in the same deep red wood. She opened the doors of the closet and found that the minibar, TV and remote were all hidden inside. On the bureau, glossy magazines, hotel guide, room service menu and brochures giving the history of the place. On a small wooden book-holder placed on top of the bureau, a selection of old books. Meredith ran her eyes along the spines—the usual thrillers and classics, a guide to some kind of hat museum in Espéraza, a couple of books on local history.

She crossed the room to the window and opened the shutters, breathing in the heady smell of the damp earth and the night air. The dark lawns stretched away for what seemed like miles. She could just make out an ornamental lake, then a tall hedge separating the formal part of the garden from the woods beyond. She was pleased she was at the back of the hotel, away from the parking lot and the sound of car doors slamming, although there was a terrace below with wooden tables and chairs and patio heaters.

Meredith unpacked, properly this time rather than leaving everything in the bag as she had in Paris—denims, T-shirts and sweaters in the drawers, and her smarter outfits in the closet. She arranged her toothbrush and makeup on the shelves in the bathroom, then tried out the fancy Molton Brown soaps and shampoo in the tub.

Thirty minutes later, feeling more like herself, she wrapped herself in a huge white bathrobe, plugged in her cell to recharge and sat down at her laptop. Discovering she couldn't get Internet access, she reached over and dialed reception.

"Hi. This is Ms. Martin. In the Yellow Room. I need to check e-mail, but I'm having trouble getting online. I'm wondering if you can give me the password or if you can organize it from your end?" Holding the receiver between her ear and her shoulder, she scribbled down the information. "Okay, that's great, thanks. Got it."

She hung up, struck by the coincidence of the password as she typed it in—CONSTANTINE—and quickly got a connection. She sent her daily e-mail to Mary, letting her know she'd arrived safely and that she'd already found the place where one of the photographs had been taken, and promising to be in touch if there was anything to report. Next she looked into her checking account and saw with relief that the money from the publisher had at last come through.

Finally.

There were a couple of personal e-mails, including an invitation to the wedding of two of her college friends in Los Angeles, which she declined, and one to a concert conducted by an old school friend, now back in Milwaukee, which she accepted.

She was about to log off when she thought she might as well see if there was anything online about the fire at the Domaine de la Cade in October 1897. There wasn't much more than she'd learned already from the hotel brochure.

Next she typed LASCOMBE into the search engine.

This did yield a little new information about Jules Lascombe. He appeared to have been some sort of amateur historian, an expert on the Visigoth era and local folklore and superstitions. He'd even had a few books, pamphlets, privately published by a local printing company, Bousquet.

Meredith's eyes narrowed. She clicked on a link and information flashed on the screen. A well-known local family, as well as being the owners of the largest department store in Rennes-les-Bains and a substantial printing business, the Bousquets were also first cousins of Jules Lascombe and had inherited the Domaine de la Cade on his death.

Meredith scrolled down the page until she found what she was looking for. She clicked, then started to read:

> The Bousquet Tarot is a rare deck, not used much outside France. The earliest examples of this deck were printed by the Bousquet publishing company, located outside Rennes-les-Bains in southwest France, in the late 1890s.
>
> Said to be based on a far older deck dating back to the seventeenth century, aspects unique to this deck include the substitution of Maître, Maîtresse, Fils and Fille for the four court cards in each suit, and the period clothing and iconography. The artist of the major arcana cards, which are contemporaneous with the first printed deck, is unknown.

Beside her on the desk, the phone rang. Meredith jumped, the sound raucously loud in the silence of the room. Without taking her eyes from the screen, Meredith flung out her hand and grabbed the receiver.

"Yes? . . . Yes, this is she."

It was the restaurant asking if she still required her table. Meredith glanced at the clock on her laptop and was amazed to find it was eight-forty.

"Actually, I think I'll get something sent up instead," she said, but was swiftly informed that room service stopped at six.

Meredith was torn. She didn't want to stop, not right now, when she was getting somewhere—although whether it mattered or what it meant was another issue. But she was ravenous. She'd skipped lunch, and she was useless on an empty stomach.

Crazy hallucinations at the river and on the road were evidence enough.

"I'll be right down," she said.

She saved the page and the links, then logged off.

31

"What the hell's wrong with you?" demanded Julian Lawrence.

"What's wrong with me?" Hal shouted. "What do you mean what's wrong with me? Apart from having just buried my father? Apart from that, you mean?"

He slammed the door of the Peugeot shut, too hard, then started to walk toward the steps, yanking off his tie and shoving it into his jacket pocket as he went.

"Keep your voice down," his uncle hissed. "We don't want another scene. There's been enough of that this evening." He locked the car and followed his nephew across the car park toward the back entrance to the hotel. "What the devil were you playing at? And in front of the whole town."

From a distance, they looked like a father and son going in to some sort of formal dinner together. Smart, dressed in black suits, polished shoes. Only the expressions on their faces and Hal's clenched fists indicated the hatred the two men felt for each other.

"That's it, isn't it?" Hal shouted. "All you care about. Reputation. What people might think." He tapped his head. "Has the fact that it was your brother—my father—in that box even penetrated your consciousness? I doubt it!"

Lawrence reached out and put his hand on his nephew's shoulder.

"Look, Hal," in a softer voice. "I understand you're upset. Everybody understands. It's only natural. But throwing around wild accusations isn't helping. If anything, it's making it worse. It's starting to make people think there is some substance to the allegations."

Hal tried to shake himself free. His uncle's grip tightened.

"The town—the commissariat, the mairie—everyone's sympathetic for your loss. And your father was well liked. But if you keep on—"

Hal glared at him. "Are you threatening me?" He jerked his shoulder, shrugging his uncle's hand away. "Are you?"

The shutters came down over Julian Lawrence's eyes. Gone was the look of compassion, familial concern. In its place, irritation and something else.

Contempt.

"Don't be ridiculous," he said in a cold voice. "For Christ's sake, pull yourself together. You're twenty-eight years old, not some spoiled public schoolboy!"

He walked into the hotel.

"Have a drink, sleep on it," he said over his shoulder. "We'll talk in the morning."

Hal strode past him. "There's nothing more to say," he said. "You know what I think. Nothing you can say or do is going to make me change my mind."

He veered to the right and headed for the bar. His uncle waited a moment, watching him until the glass door had swung shut between them. Then he walked round to the front desk.

"Evening, Eloise. Everything fine?"

"Very quiet tonight." She smiled up at him with sympathy. "Funerals are always so difficult, no?"

He rolled his eyes. "You have no idea," he said. He put his hands on the desk between them. "Any messages?"

"Only one," she said, handing him a white envelope. "But everything went all right in the church, *oui*?"

He nodded grimly. "As well as could be expected in the circumstances."

He glanced at the handwriting on the envelope. A slow smile broke across his face. It was the information he'd been waiting for about a Visigoth burial chamber discovered in Quillan, which Julian hoped might have some relevance to his excavations at the Domaine de la Cade. The Quillan site was sealed, no inventory had yet been released.

"What time did this come, Eloise?"

"At eight o'clock, Monsieur Lawrence. Delivered by hand."

He drummed his fingers on the counter in a tattoo. "Excellent. Thank you, Eloise. Have a good evening now. I'll be in my office if anyone needs me."

"*D'accord.*" She nodded, but he had already turned away.

32

By a quarter of ten, Meredith was through eating.
    She walked back into the tiled lobby. Although she was wiped out, there was no point turning in just yet. She'd never sleep, and she had too much on her mind.

She looked out through the front door to the darkness beyond.

Maybe a walk? The paths were brightly lit but deserted and quiet. She pulled her red Abercrombie & Fitch cardigan around her slim frame and dismissed the idea. Besides, she'd done nothing but walk these past couple of days.

Not after earlier.

Meredith rejected the idea. There was a murmur of noise slipping down the passageway leading to the terrace bar. She wasn't a great fan of bars, but since she didn't want to go straight up to her room and be tempted to climb into bed, it seemed the best option.

Walking past display cases filled with china and porcelain, she pushed open a glass door and walked in. The room looked more like a library than a bar. The walls were covered floor to ceiling with books in glass-fronted cabinets. In the corner there was a set of sliding wooden stairs, highly polished, for reaching the higher shelves.

Leather armchairs were grouped at low, round tables, like a gentlemen's country club. The atmosphere was comfortable and relaxed. Seated nearby were two couples, a family group and several men on their own.

There wasn't a free table, so Meredith took a stool at the counter. She put her key and the brochure down and picked up the bar list.

The bartender smiled. *"Cocktails d'un coté, vins de l'autre."*

Meredith turned the card over and read the wines by the glass on the reverse, then put the menu down.

"Quelque chose de la région?" she suggested. *"Qu'est-ce que vous recommandez?"*

"Blanc, rouge, rosé?"

"Blanc."

"Try the Domaine Begude Chardonnay," said another voice.

Surprised by both the English accent and the fact that someone was talking to her at all, Meredith turned to see a man sitting a couple of stools farther down the bar. A smart, well-cut jacket was draped over the two seats between them, and his crisp white shirt, open at the neck, black pants and shoes seemed at odds with his utterly defeated air. A mop of thick, black hair hung over his face.

"Local vineyard. Cépie, just north of Limoux. Good stuff."

He turned his head and looked at her, as if checking that she was listening to him, then went back to staring into the bottom of his glass of red wine.

Such blue eyes.

Meredith realized with a jolt that she recognized him. It was the same man she'd seen earlier in the Place des Deux Rennes, walking behind the casket in the funeral cortège. Somehow, the fact that she knew that about him made her feel uncomfortable. Like she'd been snooping, even though she hadn't meant to.

She looked at him. "Okay." Then back to the bartender. *"S'il vous plaît."*

"Très bien, Madame. Votre chambre?"

Meredith showed him the fob of her key, then glanced back at the man along the bar. "Thanks for the recommendation."

"Don't mention it," he said.

Meredith shifted on her stool, feeling a little awkward, not sure if they were going to have a conversation or not. He made the decision for her, suddenly turning round and offering his hand across the expanse of black leather and wood.

"I'm Hal, by the way," he said.

They shook. "Meredith. Meredith Martin."

The barman put a paper mat in front of her, then a glass filled with a rich, deep yellow wine. Discreetly, he slipped the check and a pen in front of her, too.

Acutely aware of Hal watching her, Meredith took a sip. Light, lemony, clean, it was reminiscent of the white wines Mary and Bill served on special occasions or when she came home on weekends.

"It's great. Good call."

The barman glanced at Hal. "*Encore un verre, Monsieur?*"

He nodded. "Thanks, Georges." He twisted round so he was half facing her. "So, Meredith Martin. You're American."

The moment the words were out of his mouth, he dropped his elbows to the bar and pushed his fingers through his unruly hair. Meredith wondered if he might be a little drunk.

"Sorry, what a ridiculous thing to say."

"It's okay." She smiled. "And yes, I am."

"Just arrived?"

"A couple of hours ago." She took another sip of wine and felt the alcohol hit her stomach. "What about you?"

"My father . . ." He stopped, a desperate expression on his face. "My uncle owns the place," he finished. Meredith figured it was Hal's father's funeral she'd witnessed, and felt even worse for him. She waited until she felt his eyes come back to her.

"Sorry," he said. "Not a great day." He drained his glass, then reached out for the refill the barman had placed in front of him. "Are you here for business or pleasure?"

Meredith felt as though she was stuck in some kind of surreal play. She knew why he was so distracted but couldn't admit it. And Hal, trying to make small talk with a total stranger, missing all his cues. The pauses between comments were all way too long, his train of thought disjointed.

"Both," she replied. "I'm a writer."

"A journalist?" he said quickly.

"No. I'm working on a book. A biography of the composer Claude Debussy."

Meredith saw the spark go out of his eyes and the same hooded look come down again. Not the reaction she was looking for.

"It's a beautiful place," she said quickly, taking in the bar with her gaze. "Has your uncle been here long?"

Hal sighed. Meredith could see the tension in his shoulders beneath the white cotton shirt.

"He and my father bought it together in 2003. Spent a fortune doing it up."

Meredith struggled with what to say next. He wasn't exactly making it easy.

"And your father?"

"Dad only came out here full time back in May. He wanted to get more involved in the day-to-day running of the ... He ..." He stopped. Meredith heard the catch in his voice. "He died in a car crash four weeks ago." He swallowed hard. "It was his funeral today."

In her relief that the information was out in the open, Meredith reached over and took Hal's hand before she even realized she'd done it.

"I'm sorry."

Meredith saw some of the tension leave his shoulders. They just sat there awhile, hand in silent hand, then she gently slid her fingers away under the cover of picking up her glass.

"Four weeks? That's quite a time before ..."

He looked at her. "It wasn't straightforward. Postmortem took a while. The body was released only last week."

Meredith nodded, wondering what the issue had been. Hal sat in silence.

"Do you live here?" she asked, trying to get the conversation going again.

Hal shook his head. "London. Investment banker, although I just handed in my notice." He hesitated. "I'd had enough anyway. Even before this. I was working fourteen-hour days, seven days a week. Great money but no time to spend it."

"Do you have other family out here? I mean, relatives in this part of France?"

"No. English through and through."

Meredith paused a moment. "What are your plans now?"

He shrugged.

"Will you stay in London?"

"Don't know," he said. "Doubt it."

Meredith took another mouthful of wine.

"Debussy," Hal said suddenly, as if it had only just registered what she'd just said. "I'm embarrassed to admit I don't know the first thing about him."

Meredith smiled, relieved he was at least making an effort.

"No reason why you should," she said.

"What's his connection with this part of France?"

Meredith laughed. "Tenuous," she said. "In August 1900, Debussy wrote a letter to a friend saying he was sending his wife, Lilly, to the Pyrenees to convalesce after an operation. Reading between the lines, a termination. So far no one's proved the story one way or the other—and if Lilly did go, it sure wasn't for long, because she was back in Paris in October."

Hal pulled a face. "It's possible. It's hard to imagine it now, but I believe Rennes-les-Bains was a very popular resort at that time."

"It was," Meredith agreed. "Particularly with Parisians. And also, partly, because it didn't specialize in treating only one kind of problem—some places were known for treatments for rheumatism; others, like Lamalou, for focusing on syphilis."

Hal raised his eyebrows but didn't pick up the thread. "You know, it seems a lot of effort to go to," he said, in the end. "Coming all this way on the off chance Lilly Debussy was here. Is it that important in the overall scheme of things?"

"If I'm honest, no, not really," she replied, surprised at how defensive she felt. As if her real motive for coming to Rennes-les-Bains was suddenly painfully transparent. "But it would be a great piece of original research, something no one else has got. That can make all the difference to making one book stand out from the others." She paused. "And it's an interesting period of Debussy's life, too. Lilly Texier was only twenty-four when she met him, working as a mannequin. They married a year later, in 1899. He dedicated a lot of his works to friends, lovers, colleagues, and it's undeniable that Lilly's name doesn't figure on many scores, songs or piano pieces."

Meredith was aware she was gabbling, but she was caught up in her own story now and couldn't stop. She leaned closer. "The way I see it, Lilly was right there during the crucial years leading up to the first performance of Debussy's only opera, *Pelléas et Mélisande,* in 1902. That was when his fortunes, his reputation, his status changed for good. Lilly was by his side when he made it. I figure that's got to count for something."

She stopped to draw breath and saw, for the first time since they'd started talking, that Hal was almost smiling.

"Sorry," she said ruefully. "I didn't mean to get so carried away, be so full-on. It's a terrible habit, assuming everyone will be as interested as I am."

"I think it's great there's something you're so passionate about," he said quietly. Caught by the shifting tone of his voice, Meredith looked across at him and saw that his blue eyes were fixed firmly on her. To her embarrassment, she felt herself coloring.

"I like the research process better than the actual writing," she said quickly. "All the mental excavation. All the obsessing over scores and old articles and letters, trying to bring to life a moment, a snapshot, from the past. It's all about reconstruction, about context, about getting under the skin of a different time and place, but with the benefit of hindsight."

"Detective work."

Meredith shot a sharp glance at him, suspecting his thoughts were on something else, but he followed through.

"When are you hoping to finish?"

"I'm due to be done April next year. I've got way too much material as it is. All the academic papers published in the *Cahiers Debussy* and the *Oeuvres complètes de Claude Debussy,* notes on every biography ever published. Added to which, Debussy himself was a prolific letter writer. He wrote for a daily newspaper, *Gil Blas,* as well as producing a handful of reviews for *La revue blanche.* You name it, I've read it."

Guilt hit her when she realized she was still doing it, going on talking when he was having such a hard time. She glanced over at him, intending to apologize for her insensitivity, but something caught her. The boyish expression, his demeanor, he suddenly reminded her of someone. She racked her brain but couldn't figure out who it was.

A wave of tiredness washed over her. She looked at Hal, lost in his own depressed thoughts and suddenly lacked the energy to keep the conversation going any longer. Time to call it a night.

She got down from the stool and gathered her things.

Hal's head snapped up. "You're not going?"

Meredith gave an apologetic smile. "It's been a long day."

"Of course." He got down from his stool, too. "Look," he said. "I know this probably sounds outrageous, I don't know, but perhaps . . . if you're around tomorrow, maybe we could go out. Or meet for a drink?"

Meredith blinked with surprise.

On the one hand, she liked Hal. He was cute and charming, and clearly needed company. On the other, she needed to focus on finding out what she could about her birth family—and in private. She didn't want anyone else tagging along. And she could hear Mary's voice in her head warning her that she knew nothing about the guy.

"Of course, if you're busy . . ." he started to say.

It was the undercurrent of disappointment in his voice that made her mind up for her. Besides, apart from the time spent with Laura during the reading—and that hardly counted—she'd not had a face-to-face conversation with anyone longer than a couple of sentences in weeks.

"Sure, why not," she heard herself say.

Hal smiled, properly this time, transforming his face. "That's great."

"But I was intending to head out pretty early. Do some research."

"I could come along for the ride," he suggested. "Might be able to help out a little. I don't know the area that well, but I've been coming here on and off for the past five years."

"It might be pretty boring."

Hal shrugged. "I can do boring. Do you have a list of places you want to visit?"

"I thought I'd play it by ear." She paused. "I had hoped to get something from the old spa buildings in Rennes-les-Bains, but they're all closed up for the winter. I'd thought maybe if I went to the mairie there might be a person who could help."

Hal's face clouded over. "They're useless," he said savagely. "Like beating your head against a brick wall."

"Sorry," she said quickly. "I didn't mean to remind you of . . ."

Hal gave a sharp shake of his head. "No, sorry. It's me." He sighed, then smiled at her again. "I have a suggestion. Given the period of time you're interested in for Lilly Debussy, you might find something useful in the museum in Rennes-le-Château. I've been there only once, but I remember it gave a pretty good account of what life might have been like round here at that time."

Meredith felt a spike of excitement. "That sounds great."

"Shall we meet in reception at ten?" he suggested.

Meredith hesitated, then decided she was being too cautious.

"Okay," she said. "Ten is good."

He stood up, and pushed his hands deep into his pockets. "Night."

Meredith nodded. "See you tomorrow."

33

Back in her room, Meredith was too wound up to sleep. She ran the conversation between them over in her mind, remembering what she'd said, what he'd said. Trying to interpret what lay between the lines.

She stared at her reflection in the mirror as she brushed her teeth, feeling desperately sorry for him. He seemed so vulnerable. She spat the toothpaste into the basin. He probably wasn't interested in her at all. He probably just needed a little company.

She climbed into bed and turned off the light, plunging the room into a soft and inky darkness. She lay staring at the ceiling awhile, until her limbs went heavy and she started to drift off to sleep.

Straightaway, the face Meredith had seen in the water, then the weird experience on the road, came rushing into her mind. Worse, the tortured, beautiful face of her birth mother, crying, begging the voices to leave her in peace.

Meredith's eyes snapped open.

No. No way. I will not let the past get to me.

She was here to find out who she was, to escape the shadow of her mother not to bring her back, more real than ever. Meredith pushed her childhood memories away, replacing them with the tarot images she'd been carrying around in her head all day. Le Mat and La Justice. The Devil with blue eyes, The Lovers chained, hopeless, at his feet.

She replayed Laura's words in her mind, let her thoughts wander from card to card, slipping down into sleep. Her eyes grew heavy. Now Meredith was thinking of Lilly Debussy, pale and with a bullet lodged for eternity in her chest. Debussy scowling and smoking at the piano as he played. Mary sitting on the porch in Chapel Hill, her chair rocking backward and forward as she read. The sepia soldier framed by the *platanes* in the Place des Deux Rennes.

Meredith heard the slam of a car door and the crunch of shoes on the gravel, the hooting of an owl setting out to hunt, the occasional judder and rattle of the hot-water pipes.

The hotel fell silent. Night wrapped its black arms around the house. The grounds of the Domaine de la Cade lay sleeping beneath a pale moon.

The hours passed. Midnight, two o'clock, four.

Suddenly, Meredith jolted awake, her eyes wide open in the dark. Every nerve in her body was vibrating, alert. Every muscle, every sinew, pulled as tight as a violin string.

Someone was singing.

No, not singing. Playing the piano. And really close.

She sat up. The room was cold. The same penetrating chill she'd felt under the bridge. The darkness was different, too, less dense, more fragmented. Meredith felt almost as if she could see the particles of light and dark and shadow breaking down in front of her. There was a breeze coming in from somewhere, even though she could swear all the windows were shut, a light breeze brushing over her shoulders and neck, skimming without touching, pressing, whispering.

There's someone in the room.

She told herself it was impossible. She'd have heard something. Yet she was gripped with an overwhelming certainty that someone was standing at the foot of the bed, watching. Two eyes burning in the darkness. Trails of sweat slid cold between her shoulder blades and into the hollow between her breasts.

Adrenaline kicked in.

Now. Do it.

She counted to three, then, with a burst of bravado, rolled over and flicked on the light.

The darkness was sent scattering. All the regular everyday objects rushed back to greet her. Nothing out of place. Closet, table, window, mantelpiece, bureau, all just as they should be. The cheval mirror, standing by the door to the bathroom, reflecting the light.

No one.

Meredith slumped back against the mahogany headboard. Relief washed over her. On the nightstand, the clock blinked the time in red. Four-forty-five. Not eyes at all, just the flashing LED of the radio alarm, reflected in the mirror.

Just a regular nightmare.

She should have expected it after the stuff that had happened today.

Meredith kicked back the covers to cool herself and lay still awhile, hands folded on her chest like a figure on a tomb, then got out of bed. She needed to move around, do something physical. Not just lie there. She grabbed a bottle of mineral water from the minibar, then walked over to the window and looked down over the silent gardens in the moonlight. The weather had broken, and the terrace below glistened with rain. There was a veil of white mist floating in the still air above the line of the trees.

Meredith pressed her warm hand against the cold glass, as if she could push the bad thoughts away. Not for the first time, doubt at what she was getting herself into slipped in. What if there was nothing to find? All the time, the idea of coming to Rennes-les-Bains, armed with only a handful of old photographs and a piece of piano music, had kept her going.

But now that she was here and could see what a small place it was, she felt less certain. The whole idea of tracing her birth family back here, without even having proper names to search for, seemed crazy. A stupid dream that belonged in a feel-good movie.

Not in real life.

Meredith had no idea of how long she stood there, just thinking, working things through at the window. Only when she realized that her toes were numb with cold did she turn and look at the clock. She gave a sigh of relief. It was past five o'clock in the morning. She'd killed enough time. Chased away the ghosts, the demons of the night. The face in the water, the figure on the road, the intimidating images on the cards.

This time when she lay down to sleep, the room was peaceful. No eyes staring at her, no shimmering presence in the darkness, just the blinking electric numbers of the alarm clock. She closed her eyes.

Her soldier melted into Debussy, became Hal.

Part V

Domaine de la Cade
September 1891

34

Monday, September 21, 1891

Léonie yawned and opened her eyes. She stretched her pale, slim arms above her head, then propped herself up on her generous white pillows. Despite the surfeit of *blanquette de Limoux* drunk last evening—or perhaps as a consequence of it—she had slept well.

The Yellow Room was pretty in the morning light. For a while, she lay in bed listening to the rare sounds that broke the deep silence of the countryside. The dawn songs of the birds, the wind in the trees. It was more pleasant by far than waking at home to a gray Parisian daybreak, the sounds of screeching metal from the Gare Saint-Lazare.

At eight o'clock, Marieta brought the breakfast tray. She placed it on the table by the window, then drew the curtains, flooding the room with the first refracted rays of sunlight. Through the imperfect glass of the old casements, Léonie could see that the sky was bright and blue, flecked with trailing wisps of purple and white cloud.

"Thank you, Marieta," she said. "I can manage."

"Very good, Madomaisèla."

Léonie threw off the covers and swung her feet down to the carpet, finding her slippers. She took her blue cashmere dressing gown from the back of the door, splashed a little of last night's water on her face, then sat down at the table in front of the window, feeling sophisticated to be breakfasting alone in her bedchamber. The only time she did so at home was when Du Pont was visiting M'man.

She lifted the lid on the pot of steaming coffee, releasing the delicious aroma of freshly roasted beans, like a genie from a lamp. Beside the silver pot stood a jug of frothy warm milk, a bowl of white sugar cubes and a pair of silver tongs. She lifted the pressed linen napkin to discover a plate of white bread, the golden crust warm to the touch, and a dish of creamy whipped butter. There were three different jams in individual china dishes and a bowl of quince and apple compote.

As she ate, she gazed out across the gardens. A white mist hung suspended over the valley between the hills, skimming the tops of the trees. The lawns lay peaceful and calm under the September sun, no evidence of the wind that had threatened the previous evening.

Léonie dressed in a plain woolen skirt and high-necked blouse, and then picked up the book Anatole had brought for her last evening. She had a fancy to see the library for herself, to investigate the dusty stacks and polished spines. If she were challenged—although she saw no reason why she should be, given that Isolde had asked them to treat the house as their own—she would have the excuse that she was returning Monsieur Baillard's pamphlet.

She opened the door and stepped out into the hall. The rest of the household appeared to be sleeping. Everything was still. No rattle of coffee cups, no whistling from Anatole's bedroom as he made his morning toilette, no sign of life at all. Downstairs, the hall also was deserted, although behind the pass door that led to the servants' quarters she could hear the sound of voices and the distant clattering of pots in the kitchen.

The library occupied the southwest corner of the house and was accessed by means of a small passageway tucked between the drawing room and the door to the study. Indeed, Léonie was surprised that Anatole had stumbled upon it at all. There had been little time to explore yesterday afternoon.

The corridor was bright and airy for all that, and wide enough to accommodate several glass cases mounted on the walls. The first displayed Marseille and Rouen china; the second a small, ancient cuirass, two sabers, a foil that resembled Anatole's favorite fencing weapon and a musket; the third case, smaller than the others, contained a selection of military medals and ribbons, laid out on blue velvet. There was nothing to indicate to whom they had been awarded or for what. Léonie presumed they belonged to Oncle Jules.

She lifted the handle of the library door and slipped inside. Instantly, she felt the room's peace and tranquility—the smell of beeswax and honey and ink, dusty velvet and blotters. It was more generous in size than she had expected, and had a dual aspect, with windows looking out to the south and the west. The curtains, fashioned from heavy gold-and-blue brocade, fell in folds from ceiling to floor.

The sound of her clipped heels was swallowed up by the thick oval rug that filled the center of the room and upon which stood a pedestal table, large enough to accommodate even the most substantial volume. There was an inkwell and pen beside a leather writing pad with a fresh blotter.

Léonie decided to start her exploration at the corner farthest from the door. She ran her eyes along each shelf in turn, reading the names on the spines, letting her fingers trail over the leather bindings, pausing from time to time when a particular volume caught her interest.

She came upon a beautiful missal with an ornate double clasp, printed in Tours, with rich green-and-gold endpapers and delicate, tissue-thin paper protecting the engravings. She read, upon the flyleaf, her late uncle's name— Jules Lascombe—inscribed with the date of his confirmation.

In the next stack she discovered a first edition of Maistre's *Voyage autour de ma chambre*. It was battered and dog-eared, unlike Anatole's pristine copy at home. In another alcove she found a collection of both religious and fervently antireligious texts, grouped together as if to cancel one another out.

In the section devoted to contemporary French literature, there was a set of Zola's *Rougon-Macquart* novels, as well as Flaubert, Maupassant and Huysmans—indeed, many of the intellectually improving texts Anatole tried in vain to press upon her, even a first edition of Stendhal's *Le rouge et le noir*. There were a few works in translation but nothing entirely to her taste except for Baudelaire's translations of Monsieur Poe. Nothing by Madame Radcliffe or Monsieur Le Fanu.

A dull collection.

In the farthest corner of the library, Léonie found herself in an alcove dedicated to books on local history, where, she presumed, Anatole had come upon Monsieur Baillard's monograph. She found her spirits quickening as she stepped from the warmth and space of the main area into the confined, somber stacks. The alcove harbored a damp mugginess that caught at the back of her throat.

She cast her eyes along the serried rows of spines and covers until she reached the letter B. There was no obviously vacant space. Puzzled, she squeezed the slim volume in where she believed it should go. Her task completed, she turned back toward the door.

Only then did she notice the three or four glass display cases high up on the wall to the right of the door, presumably to house the more valuable volumes. A set of wooden sliding steps was attached to a brass rail. Léonie took hold of the contraption with both hands and pulled as hard as she could. The steps creaked and complained but quickly surrendered. She slid them along the rail to the middle point, then, positioning the feet securely, folded them out and began to climb. Her taffeta petticoats rustled and caught between her legs.

She stopped on the second-to-top step. Bracing herself with her knees, she peered into the case. It was dark within, but by cupping her hands over the glass to shield her eyes from the light from the two tall windows, she could see just enough to enable her to read the titles on the spines.

The first was *Dogme et rituel de la haute magie* by Éliphas Lévi. Next to it was a volume titled *Traité méthodique de science occulte*. On the shelf above, several other writings by Papus, Court de Gébelin, Etteilla and MacGregor Mathers. She had never read such authors but knew they were occultist writers and considered subversive. Their names appeared regularly in the columns of newspapers and periodicals.

Léonie was on the point of descending when her attention was caught by a large, plain volume bound in black leather, less gaudy and ostentatious than the rest, displayed facing outward. Her uncle's name was written on the cover in gold embossed letters beneath the title.

Les Tarots.

35

Paris

By the time a smoggy and hesitant dawn broke over the offices of the Commissariat of Police of the eighth arrondissement in the rue de Lisbonne, tempers were already frayed.

The body of a woman identified as Madame Marguerite Vernier had been discovered shortly after eight o'clock on the evening of Sunday, September 20. The news had been telephoned in from one of the new public booths on the corner of the rue de Berlin and the rue d'Amsterdam by a reporter from *Le Petit Journal.*

Because the deceased lady had been associated with a war hero, General Du Pont, Prefect Laboughe had been summoned back from his country residence to take command.

In high ill-humor, he strode through the outer office and dropped a pile of early editions onto Inspector Thouron's desk.

Carmen Murder! War Hero Detained! Lovers' Quarrel Leads to Knife Death!

"What is the meaning of this?" Laboughe thundered.

Thouron stood and murmured a respectful greeting, then removed the other papers from the single vacant chair in the cramped and fuggy room, feeling Laboughe's simmering eyes on him. When it was done, the prefect removed his silk top hat and sat down, perching his hands on his cane. The wooden back of the chair creaked under his impressive weight but did not give way.

"Well, Thouron?" he demanded, once the inspector had returned to his seat. "How did they get so many inside details? One of your men got a loose tongue?"

Inspector Thouron bore all the marks of a man who had seen daybreak without experiencing the luxury of his own bed. He had smudged dark shadows, like half-moons, beneath his eyes. His moustache drooped, and there was stubble on his chin.

"I don't believe so, sir," he said. "The reporters were already there before we arrived on the night in question."

Laboughe stared at him from beneath white bushy eyebrows. "Tipped off?"

"It appears so."

"By whom?"

"No one will say. One of my gendarmes overheard a conversation between two of the vultures suggesting that at least two of the newspaper offices received a communication at approximately eight o'clock on Sunday evening intimating that it would be an expedient measure to dispatch a reporter to the rue de Berlin."

"The exact address? Apartment number?"

"Again, they would not disclose that information, sir, but I assume so."

Prefect Laboughe clenched his old blue-veined hands on the ivory head of his cane. "General Du Pont? Does he deny he and Marguerite Vernier were lovers?"

"He does not, although he has requested assurances that we will be discreet in the matter."

"Which you gave?"

"I did, sir. The general most vigorously denies killing her. Similar explanation to that offered by the *journalistes*. Claims that a note was passed to him as he came out of a lunchtime concert, postponing their assignation on the afternoon in question from three o'clock until later in the evening. They were due to travel to the Marne Valley this morning for a few weeks in the country. The servants were all dismissed for the duration. The apartment was certainly prepared for an absence."

"Does Du Pont still have the note in his possession?"

Thouron sighed. "Out of respect for the lady's reputation, or so he says, he claims he tore up the missive and threw it away outside the concert hall." Thouron dropped his elbows to the desk as he ran tired fingers through his hair. "I set a man on to it straightaway, but the cleaners in that arrondissement had been surprisingly assiduous."

"Evidence of relations of an intimate nature prior to her death?"

Thouron nodded.

"What does the fellow say to that?"

"Shaken by the information but held his composure. Not him, or so he says. Sticks to his story that he arrived to find her dead and a crowd of reporters milling around in the street outside."

"Was his arrival witnessed?"

"At eight-thirty it was. The issue is whether or not he was there earlier in the evening. We have only his word that he was not."

Laboughe shook his head. "General Du Pont," he muttered. "Well connected . . . always awkward." He peered at Thouron. "How did he get in?"

"He has a latchkey."

"Other members of the household?"

Thouron burrowed into one of the teetering stacks of paper on his desk, nearly upsetting an inkwell. He found the manila folder he wanted, and extracted from it a single sheet of paper.

"Apart from the servants, there's one son living there, Anatole Vernier, unmarried, aged twenty-six, an erstwhile journalist and litterateur, now on the board of some periodical dedicated to the subject of rare books, *beaux livres*, that manner of thing." He glanced down at his notes. "And one daughter, Léonie, seventeen, also unmarried and living at home."

"Have they been informed of their mother's murder?"

Thouron sighed. "Unfortunately, they have not. We have not been able to locate them."

"Whyever not?"

"It is believed they have gone to the country. My men have questioned the neighbors, but they know little."

Prefect Laboughe frowned, causing his white eyebrows to meet in the middle of his forehead. "Vernier? Why is that name familiar?"

"Could be one of a number of reasons, sir. The father, Leo Vernier, was a Communard. Arrested and brought to trial, sentenced to deportation. Died in the galleys."

Laboughe shook his head. "More recently than that."

"During the course of this year, Vernier *fils* has appeared in the newspapers on more than one occasion. Allegations of gambling, opium dens, whoring, all unproven. A suggestion of immorality, if you like, rather than evidence of it."

"Some manner of smear campaign?"

"There is a strong smell of that, yes, sir."

"Anonymous, I presume?"

Thouron nodded. "*La Croix* seems particularly to have had Vernier in its sights. They published, for example, an allegation that he had been involved in a duel on the Champs de Mars, admittedly as a second rather than as a principal, but even so . . . the newspaper printed times, dates, names. Vernier was able to prove he was elsewhere. He claimed to be ignorant as to who might be behind the slanders."

Laboughe caught his tone. "You do not believe him?"

The inspector looked skeptical. "Anonymous attacks are rarely that to those involved. Then, on the twelfth of February last, he was implicated in a scandal involving the theft of a rare manuscript from the Bibliothèque de l'Arsenal."

Laboughe slapped his knee. "That's it. That is why the name's familiar."

"Through his business activities, Vernier was a regular and trusted visitor. In February, after an anonymous tip-off, it was discovered that an extremely precious occultist text had gone missing." Thouron glanced down at his notes once more. "A work by a Robert Fludd."

"Never heard of him."

"Nothing was traced to Vernier, and the matter revealed the rather inadequate security arrangements of the Bibliothèque, so the whole business was hushed up."

"Is Vernier one of those esoterists?"

"It appears not, except in the course of his work as a collector."

"Was he questioned?"

"Again, yes. Again, it was a simple matter to prove he could not have been involved. And again, when he was asked if there were persons who might have some malicious intent toward him by suggesting otherwise, he said not. We had no choice but to let the matter drop."

Laboughe was silent for a moment as he absorbed the information.

"What about Vernier's sources of income?"

"Irregular," replied Thouron, "although by no means insignificant. He has some twelve thousand francs a year, from a variety of sources." He glanced down. "His position on the advisory board of the periodical, which pays him a retainer of some six thousand francs. Offices are in the rue Montorgueil. He supplements this with writing articles for other specialist magazines and journals and, no doubt, winnings at the *rouge et noir* tables and at cards."

"Any expectations?"

Thouron shook his head. "As a convicted Communard, his father's assets were confiscated. Vernier *père* was an only child, and his parents are long dead."

"And Marguerite Vernier?"

"We are investigating. Neighbors knew of no close relatives, but we will see."

"Does Du Pont make a contribution to the household expenses of the rue de Berlin?"

Thouron shrugged. "He claims not, although I doubt he is being entirely candid on that matter. Whether or not Vernier is party to these arrangements, I would not like to speculate."

Laboughe shifted position, causing the chair to creak and complain. Thouron waited patiently while his superior considered the facts.

"You said Vernier was unmarried," he said finally. "He has a mistress?"

"He was involved with a woman. She died in March and was buried in the cimetière de Montmartre. Medical records suggest that some two weeks previously she had undergone an operation at a clinic, the Maison Dubois."

Laboughe made an expression of distaste. "A termination?"

"Possibly, sir. The medical records have been mislaid. Stolen, the staff claim. The clinic did confirm, however, that the expenses were paid by Vernier."

"March, you say," Laboughe said. "So unlikely to be connected with Marguerite Vernier's murder?"

"No, sir," the inspector replied, then added, "I think it more likely, if indeed Vernier has been the victim of some whispering campaign, that those two things might well be connected."

Laboughe snorted. "Come, Thouron. Slandering a man is hardly the act of a person of honor. But from that to murder?"

"Quite, Monsieur le Préfet, and in usual circumstances I would agree. But there is one other occurrence that makes me wonder if there has been an escalation of ill will."

Laboughe sighed, realizing his inspector was not finished. He pulled a black meerschaum pipe from his pocket, knocked it on the corner of the desk to loosen the tobacco, then struck a match and drew until the flame took. A muggy, sour smell filled the cramped office.

"Obviously, one cannot be certain that this has any connection with the matter at hand, but Vernier himself was the victim of an assault in the Passage des Panoramas in the early hours of the seventeenth of September, last Thursday."

"The morning after the Palais Garnier riot?"

"You know the place, sir?"

"Smart arcade of shops and restaurants. The engraver, Stern, has premises there."

"That's it, sir. Vernier sustained a nasty wound just above the left eye and a good set of bruises. It was reported, again anonymously, to our colleagues in the *deuxième* arrondissement. They, in turn, informed us of the incident, knowing our interest in the gentleman. When questioned, the nightwatchman of the Passage admitted he had known of the attack—witnessed it, in point of fact—but confessed that Vernier had paid him handsomely to say nothing of it."

"Did you pursue the matter?"

"We did not, sir. Since Vernier, the victim, had chosen not to report the incident, there was little we could do. I mention it only to support the suggestion that perhaps it was an indication."

"Of what?"

"Of an escalation in hostilities," Thouron replied patiently.

"But in that case, Thouron, why is it Marguerite Vernier lying dead on a slab rather than Vernier himself? It makes no sense."

Prefect Laboughe sat back in his chair, drawing on his pipe. Thouron watched him and waited in silence.

"Do you believe Du Pont is guilty of the murder, Inspector, yes or no?"

"I am keeping an open mind, sir, until we have gathered more information."

"Yes, yes." Laboughe waved his hand impatiently. "But your instinct?"

"In truth, I do not think Du Pont is our man. Of course it seems the most likely explanation. The general was there. We have only his word for it that he arrived to find Marguerite Vernier dead. There were two Champagne glasses, but also one whiskey tumbler smashed in the grate. But there are too many things that do not seem to fit." Thouron took a deep breath, floundering for the right words. "The tip-off, for one. If indeed it was a lovers' quarrel that got out of hand, who was it that made contact with the papers? Du Pont himself?

I hardly think so. The servants had all been dismissed. It can have been only a third party."

Laboughe nodded. "Go on."

"Also, the timing, if you will, of both son and daughter being out of town and the apartment closed up for the duration." He sighed. "I don't know, sir. Something staged about the whole thing."

"You think Du Pont was set up to take the fall?"

"I think it is something we should consider, sir. If it were him, why would he only postpone the assignation? Surely he would take care to be nowhere in the vicinity?"

Laboughe nodded. "I can't deny that it would be a relief not to have to pursue an army hero through the courts, Thouron, especially one so decorated and distinguished as Du Pont." He caught Thouron's eye. "Not that it should influence your decision, Inspector. If you believe him guilty . . ."

"Of course, sir. I too would be distressed to prosecute a hero of the *patrie*!"

Laboughe glanced down at the shrill newspaper headlines. "On the other hand, Thouron, we must not forget that a woman lies dead."

"No, sir."

"Our priority must be to locate Vernier and inform him of his mother's murder. If before he was unwilling to talk to the police about the various incidents with which he has been entangled during this past year, perhaps this tragedy will loosen his tongue." He shifted position. The chair creaked under his weight. "But still no sign of him, you said?"

Thouron shook his head. "We know he left Paris four days ago, in the company of his sister. A cabman, one of the regulars who work the rue d'Amsterdam, reports picking up a fare in the rue de Berlin, a man and a girl matching the description of the Verniers, and taking them to the Gare Saint-Lazare on Friday last, shortly after nine o'clock in the morning."

"Any sightings of them once they were inside Saint-Lazare?"

"None, sir. Trains from Saint-Lazare service the western suburbs—Versailles, Saint-Germain-en-Laye, as well, of course, as the boat trains for Caen. Nothing. But then they could have disembarked at any point and transferred to a branch line. My men are on to it."

Laboughe was gazing at his pipe. He seemed to be losing interest.

"And you have the word out with the railway authorities, I presume?"

"Mainline and branch stations. Notices have been posted throughout the Ile-de-France, and we are checking the passenger lists for channel sailings, just in case they intend to travel farther afield."

The prefect drew himself heavily to his feet, wheezing at the effort of it. He put his pipe in the pocket of his coat, then picked up his top hat and gloves, and moved toward the door like a ship in full sail.

Thouron also stood.

"Pay another visit to Du Pont," Laboughe said. "He is the most obvious candidate in this unfortunate business, although I am inclined to think that your reading of the situation is the correct one."

Laboughe moved slowly across the room, his cane tapping the floor, until he reached the door.

"And Inspector?"

"*Préfet?*"

"Keep me informed. Any developments in this case, I want to hear the facts from you, not from the pages of *Le Petit Journal.* I am not interested in tittle-tattle, Thouron. Leave such things to the *journalistes* and writers of fictions. Do I make myself clear?"

"Perfectly, sir."

36

Domaine de la Cade

There was a tiny brass key in the lock of the cabinet. It was stiff and did not want to give, but Léonie rattled it until eventually it turned. She pulled open the door and lifted out the intriguing volume.

Perching on the polished top step, Léonie opened *Les Tarots,* folding back the hard cover, releasing the scent of dust and old paper and age. Inside was a slim pamphlet, hardly a book at all. No more than eight pages, jagged, as if the pages had been cut by a knife. The heavy cream paper spoke of an older age—not an antique, but not a recent publication, either. The words within were handwritten, in a clear, italic hand.

On the first page was repeated her uncle's name, Jules Lascombe, and the title, *Les Tarots*, this time with a secondary heading underneath it: *Au delà du voile et l'art musicale de tirer les cartes*. Beneath that was an illustration, much like a figure eight, lying flat on its side, like a skein of thread. At the bottom of the page was a date, presumably the year her uncle had written the monograph: 1870.

After my mother fled the Domaine de la Cade and before Isolde arrived.

The frontispiece was protected by a sheet of waxed tissue paper. Léonie lifted it, then gasped involuntarily. The illustration was a black-and-white engraving of a devil, staring malevolently up from the page with a lewd and bold stare. His body was hunched, with vulgar twisted shoulders, long arms and claws in place of hands. His head was too large, distorted, suggesting somehow a travesty of the human form.

As Léonie looked closer she saw that set within the creature's brow were horns, so small as to be almost indistinct. There was an unpleasant suggestion of fur rather than skin. Most disagreeable of all were the two clearly human figures, a man and a woman, chained to the base of the tomb on which the devil was standing.

At the bottom of the engraving was a number in roman numerals: XV.

Léonie looked to the foot of the page. No artist was credited, no information given as to the provenance or origin of the piece. Just a single word, a name inscribed in careful block capital letters beneath: ASMODEUS.

Not wishing to linger longer, Léonie turned to the next page. She was confronted with line after line of introductory explanation of the subject of the book, tightly spaced. She skimmed the text, certain words catching her eye as she read. The promise of devils and tarot cards and music set her pulse racing with a delightful frisson of horror. Deciding to make herself more comfortable, she descended from her wooden tower, jumping down the last few steps, then carried the volume to the table in the center of the library and plunged deep into the heart of the story.

Upon the scrubbed flagstones within the sepulchre was the square, painted in black by my very hand earlier that day and which, now, seemed to give a faint glowing light.

At each of the four corners of the square, like compass points, the musical note corresponding therewith. C to the north, A to the west, D to the south and E to the east. Within the square were placed the cards, into which life was to be breathed and through the power of which I would walk in another dimension.

I lit the one lamp on the wall, which cast a pallid white light.

Instantly, it seemed as if the sepulchre was filled with a mist, choking the wholesome air from the atmosphere. The wind, too, asserted its presence, for to what else could I ascribe the notes that were now murmuring inside the stone chamber, like the sound of a distant pianoforte.

Through the twilight atmosphere, the cards, or so it seemed to me, came to life. The forms, released from their prisons of pigment and paint, took form and shape and walked once more upon the earth.

There was a rushing of air and the sensation that I was not alone. Now I was certain that the sepulchre was full of beings. Spirits. I cannot say they were human. All natural rules were vanquished. The entities were all around. My self and my other selves, both past and yet to come, were equally present. They brushed my shoulders and my neck, skimmed my forehead, surrounded me without ever touching, yet always pressing closer and closer. It seemed to me they flew and swept through the air, so that I was aware always of their fleeting presence. Yet they seemed to have weight and mass. Especially in the air above my head, there seemed ceaseless movement, accompanied by a cacophony of whispering and sighing and weeping that caused me to bow my neck as if under a burden.

It became clear to me that they wished to deny me access, although I knew not why. I knew only that I must regain the square or I would be in mortal danger. I took a step toward it, whereupon instantly there descended upon me a great wind, pushing me back, shrieking and howling, a fearsome melody, if I may call it that, that seemed to be both inside my head and without. The vibrations made me fear the very walls and roof of the sepulchre would collapse.

I gathered my strength and then launched myself toward the center of the square, like a drowning man reaches in desperation for the shore. Instantly, a single creature, a devil distinct yet as invisible as its hellish companions, threw itself upon me. I felt supernatural claws upon my neck and talons on my back, its fishlike breath upon my skin, and yet not a mark was laid upon me.

I drew my arms over my head to protect myself. Perspiration flowed from my brow. My heart began to lose its rhythm, and I became aware of a growing incapacity. Breathless, shaking, with every muscle strained to the utmost, I summoned the last vestiges of courage and forced myself forward once more. The music was growing louder. I dug my nails deep into the cracks in the flagstones upon the floor and, by some miracle, succeeded in dragging myself into the square marked out.

Instantly, a terrible silence oppressed the room with the force of a mighty scream, so violent, and bringing with it the stench of Hell and the depths of the sea. I thought my head would split open with the very pressure of it. Babbling wildly, I continued to recite the names upon the cards: Fool, Tower, Strength, Justice, Judgment. Was I calling the spirits of the cards, now made manifest to aid me, or was it they who attempted to prevent me from gaining the square? My voice seemed not to be of my making but to issue from somewhere outside of me, low at first but gradually increasing in volume and intensity, growing in power and filling the sepulchre.

Then, when I believed I could withstand it no longer, something withdrew from within me, from my presence, from beneath my very skin with a scraping noise, like the claws of a wild animal along the surface of my bones. There was a rushing of air. The pressure on my failing heart was relieved.

I fell prostrate to the ground. All but unconscious, I was yet aware that the notes—those same four notes—were fading and the whisperings and sighings of the spirits growing weaker till at last I could hear nothing.

I opened my eyes. The cards were returned to their sleeping state once more. On the walls of the apse, the paintings now were inert. Then a sense of emptiness and peace suddenly came over the sepulchre, and I knew that all was finished. Darkness closed over me. I know not for how long I remained unconscious.

I have notated the music to the best of my ability. The marks on the palms of my hands, stigmata, have not faded.

Léonie let out a low whistle. She turned the page. There was no more. For a while she sat, simply staring at the last lines of the pamphlet. It was an extraordinary tale. The occult interplay of music and place had brought the images upon the cards to life and, if she had understood, summoned those who had passed over to the other side. *Au delà du voile*—beyond the veil—as the title inscribed upon the wrapper declared.

And written by my uncle.

At this moment, as much as anything, it was astounding to Léonie that there could be an author of such quality within her family and yet it never had been mentioned.

And yet . . .

Léonie paused. In the introduction her uncle claimed it to be true testimony. She sat back in the chair. What did he mean when he wrote of the power to "walk in another dimension"? What did he mean when he said "my other selves, both past and yet to come"? And had the spirits, once summoned, withdrawn whence they had come?

The hairs on the back of her neck stood on end. Léonie spun round, glancing over her shoulder to the left and the right, feeling as if there was someone standing behind her. She sent her eyes darting into the shadows of the alcoves on either side of the fireplace and the dusty corners behind the tables and curtains. Were there spirits still within the estate? She thought of the figure she had seen crossing the lawns the previous evening.

A premonition? Or something other?

Léonie shook her head, half amused that she was allowing her imagination to be the master of her, and returned her attention to the book. If she took her uncle at his word, and believed the story as fact, not fiction, then did the sepulchre stand within the Domaine de la Cade itself? She was inclined to think it did, not least because the musical notes required to summon the spirits—C, D, E, A—corresponded to the letters of the name of the estate: Cade.

And does it still exist?

Léonie dropped her chin into her hand. Her practical self took over. It should be a simple matter to ascertain if there was some manner of structure such as her uncle described within the grounds. It would be in keeping for a country estate of this size to have its own chapel or mausoleum within the park. Her mother had never spoken of such a thing, but then she had said little about the estate. Tante Isolde also had not mentioned it, but the matter had not come up during the course of the conversation last evening, and as she herself had admitted, her knowledge of the history of her late husband's family estate was limited.

If the sepulchre still stands, I shall find it.

A noise in the passageway outside caught Léonie's attention.

Immediately, she slid the volume onto her lap. She did not wish to be found reading such a book. Not out of embarrassment but because it was her private adventure and she did not wish to share it with anyone. Anatole would tease her.

The footsteps became fainter, then Léonie heard the sound of a door closing beyond the hall. She stood up, wondering if she could take *Les Tarots*. She did not think her aunt would object to the loan, given that she had invited them to treat the house as their own. And although the book had been locked within a case, Léonie was certain that was as protection against the ravages of dust and time and sunlight rather than a sense of it being forbidden. Else why should the key have been so obligingly left in the lock?

Léonie left the library, taking the purloined volume with her.

37

Paris

Victor Constant folded the newspaper and placed it on the seat beside him.

Carmen Murder—Police Seek Son!

His eyes narrowed with contempt. The Carmen Murder. It offended him, after all the help he had given them, that the gentlemen of the press were so predictable. No two women could be less alike than Marguerite Vernier and

Bizet's impetuous, flawed heroine, in terms of character or temperament, but the opera had seeped into French public consciousness to a distressing degree. All it took for the comparison to be made was a soldier and a knife, and the story was written.

In the space of hours, Du Pont had gone from prime suspect to innocent victim in the columns of the newspapers. At first, the fact that the prefect had not charged him with the murder aroused their interest and made them cast their literary nets a little wider. Now—thanks in no small part to Constant's own endeavors—the reporters had Anatole Vernier in their sights. He was not quite yet a suspect, but the fact that his whereabouts were still unknown was seen as suspicious. It was said the police were unable to locate either Vernier or his sister to inform them of the tragedy. Would an innocent man be so hard to find?

Indeed, the more Inspector Thouron denied that Vernier himself was a suspect, the more virulent the rumors grew. Vernier's absence from Paris became, de facto, a presence in the apartment on the night of the murder.

It served Constant well that journalists were lazy. Present them with a tale, neatly wrapped like a parcel, and they would offer it, with little modification, to their readers. The suggestion that they might independently verify the information they had been given or satisfy themselves as to the veracity of the facts they had been fed did not occur.

Despite his hatred for Vernier, Constant was forced to admit that the fool had been clever. Even Constant, with his deep pockets and web of spies and informants working all night, had been unable to discover where Vernier and his sister had gone.

He threw an uninterested glance out the window as the Marseille Express rattled south through the Parisian suburbs. Constant rarely ventured beyond the *banlieue*. He disliked the views, the indiscriminate light of the sun or dull, gray skies that bleached everything under their broad and ugly gaze. He disliked wild nature. He preferred to conduct his business in the twilight of artificially lit streets, in the semidarkness of concealed rooms lighted in the old-fashioned way, with tallow and wax. He despised fresh air and open spaces. His milieu was the perfumed corridors of theaters filled by girls with feathers and fans, private rooms in private clubs.

In the end, he had unraveled the maze of confusion Vernier had attempted to build around their departure. The neighbors, encouraged by a sou or two, claimed to know nothing definite but had overheard, remembered or absorbed sufficient fragments of information. Certainly enough for Constant to build a jigsaw of the day of the Verniers' flight from Paris. The *patron* of Le Petit Chablisien, a restaurant close to the Vernier apartment in rue de Berlin, had admitted to overhearing a discussion about the medieval city of Carcassonne.

With a purseful of coins, Constant's manservant had easily tracked down the cabman who had transported them to Saint-Lazare on the Friday morning, then the second fiacre that had taken them thence to the Gare Montparnasse, something he knew the gendarmes of the eighth arrondissement had thus far failed to discover.

It was not much, but it was enough to convince Constant it was worth the cost of the train ticket south. If the Verniers were staying in Carcassonne, that would be easier. With her, the whore, or without her. He did not know what name she lived under now, only that the name by which he had known her was carved upon the tombstone in the cimetière de Montmartre. A dead end.

Constant would arrive in Marseille later that day. Tomorrow he would take the coast train from Marseille to Carcassonne, and there would install himself, like a spider in the center of a web, waiting for his prey to come within range.

Sooner or later, people would talk. They always did. Whispers, rumors. The Vernier girl was striking. Among the black-haired, coal-eyed, dark-skinned people of the Midi, such white skin, such auburn curls would be remembered.

It might take time, but he would find them.

Constant took Vernier's timepiece from his pocket in his gloved hands. A gold casing with a platinum monogram, it was a distinguished and distinctive watch. It gave him pleasure simply to possess it, to have taken something of Vernier's.

Tit for tat.

His expression hardened as he pictured her smiling at Vernier, as once she had smiled for him. A sudden image flashed into his tortured mind of her uncovered before his rival's gaze. And he could not bear it.

To distract himself, Constant reached inside the leather traveling valise for something to help the journey pass. His hand brushed over the knife, concealed in a thick leather sheath, which had cut the life from Marguerite Vernier. He pulled out *The Subterranean Voyage of Nicholas Klimm* by Holberg and Swedenborg's *Heaven and Hell,* but found neither to his taste.

He chose again. This time he took out *Chiromancy* by Robert Fludd. Another souvenir. It suited his mood perfectly.

38

Rennes-les-Bains

Léonie had barely departed the library when she was accosted by the maid, Marieta, in the hall. She thrust the book behind her back.

"Madomaisèla, your brother has sent me to inform you that he is planning a visit to Rennes-les-Bains this morning and would be pleased if you would accompany him."

Léonie hesitated but only for a moment. She was excited at her plans to explore the Domaine in search of the sepulchre. But such an expedition could wait. A trip to town with Anatole could not.

"Please give my brother my compliments. Tell him I shall be delighted."

"Very good, Madomaisèla. The carriage is ordered for ten-thirty."

Taking the stairs two by two, Léonie bounded up to her chamber and cast her eyes around for some secret place to conceal *Les Tarots,* not wishing to provoke interest on the part of the servants by leaving such a volume in plain view. Her eyes fell upon her workbox. Quickly she opened up the mother-of-pearl lid and concealed the book deep within the reels of cotton and thread, the jumble of scraps of material, thimbles, pins and needlebooks.

. . .

THERE WAS NO SIGN of Anatole when Léonie descended to the hall.

She wandered out to the terrace at the back of the property and stood with her hands on the balustrade, looking out over the lawns. Broad slatted shafts of sunlight, filtered through a veil of cloud, made it difficult to see clearly in the abrupt contrast between light and shade. Léonie took a deep breath, drawing in the fresh, clean, unpolluted air. It was so unlike Paris, with its stink of soot and hot iron and the perpetual mantle of smog.

The gardener and his boy were working on the beds below, strapping the smaller bushes and trees to wooden stakes. A wooden barrow stood filled with raked red autumn leaves the color of wine. The older man wore a short brown jacket and a cap, with a red handkerchief tied at his neck. The boy, no more than eleven or twelve, was bareheaded and wearing a collarless shirt.

Léonie descended the steps. The gardener snatched his cap from his head as she approached, brown felt the color of autumn earth, and clutched it between grimy fingers.

"Good morning."

"*Bonjorn,* Madomaisèla," he mumbled.

"A beautiful day."

"Storm's coming."

Léonie looked doubtfully up at the perfectly blue sky, flecked with floating islands of cloud. "It seems so still. Settled."

"Biding its time."

He leaned toward her, revealing a mouth of blackened, crooked teeth like a row of old gravestones.

"The devil's work, the storm. All the old signs. Music over the lake last evening."

His breath was peaty and sour and Léonie instinctively pulled back, a little affected, despite herself, by the old man's sincerity.

"Whatever do you mean?" she said sharply.

The gardener crossed himself. "Hereabouts the devil walks. Each time he comes out of the Lac de Barrenc, he brings with him violent storms chasing one another across the country. The late master sent men to fill in the lake, but the devil came and told them plain that if they continued their work, Rennes-les-Bains would be drowned."

"These are just silly superstitions. I cannot—"

"A bargain was struck, not for me to say why or how, but the fact of the matter was the workmen withdrew. Lake was let be. But now, *mas ara*, the natural order again is overturned. All the signs are there. The devil will come to claim his due."

"Natural order?" she heard herself whisper. "What can you mean?"

"Twenty-one years ago," he muttered. "Late master raised the devil. Music comes when the ghosts are walking out of the tomb. Not for me to say the why and how of it. The priest came."

She frowned. "The priest? Which priest?"

"Léonie!"

With a mixture of guilt and relief, she spun round at the sound of her brother's voice. Anatole was standing, waving at her from the terrace.

"The gig is here," he shouted.

"Keep your soul close, Madomaisèla," said the gardener, under his breath. "When storms come, the spirits are released to walk."

She worked the dates out in her head. Twenty-one years ago, he had said, which would make it 1870. She shivered. In her mind's eye, she saw the same date, the year of publication, printed upon the front page of *Les Tarots*.

The spirits are released to walk.

The gardener's words, which chimed so precisely with what she had read this morning. Léonie opened her mouth to ask another question, but the old man had already pushed his hat back on his head and returned to his digging. She hesitated a moment longer, then hitched up her skirts and ran lightly up the steps to where her brother stood waiting. It was intriguing, yes. Disquieting also. But she would not permit anything to spoil her time with Anatole.

"Good morning," he said, leaning forward to plant a kiss on her flushed cheek and looking her up and down. "Perhaps a little more modesty is called for?"

Léonie glanced down at her stockings, clearly visible and flecked with touches of mud from the path. She grinned as she smoothed down her skirts with her hands.

"There," she said. "Quite respectable!"

Anatole shook his head, half frustrated, half amused.

They walked together through the house and climbed into the carriage.

"Have you been sewing already?" he asked, noticing a piece of red cotton thread stuck to her sleeve. "How very industrious!"

Léonie picked off the strand and let it drop to the ground. "I was searching for something in my workbox, that's all," she replied, not even blushing at the unrehearsed lie.

The driver cracked the whip and the carriage jerked forward and down the drive.

"Tante Isolde did not wish to accompany us?" she asked, raising her voice to be heard over the rattling of the harness and hooves.

"She had estate matters requiring her attention."

"But the supper party is settled for Saturday evening?"

Anatole patted his jacket pocket. "It is. And I have promised we will play messenger and deliver the invitations."

The night winds had shaken loose twigs and leaves from the smooth, silver trunks of the beech trees, but the track down from the Domaine de la Cade was passably clear of debris, and they covered the terrain quickly. The horses were blinkered and held steady, even though the lamps in the holders bumped and knocked against the sides of the carriage as they made the decline.

"Did you hear the thunder last night?" said Léonie. "It was so strange. Dry rumblings, then sudden outbursts, all the time the wind howling."

He nodded. "It is apparently quite commonplace to have thunderstorms with no rain, especially in the summer, when there might be a string of such storms, one after the other."

"It sounded as if the thunder was trapped in the valley between the hills. As if it was angry."

Anatole laughed. "That might have been the *blanquette* working in you!"

Léonie stuck out her tongue. "I am suffering no ill effects whatsoever," she said. "The gardener was telling me how the storms are said to come when the ghosts are walking." She paused. "Or is it the other way round? I am not certain."

Anatole raised his eyebrows. "Indeed?"

Léonie twisted round to address the driver on his bench.

"Do you know of a place called the Lac de Barrenc?" she asked.

"*Oc*, Madomaisèla."

"Is it far from here?"

"*Pas luènh.*" Not far. "For the *toristas* it is a place to visit, though I would not venture up there."

He pointed with his whip at a dense parcel of woodland and a clearing with three or four stone megaliths sticking out of the ground as if dropped there by some giant hand. "Up there is the Devil's Armchair. And, not above a morning's walk, the Étang du Diable and the Horned Mountain."

Léonie was only talking about what she feared in order to gain mastery of it, and she knew it. Even so, she turned back to face Anatole with an expression of triumph on her face.

"You see," she said. "Everywhere evidence of devils and phantoms."

Anatole laughed. "Superstition, *petite*, certainly. Hardly evidence."

The gig set them down in the Place du Pérou. Anatole found a boy willing to deliver the invitations to Isolde's guests for a sou, then they set off. They began by promenading along the Gran'Rue in the direction of the thermal establishment. They halted awhile at a small pavement café, where Léonie drank a cup of strong, sweet coffee and Anatole an absinthe. Ladies and gentlemen in frock coats and walking suits passed. A nurse pushing a baby carriage. Girls, their flowing hair decorated with silk ribbons of red and blue, and a boy in knee-length britches with a hoop and stick.

They paid a visit to the largest shop in the town, the Magasins Bousquet, which sold all manner of items from thread and ribbon, to copper pots and pans, to snares and nets and hunting guns. Anatole passed over to Léonie Isolde's list for provisions to be delivered to the Domaine de la Cade on Saturday and allowed her to place the orders.

Léonie enjoyed herself greatly.

They admired the architecture of the town. Many of the buildings on the *rive gauche* were more substantial than they appeared from the road; indeed, several were many stories taller and deeper and built down into the gorge of the river. Some were well cared for, if modest. Others were a little shabbier, the paint peeling and the walls leaning misaligned, as if time lay heavy upon them.

At the river's bend, Léonie had excellent views of the terraces of the thermal spa and the back balconies of the Hôtel de la Reine. More so than from the street, the establishment dominated the vista with its grandeur and importance, its modern buildings and pools and expansive glass windows. Narrow stone steps led down from the terraces directly to the water's edge, where stood a collection of individual bathing huts. It was a testament to progress, to science, a modern-day shrine for contemporary pilgrims in need of physical succor.

A solitary nurse, her winged white hat perched on her head like a giant sea-bird, was pushing a patient in a *chaise roulante*. By the water's edge, at the foot of the Allée des Bains de la Reine, a wrought-iron pergola in the shape of a crown provided welcome shade from the sun. Outside a small traveling kiosk, with a narrow fold-down hatch giving on to the street, a woman with a pale headscarf and broad, sun-tanned arms was selling cups of apple cider for a couple of centimes. Beside the wheeled café, in character quite like a caravan, was a wooden contraption for pressing apples, its metal teeth grinding slowly as a small boy with scarred hands and wearing a loose shirt several sizes too big for him fed apples of russet and red into it.

Anatole stood in line and purchased two cups. It was too sweet for his palate. Léonie, however, declared it delicious and drank first hers, then the last of his, spitting out the stray pips into her handkerchief.

The *rive droite*—the far bank—had a different character. There were fewer buildings, and those that did cling to the hillside, dotted amongst the trees that came down almost to the water's edge, were domestic dwellings, small and modest. Here lived the artisans, the servants, the shopkeepers whose livelihoods depended on the ailments and the hypochondrias of the urban middle classes from Toulouse, from Perpignan, from Bordeaux. Léonie could see patients sitting in the steaming, iron-rich water of the *bains forts*, accessed by means of a private covered alleyway. A line of nurses and servants waited patiently on the bank, towels draped across their arms, for their charges to emerge.

When they had explored the whole town to Léonie's satisfaction, she declared herself fatigued and complained that her boots were pinching. They returned to the Place du Pérou, via the poste restante and the telegraph office.

Anatole proposed a pretty brasserie on the south side of the square.

"Is this acceptable?" he asked, pointing at the sole free table with his walking stick. "Or would you prefer to eat inside?"

The wind was playing a gentle game of *cache-cache* between the buildings, whispering through the alleyways and causing the awnings to flutter. Léonie looked around at the gold and bronze and claret leaves, spiraling in the wind, at the delicate traces of sunlight on the ivy-covered building.

"Outside," she said. "It is charming. Quite perfect."

Anatole smiled. "I wonder if this is the wind they call the Cers," he mused, sitting down opposite her. "I believe this is a northwesterly, which comes down from the mountains, according to Isolde, as opposed to the Marin, which comes from the Mediterranean." He shook out his napkin. "Or is that the Mistral?"

Léonie shrugged.

Anatole ordered the *pâté de la maison,* a dish of tomatoes and a *bûche* of local goat cheese, dressed in almonds and honey, to share between them, with a *pichet* of mountain rosé.

Léonie broke off a morsel of bread and popped it into her mouth.

"I visited the library this morning," she said. "A most interesting selection of books, I thought. I am surprised we had the pleasure of your company at all last night."

His brown eyes sharpened. "Whatever do you mean?"

"Only that there are more than enough books to keep you occupied for some time and, indeed, that I was surprised you managed to locate Monsieur Baillard's volume among so many." Her eyes narrowed. "Why? What did you think I meant?"

"Nothing," replied Anatole, twisting the ends of his moustache.

Sensing some evasion, Léonie put down her fork. "Although now you come to mention it, I do confess I am surprised that you did not remark upon the collection when you came to my chamber last evening before dinner."

"Remark upon . . . ?"

"Why, the collection of *beaux livres,* for a start." She fixed her eyes on his face to watch his reaction. "And the occultist books also. Some of them looked to be rare editions."

Anatole did not immediately answer. "Well, you have accused me, on more than one occasion, of being somewhat tiresome on the matter of antiquarian books," he said finally. "I did not wish to bore you."

Léonie laughed. "Oh for goodness' sake, Anatole, whatever is the matter with you? I know, from what you yourself have told me, that a good many of these books are considered quite disreputable. Even in Paris. It's not what one would expect in a place like this. And for you to not even mention it, well, it is . . ."

Anatole sat drawing on his cigarette.

"Well?" she demanded.

"Well, what?"

"Well, to start with, *why* are you determined to show no interest?" She drew breath. "And why should our uncle have such a wide collection of books of such a character?"

"You seem determined to be critical of Isolde. Evidently, you do not care for her."

Léonie flushed. "You are mistaken if that is the impression you have gained. I think Tante Isolde quite charming." She raised her voice slightly, to prevent him from interrupting her. "It is not our aunt but more the character of the place that is disquieting, especially when taken together with the presence of such occultist books in the library."

Anatole sighed. "I did not notice it. You are making something over nothing. The most *obvious* explanation, to use your words, is that Oncle Jules had catholic—or, rather, liberal—tastes. Or, perhaps, that he inherited many of the books with the house."

"Some of them are very recent," she said doggedly.

She knew she was provoking him and wished to draw back, but somehow she could not check herself.

"And you are the expert on such publications," he said skeptically.

She recoiled at his cold tone. "No, but that is precisely my point. You are! Hence my surprise that you did not see fit to mention the collection at all."

"I cannot account for why you are so determined to find some mystery in this—indeed, in everything here. I really cannot comprehend it."

Léonie leaned forward. "I tell you, Anatole, there is something strange about the Domaine, whether or not you will admit it." She paused. "Indeed, I even find myself wondering if you did go into the library at all."

"That is enough," he said, his voice thick with warning. "I don't know what the devil has got into you today."

"You accuse me of wishing to inject some sort of mystery into the house. I admit that might be so. But by the same token, you appear determined to do the opposite."

Anatole rolled his eyes in exasperation. "Listen to yourself!" he threw out. "Isolde has made us both most welcome. Her position is an uncomfortable one, and if there is any awkwardness, surely this can be put down to the fact that she herself is a stranger here, living among long-established servants who probably resent an outsider coming in as mistress of the house. From what I gather, Lascombe was often absent, and I suppose that the staff had the run of the house. Such comments are not worthy of you."

Léonie pulled back, realizing she had gone too far. "I only wanted . . ."

Anatole dabbed his mouth at the corners, then tossed his napkin on the table. "All I intended was to find you some interesting volume to keep you company last evening," he said, "not wishing you to be homesick in an unfa-

miliar house. Isolde has shown you nothing but kindness, and yet you seem
determined to find fault in everything."

Léonie's desire to provoke a quarrel evaporated. She could no longer even
remember why she had been so determined to squabble in the first place.

"I am sorry if my words offended you, but . . ." she began, but it was
too late.

"Nothing I say seems to stop this childish mischief-making of yours," he
said fiercely, "so there is nothing to profit from continuing the conversation
further." He snatched up his hat and cane. "Come. The gig is waiting."

"Anatole, please," she pleaded, but he was already striding across the square.
Léonie, torn between regret and resentment, had no choice but to follow.
More than anything, she wished she had held her tongue.

But as they drove out of Rennes-les-Bains, she began to feel aggrieved. The
fault was not hers. Well, perhaps in the first instance, but she had meant no
harm. Anatole had determined to take insult when none was intended. And
hard on the heels of such excuses was another, more insidious consideration.

He defends Isolde over me.

It was most unfair after so brief an acquaintance. Worse, the thought made
Léonie quite sick with jealousy.

39

The journey back to the Domaine de la Cade was an uncomfortable one.
Léonie sulked. Anatole paid her no attention at all. As soon as they
arrived, he leapt down from the carriage and vanished into the house without
a backward glance, leaving her alone to contemplate a dull and solitary afternoon stretching out before her.

She stormed upstairs to her chamber, not wishing to see anyone, and flung

herself facedown upon the bed. She kicked off her shoes, letting them drop
with a satisfying thump to the floor, leaving her feet to dangle over the edge
as if she was floating on a raft on a river.

"*J'en ai marre.*" Bored.

The clock on the mantelshelf chimed two.

Léonie picked at the stray threads on the embroidered cover, teasing out
the emaciated shimmering strands of gold until she had made a pile worthy
of Rumpelstiltskin on the bed beside her. She threw a frustrated glance at
the clock.

Two minutes past two o'clock. Time was barely moving.

She slid off the bed and walked over to the window, lifting the corner of
the curtain with her hand. The lawns were flooded with light, rich and
golden.

Everywhere Léonie could see evidence of the damage wrought by the mischievous wind. Yet at the same time, the gardens looked serene. Perhaps she
would take a walk. Explore the grounds a little.

Her eyes alighted upon her workbox, and she burrowed through the materials and sequins to where the black book lay.

Of course.

It was the ideal opportunity to search for the sepulchre, to return to her
earlier plan for the day. Perhaps she would even find the tarot cards. She took
out the book. This time, Léonie read every word.

AN HOUR LATER, dressed in her new worsted jacket and sturdy walking
boots, her hat perched on her head, Léonie sneaked out onto the terrace.

There was nobody in the gardens, but she walked fast nonetheless, not
wishing to have to explain herself. She passed the cluster of rhododendron
and juniper bushes almost at a run, keeping up the pace until she was out of
plain view of the house. Only once she was through the opening in the high
box hedge did she slow and catch her breath. She was perspiring already. She
stopped and removed her scratchy hat, enjoying the feel of the fresh air on her
bare head, and pushed her gloves deep into her pockets. She felt exhilarated
to be so completely alone and unobserved, the mistress of herself.

At the edge of the woods she stopped, feeling the first prickings of caution.
There was a palpable sense of quiet, the scent of bracken and fallen leaves. She

glanced back over her shoulder, in the direction that she had come, then into the somber light of the woods. The house was all but out of sight.

What if I cannot find my way back?

Léonie looked up at the sky. Provided she was not too long, provided the weather held, she could simply head home to the west, in the direction of the setting sun. Besides, these were private woods, managed and tended, set within an estate. It was hardly like venturing into the unknown.

There is nothing to cause alarm.

Having talked herself into continuing, feeling much like a heroine in a serial adventure, Léonie set out along an overgrown path. Soon she found herself standing at the crossroads of two paths. To the left there was an air of neglect and stillness. The box trees and laurel seemed to drip with condensation. The downy oak and sharp needles of the *pins maritimes* seemed to bow under the unwelcome weight of time with a blighted and exhausted aspect. The right-hand path was positively mundane in comparison.

If there was a long-forgotten sepulchre within the grounds, then surely it would be deep within the woods? Far out of sight of the house itself?

Léonie took the path to the left, into the shadows. The track looked unfrequented. There were no fresh wheel ruts made by the gardener's barrow, no indication that the leaves had been raked, no sense that anyone had recently passed this way.

Léonie realized she was walking uphill. The path was growing rougher and less clear. Stones, uneven earth and fallen branches tumbled from the overgrown thicket on either side. She felt enclosed, as if the landscape was pushing in upon her, shrinking. On one side, above the path, was a steep embankment, covered with dense green undergrowth and boughs of hawthorn and an intense tangle of yew, knitted together like iron-black lace in the half-light. Léonie felt a fluttering of nerves in her chest. Every branch, every root spoke of abandonment. Even the animals seemed to have forsaken the benighted woods. No birds sang, no rabbits or foxes or mice moved in the undergrowth to their burrows.

Soon the ground beside the path fell away sharply to the right. Several times Léonie dislodged a stone with her foot and heard it tumble into the chasm below. Her misgivings grew. It required no great leap of imagination to summon the spirits or ghosts or apparitions that both the gardener and Monsieur Baillard, in his book, claimed haunted these glades.

Then she emerged onto a platform in the hillside, open on one side to reveal the panorama of the distant mountains. There was a small stone bridge over a culvert, where a strip of brown earth intersected the path beneath it at right angles, a low channel worn away by the fierce rushing of meltwaters in spring. It was dry now.

Far away through the opening, glimpsed over the heads of the smaller trees, the entire world seemed suddenly to spread out before her like a picture. The clouds scudding across the seemingly endless sky, a late summer-afternoon heat haze or mist floating in the troughs and curves of the hills.

Léonie took a deep breath. She felt magnificently distant from all of civilization, from the river and the gray and red roofs of the houses below in Rénnes-les-Bains, from the thin outline of the *cloche-mur* and the silhouette of the Hôtel de la Reine. Cocooned in her wooded silence, Léonie could imagine the noise in the cafés and bars, the clatter in the kitchens, the rattle of harness and gig in the Gran'Rue, the yell of the cabman as the *courrier* took up position in the Place du Pérou. And then the thin tolling of the church bell carried on the wind to where she stood listening.

Four o'clock already.

Léonie listened until the faint echo had died away. Her spirit of adventure faded with the sound. The words of the gardener came back to her.

Keep your soul close.

She wished she had asked him—asked somebody—for directions. Always wishing to do things for herself, she hated to ask for help. More than anything, she regretted not bringing the book itself.

But I have come too far to turn back now.

Léonie raised her chin and walked on with determination, fighting the creeping suspicion that she was going in the wrong direction entirely. Instinct had led her this way in the first place. She had no map, no words of instruction. Again she regretted the lack of forethought not to at least inquire about a map of the Domaine, or to look for one in the library.

It crossed her mind that no one knew where she had gone. If she should fall or lose her way, nobody would know where to find her. It occurred to her, too, that she should have left some sort of trail. Fragments of paper or, like Hansel and Gretel in their woods, white pebbles to mark the way home.

There is no reason you should become lost.

Léonie walked deeper, farther into the grounds. Now she found herself in a wooded glade, ringed by a circle of wild juniper bushes covered with late-ripening berries, as if birds never penetrated this deep into the forest.

Shadows, distorted shades, slipped in and out of her vision. Within the green mantle of the wood, the light was thickening, stripping away the reassuring and familiar world and replacing it with something unknowable, something more ancient. Winding through the trees, the briars, the copse, an afternoon mist had set in, stealing up without a word of warning or announcement. There was an absolute and impenetrable stillness as the sodden air muffled all sound. Léonie felt its tentacles wrapping themselves around her neck like a muffler, curling around her legs beneath her skirts like a cat.

Then suddenly ahead of her she glimpsed, through the trees, the outline of something not made of wood or earth or bark. A small stone chapel, no bigger than would accommodate six or eight worshippers, its roof steeply pitched and a small stone cross upon the arched entrance.

Léonie caught her breath.

I have found it.

The sepulchre was surrounded by a host of gnarled yew trees, their roots twisted and misshapen like an old man's hands, overshadowing the path. There were no impressions in the mud. The brambles and briars were all overgrown.

Feeling pride and anticipation in equal measure, Léonie stepped forward. Leaves rustled and twigs snapped beneath her boots. Another step. Closer, now, until she stood before the door. She tilted her head and looked up. Above the wooden arch, symmetrical and perfectly pointed, were two lines of verse painted in antique black lettering.

Aïci lo tems s'en
Va res l'Eternitat.

Léonie read the words twice aloud, rolling the strange sounds over in her mouth. She pulled her all-weather pencil from her pocket and scribbled them down on a scrap of paper.

There was a noise behind her. A rustling? A wild animal? A mountain cat or even a bear? Then a different sound, as if a rope was being drawn across the deck of a ship. A snake? Her confidence evaporated. The dark eyes of the forest seemed to be pressing in upon her. The words in the book now came back to her with a dreadful clarity. Premonitions, hauntings, a place where the veil between worlds was drawn back.

Léonie felt suddenly reluctant to enter the sepulchre. But the alternative, remaining alone, unprotected in the clearing, seemed far worse. With the blood pounding inside her head, she reached forward and grasped the heavy metal ring on the door, and pushed.

At first, nothing happened. She pushed again. This time there was the sound of metal grinding out of place, and then a sharp click as the catch gave. She put her narrow shoulder against the timber and, with the weight of her whole body, gave a sharp shove.

The door juddered slowly open.

40

Léonie stepped inside the sepulchre. Chill air rushed to meet her, together with the unmistakable scent of dust and antiquity and the memory of centuries-old incense. There was something else, too. She wrinkled up her nose. A lingering smell of fish, the sea, the salted hull of a wrecked fishing boat.

She clenched her hands at her sides to stop them from shaking.

This is the place.

Immediately to the right of the main door on the west wall was the confessional, about six feet tall by eight wide and no more than two feet deep. It was made of dark wood and was very plain, nothing like the elaborate or ornate carved versions in the cathedrals and churches of Paris. The grille was shut. A single drab curtain of purple hung in front of one of the seats. On the other side of the compartment, the curtain was missing.

To the immediate left of the main door was the *bénitier,* the stoop for holy water. Léonie recoiled. The basin was of red-and-white marble, but it was supported upon the back of a grinning, diabolic figure. Blistered red skin, clawed hands and feet, malevolent eyes of piercing blue.

I know you.

The statue was the twin of the engraving from the frontispiece of *Les Tarots.*

Despite the burden on his back, the defiance remained. Carefully, as if afraid he might come to life, Léonie edged closer. Beneath, printed on a small white card, yellowed by age, was the confirmation: ASMODÉE, MAÇON AU TEM-PLE DE SALOMON, DÉMON DU COURROUX.

"Asmodeus, builder of the Temple of Solomon, the demon of wrath," she read aloud. Standing on her cold tiptoes, Léonie peered inside. The *bénitier* was dry. But there were letters carved into the marble. She traced them with her fingers.

"*Par ce signe tu le vaincras,*" she murmured out loud. "By this sign shall you conquer him."

She frowned. To whom did "him" refer? The devil Asmodeus himself? Which had come first: the illustration in the book or the *bénitier*? Which was the copy, which the original?

All she knew was that the date in the book was 1870.

Bending down, her worsted skirts making swirling patterns in the dust on the flagstoned floor, Léonie examined the base of the statue to see if there was any date or mark upon it. There was nothing to indicate either its age or its provenance.

Not Visigoth though.

Making a mental note to research the matter further—perhaps Isolde might know—Léonie stood up and turned to face the nave. There were three rows of simple wooden pews on the south side of the sepulchre, facing front, like a classroom in elementary school but no wider than could accommodate two worshippers apiece. No decoration, no carvings, at the end of the rows, and no cushions on which to kneel, just a single thin wooden footrest running the length of each.

The walls of the sepulchre were whitewashed and peeling. Plain arched windows, no colored glass, let in the light but stripped the space of warmth. The Stations of the Cross were small illustrations set into the frame of wooden crosses, hardly paintings at all, more medallions, and all unremarkable to Léonie's untrained eye.

She began to walk slowly up the nave, like a reluctant bride, becoming more anxious the farther she traveled from the door. Once, thinking there was someone behind her, she spun.

Again, no one.

To her left, the narrow nave was flanked by statues of plaster saints, all half-sized, like malevolent children. Their eyes seemed to follow her as she passed by. She halted from time to time to read the names painted in black on wooden signs beneath each: Saint-Antoine, the Egyptian Hermit; Sainte-Germaine, her apron full of Pyrenean mountain flowers; the lame Saint-Roch with his staff. Saints of local significance, she presumed.

The last statue, closest to the altar, was of a slender and petite woman wearing a knee-length red dress, with straight black hair hanging to her shoulders. With both hands she held a sword, not threatening nor as if she was under attack but rather as if she herself was the protector.

Beneath it was a wooden sign with the words: La Fille d' Épées.

Léonie wrinkled her brow. The Daughter of Swords. Perhaps it was intended to be a representation of Sainte-Jeanne d'Arc?

There was another noise. She glanced up at the high windows. Just the branches of the sweet chestnut trees tapping like nails upon the glass. Just the sound of the somber call of the birds.

At the end of the nave, Léonie stopped, then crouched down and examined the floor, seeking evidence of the black square the author had described, and for the four letters—C, A, D, E—she believed her uncle had marked upon the ground. She could not see anything, not even the faintest memory, but she did uncover an inscription scratched into the flagstones.

"*Fujhi, poudes; Escapa, non,*" she read. She copied this too.

Léonie straightened up and stepped forward to the altar. It matched precisely, to her memory, the description in *Les Tarots*: a bare table, none of the artifacts of religion—no candles, no silver cross, no missal, no antiphoner. It was set in an octagonal apse, the ceiling above a bright cerulean blue, like the opulent roof of the Palais Garnier. Each of the eight panels was lined with a patterned wallpaper decorated with thick, faded horizontal pink stripes, divided by a frieze of red-and-white juniper flowers and a repeat detail of blue disks or coins. At the intersection of every papered section were plaster mold-ings, batons or wands, painted gold.

Within each was a single painted image.

Léonie gasped, discerning suddenly what she was looking at. Eight indi-vidual tableaux taken from the tarot, as if each figure had stepped out of its card and up onto the wall. Printed beneath each one was a title: Le Mat, Le Pagad, La Prêtresse, Les Amoureux, La Force, La Justice, Le Diable, Le Tour. Black antique ink on yellowed cards.

It is the same hand as the book.

Léonie nodded. What better evidence that her uncle's testimony was based on true events? She moved closer. The question was why these eight, of the seventy-eight cards her uncle's book had detailed, in particular? With excite-ment fluttering in her chest, she started to copy out the names. She was run-ning out of space on the tiny scrap of paper she had found in her pocket. She cast her eyes around the sepulchre, looking for something else on which to write.

Peeking out from beneath the stone feet of the altar, she noticed the corner of a sheet of paper. She pulled it out. It was a leaf of piano music, handwritten on heavy yellow parchment. Treble and bass clef, common time, with no flats or sharps. The memory of the subtitle on the front cover of her uncle's book came into her mind, and his testimony that he had written the music down.

She flattened the music sheet and attempted to sight-sing the opening bars, but could not catch the melody even though it was very plain. There were but a limited number of notes, which at first glance reminded her of nothing so much as the sort of four-finger exercises she had been obliged to struggle through in her childhood piano lessons.

Then a slow smile came to her lips. Now she could see the pattern: C-A-D-E. The same notes repeating in sequence. Beautiful. As the book had claimed, music to summon the spirits.

Now another thought, quick, following on the heels of the last.

If the music remains in the sepulchre, why not also the cards?

Léonie hesitated, then scribbled the date and the word *Sepulchre* across the top, as evidence of where she had found the music, then slipped it into her pocket and began a methodical search of the stone chapel. She pushed her fingers into dusty corners and crevices, looking for concealed spaces but find-

ing nothing. There were no pieces of furniture or furnishings behind which a
deck of cards could be hidden.

But if not here, then where?

She moved around behind the altar. Now that her eyes were accustomed to
the somber atmosphere, she fancied she could make out the outline of a small
door concealed within the eight panels of the apse. She reached out, looking
for some disturbance in the surface, and found a slight depression, perhaps
the markings of an old opening that once had done service. She pushed hard
with her hand, but nothing happened. It was quite firmly fixed. If there had
been a door here, it was no longer in use.

Léonie stood back, hands on her hips. She was reluctant to accept that the
cards were not here, but she had exhausted every possible hiding place. She
could think of nothing else for it but to go back to the book once more and
seek answers there. Now that she had seen the place, surely she would be able
to read the hidden meanings in the text.

If indeed there are any.

Léonie again glanced up at the windows. The light was fading. Shafts of
tree-filtered light had slipped away, leaving the glass dark. Now, as before, she
felt the eyes of the plaster statues were turned upon her, watching. And as she
became aware of their presence, the atmosphere within the tomb seemed to
tip, to shift.

There was a rushing of air. She could discern music, inside her head, coming from somewhere within her. Heard but not heard. Then a presence behind
her, surrounding her, skimming past without ever touching yet pressing closer,
a ceaseless movement accompanied by a silent cacophony of whispering and
sighing and weeping.

Her pulse started to race.

It is but my imagination.

She heard a different noise. She tried to dismiss it, as she had dismissed all
other sounds from within and without. But it came again. A scratching, a
shuffling. The clip of nails or claws upon the flagstones, coming from behind
the altar.

Now Léonie felt as if she was a trespasser. She had disturbed the silence of
the sepulchre and of the listeners, the watchers who inhabited its dusty stone
interior. She was not welcome. She had looked upon the painted images on

the walls and stared into the eyes of the plaster saints that kept vigil. She turned, held in the malicious blue eyes of Asmodeus. The descriptions of the demons of the book came back to her with full force. She recalled her uncle's terror as he wrote of how the black wings, the presences, bore down upon him. Tore into him.

The marks on the palms of my hands, like stigmata, have not faded.

Léonie looked down and saw, or imagined she saw, red marks spreading across her cold, upturned hands. Scars in the form of a figure eight on its side upon her pale skin.

Her courage finally abandoned her.

She picked up her skirts and bolted for the door. The malignant gaze of Asmodeus seemed to mock her as she passed, his eyes following her down the short nave. In terror, she threw the full weight of her body at the door, succeeding only in closing it more firmly shut. Frantic, she remembered it opened inward. She grabbed at the handle and pulled.

Now Léonie was certain there were footsteps behind her. Claws, nails, slipping on the flagstones, coming after her. Hunting her. The devils of the place had been released to protect the sanctuary of the sepulchre. A horrified sob escaped from her throat as she stumbled out into the darkening woods.

The door fell heavily shut behind her, rattling on its ancient hinges. She was no longer afraid of what might be lying in wait in the twilight of the trees. It was as nothing compared to the supernatural terrors within the tomb.

Léonie ran, knowing the demon's eyes were watching her still, realizing, only just in time, how the ancient gaze of spirits and demons kept guard over their domain against intruders. She plunged back through the cold dusk, dropping her hat, stumbling and half falling, retracing her steps all the way along the path, over the dry stream, through the dusk-draped woods to the safety of the lawns and the gardens.

Fujhi, poudes; Escapa, non.

For a fleeting moment, she thought she understood the meaning of the words.

41

Léonie arrived back at the house frozen to the bone, to find Anatole pacing the hall. Not only had her absence been noted, but it had also caused great consternation. Isolde threw her arms around her and then quickly withdrew, as if embarrassed by her display of affection. Anatole hugged her, then shook her. He was torn between chastising her and relief that no ill had befallen her. Nothing was said about the earlier quarrel that had driven her out alone into the grounds in the first place.

"Where have you been?" he demanded. "How could you be so thoughtless?"

"Walking in the gardens."

"Walking! It is almost dark!"

"I lost track of the time."

Anatole continued to fire question after question at her. Had she seen anyone? Had she strayed beyond the boundaries of the Domaine? Had she noticed or heard anything out of the ordinary? Under such a sustained verbal interrogation, the fear that had taken hold of her in the sepulchre loosened its grip. Léonie rallied and started to defend herself, his determination to make so much of the incident encouraging her to do the opposite.

"I am not a child," she threw back at him, thoroughly irritated by his treatment of her. "I am perfectly capable of looking after myself."

"No you are not!" he shouted. "You are only seventeen."

Léonie tossed her copper curls. "You talk as if you feared I had been kidnapped!"

"Don't be absurd," he snapped, although Léonie intercepted a glance passed between him and Isolde.

Her eyes narrowed. "What?" she said slowly. "Whatever has happened to make you overreact so? What is it that you are not telling me?"

Anatole opened his mouth, then closed it again, leaving Isolde to step in.

"I am sorry if our concern seems excessive to you. Of course you are perfectly at liberty to walk wherever you please. It is just that there have been reports of wild animals coming right down into the valley at dusk. Sightings of mountain cats—wolves, perhaps—not far from Rennes-les-Bains."

Léonie was on the point of challenging the explanation when the memory of the sound of claws on the flagstones of the sepulchre came sharply back to her. She shuddered. She could not say for certain what had turned the adventure into something altogether else, and so abruptly. Only that in the moment she began to run, she had believed herself in danger of her life. From what, she did not know.

"See, you have made yourself quite ill," Anatole raged.

"Anatole, enough," Isolde said quietly, lightly touching him on the arm.

To Léonie's astonishment, he fell silent.

With an exhalation of disgust, he spun away, his hands on his hips.

"There are also warnings of more bad weather coming in from the mountains," Isolde said. "We were fearful you would be caught out in the storm."

Her comment was interrupted by an ominous rumble of thunder. All three looked to the windows. Brooding and malevolent clouds could now be seen scudding across the tops of the mountains. A white mist, like the smoke from a bonfire, hung suspended between the hills in the distance. Another rumble of thunder, closer at hand, rattled the glass in the panes.

"Come," said Isolde, taking Léonie's arm. "I will have the maid draw you a hot bath, then we will have supper and a fire in the drawing room. And, perhaps, a game of cards? Bezique, *vingt-et-un*, whatever you wish."

Léonie remembered. She looked down at the palms of her hands, white with the cold. There was nothing there. No red marks branding her skin.

She allowed herself to be taken to her room.

IT WAS ONLY some time later, when the bell for supper had rung, that Léonie paused to contemplate her reflection in the looking glass.

She slipped onto the stool in front of her dressing table and stared with unflinching eyes at the mirror. Her eyes, although bright, were feverish. She could see plainly the memory of the fear etched upon her skin and wondered if it would be evident to Isolde or Anatole.

Léonie hesitated, not wishing to stir her unsteady nerves, but then got up

and retrieved *Les Tarots* from her workbox. With cautious fingers, she turned
the pages until she came to the passage she wanted.

> There was a rushing of air and the sensation that I was not alone. Now I was
> certain that the sepulchre was full of beings. Spirits. I cannot say they were
> human. All natural rules were vanquished. The entities were all around. My
> self and my other selves, both past and yet to come. . . . It seemed to me they
> flew and swept through the air, so that I was aware always of their fleeting pres-
> ence. . . . Especially in the air above my head, there seemed ceaseless movement,
> accompanied by a cacophony of whispering and sighing and weeping . . .

Léonie closed the book.

It so precisely matched her experience. The question was, Had the words
lodged themselves deep in her unconscious mind and thus directed her emotions and reactions? Or had she independently experienced something of
what her uncle had seen? Another thought came into her mind.

And can Isolde really know nothing of this?

That both her mother and Isolde felt something disturbing in the character
of the place, Léonie had no doubt. In their different manners they alluded to
a certain atmosphere, they hinted at a sense of disquiet, although admittedly
neither was explicit. Léonie pressed her hands together, making a steeple of
her fingers as she thought hard. She, too, had felt it on that first afternoon
when she and Anatole arrived at the Domaine de la Cade.

Still turning the matter over in her mind, she returned the book to its hiding place, slipping the sheet of piano music within the covers, then hastened
downstairs to join the others. Now her fear had retreated, she was intrigued,
determined to discover more. She had many questions she wished to ask of
Isolde, not least what she knew of her husband's activities before they were
married. Perhaps, even, she would write to M'man to inquire as to if there
were any specific incidents in her childhood that had caused her alarm. For
without knowing what she was so certain about, Léonie was sure that it was
the place itself that held captive terrors, the woods, the lake, the ancient
trees.

But then, as she closed the bedroom door behind her, Léonie realized
she could not mention her expedition for fear she would be forbidden to re-

turn to the sepulchre. For the time being at least, her adventure must remain secret.

NIGHT SLOWLY FELL over the Domaine de la Cade, bringing with it a sense of anticipation, a sense of waiting and watching.

Supper passed agreeably, with occasional rumbles of disconsolate thunder in the distance. The matter of Léonie's adventure into the grounds was not mentioned. Instead, they talked of Rennes-les-Bains and adjoining towns, of the preparations for Saturday's supper party and the guests, of how much there was to do and the enjoyment they would have doing it.

Pleasant, ordinary, domestic conversation.

After they had eaten, they withdrew to the drawing room and their moods changed. The darkness without seemed almost to be alive. It was, at last, a relief when the storm struck. The very sky itself began to growl and shudder. Brilliant and jagged forked lightning ripped silver through the black clouds. Thunder clapped, bellowed, ricocheted off rock and branch, echoing between the valleys.

Then the wind, stilled momentarily as if gathering up its strength, suddenly hit the house in full force, bringing with it the first of the rain that had threatened all evening. Gusts of hail lashed against the windows, until it seemed to those cowering within the house that an avalanche of water was cascading over the face of the building like waves breaking upon the shore.

From time to time Léonie thought that she could hear music. The notes that lay inscribed on the sheet hidden in her bedroom, taken up and sounded by the wind. As, indeed, she remembered with a shudder, the old gardener had warned.

For the most part, Anatole, Isolde and Léonie attempted to pay no heed to the tempest beyond the walls. A good fire crackled and spat in the grate. All the lamps were lit and the servants had brought extra candles. They had been made as comfortable as possible, but still Léonie feared the walls were bending, shifting, caving in under the onslaught.

In the hall, a door came unlatched, blown open by the wind, and was quickly secured. Léonie could hear the servants moving around the house, checking that all the windows were shuttered. Because there was a danger that the thin glass of the windows in the oldest casements would shatter, all the curtains had been drawn. In the upstairs corridors, they heard footsteps and the chink of pails and buckets set at intervals to catch the drips, the leaks that Isolde told them allowed rain through the loose tiles on the roof.

Confined to the drawing room, the three of them sat, strolled, paced, talked. They drank a little wine. They attempted to occupy themselves with normal evening pursuits. Anatole stoked the fire and replenished their glasses. Isolde twisted her long, pale fingers in her lap. Once, Léonie drew back the curtain and stared out into the blackness. She could see little through the slats of the ill-fitting shutters except the silhouettes of the trees in the parkland beyond, lit on the instant by a flash of lightning, plunging and tossing like unbroken horses on a rope. It seemed to her that the very woods seemed to be calling out for help, the ancient trees creaking, cracking, resisting.

At ten o'clock, Léonie suggested a game of bezique. She and Isolde settled themselves at the card table. Anatole stood, his arm resting on the mantelshelf, smoking a cigarette and holding a glass of brandy.

They spoke little. Each of them, whilst pretending to be oblivious to the storm, was listening for the subtle changes in the wind and the rain that might indicate that the worst was over. Léonie noticed how very pale Isolde had become, as if there was some further threat, some warning within the storm. As the time limped slowly on, it seemed to her that Isolde struggled for composure. Her hand strayed often to her stomach as if she was ailing from some sickness. Or else her fingers plucked at the fabric of her skirts, at the corners of the playing cards, at the green baize.

A crack of thunder struck directly overhead. Isolde's gray eyes flared wide. In a moment, Anatole was at her side. Léonie felt a spurt of jealousy. She felt excluded, as if they had forgotten she was there.

"We are quite safe," he murmured.

"According to Monsieur Baillard," Léonie interrupted, "local legend holds that the storms are sent by the devil when the world is off-kilter. When the natural order of things is disturbed. The gardener said much the same this morning. He said that music was heard over the lake last evening, which—"

"Léonie, *ça suffit!*" Anatole said sharply. "All these sorts of tales, demons and diabolic happenings, those curses and maledictions, they are merely stories to scare children."

Isolde threw another glance at the window. "How much longer can this last? I do not think I can bear it."

Anatole fleetingly let his hand drop onto her shoulder, then withdrew it, but not so quickly that Léonie did not observe the gesture.

He wishes to look after her. Protect her.

She pushed the envious thought away.

"The storm will blow itself out soon," Anatole said again. "It's just the wind."

"It's not the wind. I feel something . . . something terrible is going to happen," Isolde whispered. "I feel as if he is coming. Getting closer to us."

"Isolde, *chérie*," Anatole said, dropping his voice.

Léonie's eyes narrowed. "He?" she echoed. "Who? Who is coming?"

Neither of them paid her any attention.

Another gust of wind rattled the shutters. The sky cracked. "I am certain that this dignified old house has seen much worse than this," Anatole said, trying to inject a lightness into his voice. "Indeed, I wager it will still be standing many years after we are all dead and buried. There's nothing to fear."

Isolde's gray eyes flashed feverishly. Léonie could see his words had had the opposite effect on her to the one intended. They had not soothed but instead raised the stakes.

Dead and buried.

For a fraction of an instant, Léonie thought she saw the grimacing face of the demon Asmodeus looking out at her from the leaping flames of the fire. She felt herself start back.

She was nearly at the point of confessing to Anatole the truth of how she had passed her afternoon. What she had seen and heard. But when she turned to him, she saw he was gazing at Isolde with a look of such tenderness, such concern, that she felt almost ashamed to have witnessed it.

She closed her mouth again and said nothing.

The wind did not relent. Nor did her unquiet imagination give her any rest.

42

When Léonie woke the following morning, she was surprised to find herself on the chaise longue in the drawing room of the Domaine de la Cade rather than in her bedroom.

Shafts of golden early-morning light were slipping in through the cracks in the curtain. The fire was dead in the grate. The playing cards and empty glasses sat on the table, abandoned, where they had been left last evening.

Léonie sat for a while, listening to the silence. After all the pounding, the hammering of rain and wind, everything was now quiet. The old house no longer creaked and groaned. The storm had passed.

She smiled. Last night's terrors—thoughts of ghosts and devils—seemed quite absurd in the benign morning light. Soon, hunger drove her from the sanctuary of the sofa. She tiptoed to the door and out into the hall. The air was cool and there was a pervasive smell of damp everywhere, but there was a freshness in the air that had been lacking the previous night. She went through the pass door separating the front of the house from the servants' quarters, feeling the cold tiles through the thin soles of her *savates*, and found herself in a long flagstoned corridor. At the end, behind a second door, she could hear voices and the clattering of cooking utensils, someone whistling.

Léonie entered the kitchen. It was smaller than she had imagined, a pleasant, square room with waxed walls and black beams from which hung a variety of copper-bottomed pans and cooking implements. On the blackened top of the stove, set within a chimney large enough to accommodate a stone bench on either side, was a bubbling pot.

The cook was holding a long-handled wooden paddle in her hand as she turned toward the unexpected visitor. There was a scrape of chair legs on the flagstones as the other servants, eating breakfast at a scarred wooden table in the middle of the kitchen, rose to their feet.

"Please, don't get up," said Léonie quickly, awkward at her intrusion. "I wonder if I might have some coffee. Some bread, too, perhaps."

The cook nodded. "I will prepare a tray, Madomaisèla. In the morning room?"

"Yes, thank you. Has anybody else come down?" she asked.

"No, Madomaisèla. You are the first."

The tone was courteous but the dismissal clear.

Still, Léonie delayed. "Has there been any damage from the storm?"

"Nothing that can't be put right," the cook said.

"No flooding?" she asked, worried that perhaps Saturday's dinner party, although some days off, would be postponed if the road up from the village was damaged.

"Nothing serious reported from Rennes-les-Bains. One of the girls heard tell there's been a landslide at Alet-les-Bains. The mail coach is held over at Limoux." The cook wiped her hands on her apron. "Now, if there's nothing else, Madomaisèla, perhaps you will excuse me. There is a great deal to prepare for this evening."

Léonie had no choice but to withdraw. "Of course."

As she left the kitchen, the clock in the hall struck seven. She looked through the windows outside to see a pink sky behind white clouds. On the grounds, work had begun sweeping up the leaves and gathering the wood and branches that had blown loose from the trees.

THE NEXT FEW DAYS passed quietly.

Léonie had the run of the house and grounds. She breakfasted in her room and was free to spend the morning howsoever she chose. Often she did not see her brother or aunt until luncheon. In the afternoons, she and Isolde walked in the grounds, weather permitting, or explored the house. Her aunt was unfailingly attentive, gentle, but with a sharp and amusing wit. They played Rubinstein duets on the piano, clumsily and with more enjoyment than skill, and amused themselves with parlor games in the evenings. Léonie read and painted a landscape of the house from the small promontory overlooking the lake.

Her uncle's book and the sheet of music she had taken from the sepulchre were much on her mind, but she did not return to them. And in her peram-

bulations of the estate, Léonie deliberately did not allow her feet to take her
in the direction of the overgrown path in the woods that led to the deserted
Visigoth chapel.

SATURDAY, SEPTEMBER 26, the day of the dinner party, dawned bright
and clear.

By the time Léonie had finished eating breakfast, the first of the wooden
delivery carts from Rennes-les-Bains was rattling up the drive of the Domaine
de la Cade. A boy jumped down and unloaded two large blocks of ice. Not
long after, another arrived with the viand, cheeses and fresh milk and cream.

In every room of the house, or so it seemed to Léonie, servants polished
and primed and folded linen and set out ashtrays or glasses under the eye of
the old housekeeper.

At nine o'clock, Isolde appeared from her room and took Léonie with her
into the gardens. Armed with a pair of secateurs and thick rubber overshoes
as protection against the damp paths, they cut flowers for the table displays
while the first dew was still on them.

When they returned to the house at eleven o'clock, they had filled four flat
trug baskets with blooms. They found steaming coffee waiting for them in the
morning room and Anatole, in excellent spirits, smiling up at them from
behind the newspaper.

At noon, Léonie finished the last of the placement cards, the names printed
and designed to Isolde's specifications. She extracted a promise from her aunt
that when the table was ready, she could lay out the cards herself.

By one, there was nothing left to do. After a light lunch, Isolde announced
her intention to retire to her chamber to rest for a few hours. Anatole withdrew to attend to some correspondence. Léonie was left with no alternative
but to do the same.

In her room, she glanced to her workbox where *Les Tarots* lay sleeping
beneath red cotton and blue thread, but even though some days had passed
since her expedition to the sepulchre, she was still reluctant to disturb her own
peace of mind by getting caught up again in the mysteries of the book. Besides, Léonie was well aware that reading would not occupy her this afternoon.
Her mind was too skittish, such was her state of anticipation.

Her eyes instead darted to where her colors, brushes, easel and book of cartridge papers sat on the floor. She stood up, feeling a wave of affection for her mother. This afternoon would be the ideal opportunity to make good use of her time and paint something as a souvenir. A gift to present to her on their return to town at the end of October.

To eclipse her unhappy childhood memories of the Domaine de la Cade?

Léonie rang for the maid and instructed her to fetch a bowl of water for her brushes and a sheet of thick cotton to cover the table. Then she took out her palette and tubes of paint and began to squeeze out beads of crimson, ocher, tourmaline blue, yellow and moss green, with ebony black for edging. From her book of cartridge paper, she took a single heavy cream sheet.

She sat for a while, waiting for inspiration to strike. Without having any clear idea of what she might choose to attempt, she began to sketch the outline of a figure in thin, black strokes. As her brush glided over the paper, her mind was concentrated on the excitements of the evening ahead. The painting began to find its shape without her. She wondered how she would find the society of Rennes-les-Bains. Everyone invited had accepted Isolde's hospitality. Léonie saw herself admired and complimented, picturing herself first in her blue gown, then the red, then her green dress from La Samaritaine. She imagined her slim arms in various evening gloves, favoring the particular trim of one pair or the length of another. She imagined her copper hair held in place by mother-of-pearl combs or silver hairpins that would most flatter her coloring. She toyed with a variety of necklaces and earrings and bracelets to complete the look.

As the shadows lengthened on the lawns below, as she passed the time in pleasurable thought, stroke by stroke the colors thickened on the sheet of cartridge paper and the image came to life.

Only when Marieta had returned to clear away and quitted the room did Léonie take stock of what she had painted. What she saw astonished her. Without in the least intending to do so, she had painted a figure from one of the tarot tableaux on the wall of the sepulchre: La Force. The only difference was that she had given the girl long dark red hair and a morning dress that looked quite the copy of a gown she had hanging in her own closet in the rue de Berlin.

She had painted herself into the picture.

Caught between pride at the quality of her handiwork and her intriguing choice of subject matter, Léonie held the self-portrait up to the light. As a rule, all her characters looked rather similar and bore little relationship to the subject she had been attempting. But on this occasion, there was more than a passing resemblance.

Strength?

Was that how she saw herself? Léonie would not have said so. She examined the picture a moment longer, but, aware that the afternoon was drawing to a close, she was obliged to prop the portrait behind the clock on the mantelshelf and put it out of her mind.

MARIETA KNOCKED upon her door at seven o'clock.

"Madomaisèla?" she said, peeking her head around the half-open door. "Madama Isolde has sent me to help you dress. Are you decided upon what you will wear?"

Léonie nodded, as it was never in question. "The green gown with the square neck. And the *sous-jupe* with the broderie anglaise trim."

"Very good, Madomaisèla."

Marieta fetched the garments, conveying them over outstretched arms, and laid them carefully upon the bed. Then, with deft fingers, she helped Léonie into her corset over her chemise and undergarments, lacing it tight at the back and fastening the hooks and eyes at the front. Léonie twisted first to the left, then the right, to see her reflection in the glass, then smiled.

The maid climbed onto the chair and lowered first the petticoat, then the dress itself over Léonie's head. The green silk was cool against her skin as it fell in shimmering folds like water touched by sunlight.

Marieta jumped down and dealt with the fastenings, then sat back on her heels to arrange the hemline, while Léonie adjusted the sleeves.

"How would you like me to dress your hair, Madomaisèla?"

Léonie returned to the dressing table. Tilting her head to one side, she wound a thick handful of her tumbling curls around her hand and twisted them up onto the top of her head. "Like so."

She let the hair drop, and then pulled toward her a small brown leather jewelry case. "I have tortoiseshell combs with inlaid abalone pearls in my jewelry box, which match the earrings and pendant I intend to wear."

Marieta worked quickly but carefully. She fixed the clasp of the platinum leaf and pearl necklace around Léonie's neck, then stood back to admire her handiwork.

Léonie took a long, hard look in the cheval glass, tilting the mirror to obtain a full view. She smiled, pleased with what she saw. The gown hung well, neither too plain nor too extravagant for a private dinner. It flattered her coloring and her figure. Her eyes were clear and bright, and her complexion was excellent, neither too pale nor too high a color.

From downstairs, the raucous clamor of the bell. Then the sound of the front door being opened as the first guests arrived.

The two girls locked eyes.

"Which gloves would you like, the green or the white?"

"The green with the beading around the cuff," said Léonie. "There is a fan of much the same color in one of the hatboxes at the top of the closet."

When she was ready, Léonie swept up her chatelaine bag from the top of the chest of drawers, then slipped her stockinged feet into green silk slippers.

"You look a picture, Madomaisèla," breathed Marieta. "Beautiful."

A VOLLEY OF NOISE hit Léonie when she emerged from her room and stopped her in her tracks. She peeped over the balcony to the hall below. The servants were dressed in hired livery for the evening and looked very smart. It added to the sense of occasion. She fixed a dazzling smile onto her face, made sure that her dress was quite perfect, and then, with butterflies in the pit of her stomach, went down to join the party.

At the entrance to the drawing room, Pascal announced her in a strong and clear voice, and then rather spoiled the effect by giving her a wink of encouragement as she walked through.

Isolde was standing before the fireplace talking to an ill-complexioned young woman. With her eyes she called Léonie over to join them.

"Mademoiselle Denarnaud, may I present my niece, Léonie Vernier, the daughter of my late husband's sister."

"Enchantée," said Léonie prettily.

During the course of the short exchange, it transpired that Mademoiselle Denarnaud was an unmarried sister of the gentleman who had helped them with their luggage at Couiza on the day of their arrival. Denarnaud himself raised his hand and waved when he saw Léonie looking across the room at him. A rather more distant cousin, she learned, worked as the housekeeper to the curé of Rennes-le-Château. *Another large family,* Léonie thought, remembering how Isolde had mentioned at supper two nights ago that the Abbé Saunière himself was one of eleven siblings.

Her attempts at conversation were met with a cold stare. Although perhaps no older than Isolde, Mademoiselle Denarnaud was wearing a matronly, heavy brocade gown more suited to a woman of twice her years and a hideously old-fashioned bustle, of the kind not seen in Paris for some years. The contrast between her and their hostess could not have been greater. Isolde had dressed her hair in ringlets of yellow curls piled high on her head and held in place by pearl combs. Her golden taffeta and ivory silk gown, fine enough to Léonie's eye to have come from the latest collection by Charles Worth, was shot through with crystal and metallic thread. At her neck she wore a high choker in the same fabric, with a pearl brooch set in the middle. As she talked and moved, her dress caught the light and shimmered.

With relief, Léonie spotted Anatole standing by the windows, smoking and talking to Dr. Gabignaud. She excused herself and slipped across the room to join the gentlemen. The scent of sandalwood soap, hair oil and a freshly pressed black dinner jacket greeted her as she approached. Anatole's face lit up when he saw her.

"Léonie!" He slipped an arm around her waist and hugged her tight. "May I say, you look quite charming." He took a step back to let the doctor into the conversation. "Gabignaud, you remember my sister?"

"Indeed I do." The doctor gave a crisp bow. "Mademoiselle Vernier. And may I add my compliments to those of your brother."

Léonie blushed charmingly. "It is quite a gathering," she said.

Anatole identified the other guests for her. "You remember Maître Fromilhague? And Denarnaud and his sister, who keeps house for him."

Léonie nodded. "Tante Isolde introduced me."

"And that is Bérenger Saunière, the parish priest of Rennes-le-Château and friend of our late uncle."

He pointed to a tall and muscular man, with a high forehead and strong features rather at odds with his long black robes.

"Seems a charming fellow," Anatole continued, "although not a man given to trivialities." He nodded to the doctor. "He was rather more interested in Gabignaud's medical investigations than the mundane pleasantries I had to offer."

Gabignaud smiled, acknowledging the truth of it. "Saunière is an extremely informed man, in all manner of things. He has an appetite for knowledge. Always asking questions."

Léonie looked at the priest a moment longer, then her gaze moved on.

"And the lady with him?"

"Madame Bousquet, a distant relative of our late uncle." Anatole dropped his voice. "Had not Lascombe taken it upon himself to marry, she would have inherited the Domaine de la Cade."

"Yet she has accepted the invitation to dine?"

He nodded. "The bond between Madame Bousquet and Isolde is hardly that of sisters, but it is civilized. They receive one another. Indeed, Isolde admires her."

Only now did Léonie notice a tall, very thin man standing a little behind their small group. She half turned to observe him. He was dressed most unusually in a white suit, rather than customary black evening wear, and sported a yellow handkerchief in the breast pocket of his jacket. His waistcoat, too, was yellow.

His face was lined and his skin almost transparent with antiquity, and yet it seemed to Léonie that no great sense of age hung about him. There was, though, she thought, an underlying sadness. As if he was a man who had suffered and seen much.

Anatole turned to see who or what had so caught her attention. He leaned closer to whisper in her ear. "Ah, that is Rennes-les-Bains' most celebrated visitor, Audric Baillard, author of that strange little pamphlet that engaged you so." He smiled. "Quite the eccentric, apparently. Gabignaud's been telling me that he always dresses in that singular manner, regardless of the occasion. Always in a pale suit, always with a yellow cravat."

Léonie turned to the doctor. "Why is that?" she asked sotto voce.

Gabignaud smiled and shrugged. "I believe in memory of friends once lost, Mademoiselle Vernier. Fallen comrades, I'm not entirely certain."

"You can ask him yourself, *petite*, at dinner," said Anatole.

. . .

THE CONVERSATION prospered until the sound of the gong being struck
called the party in to dinner.

Isolde, escorted by Maître Fromilhague, led her guests from the drawing
room and across the hall. Anatole accompanied Madame Bousquet. Léonie,
on Monsieur Denarnaud's arm, kept Monsieur Baillard in her sights. Abbé
Saunière and Dr. Gabignaud brought up the rear, with Mademoiselle Denarnaud between them.

Pascal, splendid in borrowed red-and-gold livery, threw open the doors as
the party approached. There was an immediate murmur of appreciation. Even
Léonie, who had seen the dining room in various stages of preparation during
the course of the morning, was dazzled by the transformation. The magnificent glass chandelier was alive with three tiers of white wax candles. The long,
oval table was dressed with armfuls of fresh lilies, lit by three silver candelabra.
On the sideboard were serving tureens, their lids domed and gleaming like
armor. Light from the candles sent shadows dancing along the walls across the
painted faces of past generations of the Lascombe family that hung upon
the walls.

The ratio of four ladies to six gentlemen made the table a little uneven.
Isolde sat at the head, with Monsieur Baillard at the foot. Anatole was on
Isolde's left, with Maître Fromilhague to her right. Beside Fromilhague was
Mademoiselle Denarnaud, and next to her Dr. Gabignaud. Léonie was next,
with Audric Baillard on her right. She gave a shy smile as the servant pulled
out her chair and she sat.

On the far side of the table, Anatole had the pleasure of Madame Bousquet,
followed by Charles Denarnaud and Abbé Saunière beyond.

The servants poured generous measures of *blanquette de Limoux* into flat,
basin-like glasses as wide as coffee bowls. Fromilhague concentrated his attentions on his hostess, all but ignoring Denarnaud's sister, which Léonie
thought discourteous although she could not entirely blame him for it. In
their brief conversation, she had thought her a most dull woman.

After a few formal exchanges with Madame Bousquet, Léonie could hear
Anatole was already launched into animated conversation with Maître Fromilhague about literature. Fromilhague was a man of strong opinions, dismissing

Monsieur Zola's latest novel, *L'Argent*, as dreary and immoral. He condemned other habitués of Zola's erstwhile writing fraternity, such as Guy de Maupassant—who, rumor had it, having tried to take his own life, was now confined at Dr. Blanche's asylum in Paris. In vain, Anatole did try to suggest that a man's life and his work might be treated separately.

"Immorality in life debases the art" was Fromilhague's stubborn response.

Soon most of the table were engaged in the debate.

"You are quiet, Madomaisèla Léonie," came a voice at her ear. "Does literature not interest you?"

She turned to Audric Baillard. "I adore reading," she said with relief. "But in company such as this, it is difficult to make one's opinions heard."

He smiled. "Ah, yes."

"And I confess," she continued, blushing a little, "I find much contemporary literature utterly wearisome. Page after page of ideas, exquisite turns of phrase and clever ideas, but where nothing ever happens!"

A smile flickered in his eyes. "It is stories that capture your imagination?"

Léonie smiled back. "My brother, Anatole, always tells me I have rather low tastes, and I suppose he is right. The most thrilling novel I have read is *The Castle of Otranto,* but I am also a fan of Amelia B. Edwards's ghost stories and anything by Monsieur Poe."

Baillard nodded. "He was gifted. A troubled man, but so adept at capturing the dark side of our human nature, don't you think?"

Léonie felt a spike of pleasure. She had endured too many tedious soirées in Paris being all but ignored by the majority of guests, who seemed to believe that she would have no opinions worth the hearing. Monsieur Baillard appeared to be different.

"I do," she agreed. "My favorite of Monsieur Poe's stories, although I confess it gives me nightmares each time I read it, is 'The Tell-Tale Heart.' A murderer driven mad by the sounds of the beating heart of the man he has slaughtered and concealed beneath the floorboards. Quite brilliant!"

"Guilt is a powerful emotion," he said quietly.

Léonie looked at him closely for a moment, waiting for him to expound, but he said nothing more.

"May I be impertinent and ask you a question, Monsieur Baillard?"

"Of course."

"You are dressed, well . . ." She broke off, not wishing to cause offense.

Baillard smiled. "Unconventionally? Not in the usual uniform?"

"Uniform?"

"Of a gentlemen these days at dinner," he said, his eyes twinkling.

Léonie gave a sigh. "Well, yes. Although it was not that so much, as that my brother said that you were known to always wear yellow. In memory of fallen comrades, he said."

Audric Baillard's face seemed to cloud over.

"That is so," he said quietly.

"Did you fight at Sedan?" she asked, then hesitated. "Or . . . my papa fought for the Commune. I never knew him. He was deported and . . ."

For a moment Audric Baillard's hand covered hers. She felt his skin, paper thin, through the material of her glove, and the lightness of his touch. Léonie did not know what overcame her at that moment, only that an anguish she had never realized she felt was suddenly put into words.

"Is it always right to fight for what you believe in, Monsieur Baillard?" she said quietly. "I have often wondered. Even if the cost to those around you is so great?"

He squeezed her fingers. "Always," he said quietly. "And to remember those who fall."

For an instant, the noise of the room receded. All the voices, the laughter, the chink of glasses and silver cutlery. Léonie looked directly at him and felt her gaze, her thoughts, absorbed by the wisdom and experience flickering in his pale, dignified eyes.

Then he smiled. His eyes crinkled, and the intimacy was broken.

"The Good Christians, the Cathar believers, were forced to wear a yellow cross pinned to their clothing to mark them out." His fingers patted the sunflower-yellow handkerchief in his pocket. "I wear this in remembrance."

Léonie tilted her head. "You feel deeply for them, Monsieur Baillard," she said, smiling.

"Those who have gone before us are not necessarily gone, Madomaisèla Vernier." He tapped his chest. "They live here." He smiled. "You did not know your father, you say, and yet he lives in you? Yes?"

To her astonishment, Léonie felt tears spring to her eyes. She nodded, unable to trust herself to speak. It was, in some respects, a relief when Dr. Gabignaud asked her a question and she was obliged to answer.

43

Course after course was brought to the table. Fresh trout, pink and melting from the bone like butter, followed by dainty lamb cutlets served on a bed of late asparagus. The men were poured a strong Corbières, a hearty local red wine from Jules Lascombe's excellent cellar. For the ladies, a semi-sweet white wine from Tarascon, rich and dark, the color of singed onion skins.

The air grew hot with conversation and opinion, arguments of faith and politics, of north and south, of country living versus the town. Léonie glanced across at her brother. Anatole was in his element, his brown eyes sparkling, his black hair glistening. She could see how he was charming both Madame Bousquet and Isolde herself. At the same time, she could not fail to notice there were shadows beneath his eyes. And that in the dancing light of the candles, the scar across his brow looked particularly vivid.

Léonie took some time to recover from the strong emotions her conversation with Audric Baillard had aroused in her. Little by little, self-consciousness and embarrassment at having revealed herself so openly—and so unexpectedly—began to give way to curiosity that she should have done so. Having recovered her composure, she became impatient for an opportunity to rekindle their conversation. But Monsieur Baillard was deeply engaged in debate with the curé, Bérenger Saunière. To her other side, Dr. Gabignaud seemed determined to fill every moment with talking. Only with the arrival of dessert did the opportunity present itself.

"Tante Isolde says you are an expert in many matters, Monsieur Baillard. Not only the Albigensians, but Visigoth history, also Egyptian hieroglyphs. On my first evening here, I read your monograph *Diables et esprits maléfiques et phantômes de la montagne*. There is a copy here in the library."

He smiled, and Léonie felt that he, too, was pleased to return to the conversation.

"I made a gift of it to Jules Lascombe myself."

"It must have taken a long time to gather so many stories together in one volume," she continued.

"Not so long," he said lightly. "It is but a matter of listening to the landscape, to the people who inhabit this land. The stories often recorded as myth or legend, spirits and demons and creatures, are as much woven into the character of the region as the rocks and mountains and lakes."

"Of course," she said. "But do you not also think there are mysteries that cannot be explained?"

"*Oc, Madomaisèla, ieu tanben.* I believe that, too."

Léonie's eyes widened. "You speak Occitan?"

"It is my mother tongue."

"You are not French?"

He gave a sharp glance. "No, indeed not."

"Tante Isolde wishes the servants to speak French within the house, but they lapse into Occitan so frequently that she has given up reprimanding them."

"Occitan is the language of these lands. Aude, Ariège, Corbières, Razès—and beyond, into Spain and Piedmont. The language of poetry, of stories and folklore."

"So you come from this region then, Monsieur Baillard?"

"*Pas luènh,*" he replied, passing lightly over her inquiry.

The realization that he might translate for her the words she had seen inscribed above the door to the sepulchre was followed swiftly by the memory of the scratching of claws on the flagstones, like the grating of a trapped animal.

She shivered. "But are such stories true, Monsieur Baillard?" she asked. "Of evil spirits and phantoms and demons. Are they true?"

"*Vertat?*" he repeated, holding her gaze with his pale eyes for a moment longer. "True? Who is to say, Madomaisèla? There are those who believe that the veil that separates one dimension from the other is so transparent, so lucent, as to be almost invisible. Others would say that only the laws of science dictate what we may and we may not believe." He paused. "For my part, I can tell you only that attitudes change over time. What one century holds as fact, another will see as heresy."

"Monsieur Baillard," Léonie said quickly, "when I was reading your book, I found myself wondering if the legends followed the natural landscape. Were the Fauteuil du Diable or the Étang du Diable named for stories that were told in these parts, or did the stories grow up as a way of giving character to the place?"

He nodded and smiled. "That is a perceptive question, Madomaisèla."

Baillard spoke quietly, and yet Léonie felt all other sound retreat in the face of his clear, timeless voice. "What we call civilization is merely man's way of trying to impose his values upon the natural world. Books, music, painting, all these constructed things that have so occupied our fellow guests this evening are but attempts to capture the soul of what we see around us. A way of making sense, of ordering our human experiences into something manageable, containable."

Léonie stared at him for a moment. "But ghosts, Monsieur Baillard, and devils," she said slowly. "Do you believe in ghosts?"

"*Benleu,*" he said, in his soft and steady voice. Perhaps.

He turned his head to the windows, as if looking for someone beyond, then back to Léonie.

"This much I will say. Twice before, the devil that haunts this place has been summoned. Twice he has been defeated." He glanced to his right. "Most recently, with the help of our friend here." He paused. "I should not wish to live through such times again, unless there was no choice."

Léonie followed his gaze. "Abbé Saunière?"

Baillard gave no indication he had heard her. "These mountains, these valleys, these stones—and the spirit that gave life to them—existed long before people came and tried to capture the essence of ancient things with language. It is our fears that are reflected in those names to which you refer."

Léonie considered what he had said. "But I am not sure you have answered my question, Monsieur Baillard."

He placed his hands on the table. Léonie could see blue veins and the brown marks of age written upon his white skin. "There is a spirit that lives in all things. Here we sit in a house several hundred years old. It is established, one might say, antique by modern human standards. But it stands within a place that is many thousands and thousands of years old. Our influence upon the universe is nothing more than a whisper. Its essential character, its qualities of light and dark, were set millennia before man attempted to make his mark upon the landscape. The ghosts of those who have gone before are all around us, absorbed into the pattern, the music of the world, if you like."

Léonie felt suddenly feverish. She put her hand to her brow. To her surprise, it felt clammy, cold. The room was spinning, swaying, shifting. The candles, the voices, the blur of servants moving to and fro, everything was blurred around the edges.

She tried to bring her thoughts back to the matter in hand, taking another sip of wine to steady her nerves.

"Music," she said, although her voice sounded as if it came from a long way off. "Can you tell me about the music, Monsieur Baillard?"

She saw the expression on his face, and for a moment thought that he had somehow understood the unspoken question behind her words.

Why, when I sleep, when I enter the woods, do I hear music in the wind?

"Music is an art form that involves organized sounds and silence, Madomaisèla Léonie. We consider it now an entertainment, a diversion, but it is so much more than that. Think instead of knowledge expressed in terms of pitch, that is to say, melody and harmony; in terms of rhythm, that is tempo and meter; and in terms of the quality of sound, timbre, dynamics and texture. Put simply, music is a personal response to vibration."

She nodded. "I have read that it may, in certain situations, provide a link between this world and the next. That a person might pass from one dimension to another. Do you think there could be some veracity in such claims, Monsieur Baillard?"

He met her gaze. "There is no pattern the human mind can devise that does not exist already within the bounds of nature," he said. "Everything we do, see, write, notate, all are an echo of the deep seams of the universe. Music is the invisible world made visible through sound."

Léonie felt her heart contract. Now they were approaching the core of it. All along, she now knew, she had been moving toward this one moment when she would tell of how she had found the sepulchre concealed within the woods, led there by the promise of arcane secrets laid out within the book. Such a man as Audric Baillard would understand. He would tell her what she wished to know.

Léonie took a deep breath.

"Are you acquainted with the game of tarot, Monsieur Baillard?"

The expression on his face did not alter, but his eyes sharpened.

Indeed, almost as if he was expecting such a question.

"Tell me, Madomaisèla," he said at last, "is your inquiry related to matters we have been discussing previously. Or separate from it?"

"Both." Léonie felt her cheeks grow hot. "Although I ask because . . . because I came upon a book in the library. It was written in a most old-fashioned manner, the words themselves are obscure, and yet there was something . . ." She paused. "I am not certain that I divined the true meaning."

"Go on."

"This text, which purported to be a real testimony and was . . ." She stumbled, not certain if she should reveal the authorship of the text. Monsieur Baillard completed the thought for her.

"Written by your late uncle," he said, smiling at the look of surprise she could not conceal. "I am aware of the book."

"You have read it?"

He nodded.

Léonie breathed a sigh of relief. "The author—that is, my uncle—talked of music woven into the fabric of the corporeal world. Certain notes that could, or so he claimed, summon the spirits. And the cards also were associated with both the music and the place itself, pictures that came to life only during the course of . . . this communication between worlds." She paused. "A tomb within these grounds was mentioned, and claim of an event that once had taken place here." She raised her head. "Have you heard stories of such happenings, Monsieur Baillard?"

He met her green gaze with steady eyes. "I have."

Before embarking on the conversation, she had intended to conceal the fact of her expedition from him, but under his wise, searching eyes, she found she could not dissemble.

"I . . . I found it," she said. "It lies higher up, in the woods to the east."

Léonie turned her flushed face toward the open windows. She longed, suddenly, to be out of doors, away from the candles, the conversation, the stale air in the overheated room. Then she shivered, as if a shadow had stepped behind her.

"I know it, too," he said. He stopped, waited, then added, "And I believe there is a question you wish to ask of me?"

Léonie turned her head back to face him. "There was an inscription written upon the arch above the door of the sepulchre."

She recited it as best she could, the unfamiliar words clumsy in her mouth.

"Aïci lo tems s'en, va res l'Eternitat."

He smiled. "You have a good memory, Madomaisèla."

"What does it mean?"

"It is something of a corruption, but in essence it means: 'Here, in this place, time moves away toward eternity.'"

For a moment, their eyes met. Hers glassy and sparkling with the *blanquette* she had drunk, his steady and calm and wise. Then he smiled. "You remind me very much, Madomaisèla Léonie, of a girl I once knew."

"What happened to her?" Léonie asked, momentarily diverted.

He said nothing, but she could see he was remembering. "Oh, it is another story," he said softly. "One that is not yet ready for the telling."

Léonie saw him withdraw, wrapping his memories around himself. His skin seemed, suddenly, transparent, the lines on his thin face deeper, as if etched in stone.

"You were telling how you found the sepulchre," he said. "Did you enter?"

Léonie took her mind back to that afternoon. "I did."

"So you read the inscription upon the floor: *Fujhi, poudes; Escapa, non.* And now you find the words haunt you?"

Léonie eyes widened. "Yes, but how could you know? I do not even know their meaning, only that they repeat endlessly in my head."

He paused, then said: "Tell me, Madomaisèla, what do you think you found there? Within the sepulchre?"

"The place where spirits walk," she heard herself say, and knew it to be true.

Baillard was silent for what seemed like an age. "You asked me before if I believed in ghosts, Madomaisèla," he said eventually. "There are many types of ghosts. Those who cannot rest because they have done wrong, who must seek forgiveness or atonement. Also those to whom wrong has been done and who are condemned to walk until they can find an agent of justice to speak their cause."

He looked at her. "Did you look for the cards, Madomaisèla Léonie?"

She nodded, then regretted it, for the action made the room spin. "But I did not find them."

She stopped, feeling suddenly sick. Her stomach was churning, lurching, as if she was onboard a boat on a rough sea. "All I found was a sheet of music for the piano."

Her voice sounded muffled, woolen, as if she was speaking from underwater.

"Did you take it from the sepulchre?"

Léonie pictured herself thrusting the music, with the words written upon it, into the deep pocket of her worsted jacket as she ran down the nave of the sepulchre and out into the twilight of the forest. Then, later, slipping it between the pages of *Les Tarots*.

"Yes," she said, all but tripping over the word. "I did."

"Léonie, listen to me. You are steadfast and you are courageous. *Forca e vertu*, good qualities both when used wisely. You know how to love, and well." He glanced across the table to where Anatole sat, then his gaze flickered to Isolde, before returning to Léonie. "I fear there are great trials ahead for you. Your love will be tested. You will be called upon to act. The living will be in need of your services, not the dead. Do not return to the sepulchre until—*if*—it becomes absolutely necessary for you to do so."

"But I—"

"My advice, Madomaisèla, is that you return *Les Tarots* to the library. Forget all that you read within it. It is, in so many ways, an enchanting book, a seductive book, but for now, you should put the whole matter from your mind."

"Monsieur Baillard, I—"

"You said perhaps you feared you had misunderstood the words in the book." He paused. "You did not, Léonie. You understood very well."

She continued all the same. "So it is true? That the cards can summon the spirits of the dead?"

He did not reply directly. "With the correct patterning of sound and image and place, such things might happen."

Her head was spinning. She wanted to ask a thousand questions, but she could not find the words.

"Léonie," he said, drawing her back to him. "Save your strength for the living. For your brother. For his wife and child. It is they who will need you."

Wife? Child?

Her confidence in Monsieur Baillard momentarily faltered. "No, you are mistaken. Anatole has no—"

At that moment, Isolde's voice rang out from the end of the table.

"Ladies, shall we?"

Immediately, the room was filled with the scrape and slide of the chairs on the polished wooden floors as the guests rose from the table.

Léonie got unsteadily to her feet. The folds of her green dress fell like water to the floor.

"I do not understand, Monsieur Baillard. I thought I did, but now I find I was mistaken." She halted, realizing how utterly intoxicated she was. The effort of remaining upright was quite overwhelming suddenly. She put out a hand to steady herself on the back of his chair.

"And you will heed my advice?"

"I shall do my best," she said, giving a crooked grin. Her thoughts were going round in circles. She could no longer remember which words had been spoken out loud and which uttered only within her muddled head.

"*Ben, ben.* Good. I am reassured to hear it. Although . . ." He paused again, as if he was undecided whether to speak further. "If the time does come when you need the agency of the cards, Madomaisèla, then know this. You may call upon me. And I will help you."

She nodded, again making the room spin wildly.

"Monsieur Baillard," she said, "you did not tell me what the second inscription meant. Upon the floor."

"*Fujhi, poudes; Escapa, non?*"

"Those words, yes."

His eyes clouded. "Flee, you may; escape, you cannot."

Part VI

Rennes-le-Château
October 2007

44

Tuesday, October 30

Meredith woke the next morning with a thudding head after broken sleep. The combination of wine, the whispering of the wind in the trees and her crazy dreams had made her restless.

She didn't want to think about the night. Ghosts, visions. What it might mean. She had to keep focused. She was here to do a job, and that's all she should be worrying about.

Meredith stood under the shower until the water ran cold, took a couple of Tylenol, drank a bottle of water. She towel-dried her hair, dressed in comfortable blue jeans and a red sweater, then went down to breakfast. A supersize plate of scrambled eggs, bacon and baguette, washed down with four cups of strong, sweet French coffee, and she felt human again.

She checked her purse—phone, camera, notebook, pen, sunglasses and local map of the area—then went down to the lobby to meet Hal. There was a line at the desk. A Spanish couple complaining about having too few towels in their room, a French businessman challenging the additional charges on his bill and, by the concierge's station, a mountain of luggage waiting to be taken out to the coach of an English tour group en route to Andorra. The clerk looked strung out already. There was no sign of Hal.

Meredith was prepared for the fact he might not show. In the cold light of day, without the courage that comes with alcohol, he might be regretting the impulse that had led him to ask a stranger out. At the same time, she kind of hoped he would come. No big deal, all really low-key, and she wouldn't be devastated to be stood up. At the same time, there was no denying she had butterflies in the pit of her stomach.

She occupied herself by looking at the photographs and paintings hanging on the walls around the lobby. They were the standard oil paintings to be found in every countryside hotel. Rural views, misty towers, shepherds, mountains, nothing remarkable. The photographs were more interesting, clearly all chosen to reinforce the *fin de siècle* ambience. Framed portraits in sepia tones, brown and gray. Women with serious expressions, tight-nipped waists and big skirts, hair swept up. Men with moustaches and beards, in formal poses, straight-backed and staring into the lens.

Meredith ran her eyes over the walls, taking in the general impression rather than the specifics of each shot, until she came to one portrait tucked in right by the curve of the staircase, just above the piano she'd noticed last night. A formal pose in sepia and white, the black wooden frame chipped at the corners.

She recognized the square in Rennes-les-Bains. She took a step closer. In the center of the photograph, on an ornate metal chair, sat a man with a black moustache, his dark hair swept back from his forehead and his top hat and cane balanced across his knees. Behind him, to his left, was a beautiful, ethereal-looking woman, slim and elegant in a well-cut dark jacket, high-collared shirt and long skirt. Her black half-veil was lifted off her face, revealing light hair pinned back in an artful chignon. Her slim fingers, sheathed in black, rested lightly upon his shoulder. To the other side was a younger girl, her curly hair arranged beneath a felt hat and dressed in a cropped jacket with brass buttons and velvet trim.

I've seen her before.

Meredith narrowed her eyes. There was something about the girl's direct, bold gaze that drew her in, sending an echo slipping through her mind. A shadow of another photograph like it? A painting? The cards maybe? She dragged the heavy piano stool to one side and leaned in, racking her brain, but the memory refused to come. The girl was dazzlingly pretty, with tumbling copper locks, a pert chin and eyes that stared straight into the heart of the camera.

Meredith looked back to the man in the middle. There was a clear family resemblance. Brother and sister maybe? They had the same long lashes, the same unswerving focus, the same tilt of the head. The other woman seemed less definite, somehow. Her coloring, her pale hair, her slightly detached air. For all her physical proximity to the others, she seemed insubstantial. There

but not there. As if at any moment she might slip from sight altogether. Like
Debussy's Mélisande, Meredith thought, she carried a suggestion of belonging
to another time and place.

Meredith felt her heart lock down. It was the same expression she remembered, looking up into her birth mother's eyes when she was little. Sometimes
Jeanette's face was gentle, wistful. Sometimes it was angry, distorted. But always, on good or bad days, that same air of distraction, of a shifting mind
settling elsewhere, fixed on people no one else could see, hearing words no
one else could hear.

Enough of this.

Determined not to be disabled by her bad memories, Meredith reached
forward and lifted the photograph away from the wall, looking for some kind
of confirmation that it was Rennes-les-Bains, a date, any identifying marks.

The creased brown waxed paper was coming unstuck from the frame, but
the words printed on the back in block capitals were clear.

RENNES-LES-BAINS, OCTOBRE 1891, and then the studio credit, EDITIONS
BOUSQUET. Curiosity took the place of her unwelcome emotions.

Beneath that, three names.

MADEMOISELLE LÉONIE VERNIER, MONSIEUR ANATOLE VERNIER, MADAME
ISOLDE LASCOMBE.

Meredith felt the hairs on the back of her neck stand on end, remembering the tomb at the far edge of the cemetery in Rennes-les-Bains:
FAMILLE LASCOMBE-BOUSQUET. Now, on a photograph hanging on the
wall, the two names joined once more.

She was certain the two younger figures were the Verniers, brother and
sister, surely, rather than husband and wife, given the physical similarities
between them. The older woman had the air of someone who had seen more.
Lived a less sheltered existence. Then, in a shot, Meredith realized where she'd
seen the Verniers before. A snapshot of a moment in Paris, settling the check
in Le Petit Chablisien in the street in which Debussy had once lived. The
composer looking down from the frame, saturnine and discontented. And
beside him, his neighbors on the restaurant wall, a photograph of this same
man, this same striking girl, although with a different and older woman.

Meredith kicked herself for not paying more attention at the time. For a
moment she even thought about calling the restaurant and asking if they had

any information about the family portrait they displayed so prominently. Then the thought of having such a conversation in French, on the telephone, made her dismiss the idea.

As she stared at the photograph, in her mind's eye, the other portrait seemed to shimmer behind it, shadows of the girl and the boy, the people they had been once and were here. For a second she knew—*thought* she knew—how, if not yet why, the stories she had been following might be interlinked.

She hung the frame back on the wall, thinking she could borrow it later. As she pushed the heavy piano stool back to its original position, she noticed the lid of the instrument was now open. The ivory keys were a little yellow, the edges chipped like old teeth. Late nineteenth century, she reckoned. A Bluthner boudoir grand.

She pressed middle C. The note echoed clear and loud in the private space. She looked round, guilty, but no one was paying any attention. Too wrapped up in their own affairs. Still standing, as if sitting down would commit herself to something, Meredith played the scale of A minor. Just a couple of low octaves in the left hand. Then the arpeggio with her right. The chill of the keys on her fingertips felt good.

Like she had come home.

The stool was a deep mahogany with ornate carved legs and a red-velvet cushion stapled to the lid by a line of brass studs. To Meredith, snooping around in other people's music collections was as interesting as running one's fingers along a friend's bookshelves when they stepped out of the room a moment. The brass hinges creaked as she opened the lid, releasing the distinctive scent of wood, old music and pencil lead.

Inside was a neat pile of books and loose sheet music. Meredith went through the stack, smiling as she came across sheet music for Debussy's *Clair de lune* and *La Cathédrale engloutie,* in their distinctive pale yellow Durand covers. The regular collections of Beethoven and Mozart sonatas, as well as Bach's *Well-Tempered Clavier,* books one and two. European classics, exercises, a little sheet music, a couple of show tunes from Offenbach's *La vie parisienne* and from *Gigi.*

"Go ahead," said a voice at her shoulder. "I'm happy to wait."

"Hal!"

She let the lid of the stool fall shut with a guilty snap, then turned to see him smiling at her. He looked better this morning—good, in fact. The lines of worry, of misery, had gone from the corners of his eyes and he wasn't so pale.

"You sound surprised," he said. "Did you think I was going to stand you up?"

"No, not at all . . ." She stopped and grinned. "Well, yes, maybe. It crossed my mind."

He spread his arms out. "As you can see, present and correct and ready to go."

They stood, a little awkward, then Hal leaned over the piano stool and kissed her on the cheek. "I'm sorry I was late." He gestured at the piano. "Are you sure you don't want—"

"Quite sure," Meredith cut across him. "Maybe later."

They walked together across the tiled floor of the lobby, Meredith too aware of the small distance between them and the smell of his soap and aftershave.

"Do you know where you want to start looking for her?"

"Who?" she said quickly.

"Lilly Debussy," he said, looking surprised. "I'm sorry, isn't that what you said you were hoping to do this morning? A little research?"

She blushed. "Sure, yes. Absolutely."

Meredith experienced a rush of embarrassment for jumping to the wrong conclusion. She didn't want to explain her other reason for being in Rennes-les-Bains—her real reason, she guessed—it just felt too personal. But Hal didn't know what she'd been thinking about at the moment he arrived. He wasn't a mind reader.

"On the trail of the first Mrs. Debussy, absolutely. If Lilly ever was here, I'm going to find out how, why and when."

Hal smiled. "Shall we take my car? I'm happy to drive you wherever you want to go."

Meredith thought about it. It would leave her freer to take notes and look around properly, check out the map.

"Sure, why not."

As they walked out the door and down the steps, Meredith was aware of the eyes of the girl in the photograph on her back.

45

The drive and the grounds looked very different in daylight.

October sun flooded the gardens, burnishing everything with intense color. Meredith caught the smell of damp burning bonfires and the perfume of sun on wet leaves through the half-opened car window. A little farther away, a more dappled light fell on the deep green bushes and high box hedge. Everything was outlined as if in gold and silver.

"I'm taking the back way, cross-country to Rennes-le-Château. Much quicker than heading into Couiza and out again."

The road doubled back and twisted up on itself as it climbed through the wooded hills. There was every shade of green, every shade of brown, every hue of crimson and copper and gold, chestnuts, oaks, bright yellow broom, silver hazel and birch. On the ground beneath the pines, huge cones lay as if left to mark the way.

Then a final twist in the road, and suddenly they were out of the woods and into wide expanses of meadows and pasture.

Meredith felt her spirits lift at the views unfolding before her.

"It's wonderful. So amazingly beautiful."

"I remembered something I think will really interest you," Hal said. She heard the smile in his voice. "When I told my uncle I was going to be out this morning—and why—he reminded me that there are allegations of a connection between Debussy and Rennes-le-Château. He was unusually helpful, in fact."

Meredith turned to face him. "You're kidding."

"I'm assuming you know the basic stories about the place?"

She shook her head. "Don't think so . . ."

"It's the village that sparked all the *Holy Blood, Holy Grail* stuff? *Da Vinci Code? The Templar Legacy?* Ringing any bells? Bloodline of Christ?"

Meredith wrinkled her nose. "Sorry. I'm more . . . into nonfiction—biography, history, theory, that kind of stuff. Facts."

Hal laughed. "Okay, quick précis. The story is that Mary Magdalene was in fact married to Jesus and had children by him. After the Crucifixion, she fled, some say to France. Marseille, lots of places along the Mediterranean coast, all lay claim to being where she came ashore. Fast-forward nine hundred years, to 1891, when it's alleged the priest of Rennes-le-Château, Bérenger Saunière, came across parchments demonstrating this bloodline of Christ, going all the way from the present day to the first century AD."

Meredith went still. "Eighteen ninety-one?"

Hal nodded. "That's when Saunière began a massive renovation project that was to last for many years—starting with the church, but in the end the gardens, graveyard, house, everything." He stopped. Meredith felt him glance at her.

"Are you all right?" he asked.

"Sure," she said quickly. "Sorry. Go on."

"The bloodline parchments were supposed to have been hidden inside a Visigoth pillar, way back when. Most locals think the whole thing was a hoax from start to finish. Records contemporaneous with Saunière don't mention any sort of great mystery associated with Rennes-le-Château, other than a dramatic increase in Saunière's material circumstances."

"He got rich?"

Hal nodded. "The church hierarchy accused him of simony—that is, selling masses for money. His parishioners were more charitable. They thought he had discovered some cache of Visigoth treasure and didn't begrudge him, since he spent so much of it on the church and his parishioners."

"When did Saunière die?" she asked, remembering the dates on Henri Boudet's memorial in the church in Rennes-les-Bains.

Hal turned his blue eyes on her. "Nineteen seventeen," he said, "leaving everything to his housekeeper, Marie Denarnaud. It wasn't until the late 1970s that all the religious conspiracy theories began to surface."

She scribbled that information down, too. The name Denarnaud had appeared on several tombs in the graveyard.

"What does your uncle think about all the stories?"

Hal's face clouded over. "That it's good for business," he said, then lapsed into silence.

Since there was clearly no love lost between him and his uncle, Meredith wondered why Hal was sticking around now that the funeral was over. One look at his face suggested he wouldn't welcome the question, so she left it.

"So, Debussy?" she prompted in the end.

Hal seemed to pull his thoughts together. "Sorry. There was supposed to have been a secret society formed to act as guardians of the bloodline parchments, the things Saunière may or may not have found in the Visigoth pillar. This organization was alleged to have had some very famous leaders—figureheads, if you like. Newton, for one; Leonardo da Vinci, for another. And Debussy."

Meredith was so stunned, she burst out laughing.

"I know, I know," Hal said, starting to grin. "But I'm just giving you the story as my uncle told it."

"It is totally absurd. Debussy lived for his music. And he was not a clubbable person. Very private, very loyal to a small group of friends. The thought of him running some secret society . . . well, just plain crazy!" She wiped the corner of her eye with her sleeve. "What's the evidence to support this bizarre theory?"

Hal shrugged. "Saunière did entertain many important Parisians and guests at Rennes-le-Château around the turn of the last century—something else that fueled the conspiracy theories—heads of state, singers. Someone called Emma Calvé? Ring any bells?"

Meredith thought. "French soprano, around at the right sort of time, but I'm pretty certain she never sang a major role for Debussy." She pulled out her notebook and wrote down the name. "I'll check it out."

"So it could fit?"

"Any theory can be made to fit if you try hard enough. Doesn't make it true."

"Says the scholar."

Meredith could hear the gentle teasing in his voice and liked it. "Says the person who's spent half her life in a library. Real life is never so neat. It's messy. Stuff overlaps, facts contradict each other. You find one piece of evidence, think it's all going on. You've nailed it. Next thing you know, you come across something else that turns it all on its head."

For a while they drove on in companionable silence, both locked in their own thoughts. They passed a substantial farm and crossed a ridge. Meredith noticed the landscape on this side of the hill was different. Not so green. Gray rocks, like teeth, seemed to push out of the rust-colored earth as if a series of violent earthquakes had forced up the hidden heart of the world. Slashes of red soil, like wounds in the land. It was a less hospitable environment, more forbidding.

"It makes you realize," she said, "how little the essential landscape has changed. Take the cars and the buildings out of the equation, and you're left with mountains, gorges, valleys that have been here tens of thousands of years."

She felt Hal's attention sharpen. She was intensely aware of the gentle rise and fall of his breathing in the confined space.

"I couldn't see it last night. It all seemed too small, too insignificant to have been the center of anything. But now . . ." Meredith broke off. "Up here, the sheer scale of things is different. It makes it more plausible that Saunière might have found something of value." She paused. "I'm not saying he did or he didn't, only that it gives substance to the theory."

Hal nodded. "Rhedae—the old name for Rennes-le-Château—was at the heart of the Visigoth empire in the south. Fifth, sixth and early seventh centuries." He glanced at her, then back to the road. "But from your professional standpoint, doesn't it seem a long time—too long—for something to lie undiscovered? If there was anything genuine to find—Visigoth or even earlier, Roman, I guess—surely it would have come to light before 1891?"

"Not necessarily," Meredith replied. "Think of the Dead Sea Scrolls. It's surprising how some things turn up while others stay hidden for thousands of years. According to the guidebook, there are the remains of a Visigoth watchtower nearby in the village of Fa and Visigoth crosses in the cemetery at the village of Cassaignes, both discovered pretty recently."

"Crosses?" said Hal. "They were Christians? I'm not sure I knew that."

Meredith nodded. "Weird, huh. The interesting thing is that it was Visigoth practice to bury their kings and noblemen with their treasure in hidden graves rather than in graveyards round a church building. Swords, buckle clasps, jewelry, fibulae, drinking cups, crosses, you name it. Of course, this brought with it the same problems as the ancient Egyptians."

"How to deter grave robbers."

"Exactly. So the Visigoths developed a way of constructing secret chambers below riverbeds. The technique was to dam the river and temporarily divert its course while the site was excavated and the burial chamber prepared. Once the king or warrior and his treasure were safely stowed, the chamber would be sealed and camouflaged with mud, sand, gravel, whatever, then the dam demolished. The water rushes back and the king and his treasure are hidden for eternity."

Meredith turned to look at Hal, realizing her words had triggered thoughts about something else. She couldn't figure him out. Even bearing in mind what he had been through in the last few weeks, yesterday, in particular—he seemed to switch from open and relaxed one moment to a guy with the world on his shoulders the next.

Or maybe he's wishing he was someplace else?

Meredith carried on looking straight ahead through the windshield. If he wanted to confide in her, he would. No sense pushing it.

They drove on, higher up the bare mountainside, until Hal turned a final hairpin bend in the road.

"We're here," he said.

46

Meredith peered through the windshield as Hal edged the car up the last turn in the road.

Set high on the vertiginous hillside above them was a collection of houses and other buildings. There was a painted board welcoming them to Rennes-le-Château.

Son site, ses mystères.

White and purple flowers peeped out from the steep hedgerow at the side of the road, and big blooms, like giant, overblown hyacinths.

"There are poppies everywhere in the spring," Hal said, following the line of her gaze. "It's really something."

A couple of minutes later, they parked in a dusty lot with views over the entire southern expanse of the Haute Vallée and got out of the car. Meredith took in the panoramic view of the mountains and the valleys below, then turned around to look at the village itself.

Immediately behind them there was a circular stone water tower that stood in the center of the dusty parking lot. A square sundial painted on the south-facing curve marked the summer and winter solstices.

At the top, there was an inscription. She shielded her eyes to read it.

Aïci lo tems s'en
Va res l'Eternitat.

Meredith took a photograph.

At the edge of the parking lot was a map mounted on a viewing board. Hal jumped up onto the low wall and began to point things out: the mountain peaks of Bugarach, Soularac and Bézu, the towns of Quillan to the south, Espéraza to the southwest, Arques and Rennes-les-Bains to the east.

Meredith breathed out deeply. The endless sky, the outline of the peaks behind, the distinctive profile of the fir trees, the mountain flowers at the side of the road, the tower in the distance. It was awe-inspiring, reminiscent of the background she remembered on La Fille d'Épées. The tarot cards could easily have been painted with this landscape in mind.

"It says here," Hal said, "that on a clear day in the summer you can see twenty-two villages from this one point."

He smiled, then jumped down and pointed to a gravel path leading away from the car park.

"If I remember rightly, the church and museum are down that way."

"What's that?" asked Meredith, staring at a squat, crenellated tower built overlooking the valley.

"The Tour Magdala," he replied, following the direction of her glance. "Saunière built the belvedere, the stone walkway that runs along the south side of his gardens, with this incredible view, at the very end of the renovation program, 1898, 1899. The tower was to house his library."

"The original collection's not in there, surely?"

"I doubt it," he said. "I suspect they've done what my dad did at the Domaine de la Cade, put a few replacement volumes in the cases, for atmosphere. He called, really pleased with himself, after he'd managed to buy a whole load of secondhand books from a *vide grenier* in Quillan."

Meredith frowned.

"A secondhand sale," he explained.

"Right." She smiled. "So, does that mean your father was pretty involved in the day-to-day running of the place?"

Hal's face clouded over again. "Dad was the money, came over from the UK from time to time. It was my uncle's project. He found the place, persuaded my father to put up the cash, supervised the renovation, made all the decisions." He paused. "Until this year, that is. Dad retired and changed. For the better, really. Relaxed, enjoying himself. He came over quite a few times in January and February, then moved over for good in May."

"How did your uncle feel about that?"

Hal stuck his hands into his pockets and looked at the ground. "I'm not sure."

"Had your father always intended to retire to France?"

"I really don't know," he said. Meredith heard the mixture of bitterness and confusion in his voice, and felt a rush of sympathy.

"You want to piece together the last few months of your father's life," she said gently, understanding all too well.

Hal raised his head. "That's it. It's not that we were that close. My mother died when I was eight and I was packed off to boarding school. Even when I was home for the holidays, Dad was always working. I can't say we really knew each other." He paused. "But we'd been starting to see a little more of each other in the past couple of years. I feel I owe it to him."

Sensing Hal needed to go at his own pace, Meredith didn't press him on what he meant by that. Instead, she asked a perfectly innocuous question.

"What kind of business was he in? Before he retired?"

"Investment banking. With a singular lack of imagination, I followed him into the same firm after I graduated from university."

"Another reason you quit your job?" she asked. "You inherit your father's share of the Domaine de la Cade?"

"An excuse rather than a reason." He paused. "My uncle wants to buy me out. Not that he's said as much, but he does. But I keep thinking that maybe Dad would want me to get involved. Take over where he left off."

"Did you ever talk to your father about it?"

"No. There didn't seem any rush." He turned to Meredith. "You know?"

They had been walking slowly while they were talking, and were now standing outside an elegant villa giving directly onto the narrow street. Opposite was a pretty, formal garden with a generous stone pond and a café. The wooden shutters were down.

"I first came here with Dad," Hal said, "sixteen, seventeen years ago. Way before he and my uncle had ever thought of going into business together."

Meredith smiled to herself, now understanding why Hal knew so much about Rennes-le-Château when he knew pretty much nothing about the rest of the region. The place was special to him because of the bond it gave him with his father.

"It's all been completely done up now, but then it was pretty derelict. The church was open for a couple of hours a day, watched over by a terrifying *gardienne* dressed all in black who scared the living daylights out of me. The Villa Béthania here"—he pointed up at the impressive house they were stand-ing next to—"Saunière built for guests rather than for himself. When I came with Dad, it was open to the public but in a totally haphazard way. You'd wander into one of the rooms and see a waxwork figure of Saunière sitting up in bed."

"Sounds awful."

"All the papers and documents were lying about in unlocked display cases, in damp, unheated rooms beneath the belvedere."

Meredith grinned. "An archivist's nightmare."

He gestured through the railings separating the path from the formal gardens.

"Now, as you can see, the place is a major tourist attraction. The cemetery itself, where Saunière is buried next to his housekeeper, was closed to the public in December 2004, when the *Da Vinci Code* took off and the number of visitors coming to Rennes-le-Château went through the roof. It's down here."

They walked on in silence until they reached the high, solid metal gates protecting the graveyard.

Meredith tilted her head back to read the inscription in a porcelain pen-dant set above the locked gates.

"*Memento homo quia pulvis es et in pulverem reverteris.*"

"Which means?" Hal asked.

"Dust to dust," she said. A shiver went down her spine. There was some-thing about the place that made her uncomfortable. A brooding quality in the air, a watchfulness despite the deserted streets. She dug out her notepad and copied down the Latin.

"Do you write everything down?"

"Sure do. Occupational hazard."

She smiled at him and caught the smile he threw back.

Meredith was glad to leave the graveyard behind them. She followed Hal past a stone calvary, then doubled back up another tiny path to a small statue dedicated to Notre Dame de Lourdes behind wrought-iron railings.

The words PÉNITENCE, PÉNITENCE and MISSION 1891 were carved on the base of the ornate stone pillar.

Meredith stared. There was no getting away from it. That same date kept coming up.

"This is apparently the actual Visigoth pillar inside which the parchments were found," Hal said.

"Is it hollow?"

He shrugged. "I suppose it must be."

"Crazy that they would leave it sitting here," Meredith said. "If this place is such a magnet for conspiracy theorists and treasure hunters, you'd think the authorities would worry someone would take it."

Meredith looked attentively at the benign eyes and silent lips of the statue standing on top of the pillar. As she gazed at the stone features, imperceptibly at first, then deeper and more insistent, she saw scratch marks begin to appear on the gentle face. Ridges and furrows, like someone was gouging at the surface with a chisel.

What the hell?

Not trusting the evidence of her own eyes, she stepped forward, stretched out her hand and touched the stone.

"Meredith?" said Hal.

The surface was smooth. Quickly, she withdrew her fingers as if she'd been burnt. Nothing. She turned her palms over, as if expecting to see some mark there.

"Is something wrong?" he asked.

Only that I'm seeing things.

"I'm fine," she said firmly. "That sun is really bright."

Hal looked concerned, which Meredith realized she kind of liked.

"Anyhow, what happened to the parchments after Saunière found them?" she asked.

"He was supposed to have taken them to Paris to have them verified."

She frowned. "That makes no sense. Why would he go to Paris? The logical thing for a Catholic priest would be to head straight to the Vatican."

He laughed. "I can see you don't read much fiction!"

"Although, playing devil's advocate for a moment," she continued, thinking aloud, "the counter-explanation would be, presumably, that he didn't trust the Church not to destroy the documents."

Hal nodded. "That's the most popular theory. Dad made the point that if a parish priest in a far corner of France really had stumbled upon some amazing secret—such as a marriage document or proof of descendants going back to the first century AD—then it would have been simpler for the Church to get rid of him rather than go to all the trouble of paying him off."

"Good point."

Hal paused. "Although he had an entirely different theory."

Meredith turned to face him, hearing the catch in his voice. "Which was?"

"That the whole Rennes-le-Château saga was just a cover-up, a deliberate attempt to draw attention away from events going on at the same time in Rennes-les-Bains."

Meredith felt a kick in her stomach. "Covering up what?"

"Saunière was known to be a friend of the family who owned the Domaine de la Cade. There was a run of unexplained deaths in the region—some kind of wolf, mountain cat most likely, but rumors built up about there being some sort of devil marauding across the countryside."

Claw marks.

"Although the cause of the fire that destroyed much of the original house in 1897 was never proved, there's strong evidence that it was started deliberately to rid the area of this devil they believed was being harbored in the grounds of the Domaine de la Cade. There was also something about a deck of tarot cards associated with the Domaine. Saunière was supposed to have been involved in that, too."

The Bousquet Tarot.

"All I do know is that my uncle and Dad fell out over it," Hal said.

Meredith forced herself to keep her voice steady. "Fell out?"

"At the end of April, just before my dad made the decision to come out here for good. I was staying with him in his London flat and came into the room to catch the tail end of the conversation. Argument, really. I didn't hear much of it: something about the interior of Saunière's church being a copy of an earlier tomb."

"Did you ask your father what he meant?"

"He didn't want to talk about it. All he would say was that he'd learnt there was a Visigoth mausoleum within the grounds of the Domaine de la Cade, a sepulchre, which was destroyed at the same time as the house caught fire. All that is left is a few old stones, ruins."

For a second, Meredith was tempted to confide in Hal. Tell him all about the tarot reading in Paris. About her nightmare last night, about the cards sitting, right now, at the bottom of her closet. About the real reason she had come to Rennes-les-Bains. But something held her back. Hal was fighting his own demons right now. She frowned, again remembering the four-week delay between the accident and the funeral.

"What precisely happened to your father, Hal?" she asked, then stopped, thinking she'd gone too far, too fast. "I'm sorry, it was presumptuous of me to . . ."

Hal traced a pattern on the ground with his foot. "No, it's fine. His car ran off the road, on the bend to Rennes-les-Bains. Went over into the river." He spoke in a monotone, as if deliberately keeping all emotion from his voice. "Police couldn't understand it. It was a clear night. It wasn't raining or anything. The worst thing was . . ."

He broke off.

"You don't have to tell me if it's too difficult," she said softly, putting her hand in the small of his back.

"It happened in the early hours of the morning, so the car wasn't discovered until some hours later. He had been trying to get out, so the door was half open. But the animals had got to him first. His body and face were very badly scratched."

"I'm so sorry."

"No one was sure what kind of creature it was," he said, his face creasing at the thought of it. "Some sort of mountain cat was the suggestion, but . . ."

Meredith glanced back toward the statue on the path, fighting not to link in her mind a tragic accident in 2007 with the older superstitions that seemed to haunt the region. But the connections were hard to ignore.

All systems of divination, like music itself, work through patterns.

"The thing is, I could accept the situation if it was an accident. But they said he'd been drinking, Meredith. And that's the one thing I know he'd never do." He dropped his voice. "Never. If I knew for sure what had happened, one way or the other, it would be all right. Not all right, but I mean I could deal with it. But it's the not knowing. Why was he there at all, on that stretch of road, at that time? I just want to know."

Meredith thought of her birth mother's tear-stained face and the blood under her nails. She thought of the sepia photographs and the piece of music and the hollowness inside that had driven her to this corner of France.

"I can't deal with not knowing," he repeated. "Do you understand?"

She wrapped her arms around him and drew him close. He responded, putting his arms around her and folding her into him. Meredith fit perfectly beneath his broad shoulders. She could smell his aftershave and soap, the soft wool of his sweater tickling her nose. Could feel the heat of him, his anger, his rage, then the despair behind both.

"Yes," she said quietly. "I understand."

47

Domaine de la Cade

Julian Lawrence waited until the chambermaids had finished the first floor before leaving his study. The trip to Rennes-le-Château and back would take two hours at least. He had plenty of time.

When Hal told him he was going out, and with a girl, Julian's first reaction had been relief. They had even talked for a couple of minutes without Hal storming out. Maybe it meant his nephew was going to accept what had happened and get on with his life. Let his doubts go.

As things stood, there were loose ends. Julian had hinted that he'd be willing to buy his nephew out of his inherited share of the Domaine de la Cade but had not pushed it. He had expected to have to wait until after the funeral, but he could feel himself getting impatient.

Then Hal had let drop that the girl in question was a writer and Julian had started to wonder. Given Hal's behavior over the past four weeks, he wouldn't put it past the boy to try to get a journalist interested in the story of his father's accident, just for the hell of it.

Julian had checked the register and discovered she was an American, Meredith Martin, and booked until Friday. He'd no idea if she knew Hal or if his nephew was simply taking advantage of finding someone who might listen to his sob story. Either way, he couldn't risk Hal using the girl to stir up trouble. He wasn't prepared to let his plans be damaged by rumor and innuendo.

Julian went up the back stairs and along the corridor. With the master key, he let himself into Meredith Martin's room. He took a couple of Polaroids, to make certain he could return the room to the exact state in which he'd found it, then started to search, beginning with the bedside table. He went quickly through the drawers but found nothing of interest other than two plane tickets, one for Toulouse to Paris Orly on Friday afternoon, the other for her return flight to the States on November 11.

He moved to the bureau. Her laptop was plugged in. He opened the lid and booted it up. It was easy. There was no password protection on her operating system, and she had been using the hotel's wireless system.

Ten minutes later, Julian had read through her e-mails—tedious, domestic stuff, nothing relevant—tracked her online trail through recent sites she'd visited, and looked at a few of the stored files. None of it suggested she was a journalist out for a story. Local history, mostly. There were notes about research in England, then very basic stuff—addresses, dates, times—about Paris.

Next, Julian went into her picture files, going through them in date order. The first few were taken in London. There was a folder of shots from Paris— street scenes, landmarks, even one of a sign showing the opening hours of the Parc Monceau.

The final folder was marked Rennes-les-Bains. He opened it and began to peruse the images. These worried him more. There were several photographs of the riverbank at the entrance to the town to the north, specifically a couple of the road bridge and the tunnel at exactly the place where his brother Seymour's car had left the road.

There were other photographs of the graveyard at the rear of the church. One, taken from the covered porch looking back to the Place des Deux Rennes, enabled him to identify exactly when they had been taken. Julian laced his fingers behind his head. He could just make out, in the bottom right-hand corner of the picture, part of the tablecloth on which the book of condolences had sat.

His brow furrowed. Meredith Martin had been in Rennes-les-Bains last night, taking photographs of the funeral and the town.

Why?

As Julian copied the folder of images onto his memory stick, he tried to think of what innocent explanation there could be but came up blank.

He exited the program and shut the computer down, leaving everything just as he'd found it, then moved to the wardrobe. He took a couple more Polaroids, then worked methodically through every pocket, the piles of T-shirts and shoes, finding nothing of interest. At the bottom of the wardrobe, beneath a pair of boots and a pair of LK Bennett spikes, was a soft black travel bag.

Squatting, Julian undid the zipper and looked inside the main compartment. It was empty apart from a pair of socks and a bead bracelet caught in the stiff lining. He pushed his fingers into every corner but found nothing. Next he went through the outside pockets. Two large compartments at either end, both empty, then along either side three smaller compartments. He picked up the bag, turned it upside down and shook it. It seemed too heavy. He turned the bag over again and pulled at the cardboard base. With a tearing sound of Velcro, the lining came up to reveal another compartment. He reached in and drew out a square package of black silk. With his thumb and forefinger, he unfolded the four corners.

Julian froze. The face of Justice was staring up at him.

For a split second, he thought he was seeing things, then he realized it was just another reproduction set. He fanned them out to make sure, cutting the deck twice.

Printed, laminated, not the original Bousquet Tarot. Stupid that, even for a second, he'd thought it could possibly be.

He stood up, clutching the deck in the palm of his hand, flicking through the cards increasingly quickly, in case there was something unique, something different about this deck. There wasn't. It appeared to be the same as the one he had downstairs in his safe. No additional words, no variation in the images.

Julian forced himself to think. This discovery turned everything on its head, especially coming on the heels of the information from the Visigoth burial site at Quillan. With the grave goods, a slate had been found confirming the existence of other sites in the vicinity of the Domaine de la Cade. He hadn't been able to get through to his contact this morning.

But the immediate question was, Why did Meredith Martin have a reproduction set of the Bousquet deck with her? And hidden at the bottom of her bag. It couldn't be coincidence. Presumably, at the very least, she knew about the original deck of cards and their association with the Domaine de la Cade. What else? Maybe Seymour had said more to Hal than Julian had previously thought? And if Hal had brought her down here, maybe it wasn't to investigate the circumstances of the crash but had to do with the cards?

He needed a drink. He was sweating around the collar and under his arms from the shock of believing, if only for a moment, that he was holding the original cards in his hands.

Julian wrapped the replica deck in the black silk, returned the package to the bag and replaced the bag at the bottom of the wardrobe. He glanced round the room one last time. Everything looked as it had before. If anything was misplaced, Ms. Martin would put it down to the chambermaids. He let himself out into the corridor and walked briskly back toward the service stairs. The whole operation, from start to finish, had taken less than twenty-five minutes.

48

Rennes-le-Château

Hal was the first to break away. His blue eyes were bright with anticipation, perhaps surprise, too. His face was a little flushed.

Meredith also stepped back. The strength of their raw attraction to each other, now that the emotion of the moment had passed, left them both a little awkward.

"Anyway," he said, pushing his hands into his pockets.

Meredith grinned. "Anyway . . ."

Hal turned to the wooden gates at right angles to the path and pushed. He frowned, tried again. Meredith could hear the bolts rattling.

"It's closed," he said. "It's unbelievable, but the museum's closed. I'm sorry. I should have called ahead."

They looked at each other. Then they both burst out laughing.

"The spa in Rennes-les-Bains was closed, too," she said. "Until April thirtieth."

The same lock of unruly hair had fallen forward. Meredith's fingers ached to push it back from his face, but she kept her hands at her sides.

"At least the church is open," he said.

Meredith joined him, very aware of his physical presence now. He seemed to fill the entire path.

He pointed up at the triangular porch above the door.

"That inscription—TERRIBILIS EST LOCUS ISTE—is another reason all the conspiracy theories surrounding Rennes-le-Château took hold," he said, clearing his throat. "The phrase actually translates as 'This place is awe-inspiring,' *terribilis* in an Old Testament sense rather than *terrible* in a modern sense, but you can imagine how it's been interpreted."

Meredith did look, but it was the other, partially legible inscription on the apex on which she was concentrating. IN HOC SIGNO VINCES. Constantine again, the Christian emperor of Byzantium. The same inscription as on Henri Boudet's memorial in Rennes-les-Bains. She pictured Laura's spread of cards on the table. The Emperor was one of the major arcana, near the Magician and La Prêtresse, at the beginning of the deck. And the password she'd typed to access the Internet to pick up her e-mail . . .

"Who came up with the password for the hotel network?" she asked.

Hal looked surprised at the non sequitur but answered all the same.

"My uncle," he said, without hesitation. "Dad wasn't into computers." He reached out and took her hand. "Shall we?"

THE FIRST THING that struck Meredith as they walked into the church was how very small it was, as though it had been built on a three-quarter scale. The perspectives seemed all wrong.

On the wall to the right were handwritten notices, some French, some awkward English. Piped choral music, some kind of mediocre plainsong, filtered in over thin silver speakers suspended in the corners.

"They've sanitized the place," Hal said in a low voice. "To counteract all the rumors of mysterious treasure and secret societies, they've tried to inject a Catholic message into everything. Like this, for example." He tapped one of the signs. "Look. *Dans cette église, le trésor c'est vous.* In this church, the treasure is you."

But Meredith was staring at the stoup for holy water on the immediate left of the door. The *bénitier* was balanced on the shoulders of a three-foot-high statue of a devil. The malevolent red face, the twisted body, the unnerving, piercing blue eyes. She'd seen the demon before. At least, an image of him. Lying on the table in Paris as Laura spread out the major arcana at the beginning of the reading.

Le Diable. Card XV of the Bousquet Tarot.

"That's Asmodeus," said Hal. "The traditional guardian of treasure, keeper of secrets and builder of the Temple of Solomon."

Meredith touched the grimacing demon, which felt cold and chalky beneath her fingers. She looked at his hands, clawed and twisted, and couldn't help glancing back through the open door to where the statue of Notre Dame of Lourdes stood immobile upon the pillar.

She gave a small shake of her head and raised her eyes to the frieze above.

A tableau of four angels, each making one part of the sign of the cross, and Constantine's words yet again, although this time in French. The colors were faded and chipped, as if the angels were fighting a losing battle.

On the base, two basilisks framed a red inset containing the letters BS.

"The initials could stand for Bérenger Saunière," said Hal. "Or for Boudet and Saunière, or for La Blanque and Le Salz, two local rivers that meet at a pool nearby known as *le bénitier.*"

"The two priests knew each other well?" she asked.

"By all accounts, yes. Boudet was a mentor to the younger Saunière. In the early days of Boudet's ministry, when he spent some months in the parish of Durban nearby, he also became friendly with a third priest, Antoine Gélis, who subsequently took over the parish at Coustaussa."

"I drove by there yesterday," Meredith said. "It looked ruined."

"The castle is. The village is inhabited, though it's tiny. No more than a handful of houses. Gélis died in somewhat strange circumstances. Murdered on Halloween 1897."

"They never found out who was responsible?"

"Don't think so, no." Hal stopped in front of another plaster statue. "Saint Anthony, the Hermit," he said. "Famous Egyptian saint of the third, fourth century."

This information drove any thoughts of Gélis out of Meredith's mind.

The Hermit. Another card from the major arcana.

The evidence to prove that the Bousquet Tarot had been painted in the area was overwhelming. This tiny church dedicated to Mary Magdalene was testament to that. The only thing Meredith wasn't clear about was how the Domaine de la Cade fit in.

And how, if at all, this connects with my family.

Meredith forced herself to concentrate on the matter at hand. No sense muddling everything up together. What if Hal's father had been right in his suggestion that everything in Rennes-le-Château was constructed precisely to draw attention away from its sister village down in the valley? There was a logic to it, but Meredith needed to know more before jumping to any conclusions.

"Have you seen enough?" Hal asked. "Or do you want to stick around longer?"

Still thinking, Meredith shook her head. "I'm done."

. . .

THEY DIDN'T TALK MUCH as they walked back up to the car. The gravel on the path crunched loudly under their feet, like tightly packed snow. It had gotten cooler since they'd been inside, and the air was heavy with the smell of bonfires.

Hal unlocked the car, then looked back over his shoulder.

"Three corpses were found buried in the grounds of the Villa Béthania in the 1950s," he said. "All were male, aged between thirty and forty, and they had all been shot, although one of the bodies at least had been very badly mauled by wild animals. The official verdict was that they'd been killed during the war—the Nazis occupied some of this part of France, and the Resistance was pretty active down here. But local belief is that the bodies were older, from the end of the nineteenth century, that they were connected with the fire at the Domaine de la Cade and, possibly, also the murder of the priest Gélis in Coustaussa."

Meredith looked at Hal over the roof of the car.

"But if these three men were involved—in either the fire or the murder— who killed them?"

At that moment, Hal's cell phone rang. He flipped the lid and glanced at the number. His eyes sharpened.

"I need to take this," he said, covering the speaker. "Sorry."

Inwardly, Meredith groaned with frustration, but there was nothing she could do. "Of course, go ahead," she said. "I'll be fine."

She climbed into the car and watched as Hal wandered over to a fir tree near the Tour Magdala to talk.

No such thing as coincidence. Everything happens for a reason.

She leaned back against the headrest and ran through everything that had happened, the sequence of events from the moment she'd stepped off the train at the Gare du Nord. No, after that. From the moment she set foot on the colorful painted steps that led up to Laura's rooms.

Meredith pulled her notebook out of her purse and glanced over her notes, looking for answers. The real question was, which was the story she was chasing down here, which the echo? She was in Rennes-les-Bains searching for her own family history. Did the cards fit in with that in any way? Or was it a completely different, unrelated story? Of academic interest, but nothing to do with her.

What had Laura said? Meredith flipped back through her notes until she found it.

"The timeline is confused. The sequence seems to be jumping backward and forward, as if there is some blurring of events. Things slipping between past and present."

She glanced through the window at Hal, who was now walking back toward the car, holding his cell clenched in his fist. The other was dug deep into his pocket.

Where does he fit into all this?

"Hi," she said, as he opened the door. "Is everything okay?"

He got in. "Sorry, Meredith. I was going to suggest we go for lunch, but something's come up that I need to sort out first."

"Something good, by the look of it?" she said.

"The police commissariat handling the case in Couiza have finally agreed to let me have sight of the file into my father's accident. I've been asking for this for weeks, so it's a step forward."

"That's great, Hal," she said, hoping it would be and that he wasn't getting his hopes up for no reason.

"So either I can drop you back at the hotel," he continued, "or you could come with me and we'll find somewhere to eat later. Only problem with that is I'm not sure how long I'll be. They don't always move fast down here."

For a moment Meredith was tempted to tag along. Give Hal moral support. But she figured it was something he needed to do on his own. Besides, she needed to focus on her own stuff for a while, not let herself get sucked into Hal's problems.

"Sounds like you might be a while," she said. "If you don't mind dropping me back at the hotel on your way."

She was gratified to see Hal's expression falter, just for a moment.

"It's probably better I go alone in any case, since they are doing me a favor."

"That's what I guessed," she said, briefly touching his hand.

Hal fired the ignition and reversed the car.

"Then what about later?" he said, as he negotiated the narrow street out of Rennes-le-Château. "We could meet for a drink. Dinner, even? If you've not got plans."

"Sure." She smiled, keeping it cool. "Dinner would be good."

49

Julian Lawrence was standing at his study window in the Domaine de la Cade as his nephew turned the car and drove back down the long drive. He switched his attention to the woman who'd just got out and who was now waving goodbye. The American, he presumed.

He nodded his approval. Good figure; athletic but petite; straight, dark hair to her shoulders. It wouldn't be such a trial to spend a little time in her company.

Then she turned round and he got a proper look at her.

Julian recognized her, although he couldn't place her. He dug into his memory until it came to him. The pushy bitch from the traffic holdup in Rennes-les-Bains last night. The American accent.

Another flash of paranoia shot through him. If Ms. Martin was here working with Hal, and had mentioned she'd seen him driving into the town, his nephew might legitimately question where he'd been. Might realize the excuse Julian had given for being late didn't make sense.

He drained his glass, then made a snap decision. He crossed the study in three strides, pulled his jacket from the back of the door and walked out to intercept her in the lobby.

ON THE JOURNEY back from Rennes-le-Château, Meredith started to feel excited. Before, Laura's gift had felt a burden. Now the tarot cards seemed full of intriguing possibilities.

She waited until Hal's car disappeared from view, then turned and headed up the steps to the main door of the hotel. She felt nervous but fired up, too. The same contradictory feelings she'd experienced when sitting with Laura were back, and big-time. Hope versus skepticism, the prickling anticipation versus the fear that she was putting two and two together and coming up with five.

"Ms. Martin?"

Caught by surprise, Meredith turned in the direction of the voice to see Hal's uncle striding toward her across the lobby. She tensed, hoping after their bad-tempered exchange in Rennes-les-Bains last night, he wouldn't recognize her. But today he was smiling.

"Ms. Martin?" he said, holding out his hand. "Julian Lawrence. I just wanted to welcome you to the Domaine de la Cade," he said.

"Thank you."

They shook hands.

"Also." He stopped, giving a slight shrug. "Also I wanted to apologize if I was rather abrupt yesterday, in the town. If I'd known you were a friend of my nephew's, I would of course have introduced myself then."

Meredith blushed. "I didn't think you'd remember me, Mr. Lawrence. I'm afraid I was pretty rude myself."

"Not in the slightest. As I'm sure Hal told you, it was a rather difficult day for us all yesterday. It's no excuse, I know, but . . ."

He left the apology hanging. Meredith noticed how he had the same habit as Hal of staring right at a person with an unwavering gaze that seemed to blot out everything else. And although some thirty years older, he'd got that same kind of charisma as Hal, a way of filling the space. She wondered if Hal's father had been the same.

"Of course," she said. "I'm sorry for your loss, Mr. Lawrence."

"Julian, please. And thank you. It was a shock." He paused. "Speaking of my nephew, Ms. Martin, I don't suppose you know where he's disappeared off to? I was under the impression you were going to Rennes-le-Château this morning but that he would be here this afternoon. I had been hoping to have a word with him."

"We did go, but a call just came through from the police station, so he dropped me off before going to deal with things. Couiza, I think he said."

She sensed a sharpening of interest, even though Julian's expression didn't change. Immediately Meredith regretted letting the information out.

"What sort of things?" he said.

"He didn't really say," she said in a rush.

"Pity, I had hoped for a word." He shrugged. "But it's nothing that can't wait." He smiled again, but this time it failed to reach his eyes. "I trust you're enjoying your stay with us? You have everything you need?"

"Everything's great." She glanced at the stairs.

"Forgive me," he said. "I'm holding you up."

"I've got some stuff I need to . . ."

Julian nodded. "Ah, yes. Hal mentioned you were a writer. Are you here working on an assignment?"

Meredith felt pinned to the spot. Kind of trapped.

"Not really," she replied. "At least, a little research."

"Is that so?" He offered his hand. "In which case I won't delay you further."

Not wishing to be rude, Meredith took it. This time, the touch of his skin made her uncomfortable. Too personal somehow.

"If you see my nephew before I catch up with him," he said, squeezing her fingers a little too tightly, "do let him know I'm looking for him, won't you?"

Meredith nodded. "Sure."

Then he let her go. He turned and walked back across the lobby without a backward glance.

Clear message. He was confident, sure of himself, in control.

Meredith let a long breath escape from between her lips, wondering exactly what had just happened. She stood staring into the empty space where Julian had been. Then, mad at herself for letting him get to her again, she pulled herself together.

Put it out of your mind.

She glanced around. The desk clerk was dealing with a query and facing the opposite direction. From the noise coming from the restaurant, Meredith figured most guests were already in the dining room having lunch. Perfect for what she had in mind.

She walked quickly across the red and black tiles, ducked round beside the piano and reached up and took the photograph of Anatole and Léonie Vernier and Isolde Lascombe from the wall. She slipped it beneath her jacket, then doubled back and ran up the stairs, taking them two at a time.

Only when she was back in her room, with the door safely shut behind her, did her breathing return to normal. She paused a moment, narrowed her eyes and looked around the room.

There was something about the atmosphere that seemed different. An alien smell, very subtle but there all the same. She wrapped her arms around herself, remembering her nightmare. Then she shook her head. *Don't do this.* The maids had been in to make the bed. Besides, she thought, it wasn't at all like what she'd felt in the night.

Dreamed, she corrected herself.

Just a dream.

Then there had been a definite sense of someone being in the room with her. A presence, a chill in the air. Now, it was just . . .

Meredith shrugged. Polish or cleaning product, that was all. It wasn't so strong. Not really. Although she couldn't help wrinkling her nose. Like the smell of the sea washing stagnant on the shore.

50

Meredith went straight to the closet and retrieved the tarot deck, unfolding the four corners of black silk as if the cards inside were made of glass.

The unsettling image of the Tower was on the top, the brooding gray and green of the background and the trees more vivid here in the clouded afternoon than it had seemed in Paris. She paused a moment, suddenly thinking that Justice had been on the top of the pile when Laura pressed the cards upon her, then shrugged. Obviously not.

She cleared a space on the bureau and put the cards down, then pulled out her notebook from her purse, wishing she'd taken the time last night to transpose her scribbled notes about the reading from page to screen.

Meredith thought for a moment, trying to figure out if she lay out the ten cards that had come up yesterday, in case, in the peace and quiet of her own thoughts, she might see more in them. She decided against it. She was less interested in the reading per se than in the historical data she was gathering about the Bousquet Tarot and how the cards fit in to the story of the Domaine de la Cade, the Verniers and the Lascombe family.

Meredith searched the deck until she had found all twenty-two of the major arcana. Putting the remainder of the cards to one side, she then laid them out in three rows one above the other, placing the Fool at the top on his own, just like Laura had done. The cards felt different to the touch. Yesterday they'd made her nervous. As if she was committing herself to something even by handling them. Today they seemed—and she knew it sounded stupid—kind of well-meaning.

She slid the framed photograph from under her jacket, propped it on the bureau in front of her and studied the black-and-white figures, frozen in time. Then she dropped her eyes to the colorful images on the cards.

For a moment, her attention rested on Le Pagad, with his blue, blue eyes and thick black hair, gathering all the symbols of the tarot to him. An attractive image, but a man to be trusted?

Then the tingling feeling on her neck started over, licking all the way down her spine as a new idea took hold. Was it possible? She put the Magician to one side. Instead, she picked up Le Mat, and held it against the framed photograph. Now that she had them side by side, she had no doubt the man was Monsieur Vernier brought to life. The same debonair expression, the slim figure, the black moustache.

Next, card II, La Prêtresse. The ethereal, pale, distant features of Madame Lascombe, although in an evening gown, cut low at the neck, rather than the formal day clothes of the photograph. Meredith glanced back down, seeing the two figures painted together as the Lovers and chained at the feet of the Devil.

Finally, card VIII, La Force: Mademoiselle Léonie Vernier.

Meredith felt herself smiling. She felt the greatest connection with this card, almost as if she knew the girl. In a way, she guessed, it was because Léonie resembled her mental image of Lilly Debussy. Léonie was younger, but there was that same wide-eyed innocence, the same thick copper hair, although loose on the card and tumbling down over her shoulders, rather than tied up in a formal style. Most of all, that same straightforward way of gazing directly into the lens. A glint of understanding rippled beneath the surface of her conscious mind but was gone before Meredith could grasp it.

She turned her attention to the other cards of the major arcana that had come up in the course of the day: the Devil, the Tower, the Hermit, the Emperor. She studied each in turn but increasingly with the sense that they were taking her farther away from where she wanted to be, not closer.

Meredith sat back in her chair. The antique seat creaked. She put her hands behind her head and closed her eyes.

What am I not seeing?

She let her thoughts wander back to the reading. Allowed Laura's words to flow over her, in no particular order, letting the patterns emerge.

Octaves. All the eights.

Eight was the number of completion, of successful outcomes. There was also an explicit message about interference, obstacles and conflict. Both Strength and, in older packs, Justice carried the number eight. Both Le Pagad and La Force had the infinity symbol, like a sideways figure eight.

Music linked everything together. Her family background, the Bousquet Tarot, the Verniers, the reading in Paris, the sheet of piano music she'd inherited. She reached for her notebook, going back through the pages until she found the name she was looking for, the American cartomancer who'd linked the tarot with music. She switched on her laptop, tapping her fingers impatiently as it sought a connection. Finally, the search box flashed up on the screen. Meredith typed PAUL FOSTER CASE. Moments later, a list of sites appeared.

She went straight to the Wikipedia entry, which was thorough and straightforward. An American, Paul Foster Case became interested in tarot cards in the early 1900s while he was working the steamboats, playing piano and organ in vaudeville. Thirty years later in Los Angeles, he set up an organization to promote his own tarot system, the Builders of the Adytum, known as BOTA. One of the distinguishing features of BOTA was that Case went public with his philosophy, in sharp contrast to most esoteric systems of the time, which relied on absolute secrecy and the idea of an elite. It was also interactive. Unlike any other decks, the BOTA cards were black-and-white, the idea being that each individual could color them in, put their own mark on them. This, as much as anything, helped bring tarot into the U.S. mainstream.

Another of Case's innovations was the association of musical notes with certain of the major arcana. All of them, with the exception of card XIX, the Sun, and IX, the Hermit—as if those two images alone stood outside the common run of things—were linked with a specific note.

Meredith looked at the illustration of a keyboard, with arrows showing which card went with which.

The Tower, Judgement and the Emperor were all assigned to the note C; the Devil was linked with A; D connected with the Lovers and Strength; the Magician and the unnumbered Fool were E.

C-A-D-E. Domaine de la Cade.

She stared at the screen, as if it was trying to trick her in some way.

C-A-D-E, all white notes, all associated with particular cards of the major arcana that had come up already.

And more than that, Meredith saw another connection that had been staring her in the face all along. She reached for her talisman, the inherited sheet of piano music: *Sepulchre 1891*. She knew the piece backward—the forty-five bars, the change of tempo in the middle section—in style and character suggesting nineteenth-century gardens and girls in white dresses. Echoes of Debussy and Satie and Dukas.

And built around the notes of A, C, D and E.

For a moment, Meredith forgot what she was doing, picturing her fingers flying over the keyboard. Nothing but the music existed. A, C, D and E. The final split arpeggio, the last chord fading away.

She sat back in her chair. Everything fit together, sure.

But what the hell, if anything, does it mean?

In a moment, Meredith was back in Milwaukee, Miss Bridge's advanced music class in senior high, repeating the same mantra over and over. A smile came to her lips. "An octave is made up of twelve plus one chromatic tones." She could all but hear her teacher's voice in her head. "The semitone and the whole tone are the building blocks of the diatonic scale. There are eight tones in the diatonic scale, five in the pentatonic. The first, third and fifth tones in the diatonic scale are the building blocks of root chords, the formula for perfection, for beauty."

Meredith let her memories come, leading her thoughts. Music and math, seeking the connections not the coincidences. She typed FIBONACCI into the search box. Watched as new words appeared in front of her. In 1202, Leonardo of Pisa, known as Fibonacci, developed a mathematical theory in which numbers formed a sequence. After two starting values, each number was the sum of the two preceding numbers.

0, 1, 1, 2, 3, 5, 8, 13, 21, 34, 55, 89, 144, 233, 377.

The relationship between pairs of consecutive numbers was said to approach the golden proportion, the golden mean.

In music, the Fibonacci principle was sometimes used to determine tunings. Fibonacci numbers also appeared in natural settings, such as branching in trees, the curve of waves, the arrangement of a pinecone. In sunflowers, for example, there were always eighty-nine seeds. Meredith smiled.

I remember.

Debussy had flirted with the Fibonacci sequence in his great orchestral tone poem *La Mer.* It was one of the wonderful contradictions of Debussy that although he was seen as a composer primarily concerned with mood and color, some of his most popular works were in fact constructed around mathematical models. Or rather could be divided into sections that reflected the golden ratio, frequently by using the numbers of the standard Fibonacci sequence. So in *La Mer* the first movement was fifty-five bars long—a Fibonacci number—and it broke down into five sections of 21, 8, 8, 5 and 13 bars, all also Fibonacci numbers.

Meredith forced herself to slow down. To put her thoughts in order.

She went back to the Paul Foster Case site. Three of the four notes linked to the name of the Domaine—C, A and E—were Fibonacci numbers: the Fool was 0, the Magician was I, and Strength was VIII.

Only D, card VI, the Lovers, wasn't a Fibonacci number.

Meredith pushed her fingers through her black hair. Did that mean she'd got it wrong? Or that it was the exception that reinforced the rule?

She drummed her fingers on the desk as she figured it out. The Lovers did fit the sequence if they appeared as individuals rather than as a pair: Le Mat was zero, the Priestess was card II. And zero and two were both Fibonacci numbers, even if six was not.

But even so.

Even if those connections were valid, how could there be a link between the Bousquet Tarot, the Domaine de la Cade and Paul Foster Case. The dates didn't work.

Case set up BOTA in the 1930s, and in America, not Europe. The Bousquet deck dated back to the 1890s, the minor arcana cards possibly even earlier. There was no way it could have been based on Case's system.

What if I turn it on its head?

Meredith thought harder. What if Case had heard of the association of tarot with music and then refined it for his own system? What if he'd heard of the Bousquet Tarot? Or maybe the Domaine de la Cade itself? Could the ideas have passed not from America to France but the other way round?

She pulled her battered A5 envelope from her purse and extracted the picture of the young man in soldier's uniform. How had she been so blind? She had seen how the figure of Le Mat was Anatole Vernier but hadn't taken seriously the obvious resemblance between Vernier and her soldier. The family resemblance to Léonie, too? The long, dark lashes, the high forehead, the same trick of looking straight into the lens of the camera.

She glanced back to the portrait. The dates were right. The boy in the soldier's uniform could be a younger brother, a cousin. Even a son.

And through him, down the generations, to her.

Meredith felt as if a great weight was being lifted from her chest. The burden of not knowing, like Hal had said earlier, crumbling and folding in on itself as she edged closer to the truth. But instantly, the cautious voice in her head kicked in, warning her against seeing what she wanted to see rather than what was there.

Verify it. The facts are out there. Test it.

Her fingers flying over the keys in her eagerness to find out everything, anything, Meredith hammered the word VERNIER into the search box.

She got nothing. Meredith stared in disbelief at the screen.

There's got to be something.

She tried again, adding Bousquet and Rennes-les-Bains. This time, she got a few sites selling tarot cards, and a couple of paragraphs about the Bousquet deck, but nothing more than she'd already found out.

Meredith sat back in her chair. The obvious way forward was to register with family search websites in this part of France and see if she could pick her way back to the past that way. It would take a while. But maybe Mary could help out from the other end.

With impatient fingers, Meredith fired off an e-mail to Mary, asking her to check the Milwaukee local history websites and electoral rolls for the name

Vernier, aware that if the soldier was Léonie's son, rather than Anatole's, she still might not have the right name. As an afterthought, she added the name Lascombe as well, then signed off with a long line of kisses.

The phone beside the bed rang.

For a moment, she just stared at it as though she couldn't figure out what she was hearing.

It rang again. She grabbed the receiver. "Hello?"

"Meredith? It's Hal."

She could hear straight off things weren't so good. "Are you okay?"

"I was just letting you know I was back."

"How did it go?"

A pause, then, "I'll tell you when I see you. I'll wait in the bar. I don't want to drag you away from your work."

Meredith glanced at the time and was amazed to see it was a quarter after six already. She looked at the chaotic mess of cards, tagged Internet sites, photographs lying on the bureau, evidence of her afternoon's work. Her head felt as though it were about to explode. She had found out plenty but still felt she was in the dark.

She didn't want to stop, but she recognized that her brain had reached meltdown. All those high-school nights when Mary would come into her room, kiss the top of her head and tell her it was time to take a break. Tell her that everything would be clearer after a good night's sleep.

Meredith smiled. Mary was usually—always—right.

She wouldn't achieve anything much more tonight. Besides, Hal sounded as though he could do with company. Mary would approve of that, too. Putting the living before the dead.

"Actually, now is a good time to stop."

"Really?"

The relief in that one word made Meredith smile.

"Really," she said.

"You're sure I'm not interrupting anything?"

"I'm sure," she said. "I'll finish up here and be down in ten."

Meredith changed into a fresh white shirt and her favorite black skirt, nothing too dressy, and went through to the bathroom. She put a little powder on her cheeks, a couple of strokes of mascara and a little lipstick, then brushed her hair and twisted it up into a knot.

She was putting on her boots, ready to go down, when her laptop bleeped at her she'd got mail.

Meredith went into her inbox and clicked on the e-mail from Mary. Only two lines long, the message contained a name, dates, an address and the promise to e-mail again as soon as she'd got more to tell.

A grin broke out across her face.

Nailed it.

Meredith picked up the photograph, no longer an unknown soldier. There was still much more to pin down, but she was nearly there. She tucked the picture into the frame of the photograph, where it belonged. The family reunited. Her family.

Still standing, she leaned over and clicked on reply.

"You're totally amazing," she typed. "All further info gratefully received! Love you."

Meredith pressed send. Then, still smiling, she went down to find Hal.

Part VII

Carcassonne

September—October 1891

51

Sunday, September 27, 1891

The morning after the dinner party, Léonie, Anatole and Isolde rose late. The evening had been a great success. Everyone agreed. The generous rooms and passageways of the Domaine de la Cade, so long silent, had been brought back to life. The servants whistled in the pass corridor. Pascal grinned as he went about his business. Marieta skipped lightly across the hall with a smile on her face.

Only Léonie was out of sorts. She had a vicious headache and chills, brought on by the unaccustomed quantity of wine she had consumed and the aftereffects of Monsieur Baillard's confidences.

She spent much of the morning lying upon the chaise longue with a cold compress on her head. When she did feel recovered enough to eat a little toasted bread and beef consommé for luncheon, she found herself subject to the sort of malaise that inevitably follows the passing of a big event. The dinner party had loomed in her mind for so long, she felt there was no longer anything to look forward to.

Meanwhile, she saw Isolde move from room to room, in her customary calm and unhurried manner, but as if a burden had been lifted from her shoulders. The look on her face suggested that now, perhaps for the first time, she felt as if she was the chatelaine of the Domaine. That she owned the house rather than the house owning her. Anatole, too, whistled as he walked from hall to library, from drawing room to terrace, looking like a man who had the world at his feet.

. . .

LATER THAT AFTERNOON, Léonie accepted Isolde's invitation to walk in the gardens. She needed to clear her head and, feeling slightly better, was glad of the opportunity to stretch her legs. The air was still and warm, the afternoon sun gentle on her cheeks. Quickly, she felt her spirits restored.

They chatted pleasantly of the usual topics as Isolde led Léonie in the direction of the lake. Music, books, the latest fashions.

"So, now," said Isolde. "How shall we occupy your time while you are here? Anatole tells me you are interested in local history and archaeology? There are several excellent trips. To the ruined castle at Coustaussa, for example?"

"I would like that."

"And, of course, reading. Anatole always says you have a hunger for books as other women have for jewelry and clothes."

Léonie blushed. "He thinks I read too much, but only because he does not read sufficiently! He knows all about books as objects but is not interested in the stories that lie between the pages."

Isolde laughed. "Which, of course, may be why he was obliged to resit his examinations for his baccalaureate!"

Léonie shot a look at Isolde. "He told you this?" she asked.

"Of course not, no," she said quickly. "What man brags of his failures?"

"Then—"

"Despite the lack of intimacy between my late husband and your mother, Jules liked to be kept informed of the events in his nephew's education and upbringing."

Léonie glanced at her aunt with interest. Her mother had been quite clear that the communication between her and her half-brother had been minimal. She was on the point of pressing Isolde further, but her aunt was speaking again and the moment was lost.

"Have I mentioned I have recently taken out a subscription with the Société Musicale et la Lyre in Carcassonne, although so far I have been unable to attend any concerts? I am aware that it might become rather dull for you, cooped up here in the country, so far from any entertainments."

"I am perfectly content," Léonie said.

Isolde smiled her appreciation. "I am obliged to make a trip to Carcassonne some time in the next few weeks, so I thought we might make an outing of it. Spend a few days in the city. How would that be?"

Léonie's eyes widened with delight. "That would be wonderful, *Tante*. When?"

"I am waiting for a letter from my late husband's lawyers. A point of query. As soon as I receive word, we will make the arrangements to travel."

"Anatole, too?"

"Of course," Isolde replied, smiling. "He tells me you would like to see something of the restored medieval Cité. It looks quite unchanged, they say, from the thirteenth century. It is really quite remarkable what they have achieved. Until some fifty years ago, it was a ruin. Thanks to the work of Monsieur Viollet-le-Duc, and those who carry on his work, the slums have almost all been cleared. Nowadays, it is safe for tourists to visit."

They had reached the end of the path. They struck out toward the lake, then on in the direction of the small, shaded promontory that afforded a wonderful view of the water.

"So, now that we are better acquainted, would you mind if I asked you a question of a rather personal nature?" Isolde asked.

"Well, no," Léonie said cautiously, "although I suppose it would depend on the nature of the question."

Isolde laughed. "I wondered, only, if you had an admirer?"

Léonie blushed. "I . . ."

"Forgive me, have I presumed too much on our friendship?"

"No," Léonie said quickly, not wishing to appear gauche or naive, although in truth all her notions of romantic love had been acquired from the pages of books. "Not in the slightest. It is just that you . . . you took me by surprise."

Isolde turned to her. "Well, then? Is there someone?"

Léonie experienced, to her surprise, a momentary flash of regret that there was not. She had dreamed but of characters she had met between the pages of books or of heroes glimpsed upon the stage singing of love and honor. Never, yet, had her unspoken fantasies attached themselves to a living, breathing person.

"I have no interest in such things," she said firmly. "Indeed, in my opinion, marriage is a form of servitude."

Isolde hid a smile. "Once, maybe, but in these modern times? You are young. All girls dream of love."

"Not I. I have seen M'man—"

She broke off, remembering the scenes, the tears, the days when there was no money to put food on the table, the procession of men coming and going.

Isolde's serene expression was suddenly somber. "Marguerite's situation has been a difficult one. She has done what she can to make things comfortable for you and Anatole. You should try not to judge her harshly."

Léonie felt her temper flare. "I do not judge her," she said sharply, stung by the rebuke. "I . . . I just do not wish such a life for myself."

"Love—true love—is a precious thing, Léonie," Isolde continued. "It is painful, uncomfortable, makes fools of us all, but it is what breathes meaning and color and purpose into our lives." She paused. "Love is the one thing that lifts our common experience to the extraordinary."

Léonie glanced at her, then back to her feet.

"It is not only M'man who has made me turn my face away from love," she said. "I have witnessed how sorely Anatole has suffered. . . . I daresay this affects the way I see things."

Isolde turned. Léonie felt the full force of her gray eyes upon her and could not meet her gaze. "There was a girl he loved very much," she continued in a quiet voice. "She died. This past March. I do not know precisely the manner of her death, only that the circumstances were distressing." She swallowed hard, glanced at her aunt, then away. "For months afterward we feared for him. His spirit was broken and his nerves shot to pieces, so much so that he took refuge in all manner of ill . . . ill practices. He would spend whole nights away and—"

Isolde squeezed Léonie's arm against her. "A gentleman's constitution can cope with forms of relaxation that to us seem insidious. You should not take such things as an indication of a deeper malaise."

"You did not see him," she cried fiercely. "He was a man lost to himself."
To me.

"Your affection for your brother is a credit to you, Léonie," Isolde said, "but perhaps the time has come to worry less about him. Whatever was the situation, he appears to be in good spirits now. Would you not agree?"

Reluctantly, she nodded. "I admit he is much improved on the spring."

"There. So this is the time to think more of your own needs and less of his. You accepted my invitation because you, yourself, stood in need of a rest. Is that not so?"

Léonie nodded.

"So now you are here, you should think of yourself. Anatole is in safe hands."

Léonie thought of their headlong exit from Paris, her promise that she would help him, the sense of threat that came and went, the scar on his eyebrow as a reminder of the danger he faced, and in a moment felt a burden was being lifted from her shoulders.

"He is in safe hands," Isolde repeated firmly. "As are you."

They were now on the far side of the lake. It was peaceful and green, quite isolated and yet in full view of the house. The only sounds were the cracks of twigs underfoot, the occasional flurry of a rabbit in the undergrowth behind. High above the tree line, the caw of distant crows.

Isolde led Léonie to a curved stone bench set on the rise of ground. It was in the shape of a crescent moon, its edges softened by time. She sat down and patted the seat to invite Léonie to join her.

"In the days immediately after my husband's death," she said, "I came often to this spot. I find it a most restful place."

Isolde unpinned her white, wide-brimmed hat and placed it on the seat beside her. Léonie did the same, removing her gloves, too. She glanced at her aunt. Her golden hair seemed to shine bright as she sat, as ever, perfectly straight, her hands resting gently in her lap and her boots peeking out neatly from the bottom of her pale blue cotton skirt.

"Was it not rather . . . rather solitary? Being here alone?" Léonie said.

Isolde nodded. "We were married only a matter of years. Jules was a man of fixed habits and customs and, well, for much of that time we were not in residence here. At least, I was not."

"But you are happy here now?"

"I have grown accustomed to it," she said quietly.

All of Léonie's previous curiosity about her aunt, which had faded somewhat into the background during the excitements of the preparation for the dinner party, flooded back. A thousand questions leapt into her mind. Not least of them why, if Isolde did not feel entirely comfortable at the Domaine de la Cade, she chose to remain here.

"Do you miss Oncle Jules so very much?"

Above them, the leaves swayed in the wind, whispering, murmuring, eavesdropping. Isolde sighed.

"He was a considerate man," she replied carefully. "And a kind and generous husband."

Léonie's eyes narrowed. "But your words about love—"

"One cannot always marry the person one loves," Isolde cut in. "Circumstance, opportunity, need, all these things play a part."

Léonie pressed further.

"I wondered how it was that you came to make one another's acquaintance? I was under the impression that my uncle rarely left the Domaine de la Cade, so—"

"It is true that Jules disliked traveling far from home. He had everything he wished for here. He kept himself well occupied with his books and took his responsibilities for the estate seriously. However, it was his custom to pay a visit once a year to Paris as he had done when his father was still alive."

"And it was during one of those visits that you were introduced?"

"It was," she said.

Léonie's attention was caught not by Isolde's words but by her actions. Her aunt's hand had stolen to her neck, which, today, was covered by a delicate high lace collar despite the mildness of the weather. Léonie realized how habitual a gesture it was. And Isolde had turned quite pale, as if remembering some unpleasantness she would rather forget.

"So you do not miss him so much?" Léonie pressed.

Isolde gave one of her slow, enigmatic smiles.

This time, there was no doubt in Léonie's mind. The man about whom Isolde had talked with such longing, such tenderness, was not her husband.

Léonie stole a glance, trying to summon the courage to pursue the conversation further. She was hungry to know more, but at the same time she did not wish to be impertinent. For all the confidences Isolde appeared to have shared, in point of fact she had explained little of the history of her courtship and marriage. Moreover, Léonie had had the suspicion, several times during the course of the conversation, that Isolde was on the point of raising some other issue, unsaid between them, although what this could be, she did not know.

"Shall we return to the house?" said Isolde, breaking into her reflections. "Anatole will be wondering where we are."

She stood up. Léonie gathered her hat and gloves and did likewise. "So, do you think you will continue to live here, Tante Isolde?" she asked, as they made their way down from the promontory and headed back toward the path.

Isolde waited a moment before answering. "We will see," she said. "For all its undoubted beauty, this is a disquieting place."

52

Carcassonne
Monday, September 28

The porter opened the door to the first-class carriage, and Victor Constant stepped down to the station platform at Carcassonne.

Un, deux, trois, loup. Like a game of grandmother's footsteps. Coming to get you, ready or not.

The wind was ferocious. According to the porter, the region was forecast to suffer the worst series of autumn storms for many years. Another, predicted to be even more devastating than those preceding it, was expected to hit Carcassonne next week.

Constant looked around. Above the railway sidings, the trees were plunging, lunging like unbroken horses. The sky was as gray as steel. Menacing black clouds scudded across the tops of the buildings.

"This, is just the overture," he said, then smiled at his own joke.

He glanced along the platform to where his manservant had disembarked with the luggage. In silence, they made their way out through the concourse, and Constant waited while his man procured a cab. He watched with little interest as the bargemen on the Canal du Midi lashed their *péniches* to double moorings, or even to the bases of the lime trees that lined the bank. Water slapped against the brick embankments. In the kiosk selling newspapers, the headline of the *Dépêche de Toulouse,* the local journal, was that a storm would strike that very evening, with worse to come.

Constant secured lodgings in a narrow side street in the nineteenth-century Bastide Saint-Louis. Then, leaving his man to begin the tedious process of visiting every boardinghouse, every hotel, every house with private rooms, to show the portrait of Marguerite, Anatole and Léonie Vernier purloined from the apartment in the rue de Berlin, he set out immediately on foot for the old town, the medieval citadel that stood on the opposite bank of the River Aude.

Despite his loathing of Vernier, Constant could not but admire how well he had kicked over the traces. At the same time, he hoped that Vernier's apparent success in disappearing might lead him to be arrogant, foolish. Constant had paid the concierge in the rue de Berlin handsomely to intercept any communication addressed to the apartment from Carcassonne, relying on the fact that Vernier's need to remain undiscovered would mean that he did not yet know of his mother's death. The thought of how the net in Paris was tightening, even while he remained ignorant, gave Constant immense pleasure.

He crossed to the far side via the Pont Vieux. Far below, the Aude swirled black against the sodden banks and sped over flat rocks and choked river weeds. The water was very high. He adjusted his gloves, attempting to alleviate the discomfort of the soft blistering between the second and third fingers of his left hand.

Carcassonne had changed a great deal since last Constant had set foot in the Cité. Despite the inclement weather, entertainers and men with sandwich boards now handed out tourist brochures, it seemed, on every street corner. He skimmed the tawdry pamphlet, his unforgiving eyes passing over the advertisements for Marseille soaps and La Micheline, a local liqueur, for bicycles and boardinghouses. The text itself was a mixture of civic self-aggrandizement and history rewritten. Constant crumpled the cheap paper in his gloved fist and threw it to the ground.

Constant hated Carcassonne and had good cause to do so. Thirty years ago, his uncle had taken him to the slums of La Cité. He had walked among the ruins, seen the filthy *citadins* who lived within its crumbling walls. Later that same day, full of plum brandy and opium, in a damask-draped room above a bar in the Place d'Armes, he had had his first experience of a working girl, courtesy of his uncle.

That same uncle was now sequestered in Lamalou-les-Bains, infected by one *connasse* or another, syphilitic and mad, believing his brain was being sucked out through his nose. Constant did not visit. He had no desire to see how the disease might work, over time, upon him.

She was the first Constant had killed. It was unintentional, and the incident had shocked him. Not because he had taken a life but because it had been so easy to do so. The hand on the throat, the thrill of seeing the fear in the girl's eyes when she realized that the violence of their coupling was but a precursor to a possession more absolute.

Had it not been for his uncle's deep pockets and connections in the mairie, Constant would have had nothing but the galleys or the guillotine to look forward to. As it was, they had left swiftly and without ceremony.

The experience had taught him much, not least that money could rewrite history, amend the ending to any story. There was no such thing as a fact when gold was involved. Constant had learned well. He had spent a lifetime binding to him friends and enemies alike, through a combination of obligation, debt and, when that failed, fear. It was only some years later that he understood that all lessons came at a cost. The girl had her revenge after all. She had given him the sickness that was painfully leaching the life from his uncle and would from him. She was beyond his reach, many years below ground, but he had punished others in her place.

As he descended the bridge, he thought again of the pleasure of Marguerite Vernier's death. A flush of heat shot through him. She had, for a passing moment at least, obliterated the memory of the humiliation he suffered at the hands of her son. The fact remained that even after so many had passed beneath his depraved hands, the experience was the more pleasurable when the woman was beautiful. It made the game worth the candle.

Stimulated more than he wished by the memory of those hours in the rue de Berlin with Marguerite, Constant loosened his collar at the neck. He could all but smell the intoxicating mix of blood and fear, the distinctive scent of such liaisons. He clenched his fists, remembering the delicious feel of her resistance, the pull and stretch of her unwilling skin.

Breathing fast, Constant stepped down onto the rough cobbles of the rue Trivalle and waited an instant until he again was master of himself. He cast a supercilious eye over the vista before him. The hundreds, thousands of francs spent on the restoration of the thirteenth-century citadel did not seem to have affected the lives of the people of the quartier Trivalle. It was as impoverished and run-down as it had been thirty years ago. Bareheaded, barefoot children sat in filthy doorways. Walls of brick and stone bowed outward, as if pushed by the broad hand of time. A beggar, swaddled in dirty blankets, her eyes dead and unseeing, held out a grimy hand as he passed by. He paid no heed.

He crossed the Place Saint-Gimer in front of Monsieur Viollet-le-Duc's ugly new church. A pack of dogs and children were snapping at his heels, calling out for coins, offering their services as guides or messengers. He paid them no heed until one boy ventured too close. Constant struck him a blow with the metal head of his cane, splitting open his cheek, and the gaggle of urchins backed away.

He arrived at a narrow cul-de-sac on the left, little more than an alleyway, which led up to the base of the ramparts of the Cité. He picked his way up the filthy, slippery street. The surface was coated with a sheen of mud the color of gingerbread. Debris, the flotsam and jetsam of poor lives, covered the streets. Paper wrappings, animal excrement, rotting vegetables too decayed for even the mange-bitten dogs to eat. He was aware of unseen dark eyes watching him from behind slatted shutters.

He stopped before a tiny house in the shadows of the walls and rapped sharply on the door with his walking stick. To find Vernier and his whore, Constant had need of the services of the man who lived within. He could be patient. He was willing to wait for as long as it might take once he had proved to his own satisfaction that the Verniers were in the area.

A wooden hatch shot back.

Two bloodshot eyes widened first in shock, then in fear. The hatch was slammed shut. Then, after the sliding of a bolt and the painful turning of the key in the lock, the door was opened.

Constant stepped inside.

53

Domaine de la Cade

The blustery and changeable September gave way to a mild and gentle October.

It was only some two weeks since Léonie had left Paris, but already she found it hard to remember the pattern of days at home. To her surprise, she realized she did not miss a thing about her former life. Not the views, not the streets, not the company of her mother or her neighbors.

Both Isolde and Anatole appeared to have undergone something of a permanent transformation since the night of the dinner. Isolde's gray eyes were no longer clouded with anxiety, and although she tired easily and often kept to her room in the mornings, her complexion was radiant. With the success of the gathering, the genuine warmth of the letters of thanks, it was evident that Rennes-les-Bains was prepared to welcome Jules Lascombe's widow into their society.

During these peaceful weeks, Léonie spent as much of her time as possible out of doors, exploring every inch of the estate, although she avoided the abandoned path that led to the sepulchre. The combination of sun and early-autumn rain had painted the world in bright colors. Vivid reds, deep evergreens, the golden underside of branch and bough, the crimson of the copper beech trees and the yolk yellow of the late broom. Birdsong, the bark of a solitary dog carried up from the valley, the rustle of the undergrowth as a rabbit ran for cover, the heel of her boots dislodging pebbles and twigs underfoot, the growing chorus of cicadas vibrating in the trees; the Domaine de la Cade was spectacular. As time put a distance between the shadows she had perceived on her first evening and the chill of the sepulchre, Léonie felt herself absolutely at home. That her mother, as a child, had felt something disquieting about the grounds and house she now could not comprehend. Or so Léonie told herself. It was a place of such tranquillity.

Her days fell into an easy routine. Most mornings, she painted a little. She had intended to embark on a series of landscapes, undemanding and traditional, the changing character of the autumn countryside. But following her unexpected success on the afternoon of the supper party with her self-portrait, without at any stage taking a conscious decision to do so, she found herself embarking on a sequence, from her fading memory, of the remaining seven tarot tableaux from the sepulchre. Rather than a gift for her mother, she now had the idea that the paintings might be a souvenir for Anatole of their sojourn. At home in Paris, in galleries and museums, grand avenues and tended gardens, the charms of nature had hitherto left her unmoved. Yet here, now, Léonie found she had an affinity with the trees and views she saw from her window. She found herself painting the landscape of the Domaine de la Cade into each illustration.

Some of the tableaux came more readily to mind and more easily to her brush than others. The image of Le Mat took on the character of Anatole, the expression on his face, his figure, his coloring. La Prêtresse possessed an elegance, a charm that Léonie associated with Isolde.

She did not attempt Le Diable.

After luncheon, most days Léonie would read in her chamber or else walk with Isolde in the gardens. Her aunt continued to be discreet about the circumstances of her marriage, but little by little Léonie managed to acquire enough fragments of information to piece together a satisfyingly complete history.

Isolde had grown up in the Parisian suburbs in the care of an elderly relative, a cold and bitter woman to whom she was little more than an unpaid companion. Liberated by her aunt's death, and left with few means with which to support herself, she had been fortunate enough to find her way into the city, at the age of twenty-one, in the employ of a financier and his wife. An acquaintance of Isolde's aunt, the lady had lost her sight some years earlier and required day-to-day assistance. Isolde's duties were light. She took dictation of letters and other correspondences, read aloud from the newspapers and the latest novels, and accompanied her employer to concerts and the opera. From the softness of Isolde's tone as she talked of those few years, Léonie understood that she had been fond of the financier and his wife. Through them she also acquired a good working knowledge of culture and society and couture. Isolde was not explicit about the reasons for her dismissal, but Léonie inferred that inappropriate behavior on the part of the financier's son had played its part.

On the matter of her marriage, Isolde was more guarded. It was clear, however, that need and opportunity had played as significant a part in her acceptance of Jules Lascombe's proposal as had love. It was a matter of business rather than romance.

Léonie also learned more about the series of incidents in the area that had caused disquiet in Rennes-les-Bains, to which Monsieur Baillard had alluded and which had, for no clear reason she could comprehend, become associated with the Domaine de la Cade. Isolde was not clear on the specifics. There also had been, in the 1870s, allegations of depraved and inappropriate ceremonies within the deconsecrated chapel in the woods of the estate.

At this, Léonie had found it difficult to conceal her innermost feelings. The color drained from her face, then rushed back as she remembered Monsieur Baillard's comments about how Abbé Saunière had been called upon to attempt to quiet the spirits of the place. Léonie wished to know more, but it was a story told secondhand by Isolde and some time after the event, so she could not or would not tell her.

In another conversation, Isolde told her niece how Jules Lascombe was considered by the town to be something of a recluse. Alone since the death of his stepmother and the departure of his half-sister, he was content in his solitude. As Isolde explained it, he had no wish for company of any description, least of all a wife. However, Rennes-les-Bains had increasingly come to mistrust his bachelor status, and Lascombe found himself a focus of suspicion. The town questioned, vociferously, why his sister had fled the estate several years previously. If, indeed, she had ever actually left.

As Isolde explained it, the drizzle of gossip and innuendo grew stronger until Lascombe was obliged to act. It was in the summer of 1885 that the new parish priest of Rennes-le-Château, Bérenger Saunière, suggested to Lascombe that the presence of a woman at the Domaine de la Cade might go some way to reassuring the neighborhood.

A mutual friend introduced Isolde to Lascombe in Paris. Lascombe made it clear that it would be acceptable—indeed, agreeable—to him for his young wife to remain for most of the year in town at his expense, provided she was available in Rennes-les-Bains when he required it. The question flitted into Léonie's mind—although she was not bold enough to ask—whether or not the marriage had ever been consummated.

It was a pragmatic and unromantic story. And although it answered many of the questions Léonie had about the nature of her aunt and uncle's marriage, it did not explain of whom Isolde had been speaking when she had talked so tenderly on that first walk they had taken together. On that occasion, she had hinted at a grand passion straight from the pages of a novel. She had given tantalizing glimpses of experiences about which Léonie could only dream.

DURING THESE peaceful first early weeks of October, the storms forecast failed to materialize. The sun shone brightly but not too fiercely. There was a temperate but moderate breeze, nothing to disrupt the languor of their days. It was a pleasant time, with little to disturb the surface of the domestic and self-contained life they were constructing for themselves at the Domaine de la Cade.

The only shadow on the horizon was the lack of word from their mother. Marguerite was a lackadaisical correspondent, but to have received no communication whatsoever was surprising. Anatole tried to reassure Léonie that the most likely explanation was that a letter had been mislaid on the mail coach that had overturned outside Limoux on the night of the storm. The postmaster had told him that an entire consignment of letters, packages and telegrams had been lost, hurled by the force of the accident into the River Salz and carried downstream in the floods.

At Léonie's persistent prompting, Anatole agreed, albeit reluctantly, that he would write. He addressed the letter to the apartment on the rue de Berlin, thinking that perhaps if Du Pont had been obliged to return to Paris, Marguerite therefore might be there to receive the letter.

As Léonie watched Anatole seal the envelope and give it into the hands of the boy to be taken to the poste restante in Rennes-les-Bains, a feeling of dread suddenly overwhelmed her. She all but reached out a hand to stop him, but she checked herself. She was being foolish. She could not think that Anatole's creditors were still pursuing him.

What harm could come of sending a letter?

At the end of the second week of October, when the air was filled with the smell of autumn bonfires and the scent of fallen leaves, Léonie suggested to Isolde that perhaps they might pay Monsieur Baillard a visit. Or, indeed, invite him to the Domaine de la Cade. She was disappointed when Isolde informed her that she had heard it reported that Monsieur Baillard had unexpectedly quit his lodgings in Rennes-les-Bains and was not expected to return before the eve of Toussaint, the Eve of All Saints.

"Wherever has he gone?"

Isolde shook her head. "No one knows. Into the mountains, it is believed, but no one knows for certain."

Léonie still wished to go. Although Isolde and Anatole were reluctant, they capitulated finally and a visit was arranged for Friday, October 16.

THEY PASSED an agreeable morning in the town. They ran into Charles Denarnaud and took coffee with him on the terrace of the Hôtel de la Reine. Despite his bonhomie and cordiality, Léonie still could not bring herself to like him, and from Isolde's manner and reserve, she realized her aunt felt similarly.

"I do not trust him," Léonie whispered. "There is something false in his manner."

Isolde did not say anything in response but raised her eyebrows in such a manner as to confirm that she shared Léonie's misgivings. Léonie was relieved when Anatole stood up to take his leave.

"So you'll join me for a morning of shooting, Vernier?" said Denarnaud, shaking Anatole's hand. "Plenty of *sanglier* at this time of year. Woodcock and pigeon also."

Anatole's brown eyes glinted brightly at the prospect. "I would be delighted, Denarnaud, although I warn you I have more enthusiasm than skill. And, I am embarrassed to inform you, I am ill prepared. I have no gun."

Denarnaud slapped him on the back. "I'll provide the weapons and ammunition, if you stand the cost of the breakfast."

Anatole smiled. "A deal," he said, and despite her antipathy to the man, Léonie was cheered by the look of pleasure the promise of the hunt had brought to her brother's face.

"Ladies," said Denarnaud, raising his hat. "Vernier. Monday next? I'll send what you need up to the house ahead of time, if that is agreeable to you, Madame Lascombe."

Isolde nodded. "Of course."

As they promenaded, Léonie could not help but notice that Isolde attracted a certain amount of interest. There was no hostility or suspicion in the scrutiny, but there was a watchfulness. Isolde was dressed in somber clothes and wore her half-veil lowered in the street. It surprised Léonie that, even nine months after the event, she was still expected to dress as Jules Lascombe's widow. Periods of mourning in Paris were brief. Here, there was clearly a requirement for a longer observation.

The highlight for Léonie of their visit, however, was the presence of a traveling photographer in the Place du Pérou. His face was hidden beneath a thick black cloth, and the box contraption was balanced on the spindly wooden legs of a tripod with metal feet. He came from a studio in Toulouse. On a mission to record the life of the villages and towns of the Haute Vallée for posterity, he had already visited Rennes-le-Château, Couiza and Coustaussa. After Rennes-les-Bains, he was to progress to Espéraza and Quillan.

"May we? It will be a souvenir of our time here." Léonie pulled at Anatole's sleeve. "Please? A gift for M'man."

To her surprise, tears sprang into her eyes. For the first time since Anatole had sent the letter to the post, Léonie found herself sentimental at the thought of her mother's company.

Perhaps observing her high emotions, Anatole capitulated. He sat in the middle on an old metal chair, its legs uneven and wobbling on the cobbles, holding his cane across his knees and his hat in his lap. Isolde, elegant in her dark jacket and skirt, stood behind him to his left with her slim fingers in black silk on his shoulder. Léonie, pretty in her russet walking jacket with brass buttons and velvet trim, stood at his right, smiling directly into the camera.

"There," Léonie said, when it was over. "Now we shall always remember this day."

Before they departed Rennes-les-Bains, Anatole made his regular pilgrimage to the poste restante while Léonie, wishing to be convinced that Audric Baillard truly was not in residence, made her way to his modest lodgings. She had slipped the sheet of music taken from the sepulchre into her pocket, and she was determined to show it to him. She wished, too, to confide how she had begun to make a record on paper of the paintings on the wall of the apse.

And to ask him more of the rumors surrounding the Domaine de la Cade.

Isolde waited patiently as Léonie knocked on the blue wooden door, as if she could draw Monsieur Baillard out by force of will. The window boards were all closed and the flowers in the boxes on the outer sills were covered in felt, in anticipation of the autumn frosts that might soon come. An air of hibernation hung about the building, as if it was not expecting anyone to return for some time.

She knocked again.

As she gazed at the shuttered house, the strength of Monsieur Baillard's warning not to return to the sepulchre nor seek the cards came back to her more strongly than ever. Although she had spent only one evening in his company, she had complete confidence in him. Some weeks had passed since the dinner party. Now, as she stood silently waiting at a door that did not open, she realized how much she wished him to know that she had remained obedient to his wishes.

Almost completely so.

She had not retraced her steps through the woods. She had not taken steps to learn more. It was true she had not yet returned her uncle's book to the library, but she had not studied it. Indeed, she had barely even opened it since that first visit.

Now, although it frustrated her that Monsieur Baillard truly was absent, it did nonetheless strengthen her resolve to abide by his advice. The thought flashed through her mind that it would not be safe to do otherwise.

Léonie turned away and took Isolde's arm.

WHEN THEY ARRIVED back at the Domaine de la Cade some half an hour later, Léonie ran to the corner beneath the stairs and placed the sheet of music in the piano stool, beneath a moth-eaten copy of Bach's *Well-Tempered Clavier*. Now it seemed significant to her that in all that time she had possessed it, she had not ever actually tried to play it.

That night, when Léonie blew out the light in her bedchamber, for the first time she regretted that she had not previously returned *Les Tarots* to the library. She was sensitive to the presence of her uncle's book in her chamber, albeit hidden beneath her spools of cotton, thread and ribbon. Thoughts of devils slipped into her mind, of children stolen from their beds, of markings on the ground and stones that seemed to tell of some evil unchained. In the middle of the long night, she jolted awake with the image of the eight tarot tableaux pressing down upon her. She lit a candle and set the ghosts to flight. She would not allow them to draw her back.

For Léonie now understood absolutely the nature of Audric Baillard's warning. The spirits of the place had come close to claiming her. She should not give them such an opportunity again.

54

The clement weather held until Tuesday, October 20.

A gunmetal-gray sky sat low on the horizon. A damp and obscuring mist wrapped the Domaine in chill fingers. The trees were but silhouettes. The surface of the lake was choppy. The juniper and rhododendron bushes cowered in a gusting southwesterly wind.

Léonie was glad that Anatole had had his day's hunting with Charles Denarnaud before the rain set in. He had set off with a brown leather *etui à fusil* slung across his shoulder holding his borrowed guns, the buckles gleaming in the sun. Late in the afternoon he returned home with a brace of wood pigeon, a weather-beaten face and his eyes flushed with the thrill of the shoot.

As she glanced out of the window, she thought how much less pleasurable an experience it would have been today.

After breakfast, Léonie took herself into the morning room and was curled up on the chaise longue with the collected stories of Madame Oliphant when the post was delivered from the village. She listened to the front door being opened, a murmuring of greetings, then the clipped footsteps of the maid on the tiled floor crossing the hall to the study.

For Isolde, it was approaching a particularly busy time of year on the estate. Saint Martin's Day, November 11, was a month away. It was the day of annual accounting and, on certain estates, evictions. Isolde explained to Léonie that it was the day the tenants' rents were settled for the coming year, and as chatelaine, she was determined to fulfill her role. It was more a question of listening to the estate manager and acting on his advice than making decisions per se, but the matter had kept her cloistered away in her study the past two mornings.

Léonie dropped her eyes back to her book and continued reading.

A few minutes later, she heard raised voices, then the unaccustomed sound of the study bell jangling. Puzzled, Léonie put down her book and, in stockinged feet, ran across the room and opened the door a fraction. She was in time to see Anatole bounding down the stairs and disappearing into the study.

"Anatole?" she cried after him. "Is there news from Paris?"

But evidently he did not hear her as he slammed the door firmly shut behind him.

How quite extraordinary.

Léonie waited a moment longer, peering inquisitively around the door frame, hoping to glimpse her brother, but nothing further happened, and soon she grew weary of watching and returned to her settee. Five minutes passed, then ten. Léonie continued to read, even though her attention was elsewhere.

At eleven o'clock, Marieta brought a tray of coffee into the morning room and set it out on the table. There were, as usual, three cups.

"My aunt and brother will be joining me?"

"I have not been given orders to the contrary, Madomaisèla."

At that moment, Anatole and Isolde appeared together in the doorway.

"Good morning, *petite*," he said. His brown eyes were shining.

"I heard the commotion," Léonie said, leaping to her feet. "I wondered if you had received news from Paris."

His expression faltered a moment. "I'm sorry, no. Nothing from M'man."

"Then ... whatever has happened?" she asked, realizing that Isolde, too, was in a state of some excitement. Her complexion was high and her eyes, too, were bright.

She crossed the room and squeezed Léonie's hand. "This morning I received the letter I have been waiting for from Carcassonne."

Anatole had taken a position in front of the fire, his hands behind his back. "I believe Isolde may have promised a concert. . . ."

"So we are going!" Léonie leapt up and kissed her aunt. "That is perfectly wonderful!"

Anatole laughed. "We had hoped you would be pleased. It is not the best time of year for such a journey, of course, but we are at the mercy of circumstances."

"When shall we go?" Léonie asked, looking from one to the other.

"We will depart this Thursday morning. Isolde has wired to inform the lawyers she will be there at two o'clock." He paused, exchanged another glance with Isolde. Léonie caught it.

There is something more he wishes to tell me.

Her nerves again fluttered within her chest.

"In point of fact, there was one other matter we wished to raise with you. Isolde has most generously suggested that we might extend our stay here. Perhaps even until the new year. What would you say to that?"

Léonie stared at Anatole in amazement. In the first instance, she did not know quite what she thought of such a suggestion. Would the pleasures of the country pall if they remained longer?

"But . . . but your work? Can the magazine spare you for so long? Do you not need to oversee your interests from closer at hand?"

"Oh, I daresay the magazine can manage a little longer without me," he said lightly. He accepted a cup of coffee from Isolde.

"What of M'man?" Léonie said, assailed suddenly by an image of her beautiful mother sitting alone in the drawing room of the rue de Berlin.

"If Du Pont can spare her, we had thought, perhaps, to invite her to join us here."

Léonie stared hard at Anatole.

He cannot believe she will ever leave Paris. Or return here.

"I do not think that General Du Pont would wish it," she said, as an excuse for the refusal that would surely be the response to such an invitation.

"Or perhaps you are too bored with my company to wish to remain here longer?" Anatole said, coming across the room and draping his arm around her shoulders. "Does the thought of further weeks spent confined here with your brother distress you so?"

The moment stretched, taut and expectant, then Léonie giggled.

"You are a fool, Anatole! Of course I would be delighted to stay longer. I cannot think of anything I would like more, although—"

"Although?" Anatole said quickly.

The smile slipped from her lips. "I should be glad to hear from M'man."

Anatole put down his cup and lit a cigarette. "As would I," he said quietly. "I am certain it is only that she is having so agreeable a time that she has not yet found the opportunity to write. And, of course, allowing time for my letter to be forwarded to the Marne."

Her eyes narrowed. "I thought you believed they must have returned to Paris?"

"I suggested only that they *might* have done so," he said mildly. Then his expression lightened again. "But the thought of a trip to Carcassonne pleases you?"

"Indeed, yes."

He nodded. "Good. On Thursday, we will take the morning train from Couiza. The *courrier publique* leaves from the Place du Pérou at five o'clock."

"How long will we be staying?"

"Two days, maybe three."

Léonie's face fell in disappointment. "But that is hardly any time at all."

"Quite long enough." He smiled.

This time, Léonie could not fail to notice the intimate glance that passed between him and Isolde.

55

The lovers lay beneath the sheets, their faces lit only by the flickering light of a single candle.

"You should return to your rooms," she said. "It is late."

Anatole folded his arms behind his head in a gesture that clearly spoke of his determination to stay longer.

"Quite. Everyone is in bed."

Isolde smiled. "I did not believe that I could experience such happiness," she said quietly. "That we would ever be together here." Then the smile fell from her pale face. Her hand went, automatically, to the hollow of her throat. "I fear it will not last."

Anatole bent over and kissed the damaged skin. Even now he felt her desire to pull away from the touch of his lips. The scar was a constant reminder of her brief and violent affair with Victor Constant.

It was only some months into their romance, after the death of her husband, that Isolde had permitted Anatole to see her uncovered and without her customary high collar or scarf or choker concealing the ugly red scar on her neck. It was some weeks later still before he succeeded in persuading her to tell him the story of how she had come by the injury.

He had thought—mistakenly—that speaking of the past might help her gain mastery over her memories. It had not done so. Moreover, it had disturbed his peace of mind. Even now, some nine months after their first meeting and when the litany of the physical punishments Isolde had suffered at Constant's hands was familiar to him, Anatole still found himself flinching as he remembered her calm and expressionless recitation of how, in an attack of jealousy, Constant had used fire tongs to hold his signet ring to the coals, then pressed the hot metal to her throat until she passed out from the pain. He had branded her. So vivid was her description that Anatole all but felt he could smell the sickly-sweet scent of her burning flesh.

Isolde's liaison with Constant had lasted only a matter of weeks. Broken fingers had healed, the bruises had faded; only that one scar remained as a physical souvenir of the damage Constant had inflicted upon her during the course of the thirty days. But the psychological damage lasted far longer. It pained Anatole that despite her beauty, her graceful character, her elegance, Isolde was now so fearful, so lacking in all self-worth, so afraid.

"It will last," Anatole said firmly.

He let his hand move lower, smoothing over the beloved familiar bone and form until it came to rest upon the soft white skin at the top of her thighs.

"Everything is in place. We have the license. Tomorrow we will meet with Lascombe's lawyers in Carcassonne. Once we know where you stand with regard to this place, we can make our final arrangements." He snapped his fingers. *"Facile."*

He reached over to the nightstand, the muscles stretched visible beneath his bare skin. He retrieved his case and matches, lit two cigarettes, then handed one to Isolde.

"There will be those who refuse to receive us," she said. "Madame Bousquet, Maître Fromilhague."

"I daresay." He shrugged. "But do you care so greatly for their good opinion?"

Isolde did not answer the question. "Madame Bousquet has reason to be aggrieved. If Jules had not taken it upon himself to marry, she would have inherited the estate. She might even challenge the will."

Anatole shook his head. "Instinct tells me that if she had intended to do so, she would have done it when Lascombe died and the will was published. Let's see what the codicil says before we concern ourselves with imagined objections." He inhaled another mouthful of smoke. "I do concede that Maître Fromilhague might deplore the haste of our marriage. He might object, even though there is no blood tie between us, but what business is it of his?" He shrugged. "He will come round given time. When all is said and done, Fromilhague is a pragmatist. He will not wish to sever links with the estate."

Isolde nodded, although Anatole suspected it was because she wished to believe him rather than because he had convinced her.

"And are you still of the opinion we should live here? Not hide ourselves in the anonymity of Paris?" she asked.

Anatole remembered how distressed Isolde became whenever she returned to town. How she was but a shadow of herself. Every smell, every sound, every sight seemed to cause her pain and remind her of her brief liaison with Constant. He could not live like that, and he doubted she could, either.

"Yes, if we can do so, then I think we should make our home here." He broke off, then gently placed his hand upon her lightly swelling stomach. "Especially if your suspicions are correct." He looked at her, his eyes flashing with pride. "I still cannot believe I am to be a father."

"It is early days yet," she said gently. "Very early. Although for all that, I do not think I am mistaken."

She placed her hand upon his, and for a moment they were silent.

"You do not fear that we will be punished for our wickedness in March?" she whispered.

Anatole frowned, not understanding her meaning.

"The clinic. Pretending that I was obliged to . . . interrupt a pregnancy."

"Not in the slightest," he said firmly.

She fell silent once more. "Will you give me your word that your decision not to return to the capital is nothing to do with Victor," she said finally. "Paris is your home, Anatole. You wish to relinquish it for good?"

Anatole extinguished his cigarette, then pushed his fingers through his thick, dark hair.

"We have discussed this too many times already," he said. "But if it reassures you for me to say it again, I give you my word that it is my considered opinion that the Domaine de la Cade is the most appropriate domicile for us." He made the mark of a cross on his bare chest. "It is nothing to do with Constant. Nothing to do with Paris. Here, we can live simply, quietly, establish ourselves."

"And Léonie, too?"

"I hope she will make her home with us, yes."

Isolde became silent. Anatole could feel her entire body become quite still, tense, as if ready for flight.

"Why do you allow him still to have such a hold over you?"

She dropped her eyes, and immediately he regretted speaking his mind. He knew Isolde was well aware how it frustrated him that Constant was so often in her thoughts. In the early days of their liaison, he had told her how inadequate her continuing fear of Constant made him feel. As if he was not man enough to banish the specters of her past. He had allowed his irritation to show.

As a consequence, he knew that she had decided to hold her tongue. Not that her memories of the suffering she had endured troubled her less. Now he understood how the remembrance of mistreatment took longer to heal than physical evidence. But what Anatole still struggled to comprehend was why she felt so ashamed. On more than one occasion she had attempted to explain how humiliated his abuse of her made her feel. How she felt disgraced by her emotions, polluted, that she had been so deceived as to believe she could fall in love with such a man.

In his darkest hours, Anatole feared that Isolde believed she had forfeited the right to any future happiness because of that one fleeting error of judgment. And it saddened him that despite his reassurances and the extraordinary measures they had taken to escape Constant's attentions—going so far as the pantomime in the cimetière de Montmartre—she still did not feel safe.

"If Constant was looking for us, we would know of it by now. He made little attempt to conceal his malevolent intentions in the early months of the year, Isolde." He paused. "Did he ever know your real name?"

"He did not, no. We were introduced at the house of a mutal friend where Christian names alone sufficed."

"He knew you were married?"

She nodded. "He knew I had a husband in the country who, within the usual bounds of respectability, was tolerant of my need for a measure of independence provided I was discreet. It was not something we discussed. When I told him I was leaving, I cited the need to be with my husband."

She shivered, and Anatole knew she was thinking of the night he had nearly killed her.

"Constant never knew Lascombe," he said. "That is right, is it not?"

"He was not acquainted with Jules."

"And nor did he ever know of any address, any connection, other than the apartment in the rue Feydeau?"

"No." She paused. "At least, never from my lips."

"Well, then," Anatole said, as if he had proved his case. "It has been seven months since the burial, has it not? And nothing has happened to disturb our tranquility."

"Except the attack upon you in the Passage des Panoramas."

His brow furrowed. "That was nothing whatever to do with Constant," he said immediately.

"But they took only your father's timepiece," she protested. "What thief leaves a notebook full of francs?"

"I was in the wrong place at the wrong time," he said. "That's all."

He leaned toward her and stroked her cheek with the back of his hand. "Since we arrived at the Domaine de la Cade, I have kept my ears and eyes open, Isolde. I have heard nothing, seen nothing untoward. Nothing that could cause us a moment's disquiet. No questions have been asked in the village. No strangers have been reported around the estate."

Isolde sighed. "Does it not concern you that there has been no word from Marguerite?"

His frown deepened. "I admit, it does. I was reluctant to write, after all the efforts we went to, to obscure our whereabouts. I can only assume it is because she is engaged with Du Pont."

Isolde smiled at his ill-concealed dislike. "His only crime is to love your mother," she rebuked him gently.

"Then why does he not marry her?" he said, more sharply than he had intended.

"You know why," she said gently. "She is the widow of a Communard. He is not the sort of man to flout convention."

Anatole nodded, then sighed. "The simple truth is that he occupies her time and, God help me, despite my antipathy to the man, I worry less about M'man knowing she is in his company in the Marne than if she were alone in Paris."

Isolde took her peignoir from the chair beside the bed and draped it over her shoulders.

Concern flickered in his eyes. "Are you cold?"

"A little."

"Is there anything I can fetch you?"

Isolde put her hand on his arm. "I am fine." She smiled.

"But in your condition, you should—"

"I am not ill, Anatole," she teased. "My condition, as you put it, is perfectly natural. Please, do not worry so." The smile slid from her lips. "But on the question of family, I am still of the view that we should confide the real reason for our visit to Carcassonne to Léonie. Tell her what we intend."

Anatole ran his fingers through his hair. "And I still am of the opinion it is better she does not know until after the event."

He lit another cigarette. White wisps floated up into the room, like writing in the air.

"Can you really believe, Anatole, that Léonie will forgive you for keeping her so in the dark?" Isolde paused. "Forgive us."

"You are fond of her, are you not?" he said. "I am glad of it."

Isolde nodded. "It is why I balk at deceiving her further."

Anatole drew deeply on his cigarette. "She will understand that we considered it too great a burden to place upon her to involve her in our plans beforehand."

"I hold the opposite opinion. I believe that Léonie would do anything for you, accept anything you confided in her. However . . ." She gave a slight shrug of her shoulders. "If she feels slighted, if she—indeed, rightly—thinks we do not trust her, then I fear that her anger might lead her to behave in ways that she—and we, too—might very much regret."

"What do you mean?"

She took his hand. "She is not a child, Anatole. Not any longer."

"She is only seventeen," he protested.

"She is already jealous of the attention you pay to me," she said quietly.

"Nonsense."

"How do you think she will feel when she discovers we—you—have deceived her?"

"It is not a question of deceit," he said. "It is a question of discretion. The fewer people who are aware of what we intend, the better."

He placed his hand on Isolde's belly, making it clear he considered the subject closed.

"Soon, my love, it will all be over."

He cupped her head with the other hand and drew her to him, kissing her lips. Then, slowly, he slipped the peignoir from her shoulders, revealing her full breasts. Isolde closed her eyes.

"Soon," he murmured into her milky skin, "everything will be out in the open. We can start a new chapter of our lives."

56

Thursday, October 22

At half past four, the gig pulled away down the long drive of the Domaine de la Cade with Anatole, Léonie and Isolde inside. Marieta sat up front with Pascal driving, a single blanket draped over their knees.

The carriage was closed, but the cracked leather hood was inadequate protection against the cold early morning. Léonie was swaddled in her long black cloak, drawn up over her head, squashed warmly between her brother and her aunt. She could smell the must and mothballs of the fur throws, used for the first time this autumn, which covered them from chin to toe.

For Léonie, the blue light of the early hour and the cold only added to the adventure. The romance of setting out before dawn, the prospect of two days in Carcassonne to explore and go to a concert and eat in restaurants, she could not wait.

The lamps clinked and knocked against the cab as they made their way down to the Sougraigne road, two points of light in the darkness. Isolde admitted she had slept badly and consequently felt a little nauseated. She said little. Anatole, too, was silent.

Léonie was wide awake. She had the early-morning scent of the heavy, damp earth in her nose and the fragrant mingling scents of cyclamen and box, the mulberry bushes and sweet chestnut trees. It was too early, yet, for sound of lark or pigeon, but she heard the hoot of owls returning from a night's hunting.

DESPITE THEIR EARLY START, the blustery weather conditions resulted in the train arriving more than an hour late into Carcassonne.

Léonie and Isolde waited while Anatole hailed a cab. Within moments they were flying across the Pont Marengo to a hotel in the northern quartier of the Bastide Saint-Louis, recommended by Dr. Gabignaud.

Situated in the rue du Port, on the corner of a quiet side street close to the église Saint-Vincent, it was modest yet comfortable. A semicircle of three stone steps led up from the pavement to the entrance, a black-painted door framed in chiseled stone. The pavements were raised above the cobbled street. Ornamental trees stood along the outer wall in terra-cotta pots, like a line of sentries on duty. Window boxes upon the sills cast their green-and-white shadows against freshly painted shutters. On the side wall, the words HÔTEL ET RESTAURANT were painted in high block capital letters.

Anatole took care of the formalities and oversaw the bags being carried to the rooms. They took a first-floor suite for Isolde, Léonie and the maid, with a single room for himself across the corridor.

After a light lunch in the brasserie of the hotel, they agreed to rendezvous at the hotel at half past five in time for an early supper before the concert.

Isolde's appointment with her late husband's lawyers was fixed for two o'clock in the road called Carriere Mage. Anatole had offered to accompany her. As they departed, he exacted a promise from Léonie that she would go nowhere without Marieta and that she would not venture unchaperoned across the river and beyond the boundaries of the Bastide.

It was raining again. Léonie occupied herself talking to another guest, an elderly widow, Madame Sanchez, who had been visiting Carcassonne for many years. She explained how the lower town—the Basse Ville, she termed it—was constructed on a grid system, much like the modern American cities. Availing herself of Léonie's all-weather pencil, Madame Sanchez ringed the hotel and central square on the *plan de la ville* provided by the proprietor. She also warned how many of the street names were out of date.

"Saints have yielded to generals," she said, shaking her head. "So now we listen to the band in the Square Gambetta rather than the Square Sainte-Cécile. All I can tell you is that the music sounds exactly the same!"

Noticing the rain was easing and impatient to begin her explorations, Léonie excused herself, reassuring Madame Sanchez that she would manage perfectly well, and made hasty preparations to go.

With Marieta struggling to keep up, she headed for the main square, La Place aux Herbes, led by the shouts of the hawkers and market traders, the rattling of cartwheels and harness filtering up the narrow street. As Léonie drew closer, she could see that many of the stalls were already in the process of being dismantled. But there was a delicious smell of roasting chestnuts and freshly baked bread. Punch flavored with sugar and cinnamon was being ladled from steaming metal containers hanging from the back of a wooden handcart.

The Place aux Herbes was an unassuming but well-proportioned square, lined on all four sides by six-story buildings and with small roads and passageways leading in from each corner. The center was dominated by an ornate eighteenth-century fountain dedicated to Neptune. From beneath the rim of her hat, Léonie read the label out of duty but thought the work vulgar and did not linger.

The branches of the spreading *platanes* were losing their leaves, and what remained was painted in tones of copper, pale green and gold. Everywhere were umbrellas and brightly colored parasols, sheltering from the wind and the rain that came and went, willow *paniers* containing fresh vegetables, fruit, garden herbs and the autumn flowers. From wicker *corbeilles,* black-draped women with weather-beaten faces sold bread and chèvres.

To Léonie's surprise and delight, almost the entire façade of one side of the square was occupied by a department store. Its name in bold letters was attached by twisted threads of wire to the wrought-iron balcony railings: PARIS CARCASSONNE. Although it was only just past two-thirty, the trays of bargain goods—*solde d'articles, réclame absolûment sacrifiés*—were being laid out on tables at the front of the store. Hanging from the awnings on metal display hooks were hunting guns, prêt-à-porter dresses, baskets, all manner of household objects, frying skillets, even stoves and ovens.

I could purchase some item of hunting equipment for Anatole.

The thought flashed in and then out of her mind. She had only a little money and no possibility of acquiring credit. Besides, she would not know where to start. Instead she strolled with fascination around the *marché.* Here, or so it seemed to her, the women and few men selling their produce had smiling and open faces. She picked up vegetables, rubbed herbs between her fingers, breathed in the scent of tall-stemmed flowers, in a manner she would never have done in Paris.

When she had seen all the Place aux Herbes had to offer, she decided to venture into the side streets surrounding the square. She walked west and found herself in Carriere Mage, the street where Isolde's lawyers were situated. At the top end were mostly offices and *ateliers de couturières.* She paused awhile outside the workshops of Tissus Cathala. Through the glass door she could see displays of cloth of every color, as well as all manner of sewing materials. On the wooden shutters on either side of the entrance, paper drawings of *les modes masculine et féminine* were tacked up with pins, from gentlemen's morning suits to ladies' tea dresses and capes.

Léonie occupied herself by examining the sewing patterns, regularly glancing up the street toward the lawyer's offices, thinking perhaps to see Isolde and Anatole emerge. But as the minutes passed and there was no sign of them, the lure of the shops farther down the street drew her instead.

With Marieta trailing behind, she walked in the direction of the river. She stopped to look through the plate-glass windows of the several establishments trading in antiquaries. There was a *librairie,* its windows filled with dark wooden bookcases and bound red and green and blue leather spines. At number 75, an *épicerie fine*, there was the enticing smell of strong and bitter ground and roasted coffee. For a moment, she stood on the pavement looking in through the three tall windows. Inside, shelves of glass and wood displayed examples of beans, paraphernalia and pots for the stove and for the fire. The letters above the door read *ÉLIE HUC*. Inside, strings of dried sausage hung on hooks to one side of the store. On the other, bundles of wild thyme, sage and rosemary, and a table covered with dishes and jars filled with pickled cherries and sweet glacé plums.

Léonie decided she would make a purchase for Isolde, a gift to thank her for arranging this trip to Carcassonne. She stepped inside the Aladdin's cave, leaving Marieta to twist her anxious hands on the pavement, returning some ten minutes later holding a white paper packet containing the finest Arabian coffee beans and a tall glass jar of crystallized fruit.

She was becoming bored with Marieta's anxious face and doglike presence.

Dare I?

Léonie felt a spark of excitement at the mischievous idea that had slipped, unbidden, into her mind. Anatole would scold her badly. But there was no need for him to find out if she was quick and if Marieta held her tongue. Léonie glanced up and then down the street. There were some unaccompanied women of her class out taking the air. Admittedly, it was not the norm, but there were a few. And no one seemed to pay the slightest attention. Anatole fussed too much.

In such an environment, I do not need a guard dog.

"I do not wish to carry these," she said, thrusting the packages at Marieta, then making a show of staring up at the sky. "I fear it might rain again," she said. "The best thing would be for you to take the packages back to the hotel and acquire an umbrella at the same time. I will wait for you here."

Worry sparked in Marieta's eyes. "But Sénher Vernier said to stay with you."

"It is a task that will take no more than ten minutes," Léonie said firmly. "You will be there and back without him ever knowing." She patted the white package. "The coffee is a gift for my aunt, and I do not wish it to spoil. Bring the umbrella back with you. We will have the reassurance of protection from the rain, should we need it." She drove home her final point. "My brother would not thank you were I to catch a cold."

Marieta hesitated, looking down at the packages.

"Hurry," said Léonie impatiently. "I will wait for you here."

With a doubtful glance behind her, the girl scurried away back up Carriere Mage, repeatedly looking over her shoulder to reassure herself that her young mistress had not vanished.

Léonie smiled, delighted by her harmless subterfuge. She did not intend to go against Anatole's instructions and leave the Bastide. Conversely, she did feel she could, with clear conscience, walk as far as the river and catch her first glimpse of the medieval citadel from the right bank of the Aude. She was inquisitive to see the Cité about which Isolde had spoken and for which Monsieur Baillard had such affection. She removed the map from her pocket and studied it.

It cannot be so far.

If Marieta did, by bad luck, arrive back before she did, Léonie could simply explain that she had taken it upon herself to seek out the lawyers' offices in order to be able to walk back with Isolde and Anatole, and had thus become separated from the maid.

Pleased with her plan, she crossed the rue Pelisserie, her head held high. She felt quite independent, adventurous, and liked the sensation. She passed the marble columns of the Hôtel de Ville, flying a pristine *tricolore,* and walked toward what she identified from the *plan* to be the ruins of the ancient monastère des Clarisses. At the top of the single remaining tower, a decorative cupola covered a solitary bell.

Léonie exited the tight grid of bustling streets and entered the tree-lined calm of the Square Gambetta. A plaque commemorated the work of the Carcassonnais architect, Léopold Petit, who had designed and supervised the gardens. There was a lake in the center of the park, with single jets of water shooting to the heavens from beneath the surface, creating a white haze all round. A bandstand in the Japanese style was surrounded by white chairs. The ramshackle arrangement of the seating, the debris of ice-cream biscuits and waxed paper and the wet ends of cigars suggested that the concert had finished some time ago. The ground was littered with discarded flyers for the concert, muddy footprints upon the white paper. Léonie bent down and picked one up.

From the green and pleasant spaces of Gambetta, she turned right along a rather dull cobblestoned street that ran down the side of the hospital and promised to lead to a panoramic viewpoint at the foot of the Pont Vieux.

A brass figure was mounted on top of the fountain set at the crossroads where three roads met. Léonie rubbed the plaque to read the inscription. She was variously La Samaritaine or Flore or even Pomone.

Keeping watch over the classical heroine was a Christian saint, Saint Vincent de Paul, who surveyed the scene from the Hôpital des Malades at the approach to the bridge. His benign stone gaze and open arms seemed to gather in the chapel alongside, with its high arched stone doorway and rose window above.

The whole spoke of beneficence, money, affluence.

Léonie turned full square and had her first uninterrupted sight of La Cité, the citadel set high on a hill on the opposite bank of the river. She caught her breath. It was both more magnificent and more human in scale than she had pictured. She had seen the popular postcards of the Cité that carried the famous words of Gustave Nadaud: *"Il ne faut pas mourir sans avoir vu Carcassonne"*—One must not die without having seen Carcassonne—but had thought it no more than an advertising slogan. Now that she was here, it seemed a true reflection of fact.

Léonie could see that the water was very high. Indeed, in places it was lapping over the bank and up on the grass, washing against the stone foundations of the chapelle de Saint-Vincent-de-Paul and the hospital buildings. She had no intention of disobeying Anatole further, and yet she found herself stepping up onto the gentle slope of the bridge, which spanned the river in a series of stone arches.

A few steps farther and I will turn back.

The far bank was mostly wooded. Through the treetops and branches Léonie could see watermills, the flat roofs of the distilleries and the textile workshops with their *filatures mécaniques.* It was surprisingly rural, she thought, remnants of another, older world.

She looked up to see a battered stone Jesus hanging upon a cross in the central *bec* of the bridge, a niche in the low wall where travelers could sit awhile or remove themselves from the path of carriages or draymen's carts.

Léonie took another step, and so, without ever actually deciding to do so, crossed from the safety of the Bastide to the romance of the Cité.

57

A natole and Isolde stood before the altar.
An hour past, all the papers had been signed. The conditions of Jules Lascombe's will, after the delays of the summer, had finally been verified.

Lascombe had left his estate to his widow for her lifetime. In an unexpected twist of fortune, he had willed that in the event of her remarrying, the property should pass to the son of his half-sister, Marguerite Vernier, née Lascombe.

When the lawyer had read the terms out loud in his dry and scratchy voice, it had taken a moment for Anatole to realize that it was to him that the document referred. It was all he could do not to laugh out loud. The Domaine de la Cade, one way or another, would belong to them.

Now, half an hour later, as they stood in the small Jesuit chapel and the priest spoke the closing words of the brief ceremony that joined them together as man and wife, Anatole reached out and took Isolde's hands.

"Madame Vernier, *enfin*," he whispered. "*Mon coeur.*"

The witnesses, chosen at random on the street, smiled at their open signs of affection, although they considered it a pity it was such a modest affair.

Anatole and Isolde stepped out into the street to the peal of bells. They heard the thunder. Wishing to spend the first hour of their married life alone—and reassured that Léonie and Marieta were comfortably awaiting their return in the hotel—they ran down the street and ducked into the first suitable establishment they came to.

Anatole ordered a bottle of Cristal, the most expensive Champagne on the menu. They exchanged gifts. Anatole gave Isolde a silver locket with a miniature of her on one side, him on the other. She presented him with a fine gold-plate timepiece with his initials engraved on the top to replace the one stolen in the attack in the Passage des Panoramas.

For the next hour, they drank and talked, happy in each other's affectionate company, as the first spots of heavy rain struck the wide plate-glass windows.

58

Léonie felt a moment of disquiet as she descended the bridge. She could no longer pretend that she was not disobeying Anatole's express instructions. She pushed the thought from her mind, then looked back over her shoulder to observe that black storm clouds were massing over the Bastide.

At this instant, she told herself, it would be wiser to remain on the far side of the river away from the worst of the weather. Indeed, it would be inadvisable to return to the Basse Ville quite yet. Besides, an adventuress, a lady explorer, would not give up the chase simply because her brother told her so.

The quartier Trivalle was more unnerving, far poorer than she had imagined. All the children were barefoot. At the side of the road, a blind beggar with milky, dead eyes sat swaddled in a cloth the color of the damp pavement. With hands streaked black with grime and poverty, he held out a filthy cup as she passed by. She dropped a coin into it and picked her way cautiously up the cobblestone road, which was lined with plain buildings. The shutters all were peeling and in a state of disrepair. Léonie wrinkled her nose. The street smelled of overcrowding and neglect.

It will be better within the Cité.

The road sloped gently upward. She found herself clear of the buildings and in the open air, the beginning of the green approach to the Cité itself. To her left, at the top of a crumbling set of stone steps, she glimpsed a heavy wooden door set deep within ancient gray walls. The sign, battered and worn, announced that this was the Capuchin convent.

Had once been.

Neither Léonie nor Anatole had been brought up in the repressive shadow of the Church. Her mother was too free a spirit, and her father's Republican sympathies meant that, as Anatole had once explained it to her, Leo Vernier considered clerics as much of an enemy to the establishment of a true Republic as the aristocracy. Nevertheless, Léonie's romantic imagination caused her to regret the intransigence of politics and progress that demanded all beauty should be sacrificed for principle. The architecture spoke to her, even if the words echoed within the convent did not.

In a reflective mood, Léonie continued past a rather fine landmark, the Maison de Montmorency, with exterior wooden beams and mullioned windows, the diamond panes of glass catching the light in prisms of blue and pink and yellow, despite the dullness of the sky.

At the top of the rue Trivalle, she turned to the right. Straight ahead, she could see the high and narrow sand-colored towers of the Porte Narbonnaise, the primary entrance into the Cité. Her heart lurched with excitement at the double ring of walls, punctuated by towers, some with red-tiled roofs, some with gray slates, all in silhouette against the glowering sky.

Holding her skirts in one hand to make the climbing easier, she fared forward with renewed vigor. As she drew closer, she saw the tops of gray tombstones with soaring angels and monumental crosses behind the high walls of a cemetery.

Beyond, all was pasture and grasslands.

Léonie paused a moment to catch her breath. The approach into the citadel was by means of a cobblestoned bridge over a grassy moat, flat and wide. At the head of the bridge was a small rectangular toll office. A man wearing a battered top hat and old-fashioned whiskers stood, hands in his pockets, looking out and claiming payment from the drivers of goods carts, merchants carrying barrels of ale for the Cité.

Perched on the wide and low stone wall of the bridge was a man, in the company of two soldiers. He was wearing an old blue Napoleonic cape and smoking a long-stemmed pipe as black as his teeth. All three men were laughing. For a moment, Léonie fancied his eyes widened a fraction as he caught sight of her. He held her in his gaze a moment, his stare a little impertinent, then looked away. Unnerved by his attention, she walked quickly past.

As she stepped out onto the bridge, the direct force of the northwesterly wind struck her. She was obliged to put one hand on her hat to hold it in place, and the other kept her swirling skirts free from tangling round her legs. She fought her way forward, eyes screwed tightly against the dust and grit thrown up into her face.

But the instant she passed into the Cité, she was sheltered from the wind. She paused a moment to adjust her clothing, then, taking care not to dampen her boots in the stream of water running down the gutter in the center of the cobbles, she made her way through into the open space between the inner and outer fortifications. There was a pump, with two boys powering the metal arm up and down, spitting water into a metal pail. To left and right she saw the remains of the humble shanty houses that had recently been demolished. At upper-story height, hanging in midair, was a hearthstone, black with soot, left behind when the lodgings had been torn down.

Wishing she had had the foresight to conceal her guidebook in her pocket before departing the hotel, rather than the map of the Bastide only, Léonie asked for directions and was informed that the castle was straight ahead, set into the western walls of the fortification. As she walked on, she felt a flutter of misgiving. After the distant grandeur of the exterior and the windswept spaces of the *hautes lices,* the space between the inner and outer walls, the interior, was darker and more somber than she had expected. And it was dirty. Mud covered the slippery cobbles. Debris and detritus of all kinds littered the gutters.

Léonie picked her way up the narrow street, following a hand-painted wooden sign for the Château Comtal, where the garrison was quartered. This, too, disappointed. From previous reading, she knew it had once been the home of the Trencavel dynasty, lords of the Cité many hundreds of years ago. Léonie had imagined a fairy-tale castle, such as those that stood on the banks of the Rhône or the Loire. She had pictured courtyards and great halls, filled with ladies in sweeping dresses, and chevaliers riding out to battle.

The Château Comtal looked like what it now was, a plain military building, efficient, workaday, drab. The Tour de Vade, in the shadow of the walls, was a powder depot. A single sentinel stood guard, picking his teeth. The place wore a mantle of neglect, a building tolerated but not cherished.

Léonie looked for a while from beneath the wide brim of her hat, attempting to see some romance in the plain bridge and the functional narrow gateway into the château itself, but could find none. As she turned away, the thought came into her mind that attempts to rejuvenate the Cité as a tourist landmark were likely to fail. She could not imagine streets such as these thronged with visitors. It was too dull, not designed to appeal to contemporary tastes and fashions. The newly repaired walls, the machine-cut stone and tiles only emphasized how ruined were the authentic surroundings. She could only assume the hope was that when the works were finished, the atmosphere would change. That new restaurants, shops, perhaps even a hotel, would bring life again to the winding streets. Léonie strolled up and down the passageways. A few fellow travelers, ladies with their hands warm in fur muffs, gentlemen with walking sticks and top hats, bade her good afternoon.

The wind was even stronger here, and Léonie was obliged to retrieve her handkerchief from her pocket and hold it across her mouth and nose as protection against the worst of the damp air. She picked her way through a complicated chicane, and found herself standing beside an old stone cross looking out over terraced market gardens, with vegetable plots, vines, chicken coops and rabbit hutches. Below was a cluster of small, cramped houses.

From this vantage point, she could see clearly how very high the river was. A restless, swirling black mass of water, speeding through the mills, setting the blades spinning. Beyond, the Bastide lay spread out before her. She could pick out the spire of the cathedral of Saint-Michel and the tall, thin bell tower of the église Saint-Vincent, hard by their hotel. Léonie felt a spike of anxiety. She glanced up at the threatening sky and realized she could find herself confined on the far side of the river, trapped by the water levels rising. The Basse Ville seemed suddenly some distance off. The story she had concocted in her mind to tell Anatole of how she had become disoriented and lost in the narrow streets of the Bastide would be of no matter if she was caught by flooding.

A movement above her head made her glance up. A flock of autumn crows, black against the gray sky, flew up over the turrets and battlements, fighting against the wind. Léonie started to hurry. The first spot of rain landed on her cheek. Then another and another, faster, heavier, colder. Then a rattle of sleet and a single, abrupt crack of thunder. Suddenly, all round was water.

The storm, so long threatened, had arrived.

59

Léonie cast around urgently for shelter, but there was nothing. Caught halfway down the steep and cobbled path that linked the citadel to the quartier Barbacane below, there were no trees, no buildings, no dwellings. Her tired legs protested at the thought of climbing back up to the Cité.

Nothing but to continue down.

She stumbled down the *calada*, holding her skirts above her ankles to prevent them being soaked by the water cascading over the cobbles like a millrace. The wind boxed her ears and blew the rain beneath the brim of her hat, and caused her coat to flap and catch round her legs.

She did not see the two men watching her beside the stone cross at the top of the ramp. One was well dressed, imposing and stylish, a person of some means and status. The other was short and dark, wrapped in a thick Napoleonic cloak. They exchanged a few words. There was a glint of coins passing from one gloved hand to the dirty palms of the old soldier, then the two men parted company. The soldier vanished into the Cité.

The gentleman followed Léonie down.

BY THE TIME Léonie reached the Place Saint-Gimer, she was drenched.

In the absence of any sort of public restaurant or café, her only option was to take shelter in the church itself. She hurried up the charmless modern steps and through the metal gate standing partly open in the black railings.

Léonie pushed open the wooden door and stepped inside. Although the candles were lit on the altar and in the side chapels, she shivered. It was colder inside than out. She stamped her feet to shake off what rain she could, breathing in the scent of wet stone and incense. She hesitated, then, realizing she could be stranded within the église de Saint-Gimer for some time, decided that not catching a chill was of more importance than her appearance, and removed both her gloves and her sodden hat.

As her eyes became accustomed to the gloom, Léonie realized with relief that others had been drawn to the church to shelter from the storm. It was a strange congregation. In the nave and side chapels, people milled quietly about. A gentleman in a top hat and greatcoat, with a lady on his arm, sat bolt upright in one of the pews as if they had an unpleasant smell beneath their noses. Local residents of the quartier, many without boots and inadequately dressed, squatted on the flagstones. There was even a donkey, and a woman clutching two chickens, one under each arm.

"An extraordinary sight," said a voice at her ear. "But then one must remember that sanctuary welcomes all those who seek it."

Startled to be directly addressed, Léonie spun around to see a gentleman standing at her elbow. His gray top hat and frock coat marked his class, as did the silver head and tip of his cane and his kid-leather gloves. The traditional elegance of his attire made his blue eyes all the more startling. For an instant, Léonie thought she might have seen him before. Then she realized it was just that, although broader and more substantial, there was some resemblance in coloring and features to her brother.

There was something else about him, something about his direct gaze and his vulpine features that caused a quite unexpected tumult in Léonie's chest. Her heart began to beat a little harder, and she felt her skin suddenly warm beneath her sodden clothes.

"I . . ." She blushed prettily, and looked down.

"Forgive me, I did not mean to offend you," he said. "In normal circumstances I would not, of course, address a lady without introduction. Even in such a place." He smiled. "But these are somewhat unusual circumstances, no?"

His courtesy reassured her.

Léonie raised her eyes. "Yes," she agreed. "They are rather."

"So here we are, fellow travelers seeking refuge from the storm. I felt that perhaps normal rules of etiquette and behavior might be suspended." He tipped his hat to reveal a high forehead and glossy hair, precisely cut to the top of his high collar. "So, can we be friends for the duration? I do not offend you to make such a request?"

Léonie shook her head. "Not in the slightest," she said clearly. "Besides, we might find ourselves here, after all, for quite some time."

She regretted that to her ears her voice sounded strained, too high, too thin to be pleasing. But the stranger was smiling still and did not seem to notice.

"Quite." He looked around. "But bearing in mind the proprieties, perhaps if I might make so bold as to introduce myself to you, then we will no longer be strangers. And your guardians need not worry."

"Oh, I am . . ." Léonie stopped. It might not be prudent to reveal that she was alone. "I should be delighted to accept your introduction."

With a half-bow, he pulled a calling card from his pocket. "Victor Constant, Mademoiselle."

Léonie accepted the elegant embossed card with a frisson of excitement, which she attempted to mask by studying the name upon the card. She tried to think of something amusing to say. She wished, too, she had not previously removed her gloves. Beneath his turquoise stare, she felt quite undressed.

"And may I be so impertinent as to ask your name?"

A laugh slipped out from between her lips. "Of course. How stupid of me. I regret that I do not . . . I have neglected to bring any visiting cards," she lied, without questioning why. "I am Léonie Vernier."

Constant took her bare hand and raised it to his lips. *"Enchanté."*

Léonie felt a jolt as his lips grazed her skin. She heard herself gasp, then felt the red rush into her cheeks, self-conscious at so obvious a reaction, and pulled her fingers away.

Gallantly, he affected not to notice. Léonie liked him for it.

"Why did you assume I am under the care of a guardian?" she said, when she could trust herself to speak. "I might be accompanied by my husband."

"Indeed you might," he said, "but for one thing. I cannot believe that any husband would be so lacking in chivalry as to leave so beautiful a young wife alone." He glanced around the church. "And in such company."

They both cast their eyes around the bedraggled collection of people.

Léonie felt a spurt of pleasure at the compliment but hid her smile.

"My husband might have gone simply to summon assistance."

"No man would be such a fool," he said, and there was something passionate, almost savage, in the way he said the words that caused Léonie's heart to somersault.

He glanced down at her bare hand, devoid of any marriage band.

"Well, I admit you are quite perspicacious, Monsieur Constant," she replied. "And you are indeed correct in your assumption that I have no husband."

"What husband would wish to be parted from such a wife, even for an instant."

She tilted her head. "For you, of course, would not treat your wife in such a manner?" she said, the bold words slipping out before she could check herself.

"Alas, I am not married," he said with a slow smile. "I meant merely that if I were lucky enough to enjoy such a precious possession, I would take greater care."

Their eyes collided, the green and the blue. To cover the surge of emotion she was experiencing, Léonie laughed, causing several of the temporary citizens of Saint-Gimer to turn and stare.

Constant placed his finger to his lips. "Shush," he said. "Our levity, clearly, is not appreciated."

He had lowered his voice yet further, so she was obliged to draw nearer. Indeed, they were so close as to be almost touching. Léonie could feel the heat of him beside her, as if the entire right side of her body was facing an open fire. She remembered Isolde's words about love as they had sat on the promontory overlooking the lake and, for the first time, had a glimpse into what such a feeling might be like.

"Shall I tell you a secret?" he asked.

"By all means."

"I believe I know what drew you to this place, Mademoiselle Vernier."

Léonie raised her eyebrows. "Indeed?"

"You have the air of a young lady upon a solitary adventure. You entered the church alone, drenched from the downpour, which suggests you have no servant with you, for certainly they would have been equipped with an umbrella. And your eyes, quite like emeralds, dazzle with the excitement of the moment."

A burst of loud and angry words came from a Spanish family close by, drawing Constant's attention. Léonie felt quite unlike herself, but she was not so far lost as to not realize the danger. That, in the intensity of the moment, she might say things she would subsequently wish she had not.

She turned his compliment over in her mind.

Your eyes dazzle quite like emeralds.

"There are many Spanish textile workers in this quartier," Constant said, as if sensing her discomfort. "Until the renovations of the medieval fortress were commenced in 1847, the Cité was the center of the local cloth industry."

"You are well informed, Monsieur Constant," she said, trying to keep her concentration. "Are you involved with the restoration? You are an architect, perhaps?"

She fancied his blue eyes flared with pleasure. "You flatter me, Mademoiselle Vernier, but no. Nothing so celebrated. I have merely an amateur interest."

"I see."

Léonie found that she could not think of a single amusing thing to say. Eager to keep the conversation alive, she cast round for a topic of conversation with which to engage him. She wished him to think her witty, intelligent, charming. Fortunately, Victor Constant continued to talk unaided by her.

"There has been a church dedicated to Saint-Gimer close by this site since the end of the eleventh century. This particular building was consecrated in 1859, after it had become clear that such was the state of disrepair of the original that it would be advisable to build a new church rather than attempt a restoration."

"I see," she said, then winced.

How dull I sound. How stupid.

"The church was begun under the auspices of Monsieur Viollet-le-Duc," Constant continued, "although the construction was quickly handed over to a local architect, Monsieur Cals, to complete his designs."

He placed his hands upon her shoulders and turned her round so she was facing up the nave. Léonie caught her breath as a shot of heat surged through her.

"The altar, the pulpit, the chapels and the screens are all Viollet-le-Duc's work," he said. "Quite typical. A blend of styles, north and south. They transferred many of the objects from the original building to here. And although it is rather modern for my tastes, it is nonetheless a place of some character. Do you not agree, Mademoiselle Vernier?"

Léonie felt his hands slip from her shoulders, brushing against the small of her back as they did so. She could only nod, not trusting herself to speak.

A woman sitting in the side aisle on the floor, in the golden shadow of a reliquary casket set into the wall, began to sing a lullaby to still the restless baby in her arms.

Grateful for the diversion, Léonie turned to look.

"Aquèla Trivala
Ah qu'un polit quartier
Es plen de gitanòs."

The words floated across the church to the nave where Léonie and Constant were standing.

"There is a great charm in simple things," he said.

"That is the language of Occitan," she said, wishing to impress. "The maids at home speak it when they believe no one is listening."

She felt his attention sharpen.

"At home?" he said. "Forgive me, from your clothes and your bearing I assumed you were but traveling in this region. I had taken you for *une vraie Parisienne.*"

Léonie smiled at the compliment. "Again, Monsieur Constant, your perspicacity does you credit. My brother and I are indeed only guests in the Languedoc. We live in the eighth arrondissement, not far from the Gare Saint-Lazare. Do you know the quartier?"

"Only from the paintings of Monsieur Monet, I regret."

"The Place d'Europe is visible from our drawing-room windows," she said. "If you knew the area, you could place our lodgings precisely."

He gave a regretful shrug. "In which case, if it is not too impertinent a question, Mademoiselle Vernier, what brings you to the Languedoc? It is late in the season to be traveling."

"We are staying with a relative for a month. An aunt."

He pulled a face. "My commiserations," he said.

It was a moment before Léonie realized he was teasing her.

"Oh." She laughed. "Isolde is not at all that kind of aunt. All mothballs and eau de cologne. She is beautiful and young, also from Paris in the first instance."

She saw something flash in his eyes—satisfaction, delight even. She blushed with pleasure, that he was evidently enjoying their flirtation as much as she.

It is perfectly harmless.

Constant placed his hand on his heart and gave a half-bow.

"I stand corrected," he said.

"I forgive you for it," she replied prettily.

"And your aunt," he said, "this beautiful and charming Isolde, previously of Paris, she is now resident in Carcassonne?"

Léonie shook her head. "No. We are in town for a few days. My aunt has business to attend to, concerning her late husband's estate. We are to go to a concert this evening."

He nodded. "Carcassonne is a charming city. Much improved in the past ten years. There are now many excellent restaurants and shops. Hotels, too." He paused. "Or have you taken lodgings, perhaps?"

Léonie laughed. "We are here only for a matter of days, Monsieur Constant. The Hôtel Saint-Vincent is more than adequate for our needs!"

The door to the church opened with a gust of cold air as more travelers came in from the rain. Léonie shivered as her wet skirts wrapped themselves around her cold legs.

"The storm distresses you?" he asked quickly.

"No, not in the slightest," she said, although pleased at his concern. "My aunt's estate is high in the mountains. In the past two weeks we have experienced thunder and lightning considerably more severe than this."

"So you are some distance outside Carcassonne?"

"We are situated south of Limoux, in the Haute Vallée. Not far from the spa town of Rennes-les-Bains." She smiled up at him. "Do you know it?"

"I regret I do not," he said. "Although, I admit, the region suddenly holds considerable interest for me. Perhaps I will be moved to pay a visit in the not-too-distant future."

Léonie blushed at the charming compliment. "It is rather isolated, but the countryside is magnificent."

"Is there much society in Rennes-les-Bains?"

She laughed. "No, but we are quite happy with the quiet life. My brother leads a busy existence in town. We are here to rest."

"Well, I trust that the Midi will have the pleasure of your company for a while longer," he said softly.

Léonie struggled to maintain her calm expression.

The Spanish family, still arguing, suddenly got to their feet. Léonie turned round and saw that the main doors were now standing open.

"The rain appears to be stopping, Mademoiselle Vernier," said Constant. "A pity."

The last word was spoken so quietly that Léonie threw a sideways glance at him, wondering at so open a declaration of interest. But his face was quite innocent, and she was left wondering if she had mistaken his meaning. She looked back to the doors and saw that the sun had come out, flooding the wet steps with a bright and blinding light.

The gentleman in the top hat helped his companion to her feet. They stepped carefully out of their pew into the nave and walked out. One by one, everyone else started to follow. Léonie was surprised to realize how large the congregation had become. She had barely noticed them.

Monsieur Constant held out his arm. "Shall we?" he said.

His voice sent a shiver down her spine. Léonie hesitated for only a moment. Then, as if in slow motion, she saw herself reaching out her ungloved hand and resting it upon his gray sleeve.

"You are most kind," she said.

Together, Léonie Vernier and Victor Constant left the church and processed into the Place Saint-Gimer.

60

Despite her disheveled appearance, Léonie felt the most fortunate person in the Place Saint-Gimer. Having often imagined a moment as this, it was nonetheless extraordinary that it felt so natural to be walking, arm in arm, with a man.

And not in a dream.

Victor Constant continued to be the perfect gentleman, attentive but not inappropriately so. He asked her permission to smoke, and when Léonie granted it, did her the honor of offering her one of his Turkish cigarettes, thick and brown, unlike those Anatole favored. She declined but was flattered to be treated as an adult.

The conversation between them continued along predictable lines—the weather, the delights of Carcassonne, the splendor of the Pyrenees—until they reached the far side of the Pont Vieux.

"This is, I regret, where I must leave you," he said.

Disappointment swooped over her, but Léonie succeeded in keeping her expression perfectly composed.

"You have been most kind, Monsieur Constant, most solicitous." She hesitated, then added, "I, too, must return. My brother will be wondering what has become of me."

For a moment, they stood awkwardly together. It was quite one thing to make each other's acquaintance in so unorthodox a manner owing to the peculiarities of the circumstances of the storm. It was quite another to take the association a step further.

Although she liked to think herself not bounded by convention, Léonie nonetheless waited for him to speak first. It would be perfectly improper for her to suggest a further meeting. But she smiled at him, hoping to make it clear she would not rebuke him should he issue some kind of invitation.

"Mademoiselle Vernier," he said. Léonie heard a tremor in his voice and liked him the more for it.

"Yes, Monsieur Constant?"

"I hope you will forgive me if this seems too bold a comment, but I was wondering if you yet had had the pleasure of visiting Square Gambetta," he said, gesturing to the right. "No more than two or three minutes from here."

"I walked there earlier," she said.

"Should you happen to enjoy music, there is an excellent concert every Friday morning at eleven o'clock." He turned the full force of his blue eyes upon her. "Certainly, I shall attend tomorrow."

Léonie hid a smile, admiring the finesse with which he had invited her to meet him without transgressing the bounds of social proprieties.

"My aunt had intended for me to enjoy a range of musical activities while we are in Carcassonne," she said, tilting her head to one side.

"In which case, perhaps I may be fortunate and find that our paths cross again tomorrow, Mademoiselle," he said, raising his hat. "And to have the pleasure of meeting your aunt and brother." He fixed her with a look, and for a fleeting instant, Léonie felt they were bound together, as if she was being inexorably drawn toward him, reeled in like a fish on a line. She caught her breath, wishing for nothing more at that moment than that Monsieur Constant would, with his hands around her waist, kiss her.

"*A la prochaine,*" he said.

His words broke the spell. Léonie blushed, as if he could read her innermost thoughts.

"Yes, indeed," she stammered. "Until the next time."

Then she turned and walked briskly away up the rue du Pont Vieux before she shamed herself by revealing the extent of the hopes playing within her.

CONSTANT WATCHED HER GO, seeing from her posture, her pretty step, the way she held her head high, that she was more than aware of his eyes upon her retreating back.

Like mother, like daughter.

In truth, it was almost too easy. The schoolgirl blushes, her widening eyes, the way she parted her lips revealing the tip of a pink tongue. He could have enticed her away there and then, had he so wished. That did not suit his purposes. It was infinitely more satisfying to play with her emotions. Ruin her certainly, but by making her fall in love with him. That knowledge would torment Vernier more than the idea of her being taken by force.

And she *would* fall in love him. She was impressionable and young, ripe for the taking.

Pitiable.

He clicked his fingers. The man in the blue cloak, following at some distance behind, appeared instantly at his side.

"Monsieur."

Constant penned a curt note and gave instructions for it to be delivered to the Hôtel Saint-Vincent. The thought of Vernier's face when he read the letter was too much to resist. He wanted to make him suffer. Both of them, Vernier and his whore. He wanted them to spend the next few days looking over their shoulders, waiting, haunted, always wondering when the blow would fall.

He thrust a purse of money into the man's greasy hands.

"Follow them," he said. "Stay with them. Send word in the usual manner to let me know precisely where they go. Is that clear? You think you can deliver the note before the girl arrives back at the hotel?"

The man looked offended. "It is my town," he muttered, then turned on his heel and vanished into a narrow *allée* running along the back of the Hôpital des Malades.

Constant put the girl out of his mind and considered his next move. During the course of the tedious flirtation in the church, she had not only given him the name of the hotel in which they were staying in Carcassonne but, more important, had told him where Vernier and his whore had gone to ground.

He was acquainted with Rennes-les-Bains and its therapeutic treatments. The location suited his purposes well. He could not move against them in Carcassonne. The city was too crowded, and a confrontation here would attract too much attention. But an isolated estate in the country? He had some connections in the town, one man in particular, a person of few scruples and a cruel temperament to whom he had once been of service. Constant did not foresee any difficulties in persuading him that the time had come for the debt to be repaid.

Constant took a fiacre back into the heart of the Bastide, then threaded his way through the network of streets behind the Café des Négociants on the Boulevard Barbès. There the most exclusive of private clubs was to be found. Champagne, perhaps a girl? There was mostly only dark meat this far south, not the pale skin and blond hair he preferred. But today he was prepared to make an exception. He was in the mood to celebrate.

61

Léonie rushed through the Square Gambetta, its pathways and borders glinting with pools of rainwater reflecting the pale rays of the sun, then past an ugly municipal building and into the heart of the Bastide.

She was all but oblivious to the rush of the world about her. The pavements were crowded; the streets swirled with black water and debris carried from the top of the town by the force of the storm.

The consequences of her afternoon's excursion were only now hitting her. Thoughts of how Anatole would chastise her filled her head as she half walked, half ran, picking her way through the drenched streets, her nerves stretched to breaking point.

Although I do not regret it.

She would be punished for her disobedience, she had no doubt, but she could not say that she wished she had never gone.

She looked up at the street sign and found she was in the rue Courtejaire, not in Carriere Mage as she had supposed. Indeed, she was quite lost. The *plan de la ville* was soaking wet and disintegrated in her hands. The ink had run, and the street names now were all but illegible. Léonie turned to the right first, then to the left, looking for a landmark she might recognize, but all the shops were boarded up against the ill weather and the narrow streets in the Bastide all looked the same.

She mistook her way several times, so it was the best part of another hour before she managed to locate the church of Saint-Vincent and, from there, the rue du Port and their hotel. As she charged up the steps of the main entrance, she heard the bells of the cathedral strike six.

She burst into the lobby, still at a run, hoping at the very least to be able to regain the privacy of her room and change into dry clothes before facing her brother. But Anatole was standing in the reception hall, pacing up and down, a cigarette wedged deep between his fingers. She stopped dead in her tracks. When he saw her, he stormed across the floor, took her shoulders and shook her hard.

"Where in the blazes have you been?" he shouted. "I have been going out of my mind!"

Léonie stood fixed to the spot, struck dumb in the face of his anger.

"Well?" he demanded.

"I—I am so sorry. I got caught out in the storm."

"Do not play with me, Léonie," he yelled. "I expressly forbade you to go out alone. You dismissed Marieta under some absurd pretext, and then disappeared. Where in God's name have you been? Tell me, damn you!"

Léonie's eyes widened. He had never sworn at her before, not once. Not ever.

"Anything could have happened to you! A young girl alone in an unfamiliar place. Anything!"

Léonie glanced at the *patron*, who was listening with undisguised interest.

"Anatole, please," she whispered. "I can explain. If we could go somewhere more private. To our rooms. I—"

"Did you disobey me and go beyond the Bastide?" He shook her again. "Well? Did you?"

"No," she lied, too frightened to tell the truth. "I enjoyed the Square Gambetta and admired the wonderful architecture of the Bastide. I admit I did send Marieta back to fetch an umbrella—and I should not have done that, I know—but when the rain started, I thought you would rather I took shelter than remain in the open. Did she tell you we went to the Carriere Mage to find you?"

Anatole's expression darkened yet further.

"She did not inform me of that, no," he said curtly. "And did you see us?"

"No, I—"

Anatole renewed his assault. "Even so, the rain stopped more than an hour ago. We agreed that we would meet at half past five. Or did you put that out of your mind?"

"I remembered, but—"

"One cannot fail but to be aware of the time in this city. One cannot take a single step without being assailed by bells. Do not lie to me, Léonie. Do not pretend you did not know how late it was, for I shall not believe it."

"I was not intending to offer such an excuse," she said in a small voice.

"Where did you take shelter?" he demanded.

"In a church," she replied quickly.

"Which church? Where?"

"I do not know," she said. "Near the river."

Anatole grabbed her arm. "Are you telling me the truth, Léonie? Did you cross the river to the Cité?"

"The church was not in the Cité," she cried truthfully, distressed at the tears that had sprung to her eyes. "Please, Anatole, you're hurting me."

"And nobody approached you? Nobody tried to harm you?"

"You can see they did not," she said, trying to pull her arm free.

He stared at her, his eyes blazing with a fury she had rarely provoked before. Then, without warning, he let her go, all but pushing her away from him.

Léonie's cold fingers stole to the pocket in which she had put Monsieur Constant's calling card.

If he should find this now . . .

He took a step away from her. "I am disappointed in you," he said. The coldness and lack of affection in his voice chilled Léonie to the core. "Always I expect better of you, then you go and behave in this manner."

Temper flared in her and she was on the point of exclaiming that she had done nothing more than go for a walk unaccompanied, but she bit her tongue. There was no sense in inflaming him further.

Léonie dropped her head. "Forgive me," she said.

He turned away. "Go to your room and pack."

No, not that.

Her eyes snapped up. Straightaway, her fighting spirit rushed back.

"Pack? Why must I pack?"

"Don't question me, Léonie, just do as you are told."

If they left this evening, she would not be able to meet Victor Constant tomorrow in the Square Gambetta. Léonie had not determined she would go, yet she did not want the decision taken out of her hands.

What will he think if I do not attend the concert?

Léonie rushed to Anatole and seized his arm. "Please, I beg you, I have said I am sorry. Punish me if you like, but not in such a manner. I don't want to leave Carcassonne."

He shook her off. "There are warnings of further storms and flooding. This is nothing to do with you," he said savagely. "Thanks to your disobedience, I have been obliged to send Isolde ahead to the station with Marieta."

"But the concert," Léonie cried. "I want to stay! Please! You promised."

"Go—and—pack!" he shouted.

Even now, Léonie could not bring herself to accept the situation.

"What has happened to make you wish to leave so abruptly?" she demanded, her voice rising to match his. "Is it something to do with Isolde's meeting with the lawyers?"

Anatole stepped back as if she had struck him. "Nothing has happened."

Without warning, he suddenly stopped shouting. His expression softened.

"There will be other concerts," he said, his voice more gentle. He tried to put his arm around her, but she pushed him away.

"I hate you!" she cried.

With tears stinging her eyes and not caring in the least who saw her, Léonie ran up the stairs, along the passageway into her room and threw herself face-down on the bed in a storm of weeping.

I will not go. I will not.

But she knew there was nothing she could do. She had little money of her own. Whatever the true reason for their sudden departure—she did not be-lieve in the excuse of the worsening weather—she had no choice. He was determined to punish her for her willfulness and had chosen the surest way to do it.

Her fit of sobbing over, Léonie went to the wardrobe to pick out something dry to wear and was astonished to find it empty of all but her traveling cloak. She burst through the communicating door into the common part of the suite to find it deserted, and realized Marieta had taken almost everything.

Thoroughly miserable, her heavy, damp clothes scratchy and uncomfort-able, she gathered the few private items the maid had left on the dressing table, then snatched up her cloak and stormed into the corridor, where she encoun-tered Anatole.

"Marieta has left nothing whatever for me to wear," she protested, her eyes flashing with fury. "My clothes are wet and I am cold."

"Good," he said, walking into his room opposite and slamming the door.

Léonie turned on her heel and stamped back into her own room.

I hate him.

She would show him. She had been careful to behave properly and with decorum, but Anatole was forcing her to take more drastic measures. She would send word to Monsieur Constant explaining why she could not honor their arrangement in person. At least then he would not think ill of her. Per-haps he might even write to express his sadness at their friendship being cut short.

Her complexion flushed with defiance, with determination, Léonie rushed to the bureau and took out a sheet of writing paper. Quickly, before she lost her nerve, she scribbled a few lines of regret, suggesting that letters sent care of the poste restante in Rennes-les-Bains would find her in the event he might wish to put her mind at rest by confirming receipt of this note. She did not feel she could so far forget herself as to give the address of Domaine de la Cade itself.

Anatole would be furious.

Léonie did not care. It served him right. If he insisted on treating her like a child, then she would behave like one. If he would not allow her to make her own decisions, then she would henceforth take no account of his wishes.

She sealed the envelope and addressed it. After a moment's pause, she took her glass bottle of perfume from her bag and sprinkled a few drops over the letter, as the heroines of her favorite novels would have done. Then she held it to her lips, as if she could imprint a little of herself upon the white paper.

There. It is done.

Now all she had to do was find a way to leave it with the *patron* of the hotel without Anatole's knowledge, to be delivered at the appointed hour tomorrow morning to Monsieur Constant in the Square Gambetta.

Then, she could only wait and see what came of it.

IN HIS BEDROOM OPPOSITE, Anatole sat with his head in his hands. Screwed in his fist he held a letter that had been delivered by hand to the hotel some half an hour before Léonie had reappeared.

It was barely a letter. Just five words that struck iron into his soul.

CE N'EST PAS LA FIN. It is not the end.

There was no signature, no return address, but Anatole understood the meaning well enough. It was a response to the single word he had written on the final page of the journal he had left in Paris.

FIN.

He raised his head in desperation, his brown eyes burning bright. His cheeks were hollow and white with the shock.

Somehow, Constant knew. He knew both that the burial in the cimetière de Montmartre had been a hoax and that Isolde was alive, even that she was here, with him, in the Midi. Anatole ran his fingers through his hair. How? How had Constant learned they were in Carcassonne? Nobody but he, Léonie, Isolde and the household servants knew that they were even in the town, let alone at this hotel in particular.

The lawyer knew. And the priest.

But not that they were staying at this very hotel.

Anatole forced himself to concentrate. He could not afford to indulge himself in wondering how they had been discovered. This was not the time to concern himself with how Constant had found them—there would be time enough for such morbid analysis later—but rather to decide what they should do now.

His shoulders slumped as the memory of Isolde's broken expression came back into his mind. He would have given anything to have kept it from her, but she had come upon him moments after the letter had arrived, and he had been unable to hide the truth.

The joy of the afternoon had turned to ashes in their hands. The promise of a new life together, neither hiding nor fearful, slipped out of their grasp.

He had intended to tell Léonie their happy news this evening. He frowned. After her outrageous performance this afternoon, he decided against it. His decision not to involve her in the wedding was vindicated. She had proved she could not be trusted to behave properly.

Anatole strode to the window, parted the wooden slats of the blinds and looked out. There was no one in the street, except for one drunken fellow, wrapped in an old soldier's cloak, knees drawn up and slumped against the wall opposite.

He let the blind snap shut.

He had no way of knowing if Constant himself was actually present in Carcassonne. Or if not, how close at hand he might be. His instinct was that their best hope was to return immediately to Rennes-Les-Bain.

He had to hold to the slim hope that if Constant had known of the Domaine de la Cade, he would have sent the letter there instead.

62

Léonie waited for Anatole in the lobby, standing with her hands clasped in front of her and in silence. Her eyes were defiant, but her nerves were cracking for fear the *patron* would give her away.

Anatole descended the stairs without a word to her. He went to the desk, spoke briefly with the *patron*, then strode past her and out into the street where the fiacre was standing in readiness to convey them to the railway station.

Léonie gave a sigh of relief. "My thanks, Monsieur," she said quietly.

"*Je vous en prie*, Mademoiselle Vernier," he said, winking at her. He patted his breast pocket. "I will see the letter delivered as you wish."

Léonie nodded her farewell, then hurried down the steps to catch up with Anatole.

"Get in," he ordered in a cold voice as she climbed into the carriage, as if he was speaking to a lazy servant. She flushed.

He leaned forward and slipped a silver coin to the driver. "Fast as you can."

He did not address another word to her during the short ride to the railway station. Indeed, he did not even look at her.

THE TRAFFIC THROUGH the town was slow in the drenched and sodden streets, and they made the train with only moments to spare, rushing along the slippery platform to the first-class carriages at the front. The guard held the door for them and ushered them on.

The door slammed shut. Isolde and Marieta were settled in the corner.

"Tante Isolde," Léonie cried, forgetting her ill humor at the sight of her. There was not a drop of color in her cheeks, and her gray eyes were rimmed red. Léonie was certain she had been crying.

Marieta stood up. "I thought it better to stay with Madama," she murmured to Anatole. "Rather than withdraw to my carriage."

"Quite right," he said, not taking his eyes off Isolde. "I'll settle it with the guard."

He sat down on the banquette beside Isolde and took her limp hand.

Léonie, too, drew closer. "Whatever is the matter?"

"I fear I have caught a chill," she said. "The journey, the weather also, has quite worn me out." She looked at Léonie with her gray eyes. "I am so very sorry that, for my sake, you should miss the concert. I know how much you were looking forward to it."

"Léonie accepts that your health comes first," Anatole said sharply, not allowing her the chance to answer for herself. "Also that we cannot risk being stranded this far from home, despite her inconsiderate perambulations this afternoon."

The unfairness of his rebuke stung her, but Léonie managed to hold her tongue. Whatever the real reason for their hasty departure from Carcassonne, Isolde was clearly sickening. There was no doubt that she needed to be in the comfort of her own home.

Indeed, if Anatole had said as much, I would have made no complaint.

Resentment at how he had put her in the wrong pricked at her. She would not forgive him. She persuaded herself that Anatole had provoked the quarrel and that she, in fact, had really done nothing.

So she sighed and sulked and looked pointedly out of the window.

But when she stared at Anatole, to see if he was observing her displeasure, her mounting concern for Isolde started to eclipse the memory of her quarrel with her brother.

The whistle blew. Steam exhaled into the damp and blustery air. The train juddered forward.

ON THE OPPOSITE PLATFORM, a matter of minutes later, Inspector Thouron and two Parisian officers disembarked the train from Marseille. They were some two hours late, having been held up by a landslide brought on by heavy rain on the track outside Béziers.

Thouron was greeted by Inspector Bouchou of the Carcassonne gendarmerie. The two men shook hands. Then, holding their flapping coats tight about them and clasping their hats firmly on their heads, they battled their way down the squally concourse into the fierce headwind.

The foot tunnel linking one side of the station to the other was flooded, so the stationmaster was waiting at a small side gate that gave onto the street, holding the chain hard for fear it would fly back in the storm and break at the hinges.

"Good of you to meet me, Bouchou," said Thouron, tired and ill-tempered after his long and uncomfortable journey.

Bouchou was a corpulent, red-faced man, close to the age of retirement, with the dark coloring and stocky physique Thouron associated with the Midi. But on first acquaintance, he seemed an amiable enough fellow, and Thouron's concerns that as northerners—worse still, Parisians—he and his men might be treated with suspicion seemed ill founded.

"Delighted to be of assistance," Bouchou shouted to make himself heard over the wind. "Although I confess I'm puzzled as to why someone of your standing should make such a journey in person. It is only a matter of finding Vernier to inform him of the murder of his mother, è?" He turned a shrewd eye on Thouron. "Or is there more to it?"

The inspector sighed. "Let's get out of this wind and I'll tell you."

Ten minutes later, they were established in a small café hard by the Cour de Justice Présidiale where they could talk without fear of being overheard. Most of the clientele were either fellow officers from the gendarmerie or personnel from the prison.

Bouchou ordered two glasses of a local liqueur, La Micheline, then pulled up his chair to listen. Thouron found it a fraction too sweet for his taste but drank gratefully all the same as he explained the bare bones of the case.

Marguerite Vernier, widow of a Communard and more recently the mistress of a prominent and highly decorated war hero, had been found murdered in the family apartment on the evening of Sunday, September 20. Since then, a month had passed and yet they had still been unable to trace either her son or her daughter, as next of kin, to inform them of their loss.

Indeed, although there was no reason to consider Vernier a suspect, at the same time a number of points of interest, irregularities *quand même,* had come to light. Not least the growing evidence that he and his sister had deliberately taken steps to cover their traces. This meant it had taken Thouron's men some time to discover that Monsieur and Mademoiselle Vernier had traveled south from the Gare Montparnasse, rather than west or north from the Gare Saint-Lazare, as previously believed.

"In truth," Thouron admitted, "if one of my men had not been on his toes, we would have got no further than that."

"Go on," said Bouchou, his eyes sharp with interest.

"After four weeks, you understand," explained Thouron, "I could no longer justify a full-time watch on the apartment."

Bouchou shrugged. *"Bien sûr."*

"However, in the way of these things, one of my officers—sharp boy, Gaston Leblanc—has become friendly with a maid in the Debussy household, the family which resides in the apartment below the Verniers in the rue de Berlin. She told Leblanc that she had seen the concierge accepting money from a man and, in return, handing over some sort of envelope."

Bouchou dropped his elbows to the table. "The concierge admitted it?"

Thouron nodded. "At first he denied it. These people always do. But under threat of arrest, eventually he admitted that he had been paid—and handsomely—to pass over any correspondence addressed to the Vernier apartment."

"By whom?"

Thouron shrugged. "He claimed not to know. The transactions were always done with a servant."

"And you believed him?"

"Yes," he said, draining his glass. "On balance, I did. The long and the short of it was that the concierge claimed, although he could not be certain, that the handwriting resembled that of Anatole Vernier. And that the postmark was Aude."

"Et voilà, so you are here."

Thouron pulled a face. "It is not much, I know, but it is the only lead we have."

Bouchou raised his hand to order another round of drinks. "And the matter is sensitive because of Madame Vernier's romantic liaison."

Thouron nodded. "General Du Pont is a man of some reputation and influence. He is not suspected of the crime, but—"

"And you are certain of that?" Bouchou interrupted. "It is not just that your *Préfet* does not wish to find himself embroiled in some scandal?"

For the first time, Thouron allowed a smile to flicker across his lips. It transformed his face, making him seem younger than his forty years.

"I do not deny that my superiors would have been rather . . . disquieted, shall we say, should there have been a case against Du Pont," he replied carefully. "But fortunately for all concerned, there are too many mitigating factors against the general being responsible. He is, however, anxious not to have this shadow hanging over him. Understandably, he believes that until the killer is caught and brought to justice, there will be rumors, the possibility of a stain on his character."

Bouchou listened in attentive silence as Thouron went through his reasoning for believing Du Pont innocent—the anonymous tip-off, the fact that the medical examiner's estimated time of death was some hours earlier than the body was found when Du Pont was attending a concert and in plain view, the issue of who had been bribing the concierge.

"A rival lover?" he suggested.

"I wondered about that, yes," Thouron admitted. "There were two Champagne glasses, but also a whiskey glass broken in the grate. Also, although there was some evidence that Vernier's room had been searched, the servants are adamant that the only thing taken was a framed family portrait that resided on the sideboard."

Thouron produced a similar photograph from his pocket, from the same sitting at the Parisian studio. Bouchou looked at it without comment.

"I appreciate," continued Thouron, "that even if the Verniers were in the Aude, they might not be so now. It is a large area, and if they are here in Carcassonne, or in a private house in the country, then it might be very difficult to gain information about their whereabouts."

"Do you have copies?"

Thouron nodded.

"I will put out an alert in the hotels and boardinghouses in Carcassonne in the first instance, then perhaps the major tourist towns to the south. They would stand out less in an urban environment than in the country." He looked down at the photograph. "The girl is striking, is she not? Such coloring is uncommon." He slipped the image into his waistcoat pocket. "Leave it with me, Thouron. I'll see what we can do."

The inspector gave a deep sigh. "I am most grateful, Bouchou. This case . . . drags on."

"*Je vous en prie,* Thouron. Now, some supper, I think?"

They ate a plate of chops each, followed by steamed plum pudding, washed down with a *pichet* of robust red wine from the Minervois. The wind and rain continued to batter the building. Other customers came and went, stamping the wet from their boots and shaking their hats. Word went round that the mairie had issued a flood warning that the River Aude was close to bursting its banks.

Bouchou snorted. "Every autumn they say the same thing, but it never happens!"

Thouron raised his eyebrows. "Never?"

"Well, not for some years," Bouchou conceded with a grin. "I think, tonight, the defenses will be sufficient to hold."

THE STORM HIT the Haute Vallée at a little after eight o'clock in the evening, just as the train carrying Léonie, Anatole and Isolde south approached the station at Limoux.

Thunder, then a jagged fork of lightning slashed the purple sky. Isolde cried out. Instantly, Anatole was at her side.

"*Je suis là,*" he soothed.

Another crack split the air, making Léonie jolt in her seat, followed by a second burst of lightning as the storm rolled ever closer across the plains. The *pins maritimes,* the *platanes,* the beech trees swayed, then lunged, in the gusting crescendo of the wind. Even the vines, regimented in neat rows, shook with the ferocity of the tempest.

Léonie rubbed at the steamy glass and watched, half horrified, half exhilarated, as the elements raged about them. The train continued on its laborious way. Several times they were obliged to stop between halts while the rails were cleared of fallen branches and even small trees, loosened from the steep slopes of the gorges.

At every station, more and more people seemed to board the train, replacing twice over those who were alighting. Hats were pulled low over brows, collars turned up to provide protection against the rain that was driving into the thin glass of the carriage windows. The period of delay at each station became more and more interminable, the carriages increasingly crowded with refugees from the storm.

Some hours later, they arrived in Couiza. The weather was less ferocious in the valleys, but still there was no cab for hire and the *courrier publique* had long departed. Anatole was obliged to round up one of the shopkeepers to send his boy by mule up the valley to fetch Pascal to bring the gig to collect them.

While they waited, they took shelter in a miserable restaurant building adjoining the *gare*. It was too late for dinner, even had the conditions not been so dreadful. But on seeing Isolde's ghostly complexion and Anatole's undisguised anguish, the owner's wife took pity on their bedraggled party and provided cups of steaming oxtail soup and chunks of dry black bread, together with a bottle of strong Tarascon wine.

Two men joined them, also seeking refuge from the storm, bringing with them news that the River Aude was said to be close to bursting its banks in Carcassonne. There were already pockets of flooding in the quartiers Trivalle and Barbacane.

Léonie went pale, picturing the black water lapping at the steps of the église de Saint-Gimer. How easily she could have been trapped. The streets through which she had walked were now, if the accounts were to be believed, submerged. Then another thought shot into her mind. Was Victor Constant safe?

The torment of imagining him in danger played on her nerves all the way back to the Domaine de la Cade, making her oblivious to the rigors of the journey and the struggle of the weary horses along the slippery and perilous roads leading home.

By the time they drove up the long graveled drive, the wheels sticking on the wet stones and mud, Isolde was all but insensible. Her eyelids fluttered as she struggled to stay conscious. Her skin was cold to the touch.

Anatole charged into the house, shouting instructions. Marieta was sent to mix a powder to help her mistress sleep, another maid to fetch the *moine*, the bedwarmer and frame, to take the chill from Isolde's sheets, a third to stoke the fire already burning in the grate. Then, seeing Isolde was too weak to walk, Anatole swept her up in his arms and carried her up the stairs. Strands of her blond hair, trailing loose now down her back, hung like pale silk against his black jacket sleeves.

Astounded, Léonie watched them go. By the time she had rallied her thoughts, everyone had disappeared, leaving her to fend for herself.

Frozen to her bones and out of sorts, she followed them up to the first floor. She undressed and climbed into her bed. The covers seemed damp. No fire burned in her grate. The room was unwelcoming and cheerless.

She attempted to sleep, but all the time she was aware of Anatole pacing the corridors. Later, she heard the clip of his boots on the tiles of the hall below, marching up and down like a soldier on the night watch, and the sound of the front door opening.

Then silence.

At last, Léonie fell into a restless half-sleep, dreaming of Victor Constant.

Part VIII

Hôtel de la Cade
October 2007

63

Tuesday, October 30, 2007

Meredith saw Hal before he saw her. Her heart skipped a beat at the look of him. He was sprawled in one of three low armchairs set around a small table, wearing much the same clothes he'd had on earlier, blue jeans and white T-shirt, but had swapped his blue sweater for a pale brown one.

As she watched, he lifted his hand and pushed his unruly hair off his face. She smiled at the already familiar gesture. Letting the door swing shut behind her, she walked across the room toward him.

He stood up as she drew close.

"Hi," she said, putting her hand on his shoulder. "Tough afternoon?"

"I've had better," he said, kissing her on the cheek, then turning round to summon the waiter. "What can I get you?"

"The wine you recommended last night was pretty good."

Hal ordered. *"Une bouteille du Domaine Begude, s'il vous plaît, Georges. Et trois verres."*

"Three glasses?" Meredith queried.

Hal's face clouded over. "I bumped into my uncle coming in. He seemed to think you wouldn't mind. Said you were talking earlier. When I said we were meeting for a drink, he invited himself."

"No way," she said, keen to counteract the impression Hal had got. "He asked me if I knew where you had gone after you dropped me back here. I said I wasn't sure. That was the extent of it."

"Right."

"Not what you'd call a conversation," she said, driving the point home. She leaned forward, hands on her knees. "What happened this afternoon?"

Hal glanced at the door, then back to her.

"I tell you what, why don't I reserve us a table for dinner? I don't want to start, then have to break off in a few minutes when my uncle gets here. It brings things to a natural close without being too obvious about it. How does that sound?"

Meredith grinned. "Dinner sounds great," she said. "I skipped lunch. I'm ravenous."

Looking pleased, Hal stood up. "Be back in a moment."

Meredith watched him walk across the room to the door, liking the way he seemed to fill the space with his broad shoulders. She saw him hesitate, then turn, as if he could feel her gaze on his back. Their eyes collided in midair, held for a moment. Then Hal gave a slow half-smile and disappeared into the corridor.

It was Meredith's turn to push her black bangs off her face. She felt her skin flush hot in the hollow of her throat, her palms grow damp, and shook her head at such schoolgirl silliness.

Georges brought the wine in an ice bucket on a stand and poured her a large tulip-shaped glass. Meredith drank several mouthfuls in one go, like it was soda, and fanned herself with the cocktail list on the table.

She cast her eyes around the bar at the floor-to-ceiling shelves of books, wondering if Hal knew which—if any—had survived the fire and were part of the original library. It occurred to her that here there might be some kind of link involving the Lascombe family and the Verniers, especially given the connection with printing through the Bousquet family. On the other hand, the books could all be from the *vide-grenier* sale.

She looked out of the window to the darkness beyond. On the farthest edges of the lawns she could see the shapes of the trees, swaying, moving, like an army of shadows. She felt eyes upon her, fleetingly, as if someone had passed just in front of the window and was looking in. Meredith narrowed her gaze but couldn't see anything.

Then she became aware that someone was in fact coming up behind her. She could hear footsteps. A trickle of anticipation slithered down her spine. She smiled, then turned, her eyes bright.

She found herself looking up not at Hal but into the face of his uncle, Julian Lawrence. There was a faint smell of whiskey on his breath. Embarrassed, she adjusted the expression on her face and started to get to her feet.

"Ms. Martin," he said, lightly putting his hand on her shoulder. "Please, don't get up."

Julian threw himself into the leather armchair to Meredith's right, leaned forward, poured himself some wine and sat back before she had the chance to tell him he was in Hal's chair.

"*Santé*," he said, raising his glass. "My nephew's done another vanishing act?"

"He's gone to get us a reservation for dinner," she replied.

Polite, to the point, but nothing more.

Julian just smiled. He was dressed in a pale linen suit and blue shirt, open at the neck. As every time she'd seen him, he looked comfortable and in control, although he was a little flushed. Meredith found her eyes drawn to his left hand resting on the arm of the chair. It betrayed his age, late fifties rather than the mid-forties she would have given him, but his skin was tanned and his grip looked strong against the red leather. He wore no ring.

Feeling the silence pressing on her, Meredith looked back up to his face. He was still staring right at her in the same direct manner.

Like Hal's eyes.

She pushed the comparison from her mind.

Julian put his glass back on the table. "What do you know about tarot cards, Ms. Martin?"

His question took her totally by surprise. Taken aback, she stared dumbly at him, wondering how the hell he'd struck upon that subject in particular. Her thoughts flew to the photograph she'd stolen from the wall of the lobby, the deck of cards, the tagged sites on her laptop, the musical notes overlapping. He couldn't know about it, any of it, but she felt herself coloring with embarrassment at having been caught out, all the same. Worse, she could see he was enjoying her discomfort.

"Jane Seymour in the movie *Live and Let Die*," she said, trying to make a joke of it. "That's about it."

"Ah, the beautiful Solitaire," he said, raising his eyebrows.

Meredith met his gaze and said nothing.

"Personally," he continued, "I find myself attracted by the history of the tarot, although I do not for a moment believe that fortune-telling is any sort of way to plan one's life."

Meredith realized how similar his voice was to Hal's. They had the same habit of rolling their words as if every one was special. But the key difference was that Hal wore his heart on his sleeve, every emotion laid bare. Julian, on the other hand, always sounded faintly mocking. Sarcastic. She glanced at the door, but it remained resolutely shut.

"Are you aware of the principles behind the interpretation of tarot cards, Ms. Martin?"

"It's not something I know much about," she said, wishing he'd get off the subject.

"Really? My nephew gave me the impression that it was an interest of yours. He said tarot cards had come up when you were walking around Rennes-le-Château this morning." He shrugged. "Perhaps I misunderstood."

Meredith racked her brains. Tarot had never been far from her mind, sure, but she didn't remember actually discussing it with Hal. Julian was still staring right at her, a hint of challenge in his unwavering scrutiny.

In the end, Meredith found herself responding, just to cover the awkward silence. "I think the idea is that although it seems as if the cards are laid at random, in fact the process of shuffling is merely a way of allowing invisible connections to be made visible."

He raised his eyebrows. "Well put." He kept staring. "Have you ever had your cards read, Ms. Martin?"

A strangled laugh escaped her. "Why do you ask?"

He raised his eyebrows. "Just interested."

Meredith glared at him, pissed at him for making her feel so uncomfortable, and at herself for letting him do it.

At that instant, a hand fell on her shoulder. She jumped, looked round with alarm, this time to see Hal smiling down at her.

"Sorry," he said. "I didn't mean to surprise you."

Hal nodded at his uncle, then sat down in the vacant seat opposite Meredith. He took the bottle from the ice bucket and poured himself some wine.

"We were just talking about tarot cards," Julian said.

"Really?" said Hal, glancing from one to the other. "What were you saying?"

Meredith looked into his eyes and read the message in them. Her heart sank. She did not want to get caught up in a discussion about tarot, but she could see Hal saw it as a good way of keeping his uncle off the subject of his visit to the police commissariat.

"I was just asking Ms. Martin if she had ever been to a tarot reading," Julian said. "She was about to answer."

She looked at him, then to Hal, and realized that unless she could think of an alternative topic of conversation in the next couple of seconds, she was going to have to go with it.

"Actually, I did have a reading," she said in the end, trying to make it sound as dull as possible. "In Paris, in fact, a couple of days ago. First—and last—time."

"And was it a pleasurable experience, Ms. Martin?"

"It was interesting, certainly. What about you, Mr. Lawrence? Have you ever had your cards read?"

"Julian, please," he said. Meredith caught a look of amusement flicker across his face, amusement mixed with something else. A sharpening of interest?

"But, no," he said. "Not my kind of thing, although I confess I am interested in some of the symbolism associated with tarot cards."

Meredith felt her nerves tighten at having her suspicions confirmed. This wasn't small talk. He was after something specific. She took another mouthful of wine and fixed a bland expression on her face. "Is that right?"

"The symbolism of numbers, for example," he continued.

"Like I said, it's not something I know much about."

Julian reached into his pocket. Meredith tensed. It would be too appalling if he produced a deck of tarot cards, cheap. He held her gaze a moment, as if he knew exactly what was going through her mind, then pulled a packet of Gauloises and a Zippo from his pocket.

"Cigarette, Ms. Martin?" he said, offering her the packet. "Although it will have to be outside, I'm afraid."

Mad that she was making such a fool of herself—worse, that she was letting it show—she shook her head. "I don't smoke."

"Very wise." Julian placed the packet, the lighter on top, on the table between them, then carried on talking. "The number symbolism in the church at Rennes-le-Château, for example, is quite fascinating."

Meredith glanced over at Hal, willing him to say something, but he was sitting looking resolutely into the middle distance.

"I didn't notice."

"Did you not?" he said. "The number twenty-two, in particular, comes up surprisingly often."

Despite the antipathy she felt for Hal's uncle, Meredith found herself being drawn in. She wanted to hear what Julian had to say. She just didn't want to give the impression she was interested.

"In what form?" The words slipped out, a little abrupt. Julian smiled.

"The baptismal font in the entrance, the statue of the devil Asmodeus. You must have seen it?"

Meredith nodded.

"Asmodeus was supposed to be one of the guardians of the Temple of Solomon. The Temple was destroyed in 598 BC. If you add each digit to the next—five plus nine plus eight—you get twenty-two. You know, I presume, Ms. Martin, that there are twenty-two cards in the major arcana?"

"I do."

Julian shrugged. "Well then."

"I presume there are other occurrences of the number?"

"The twenty-second of July is the feast day of Saint Mary Magdalene, to whom the church is dedicated. There is a statue of her between paintings thirteen and fourteen of the Stations of the Cross; she is also depicted in two of the three stained-glass windows behind the altar. Another link is with Jacques de Molay, the last leader of the Templars—there are supposed to be Templar links at Bézu, across the valley. He was the twenty-second Grand Master of the Poor Knights of the Temple, to give the outfit its full name. Then the French transliteration of Christ's cry from the cross: *Elie, Elie, lamah sabactani*—my God, my God, why hast thou forsaken me—has twenty-two letters. It's also the opening verse of Psalm twenty-two."

This was all interesting, in a kind of abstract way, although Meredith couldn't figure out why he was telling her. Just to see her reaction? To find out how much she did know about tarot?

And more to the point, why?

"Finally, the priest of Rennes-le-Château, Bérenger Saunière, died on the twenty-second of January 1917. An odd story attached to his death. Allegedly, his body was placed on a throne on the belvedere of his estate, and the villagers filed past and each plucked a tassel from the hem of his robe. Much like the image of the King of Pentacles in the Waite Tarot, in fact." He shrugged. "Or, if you add two plus two, plus the year of his death, you end up with—"

Meredith's patience ran out. "I can do the math," she muttered under her breath, then turned to Hal. "What time is our reservation for dinner?" she said pointedly.

"Seven-fifteen. Ten minutes."

"Of course," Julian said, ignoring her interruption, "playing devil's advocate, one could just as easily take any number and find a whole string of things that suggested there was some special significance."

He picked up the wine bottle and leaned forward to top Meredith up. She covered her glass with her hand. Hal shook his head. Julian shrugged, then emptied the remains of the wine into his own glass.

"It's not as if any of us have to drive," he said casually.

Meredith saw Hal clench his fists.

"I don't know if my nephew mentioned it, Ms. Martin, but there is a theory that the design of the church at Rennes-le-Château is in fact based on a building that once stood within our grounds here."

Meredith forced her attention back to Julian.

"Is that right?"

"There's a significant amount of tarot imagery within the church," he continued. "The Emperor, the Hermit, the Hierophant—who is, as I'm sure you remember, the symbol of the established church in tarot iconography."

"I really don't know—"

He carried on talking. "Some would say the Magician is suggested, in the form perhaps of Christ, and of course four of the paintings of the Stations of the Cross have towers in them, not to mention the Tour Magdala on the belvedere."

"But that looks nothing like it," she said, before she could stop herself.

Julian leaned sharply forward in his chair. "Like what, Ms. Martin?" he said. She could hear excitement in his voice, as if he thought he'd caught her out.

"Jerusalem," she said, the first thing that came into her mind.

He raised his eyebrows. "Or perhaps like any tarot card you've seen," he said.

A silence fell over the table. Hal was frowning. Meredith couldn't figure out if he was embarrassed or had picked up the tension between her and his uncle and misunderstood it.

Julian suddenly drained his wine, placed his glass on the table, pushed back his chair and stood up.

"I'll leave you two to it," he said, smiling at them as if they'd just passed the most pleasant half-hour in one another's company. "Ms. Martin. I hope you enjoy the rest of your stay with us." He put his hand on his nephew's shoulder. Meredith could see Hal struggling not to pull away. "Can you pop your head into my study when you're finished with Ms. Martin? There are a couple of things I need to discuss with you."

"Tonight?"

Julian held Hal's gaze. "Tonight," he said.

Hal hesitated, then gave a sharp nod.

They sat in silence until Julian had gone.

"I don't know how you can . . ." Meredith began, then stopped. Rule number one: never criticize anyone else's family.

"How I can put up with it?" Hal said savagely. "Answer, I can't. As soon as I've sorted things, I'm out of here."

"And are you any closer to that?"

Meredith saw the belligerence go out of him as his thoughts switched from loathing his uncle to grieving his father. He stood up, hands buried deep in his pockets, and looked at her through clouded eyes.

"I'll tell you at dinner."

64

Julian broke the seal on a new bottle, poured a generous measure, then sat heavily down at his desk with the reproduction pack in front of him.

Pointless exercise.

He'd studied the reproduction Bousquet Tarot deck over many years, always looking for something, a hidden key or a code he might have missed. All the time, the search for the original cards had occupied him ever since he'd first come to the Aude valley and heard the rumors about the undiscovered caches of treasure buried beneath the mountains, the rocks, even the rivers.

Having acquired the Domaine de la Cade, Julian had quickly come to the conclusion, like many before him, that all the stories surrounding Rennes-le-Château were a hoax and the renegade nineteenth-century priest at the heart of the rumors—Saunière—was prospecting more for material than spiritual treasures.

Then Julian started to pick up stories about how a deck of cards revealed the location not of a single tomb but allegedly of the entire treasury of the Visigoth empire. Perhaps even the contents of the Temple of Solomon, looted by the Romans in the first century AD, then in turn plundered when Rome itself fell in the fifth century to the Visigoths.

The cards were rumored to be hidden within the estate itself. Julian had sunk every penny into trying to find them through systematic searching and excavation, starting with the area around the ruins of the Visigoth sepulchre and working out from it. It was difficult terrain, and the effort was extremely labor-intensive—and therefore expensive.

Still nothing.

When he'd exhausted his credit at the bank, he'd begun borrowing from the hotel. It was useful that the hotel was—at least in part—a cash business. But it was also a tough market in which to make money. The overhead was high. The place was still finding its feet when the bank called in its loans. But he kept taking money out all the same—gambling that soon he'd find what he was looking for and everything would be all right.

Julian drained his glass in one.

Only a matter of time.

It was his brother's fault. Seymour could have been patient. Should have trusted him. Not interfered. He knew he was nearly there.

I would have repaid the money.

Nodding to himself, Julian flipped the lid of his Zippo with a snap. He took out a cigarette, lit it and inhaled deeply. Just after Hal had left the station, Julian had spoken with the police commissariat in Couiza, who had suggested that it would be better if the boy stopped asking questions. Julian had promised to have a word and invited the commissaire for a drink the following week.

He reached for the bottle, pouring himself another two fingers. He cast his mind back over the conversation in the bar. He had been deliberately clumsy, hardly subtle in his technique, but it had seemed the easiest way to flush the

American out. She had been reluctant to talk about the tarot. The girl was sharp. Attractive, too.

What? What does she know?

He realized the sound he could hear was the sound of his fingers drumming on the desk. Julian looked down at his hand as if it didn't belong to him, then forced it to be still.

In a drawer of his locked desk, the deeds of the transfer of ownership lay ready to sign and return to the *notaire* in Espéraza. The boy wasn't stupid. He didn't want to stay at the Domaine de la Cade. He and Hal couldn't work together anymore than he and Seymour had been able to. Julian had been leaving a decent interval before talking any further to Hal about his plans.

"It wasn't my fault," he said. There was a slur in his voice.

He should talk to her again, the American girl. She must know something about the original Bousquet deck. Why else was she here? Her presence had nothing to do with Seymour's accident or his pathetic nephew or the hotel finances, he could see that now. She was here for the same reason he was. He hadn't done all the dirty work to see some American bitch come in and take the cards from him.

He gazed out at the darkened woods. Night had fallen. Julian reached out and turned on the lamp, then screamed.

His brother was standing right behind him. Seymour, waxy and lifeless as Julian had seen him in the morgue, the skin on his face scarred from the crash, lined, his eyes bloodshot.

He leapt up out of his chair, sending it hurtling back behind him to the ground. The whiskey glass went flying across the polished wood of the desk.

Julian spun round.

"You can't be . . ."

The room was empty.

He stared, uncomprehending, his eyes darting around the room into the shadows, back to the window, until he realized. It was his own pallid reflection, stark in the darkened glass. It was his eyes, not his brother's.

Julian took a deep breath.

His brother was dead. He knew. He had spiked his drink with Rohypnol. He had driven the car to the bridge outside Rennes-les-Bains; struggled to maneuver Seymour into the driver's seat; released the hand brake. He had seen the car fall.

"You made me do it," he muttered.

He lifted his eyes to the window, blinked. Nothing there.

He exhaled a long, exhausted breath, then bent down and righted the chair. For a moment he stood with his hands gripping the back, knuckles white, his head bowed. He could feel the sweat running down his back, between his shoulder blades.

Then he pulled himself together. He reached for his cigarettes, needing the hit of the nicotine to calm his nerves, and looked back out to the black woods beyond.

The original cards were still out there, he knew it.

"Next time," he murmured. He was so close. He could feel it. Next time, he'd be lucky. He knew it.

The spilled whiskey reached the edge of the desk and started to drip, slowly, onto the carpet.

65

O kay, shoot," Meredith said. "Tell me what happened."

Hal put his elbows on the table. "Bottom line, they don't see any grounds for opening things up. They are satisfied with the verdict."

"Which is?" she gently pushed him.

"Accidental death. That Dad was drunk," he said bluntly. "That he lost control of the car, went over the bridge into the River Salz. Three times over the limit, that's what the tox report claims."

They were sitting in one of the window alcoves. The restaurant was quiet this early so they could talk without being overheard. Across the white linen tablecloth, in the light of the candle flickering on the table, Meredith reached out and covered his hands with her own.

"There was a witness, apparently. An English woman, a Dr. Shelagh O'Donnell, who lives locally."

"That's helpful, isn't it? Did she see the accident?"

Hal shook his head. "That's the problem. According to the file, she heard brakes, the sound of tires. She didn't actually see anything."

"Did she report it?"

"Not straightaway. According to the commissaire, lots of people take the road too fast on the bend coming into Rennes-les-Bains. It was only the following morning when she saw the ambulance and the police recovering the car from the river that she put two and two together." He paused. "I thought I might talk to her. See if there's anything that's come back to her."

"Wouldn't she have told the police everything already?"

"I didn't get the impression they thought her a reliable witness."

"In what way?"

"They didn't say it in so many words, but they implied that she was drunk. Also, there were no tire marks on the road, so it's unlikely she could have heard anything. According to the police, that is." He paused. "They wouldn't give me her address, but I managed to copy down her number from the file. In fact . . ." He hesitated. "I invited her up here tomorrow."

"Is that such a great idea?" said Meredith. "If the police think you're interfering, won't that make them less rather than more likely to help?"

"They're already pissed off with me," he said fiercely, "but to tell you the truth, I feel like I'm hitting my head against a brick wall. I don't care anymore. For weeks I've been trying to get the police to take me seriously, sitting around here, being patient, but it's got me nowhere." He stopped, his cheeks flushed. "Sorry. This can't be much fun for you."

"It's okay," she said, thinking how similar Hal and his uncle were in some ways—both quick to flare up—then felt guilty, knowing just how much Hal would hate such a comparison being made.

"I appreciate there's no reason for you to take what I say at face value, but I just don't believe the official version of events. I'm not saying my dad was perfect—to be honest, we didn't have much in common. He was distant and quiet, not the sort of man to make a fuss—but there's just no way he would drink and drive. Even in France. No way."

"It's easy to misjudge that sort of thing, Hal," she said gently. "We've all done it," she added, although she never had. "Had one too many. Played the odds."

"I'm telling you, not Dad," he said. "He liked his wine, but he was fanatical about not getting behind the wheel if he'd been drinking. Not even one glass." He dropped his shoulders. "My mother was killed by a drunk driver," he continued in a quieter voice. "On her way to pick me up from school in the village we lived in, half past three in the afternoon. An idiot in a BMW, on his way back from the pub, tanked up on Champagne and driving too fast."

Now Meredith totally understood why Hal couldn't bring himself to accept the verdict. But wishing things were different didn't make them so. She'd been there herself. If wishes were promises, her birth mother would have gotten healthy. All the scenes and fights would never have happened.

Hal raised his eyes and stared at her. "Dad wouldn't drive if he was drunk."

Meredith gave a noncommital smile. "But if the tox screen came back positive for alcohol . . ." She left the question floating. "What did the police say when you raised that?"

Hal shrugged. "It was obvious they thought I was just too fucked up by the whole situation to think straight."

"Okay. Let's come at it from other directions. Could the tests be wrong?"

"The police say no."

"Did they search for anything else?"

"Like what?"

"Drugs?"

Hal shook his head. "Didn't think there was any need."

Meredith thought. "Well, could he have been driving too fast? Just lost control on the bend?"

"Back to the lack of skid marks on the road and, in any case, that doesn't account for the alcohol in his bloodstream."

Meredith fixed him with her gaze. "Then what, Hal? What are you saying?"

"That either the tests are fake, or someone spiked his drink."

Her face gave her away.

"You don't believe me," he said.

"I'm not saying that," she said quickly. "But think about it, Hal. Even supposing it was possible, who would do such a thing? Why would they?"

Hal held her gaze until Meredith realized what he was getting at.

"Your uncle?"

He nodded. "Got to be."

"You can't be serious," she objected. "I mean, I know you don't see eye to eye, but even so . . . to accuse him of—"

"I know it sounds ridiculous, but think about it, Meredith. Who else?"

Meredith was shaking her head. "Did you make this accusation to the police?"

"Not in so many words, but I did request that the *gendarmerie nationale* were shown the file."

"Which means?"

"They investigate actual crimes. At the moment, the crash is being treated as a traffic accident. But if I can find some sort of evidence linking it to Julian, then I could make them reconsider." He looked at her. "If you would talk to Dr. O'Donnell, I'm sure she'd be more likely to open up."

Meredith sat back in her chair. The whole scenario was crazy. She could see Hal had talked himself into believing it one hundred percent. She really felt for him, but she was sure he was wrong. He needed someone to blame, needed to do something with his anger and his sense of loss. And she knew from her own experience that however bad the truth turned out to be, not knowing was worse. It made it impossible to put the past behind and move on.

"Meredith?"

She realized Hal was staring at her. "Sorry," she said. "Just thinking."

"Would you be able to be here when Dr. O'Donnell comes tomorrow?"

She hesitated.

"I'd really appreciate it."

"I guess," she said in the end. "Sure."

Hal gave a sigh of relief. "Thank you."

The waiter came over and straightaway the mood changed, became less intense, more like a regular date. They both ordered steak and Hal chose a bottle of local red to go with it. For a moment, they sat half looking at each other, catching each other's eye, smiling awkwardly, not sure what to say.

Hal broke the silence. "Anyway," he said, "enough of my problems. Are you going to tell me now why you're really here?"

Meredith went still. "Excuse me?"

"It's obviously not for the Debussy book, is it? Or, at least, not only."

"Why do you say that?" It came out snappier than she'd intended.

He flushed. "Well, for a start, the stuff you were interested in today didn't seem to have much to do with Lilly Debussy. You seem more into the history of this place, Rennes-les-Bains, and the people here." He grinned. "Also, I noticed that the photograph hanging above the piano has disappeared. Someone's borrowed it."

"You think I took it?"

"You were looking at it this morning, so . . ." he said, pulling an apologetic smile. "And, well, with my uncle . . . I don't know, probably my mistake, but I got the idea you might be here checking up on him . . . You certainly didn't seem to like each other."

He stumbled to a standstill.

"You think I'm here to check up on your uncle? You're kidding, right?"

"Well, possibly, maybe." He shrugged. "I don't know, no."

She took a sip of her wine.

"I didn't mean to piss you—"

Meredith held up her hand. "Let me see if I've got this straight. Because you don't believe your father's accident was, in fact, an accident, and because you think the results might have been tampered with or his drink was spiked and the car forced from the road—"

"Yes, although—"

"Bottom line, you suspect your uncle was involved in your father's death. Right?"

"Well, put like that, it sounds—"

Meredith kept right on talking, her voice rising. "And so because of all this, for some crazy reason, when I turn up you jump to the conclusion that I'm somehow involved? Is that what you think, Hal? That I'm some kind of, what, Nancy Drew?"

She sat back in her chair and stared at him.

He had the grace to blush. "I didn't mean to offend you," he said. "But, well, it was something Dad said in April—after that conversation I was telling you about earlier—that gave me the impression that he was unhappy with the way Julian was running things out here and was going to do something."

"If that was the case, wouldn't your father have just come right out and told you? If there was a problem, it would have affected you, too."

Hal shook his head. "Dad wasn't like that. He hated gossip, rumor. He'd never say anything, even to me, until he was completely certain of his facts. Innocent until proved guilty."

Meredith thought about it. "Okay, I can see that. But you still picked up on the feeling something was wrong between them?"

"It might have been something trivial, but I got the impression it was serious. Something to do with the Domaine de la Cade and its history, not just money." He shrugged. "Sorry, Meredith, I'm not being clear."

"He didn't leave you anything? A file? Notes?"

"Believe me, I've looked everywhere. There's nothing."

"And when you put all this together, you started to think he might have employed someone to dig around your uncle. See if anything turned up." She stopped, looked at him across the table. "Why didn't you just ask me?" she said, eyes flashing, although she could see perfectly well why not.

"Well, because I only started to think you might be here for . . . because of my dad when I was thinking about it this afternoon."

Meredith folded her arms. "So it's not why you started talking to me in the bar last night?"

"No, of course not!" he said, looking genuinely appalled.

"Then why?" she demanded.

Hal turned red. "Christ, Meredith, you know why. It's obvious enough."

This time, it was Meredith's turn to blush.

66

Hal insisted on signing for dinner. As she watched him, Meredith wondered if his uncle would make him settle up, given that he technically owned half the place. Straight off, her worries for him came flooding back.

They left the restaurant and walked out into the lobby. At the bottom of the staircase, Meredith felt Hal's fingers wrap around hers.

Hand in silent hand, they walked up the stairs. Meredith felt totally calm, not nervous or ambivalent at all. She didn't have to think about whether this was what she wanted. It felt good. They didn't even need to discuss where to go, automatically both understanding that Meredith's room was better. Right for them, right now.

They reached the end of the first-floor passageway without meeting any other guests. Meredith turned the key, loud in the hushed corridor, and pushed open the door. Almost formal, they walked in still holding hands.

Slats of white light from a harvest moon shone in through the windows and patterned the surface of the floor. Rays refracted and glinted on the reflective surface of the mirror, on the glass of the framed portrait of Anatole and Léonie Vernier and Isolde Lascombe, propped on the desk.

Meredith reached out to put on the light.

"Don't," Hal said quietly.

He cupped his hand behind her head and drew her to him. Meredith breathed in the smell of him, just like at Rennes-le-Château outside the church, a mixture of wool and soap.

They kissed, their lips carrying the trace of red wine, softly at first, tentatively, the mark of friendship moving into something else, something more urgent. Meredith felt comfort give way to desire, a heat that spread through her, up from the soles of her feet, between her legs, to the pit of her stomach, to the palms of her hands, to a rush of blood to the head.

Hal bent over and picked her up, sweeping her into his arms in one movement, and carried her to the bed. The key dropped from Meredith's hand, landing with a heavy thump on the thick pile carpet.

"You're so light," he whispered, kissing her neck.

He placed her carefully down, then sat beside her, his feet still firmly planted on the floor, like a Hollywood matinee idol under fear of the censor.

"Are you ..." He started, stopped, then tried again. "Are you sure you want—"

Meredith laid a single finger across his mouth. "Ssshh."

Slowly she began to undo the buttons of her shirt, then guided his hand to her. Half invitation, half instruction. She heard Hal catch his breath, and then the rise and fall of his breath in the dappled silver light of the room. Sitting cross-legged on the edge of the mahogany bed, Meredith leaned forward to kiss him, her dark hair falling over her face, the difference in their heights eliminated now.

Hal struggled to remove his sweater and became tangled as Meredith pushed her hands beneath the cotton of his T-shirt. They both laughed, a little shy, then stood up to finish undressing.

Meredith didn't feel self-conscious. It seemed totally natural, the right thing to do. Being in Rennes-les-Bains, all of it felt like time out of time. As if for a few days she had stepped out of her regular life—the person she was, thinking of consequences, life running on in the same kind of way—to a place where different rules applied.

She removed her last piece of clothing.

"Wow," Hal said.

Meredith took a step toward him, their bare skin touching, top to toe, so intimate, so startling. She could feel how much he wanted her, but he was happy to wait, to let her lead the way.

She took his hand and led him down to the bed. She lifted up the covers and they slipped in between the sheets, the linen crisp and cool and impersonal against the heat generated by their bodies. For a moment they lay side by side, arm to arm, like a knight and his lady on a stone tomb, then Hal propped himself on one elbow and with his other hand started to stroke her head.

Meredith breathed deeply, relaxing under his touch.

Now his hand was moving lower, smoothing over her shoulders, to the hollow of her throat, skimming her breasts, winding her fingers with his, his lips and his tongue whispering over the surface of her skin.

Meredith felt desire burn in her, red hot, as if she could trace it along the lines of her veins, her arteries, her bones, every part of her. She raised herself toward him, her kisses hungry now, wanting more. Just when the waiting was becoming intolerable, Hal shifted position and lowered himself into the space between her naked legs. Meredith looked up into his ice-blue eyes and saw every possibility reflected, for an instant, in them. The best of her, and the worst.

"You're sure?"

Meredith smiled and reached down to guide him. Carefully, Hal eased himself inside her.

"It's okay," she murmured.

For a moment they lay still, celebrating the peace of being in each other's arms. Then Hal began to move, slowly at first, then a little more urgently.

Meredith placed her hands firmly on his back, her body filled with the hammering of her own blood running through her. She could feel the power of him, the strength in his arms and hands. Her tongue darted between his lips, wet and devoid of speech.

Hal was breathing harder, moving harder, as desire, need, the ecstasy of the automatic movement drove him on. Meredith held him to her, tighter, rising to meet him, possessing him, also caught by the moment. He cried out her name, shuddered, and they both fell still.

The rushing in her head faded away. She felt the full weight of him come back, squeezing the air from her body, but she did not move. She stroked his thick black hair and held him in her arms. It was a moment before she realized his face was wet, that he was silently crying.

"Oh, Hal," she murmured in pity.

"Tell me something about yourself," he said a little later. "You know so much about me, what I'm doing here—too much, probably—but I know next to nothing about you, Ms. Martin."

Meredith laughed. "How very formal, Mr. Lawrence," she said, moving her hand across his chest and lower.

Hal grabbed her fingers. "I'm serious! I don't even know where you live. Where you come from. What your parents do. Come on, tell."

Meredith knitted her fingers through his. "Okay. One résumé coming right up. I grew up in Milwaukee, stayed there until I was eighteen, then went to college in North Carolina. I stayed on and did post-grad research there, had a couple of teaching jobs at graduate colleges—one in Saint Louis, one outside Seattle—all the time trying to get funding to finish my Debussy biography. Fast-forward a couple of years. My adoptive parents upped sticks, left Milwaukee and moved to Chapel Hill, close by my old college. Earlier this year I was offered a job in a private college not far from UNC and, at last, a publishing deal."

"Adoptive parents?" said Hal.

Meredith sighed. "My birth mother, Jeanette, was not able to take care of me. Mary is a distant cousin, a kind of aunt a couple of times removed. I'd spent time with them, on and off, when Jeanette was sick. When things finally got too bad, I went to live with them for good. They formally adopted me a couple of years later, when my birth mom . . . died."

The plain, carefully chosen words did not do justice to the years of late-night phone calls, the unannounced visits, the shouting in the street, the burden of responsibility the child Meredith had felt for her damaged and volatile mother. Nor did her matter-of-fact recitation of the facts hint at the guilt she carried with her still, all these years later, that her first reaction on hearing her mother was dead was not one of grief but relief.

She couldn't forgive herself for that.

"Sounds tough," Hal said.

Meredith smiled at his British understatement and shifted closer against his warm body beside her in the bed.

"I was lucky," she said. "Mary is an amazing lady. It was she who got me started on the violin, then the piano. I owe everything to her and Bill."

He grinned. "So you really are writing a biography of Debussy?" he teased.

Meredith hit him playfully on the arm. "Sure am!"

For a moment, they lay in companionable silence, still and touching.

"But there is something more to you being here than that," Hal said in the end. He turned his head on the pillow toward the framed portrait across the other side of the room. "I'm not wrong about that, am I?"

Meredith sat up, pulling the sheet up with her, so only her shoulders were uncovered.

"No, you're not wrong."

Picking up that she wasn't quite ready to speak, Hal sat up, too, and swung his legs to the floor. "Is there anything I can get you? A drink? Anything?"

"A glass of water would be good," she said.

She watched as he disappeared into the bathroom, emerging seconds later with two tooth mugs, then grabbed a couple of bottles from the minibar before climbing back into bed.

"Here you go."

"Thanks," Meredith said, taking a mouthful from the bottle. "Until now, all I knew about my birth mother's family was that they might have come from this part of France during—or just after—World War I and settled in America. I have a photograph of, I'm pretty sure, my great-grandfather, in French army uniform, taken in the square in Rennes-les-Bains in 1914. The story was he ended up in Milwaukee, but since I didn't have a name, I couldn't get much further. The city had a large European population from the early nineteenth century. The first permanent European resident was a French trader, Jacques

Vieau, who established a trading post on the bluffs where the three rivers—the Milwaukee, the Menomonee and the Kinnickinnic—meet. So, it was plausible enough."

For the next few minutes, she gave Hal a skeleton version of what she'd discovered since arriving at the Domaine de la Cade, keeping to the hard facts, all pretty straightforward. She told him why she'd taken the portrait from the lobby and the piece of music that she'd inherited from her grandmother, Louisa Martin, but did not mention the cards. There had been more than enough uncomfortable discussion in the bar earlier, and Meredith sure didn't want to remind Hal of his uncle now.

"So you think your unknown soldier is a Vernier," Hal said, when Meredith had talked herself to a standstill.

She nodded. "The physical resemblance is overwhelming. Coloring, features. He could be a younger brother or a cousin, I guess, but taking the dates and his age into consideration, I'm thinking he could be a direct descendant." She stopped, letting a smile break out on her face. "Then, just before I came down to supper, I got an e-mail from Mary saying that there was a record of a Vernier in the graveyard at Mitchell Point, Milwaukee."

Hal smiled. "So you think Anatole Vernier was his father?"

"I don't know. That's the next step." She sighed. "Maybe Léonie's son?"

"Then he wouldn't be a Vernier, would he?"

"He would if she wasn't married."

Hal nodded. "Fair enough."

"So, here's the deal. Tomorrow, after we've visited with Dr. O'Donnell, you help me do a little research into the Verniers."

"Deal," he said lightly, but Meredith could feel he'd tensed again. "I know you think I'm making too much of it, but I'd really appreciate you being here. She's coming at ten."

"Well," she murmured softly, feeling herself growing sleepy. "As you said, she's more likely to talk with another woman there."

She was struggling to keep her eyes open. Slowly, Meredith felt herself drifting away from Hal. The silver moon made her progress across the black Midi sky. Below in the valley, the bell tolled the passing of the hours.

67

In her dream, Meredith was sitting at the piano at the foot of the stairs. The chill of the keys and the melody were familiar beneath her fingers. She was playing Louisa's signature piece, better than she had ever played it before, sweet and yet haunting.

Then the piano vanished and she was walking along a narrow and empty corridor. There was a patch of light at the end and a set of stone stairs, dipped and worn away in the center by the passage of feet and time. She turned to go, but found herself always standing in the same place. It was somewhere within the Domaine de la Cade, she knew, but not a part of the house or grounds she recognized.

The light, a perfect square, was coming from a gas jet on the wall, which hissed and spat at her as she passed. Facing her at the top of the steps was an old and dusty tapestry of a hunt. She stared a moment at the cruel expressions of the men, the smears of red blood on their spears. Except, as she looked with her dream eyes, she realized it was not an animal they were hunting. Not a bear, not a wild boar, not a wolf. Instead, a black creature, standing on two legs with cloven feet, an expression of rage on its almost-human features. A demon, his claws tipped red.

Asmodeus.

In the background, flames. The wood was burning.

In her bed, Meredith moaned and shifted position as her dreaming hands, both weighted and weightless, pushed at an old wooden door. There was a carpet of silver dust on the ground, glinting in the moonlight or the halo from the gaslight.

The air was still. At the same time, the room wasn't damp or cold like a space left empty. Time jumped forward. Now Meredith could hear the piano again, but this time distorted. Like the sound of a fairground or a carousel, menacing and sinister.

Her breath came faster. Her sleeping hands clutched at the covers as she reached out and grasped the cold metal latch.

She pushed open the door. Stepped over the stone step.

No birds flew up, there was no whispering of voices, hidden, behind the door. Now she was standing inside some kind of chapel. High ceilings, flagstone floors, an altar and plain glass windows. Paintings covering the walls, immediately recognizable as the characters from the cards. A sepulchre.

It was utterly silent. Nothing but the echo of her footsteps disturbed the hush. And yet little by little, the air began to whisper. She could hear voices, noises in the darkness. At least voices behind the silence. And singing.

She moved forward and felt the air part, as if unseen spirits lost in the light were standing back to let her pass. The very space itself seemed to be holding its breath, beating in time with the heavy thump of her heart.

Meredith kept walking until she stood before the altar, placed an equal distance from each of the four windows set inside the octagonal walls. She was standing now inside a square, marked in black upon the stone floor. Around it, letters inscribed on the ground.

Help me.

Someone was there. In the darkness and the silence, something was moving. Meredith felt the space around her shrinking, folding in upon itself. She could see nothing, yet she knew she was there. A living, breathing presence in the fabric of the air. And she knew she had sensed her before—beneath the bridge, on the road, at the foot of her bed. Air, water, fire and now earth. The four suits of the tarot, containing within them all the possibilities.

Hear me. Listen to me.

Meredith felt herself falling down into a place of stillness and peace. She was not afraid. She was no longer herself but instead standing outside, looking in. And clear in the darkness, she heard her own sleeping voice speak calmly out.

"Léonie?"

It seemed to Meredith now that there was a different quality in the darkness and in the air around the shrouded figure, a shifting of the air, almost like a wind. The figure gave a slight movement of her head. Long copper curls, color without substance, unveiled as the hood fell from her hair. Skin translucent. Green eyes, although transparent. Form without substance. A long black dress beneath the cloak. Shape without form.

I am Léonie.

Meredith heard the words inside her head. A young girl's voice, a voice from an earlier time. Again, the atmosphere in the room seemed to shift. As if the space itself gave a sigh of relief.

I cannot sleep. Until I am found, I can never sleep. Hear the truth.

"The truth? About what?" Meredith whispered. The light was changing, loosening.

The story is in the cards.

There was a rushing of air, a shifting of the light, a shimmering of something—someone—withdrawing. The atmosphere was different again now. There was a threat in the darkness, which Léonie had held at bay. But the gentle presence of the ghost had vanished, replaced by something destructive. A malevolence. The air was now oppressively cold, pushing in on Meredith. Like an early-morning mist at sea, the sharp tang of salt and fish and smoke. She felt the need to run, although she did not know from what. She felt herself edging toward the door.

There was something behind her. A black figure or some kind of creature. Meredith could almost feel its breath on the back of her neck, puffs of white clouds in the frigid air. But the passage to the sepulchre was receding. The wooden door was getting smaller and more distant.

Un, deux, trois, loup! Coming to get you, ready or not.

Something snapping at heels, gaining speed in the shadows, getting ready to leap. Meredith started to run, fear giving power to her shaking legs. Her sneakers were skidding, sliding, on the flagstone floor. Always behind her, the breathing.

Nearly there.

She threw herself at the wooden door, feeling her shoulder crashing into the frame, sending pain ricocheting down her arm. The creature was right behind, the bristling of its fur, the stench of iron and blood melting into her skin, the surface of her scalp and the soles of her feet. She fumbled at the latch, rattling, tugging, jerking it toward her, but it wouldn't open.

She started to bang on the door, trying not to look over her shoulder, trying not to be caught in the gaze of its hideous blue eyes. She could feel the silence deepen around her. Could feel its malevolent arms coming down around her neck, wet and cold and rough. The smell of the sea, dragging her down into its fatal depths.

68

Meredith! Meredith. It's all right. You're safe, it's all right."
She called out, waking with a massive jolt that left her gasping for breath. Every muscle in her body was alert, every nerve screaming. The cotton sheets were tangled and mussed. Her fingers were locked rigid. For a moment she was subsumed by a devouring anger, as if the rage of the creature had forced its way through the surface of her skin.

"Meredith, it's okay! I'm here."

She was trying to pry herself free, disoriented, until gradually she realized that she felt warm skin holding her tight to save her, not to harm her.

"Hal."

The tension fell from her shoulders.

"You were having a nightmare," he said, "that's all. It's all right."

"She was here. She was here . . . then . . . it came and . . ."

"Ssh, it's okay," he said again.

Meredith stared at him. She reached up her hand and with her fingers traced the contours of his face.

"She came . . . and then, behind her, coming to . . ."

"There's no one here but us. Just a nightmare. It's all over now."

Meredith looked round the room, as if expecting at any moment someone to step out of a black corner. At the same time, she knew the dream had passed. Slowly, she let Hal take her in his arms. She felt the warmth and the strength of him pulling her closer, holding her safe, tight against his chest. She could feel the bones of her rib cage as they rose and fell, rose and fell, her heart thumping.

"I saw her," she murmured, although she was talking to herself now, not Hal.

"Who?" he whispered.

She didn't answer.

"It's all right," he repeated gently. "Go back to sleep."

He began to stroke her head, smoothing her bangs back from her forehead like Mary used to do when Meredith first went to live with her, soothing away the nightmares.

"She was here," Meredith said again.

Gradually, beneath the repetitive and gentle motion of Hal's hand, the terror faded away. Her eyelids became heavy, her arms and legs and body, too, as the warmth and feeling came back.

Four o'clock in the morning.

Clouds had covered the moon, and it was completely dark. The lovers, learning to know each other, fell back to sleep in each other's arms, shrouded in the deep blue of early morning before the day comes.

Part IX

The Glade
October—November 1891

69

Friday, October 23, 1891

When Léonie woke the following morning, the first thought that came to her mind was of Victor Constant, as it had been the last before she went to sleep.

Wishing to feel the fresh air on her face, she dressed quickly and let herself out into the early morning. Evidence of yesterday's storm was all around, broken branches, leaves sent flying by the agitating wind. Everything was quite still now, and the pink dawn sky was clear. But in the distance, over the Pyrenees, a gray bank of storm clouds threatened more bad weather to come.

Léonie took a turn around the lake, pausing awhile on the small promontory that overlooked the choppy waters, then walked slowly back toward the house across the lawns. The hem of her skirts glistened with the dew. Her feet left barely an imprint on the wet grass.

She walked round to the front door, which she had left unbolted when she had slipped out, then stepped into the hall. She stamped her boots on the rough-haired mat. Then she pushed the hood from her face, unhooked the clasp and hung her cloak back on the metal hook from which she had taken it earlier.

As she walked across the red and black tiles toward the dining room, she realized that she hoped Anatole had not yet descended for breakfast. Although she worried for Isolde's health, Léonie was still sulking about their headlong and premature departure from Carcassonne the previous evening, and did not wish to be obliged to be civil to her brother.

She opened the door and found the room deserted apart from the maid, who was setting the enamel red-and-blue patterned coffeepot on the metal trivet in the center of the table.

Marieta gave a half-bob. "Madomaisèla."

"Good morning."

Léonie walked round to take her customary seat on the far side of the long oval table, so that she was facing the door.

Two thoughts preyed on her mind. That if the ill weather was continuing in Carcassonne without respite, then the *patron* of the hotel might be unable to deliver her letter to Victor Constant in the Square Gambetta. Or if, due to the torrential rain, the concert would be canceled. She felt helpless and thoroughly frustrated at the realization that she had no way of being certain whether or not Monsieur Constant had received her communication.

Not unless he chooses to write to tell me so.

She sighed and shook out her napkin. "Has my brother come down, Marieta?"

"No, Madomaisèla. You are the first."

"And my aunt? Is she recovered after last evening?"

Marieta paused, then dropped her voice, as if confiding a great secret. "Do you not know, Madomaisèla? Madama was taken that bad in the night that Sénher Anatole was obliged to send to town for the doctor."

"What?" Léonie gasped. She rose from her seat. "I had no idea. I should go to her."

"Best to leave her," Marieta said quickly. "Madama was sleeping like a baby not thirty minutes past."

Léonie sat down again. "Well, what did the doctor say?" she questioned. "Dr. Gabignaud, was it?"

Marieta nodded. "That Madama had caught a chill, which was threatening to develop into something worse. He gave her a powder to bring down the fever. He stayed with her, your brother, too, all night."

"What is the diagnosis now?"

"You will have to ask Sénher Anatole, Madomaisèla. The doctor spoke with him in private."

Léonie felt dreadful, guilty about her previous uncharitable thoughts and that she had somehow slept through the night without having the first idea of the crisis taking place elsewhere in the house. Her stomach was full of knots, like a ball of thread tangled and twisted out of shape. She doubted that she would be able to let even the smallest morsel pass her lips.

However, when Marieta returned and placed in front of her a plate of salted mountain bacon, fresh eggs from the pullets and warm white bread with a turned roll of churned butter, she felt she might manage a little.

She ate in silence, her thoughts flipping backward and forward like a fish thrown upon the riverbank, first worrying about her aunt's health, then more pleasurable thoughts of Monsieur Constant, then back to Isolde.

She heard the sound of footsteps crossing the hall. Tossing her napkin to the table, she leapt to her feet and ran to the door, coming face to face with Anatole in the hall.

He was pale and had hollow circles under his eyes, like black finger marks, betraying the fact that he had not slept.

"Forgive me, Anatole, I have only just heard. Marieta suggested it would be better to leave Tante Isolde to sleep than disturb her. Is the doctor returning this morning? Is—"

Despite his wretched appearance, Anatole smiled. He held up his hand, as if to deflect the volley of questions.

"*Calme-toi*," he said, placing his arm around her shoulder. "The worst is over."

"But—"

"Isolde will be fine. Gabignaud was excellent. Gave her something to help her sleep. She is weak, but the fever has gone. It's nothing that a few days' bed rest will not cure."

Léonie shocked herself by bursting into tears. She had not realized how much affection she had come to feel for her quiet, gentle aunt.

"Come, *petite*," he said affectionately. "No need to cry. Everything will be fine. Nothing to get worked up about."

"Let's not ever argue again," Léonie wailed. "I cannot bear it when we are not friends."

"Nor I," he said, pulling his handkerchief from his pocket and handing it to her. Léonie wiped her tear-stained face, then blew her nose.

"How very unladylike!" He laughed. "M'man would be most displeased with you." He grinned down at her. "Now, have you breakfasted?"

Léonie nodded.

"Well, I have not. Will you keep me company?"

FOR THE REST of the day, Léonie stayed close to her brother, all thoughts of Victor Constant pushed to the side for the time being. For now, the Domaine de la Cade and the love and affection of those sheltering within it were the sole focus of her heart and mind.

Over the course of the weekend, Isolde kept to her bed. She was weak and tired easily, but Léonie read to her in the afternoons, and little by little the color came back to her cheeks. Anatole busied himself with matters concerning the estate on her behalf and even sat with her in her chamber in the evenings. If the servants found such familiarity surprising, they did not remark upon it in Léonie's hearing.

Several times, Léonie caught Anatole looking at her as if he was on the point of confiding something. But whenever she questioned him, he smiled and said it was nothing, then dropped his eyes and carried on with what he was doing.

By Sunday evening, Isolde's appetite had returned sufficiently for a supper tray to be taken to her room. Léonie was pleased to see that the hollow, drawn expression had gone and she no longer looked so thin. Indeed, in some respects, she looked in better health than before. There was a glow to her skin, a brightness to her eyes. Léonie knew that Anatole had noticed it, too. He walked around the house whistling and looking much relieved.

The main topic of conversation in the servants' quarters was the severe flooding in Carcassonne. From Friday morning to Sunday evening, town and countryside alike had been racked by the sequence of storms. Communications were disrupted and in some areas suspended altogether.

The situation around Rennes-les-Bains and Quillan was bad, certainly, but no more than one might expect during the autumn season of storms. But by Monday evening, news of the catastrophe that had struck Carcassonne reached the Domaine de la Cade. After three days of relentless rain, worse on the plains than in the villages higher up in the mountains, in the early hours of Sunday morning, the River Aude had finally burst its banks, flooding the Bastide and the low-lying river areas. Early reports had it that much of the quartier Trivalle and the quartier Barbacane were completely underwater. The Pont Vieux, linking the medieval Cité to the Bastide, was submerged although passable. The gardens of the Hôpital des Malades were knee-deep in black floodwaters. Several other buildings on the left bank had fallen into the torrent.

Farther up the swollen river, toward the weir at Païchérou, whole trees had been uprooted, twisted and clinging desperately to the mud.

Léonie listened to the news with increasing anxiety. She feared for the well-being of Monsieur Constant. There was no reason to believe any ill had befallen him, but her worries played remorselessly upon her. Her anguish was all the worse for being unable to admit to Anatole that she knew the flooded neighborhoods or that she had some specific interest in the matter.

Léonie reprimanded herself. She knew it was perfectly absurd to feel so strongly for a person in whose company she had spent little more than an hour. Yet Monsieur Constant had taken residence in her romantic mind, and she could not shake her thoughts free of him. So whereas in the early weeks of October she had sat in the window and waited for a letter from her mother from Paris, now, at the tail end of the month, she instead wondered if there was a letter from Carcassonne lying unclaimed in the boxes at the poste restante in Rennes-les-Bains.

The question was how she could make the trip to town in person? She could hardly entrust so delicate a matter to one of the servants, not even the amiable Pascal or sweet Marieta. And there was another concern: if the *patron* of the hotel had not delivered her note to the Square Gambetta at the appointed time, in the event the concert had not been postponed, then Monsieur Constant—who was clearly a principled man—would be honor-bound to let the matter drop.

The thought that he would not know where to find her—or equally, that he might be thinking ill of her for her discourtesy in not keeping to their discreet arrangement—played endlessly on her mind.

70

H er chance came three days later.

On Wednesday evening, Isolde was improved enough to join Anatole and Léonie for dinner in the dining room. She ate little. Or, rather, she sampled many dishes, but none seemed to her liking. Even the coffee, freshly brewed from the beans Léonie had purchased for her in Carcassonne, was not to her taste.

Anatole fussed around her, endlessly suggesting different collations that might tempt her, but in the end only succeeded in persuading her to eat a little white bread and churned butter, with a little *chèvre trois jours* and honey.

"Is there anything? Whatever it is, I will endeavor to get it for you."

Isolde smiled. "Everything tastes so peculiar."

"You must eat," he said firmly. "You need to recover your strength and . . ."

He stopped short. Léonie noticed a look pass between them and again wondered what he had been about to say.

"I can go down into Rennes-les-Bains tomorrow and purchase whatever you would like," he continued.

Léonie suddenly had an idea. "I could go," she said, trying to keep her voice light. "Rather than tear you away, Anatole, it would be my pleasure to go down to the town." She turned to Isolde. "I am well acquainted with your tastes, *Tante*. If the gig could be spared in the morning, Pascal could drive me." She paused. "I could bring back a tin of crystallized ginger from the Magasins Bousquet."

To her delight and excitement, Léonie saw a spark of interest flare in Isolde's pale gray eyes.

"I confess, that is something I could manage," she admitted.

"And perhaps also," Léonie added, quickly running through Isolde's favorite treats in her mind, "I could visit the *patissier* and purchase a box of Jesuites?"

Léonie detested the heavy, sickly cream cakes but was aware that Isolde could be occasionally persuaded to indulge herself.

"They might be a little rich for me at present." Isolde smiled. "But some of those black-pepper biscuits might be quite the thing."

Anatole was smiling at her and nodding.

"Very well," he said. "That is settled then." He covered Léonie's small hand with his. "I am more than happy to come with you, *petite*, if you wish it."

"Not at all. It will be an adventure. I am certain there are plenty of things to occupy your time here."

He glanced across at Isolde. "True," he concurred. "Well, if you are certain, Léonie."

"Quite certain," she said briskly. "I will leave at ten o'clock, so as to be back in good time for luncheon. I shall compile a list."

"You are kind to go to so much trouble," Isolde said.

"It is my pleasure," Léonie replied, truthfully.

She had done it. Provided she could slip away to the poste restante without Pascal's knowledge sometime during the course of the morning, she would be able to put her mind at rest as to Monsieur Constant's intentions toward her, for good or ill.

When Léonie retired for the evening, she was dreaming of how it might feel to hold his letter in her hand, what such a billet-doux might say, the feelings that might be expressed therein.

Indeed, by the time she finally fell asleep, she had already composed, a hundred times over, a beautifully drafted response to Monsieur Constant's— imagined—elegantly stated protestations of affection and regard.

THE MORNING OF Thursday, October 29, was glorious.

The Domaine de la Cade was bathed in a soft copper light, beneath an endless blue sky, spotted here and there with generous white clouds. And it was mild. The days of storms had gone out, bringing in their place the memory of the scent of summer breezes. An *été indien*.

At a quarter past ten, Léonie stepped down from the gig in the Place du

Pérou, dressed for the occasion in her favorite crimson day dress, with matching jacket and hat. With her shopping list in her hand, she promenaded along the Gran'Rue, visiting each of the shops in turn. Pascal accompanied her to carry her various purchases from the Magasins Bousquet; from Les Frères Marcel Pâtisserie et Chocolaterie, *boulangerie artisanale;* and from the haberdashery where she purchased some thread. She paused for a *sirop de grenadine* at the street-side café adjoining the Maison Gravère, where she and Anatole had taken coffee on their first expedition, and felt quite at home.

Indeed, Léonie felt as if she belonged to the town and the town to her. And although one or two people with whom she had a passing acquaintance were a little cold to her, or so it seemed—the wives looking away and the husbands barely lifting their hats as she passed—Léonie dismissed the notion that she could have given some offense. She now believed wholeheartedly that although she considered herself thoroughly Parisian, in point of fact she felt more alive, more vital in the wooded landscape of the mountains and lakes of the Aude than ever she had in the city.

Now the thought of the dirty streets and soot of the eighth arrondissement, not to mention the limitations placed on her freedom, appalled her. Certainly, if Anatole could persuade their mother to join them for Christmas, then Léonie would be more than content to remain at the Domaine de la Cade until the New Year and beyond.

Her tasks were quickly accomplished. By eleven o'clock, all that remained was to slip away from Pascal for long enough to make her detour to the poste restante. She asked him to convey the packages back to the gig, which had been left in the care of one of his many nephews by the drinking trough a little to the south of the main square. She then declared that she intended to pay her respects to Monsieur Baillard.

Pascal's expression hardened. "I was not aware he had returned to Rennes-les-Bains, Madomaisèla Léonie," he said.

Their eyes met. "I do not know for certain that he has," she admitted. "But it is no trouble to walk there and back. I shall meet you in the Place du Pérou presently."

As she was speaking, Léonie suddenly realized how she could engineer an opportunity to read the letter in private. "In point of fact, Pascal," she added quickly, "you may leave me. I believe I shall walk all the way back to the Domaine de la Cade instead. You need not wait."

Pascal's face flushed red. "I am certain Sénher Anatole would not wish me to abandon you here to make the return journey on foot," he said, his expression making it clear that he knew how her brother had scolded Marieta for letting Léonie slip from her charge in Carcassonne.

"My brother did not give you instructions that I should not be left unaccompanied," she said immediately, "did he?"

Pascal was forced to concede that he had not.

"Well, then. I am confident of the path through the woods," she said firmly. "Marieta brought us through the rear entrance to the Domaine de la Cade, as you know, so it is not unknown to me. It is such a fine day, possibly the last of this year's sun, I cannot believe my brother would not wish me to take advantage of the good air."

Pascal did not move.

"That will be all," Léonie said, more sharply than she intended.

He stared at her a moment longer, his broad face impassive, then suddenly he grinned. "As you wish, Madomaisèla Léonie," he said in his calm, steady voice, "but you shall answer to Sénher Anatole, not I."

"I shall tell him that I insisted you left me, yes."

"And, by your leave, I shall send Marieta to unlock the gates and walk to meet you halfway down. In case you mistake the path."

Léonie felt humbled, both by Pascal's good nature in the face of her ill temper and by his concern for her well-being. For the truth was that despite her fighting talk, she was a little anxious at the thought of going alone all the way through the woods.

"Thank you, Pascal," she said softly. "I promise I will be quick. My aunt and brother will not even notice."

He nodded, then, with his arms full of the packages, turned on his heel and walked away. Léonie watched him go. As he turned the corner, something else caught her eye. She glimpsed a person in a blue cape darting into the passageway that led to the church, as if he did not wish to be seen. Léonie frowned but put it out of her mind as she retraced her steps back toward the river.

As a precaution in case Pascal should take it upon himself to follow her, she had decided to walk to the poste restante via the road in which Monsieur Baillard's lodgings were to be found.

She smiled at a couple of Isolde's acquaintances but did not stop to pass the time of day. Within minutes, she had reached her destination. To her intense surprise, the blue shutters of the tiny house were pinned back.

Léonie stopped. Isolde had been certain Monsieur Baillard had quit Rennes-les-Bains for the foreseeable future. At least until Toussaint, All Saints' Day, or so she had been told. Had the house been let to someone else for the interim? Or had he returned ahead of time?

Léonie glanced down the rue de l'Hermite, which led, at the river end, to the street where the poste restante was situated. She was in a fever of excitement about the possibility of receiving her letter. She had thought of little else for days. But having enjoyed a period of exquisite anticipation, she was suddenly fearful that her hopes might be on the point of being dashed. That there might be no communication from Monsieur Constant.

And she had been regretting the absence of Monsieur Baillard now for some weeks. If she passed by without stopping and later discovered she had missed an opportunity to renew her acquaintance with him, she would never forgive herself.

If there is a letter, it will still be there in ten minutes' time.

Léonie stepped forward and rapped on the door.

For a moment, nothing happened. She leaned her ear closer to the painted panels and could just pick out the sound of feet walking across a tiled floor.

"*Oc?*" came a child's voice.

She took a step back as the door was opened, suddenly shy that she had taken it upon herself to call uninvited. A small dark-haired boy with eyes the color of blackberries stood looking up at her.

"Is Monsieur Baillard at home?" she said. "It is Léonie Vernier. The niece of Madame Lascombe. From the Domaine de la Cade."

"He is expecting you?"

"He is not. I was passing so I took the liberty of paying an impromptu visit. If it is inconvenient . . ."

"*Que ès?*"

The boy turned. Léonie smiled with pleasure at the sound of Monsieur Baillard's voice. Emboldened, she called out.

"It is Léonie Vernier, Monsieur Baillard."

Moments later, the distinctive figure in the white suit she remembered so clearly from the evening of the dinner party appeared at the end of the passageway. Even in the gloom of the narrow entrance, Léonie could see he was smiling.

"Madomaisèla Léonie," he said. "An unexpected pleasure."

"I have been undertaking certain tasks for my aunt—she has been unwell—and Pascal has gone ahead. I had thought you were away from Rennes-les-Bains at present, but when I saw the shutters pinned back, I . . ."

She realized she was gabbling, and checked her tongue.

"I am delighted you did so," Baillard said. "Please, do come in."

Léonie hesitated. Although he was a man of some reputation, an acquaintance of Tante Isolde and on visiting terms with the Domaine de la Cade, she was aware it might be considered inappropriate for a young girl to enter the house of a gentleman alone.

But then who is here to witness it?

"Thank you," she said. "I should be delighted."

She stepped over the threshold.

71

Léonie followed Monsieur Baillard down the passageway, which opened into a pleasant room at the rear of the tiny house. A single large window dominated the whole of one wall.

"Oh," she exclaimed. "The view is quite as perfect as a picture."

"It is." He smiled. "I am fortunate."

He rang a small silver bell that sat on a low side table next to the wing armchair in which he had clearly been sitting, beside the wide stone fireplace. The same boy reappeared. Léonie discreetly cast her eyes around the room. It was a plain and simple chamber, with a selection of mismatched chairs, a boudoir table behind the sofa. Bookcases covered the length of the wall opposite the fireplace, every inch of them filled.

"There, now," he said. "Please, take a seat. Tell me your news, Madomaisèla Léonie. I trust all is well at the Domaine de la Cade. You said your aunt was indisposed, Nothing serious, I hope?"

Léonie removed her hat and gloves, then settled herself opposite him.

"She is much improved. We were caught out in the ill weather last week and my aunt developed a chill. The doctor was called, but the worst is over and every day she grows stronger."

"Her condition hangs in the balance," he said, "and it is early days. But all will be well."

Léonie looked at him, puzzled at this non sequitur, but at that moment the boy returned carrying a brass tray with two ornate glass goblets and a silver jug on it, much like a coffee pot but with swirling diamond patterns, and the question died on her lips.

"It comes from the Holy Land," her host told her. "A gift from an old friend, many years ago now."

The servant handed her a glass filled with a thick red liquid.

"What is this, Monsieur Baillard?"

"A local cherry liqueur, *guignolet*. I admit, I am rather partial to it. It is particularly good when taken with these black-pepper biscuits." He nodded, and the boy offered the plate to Léonie. "They are a local speciality and can be purchased everywhere, but I judge those baked here at the Frères Marcel quite the best I have tasted."

"I bought some myself," Léonie replied. She took a mouthful of *guignolet,* then immediately coughed. It was sweet, tasting intensely of wild cherries, but very strong indeed.

"You have returned earlier than we were expecting," she said. "My aunt led me to believe that you would be away until November at least, perhaps even until Noel."

"My business was quicker to conclude than I had expected, so I returned. There are stories coming up from the town. I felt here I might be of more use."

Use? Léonie thought it an odd word but said nothing of it.

"Where did you go, Monsieur?"

"To visit old friends," he said quietly. "Also, I have a house some way into the mountains. In a tiny village called Los Seres, not so far from the old fortress citadel of Montségur. I wished to ensure that it was ready, should I need to repair there in the foreseeable future."

Léonie frowned. "Is that likely, Monsieur? I was under the impression that you had taken lodgings here in town in order to avoid the rigors of winter in the mountains."

His eyes sparkled. "I have lived through many mountain winters, Madomaisèla," he said softly. "Some hard, others less so." He fell silent a moment and seemed to drift into thought. "But, tell me," he said finally, gathering himself together once more, "what of you these past weeks? Have you had any further adventures, Madomaisèla Léonie, since last we met?"

She met his gaze. "I have not returned to the sepulchre, Monsieur Baillard," she said, "if that is your meaning."

He smiled. "That was indeed my meaning."

"Although, I must confess, the subject of tarot has continued to hold some interest for me." She scrutinized his expression, but his timeworn face gave nothing away. "I have begun a sequence of paintings also." She hesitated. "Reproductions of the images from the walls."

"Is that so?"

"They are studies, I suppose. No, in point of fact, they are rather copies."

He leaned forward in his chair. "And you have attempted all of them?"

"Well, no," she answered, although thinking it a singular question. "Just those at the beginning. What they term the major arcana, and even then, not each character. I find that I am disinclined to attempt certain of the images. For example, Le Diable."

"And La Tour?"

Her green eyes narrowed. "Quite. Nor the Tower. How did—"

"When did you begin these paintings, Madomaisèla?"

"The afternoon of the supper party. I wished only to occupy myself, to fill the empty hours of waiting. Without the slightest conscious design, I found I had painted myself into the picture, Monsieur Baillard, so I felt moved to continue."

"May I ask within which of them?"

"La Force." She paused, then shivered as she recollected the complication of emotions that had swept over her at that moment. "The face was my face. Why do you think that should be?"

"The most obvious explanation would be that you see the characteristic of strength within yourself."

Léonie waited, expecting more, until it became clear that again Monsieur Baillard had said all he intended to on the matter.

"I admit I find myself increasingly intrigued by my uncle and the experiences of which he writes in his monograph *Les Tarots*," Léonie continued. "I do not wish to press you against your better judgment, Monsieur Baillard, but I have wondered if you knew my uncle at the time of the events detailed in the book?" She scanned his face, looking for signs of encouragement or else displeasure at the line of questioning, but his expression remained unreadable. "I have realized the . . . situation sits precisely within the period of time after my mother had left the Domaine de la Cade and yet before my aunt and uncle married." She hesitated. "I imagine, without intending to be disrespectful in any way, that he was by nature a solitary man. Not drawn much to the company of others?"

She stopped once more, giving Monsieur Baillard the opportunity to make some response. He remained perfectly still, his veined hands in his lap, seemingly content to listen.

"From comments Tante Isolde has made," Léonie ploughed on, "I gained the impression that you had been instrumental in effecting an introduction between my uncle and Abbé Saunière, when he was appointed to the parish at Rennes-le-Château. She also hinted at some unpleasantness, rumors, incidents traced back to the sepulchre, which required the intervention of a priest. As you had."

"Ah." Audric Baillard pressed the tips of his fingers together.

She took a deep breath. "I have . . . Did the Abbé Saunière perform an exorcism on behalf of my uncle, is that it? Did such an . . . an event take place within the sepulchre?"

This time, having asked the question, Léonie did not rush in. She allowed the silence to do the work of persuasion. For an endless time, or so it seemed, the only sound was the ticking of the clock. In a room beyond the passageway, she could just discern the chinking of crockery and the distinctive rough scratching of a broom on the wooden boards.

"To rid the place of evil," she said eventually. "Is that so? Once or twice I have glimpsed it. But I realize now that my mother might have felt its presence, Monsieur, when she was a girl. She quitted the Domaine as soon as she was able."

72

In certain decks of tarot cards," Baillard said eventually, "the card representing the Devil is modeled upon the head of Baphomet, the idol the Poor Knights of the Temple of Solomon were accused—falsely—of worshipping."

Léonie nodded, pleased he was speaking, although it was not clear to her how this digression might be of relevance.

"There was said to be a Templar presbytery not far from here, at Bézu," he continued. "No such thing existed, of course. In the matter of historical record, there has been confusion in the collective memory, a conflation of the Albigensians and the Poor Knights. They did bestride the earth contemporaneously but were little connected one with the other. A coincidence of timing, not an overlapping."

"But how does this connect to the Domaine de la Cade, Monsieur Baillard?"

He smiled. "You observed, on your visit, the statue of Asmodeus in the sepulchre, è? Bearing the burden of the *bénitier*?"

"I did."

"Asmodeus, also known as Ashmadia or Asmodai, is most likely derived from a form of Persian, the phrase *aeshma-daeva*, meaning demon of wrath. Asmodeus appears in the deuterocanonical Book of Tobit and, again, in the Testament of Solomon, which is a pseudepigraphical work of the Old Testament. That is, a work purportedly written by and attributed to Solomon but unlikely to have been so in historical truth."

Léonie nodded, even though her knowledge of the Old Testament was somewhat limited. Neither she nor Anatole had attended Sunday school or learned their catechism. Religious superstition, their mother claimed, sat ill with modern sensibilities. Traditional in ways of society and manners, Marguerite was a vehement opponent of the Church. Léonie suddenly wondered, for the first time, if the violence of her mother's feelings could be traced back to the atmosphere of the Domaine de la Cade, where she had endured her childhood, and made a note to ask her at the earliest opportunity.

Monsieur Baillard's calm voice called her back from her reflections.

"The story tells of how King Solomon invokes Asmodeus to aid in the construction of the Temple—the great Temple. Asmodeus, a demon most particularly associated with lust, does appear, but his presence is disturbing. He predicts that Solomon's kingdom will one day be divided."

Baillard stood up, crossed the room and took from a shelf a small brown leatherbound book. He turned the tissue-thin pages with his delicate fingers until he found the passage he wanted.

"It reads: 'My constellation is like an animal which reclines in its den,' spake the demon. So do not ask me so many things, Solomon, for eventually your kingdom will be divided. This glory of yours is temporary. You have us to torture for a little while; then we shall disperse among human beings again with the result that we shall be worshipped as gods because men do not know the name of the angels who rule over us.'" He closed the book and looked up. "Testament of Solomon, chapter five, verses four and five."

Léonie did not know how she should react to this, so she remained silent.

"Asmodeus, as I said previously, is a demon associated with carnal desires," Baillard continued. "He is most especially an enemy of newlyweds. In the apocryphal Book of Tobit, he torments a woman called Sarah, killing each of her seven husbands before the marriages can be consummated. On the eighth occasion, the angel Raphaël instructs Sarah's latest suitor to place the heart and liver of a fish on red-hot cinders. The smoky, foul-smelling vapor repels Asmodeus and causes him to flee to Egypt, where Raphaël binds him, his power broken."

Léonie shivered, not at his words but at the sudden memory of the faint but disgusting stench that had assailed her senses in the sepulchre. An inexplicable scent of damp, smoke and the sea.

"These parables seem rather archaic, do they not?" said her host. "They are intended to convey some larger truth but so often serve only to obscure." He tapped the leather book with his long, thin fingers. "In the Book of Solomon, it is also said that Asmodeus detests being near water."

Léonie sat up straighter. "Hence perhaps the holy water stoup being set upon his shoulders? Could that be, Monsieur Baillard?"

"It could," he agreed. "Asmodeus appears in other works of religious commentary. In the Talmud, for example, he corresponds with Ashmedai, a far less malevolent character than the Asmodeus of Tobit, although his desires are focused on Solomon's wives and Bathsheba. Some years later, in the middle of the fifteenth century, Asmodai appears as the demon of lust in the *Malleus Maleficarum*, a rather simplistic catalogue, to my mind, of demons and their ill works. As a collector, it is a book perhaps your brother would know?"

Léonie shrugged. "He might well, yes."

"There are those who believe that different devils have particular potency at different times of the year."

"And when is Asmodeus considered to be at his most powerful?"

"During the month of November."

"November," she echoed. She thought a moment. "But what does it mean, Monsieur Baillard, this marriage of superstition and supposition—the cards, the sepulchre, such a demon with his fear of water and hatred of marriage?"

He returned the book to the shelf, then walked over to the window and placed his hands on the sill, with his back to her.

"Monsieur Baillard?" she prompted.

He turned round. For a moment, the brilliant sun coming in through the wide window seemed to cast a halo of light around him. Léonie had the impression that she was looking at an Old Testament prophet such as one might see in an oil painting.

Then he stepped back into the center of the room, and the illusion was lost.

"It means, Madomaisèla, that when village superstitions talk of a demon walking these valleys and wooded hillsides, when the times are out of joint, we should not dismiss them as stories only. There are certain places—the Domaine de la Cade is one—where older forces are at work." He paused. "Alternatively, there are those who choose to raise such a creature, to commune with such spirits, failing to understand that evil cannot be mastered."

She didn't believe it, yet at the same time her heart skipped a beat.

"And my uncle did this, Monsieur Baillard? Are you asking me to accept that my uncle, through the agency of the cards and the spirit of the place, called forth the devil Asmodeus? And then found himself unable to master him? That all those stories of a beast are, in point of fact, true? That my uncle was responsible—morally, at least—for the killings in the valley? And knew this?"

Audric Baillard held her gaze. "He knew it."

"And so that was why he was obliged to seek the services of Abbé Saunière," she continued, "to banish the monster he had released?" She stopped. "Did Tante Isolde know of this?"

"It was before her time here. She did not."

Léonie stood up and walked to the window. "I do not believe it," she said abruptly. "Such stories. Devils, demons. Such tales cannot be credited in the modern world." Then her voice dropped, thinking of the pity of it. "Those children," she whispered. She resumed her pacing, causing the floorboards to creak and groan in protest. "I do not believe it," she repeated, but her voice was less certain.

"Blood will attract blood," Baillard said quietly. "There are some things that draw evil to them. A place, an object, a person may, by force of their ill will, draw to them ill circumstances, wrongdoings, sins."

Léonie came to a halt, her thoughts running along other pathways. She looked at her gentle host, then threw herself back into her chair.

"Even supposing I could accept such things, what of the deck of cards, Monsieur Baillard? Unless I mistake your meaning, you are suggesting that they might be a force for good or for ill, depending on the circumstances of their use."

"That is so. Consider how a sword is an instrument either for good or for bad. It is the hand that wields it that makes it so, not the steel."

Léonie nodded. "What is the provenance of the cards? Who painted them in the first instance? And for what purpose? When I first read my uncle's words, I understood him to be saying that the paintings upon the wall of the sepulchre might somehow step down and imprint themselves upon the cards."

Audric Baillard smiled. "If that were the case, Madomaisèla Léonie, there would be only eight cards, whereas there is a full deck."

Her heart sank. "Yes, I suppose so. I had not considered that."

"Although," he continued, "it does not mean that there is not some kernel of truth in what you say."

"In which case, Monsieur Baillard, tell me, why those eight tableaux in particular?" Her green eyes were sparkling as a new idea came to her. "Could it be that the images that remain imprinted upon the wall are those very same that my uncle drew to him? That in another situation, another such communication between the worlds, it might be other tableaux, images from other cards, visible upon the walls?" She paused. "From paintings, perhaps?"

Audric Baillard allowed a faint smile to play across his lips. "The lesser of the cards, simple playing cards, if you will, date from that unhappy time when, once more, men driven by faith to murder and to oppress and to extirpate heresy plunged the world into blood."

"The Albigensians?" Léonie said, remembering conversations between Anatole and Isolde about the tragic thirteenth-century history of the Languedoc.

He gave a resigned shake of his head. "Ah, if only lessons were learnt so quickly, Madomaisèla. But I fear they are not."

In the gravitas of his voice, it seemed to Léonie that behind his words lay a wisdom that spanned centuries. And she, who had never taken the slightest interest in the events of the past, found herself wishing to understand how one consequence led to another.

"I speak not of the Albigensians, Madomaisèla Léonie, but instead of the later wars of religion, the conflicts of the sixteenth century between the Catholic house of Guise and what we might call, for sake of clarity, the Huguenot house of Bourbon." He raised his hands and then let them drop. "As always, perhaps it will be ever thus, how the demands of faith so quickly become inextricably bound to those of territory and control."

"And the cards date from this period?" she urged.

"The original fifty-six of the cards, intended simply to help pass a long winter's evening, followed much in the tradition of the Italian game of *tarrochi*. A hundred years prior to the time of which I speak, the Italian court and nobility had given birth to a fashion for such entertainments. When the Republic was born, the court cards were replaced by *Maître* and *Maîtresse, Fils* and *Fille*, as you have seen."

"La Fille d'Épées," she said, remembering the painting on the wall of the sepulchre. "By when?"

"That is not so clear. It was at much the same time, on the eve, indeed, of the Revolution, that in France the harmless game of tarot was transformed into something other. A system of divination, a way of linking the seen and known to the unseen and unknown."

"So the deck of cards was already at the Domaine de la Cade?"

"The fifty-six cards were the possession of the house, if you like, rather than the individuals within it. The ancient spirit of the place worked upon the deck; the legends and rumors invested the cards with some further meaning and purpose. The cards were waiting, you see, for one who would complete the sequence."

"My uncle," she said, a statement, not a question.

Baillard nodded. "Lascombe read the books being published by the carto-mancers in Paris—the antique words of Antoine Court de Gébelin, the contemporary writings of Eliphas Lévi and Romain Merlin—and was seduced by them. To the deck of cards he had inherited he added the twenty-two greater arcana—those speaking of the fundamental turns of life and what lies beyond—and fixed those he wished to summon to him upon the wall of the sepulchre."

"My late uncle painted the twenty-two additional cards?"

"He did." He paused. "You believe absolutely, then, Madomaisèla Léonie, that through the agency of the tarot cards—in the specific place and with the conditions that make such things possible—demons, ghosts might be summoned?"

"It does not credit belief, Monsieur Baillard, yet I find I do believe it." She paused and thought for a moment. "What I do not understand, however, is how the cards control the spirits."

"Ah, no," Baillard said swiftly. "That was the mistake your uncle made. The cards may summon the spirits, yes, but never control them. All possibilities are contained within the images—all character, all human desire, good and ill, all of our long and overlapping stories—but should they be released, they take on a life of their own."

Léonie frowned. "I don't understand."

"The tableaux upon the wall are the imprints of the last cards summoned in that place. But if one were to alter, through the touch of a brush, the fea-tures on one or other of the cards, they would take on other characteristics instead. The cards can tell different stories," he said.

"Would this be true of these cards anywhere?" she asked. "Or only in the Domaine de la Cade, in the sepulchre?"

"It is the unique combination, Madomaisèla, of image and sound and the spirit of the place. That one place," he replied. "At the same time, the place works upon the cards. So, for example, it might be that La Force now attaches itself specifically to you. Through your artistry."

Léonie looked at him. "But I have not seen the cards themselves. Indeed, I have not painted cards, only imitations on common paper of what I saw on the walls."

He gave a slow smile. "Things do not always hold fast, Madomaisèla. And besides, you have painted more than yourself into the cards, have you not? You have painted your brother and your aunt into these pictures also."

She blushed. "They are just paintings intended as a memento of our time spent here."

"Perhaps." He inclined his head to one side. "Through such pictures your stories will endure longer than you have tongue to tell them."

"You are frightening me, Monsieur," she said sharply.

"That is not my intention."

Léonie paused before asking the question that had been on her lips since the very first moment she heard of the tarot cards. "Does the deck exist still?"

He fixed her with his wise eyes. "The deck survives," he said finally.

"Within the house?" she asked quickly.

"The Abbé Saunière begged your uncle to destroy the cards, to burn them, so that no other man would be tempted to make use of them. The sepulchre, too." Baillard shook his head. "But Jules Lascombe was a scholar. He could no more destroy something of such ancient origin than the Abbé himself could denounce his God."

"Are the cards hidden within the grounds, then? I am certain they are not in the sepulchre."

"They are safe," he said. "Concealed where the river runs dry, in a place where once the ancient kings were buried."

"But if that is the case, then—"

Audric Baillard raised his finger to his lips. "I have told you all this as a way to curb your inquisitive nature, Madomaisèla Léonie, not to fan your curiosity. I understand how you have been drawn into this story, how you wish to have some more explicit understanding of your family and the events that have shaped their lives. But I repeat my warning: no good will come of trying to find the cards, especially at such a time, when matters hang so delicately balanced."

"At such a time? What do you mean, Monsieur Baillard? Because November approaches?"

But it was clear from the expression that had come over his face that he was prepared to say nothing further. Léonie tapped her foot. She had so many questions she wished to ask. She drew breath, but he spoke before she could say more.

"It is enough," he said.

Through the open window came the sound of the bell of the tiny church of Saint-Celse and Saint-Nazaire tolling out the midday. An emaciated single note marking the passing of the morning.

The sound jerked Léonie's attention back into the present. She had quite forgotten her task. She leapt to her feet.

"Forgive me, Monsieur Baillard, I have taken up more than enough of your time." She pulled her gloves on. "And in so doing have quite forgotten my own responsibilities this morning. The bureau de poste . . . If I hurry, I might still . . ."

Clutching her hat, Léonie ran across the room to the door. Audric Baillard drew himself to his feet, an elegant and timeless figure.

"If I may, Monsieur, I will call again. *Au revoir.*"

"Of course, Madomaisèla. The pleasure will be mine."

Léonie waved, then quitted the room, rushing down the passageway and out of the front door into the street, leaving Audric Baillard alone in the quiet room deep in reflection. The boy slipped out of the shadows and closed the door behind her.

Baillard sat down once more in his chair.

"*Si es atal es atal,*" he muttered, in the old language. Things will be as they will be. "But with this child, I wish it were not so."

73

Léonie ran along the rue de l'Hermite, dragging her gloves up over her wrists and struggling with the buttons. She turned sharply right and along to the poste restante.

The double wooden door was closed and barred. Léonie hammered on it with her fist and called out.

"*S'il vous plaît?*" It was only three minutes past midday. Surely there must still be someone inside. "*Il y a quelqu'un? C'est vraiment important!*"

There was no sign of life. She knocked and called out again, but nobody came. An ill-tempered woman with two thin gray plaits leaned out of the window opposite and shouted at her to stop her banging.

Léonie apologized, realizing how stupid she was being by drawing attention to herself in such a manner. If there was a letter waiting for her from Monsieur Constant, it was now destined to remain there for the time being. She could hardly remain in Rennes-les-Bains until such time as the poste restante reopened later that afternoon. She would simply have to return on another occasion.

Her emotions were muddled. She was vexed at herself for having failed to achieve the one thing she had set out to do. At the same time, she felt she had been granted a reprieve.

At least I do not know that Monsieur Constant has not *written.*

Her confused reasoning, in some strange way, cheered her.

Léonie crossed the river. Away to the left, she saw the patients of the thermal spa sitting in the steaming, iron-rich water of the *bains forts*. Behind them a row of nurses in white uniforms, their wide, sweeping hats perched upon their heads like giant seabirds, stood waiting patiently for their charges to emerge.

She found the path along which Marieta had taken them easily enough. In one month and more, the character of the wood had changed a great deal. Some of the trees had lost their leaves, due to either the natural approach of autumn or the ferocity of the storms that had battered the hillside. The ground beneath Léonie's feet was carpeted in wine-colored foliage, golden and claret and copper. She stopped for a moment, thinking of the watercolor sketches she was working on. The image of Le Mat came into her mind, and she thought perhaps she would amend the background colors to suit the autumn hues of the forest.

She walked on, wrapped in the green mantle of the evergreen wood higher up. Twigs, fallen branches, stones shaken loose from the banks on either side rattled and snapped under her feet. Everywhere were fallen pinecones and shiny brown fruit from the horse chestnut trees. For a moment, she had a pang of homesickness. She thought of her mother and how, each October, she had taken Anatole and Léonie to the Parc Monceau to gather horse chestnuts. She rubbed her fingers together, remembering the feel and texture of childhood autumns.

Rennes-les-Bains had vanished from sight. Léonie walked a little faster, knowing that the town was still within hailing distance but at the same time feeling she was suddenly a very long way indeed from civilization. A bird flew up, its wings beating heavily on the air, making her jump. She laughed nervously when she realized it was only a tiny wood pigeon. In the distance she heard the shots from hunting guns and wondered if Charles Denarnaud's was one of them.

Léonie pressed on and soon reached the estate. When the rear gates of the Domaine de la Cade came into view, she felt a rush of relief. She hurried forward, expecting at any moment to see the maid step out with the key.

"Marieta?"

Only the sound of her own voice echoed back. By the quality of the silence, Léonie knew there was no one there. She frowned. It was unlike Pascal not to do what he said he would. And although Marieta was easily flustered, she was reliable as a rule.

Or perhaps she came and has given up waiting?

Léonie rattled the gates and found them locked. She felt a burst of ill temper and then frustration as she stood a moment, hands on her hips, considering her situation.

She did not wish to have to walk the entire perimeter to enter by the front gates. She was fatigued from her morning's experiences and the demands of the walk up the hill.

There must be some other way into the grounds.

Léonie could not believe the small outside staff Isolde kept could possibly maintain the boundaries of so large a property in perfect condition. She was slightly built. She was certain if she looked hard enough, she would find an opening wide enough for her to slip through. From there, it would be a simple matter to find her way back to familiar paths.

She looked to left and right, trying to decide which way was likely to best serve her purpose. In the end, she reasoned that the sections in the greatest state of disrepair were likely to be farthest from the house. She turned to the east. If the worst came to the worst, she would simply follow the line of the boundary all the way around. She hoped it would not.

Léonie walked briskly, peering through the hedge growth, pulling at briars and avoiding the vicious tangle of blackberry bushes, looking for any sort of break in the wrought-iron railings. The section immediately surrounding the gate was secure, but as she remembered from their first arrival at the Domaine de la Cade, the sense of dereliction and abandonment intensified the farther she walked.

She had not been searching for more than five minutes when she did come across an interruption in the fencing. She removed her hat, crouched down and, breathing in deeply, slipped through the narrow opening with a sense of relief. Once through, she picked the thorns and foliage from her jacket, brushed the mud from the hem of her skirts, then stepped forward with re-newed energy, pleased to be not far from home.

The land here was steeper, the canopy overhead darker and more oppressive. It was not long before Léonie realized that she was on the far side of the beech woods, and that if she were not careful, her route would take her past the site of the sepulchre. She frowned. Was there another way?

There was a crisscross of small tracks rather than one clear path to follow. All the clearings and copses looked the same. Léonie had no way of plotting her course other than to rely on the sun shining high above the canopy of leaves, but that was an unreliable guide deep in the shadows. But, she told herself, provided she kept walking forward, then she would come upon the lawns and the house soon enough. She just had to hope that she would bypass the sepulchre.

She set off across the slope, on a vague track that led to a small clearing. Suddenly, through a break in the trees, she saw the parcel of woodland on the

opposite bank of the River Aude within which stood the group of stone megaliths Pascal had previously pointed out to her. Then she realized with a jolt
that all the places with diabolic names round about were visible from the
Domaine de la Cade: the Devil's Armchair, the Étang du Diable, the Horned
Mountain. She scanned the horizon. And so, too, was the point at which the
rivers La Blanque and La Salz met, a spot known locally, Pascal had told her,
as *le bénitier.*

Léonie forced herself to suppress the image interposing itself into her mind
of the twisted body of the demon and his malevolent blue eyes. She hurried
on, striding out across the uneven ground, telling herself how absurd it was
to be disturbed by a statue, by a picture in a book.

The hillside rose sharply. The quality of the surface beneath her boots
changed, and soon she found herself walking over bare earth rather than
bracken or pinecones, bordered by bushes or trees but empty of them. It was
like a strip of brown paper torn at right angles out of the green landscape.

Léonie stopped and looked ahead. Above her was a steep wall of hillside,
like a barrier set across her path. Directly over her head was a natural platform, almost like a bridge arching over the patch of ground on which she
stood. She suddenly realized she was standing in a dry riverbed. Once a torrent of water, thundering down from one of the ancient Celtic springs higher
up in the hills, had forged this deep depression through the hillside.

Monsieur Baillard's words came back to her.

*Concealed where the river runs dry, in a place where once the ancient kings
were buried.*

Léonie cast her eyes about her, searching for anything out of the ordinary,
looking at the shape of the land, the trees, the undergrowth. Her attention was
drawn by a shallow depression in the ground and, beside it, a flat gray stone,
just visible beneath the tangled skirts and roots of a wild juniper bush.

She walked over to it and crouched down. She reached in, pulled at the
knotted undergrowth and peered into the damp green space around the roots.
Now she could see that there was a ring of stones, eight in all. She thrust her
hands into the foliage, staining the tips of her gloves with green slime and
mud, trying to see if anything was hidden beneath them.

The largest was quickly dislodged. Léonie sat back on her heels, resting it
in her lap. There was something painted on the surface in black tar or paint,
a five-pointed star set within a circle.

In her eagerness to discover if she had stumbled upon the place where the tarot cards were concealed, Léonie put the stone to one side. Using a piece of wood, she dug around each of the others in turn, piling the earth alongside. She saw a fragment of heavy material concealed in the mud and realized that the stones were holding it in place.

She continued digging, using the piece of fallen timber like a shovel, scraping against stones and shards of tile until she was able to pull the material free from the earth. It was covering a small hole. Excited, she jabbed at it, trying to loosen what was buried beneath, scraping the mud and worms and black beetles away, until she hit something solid.

A little more, and she could see she was looking at a plain wooden casket with metal handles at each end. Fixing her filthy gloves on the clasps, she pulled. The ground was reluctant to yield, but Léonie wrenched and twisted until, finally, it gave up its treasure with a wet sucking sound.

Breathing hard, Léonie dragged the box out of the depression to an area of dry ground and placed it on top of the cloth. She sacrificed her gloves to rub the surface clean and slowly opened the wooden lid. Inside the chest was another container, a metal strongbox of the kind in which M'man kept her most valuable possessions.

She removed the strongbox, closed the chest and placed the metal one on top. It was fitted with a tiny padlock, which, to Léonie's surprise, hung open. She tried to raise the lid, inching it up fraction by fraction. It creaked but gave easily enough.

The light was dim beneath the trees, and whatever was inside the strongbox was dark. As her eyes adjusted, she thought she could make out a package wrapped in some dark fabric. No doubt it was of the right size and proportion to be the deck of cards. She wiped her clammy palms on her clean, dry petticoats, then carefully folded back the corners of the fabric.

She was looking at the reverse side of a playing card, larger than those she was accustomed to. The back was painted a rich forest green, decorated with a swirling pattern of silver and gold filigree lines.

Léonie paused, gathering her courage. She exhaled, then counted to three in her head and turned over the top card. A strange image of a dark man, attired in a long red, tasseled robe and sitting on a throne on a stone belvedere, looked up at her. The mountains in the distance seemed familiar. She read the inscription at the bottom: Le Roi des Pentacles.

She looked more closely, realizing the figure of the King was in point of fact familiar. Then it came to her. It was the image of the priest called upon to banish the demon from the sepulchre and who had begged her uncle to destroy the deck of cards: Bérenger Saunière.

Surely this was proof, as Monsieur Baillard had told her but half an hour earlier, that her uncle had not taken his advice.

"Madomaisèla. Madomaisèla Léonie?"

Léonie spun round in alarm at the sound of her name being called.

"Madomaisèla?"

It was Pascal and Marieta. Evidently, Léonie realized, she had been so long absent that they had come out to find her. Quickly she wrapped the cards up once more. She wanted to take them with her, but there was nowhere at all she could conceal them about her person.

With great reluctance but seeing no alternative since she did not wish anyone to know what she had found, she put the cards back inside the inner box, then the box into the chest, which she slid back into the hole. Then she stood up and started to kick the earth back with the already muddy soles of her boots. When it was nearly done, she dropped her stained and spoiled gloves into the ground, too, and covered them over.

She had to trust the fact that no one had discovered the deck previously and therefore no one was likely to now. She would return, under cover of dark, and take the cards when it was discreet and safe to do so.

"Madomaisèla Léonie!"

She could hear the panic in Marieta's voice.

Léonie retraced her steps, climbed onto the platform and ran back down the woodland path in the direction from which she had come, toward the sound of the servants' voices. She struck out into the woods themselves, leaving the path so as not to give any hint of her starting point. Finally, when she thought she had put enough distance between herself and the treasure, she stopped, caught her breath and then called out.

"I am here," she cried. "Marieta! Pascal! Over here."

Within moments, their concerned faces burst through the opening in the trees. Marieta stopped dead, unable to hide her surprise or worry at the condition of Léonie's garments.

"I mislaid my gloves." The spontaneous lie rose easily to her lips. "I was obliged to go back to search for them."

Marieta looked hard at her. "And did you find them, Madomaisèla?" she said.

"Sadly, I did not."

"Your clothes."

Léonie looked down at her muddy boots, her stained petticoats and skirts streaked with mud and lichen. "I mistook my step and slipped on the damp ground, that is all."

She could see Marieta doubted the explanation, but the girl wisely held her tongue. They walked back to the house in silence.

74

Léonie barely had time to wash the dirt from under her fingernails and change her clothes before the bell for luncheon sounded.

Isolde joined them in the dining room. She was delighted with what Léonie had brought for her from the town and managed to eat a little soup. After they had finished, she requested Léonie keep her company. Léonie was pleased to do so, although whilst they were talking and playing cards, her thoughts were elsewhere. She was plotting both how to return to the woods and retrieve the cards. Also, how to engineer another visit to Rennes-les-Bains.

The remainder of the day passed peacefully. The skies clouded over at dusk and there was a flurry of rain down in the valley and over the town, but the Domaine de la Cade was little disturbed.

THE FOLLOWING MORNING, Léonie slept later than usual.

As she emerged onto the landing, she saw Marieta carrying the letter tray across the hall to the dining room. There was no reason whatsoever to presume that Monsieur Constant could somehow have acquired her address and written to her directly. Indeed, her fear was the opposite—that he had forgotten about her altogether. But because Léonie lived in a perpetual fog of longing and romantic possibility, she imagined easily troublesome and awkward circumstances.

So without the least hope of there being a letter from Carcassonne addressed to her, at the same time she found herself flying down the stairs with the sole intention of intercepting Marieta. She feared to see—and yet, in contradiction, hoped to see—the coat of arms familiar from the card Victor Constant had presented to her in the church and which she had committed to memory.

She pressed her eye close to the crack between wood and jamb, at the moment that Marieta opened the door from the inside and emerged with the empty salver.

They both squealed in surprise.

"Madomaisèla!"

Léonie pulled the door shut to stop their noise from drawing Anatole's attention.

"I do not suppose you happened to observe if there were any letters from Carcassonne, Marieta?" she said.

The maid gave her an inquiring look. "Not that I noticed, Madomaisèla."

"You are certain?"

Marieta now looked mystified. "There were the usual circulars, a letter from Paris for Sénher Anatole, and a letter apiece for your brother and for Madama that came up from the town."

Léonie gave a sigh of relief tinged with disappointment.

"Invitations, I daresay," Marieta added. "Very fine-quality envelopes they were, and addressed in a most elegant hand. A distinguished family crest also. Pascal said they were hand-delivered. Strange fellow in an old cloak."

Léonie grew still. "What color was the cloak?"

Marieta looked at her with surprise. "I'm sure I don't know, Madomaisèla. Pascal did not say. Now, if you will excuse me . . ."

"Of course." Léonie stood back. "Yes, of course."

She hesitated on the threshold for a moment, uncertain as to why she should suddenly be so anxious about going into her brother's company. It was her guilty conscience that made her think the letters might have anything whatsoever to do with her, nothing more. Wise counsel, she knew, but still she felt uneasy.

She turned away and ran lightly back up the stairs.

75

Anatole sat at the breakfast table, staring blindly at the letter. His hand shook as he lit a third cigarette from the stub of his second. The air in the closed room was thick with smoke. There were three envelopes on the table. One—unopened—had a Paris postmark. The other two bore an embossed crest of the type that adorned the display cases of Stern's plate-glass windows. A sheet of writing paper with the same aristocratic family emblem lay on the empty plate in front of him.

The truth was that Anatole had known that such a letter, one day, would find him. However much he had tried to reassure Isolde, ever since the attack in the Passage des Panoramas back in September he had expected it. The taunting communication they had received in the hotel in Carcassonne a week past had merely confirmed that Constant knew of the hoax and—worse—had hunted them down.

Although Anatole had attempted to make light of Isolde's fears, everything she had told him about Constant had led him to fear what he might do. The pattern of Constant's illness and the nature of it, his neuroses and paranoias, his ungoverned temper, all spoke of a man who would do anything to be revenged upon the woman he believed had wronged him.

Anatole looked down again at the formal letter in his hand, exquisitely insulting whilst being perfectly polite and proper. It was a formal challenge by Victor Constant to a duel to be fought tomorrow, Saturday, October 31, at dusk. Constant elected they should fight with pistols. He would leave it to Vernier to propose some appropriate plot of land within the Domaine de la Cade—private land, so that their illegal combat would pass unobserved.

He concluded by informing Vernier that he was at the Hôtel de la Reine in Rennes-les-Bains and awaiting his confirmation that he was a man of honor and would accept the challenge.

Not for the first time, Anatole regretted the impulse that had stayed his hand at the cimetière de Montmartre. He had felt Constant's presence in the graveyard. It had taken all of his strength not to turn round and shoot him then, in cold blood, and hang the consequences. When, this morning, he had opened the letter, his first thought had been to go to town and confront Constant in his lair.

But such an ungoverned response would not end the matter.

For some time, Anatole sat silently in the dining room. His cigarette burnt down and he lit another, but he felt too consumed with lethargy to smoke it.

He would need a second for the duel, someone local, obviously. Perhaps he could ask Charles Denarnaud? He at least had the virtue of being a man of the world. Anatole thought he might be able to prevail on Gabignaud to attend in his capacity as a medical man. Although he was certain the young doctor would balk at the request, he did not think he would refuse him. Anatole had been obliged to take Gabignaud into his confidence about the situation between him and Isolde, for the sake of Isolde's condition. He thought the doctor would agree, therefore, for her sake, if not for his own.

He tried to persuade himself of a satisfactory outcome. Constant wounded, forced to shake his hand, calling the feud to an end. But somehow he could not. Even if he was the victor, he was by no means convinced that Constant would abide by the rules of engagement.

Of course he had no alternative but to accept the challenge. He was a man of honor even if his actions this past year had been far from honorable. If he did not fight Constant, nothing would ever change. Isolde would live under an intolerable strain, always waiting for Constant to strike. So would they all. The man's appetite for persecution, if this letter was anything to judge by, showed no signs of abating. If he refused to meet him, Anatole knew Constant's campaign against them—against everyone close to them—would intensify.

In the past days, Anatole had heard gossip from the servants' hall that there were stories about the Domaine de la Cade circulating in the town. Disturbing suggestions that the beast that had so terrorized the neighborhood in Jules Lascombe's day had once more returned. It had made no sense to Anatole that such scandal should be resurrected, and he had been inclined to dismiss it. Now he suspected Constant's hand behind the malicious rumors.

He screwed the paper tightly in his fist. He would not have his child grow up in the knowledge that his father was a coward. He had to accept the challenge. He had to shoot to win.

To kill.

Anatole drummed his fingers on the table. He was not short of courage. The problem lay in the fact that he was far from being an assured shot. His skill lay with rapier and foil, not pistol.

He pushed that thought to one side. He would address that, with Pascal and perhaps with the assistance of Charles Denarnaud, in due course. At this instant, there were more immediate decisions to be taken, not least the question of whether or not he should confide in his wife.

Anatole extinguished another cigarette. Might Isolde somehow find out about the duel for herself? Such news might bring on a relapse and threaten the health of the baby. No, he could not tell her. He would ask Marieta not to mention this morning's post.

He slipped the letter addressed to Isolde by Constant's hand, the mirror of his own, into the breast pocket of his jacket. He could not hope to conceal the situation for long, but he could protect her peace of mind for a few hours more.

He wished he could send Isolde away. He gave a resigned smile, aware that there would be no possibility of persuading her to quit the Domaine de la Cade without adequate explanation. And since that was the one thing he could not furnish her with, there was no future in that train of thought.

Less simple to resolve was whether or not he should confide in Léonie.

Anatole had come to realize Isolde was right. His attitude toward his little sister was based more on the child she had once been than the young woman she had become. He still thought her impetuous and often childish, unable or unwilling to hold her temper in check or guard her tongue. Against that was her undoubted affection for Isolde and the solicitous way in which, over the past few days since their return from Carcassonne, she had cared for her aunt.

Anatole had resolved to speak to Léonie over the course of last weekend. He had intended to tell her the truth, from the beginning of his love affair with Isolde to the situation in which they now found themselves.

Isolde's fragile health had delayed matters, but now the receipt of the challenge had brought the pressing need for the conversation to the fore. Anatole tapped his fingers on the table. He decided that he would confide the story of his marriage this morning. Depending on Léonie's reactions, he would either tell her of the challenge or not tell her, as seemed appropriate.

He got to his feet. Taking all the letters with him, he strode across the dining room into the hall and rang the bell.

Marieta appeared.

"Will you invite Mademoiselle Léonie to join me in the library at midday? I would like to talk to her in private, so if she could keep the matter to herself? Please impress upon her, Marieta, the importance of that. Also, there is no need to mention the letters received this morning to Madame Isolde. I will appraise her of them myself."

Marieta looked puzzled but did not question his orders.

"Where is Pascal at present?"

To his surprise, the maid blushed. "In the kitchen, I believe, Sénher."

"Tell him to meet me at the rear of the house in ten minutes," he instructed.

Anatole returned to his room to change into outdoor clothes. He wrote a curt and formal reply to Constant, blotting the ink, then sealed the envelope to make it safe from prying eyes. Pascal could deliver the response this afternoon. Now the only thought in his mind was how, for Isolde's sake and for that of their child, he could not afford to miss.

The letter from Paris remained unopened in his waistcoat pocket.

LÉONIE PACED up and down in her bedroom, turning over in her mind why Anatole had requested to see her at noon, and privately. Could he have discovered her subterfuge? Or that she had dismissed Pascal and returned alone from the town?

The sound of voices below her open window drew her attention. She leaned out, both hands on the stone sill, to observe Anatole striding across the lawns with Pascal, who was carrying a long wooden box in both hands. It looked much like a pistol case. Léonie had never observed such equipment in the house, but she supposed her late uncle had possessed such weapons.

Perhaps they are going to hunt?

She frowned, realizing that could not be the case. Anatole was not dressed for hunting. Besides, neither he nor Pascal was carrying a shotgun. Only pistols.

Dread suddenly swooped down upon her, all the more potent for being unnamed. She snatched her hat and jacket, and pushed her hurrying feet into outdoor shoes, intending to follow him.

Then she checked her step.

Too often Anatole accused her of acting without thinking. It went against her nature to sit idle and wait, but what good would it do to go after him? If his purpose was quite innocent, then her trailing him like some tame dog would at the very least vex him. He could not intend to be long, having fixed an appointment with her at noon. She glanced at the clock on the mantelshelf. Two hours away.

She threw her hat on the bed and kicked off her shoes, then looked around the chamber. She would do better to stay put and to find some entertainment to pass the time before the rendezvous with her brother at midday.

Léonie looked at her painting equipment. She hesitated, then went to the bureau and began to unpack her brushes and papers. This would be the ideal opportunity to continue her sequence of illustrations. She had but three left to complete.

She fetched water, dipped her brush, then began to sketch with black ink the outlines of the sixth of the eight tableaux from the wall of the sepulchre.

Card XVI: La Tour.

76

In the private drawing room on the first floor of the Hôtel de la Reine in Rennes-les-Bains, two men were seated in front of a fire lit to take the edge off the damp morning. Two servants, the one Parisian, the other Carcassonnais, stood behind at a respectful distance. From time to time, when they thought their masters were not watching, they darted mistrustful glances at each other.

"You think he will seek your service in this matter?"

Charles Denarnaud, his face still flushed from the quantity of excellent brandy consumed last evening at dinner, drew deeply on his cigar, puffing until the sour, expensive leaves caught. There was an expression of complacency on his mottled face. He tilted his head back and blew a white ring of smoke up to the ceiling.

"Sure you won't join me, Constant?"

Victor Constant held up his hand, his angry skin hidden beneath gloves. He felt unwell this morning. The anticipation of the hunt coming to an end was playing on his nerves.

"You are confident Vernier will petition you?" he repeated.

Denarnaud heard the iron in Constant's voice and sat up straight. "I do not think I have mistaken the man," he said quickly, aware he had caused offense. "Vernier has few associates in Rennes-les-Bains, certainly no others with whom he is on such terms as to request such a service and in such a matter. I am certain he will make representation to me. The timings involved do not allow him the opportunity to send further afield."

"Quite," Constant said drily.

"My guess would be that he will approach Gabignaud, one of the resident doctors in the town, to be the medical man present."

Constant nodded. He turned to the servant standing closest to the door.

"The letters were delivered this morning?"

"Yes, Monsieur."

"You did not make yourself known to the household?"

He shook his head. "I passed them into the hands of a footman to be taken in with this morning's post."

Constant thought a moment. "And no one is aware you are the source of the stories circulating?"

He shook his head. "I have simply dropped a word or two in the ears of those most likely to repeat them, that the beast raised by Jules Lascombe has again been sighted. Spite and superstition have done the rest. The storms are seen as evidence enough that all is not well."

"Excellent." Constant gestured with his hand. "Return to the grounds of the Domaine and observe what Vernier does. Report at dusk."

"Very good, Monsieur."

He backed toward the door, pulling his blue Napoleonic cloak from the back of the chair as he did so, then slid out into the overcast street.

As soon as Constant heard the sound of the door closing, he stood up.

"I wish the matter resolved quickly, Denarnaud, and with the minimum of attention. Is that clear?"

Surprised at the abrupt end to the interview, Denarnaud struggled to his feet.

"Of course, Monsieur. Everything is in hand."

Constant clicked his fingers. His manservant stepped forward, holding out a drawstring bag. Denarnaud could not help but take a step back in disgust at the man's troubled skin and complexion.

"This is half of what you are promised," said Constant, handing across the money. "The remainder will follow once the business is concluded and to my satisfaction. You understand me?"

Denarnaud's voracious hands closed round the purse.

"You will confirm I am not in possession of any other weapon," Constant said, in a cold, hard voice. "You are quite clear on this."

"There will be a pair of dueling pistols, Monsieur, each with a single shot. Should you be carrying another instrument, I will fail to find it." He gave an ingratiating smile. "Although I cannot believe such a man as you, Monsieur, would fail to hit your target on the first attempt."

Constant looked contemptuous at the craven flattery.

"I never miss," he said.

77

D amn and blast it to hell," Anatole shouted, kicking the ground with the heel of his boot.

Pascal walked over to the makeshift shooting gallery he had set up in the clearing in the woods ringed by wild juniper bushes. He set up the bottles again in a row, then returned to Anatole and reloaded the pistol for him.

Of the six shots, two had gone wide, one had hit the trunk of a beech tree and two the wooden fencing, dislodging three bottles through the vibration. Only one had hit its target, although just nicking the base of the thick glass bottle.

"Try again, Sénher," Pascal said quietly. "Keep your eye steady."

"That's what I'm doing," Anatole muttered with ill temper.

"Raise your eye to the target, then drop it again. Imagine the shot as it travels down the barrel." Pascal stepped away. "Steady, Sénher. Take your aim. Don't rush."

Anatole raised his arm. This time he imagined that instead of a bottle that once had held ale, it was Victor Constant's face in front of him.

"Now," said Pascal softly. "Hold steady, hold steady. Fire."

Anatole hit it full square. The bottle shattered, exploding in a shower of glass like a cheap firework. The sound ricocheted off the trunks of the trees, sending birds flapping up in alarm from their nests.

A tiny puff of smoke slipped from the end of the barrel. Anatole blew across the top, then turned to face Pascal with his eyes glinting with satisfaction.

"Good shot," the servant said, his broad, impassive face for once the mirror to his thoughts. "And . . . when is this engagement?"

The smile faded from Anatole's face. "Tomorrow at dusk."

Pascal walked across the glade, the twigs cracking underfoot, and lined up the remaining bottles once again. "Shall we see if you can hit a second time, Sénher?"

"God willing, I shall have to do it only once," Anatole said to himself under his breath.

But he permitted Pascal to reload the pistol and keep him at it until every last bottle had been struck and a smell of powder, gunshot and old ale hung in the air of the clearing.

78

At five minutes before midday, Léonie quit her chamber and walked along the passageway and down the main staircase. She appeared composed and the mistress of her emotions, but her heart was beating like a toy soldier's tin drum.

As she crossed the tiled hall, her heels seemed to strike ominously loudly, or so it seemed, in the silent house. She glanced down at her hands and noticed there were flecks of paint, green and black, on her nails. She had, during the course of her anxious morning, completed the illustration of La Tour, but she was not satisfied with it. However lightly she had flecked the leaves on the trees or tried to color the sky, there was an unnerving and brooding presence that spoke through the strokes of her brush.

She walked past the glass display cases that led to the door of the library. The medals, curiosities and mementos barely registered in her mind, so absorbed was she in anticipating the interview to come.

On the threshold, she hesitated. Then she lifted her chin high, raised her hand and knocked sharply on the door with more courage than she felt.

"Come."

At the sound of Anatole's voice, Léonie opened the door and stepped inside.

"You wished to see me?" she said, feeling as if she had been summoned before the magistrates' bench rather than into the company of her beloved brother.

"I did," he said, smiling at her. The expression on his face relieved her, although she realized that he, too, was anxious. "Come in, Léonie. Sit down."

"You are scaring me, Anatole," she said quietly. "You seem so grave."

He put his hand on her shoulder and steered her to a chair with a tapestry seat. "It is a serious matter about which I wish to speak to you."

He pulled out the chair for her to sit, then walked some distance off and turned to face her, hands behind his back. Now Léonie noticed he was holding something between his fingers. An envelope.

"What is it?" she said, her spirit lurching at the thought that her worst fears might be about to be realized. What if Monsieur Constant had, by some skill and effort, acquired the address and written directly to her? "Is it a letter from M'man? From Paris?"

A strange look came over Anatole's face, as if he had just remembered something that had slipped his mind, but it was quickly covered.

"No. At least, yes, it is a letter, but it is one I have myself written. To you."

Hope sparked inside her chest that all might yet be well. "To me?"

Anatole smoothed his hand over his hair and sighed. "It is an awkward situation in which I find myself," he said quietly. "There are . . . matters of which we must speak, but now that the moment is here, I find myself humbled, tongue-tied in your presence."

Léonie laughed. "I cannot see how that could be," she said. "You would not be embarrassed in front of me, surely?"

She had intended her words to tease, but the very somber expression on Anatole's face froze the smile on her lips. She leapt out of her chair and ran over to him.

"Whatever is it?" she demanded. "Is it M'man? Isolde?"

Anatole looked down at the letter in his hand. "I have taken the liberty of committing the confession to paper," he said.

"Confession?"

"Contained within is information that I should—that *we* should—have shared with you some time ago. Isolde would have done so, but I believed I knew best."

"Anatole!" she cried, shaking his arm. "Tell me."

"It is better you read it in private," he said. "There is a situation that has arisen, far more serious, which requires my immediate attention. And your help." He slipped his arm out of Léonie's small hand and pushed the letter toward her. "I hope you can forgive me," he said, his voice breaking. "I shall wait outside."

Then, without further word, he strode across the room to the door, pulled it open and was gone.

The door rattled shut. Then the silence rushed back.

Bewildered by what had just taken place, and distressed by Anatole's evident anguish, Léonie looked down at the envelope. Her own name was printed in black ink in Anatole's elegant, romantic hand.

She stared at it, fearful of what might be inside, then ripped it open.

Vendredi, le 30 octobre

Ma chère petite Léonie—

Always, you accused me of treating you like a child. Even when you were still in ribbons and short skirts and I struggling with my lessons. This time, the charge is fair. For tomorrow evening at dusk, I shall be in the clearing in the beech woods preparing to face the man who has made every attempt to ruin us.

If it does not fall out in my favor, then I do not wish you to be left without explanation to all those questions you would surely ask of me. Whatever the outcome of the duel, I wish you to know the truth of the matter.

I love Isolde with my heart and soul. It was she at whose graveside you stood in March, a desperate attempt for her—for us—to seek safety from the violent intentions of a man with whom she had a brief, ill-judged liaison. To dissemble her death and her burial seemed the only way for her to escape from the shadow under which she lived.

Léonie reached out and found the back of the chair. Carefully, she sat herself down upon it.

I admit that I expected you to uncover our deception. During those difficult spring months and the early summer, even while the attacks upon me in the newspapers continued, at every turn, I expected you to tear off the mask and denounce me, but I played my part too well. You, who are so true of heart and purpose, why would you doubt that my pinched lips and haggard eyes were the consequences not of dissipation but of grief?

I must tell you that Isolde never wished to deceive you. From the moment we arrived at the Domaine de la Cade and she made your acquaintance, she had faith that your love for me—and she hoped in time that this same love would extend to her as a sister—would allow you to put moral considerations aside and support us in our deception. I disagreed.

I was a fool.

As I sit writing this, on what might be the eve of my last day upon this earth, I admit that my greatest fault was moral cowardice. One fault among many.

But these have been glorious weeks here, with you and Isolde, in the peaceful paths and gardens of the Domaine de la Cade.

There is more. A final deception, for which I pray you can find it in your heart if not to forgive, at least to understand. In Carcassonne, while you explored the innocent streets, Isolde and I were married. She is now Madame Vernier, your sister by the bonds of law as well as affection.

I am also to be a father.

But on that same happiest of days, we learned that he had discovered us. This is the true explanation for our abrupt departure. It is too the explanation for Isolde's decline and fragility. But it is clear that her health cannot withstand the assaults upon her nerves. The matter cannot remain unresolved.

Having discovered the deception of the funeral, somehow he has hunted us, first to Carcassonne, and now to Rennes-les-Bains. It is why I have accepted his challenge. It is the only way to settle the issue for good.

Tomorrow evening, I will face him. I seek your help, petite, as I should have sought it many months previously. I have great need of your service, to keep the particulars of the duel from my beloved Isolde. Should I not return, I commend the safety of my wife and child to you. The house is secure in possession.

Your affectionate and loving brother
A

Léonie's hands dropped into her lap. The tears she had struggled to keep at bay began to roll silently down her cheeks. She wept for the pity of it, for the deception and the misunderstandings that had kept them apart. She cried—for Isolde, for the fact that she and Anatole had deceived her, that she had ever deceived them—until all her emotion was spent.

Then her thoughts sharpened. The reason for Anatole's untimely expedition from the house this morning was now explained.

In a matter of days—hours—he could be dead.

She ran to the window and threw the casement wide. After the brilliance of the early morning, the day was now overcast. Everything was still and damp beneath the ineffective rays of the weak sun. An autumn fog was floating over the lawns and gardens, shrouding the world in a deceptive calm.

Tomorrow at dusk.

She looked at her reflection in the tall library window, thinking how strange it was that she could appear the same yet be so utterly changed. Eyes, face, chin, mouth, all in the same place they had been but three minutes earlier.

Léonie shivered. Tomorrow was the eve of Toussaint, the Eve of All Saints, a night of terrible beauty, when the veil between good and ill was at its slightest. It was a time when such events could take place. A time, already, of demons and evil deeds. The duel must not be allowed to go ahead. It was down to her to prevent it. So dreadful a charade could not be permitted to continue. But even as the thoughts raced furiously round in her head, Léonie knew it was no use. She could not deflect Anatole from his chosen course of action.

"He must not miss his target," she muttered under her breath. Ready to face him now, she went to the door and pulled it open.

Her brother was standing outside in a fug of cigarette smoke, the anguish of the waiting minutes while she had been reading carved clearly upon his face.

"Oh, Anatole," she said, throwing her arms around him.

His eyes filled with tears. "Forgive me," he whispered, allowing himself to be held. "I am so very sorry. Can you forgive me, *petite?*"

⁓

79

Léonie and Anatole spent much of the rest of that day in each other's company. Isolde rested in the afternoon, giving them time together to talk. Anatole was so bowed down by the burden of anticipation and how circumstances had conspired against him that Léonie felt herself the older sibling.

She alternated between rage at having been so deceived, and for so many months, and affection for the evident love he had for Isolde and the lengths he had gone to protect it.

"Did M'man know of the deception?" she challenged several times, haunted at the memory of herself standing beside an untenanted casket in the ci-metière de Montmartre. "Was I the only one not party to the hoax?"

"I did not confide in her," he replied. "Although I believe she understood that there was more to the matter than met the eye."

"No death," she said quietly. "And the clinic? Was there a child?"

"No. Another lie to shore up our deception."

It was only in the quiet moments, when Anatole had momentarily taken his leave of her, that Léonie allowed what the following day might bring. He would say little of his enemy, suffice that he had damaged Isolde greatly in the short time they had been acquainted. Anatole did admit that the man was a Parisian and that he had clearly been successful in unpicking the false trail laid for him and tracking them to the Midi. However, he professed to be at a loss as to how he had made the leap from Carcassonne to Rennes-les-Bains. Nor would he utter his name.

Léonie listened to the story of the obsession, the desire for revenge that drove their enemy—the attacks upon her brother in the columns of the news-papers, the assault upon his person in the Passage des Panoramas, the efforts to which he was prepared to go to ruin both Isolde and Anatole—and heard the real fear behind her brother's words.

They did not discuss the outcome should Anatole miss his target. Pressed by her brother, Léonie gave her word that should he fail in his task and be unable to protect them, she would find some immediate way of leaving the Domaine de la Cade under cover of night with Isolde.

"He is not a man of honor, then?" she said. "You fear he will not abide by the rules of engagement?"

"I fear he will not," he replied gravely. "Should things go ill tomorrow, I would not wish Isolde to be here when he comes to find her."

"He sounds a devil."

"And I a fool," said Anatole quietly, "for thinking it could end in any other way than this."

LATER THAT EVENING, after Isolde had retired for the night, Anatole and Léonie met in the drawing room to agree on a plan of campaign for the following day.

She disliked being party to a deception—especially having been the victim of such concealment herself—but she accepted that in her condition Isolde could not know of what was to happen. Anatole tasked her with occupying his wife so that at the appointed hour he and Pascal could slip away. He had sent word to Charles Denarnaud inviting him to be his second, a request that had been accepted without hesitation. Dr. Gabignaud, an unwilling participant, was to provide medical assistance should it be required.

Though she nodded with apparent acquiescence, Léonie had not the slightest intention of abiding by Anatole's wishes. She could not contemplate sitting idly in the drawing room, watching the hands of the clock make their slow march, knowing that her brother was engaged in such a combat. She knew she would have to find some way of passing off responsibility for Isolde between the hours of dusk and nightfall, although she could not yet conceive of how this might be achieved.

But she gave no indication of her intended disobedience, in either word or deed. And Anatole was so absorbed in his fevered plannings that he did not think to doubt her compliance.

When he, too, retired for the night, quitting the drawing room with a single candle to light his way to bed, Léonie remained behind for some time, thinking, deciding how to arrange things for the best. She would be strong. She would not permit her fears to master her. All would be well. Anatole would wound or kill his enemy. She refused to entertain an alternative.

But even as the hours of night slipped by, she was aware that wishing would not make it so.

80

Saturday, October 31

The Eve of All Saints came with a chill and pink dawn.

Léonie had barely slept, so felt the weight of the passing minutes pressing down upon her. After breakfast, when neither she nor Anatole could manage to eat much, he spent the morning time closeted with Isolde.

As she sat in the library, she could hear them laughing, whispering, planning. Isolde's joy at her brother's company made all the more painful Léonie's awareness of how easily such happiness might be snatched away.

When she joined them for coffee in the morning room, Anatole raised his head, his gaze for an instant unguarded. His anguish, the dread, the misery laid bare in his eyes made her turn away, for fear her countenance would give him away.

After lunch, they passed the afternoon in playing cards and reading stories aloud, thereby contriving to delay Isolde's afternoon rest, as Léonie and Anatole had previously planned. It was not until four o'clock that Isolde declared her intention to withdraw to her chamber until supper. Anatole returned some quarter of an hour later with sorrow etched upon his face.

"She is sleeping," he said.

They both looked out at the apricot sky, the last vestiges of sun flecked bright behind the clouds. Léonie's strength finally deserted her. "It is not too late," she cried. "There is still time to call it off." She grabbed hold of his hand. "I beg you, Anatole, do not go through with this."

He put his arms around her and drew her to him, enveloping her in the familiar scent of sandalwood and hair oil.

"You know I cannot refuse to meet him now, *petite*," he said softly. "It will never end else. Besides, I would not have my son grow up believing his father a coward." He squeezed her tighter. "Nor, indeed, my courageous and steadfast little sister."

"Or daughter," she said.

Anatole smiled. "Or daughter."

The sound of footsteps on the tiled floor made them both turn.

Pascal stopped at the bottom of the stairs, holding Anatole's greatcoat over his arm. The expression on his face betrayed how little he wished to be part of the matter.

"It is time, Sénher," he said.

Léonie held on tightly. "Please, Anatole. Please, do not go. Pascal, do not let him go."

Pascal looked on with sympathy as Anatole gently prised her fingers from his sleeve.

"Look after Isolde," he whispered. "My Isolde. I have left a letter in my dressing room, should things . . ." He broke off. "She must not want for anything. Neither she nor the child. Keep them safe."

Léonie watched, dumb with despair, as Pascal helped him into his coat, then the two men walked briskly to the front door. On the threshold, Anatole turned. He raised his hands to his lips.

"I love you, *petite*."

There was a rush of damp evening air, then the door shuddered to a close behind them and they were gone. Léonie listened to the muffled crunch of their boots upon the gravel until she could hear them no more.

Then the truth of it hit her. She sank onto the bottom step, rested her head on her arms and sobbed. From the shadows beneath the stairs, Marieta crept out. The girl hesitated, then, deciding to forget herself, sat down on the step beside Léonie and put her arm around her shoulder.

"It will be all right, Madomaisèla," she murmured. "Pascal will not let any harm come to the master."

A wail of grief, of terror, of hopelessness, burst out from between Léonie's lips, like the howl of a wild animal caught in a trap. Then, remembering how she had promised not to wake Isolde, she muted her tears.

Her fit of weeping quickly subsided. She felt light-headed, curiously empty of emotion. She felt as if there was something caught in her throat. She rubbed her eyes hard with the cuff of her sleeve.

"Is my . . ." She paused, suddenly realizing that she no longer knew quite how she should refer to Isolde. "Is my aunt still sleeping?" she asked.

Marieta got to her feet and smoothed down her apron. The look on her face suggested that Pascal had confided the whole business to her.

"Do you wish me to go and see if Madama has woken?"

Léonie shook her head. "No, let her be."

"Can I fetch you something? A tisane, perhaps."

Léonie also stood up. "No, I will be perfectly fine now." She gave a smile. "I am sure you have enough to occupy you. Besides, my brother will need refreshment when he returns. I would not have him wait."

For a moment, the eyes of the two girls met.

"Very good, Madomaisèla," Marieta said in the end. "I shall make certain the kitchen is prepared."

Léonie remained awhile in the hall, listening to the sounds of the house, satisfying herself that there were no witnesses to what she was about to do. When she was certain all was quiet, she ran quickly up the stairs, running her hand along the mahogany banister rail, and lightly along the passageway toward her room.

To her confusion, she could hear noises coming from Anatole's chamber. She froze, mistrusting the evidence of her own ears, having seen him depart the house half an hour previously and in the company of Pascal.

She was on the point of continuing when the door flew open and Isolde all but fell into her arms. Her blond hair was loose and her shift open at the neck. She looked quite deranged, as if shocked out of sleep by some demon or ghost. Léonie could not help but notice the raw, red scarring at her throat. Her shock at seeing her elegant, controlled and self-possessed aunt in the throes of such hysteria made her voice sharper than intended.

"Isolde! Whatever is it? What has happened?"

Isolde was twisting her head from side to side, as if in violent disagreement, and waving a piece of paper in her hand.

"He has gone! To fight!" she cried. "We must prevent it."

Léonie turned cold, realizing Isolde had laid her hands prematurely on the letter that Anatole had left for her in his dressing room.

"I could not sleep, so I went to find him. Instead, I found this." Isolde stopped abruptly and looked Léonie in the eyes. "You knew," she said softly, her voice suddenly calm.

For a fleeting instant, Léonie forgot that even as she spoke, Anatole was striding through the woods to fight a duel. She tried to smile as she reached out and took Isolde's hand.

"I know of the steps you have taken. The marriage," she said quietly. "I wish I could have been there."

"Léonie, I wish . . ." Isolde paused. "We wished to tell you."

Léonie put her arms around her. In an instant, their roles reversed.

"And that Anatole is to be a father?" Isolde said, almost whispering.

"That, too," Léonie said. "It is the most wonderful news."

Isolde suddenly pulled away. "But you knew of this duel also?"

Léonie hesitated. She was on the point of evading the question but then stopped. There had been enough dishonesty between them. Too many destructive lies.

"I did," she admitted. "The letter was delivered by hand yesterday. Denarnaud and Gabignaud have accompanied him."

Isolde went white. "By hand, you say," she whispered. "So he is here, then. Even here."

"Anatole will not miss his mark," Léonie said, with a conviction she did not feel.

Isolde put her head up and pushed her shoulders back. "I must go to him."

Taken by surprise at her abrupt change of mood, Léonie fumbled for a response.

"You cannot," she objected.

Isolde took not the slightest bit of notice. "Where is the contest to take place?"

"Isolde, you are unwell. It would be foolish to attempt to follow him."

"Where?" she said.

Léonie sighed. "A clearing in the beech woods. I do not know precisely where."

"Where the wild juniper grows. There is a clearing there where my late husband would sometimes go to practice."

"It may be. He said nothing more."

"I shall dress," Isolde said, slipping from Léonie's clasp.

Léonie had no choice but to follow. "But even if we leave now, and we find the precise location, Anatole left with Pascal more than half an hour ago."

"If we go now, we may yet stop it."

Not wasting time with her corset, Isolde pulled on her gray walking dress and outdoor jacket, pushed her elegant feet into boots, her fingers falling over each other as she laced each hook and eye haphazardly, then ran toward the stairs, Léonie on her heels.

"Will his opponent abide by the result?" Léonie suddenly asked, hoping for a different answer than the one with which Anatole had earlier furnished her.

Isolde stopped and looked up at her, despair in her gray eyes.

"He is . . . he is not a man of honor."

Léonie grasped her hand, seeking reassurance as much as to give comfort, as another question came into her mind. "When is the child due?"

For a moment, Isolde's eyes softened. "All being well, June. A summer baby."

As they stole through the hall, it seemed to Léonie that the world had taken on a harsher hue. Things once familiar and precious—the polished table and doors, the pianoforte and tapestried stool, within which Léonie had placed the music taken from the sepulchre—seemed to have turned their back on them. Cold, dead objects.

Léonie took down the heavy garden cloaks from the hooks inside the entrance, handed one to Isolde, wrapped the other around herself, then pulled open the door. Chill dusk air slipped around her legs like a cat, wrapping itself round her stockings, her ankles. She took the lighted lamp from the stand.

"At what time is the engagement due to take place?" Isolde asked in a quiet voice.

"Dusk," Léonie replied. "Six o'clock."

They looked up at the sky, a deep and darkening blue above them.

"If we are to be there in time," Léonie said, "we must hurry. Quick, now."

81

❧

"I love you, *petite,*" Anatole repeated to himself, as the front door juddered shut behind him.

He and Pascal, holding a lantern aloft, walked in silence to the end of the drive, where Denarnaud's carriage was waiting for them.

Anatole nodded at Gabignaud, whose expression revealed how little he wished to be a part of the proceedings. Charles Denarnaud clasped Anatole's hand.

"The principal and the doctor in the back," Denarnaud announced, his voice clear in the chill dusk air. "Your man and I will ride at the front."

The hood was up. Gabignaud and Anatole climbed in. Denarnaud and Pascal, looking uncomfortable in such company, faced them, balancing the long wooden pistol case between them on their laps.

"You know the appointed place, Denarnaud?" Anatole asked. "The glade in the beech wood to the east of the property?"

He leaned out and gave the instructions. Anatole heard the driver flick his reins and the gig moved off, the harness and bridle rattling in the still, evening air.

Denarnaud was the only one with an appetite for talk. Most of his stories involved duels with which he had been involved, close shaves all but always ending well for his principal. Anatole understood Denarnaud was trying to put him at ease but wished he would hold his tongue.

He sat bolt upright, looking out at the late fall countryside, thinking that perhaps it was the last time he would see the world. The avenue of trees lining the drive was covered in hoar frost. The heavy fall of the horses' hooves on the hard ground echoed around the park. The darkening blue sky above seemed to glint like a mirror as a pale moon rose in white splendor.

"These are my own pistols," Denarnaud explained. "I loaded them myself. The case is sealed. You will draw lots to decide whether we use these or your opponent's."

"I know that," Anatole said, then, regretting that he sounded abrupt, added, "My apologies, Denarnaud. My nerves are on edge. I am most grateful for your careful attention."

"Always worth running through the etiquette," he replied in a voice louder than the confined space of the carriage and the situation required. Anatole realized that Denarnaud, too, for all his bluster, was nervous. "We don't want any misunderstandings. For all I know, matters are conducted differently in Paris."

"I do not think so."

"You have been practicing, Vernier?"

Anatole nodded. "With the pistols from the house."

"Are you confident with them? Is the sighting good?"

"I would have had more time," he said.

The carriage turned and started to move across the rougher ground.

Anatole tried to picture his cherished Isolde, sleeping upon the bed with her hair fanned out on the pillow, her willowy white arms. He thought of Léonie's bright, questioning green eyes. And the face of a child not yet born. Tried to fix their beloved features in his mind.

I am doing this for them.

But the world had shrunk to the rattling carriage, the wooden box on Pascal's and Denarnaud's laps, the fast, nervous breathing of Gabignaud beside him.

Anatole felt the fiacre swing again to the left. Beneath the wheels, the ground became more rutted and uneven. Suddenly, Denarnaud banged on the side of the carriage and shouted to the driver to take a small lane on the right.

The gig turned into the unmade track running between the trees, then emerged into a clearing. On the far side stood another carriage. With a jolt, although it was what he knew he would see, Anatole recognized the crest of Victor Constant, Comte de Tourmaline, gold upon black. Two bay horses, plumed and blinkered, were stamping their hooves on the hard, cold ground. Beside them stood a knot of men.

Denarnaud alighted first, Gabignaud followed, then Pascal with the pistol case. Finally, Anatole stepped down. Even from this distance, with their opposite numbers dressed in black, he could identify Constant. With a shudder of revulsion, he also recognized the red-raw, pockmarked features of one of the two men who had set about him on the night of the riot at the Opéra in the Passage des Panoramas. Beside him was a dissolute-looking old soldier, shorter and of poor appearance, in an archaic Napoleonic cloak. He, too, seemed familiar.

Anatole drew his breath. Even though Victor Constant had been in residence in his thoughts from the moment he had met and fallen in love with Isolde, the two men had not been in each other's company since their one and only quarrel in January.

He was taken by surprise at the rage that rushed through him. He balled his hands into fists. A cool head was what was required, not an impetuous desire for revenge. But suddenly the wood seemed too small. The bare trunks of the beech trees appeared to be closing in on him.

He stumbled on an exposed root and nearly fell.

"Steady, Vernier," murmured Gabignaud.

Anatole gathered his thoughts to him and watched as Denarnaud walked toward Constant's party, Pascal trailing behind him, carrying the pistol box across his arms as if it was a child's coffin.

The seconds greeted one another formally, each bowing briefly, sharply, then they walked farther up into the clearing. Anatole was aware of Constant's cold eyes on him, piercing, straight as an arrow, across the frozen earth. He noted, too, that Constant looked unwell.

They moved to the center of the clearing, not far from where Pascal had set up the makeshift shooting gallery the day before, then measured the paces from where each man would take aim. Pascal and Constant's man hammered two walking sticks into the damp ground to mark precisely the spot.

"How are you holding up?" Gabignaud murmured. "Can I fetch any—"

"Nothing," Anatole said quickly. "I need nothing."

Denarnaud returned. "I regret we lost the toss for the pistols." He slapped Anatole on the shoulder. "It will make no difference, I am certain. It's the aim that counts, not the barrel."

Anatole felt he was a man walking in his sleep. Everything around him seemed to be muffled, happening to someone else. He knew he should be concerned about the fact that he was to use his opponent's pistols, but he was numb.

The two groups moved closer to one another.

Denarnaud removed Anatole's greatcoat. Constant's second did the same for him. Anatole watched as Denarnaud ostentatiously patted down Constant's jacket pockets, his waistcoat pockets, to make sure he had no pocketbook, no papers that might act as a shield, no other weapons.

Denarnaud nodded. "Nothing amiss."

Anatole lifted his arms while Constant's man ran his hands over his body to check that he, too, had no concealed advantage. He felt his watch fob being taken from his pocket and unchained.

"A new watch, Monsieur? Monogrammed. Nice piece of workmanship."

He recognized the rasping voice. It was the same man who had stolen his father's timepiece from him during the attack in Paris. He balled his fists to prevent him from striking the man down.

"Leave it," he muttered viciously.

The man glanced at his master, then shrugged and walked away.

Anatole felt Denarnaud take his elbow and lead him to one of the walking sticks. "Vernier, this is your mark."

I cannot miss.

He was handed a pistol. It was cold and heavy in his hand, a far finer weapon than those belonging to his late uncle. The barrel was long and polished, with Constant's gold monogrammed initials stamped into the handle.

Anatole felt as if he was looking down on himself from a great height. He could see a man who much resembled him, the same jet-black hair, the same moustache, the pale face and nose tipped red from the cold.

Facing him, at some paces hence, he could see the man who had persecuted him from Paris to the Midi.

Now, as from a distance, came a voice. Abruptly, absurdly quickly, the business was to be concluded.

"Are you ready, gentlemen?"

Anatole nodded. Constant nodded.

"One shot apiece."

Anatole raised his arm. Constant did the same.

Then the same voice again. "Fire."

Anatole was aware of nothing, no sights, no sounds, no smells; he experienced a total absence of emotion. He believed himself to have done nothing, and yet the muscles in his arm contracted and his fingers squeezed, pressing the trigger, and there was a snap as the catch released. He saw the powder flare in the pan and the puff of smoke bloom in the air. Two reports echoed around the glade. The birds flew up out of the tops of the surrounding trees, their wings beating the air in their panic to get away.

Anatole lost the air in his lungs. His legs went from under him. He was falling, falling to his knees on the hard earth, thinking of Isolde and Léonie, then a warmth spread over his chest, like the soothing ministrations of a hot bath.

"Is he struck?" Gabignaud's voice, perhaps? Perhaps not.

Dark figures gathered around him, no longer identifiable as Gabignaud or Denarnaud, just a forest of black-and-gray-striped trouser legs, hands encased in thick fur gloves, heavy boots. Then he heard something. A wild shrieking, his name carried in agony and despair through the chill air.

Anatole slumped sideways onto the ground. He was imagining he could hear Isolde's voice calling to him. But almost simultaneously, he realized that others could hear the shouting, too. The crowd surrounding him parted and stood back, far enough for him to see her running toward him from the cover of the trees, with Léonie hard on her heels.

"No. Anatole, no!" Isolde was shouting. "No!"

In that instant, something else caught his attention, just outside his line of vision. His eyes were darkening. He tried to sit, but a sharp pain in his side, like the stab of a knife, caused him to gasp. He reached out his hand but had no strength and felt himself slumping back down to the ground.

Everything started to move in slow motion. Anatole realized what was going to happen. At first, his eyes could not accept it. Denarnaud had checked that the rules of engagement were met. One shot and one shot only. And yet as he watched, Constant dropped the dueling pistol to the ground, reached into his jacket and pulled out a second weapon, so small that the barrel fitted between his second and third fingers. His arm continued its upward arc, then swung to the right and fired.

A second gun when there should have been only one.

Anatole shouted, at last finding his voice. But he was too late.

Her body came to a standstill, as if hanging momentarily in the air, then was thrown backward by the force of the bullet. Her eyes flared wide, open first with surprise, then shock, then pain. He watched her fall. Like him, down to the ground.

Anatole felt a cry rip from his chest. All around him was chaos, yelling and shouting and pandemonium. And in the center of it all, although it could not be, he thought he heard the sound of someone laughing. His vision faded, black replacing white, stripping the color from the world.

It was the last sound he heard before the darkness closed over him.

82

A howl split the air. Léonie heard it but was at first unaware that the cry had issued from her own lips.

For a moment, she stood rooted to the spot, unable to accept the evidence of her own eyes. She fancied she looked at a stage set, the glade and each person captured in time with brush and paint or the shutter of a lens. Lifeless, motionless, a postcard image of their real, flesh-and-blood selves.

Then, with a kick, the world rushed back. Léonie cast her gaze into the darkness, the truth imprinting its bloody handprint upon her mind.

Isolde, lying upon the damp earth, her gray dress stained red.

Anatole, struggling to raise himself on one arm, his face creased with pain, before collapsing back to the ground. Gabignaud crouched at his side.

Most shocking, the face of their murderer. The man who Isolde so feared and Anatole so detested, revealed in plain sight.

Léonie turned cold, her courage ripped from her.

"No," she whispered.

Guilt, sharp as glass, pierced her defenses. Humiliation, then anger following on its heels, swept through her like a river bursting its banks. Here, but a couple of steps away from her, was the man who had taken up residence in her private thoughts, about whom she had dreamed since Carcassonne. Victor Constant.

Anatole's assassin. Isolde's persecutor.

Was it she who had led him here?

Léonie raised her lamp higher until she could clearly see the crest on the side of the carriage standing some way off to the side, although she did not need confirmation that it was he.

Rage, sudden and violent and all-encompassing, swooped down over her. Insensible of her own safety, she charged out of the shadows of the trees and into the glade, running forward toward the knot of men standing around Anatole and Gabignaud.

The doctor seemed paralyzed. Shock at what had transpired had stolen from him the ability to act. He lurched, nearly losing his footing on the hardening ground, looking wildly to Victor Constant and his men, then in bewilderment at Charles Denarnaud, who had checked the guns and pronounced that the conditions for the duel had been met.

Léonie reached Isolde first. She threw herself down on the ground beside her and lifted her cloak. The pale gray material on the left side of her dress was soaked crimson, like an obscene hothouse bloom. Léonie pulled off her glove and, pushing Isolde's cuff higher up her arm, felt for a pulse. It was faint but there. Some slight measure of life remained. Quickly she ran her hands over Isolde's prostrate body and realized the bullet had hit her arm. Provided she did not lose too much blood, she would survive.

"Dr. Gabignaud, *vite*," she cried. "*Aidez-la.* Pascal!"

Her thoughts leapt to Anatole. The slightest frosting of white breath around his mouth and nose in the twilight gave her hope that he, too, was not mortally wounded.

She stood up and took a step toward her brother.

"I will thank you to stay where you are, Mademoiselle Vernier. You, too, Gabignaud."

Constant's voice stopped her in her tracks. Only now did Léonie register that he was still holding his weapon raised, finger on the trigger, ready to squeeze, and that it was not a dueling pistol. In fact, she recognized *Le Protector*, a gun designed to be carried in the pocket or a purse. Her mother possessed just such a weapon.

He had more shots.

Léonie was disgusted at herself, for the pretty endearments she had imagined him whispering in her ear. For how she had encouraged—with no modesty or care of her reputation—his attentions.

And I led him to them.

She forced herself to hold her nerve. She raised her chin and looked him straight in the eye.

"Monsieur Constant," she said, his name like poison on her tongue.

"Mademoiselle Vernier," he replied, still holding the gun on Gabignaud and Pascal. "This is an unexpected pleasure. I had not thought Vernier would expose you to such ugliness."

Her eyes darted to where Anatole lay on the ground, then back to Constant.

"I am here of my own accord," she said.

Constant jerked his head. His manservant stepped forward, followed by the filthy soldier whom Léonie recognized as the same creature who had followed her with his impertinent eyes as she walked into the medieval Cité of Carcassonne. With despair, she realized how complete had been Constant's planning.

The two men seized Gabignaud and pulled his arms behind his back, throwing his lamp to the ground. Léonie heard the glass smash as the flame was extinguished with a hiss in the damp leaves. Then, before she realized what was happening, the taller of the men drew a gun from beneath his coat, put it to Gabignaud's temple and pulled the trigger.

The force of the shot lifted Gabignaud from the ground. The back of his head exploded, showering his executioner with blood and bone. His body twitched, jerked, then lay still.

How little time it takes to kill a man, to sever soul from body.

The thought swooped in, then out of her mind. Léonie clamped her hands to her mouth, feeling the nausea rising in her throat, then doubled over and vomited on the damp ground.

Out of the corner of her eye, she saw Pascal taking a small step backward, then another. She could not believe he was preparing to flee—she had never had doubt to question his loyalty and his steadfastness before—but what else could he be doing?

Then he caught her eye and glanced down to signal his intention.

Léonie straightened up and turned to Charles Denarnaud. "Monsieur," she said loudly, creating a diversion, "I am surprised to find you an ally of this man. You will be condemned when news of your duplicity is reported."

He gave a complacent grimace. "From whose mouth, Mademoiselle Vernier? There is none but us here."

"Hold your tongue," commanded Constant.

"Do you care nothing for your sister," Léonie challenged, "your family, that you would disgrace them in such a manner?"

Denarnaud patted his pocket. "Money speaks louder and longer."

"Denarnaud, *ça suffit!*"

Léonie glanced at Constant, noticing for the first time how his head seemed to tremble in permanent motion, as if he had difficulty controlling his movements.

But then she saw Anatole's foot twitch on the ground.

Was he alive? Could he be? Relief bubbled up, replaced immediately by dread. If he was yet alive, he would remain so only as long as Constant thought him dead.

Night had fallen. Though the doctor's lamp was broken, the remaining lanterns cast uneven pools of yellow light on the ground. Léonie forced herself to take a step toward the man she had thought she might love. "Is it worth it, Monsieur? Damning yourself? And for what root cause? Jealousy? Revenge? For it is certainly not for honor." She took another pace, a little to the side this time, hoping to shield Pascal. "Let me tend to my brother. To Isolde."

She was now close enough to see the look of contempt on Constant's face. She could not believe she had ever thought his features distinguished, noble. He seemed so evidently vile, his mouth cruel and his pupils no more than pinpricks in his bitter eyes. He repelled her.

"You are hardly in a position to issue orders, Mademoiselle Vernier." He turned his head to where Isolde lay folded within her cloak. "And the whore. A single shot was too good for her. I would wish that she had suffered as she has made me suffer."

Léonie met his blue eyes without flinching. "She is beyond your reach now," she said, the lie coming without hesitation to her lips.

"You will forgive me, Mademoiselle Vernier, if I do not take your word for that. Besides, there is not a single tear on your cheek." He glanced at Gabignaud's body. "You have strong nerves, but I do not believe you are so hardhearted."

He hesitated, as if preparing to deliver the *coup de grâce*. Léonie felt her body tense, waiting for the shot she thought must surely now find her. She realized Pascal was almost ready to act. It took great effort of will not to look in his direction.

"In point of fact," Constant said, "in character you remind me much of your mother."

Everything stilled, as if the world was holding its breath. White clouds, cold on the evening air, the shivering of the wind in the bare branches of the trees, the rustling of the juniper bushes. At last Léonie found her tongue.

"What do you mean?" she said. Each word seemed to drop like lead into the cold air.

She could sense his satisfaction. It rose from him like the stench from a tannery, acrid, pungent.

"You still do not know what has befallen your mother?"

"What are you saying?"

"It has been quite the talk of Paris," Constant said. "I am told one of the worst murders the pedestrian minds of the gendarmes of the eighth arrondissement have been obliged to deal with for some time."

Léonie stepped back as if he had struck her. "She is dead?"

Her teeth started to chatter. She could hear the truth of what Constant claimed in the quality of his silence, but her mind could not let her accept it. If she did, she would falter and fall. And all the time, Isolde and Anatole both were growing weaker.

"I do not believe you," she managed to articulate.

"Ah, but you do, Mademoiselle Vernier. I can see it in your face." He let his arm drop, taking the gun off Léonie for an instant. She took a step backward. Behind her, she felt Denarnaud shifting, moving closer, blocking her path. In front of her, Constant stepped toward her, quickly covering the distance between them. Then, from the corner of her eye, she saw Pascal crouch and snatch up the spare pistols from the box they had brought from the house.

"*Attention!*" he shouted to her.

Léonie reacted without hesitation, throwing herself down to the ground as a shot whistled over her head.

Denarnaud fell, struck in the back.

Constant retaliated instantly, firing into the darkness but going wide of his target. Léonie could hear Pascal in the undergrowth and realized he was moving round behind Constant.

On Constant's command, the old soldier was advancing on where Léonie lay on the ground. The other man was running toward the edge of the glade, looking for Pascal, firing at random.

"*Il est ici!*" he shouted to his master.

Constant fired again. Again, the shot went wide.

Suddenly, the vibration of running feet echoed through the ground. Léonie raised her head in the direction of the noise and heard shouting.

"*Arèst!*"

She recognized Marieta's voice, calling through the darkness, and others, too. She narrowed her eyes and now could make out the glow of several lanterns getting closer, larger, jolting in the darkness. Then the gardener's boy, Emile, burst into sight on the far side of the clearing, holding a flaming torch in one hand and a stick in the other.

Léonie saw Constant take in the situation. He fired, but the boy was quicker and stepped back behind the shelter of a beech tree. Constant raised his arm, dead straight, and fired again into the darkness. Léonie saw that his face was twisted in madness as he turned the gun and sent two bullets slamming into Anatole's torso.

Léonie screamed. "No!" she cried, crawling desperately on her hands and knees over the muddy ground to where her brother lay. "No!"

The servants, some eight of them, including Marieta, rushed forward.

Constant delayed no longer. Tossing his coat behind him, he strode out of the glade and into the shadows, heading to where his fiacre still stood in readiness to depart.

"No witnesses," he said.

Without a word, his manservant turned and fired a bullet into the old soldier's head. For a moment, the dying man's face was fixed in an expression of bewilderment. Then he dropped to his knees and fell forward.

Pascal stepped out of the shadows and fired the second pistol. Léonie saw Constant stumble, his legs nearly buckling under him, but he kept walking, limping, away from the glade. Through the mayhem and chaos, she heard the slamming of the carriage doors, the rattling of the harness and the chink of the lamps as the conveyance vanished uphill into the woods, in the direction of the rear gate.

Marieta was already tending to Isolde. Léonie felt Pascal run and crouch beside her. A sob slipped from her lips. She struggled to her feet and stumbled across the last few yards to her brother.

"Anatole?" she whispered. Her arm tightened around his broad shoulders, shaking him, trying to wake him. "Anatole, please."

The stillness seemed to deepen.

Léonie grasped the thick material of Anatole's greatcoat and rolled him over. She caught her breath. So much blood, pooled on the ground where he had been lying, the holes in his body where the bullets had penetrated. She cradled his head in her arms and brushed his hair back from his face. His brown eyes were wide open, but the life was extinguished.

83

After Constant had fled, the glade quickly cleared.

With Pascal's help, Marieta led the barely conscious Isolde to Denarnaud's carriage to take back to the house. Although the wound on her arm was not serious, she had lost a lot of blood. Léonie spoke to her, but Isolde made no answer. She allowed herself to be led, but she seemed to know no one, recognize nothing. She was yet in the world but removed from it.

Léonie was cold and shivering, her hair and clothes infused with the stench of blood and gunshot and damp earth, but she refused to leave Anatole's side. The gardener's boy and ostlers from the stables constructed a makeshift bier with their coats and the wooden handles of the weapons with which they had driven off Constant and his men. They carried Anatole's prostrate body on their shoulders back across the grounds, the torches burning fiercely in the cold, black air. Léonie followed behind, a solitary mourner at an unannounced funeral.

Behind them was fetched Dr. Gabignaud. The dogcart would be sent to bring the bodies of the old soldier and the traitor Denarnaud.

News of the tragedy that had overtaken the Domaine de la Cade had spread by the time Léonie regained the house. Pascal had dispatched a messenger to Rennes-le-Château to inform Bérenger Saunière of the catastrophe and to request his presence. Marieta had sent to Rennes-les-Bains for the services of the local woman who sat with the dying and laid out the dead.

Madame Saint-Loup arrived with a small boy, carrying a large cotton bag twice his size. When Léonie, remembering herself, tried to agree rates with the woman, she was informed that costs had been met already by her neighbor, Monsieur Baillard. His kindness, so generously given, brought tears to Léonie's numbed eyes.

The bodies were placed in the dining room. Léonie watched in mute disbelief as Madame Saint-Loup filled a china bowl with water from a glass bottle she had brought with her.

"Holy water, Madomaisèla," she muttered in response to Léonie's unasked question. Into it she dipped a sprig of boxwood, then lit two scented candles, one for each, and began to recite her prayers for the dead. The boy bowed his head.

"*Peyre Sant,* Holy Father, take this thy servant . . ."

As the words washed over her, a mixture of old and new traditions, Léonie felt nothing. There was no moment of grace descending, no sense of peace in Anatole's passing, no light entering the soul and drawing together in a common circle. There was no consolation, no poetry to be found in the old woman's offerings, only a vast and echoing loss.

Madame Saint-Loup stopped. Then, after gesturing to the boy to pass her a pair of large-bladed scissors from her bag, she began to cut away Anatole's blood-sodden clothes. The cloth was matted and filthy with the forest and his jagged wounds, and the process was painstaking and difficult.

"Madomaisèla?"

She handed Léonie two envelopes from Anatole's pockets. The silver paper and black crest of the letter from Constant. The second, with a Parisian postmark, was unopened. Both were edged in rust-red, as if a border had been painted across the thick weave of the paper.

Léonie opened the second letter. It was formal and official notification from the gendarmerie of the eighth arrondissement informing Anatole of their mother's murder, on the night of Sunday, September 20. No criminal had yet been apprehended for the crime. The letter was signed by an Inspector Thouron and had been forwarded via a number of addresses before finally finding Anatole in Rennes-les-Bains.

The letter requested him to make contact at the earliest convenience.

Léonie screwed the page in her chilled fist. She had not doubted for a moment Constant's cruel words, thrown at her in the glade but an hour previously, but only now, with the black-and-white official words, did she accept the truth of the matter. Her mother was dead, and had been for more than a month.

This fact—that her mother had been unmourned and unclaimed—twisted at Léonie's bereaved heart. With Anatole gone, such matters would fall to her. Who else was there?

Madame Saint-Loup began to clean the body, wiping Anatole's face and hands with such tenderness that it pained Léonie to witness it. Finally, she pulled out several linen sheets, each yellowing and crisscrossed with black looped stitching, as if they had done service many times before.

Léonie could no longer bear to watch.

"Send word when Abbé Saunière comes," she said, quitting the room and leaving the woman to the grim process of sewing Anatole's body into his shroud.

Slowly, as if her legs were weighted down by lead, Léonie climbed the stairs and made for Isolde's chamber. Marieta was at her mistress's side. A doctor Léonie did not recognize, in a high black top hat and a modest tipped collar, had arrived from the village, accompanied by a matronly nurse in a white starched apron. Resident staff from the thermal spa, they, too, had been engaged by Monsieur Baillard.

As Léonie entered the room, the doctor was administering a sedative. The nurse had rolled up Isolde's sleeve, and he pushed the needle of the thick silver syringe into her thin arm.

"How is she?" Léonie whispered to Marieta.

The maid gave a small shake of her head. "She struggles to stay with us, Madomaisèla."

Léonie stepped closer to the bed. Even to her untrained eyes, it was clear how Isolde hovered between life and death. She was gripped by a fierce, consuming fever. Léonie sat down and took her hand. As the hours passed, the sheets beneath Isolde became sodden and were changed. The nurse laid strips of cold linen cloth across her blazing forehead, which cooled her skin for no more than a moment.

When the doctor's medicine took effect, heat turned to cold and Isolde's frame shook beneath the covers, as one afflicted with Saint Vitus' dance.

Léonie's feverish flashbacks to the violence she had witnessed were kept at bay by her fears for Isolde's health. So, too, the weight of loss threatening to overwhelm her. Her mother dead. Anatole dead. Isolde's life and that of her unborn child hanging in the balance.

The moon rose in the sky. The Eve of All Saints.

SHORTLY AFTER THE CLOCK had struck eleven, there was a knock at the door and Pascal appeared.

"Madomaisèla Léonie," he said in hushed tones. "There are . . . men here to see you."

"The priest? Abbé Saunière is here?" she queried.

He shook his head. "Monsieur Baillard," he said. "And also the police."

Taking her leave of the doctor, and promising Marieta she would return as soon as she could, Léonie quit the chamber and quickly followed Pascal along the passageway.

At the top of the staircase, she halted and looked down at the collection of black top hats and greatcoats in the hall. Two wore the uniform of the Parisian gendarme, a third a shabby provincial version of it. In the forest of dark and somber clothes, a pale suit on a lean figure.

"Monsieur Baillard," she cried, running down the stairs and taking his hands in hers. "I am so glad you are here." She looked at him. "Anatole . . ."

Her voice broke. She was unable to pronounce the words.

Baillard nodded. "I have come to pay my respects," he said formally, then lowered his voice so that his companions could not overhear. "And Madama Vernier? How goes it with her?"

"Badly. If anything, the state of her mind is of more concern to the doctor at present than the consequences of her wound. Although it is important to ensure her blood does not become infected, the bullet only nicked the inside of her arm." Léonie stopped abruptly, only now realizing what Monsieur Baillard had said. "You knew they were married?" she whispered. "But I did not . . . How—"

Baillard put his finger to his lips. "This is not a conversation to be had now and in such company." He threw her a smile, then raised his voice. "By happenstance, Madomaisèla Léonie, these gentlemen and I found ourselves traveling the drive to the Domaine de la Cade. A coincidence of timing."

The younger of the two officers removed his hat and stepped forward. He had black smudged rings under his eyes, as if he had not slept for days.

"Inspector Thouron," he said, offering his hand. "From Paris, the commissariat of the eighth arrondissement. My condolences, Mademoiselle Vernier. And I regret I am also the bearer of bad news. Worse still, it is old news. For some weeks, I have been seeking your brother to inform him—indeed, you yourself also—that—"

Léonie withdrew the letter from her pocket. "Do not distress yourself, Monsieur l'Inspecteur," she said dully. "I know of my mother's death. This arrived yesterday, albeit by a most circuitous route. Also, this evening, Vic—"

She broke off, not wishing to speak his name.

Thouron's eyes narrowed. "You and your late brother have been most difficult to locate," he said.

Léonie was aware of a quickness and intelligence behind the disheveled appearance and exhausted features.

"And in the light of the . . . tragedy of this evening, it leads me to wonder if perhaps the events of Paris a month ago and what happened here tonight are in some way connected?"

Léonie darted a glance at Monsieur Baillard, then at the older man standing beside Inspector Thouron. His hair was flecked with gray, and he had the strong, dark features characteristic of the Midi.

"You have not introduced me, as yet, Inspector Thouron, to your colleague," she said, hoping to delay a little longer the formal interview.

"Forgive me," he said. "This is Inspector Bouchou of the Carcassonne gendarmerie. Bouchou has been assisting me in locating you."

Léonie looked from one to the other. "I do not understand, Inspector Thouron. You sent a letter from Paris yet have come in person also? And you are here tonight. How is this?"

The two men exchanged a look.

"May I suggest, gentlemen," Audric Baillard said quietly but in a tone of authority that invited no disagreement, "that we continue this conversation in some more private setting?"

Léonie felt the touch of Baillard's fingers on her arm and realized a decision was required of her.

"There is a fire in the drawing room," she said.

THE SMALL GROUP crossed the checkerboard hall, and Léonie pushed open the door.

The memory of Anatole held within the drawing room was so strong that she faltered. In her mind's eye, she saw him standing before the fire, his coat-tails held up to let the heat of the flames warm his back, his hair glistening. Or by the window, a cigarette wedged deep between his fingers, talking to Dr. Gabignaud the night of the supper party. Or leaning over the green baize card table, watching while she and Isolde played vingt-et-un. He seemed to have written himself into the fabric of the room, although Léonie had never known it until this second.

It was left to Monsieur Baillard to invite the officers to take a seat and to steer her to a corner of the chaise longue, where she sat, as if half asleep. He remained standing behind her.

Thouron explained the sequence of events, as they had pieced them together, of the night of her mother's murder on September 20, the discovery of the body, and the gradual steps the investigation had taken that had led them to Carcassonne, and from there to Rennes-les-Bains.

Léonie heard the words as if they were coming from a long way away. They did not penetrate her mind. Even though it was her mother of whom Thouron spoke—and she had loved her mother—the loss of Anatole had set a wall of stone around her heart that allowed no other emotion to enter. There would be time enough to grieve for Marguerite. For the gentle and honorable doctor, too. But for now, nothing but Anatole—and the promise she had made to her brother to protect his wife and child—had any purchase in her mind.

"So," Thouron was concluding, "the concierge admitted he had been paid to pass on any correspondence. The maid in the Debussy household confirmed that she, too, had seen the man loitering around the rue de Berlin in the days leading up to and after the ... the incident." Thouron paused. "Indeed, had it not been for the letter your late brother wrote to your mother, I cannot see how we would have found you yet."

"Have you identified the man, Thouron?" inquired Baillard.

"By sight only. An unfortunate-looking individual. A raw and angry complexion, with little or no hair on a blistered scalp."

Léonie started. Three pairs of eyes looked to her.

"Do you know him, Mademoiselle Vernier?" Thouron asked.

An image of him holding the muzzle of his gun to Dr. Gabignaud's temple and pulling the trigger. The explosion of bone and blood staining the forest floor.

She took a deep breath. "He is Victor Constant's man," she said.

Thouron exchanged another look with Bouchou. "The Comte de Tourmaline?"

"I beg your pardon?"

"It is the same man, Constant, Tourmaline. He goes under either name, depending on the circumstances or the company he is keeping."

"He gave me his card," she said in a hollow voice. "Victor Constant."

She felt the reassuring pressure of Audric Baillard's hand on her shoulder. "Is the Comte de Tourmaline a suspect in this matter, Inspector Thouron?" he inquired.

The officer hesitated, then, clearly deciding that there was no benefit to concealment, nodded. "And he, too, we discovered, had traveled from Paris to the Midi some days after the late Monsieur Vernier."

Léonie did not hear. All she could think about was the way her heart had leapt when Victor Constant took her hand. How she had kept his card safe, deceiving Anatole. How, in her imagination, she had allowed him into her company by day and in her dreams at night.

She had led him to them. Because of her, Anatole lay dead.

"Léonie," Baillard asked softly. "Was Constant the man from whom Madama Vernier fled? With whom Sénher Anatole dueled this evening?"

Léonie forced herself to reply. "It was he," she said in a dead voice.

Baillard walked across the room to the small, round drinks table and poured Léonie a glass of brandy, then came back.

"From your expressions, gentlemen," he said, pressing the glass into her cold fingers, "I think this man is known to you."

"He is," Thouron confirmed. "Several times his name came up in the inquiry but never with evidence enough to associate him with the crime. He appears to have nursed a vendetta against Monsieur Vernier, a clever and sly campaign until these last weeks, when he has become less careful."

"Or more arrogant," put in Bouchou. "There was an incident at a . . . house of recreation in the quartier Barbès in Carcassonne, which left a girl badly disfigured."

"We believe his increasingly erratic behavior is, in part, due to the aggressive acceleration of his illness. It has begun to affect his brain." Thouron broke off and mouthed the word so that Léonie would not hear. "Syphilis."

Baillard came round from behind the settee and sat down beside Léonie.

"Tell Inspector Thouron what you know," he said, taking her hand.

Léonie raised the glass to her lips and took another drink. The alcohol burned her throat, but it killed the sour taste in her mouth.

What need for concealment now?

She began to talk, holding nothing back, detailing everything that had happened—from the burial in Montmartre and the attack in the Passage des Panoramas to the moment she and her beloved Anatole disembarked the *courrier publique* in the Place du Pérou and the bloody events of this evening in the woods of the Domaine de la Cade.

March, September, October.

UPSTAIRS, ISOLDE WAS STILL held captive by the brain fever that had overtaken her on the instant she saw Anatole fall.

Images, thoughts glided in and out of her mind. Her eyes flickered half open. For a fleeting, joyful moment, she thought herself lying in Anatole's arms with the flickering light of the candle reflected in his brown eyes, but the vision faded. The skin began to slip from his face, revealing the skull beneath, leaving only a death's head of bone and teeth and black holes where his eyes had been.

And always the whisperings, the voices, Constant's malicious silver tones insinuating themselves into her overheated brain. She felt herself tossing and turning on the pillow, trying to rid the echo from her head but succeeding only in making the cacophony louder. Which the voice, which the echo?

She dreamed she saw their son, crying for the father he had never known, separated from Anatole as if behind a sheet of glass. She cried out to them both, but no sounds came from her lips and they did not hear her. When she reached out, the glass shattered in myriad sharp pieces and she was left touching skin as cold and unyielding as marble. Statues only.

Memories, dreams, premonitions. A mind shaken loose from its moorings.

AS THE CLOCK TICKED down the minutes to midnight, the witching hour, the wind began to whistle and howl and rattle the wooden frames of the windows of the house.

A restless night. Not a night to be abroad.

Part X

The Lake
October 2007

84

⚮

Wednesday, October 31, 2007

When Meredith woke again, Hal was gone.

She put out her hand to the empty space in the bed where he had slept beside her. The sheet was cold, but the soft smell of him on the pillow and the impression where his head had rested remained.

The shutters were closed and it was dark in the room. Meredith looked at the time. Eight o'clock. She guessed Hal didn't want the maids to see him and had gone back to his own room. Her hand stole to her cheek, as if her skin held the recollection of where his lips had kissed her goodbye, even if she could not remember.

For a while, she lay burrowed deep in the covers, thinking about Hal, thinking about the feel of him beside her, within her, the emotions she had allowed to come flooding out last night. From Hal, her thoughts drifted to Léonie, the girl with the copper hair, her other nighttime companion.

I cannot sleep.

The words Meredith remembered from her dream, heard and yet not spoken. The sense of pity, of restlessness, the fact that Léonie wanted something of her.

Meredith slipped out of bed. She pulled on a pair of thick socks to keep her feet warm. Hal had forgotten his sweater, lying in a heap by the chair where he had tossed it last night. She held it to her face, breathing in the scent of him. Then she put it on, way too big and baggy, and found some sweats.

She looked at the portrait. The photograph of the sepia soldier, great-grandfather Vernier, was tucked into the corner of the frame where she'd put it last night. Meredith felt the tug of possibility. The mismatched ideas that had been massing in her mind had settled during the course of the night.

The obvious first step was to find out if Anatole Vernier had been married, although it was easier said than done. She also needed to find out how he and Léonie Vernier were connected to Isolde Lascombe. Had they lived in the house in 1891, around the time the photograph had been taken, or were they just visitors that fall? As her online detective work yesterday had reminded her, ordinary people didn't just appear on the Internet. You had to trawl through genealogy sites, you needed names and dates and towns of birth and death to even have a chance of getting the information.

She booted up the computer and logged on. She was disappointed, but not surprised, to find there was nothing more from Mary, but she fired off another e-mail to Chapel Hill, filling her in on the last twenty-four hours and asking if she could check out a couple more things. She said nothing about Hal. She said nothing about Léonie. No sense in giving her cause to worry. She signed off, promising to keep in touch, and pressed send.

A little cold and realizing she was thirsty, Meredith went to the bathroom to fill the kettle. While she was waiting for the water to boil, she ran her eyes along the spines of the books on the shelf above the bureau. Her attention was caught by one titled *Diables et Esprits Maléfiques et Phantômes de la Montagne*. She took it out and opened it. The flyleaf told her it was a new edition of an earlier book by a local author, Audric S. Baillard, who had lived in a village in the Pyrenees, Los Seres, and died in 2005. There was no date of original publication, but it was obviously a local classic. According to the reviews on the back, it was considered the definitive text on Pyrenean mountain folklore.

Meredith glanced down the index and saw the book was divided into stories by region—Couiza, Coustaussa, Durban, Espéraza, Fa, Limoux, Rennes-les-Bains, Rennes-le-Château, Quillan. The illustration gracing the section on Rennes-les-Bains was a black-and-white photograph of the Place des Deux Rennes, taken about 1900, when it was known as the Place du Pérou. Meredith smiled. It seemed so familiar. She could even pick out the exact spot, beneath the spreading branches of the *platanes*, where her ancestor had stood.

The kettle whistled and clicked off. She poured a packet of hot chocolate into a cup, then took the drink and the book to the chair at the window and began to read.

The stories in the collection were similar from place to place—myths of demons and devils, generations, even millennia old, a linking of folklore with natural phenomena: the Devil's Armchair, the Horned Mountain, the Devil's Lake, all the names she'd already come across on the map. She flicked back to the imprint page again, checking that there really was no clue as to when the book had first been published. The information wasn't there. The latest story she noticed was from the early 1900s, although, given that the author had only died a couple of years ago, she assumed he'd gathered the stories more recently.

Baillard's style was clear and sparse, giving the factual information with the minimum of embellishment. With excitement, Meredith discovered that there was a whole section on the Domaine de la Cade. The property had come into the hands of the Lascombe family during the Wars of Religion, a series of conflicts fought between Catholics and Huguenots from 1562 to 1568. Ancient families had fallen, replaced by *parvenus* rewarded for their loyalty to either the Catholic House of Guise or the Calvinist House of Bourbon.

She read quickly. Jules Lascombe had inherited the property on the death of his father, Guy Lascombe, in 1865. He had married an Isolde Labourde in 1885, and died without issue in 1891. She smiled at another piece of the puzzle falling into place, looking over at the ageless Isolde, Jules's widow, behind the glass of the portrait. Then it occurred to her that she hadn't noticed Isolde's name on the Lascombe-Bousquet family tomb in Rennes-les-Bains. Meredith wondered why not.

Something else to check out.

She dropped her eyes back to the page. Baillard moved to the legends associated with the Domaine. There had been, for many years, rumors of a terrifying and vicious wild beast that terrorized the countryside around Rennes-les-Bains, attacking children and land workers on isolated farms. The distinguishing feature of the attacks was claw marks, three wide gashes across the face. Unusual marks.

Meredith stopped again, thinking of the injuries sustained by Hal's father while his car lay in the river gorge. And the defaced statue of Mary set on the Visigoth pillar in the approach to the church in Rennes-le-Château. Hard on its heels, the memory of a fragment of her nightmare came back to her—the image of a tapestry hanging on a poorly lit stair. The sensation of being chased, claws and black fur touching her skin, sliding over her hands.

Un, deux, trois, loup.

And back to the graveyard in Rennes-les-Bains and the recollection of one of the names on the war memorial to the dead of World War I: Saint-Loup.

Coincidence?

Meredith stretched her arms above her head, trying to get rid of the cold and the early-morning stiffness and her memories of the nightmare, then dropped her eyes back to the page. There were many deaths and disappearances between 1870 and 1885. A period of relative calm followed, then there was an intensification of rumors from the autumn of 1891 onward and a growing belief that the creature—a demon, in local folklore—was harbored within a Visigoth sepulchre that lay within the grounds of the Domaine de la Cade. There were deaths—unattributed attacks—intermittently over the next six years, then the attacks came to an abrupt end in 1897. The author didn't actually say so, but he implied that the end of the terror was connected to the fact that parts of the house were ruined by fire and the sepulchre destroyed.

Meredith closed the book and curled up tight in the chair. She sipped her hot chocolate as she tried to marshal her thoughts, realizing what was bugging her. How weird was it that in a work devoted to folklore and legend, there was no reference to the tarot deck? Audric Baillard must have heard about the cards during his research. The deck was not only inspired by the local landscape and printed by the Bousquet family but also fell within the exact period of time covered by the book.

A deliberate omission?

Then, suddenly, she felt it again. A chillness, a density in the air that had not been there before. The sense of there being someone there, not far away, not in the room but close by. Fleeting, an imprint only.

Léonie?

Meredith stood up, finding herself drawn to the window. She unfastened the long metal catch, pulled back the two tall panes of glass and pushed open the shutters, letting them fall back against the wall. It was cold, which made her eyes water. The tops of the trees were swaying, whistling and sighing as the wind wound itself around the ancient trunks, through the tangle of leaf and bark. The air was restless, carrying the memory of the echo of the music within it. Notes drifting on the breeze. The melody of the place itself.

As Meredith cast her eyes over the grounds spread out before her, she caught a movement out of the corner of her eye. She looked down and saw a lithe, graceful figure in a long cloak with the hood pulled up over its head emerge from the lee of the building.

It seemed to her that the wind was gathering force, racing now through the arched opening cut into the high box hedge that led to the wild meadows and rough grass beyond. Distant as it was, she could just make out the white crests as it sent the water of the lake lapping up over the edge.

The outline, the impression, the figure kept to the shadows, skimming beneath the rising gaze of the pale sun, which darted in and out of a thin strata of clouds that chased across the pink sky. She seemed to glide over the damp grass, covered with the slightest sheen of dew. Meredith caught the smell of earth, of autumn, of damp soil, of burned stubble, of bonfires. Of bones.

She watched in captivated silence as the figure made its way—*her* way, Meredith felt sure—to the far side of the ornamental lake. For a moment it stopped and stood on a small promontory overlooking the water. Meredith's vision seemed to narrow right in, impossibly close, like a camera close-up. She imagined the hood falling back from the girl's face. It was pale and perfectly symmetrical, with green eyes that once had glinted as clear as emeralds. Shade without color. The skein of tumbling curls fell, like twists of beaten copper, transparent in the moonlight, over the slim shoulders of her red dress and down to her narrow waist. Shape without form. She seemed to hold Meredith's gaze with her own, reflecting back at her her own hopes and fears and imaginings.

Then she slipped away into the woods.

"Léonie?" Meredith whispered into the silence.

For a while longer she kept vigil at the window, staring at the place on the far side of the lake where the figure had stood. The distant air was still. Nothing stirred in the shadows.

Finally, she pulled back inside and shut the window.

A few days ago—no, hours, even—she would have been freaked out. Would have feared the worst. Would have looked at her reflection in the mirror and seen instead Jeanette's face staring out at her.

Not now.

Meredith couldn't account for it, but everything had changed. Her mind felt totally clear. She was fine. She wasn't frightened. She wasn't going crazy. The sightings, the visitations, were a sequence, like a piece of music. Beneath the bridge in Rennes-les-Bains—water. On the Sougraigne road—earth. Here in the hotel—particularly in this specific room, where her presence was strongest—air.

Swords, the suit of air, represented intelligence and intellect. Cups, the suit associated with water, the emotions. Pentacles, the suit of earth, of physical reality, of treasure. Of the four suits, only fire was missing. Wands, the suit of fire, energy and conflict.

The story is in the cards.

Or maybe the quartet was completed in the past and not the present? In the fire that had destroyed much of the Domaine de la Cade more than a hundred years ago?

Meredith went back to the replica deck Laura had given her, turning over each card in turn and staring again at the images, as she had done last night, willing them to give up their secrets. As she laid them out, one by one, she set her thoughts free. She thought of what Hal had told her on the way to Rennes-le-Château, of how the Visigoths buried their kings and noblemen, with their treasure, in hidden graves rather than in graveyards. In secret chambers below the river, after diverting the river's course for long enough to excavate the site and prepare the burial chamber.

If the original deck had survived the fire, hidden safe within the grounds of the Domaine de la Cade, then where more secure than an ancient Visigoth burial site? The sepulchre itself, according to Baillard's book, dated back to that same period. If there was a river in the grounds, it would be the perfect hiding place. In plain view yet totally inaccessible.

Outside, finally, sunlight split through the clouds.

Meredith yawned. She felt dizzy from lack of sleep, but she was buzzing with adrenaline. She glanced at the clock. Hal had said Dr. O'Donnell was coming at ten, but that was still an hour away.

Plenty of time for what she had in mind.

HAL WAS STANDING in his bedroom in the staff quarters, thinking of Meredith.

After he'd helped her get back to sleep after her nightmare, he'd found himself wide awake. Not wanting to disturb her by turning on the light, in the end he'd decided to slip away back to his own room to go over his notes before the meeting with Shelagh O'Donnell. He wanted to be prepared.

He glanced at his watch. Nine o'clock. An hour to wait before he saw Meredith again.

His windows, on the top floor, looked out to the south and to the east, giving him an uninterrupted view over the lawns and the lake at the back, and the kitchen and service areas to the side. He watched one of the porters throw a black refuse bag into the bin. Another was standing, his arms crossed to keep away the cold, smoking a cigarette. His breath puffed white clouds into the clear morning air.

Hal sat down on the sill, then got up and walked across the room to get some water, then changed his mind. He was too anxious to settle. He knew he shouldn't get his hopes up that Dr. O'Donnell was going to have all the answers. But he still couldn't help himself believing that she would at least be able to give him some information about the night his dad died. She might remember something that would force the police to treat it as a suspicious death rather than a traffic accident.

He ran his fingers through his hair.

His thoughts strayed back to Meredith again. He smiled. Maybe, when it was all over, she wouldn't mind if he went to visit her in the States. He brought himself up short. It was ridiculous to be thinking along such lines after only a couple of days, but he knew. He hadn't felt so strongly about a girl for a long time. Ever.

And what was to stop him? No job, an empty flat in London. He might as well be in America as anywhere. He could do whatever the hell he liked. He'd have money. He knew his uncle would buy him out.

If Meredith would like him there.

Hal stood at his high window, watching the life of the hotel go on silently below. He flexed his arms above his head and yawned. A car was slowly driving up the long drive. He watched as a tall, thin woman with cropped dark hair got out and then walked tentatively up the front steps.

Moments later, the phone on his bedside table rang. It was Eloise in reception, telling him his guest had arrived.

"What? She's nearly an hour early."

"Shall I ask her to wait?" Eloise asked.

Hal hesitated. "No, it's fine. I'll be right down."

He dragged his jacket from the back of the chair, then rushed down two flights of narrow service stairs. At the bottom, he paused to slip his arms into his jacket and to make a call from the staff phone.

. . .

MEREDITH PUT Hal's pale brown sweater over her blue jeans and long sleeved T-shirt, pushed her feet into her boots, then grabbed her denim jacket, a scarf and a pair of wooly gloves, figuring it would still be cold outside. Her hand was already on the door handle when the phone rang.

She rushed to answer. "Hi, you," she said, experiencing a kick of pleasure at the sound of Hal's voice.

But his reply was sharp and to the point. "She's here."

85

Who? Léonie?" Meredith stammered, her thoughts short-circuiting for a moment.

"Who? No, Dr. O'Donnell. She's already here. I'm in reception now. Can you come down and join us?"

Meredith threw a glance at the window, realizing that her expedition to the lake would have to wait a little while longer.

"Sure." She sighed. "Give me five."

She peeled off her extra layers, replaced Hal's sweater with a red crew-neck of her own, brushed her hair, then let herself out of her room. As she emerged onto the landing, she paused to look down on the checkerboard entrance hall. She could see Hal talking with a tall, dark-haired woman she kind of recognized. It took a moment to place her, then she remembered. The Place des Deux Rennes the night she arrived, leaning against the wall, smoking.

"How about that," she muttered to herself.

Hal's face lit up as she approached.

"Hi," she said, giving him a quick kiss on the cheek, then offering her hand to Dr. O'Donnell. "I'm Meredith. Sorry to keep you waiting."

The woman's eyes narrowed. She was clearly having trouble placing Meredith.

"We exchanged a couple of words the night of the funeral," Meredith said, helping her out. "Outside the pizzeria in the square?"

"We did?" Then her face relaxed. "That's right."

"I'll get us coffee brought to the bar," Hal said, leading the way. "It will be quiet enough for us to talk there."

Meredith and Dr. O'Donnell followed him, Meredith asking the other woman polite questions to break the ice. How long she'd lived in Rennes-les-Bains, what her connection with the area was, what she did for a living. The usual sort of stuff.

Shelagh O'Donnell answered easily enough, but there was a nervous tension behind everything she said. She was very thin. Her eyes were constantly in motion, and she repeatedly rubbed her fingertips against her thumb. Meredith guessed she was not more than early thirties, but she had the lined skin of someone older. Meredith could see why the police might not have taken her late-night observations seriously.

They sat at the same table in the corner that they had occupied the previous evening with Hal's uncle. The atmosphere was very different in the daytime. It was hard to remember the wine and cocktails from the night before given the smell of beeswax polish and fresh flowers on the bar and the stack of boxes waiting to be unpacked.

"*Merci,*" Hal said, as the waitress put the tray of coffee in front of them.

There was a pause while he poured. Dr. O'Donnell took hers black. As she stirred in her sugar, Meredith noticed the same red scars on her wrists she'd seen the first time round, and wondered what had happened to cause them.

"Before anything," Hal said, "I want to thank you for agreeing to see me."

Meredith was relieved that he sounded calm, collected and rational.

"I knew your father. He was a good man, a friend. But I've got to tell you, I really don't have anything more I can tell you."

"I understand," Hal replied, "but if you could just bear with me while I run through things. I appreciate the accident was more than a month ago, but there are things about the investigation I'm not happy with. I was hoping you might be able to tell me a little about the actual night. I think the police said you thought you had heard something?"

Shelagh darted her eyes to Meredith, then to Hal, then away again. "They're still saying Seymour went off the road because he was drunk?"

"That's what I find hard to accept. I just can't see Dad doing that."

Shelagh picked at a thread on her pants. Meredith could see how nervous she was.

"How did you meet Hal's father?" she said, hoping to give her a bit of confidence.

Hal looked surprised at her interruption, but Meredith gave a tiny shake of the head, so he let her run with it.

Dr. O'Donnell smiled. It transformed her face and, for a moment, Meredith could see how attractive she would be if she were less beaten down by life.

"That night in the square, you asked me what *bien-aimé* meant."

"That's right."

"Well, Seymour was just that. Someone everyone liked. Everyone respected him, too, even if they didn't really know him. He was always polite, courteous to waiters, shopkeepers, treated everybody with respect, unlike . . ." She broke off. Meredith and Hal exchanged a look, both thinking the same thing—that Shelagh was comparing Seymour to Julian Lawrence. "He wasn't here much, of course," she continued quickly, "but I got to know him when . . ."

She paused and messed with a button on her jacket.

"Yes?" encouraged Meredith. "You got to know him when . . . ?"

Shelagh sighed. "I went through a . . . tricky time in my life a couple of years back. I was working on an archaeological dig not far from here, in the Sabarthès Mountains, and got drawn into something. Made some bad decisions." She paused. "The long and the short of it is, things have been difficult since then. My health's not so good, so I can manage only a few hours a week, doing a little valuation work at the ateliers in Couiza." She stopped again. "I came to Rennes-les-Bains to live about eighteen months ago now. I have a friend, Alice, who lives in a village not far from here, Los Seres, with her husband and daughter, so it was a logical place to come."

Meredith recognized the name. "Los Seres is where the author Audric Baillard came from, right?"

Hal raised his eyebrows.

"I was reading a book of his earlier. Up in my room. One of your father's *vide-grenier* bargains."

Now he smiled, obviously pleased she'd remembered.

"That's the man," Shelagh said. "My friend Alice knew him well." Her eyes darkened. "I met him, too."

Meredith could see from the look on Hal's face that the conversation had brought something back to him, but he didn't say anything.

"The point is, I had been having problems. Drinking too much." Shelagh turned to Hal. "I met your dad in a bar. In Couiza, actually. I was tired; I'd probably had one too many. We got talking. He was kind, a little worried about me. Insisted he drive me back to Rennes-les-Bains. Nothing dodgy about it. Next morning, he turned up and took me back to Couiza to pick up my car." She paused. "Never mentioned it again, but after that, he always popped in when he was over here from England."

Hal nodded. "So you don't believe he would have got behind the wheel if he was in no state to drive?"

Shelagh shrugged. "I can't say for certain, but no, I just can't see it."

Meredith still thought they were both a little naive. Plenty of people said one thing and did another, but Shelagh's evident admiration and respect for Hal's father impressed her all the same.

"The police told Hal that you think you heard the accident but didn't realize what it was until the next morning," she said gently. "Is that right?"

Shelagh raised her coffee cup to her mouth with a shaky hand, took a couple of sips, then put it back in the saucer with a rattle.

"To be honest, I don't know what I heard. If it was connected at all."

"Go on."

"Definitely something, not the usual screech of brakes or tires when people take the bend too fast but just a kind of rumbling, I guess." She paused. "I was listening to John Martyn, *Solid Air*. It's pretty mellow, but even so, I wouldn't have heard the sound outside if it hadn't been in the pause between the end of one track and the start of the next."

"What time was this?"

"About one or thereabouts. I got up and looked out of the window, but I couldn't see anything at all. It was completely dark, completely quiet. I just assumed the car had gone past. It was only in the morning when I saw the police and ambulance down at the river that I wondered."

Hal's face made it clear he didn't know where Shelagh was going with this. Meredith, however, did.

"Wait up," she said, "let me get this straight. You're saying you looked out and there were no headlights. Right?"

Shelagh nodded.

"And you told the police this?"

Hal was looking from one to the other. "I'm not sure I see why this is so significant."

"It might not be," Meredith said quickly. "It's just weird. First, even if your father was way over the limit—I'm not saying he was—would he really be driving with no lights?"

Hal frowned. "But if the car went over the bridge into the water, they could have been smashed."

"Sure, but from what you said earlier, it wasn't particularly badly damaged." She carried on. "Also, according to what the police told you, Hal, Shelagh heard a screech of brakes, et cetera, right?"

He nodded.

"Except Shelagh's just told us that's precisely what she didn't hear."

"I still don't—"

"Two things. First, why is the police report inaccurate? Second—and, I admit, this is speculation—if your father did lose control on the bend and went over, surely there would have been (a) more noise and (b) something to see. I can't believe all the lights would have blown."

Hal's expression started to change. "Are you suggesting the car might have been rolled over the edge? Rather than driven?"

"It's an explanation," Meredith said.

For a moment they stared at each other, their roles reversed—Hal skeptical, Meredith building a case.

"There is something else," Shelagh put in. They both turned to her, for a moment almost having forgotten she was there. "When I turned in, maybe a quarter of an hour later, I heard another car on the road. Because of earlier, it made me look out."

"And?" said Hal.

"It was a blue Peugeot, heading south in the direction of Sougraigne. It only occurred to me in the morning that this was after the accident, about one-thirty by then. If they'd come through the town, the driver couldn't have failed to see the car crashed into the river. Why didn't they notify the police?"

Meredith and Hal looked at each other, thinking of the car parked round the back in the staff lot.

"How could you be sure it was a blue Peugeot?" Hal asked, keeping his voice level. "It was dark."

Shelagh flushed. "It's the exact same type and model as my car. Everyone's got one round here," she said defensively. "Besides, there's a streetlamp outside my bedroom window."

"What did the police say when you told them?"

"They didn't seem to think it was important." She glanced at the door. "I'm sorry, I've got to make a move."

She stood up. Meredith and Hal did the same.

"Look," he said, pushing his hands into his pockets, "I know this is a terrible imposition, but is there any way I could persuade you to come to the police station in Couiza with me? Tell them what you've just told us."

Shelagh started to shake her head. "I don't know," she said. "I've already made a statement."

"I know. But if we went together . . ." he persisted. "I've seen the accident report and most of what you've told me isn't in the file. I'll run you over there." He fixed her with his blue gaze. "I just want to get to the bottom of it. For my dad's sake."

From the anguished expression on her face, Meredith could see how hard Shelagh was finding it. She clearly wanted nothing to do with the police. But her affection for Hal's father won out. She gave a sharp nod.

Hal sighed with relief. "Thank you," he said. "Thank you so much. I'll pick you up at, say, twelve. Give you the chance to get things sorted. Is that convenient?"

Shelagh nodded. "I have a couple of urgent errands to run this morning—it's why I was early coming up here—but I'll be home by eleven."

"Right you are. And home is?"

Shelagh gave her address. They all shook hands, a little awkward under the circumstances, then made their way back to the lobby. Meredith headed back to her room, leaving Hal to walk Dr. O'Donnell to her car.

Neither of them heard the sound of another door—the door separating the bar from the offices at the back—click shut.

86

Julian Lawrence was breathing fast and his blood was pounding in his head. He strode into his study, slamming the door behind him so hard that the reverberation made the glass in the bookcases rattle.

He rummaged in his jacket pocket for his cigarettes and lighter. His hand was shaking so badly, it took several attempts to light it. The commissaire had mentioned that someone had come forward, an Englishwoman called Shelagh O'Donnell, but that she hadn't seen anything. The name had rung a bell, but he'd let it go. Since the police didn't seem to take her seriously, it hadn't seemed important. They told him she was an *ivrogne,* a drunk.

When she'd turned up at the hotel this morning, even then he hadn't put two and two together. The irony was that he'd slipped into the office at the back of the bar to listen to the conversation between her, Hal and Meredith Martin only because he had recognized her from one of the antiques dealerships in Couiza. He had jumped to the conclusion that Ms. Martin had invited her here to discuss the Bousquet Tarot.

Having listened in, he realized why O'Donnell's name was familiar. In July 2005, there'd been an incident at an archaeological dig site in the Sabarthès Mountains. Julian couldn't remember the exact details, but several people had been killed, including a well-known local author whose name escaped him. None of that mattered.

What did matter was that she had seen his car. Julian was sure it would be impossible to prove it was his rather than any one of many identical vehicles, but it might be just enough to tip the balance. The police hadn't treated O'Donnell seriously as a witness before but, if Hal kept pushing it, they might.

He couldn't believe O'Donnell had not yet associated the Peugeot with the Domaine de la Cade, otherwise she would hardly have come up here this morning. But he couldn't risk her making the connection.

He would have to do something. Yet again, his hand was being forced, just as his brother had done. Julian glanced up at the painting on the wall above his desk: the old tarot symbol, offering infinite possibilities, while he felt increasingly trapped.

On the shelf below it were objects he had found during his excavations of the estate. He had been slow to accept that the ruined sepulchre was just that, a few old stones, nothing else. But he had turned up one or two items. An expensive, although damaged, timepiece bearing the initials AV and a silver locket with two miniatures inside, both taken from graves he had discovered by the lake.

This was what he cared about, the past. Finding the cards. Not sorting out the problems of the present.

Julian went to the tantalus on the sideboard and poured himself a brandy to steady his nerves. He drained it down in one gulp, then glanced at the clock.

Ten-fifteen.

He took his jacket from the back of the door, put a mint in his mouth, grabbed his car keys and headed out.

87

Meredith left Hal talking on the phone, trying to fix the meeting at the commissariat in Couiza before going to call for Dr. O'Donnell at midday as promised.

She kissed him on the cheek. He raised a hand, mouthed that he'd see her later, then went back to his one-sided conversation. Meredith paused to ask the nice receptionist if she knew where she might borrow a shovel. Eloise made no reaction to this odd request but simply suggested that the gardener should be working in the gardens and might be able to help.

"Thank you. I'll ask him," Meredith said, then wrapped her scarf around her neck and went through the glass doors and onto the terrace. The early-morning mist had almost burnt away, although the grass was glistening with a silver dew. Everything was bathed in a copper and gold light, set against a chill sky flecked with pink-and-white clouds.

There was already a heady smell of Halloween bonfires in the air. Meredith breathed it in, the smell of fall taking her back to her childhood. She and Mary religiously carving faces in pumpkins for lanterns. Getting her trick-or-treat costume ready. She usually went out with her friends dressed as a ghost, a white bedsheet with two holes cut for the eyes and a scary mouth painted on in black marker.

As she ran lightly down the steps to the gravel path, she wondered what Mary was doing right now. Then she pulled herself up. Only a quarter after five back home. Mary would still be asleep. Maybe she'd call her later to wish her a happy Halloween.

The gardener was nowhere to be seen, but his barrow was there. Meredith looked around, however, there was no sign. She hesitated, then took the small trowel lying on the top of the leaves, tucked it in her pocket and struck out across the lawns toward the lake. She'd bring it back as soon as she could.

It was an odd sensation, but she felt she was following in the footsteps of the figure she'd seen on the lawns earlier.

Seen? Imagined?

She found herself glancing back at the facade of the hotel, at one point stopping to figure out which was her window, and whether she could possibly have seen what she thought she had from such a long way off.

As she completed the path around the left-hand side of the lake, the ground began to rise. She climbed up a grassy slope to a small promontory that over-looked the water, straight back at the hotel. It seemed crazy, but she was con-vinced this was precisely where she had seen the figure standing earlier.

Imagined.

There was a curved stone bench in the shape of a crescent moon. The sur-face glistened with dew. Meredith wiped it with her gloves, then sat down. As always, by deep water, thoughts of Jeanette rushed into her mind, and the way she had chosen to end her life. Walking into Lake Michigan with her pockets weighted down with stones. Like Virginia Woolf, Meredith had learned years later in high school, although she doubted her mother had known that.

But as Meredith sat looking out over the lake, she surprised herself by feeling peaceful. She was thinking of her birth mother, but it wasn't accompanied by the usual feelings of guilt. No thumping heart, no rush of shame, no regret. This was a place of reflection, to be calm and private. The rattling of the crows in the trees, the higher-pitched twitterings of thrushes in the thick, high box hedge at her back, isolated from the hotel by the expanse of water yet still in plain view.

She lingered awhile longer, then decided to carry on walking. Two hours earlier, she had been frustrated not to be able to rush out and start looking for the ruins of the sepulchre. Given how Shelagh O'Donnell had been in the hotel, she figured Hal would have his hands full. She didn't expect him back much before one.

She pulled out her cell and checked that she had a signal, then put it away. He could call if he needed to get in touch with her.

Careful not to slip on the wet grass, she made her way back down to the level ground close to the side of the lake and took stock of her surroundings. In one direction the path led around the lake and back toward the house. In the other, a more overgrown track went into the beech woods.

Meredith took the left-hand path. Within minutes she was deep into the trees, winding through the dappled sunlight. The track led to a crisscross of interconnecting paths, all pretty similar. Some led uphill, others seemed to slope down toward the valley. She was intending to track down the ruins of the Visigoth sepulchre, then, working out from there, to look for a place where the cards could be hidden. Anything too obvious and they would have been found years ago, but she figured it was as good a place to start as any.

Meredith set off down a path that led to a small clearing. After a few minutes, the hillside dipped away sharply. The ground beneath her feet changed. She braced her legs, taking it slow on the slippery stones and gravel, jolting down, dislodging pinecones and fallen twigs until finally she found herself standing on some kind of natural platform, almost like a bridge. And underneath, intersecting it at right angles, was a strip of brown earth leading down through the green woodland all around it.

In the distance through a break in the trees, Meredith could pick out on the far hill a cluster of stone megaliths, gray among the wooded green, possibly the same ones Hal had pointed out to her on their way to Rennes-le-Château.

The hairs on the back of her neck stood on end.

She realized that, unless she was misremembering pretty much all the natural landmarks Hal had mentioned—the Fauteuil du Diable, the *bénitier,* the Étang du Diable—were visible. More than that, from this one spot, all the locations used as backdrops for the cards were also evident.

The sepulchre dated back to Visigoth times. So it stood to reason there might be other Visigoth burial sites within the grounds. Meredith looked around. And this, to her inexpert eye at least, looked much like a dry riverbed.

Trying to keep her excitement in check, she looked around for a way down. There wasn't an obvious one. She hesitated, crouched, and maneuvered herself round, then lowered herself over the edge. For a moment, there was nothing, as she hung suspended in the air on her elbows. Then she let herself go, dropping for a fraction of a heart-stopping second, until her feet found the ground.

She took the impact in her knees, then straightened up and started to make her way down. It looked like the bed of a winterbourne at the end of a dry summer but slick with light autumn drizzle. Meredith, working hard not to slip on the loose stones and film of wet topsoil, cast her eyes about her for anything out of the ordinary.

At first there seemed no break in the undergrowth, all tangled and dripping with dew. Then, a little farther, just before the track took another sharp dive down like a helter-skelter at a fairground, Meredith noticed a shallow depression. She moved closer until she could make out a flat gray stone peeking out from beneath the tangled roots of a spreading juniper bush, with its scratchy, needlelike leaves and green and purple fruit. The depression wasn't big enough to be a grave itself, but the stone didn't look as though it had been put there by chance. Meredith got out her cell and took a couple of photos.

She put her cell away, then reached in and pulled at the knotted undergrowth. The thin branches were strong and wiry, but she succeeded in pulling them far enough apart to peek into the damp green space around the roots.

She felt a spark of adrenaline. There was a ring of stones, eight in all. The pattern set a memory chasing in her mind. She narrowed her eyes, then realized the shape of the stones echoed the crown of stars on the image of La Force. And now that she came to think about it, she could see that the landscape right here was especially reminiscent in color and tone of that card.

With growing anticipation, Meredith thrust her hands into the foliage, feeling the green slime and mud seeping through the tips of her cheap woolen gloves, and dragged clear the biggest of the stones. She wiped the surface clean, then gave a sigh of satisfaction. Painted in black tar or paint was a five-pointed star set within a circle.

The symbol for the suit of pentacles. The treasure suit.

She took a couple more photos, then put the stone to one side. She pulled the stolen trowel from her pocket and started to dig, scraping against stones and shards of unfired clay tiles. She pulled out one of the larger pieces and examined it. It looked like a roof tile, although she wondered why such a thing would be buried out here, so far from the house.

Then the metal head of the trowel hit something substantial. Not wanting to damage anything, Meredith put the trowel to one side and finished the job by hand, burrowing at the mud and worms and black beetles, pulling off her gloves and letting her fingers be her eyes.

Finally, she felt a piece of heavy material, a waxed cloth. She pushed her head under the leaves to look and peeled the corners back to reveal the beautiful lacquered lid of a small chest with a crosshatch of mother-of-pearl inlay. It looked like a jewelry case or a lady's workbox, pretty and clearly expensive. On the top were two initials in dull corroded brass.

LV.

Meredith smiled. Léonie Vernier. It had to be.

She went to open the lid, then hesitated. What if the cards were inside? What would it mean? Did she even want to see them?

In a rush, she felt the solitude press down upon her. The sounds of the woods that had been so gentle, so reassuring, now seemed oppressive, threatening. She pulled her phone from her pocket, checked the time. Maybe she should give Hal a call? The desire to hear another human voice—his voice—stabbed at her. She thought better of it. He wouldn't want to be disturbed in the middle of his meeting with the police. She hesitated, then sent an SMS and straightaway regretted it. Displacement activity. And the last thing she wanted was to come across as needy.

Meredith looked back down at the box in front of her.

The story is in the cards.

She wiped her palms, greasy with exertion and anticipation, once more on her blue jeans. Then slowly she opened the lid. The box was full of spools of cotton thread, ribbons and thimbles. The inside of the padded lid was studded with needles and pins. With grimy fingers, raw from the cold and the digging, Meredith removed some of the cotton reels, burrowing through felt and cloth, as she had previously dug through the earth and dirt.

Then there they were. She saw the top card with the same green back, the delicate patterns of tree branches threaded through in gold and silver, although the color was chalkier, clearly painted by hand with a brush rather than made by a machine. She ran her fingers over the surface. A different texture, rough not smooth. More like parchment than the modern laminated deck.

Meredith made herself count to three, summoning the courage to turn the top card over.

Her own face stared up at her. Card XI. La Justice.

As she gazed at the hand-painted image, once more she was aware of whispering inside her head. Not like the voices that had hounded her mother but gentle and soft, the voice she had heard in her dream, carried on the air, slipping between the branches and trunks of the autumn trees.

Here, in this place, time moves away toward eternity.

Meredith stood up. The most logical move now would be to take the cards and go back to the house. Study them in the comfort of her own room, with all her notes, access to the Internet, the reproduction deck on hand to compare them with.

Except now she could hear Léonie's voice again. In the turning of a moment, the whole world seemed to have shrunk to this one place. The smell of the earth in her nostrils, the grit and soil under her nails, the dampness that seeped from the earth and into her bones.

Except this is not the place.

Something was calling her on deeper into the woods. The wind was getting louder, more forceful, carrying something more than just the noises of the forest. Music heard but not heard. She could pick out a faint melody in the rustling of the fallen leaves, the tapping of the bare branches of the beech trees a little farther off.

Single notes, a mournful melody in a minor key, and always the words in her head leading her on to the ruined sepulchre.

Aïci lo tems s'en, va res l'Eternitat.

. . .

Julian left the car unlocked in the parking area on the out-skirts of Rennes-les-Bains, then walked quickly down to the Place des Deux Rennes, diagonally across the square and into the small side street where Dr. O'Donnell lived.

He loosened the tie at his neck. There were patches of sweat under his arms. The more he'd thought about the situation, the more his concern had grown. He just wanted to find the cards. Anything that prevented that or delayed it was intolerable. No loose ends.

He hadn't thought about what he was going to say. He just knew that he could not allow her to go with Hal to the commissariat.

Then he turned the corner and saw her, sitting cross-legged on the low wall that separated the terrace of her property from the deserted public footpath that led along the river. She was smoking and pushing her hands through her hair, talking on a cell phone.

What was she saying?

Julian stopped, suddenly dizzy. Now he could hear her voice, a grating accent, all flat vowels, the one-sided conversation muffled by the pounding of the blood in his head.

He took a step closer, listening. Dr. O'Donnell leaned forward, and with sharp stabbing movements extinguished a cigarette in a silver ashtray. Certain words leapt out at him.

"I've got to see about the car."

Julian put his hand out to steady himself against the wall. His mouth felt dry, like salted fish, unpleasant and sour. He needed a drink to take away the taste. He looked round, no longer thinking straight. There was a stick lying on the ground, half poking out of the hedge. He picked it up. She was still talking, on and on, telling lies. Why wouldn't she stop talking?

Julian lifted the stick and brought it down, hard, upon her head.

Shelagh O'Donnell cried out in shock, so he hit her again to stop her from making any noise. She fell to her side on the stones. Then there was silence.

Julian dropped the weapon. For a moment, he stood dead-still. Then, horrified, disbelieving, he kicked the stick back into the hedge and started to run.

Part XI

The Sepulchre
November 1891—October 1897

88

Domaine de la Cade
Sunday, November 1, 1891

Anatole was buried in the grounds of the Domaine de la Cade. The spot chosen was the little promontory overlooking the valley at the far side of the lake, in the green shade, close by the crescent stone bench where Isolde often sat.

Abbé Saunière officiated at the meager ceremony. Léonie—on the arm of Audric Baillard—Maître Fromilhague and Madame Bousquet were the only mourners.

Isolde remained under constant watch in her chamber, unaware even that the funeral was taking place. Locked within her silent and suspended world, she did not know how fast or how slowly time was passing, if indeed time had ceased or if all experience was contained in the chime of a single minute. Her existence had shrunk to the tormented space of her mind. She knew light and dark, that sometimes the fever burned in her and sometimes the cold tore at her, but also that she was trapped somewhere between two worlds, shrouded in a veil she could not draw aside.

The same group paid their respects a day later to Dr. Gabignaud in the graveyard of the parish church in Rennes-les-Bains, this time the congregation swelled by the people of the town who had known and admired the young man. Dr. Courrent gave the address, praising Gabignaud's hard work, his passion, his sense of duty.

After the burials, Léonie, numb with grief and the responsibilities thrust suddenly on her young shoulders, withdrew to the Domaine de la Cade and ventured little out. The household fell into a joyless routine, day after endless day the same.

In the bare beech woods, snow fell early, blanketing the lawns and the park in white. The lake froze and lay, a mirror of ice, beneath the lowering clouds.

A new medical recruit, Gabignaud's replacement as Dr. Courrent's assistant, came daily from the town to monitor Isolde's progress.

"Madame Vernier's pulse is fast tonight," he said gravely, packing away his equipment into his black leather bag and unhooking his stethoscope from his neck. "The severity of grief, the strain upon her due to her condition, well, I fear for the full restoration of her faculties the longer this state persists."

THE WEATHER DEEPENED in December. Blustery winds drove in from the north, bringing with them hail and ice that assaulted the roof and windows of the house in waves.

The Aude valley was frozen in misery. Those without shelter, if fortunate, were taken in by their neighbors. Oxen starved in the fields, their hooves caught in the mud and ice, rotting. The rivers froze. The tracks were impassable. There was no food, for man or beast. The tinkling bell of the sacristan rang out over the fields as Christ was carried through the countryside to grace the lips of another dying sinner, over paths concealed and made treacherous beneath snow. It seemed that all living things would, one by one, simply cease to exist. No light, no warmth, like candles blown out.

In the parish church of Rennes-les-Bains, Curé Boudet preached masses for the dead and the bell tolled out its mournful passing note. In Coustaussa, Curé Gélis opened his doors and offered the cold flagstones of the presbytery floor to the homeless as shelter. In Rennes-le-Château, Abbé Saunière preached of the evil stalking the countryside and urged his congregation to seek salvation in the arms of the one true Church.

At the Domaine de la Cade, the staff, although shaken by what had taken place and their part in the matter, remained steadfast. In Isolde's continuing indisposition, they accepted Léonie as mistress of the house. But Marieta grew alarmed as sorrow stole from Léonie her appetite and rest, and as Léonie grew thin and pale. Her green eyes lost their shine. But her courage held. She remembered her promise to Anatole that she would protect Isolde and their child and was determined not to let down his memory.

Victor Constant stood accused of the murder of Marguerite Vernier in Paris, the murder of Anatole Vernier in Rennes-les-Bains and the attempted murder of Isolde Vernier, formerly Lascombe. There was also a prosecution pending arising out of the attack on the prostitute in Carcassonne. It was suggested—and accepted without further investigation—that Dr. Gabignaud, Charles Denarnaud and a third comrade in the sorry business had been killed on the orders of Victor Constant, even if it had not been his finger on the trigger.

The town disapproved of the news that Anatole and Isolde had married in secret, more at the haste of it rather than the fact that he was the nephew of her first husband. But it seemed that, given time, the arrangements at the Domaine de la Cade would come to be accepted.

The log pile against the scullery wall diminished. Isolde showed little sign of recovering her mental faculties, although the baby grew and flourished inside her. Day and night, in her chamber on the first floor of the Domaine de la Cade, a good fire crackled and spat in the hearth. The hours of sunlight were short, barely warming the sky before dark fell over the land once again.

Enslaved by grief, Isolde stood yet at a crossroads between the world from which she had taken temporary leave and the undiscovered country beyond. The voices that were with her always whispered to her that if she fared forward she would find those she loved waiting for her in the glades. Anatole would be there, bathed in gentle, welcoming tones. There was nothing to fear. In moments of what she believed were grace, she longed to die. To be with him. But the spirit of his child wishing to be born was too strong.

On a dull and soundless afternoon, with nothing to mark it from those days that had come before or those that were to follow, Isolde felt sensation return to her delicate limbs. At first, it was her fingers, so subtle as to be almost mistaken for something else. An automatic response, not one of purpose. A tingling at the tips of and beneath her almond-shaped nails. Then a twitching of her pale feet beneath the covers. Then a pricking on the skin at the base of her neck.

She moved her hand and the hand obeyed.

Isolde heard a noise. Not, this time, the ceaseless whispering that was always with her, but the normal, domestic sound of a chair leg against the floor. For the first time in months, it was not distorted or amplified or subdued by time or light but knocking on her consciousness without refraction.

She sensed someone leaning over her, the warmth of breath on her face.

"Madama?"

She allowed her eyes to flutter open. She heard the intake of breath, then feet running and a door flung open, shouting in the passageway, coils of sound winding up from the hall below, growing in intensity, growing in certainty.

"Madomaisèla Léonie! Madama *s'éveille!*"

Isolde blinked at the brightness. More noise, then the touch of cold fingers taking her hand. Slowly she turned her head to one side and saw her niece's thoughtful young face looking down at her.

"Léonie?"

She felt her fingers being squeezed. "I am here."

"Léonie . . ." Isolde's voice faltered. "Anatole, he . . ."

ISOLDE'S CONVALESCENCE was slow. She walked, raised a fork to her mouth and slept, but her physical progress was unsteady and the light had gone from her gray eyes. Grief had detached her from herself. Everything she thought and saw, felt and smelled touched chords of painful remembrance.

Most evenings she sat with Léonie in the drawing room with the curtains drawn, her slim, white fingers resting on her growing stomach, talking of Anatole. Léonie would listen while Isolde recited the whole story of their love affair, from the instant of their first meeting, to the hoax at the cimetière de Montmartre and the short-lived happiness of their intimate wedding in Carcassonne on the eve of the great storm.

But however many times Isolde told the story, the ending remained the same. A once upon a time, a fairytale romance, but cheated of its happy ending.

THE WINTER PASSED, at last. The snow melted, although by February a crisp frost still covered the morning in sharp whiteness.

At the Domaine de la Cade, Léonie and Isolde remained locked together in their sorrow, bereaved, watching the shadows on the lawns. They had few visitors, save for Audric Baillard and Madame Bousquet, who, despite having lost the estate on Jules Lascombe's marriage, proved to be both a generous friend and a kind neighbor.

Monsieur Baillard, from time to time, brought news of the police hunt for Victor Constant, who had disappeared from the Hôtel de la Reine in Rennes-les-Bains under cover of darkness on the night of October 31 and had not been seen since in France.

The police had inquired for him in the various health spas and asylums specializing in treating men with his condition but met with no luck. Attempts were made by the state to seize his considerable assets. There was a price on his head. Even so, there were no sightings, no rumors.

On March 25, by unhappy coincidence the anniversary of Isolde's false burial in the cimetière de Montmartre, Léonie received an official letter from Inspector Thouron. He informed her that since they believed Constant had fled the country, perhaps over the border into Andorra or Spain, they were scaling down the manhunt. He reassured her that the fugitive would be arrested and guillotined should he ever return to France and hoped, therefore, that Madame and Mademoiselle Vernier would feel no alarm that Constant would concern them further.

At the tail end of March, when inclement conditions had kept them inside for some days, Léonie found herself taking up her pen to write to Anatole's former friend and neighbor, Achille Debussy. She knew he was now going by the name of Claude Debussy, although she could not bring herself to address him so.

The correspondence both filled an absence in her confined life and, more important for her fractured heart, helped keep a link with Anatole. Achille told her what was happening in the streets and boulevards she and Anatole had once called home, gossip about who was in conflict with whom, all the petty rivalries at the Académie, the authors in favor or disgraced, the artists fighting, the composers snubbed, the scandals and the affairs.

Léonie did not care for a world that was now so distant, so closed to her, but it reminded her of her conversations with Anatole. Sometimes, in the old days, when he returned home after a night out with Achille at Le Chat Noir, he had come into her room and thrown himself into the old armchair at the foot of her bed, and she, with her covers drawn up to her chin, would listen to his stories. Debussy wrote mostly of himself, covering page after page with his spidery writing. Léonie did not mind. It took her thoughts away from her own predicament. She smiled when he wrote of his Sunday-morning visits to the church of Saint-Gervais to listen to the Gregorian chant with his atheistic friends, sitting with their defiant backs to the altar, thereby offending both the congregation and the officiating priest.

Léonie could not leave Isolde, and, even had she been free to travel, the thought of returning to Paris was too painful. It was too soon. At her request, Achille and Gaby Dupont made regular visits to the cimetière de Passy in the sixteenth arrondissement to lay flowers on the grave of Marguerite Vernier. The tomb, paid for by Du Pont as a last act of generosity, was close to that of the painter Édouard Manet, Achille wrote. A peaceful, shaded spot. Léonie thought her mother would be content to lie among such company.

The weather changed as April came in, arriving like a general upon the battlefield. Aggressive, loud, bellicose. Squalls of scudding clouds skated across the peaks of the mountains. The days grew a little longer, the mornings a little lighter. Marieta got out her needles and threads. She put generous pleats into Isolde's chemises and let out the panels on her skirts to accommodate her changing shape.

Purple, white and pink valley flowers pushed tentative shoots through the crusted rim of the earth, raising their faces to the light. The smatterings of color, like dabs of paint dripped from a brush, grew stronger, more frequent, vibrating in the green of the borders and the paths.

May tiptoed shyly in, hinting at the promise of longer summer days to come, of dappled sunlight on still water. In the streets of Rennes-les-Bains, Léonie often ventured to visit Monsieur Baillard or met with Madame Bousquet to take afternoon tea in the salon of the Hôtel de la Reine. Outside the modest town houses, canaries sang in cages now hung out of doors. The lemon and orange trees were in blossom, their sharp scents filling the streets. On every corner, early fresh fruits brought over the mountains from Spain were sold from wooden carts.

The Domaine de la Cade was suddenly glorious beneath an endless blue sky. The bright June sun struck the gleaming white peaks of the Pyrenees. Summer, at last, had come.

From Paris, Achille wrote that Maître Maeterlinck had granted permission to set his new drama, *Pelléas et Mélisande,* to music. He also sent a copy of Zola's *La Débâcle,* which was set during the summer of 1870 and the Franco-Prussian War. He enclosed a personal note saying he knew it would have been of interest to Anatole, as it was to him, as sons of convicted Communards. Léonie struggled with the novel but appreciated the sentiment that had caused Achille to make her so thoughtful a gift.

She did not allow her thoughts to return to the tarot cards. They were tied up with the grim events of Halloween, and although she could not persuade Abbé Saunière to talk to her of those things he had seen or done in the service of her uncle, she remembered Monsieur Baillard's warnings that the demon, Asmodeus, walked the valleys when times were troubled. Although she did not believe such superstitions, or so she told herself, she did not wish to risk provoking a recurrence of such terror.

So she packed away her incomplete set of drawings. They were too painful a reminder of her brother and her mother. Le Diable and La Tour were left unfinished. Nor did Léonie return to the glade ringed with the wild juniper. Its proximity to the clearing where the duel had taken place, where Anatole had fallen, made her heart crack. Too much so to contemplate ever walking that way.

ISOLDE'S PAINS started early on the morning of Friday, June 24, the feast day of Saint John the Baptist.

Monsieur Baillard, with his hidden networks of friends and comrades, secured the services of a *sage-femme* from his native village of Los Seres. Both she and the lying-in nurse arrived in good time for the birth.

By lunchtime, Isolde was considerably advanced. Léonie bathed her forehead with cold cloths and opened the windows to let into the chamber the fresh air and the scent of the juniper and honeysuckle from the gardens below. Marieta dabbed her lips with a sponge soaked in sweet white wine and honey.

By teatime, and without complications, Isolde had delivered a boy, in good health and with an impressive pair of lungs.

Léonie hoped that the birth would mark the beginning of Isolde's return to full health. That she would become less listless, less fragile, less separate from the world around her. Léonie—indeed, the whole household—expected that a child, Anatole's child, would bring with it the love and purpose Isolde so needed.

But a black shadow descended over Isolde some three days after the birth. She made inquiries as to her son's condition and welfare but was struggling to save herself from falling into the same distant, stricken state that had afflicted her in the immediate aftermath of Anatole's murder. Her tiny son, so much the mirror of his father, served more to remind her of what she had lost than to give her reason to continue.

The services of a wet nurse were employed.

As the summer progressed, Isolde showed no signs of improvement. She was kindly, did her duty by her son when called upon to do so, but otherwise lived in the world of her mind, persecuted endlessly by the voices in her head.

Where Isolde was distant, Léonie fell in love with her nephew without reservation or condition. Louis-Anatole was a sunny-natured baby, with Anatole's black hair and long lashes rimming startling gray eyes inherited from his mother. In the delight of the child's company, Léonie forgot, sometimes for hours at a time, the tragedy that had overtaken them.

As the fearsomely hot July and August days marched on, from time to time Léonie would awake in the morning with a sense of hope, a lightness in her step, before she remembered and the shadows fell over her again. But her love and her determination to keep any harm from coming to Anatole's son helped her to recover her spirits.

89

Autumn 1892 tipped into spring 1893, and still Constant did not return to the Domaine de la Cade. Léonie allowed herself to believe he was dead, although she would have been grateful for confirmation of it.

August of 1893 was, like the previous year, as hot and dry as the African deserts. The drought was followed by torrential inundations throughout the Languedoc, washing away sections of land on the plains, revealing long-hidden caves and *cachettes* beneath the mud.

Achille Debussy remained a regular correspondent. In December he wrote with Christmas greetings and to tell Léonie that the Société Nationale was to present in concert a performance of *L'Après-midi d'un faune*, a new composition intended as the first of a suite of three pieces. As she read his naturalistic descriptions of the fawn in his glade, Léonie was put in mind of the clearing within which she had, two years before, discovered the deck of cards. For an instant she was tempted to retrace her steps to the spot and see if the tarot was still there.

She did not do so.

Rather than the boulevards and avenues of Paris, her world continued to be bounded by the beech woods to the east, the long driveway to the north, the lawns to the south. She was sustained only by the love of one little boy and her affection for the beautiful but damaged woman for whom she had promised to care.

Louis-Anatole became a favorite with the town and the household, who nicknamed him *pichon,* little one. He was mischievous but always charming. He was full of questions, more like his aunt than his dead father, but capable of listening also. As he grew taller, he and Léonie walked the pathways and woods of the Domaine de la Cade. Or else he was taken fishing by Pascal, who also taught him to swim in the lake. From time to time, Marieta would permit him to scrape the mixing bowl and lick the wooden spoon when she had been cooking—raspberry soufflé, chocolate puddings. He would balance on the old three-legged stool set hard against the rim of the kitchen table, one of the maid's crisp white aprons reaching down to his ankles, and Marieta, standing behind him to be sure he didn't fall, would teach him to knead dough for bread.

When Léonie took him to visit in Rennes-les-Bains, his favorite treat was to sit at the pavement café that Anatole had so loved. With his tumbling curls, white ruffed shirt and nut-brown velvet trousers drawn tight at the knee, he sat with his legs hanging down from the high wooden stool. He drank cherry syrup or freshly pressed cider and ate chocolate creams.

On his third birthday, Madame Bousquet presented Louis-Anatole with a bamboo fishing rod. The following Christmas, Maître Fromilhague sent a box of tin soldiers to the house and presented the compliments of the season to Léonie.

He was a regular visitor, too, to the house of Audric Baillard, who told him stories of medieval times and the honor of the chevaliers who had defended the independence of the Midi against the northern invaders. Rather than plunge the boy into the pages of sooty history books gathering dust in the library of the Domaine de la Cade, Monsieur Baillard brought the past to life. Louis-Anatole's favorite story was the siege of Carcassonne in 1209 and the brave men, women, even children little older than he, who had fled to the hidden villages of the Haute Vallée.

When Louis-Anatole was four years old, Audric Baillard gave him a replica of a medieval battle sword, its hilt engraved and carved with his initials. Léonie purchased for him from Quillan, with the assistance of one of Pascal's many cousins, a small copper pony, chestnut, with a thick white mane and tail and a white flash on its nose. For the duration of that hot summer, Louis-Anatole was a chevalier, fighting the French or victorious at the joust, knocking tin cans from a wooden fence set up by Pascal for the purpose on the rear lawns. From the drawing-room window, Léonie would watch, remembering how, as a little girl, she had watched Anatole run and hide and climb trees in the Parc Monceau with much the same sense of awe and envy.

Louis-Anatole also showed a marked talent for music, the money wasted on keyboard lessons for Anatole in his youth paying dividends in his son. Léonie engaged a piano teacher from Limoux. Once a week, the professor would rumble up the long drive in the dogcart, with his white neckerchief and pinned stocks and untrimmed beard, and for two hours would drill Louis-Anatole in five-finger exercises and scales. Each week, as he took his departure, he would press Léonie to make the boy practice with glasses of water balanced upon the backs of his hands to keep the touch. Léonie and Louis-Anatole would nod and, for a day or two following, he would attempt to do so. But then the water would spill, soaking Louis-Anatole's velvet breeches or staining the wide hems of Léonie's skirts, and they would laugh and play noisy duets instead.

When he was alone, often the boy would tiptoe to the piano and experiment. Léonie would stand on the landing at the top of the stairs, unobserved, and listen to the gentle, haunting melodies his child's fingers could create. Wherever he started, most frequently he would find his way to the key of A minor. And then Léonie would think of the music she had stolen so long ago from the sepulchre, concealed still in the piano stool, and wonder if she should take it out for him. But fearing the power of it and its actions upon the place itself, she stayed her hand.

Throughout this time, Isolde lived in a twilight world, drifting through the rooms and the passageways of the Domaine de la Cade like a wraith. She spoke little; she was kind to her son and much loved by the servants. Only when she looked into Léonie's emerald eyes did something deeper spark inside her. Then, for a fleeting second, grief and memory would blaze in her eyes before a cloak of darkness came down over them once more. Some days were better than others. On occasion, Isolde would emerge from her shadows, like the sun coming out from behind the clouds. But then the voices would start once more and she would clasp her hands over her ears and weep, and Marieta would gently lead her back to the privacy and half-light of her chamber until better times returned. The periods of peace grew shorter. The darkness around her grew deeper. Anatole was never far from her mind. For his part, Louis-Anatole accepted his mother as she was—he had never known her to be any different.

All in all, it was not the life Léonie had imagined for herself. She would have wished for love, for a chance to see more of the world, to be herself. But she loved her nephew and pitied Isolde and, determined to keep her word to Anatole, did not waver in her duty.

Bronze autumns gave way to chill white winters, when the snow lay thick on the tomb of Marguerite Vernier in Paris. Green springs gave way to blazing golden skies and scorched pasture, and the briars grew tangled around the more modest grave of Anatole overlooking the lake at the Domaine de la Cade.

Earth, wind, water and fire, the unchanging pattern of the natural world.

THEIR PEACEFUL EXISTENCE was not to last for much longer. Between Christmas and the New Year of 1897, there was a succession of signs—omens, warnings, even—that things were not right.

In Quillan, a chimney sweep's boy fell and broke his neck. In Espéraza, fire broke out in the hat factory, killing four of the Spanish female workers. In the atelier of the Bousquet family, an apprentice became trapped in the hot metal printing press and lost all four fingers on his right hand.

For Léonie, the general disquiet became specific when Monsieur Baillard came to give her the unwelcome news that he was obliged to quit Rennes-les-Bains. It was the time of local winter fairs—in Brenac on January 19,

Campagne-sur-Aude on the 20th and Belvianes on the 22nd. He was to pay his visits to those outlying villages, then make his way higher into the mountains. His eyes veiled with concern, he explained that there were obligations, older and more binding than his unofficial guardianship of Louis-Anatole, which he could delay no longer. Léonie regretted his decision but knew better than to question him. He gave his word that he would return before the feast day of Saint Martin in November, when the rents were collected.

She was dismayed that his *séjour* was to be of so many months' duration, but she had learned long ago that Monsieur Baillard would never be deflected from any purpose once a decision had been made.

His imminent departure—and the unexplained reasons for it—reminded Léonie once more of how little she knew of her friend and protector. She did not even know for certain how old he was, although Louis-Anatole had declared that he must be at least seven hundred years old to have so many stories to tell.

Mere days after Audric Baillard's departure, scandal erupted in Rennes-le-Château. The Abbé Saunière's restoration of his church was all but completed. In the early cold months of 1897, the statuary ordered from a specialist supplier in Toulouse was delivered. Among them was a *bénitier*—a stoup for holy water—resting on the shoulders of a twisted demon. Voices were raised in objection, vociferous, insisting that this and many other of the statues were unsuitable for a house of worship. Letters of protest were sent to the mairie and to the bishop, some anonymous, demanding that Saunière be brought to account. Demanding, too, that the priest no longer be permitted to dig in the graveyard.

Léonie had not known about the nighttime excavations around the church, nor that Saunière was said to spend the hours between dusk and dawn walking the nearby mountainside, looking for treasure, or so it was rumored. She did not involve herself in the debate nor in the growing tide of complaint against a priest she had considered devoted to his parish. Her unease came from the fact that certain of the statues were so precisely a match for those within the sepulchre. It was as if someone was guiding Abbé Saunière's hand and, at the same time, working to cause trouble against him.

Léonie knew that he had seen the statues in her late uncle's time. Why, some twelve years after the event, he should choose to replicate images that had caused such harm before she did not understand. With her friend and guide Audric Baillard absent, there was no one with whom she could discuss her fears.

The discontent spread down the mountain to the valley and Rennes-les-Bains. Suddenly there were whisperings that the troubles that had beset the town some years back had returned. There were rumors of secret tunnels running between Rennes-le-Château and Rennes-les-Bains, of Visigoth burial chambers. Allegations that, as before, the Domaine de la Cade was the refuge of a wild beast, started to gather force. Dogs, goats, even oxen were attacked by wolves or mountain cats that appeared to be afraid of neither the traps nor the hunters' guns. It was an unnatural creature, or so the rumors spread, not one governed by the normal laws of nature.

Although Pascal and Marieta tried hard to keep the gossip from reaching Léonie's ears, some of the more malicious stories pierced her consciousness all the same. The campaign was subtle, no allegations were made out loud, so it was not possible for Léonie to answer the mounting drizzle of complaint directed against the Domaine de la Cade and the household.

There was no way of identifying the source of the spiteful rumors, only that they were intensifying. As winter went out and a cold and wet spring arrived, the allegations of supernatural occurrences at the Domaine de la Cade grew more frequent. Sightings of ghosts and demons, it was said, even of satanic rituals conducted under cover of night in the sepulchre. It was a return to the dark days of Jules Lascombe's time as master of the house. The bitter and the jealous pointed to the events of Halloween 1891 and claimed that the ground was restless, seeking retribution for past sins.

Old spells, ancient words in the traditional language, were scratched on rocks at the roadside to ward off the demon that now, as before, stalked the valley. Pentagrams were daubed in black tar on stones at the roadside. Votive offerings of flowers and ribbon were left at unmarked shrines.

One afternoon, when Léonie was sitting with Louis-Anatole in his favorite spot beneath the *platanes* in the Place du Pérou, a phrase sharply uttered caught her attention.

"*Lou Diable se ris.*"

When she returned to the Domaine de la Cade, she asked Marieta what the words meant.

"The devil is laughing," she reluctantly translated.

Had Léonie not known that such a thing was impossible, she would have suspected the hand of Victor Constant in the rumors and gossip. She chastised herself for such thoughts.

Constant was dead. The police thought so. He had to be dead. Otherwise, why would he have let them be for nearly six years, only to return now?

90

Carcassonne

When the heat of July had turned the green pastures between Rennes-le-Château and Rennes-les-Bains to brown, Léonie could bear her confinement no longer. She stood in need of a change of scene.

The stories about the Domaine de la Cade had intensified. Indeed, the atmosphere on the last occasion she and Louis-Anatole went down into Rennes-les-Bains had been so unpleasant that she had resolved not to visit for the foreseeable future. Silence or suspicious glances, where once there had been greetings and smiles. She did not wish Louis-Anatole to witness such unpleasantness.

The occasion Léonie chose for the excursion was the *fête nationale*. As part of the celebrations of the anniversary of the storming of the Bastille more than one hundred years before, there was to be a display of fireworks in the medieval citadel of Carcassonne on the fourteenth day of July. Léonie had not set foot in the city since the short-lived and painful visit with Anatole and Isolde, but for her nephew's sake—it was a belated treat for his fifth birthday—she put her misgivings to one side.

She was determined to persuade Isolde to accompany them. Her aunt's nerves had been worse of late. She had taken to insisting that there were people following her, watching her from the far side of the lake, that there were faces under the water. She saw smoke in the woods even when no fires were set. Léonie did not wish to leave her, even in Marieta's capable hands, for so many days unaccompanied.

"Please, Isolde," she whispered, stroking her hand. "It would do you good to be away from here for a while. To feel the sun on your face." She squeezed her fingers. "It would mean so much to me. And for Louis-Anatole. It would be the best birthday gift you could give him. Come with us, please."

Isolde looked up at her with her deep gray eyes, which seemed both to carry great wisdom and to see nothing.

"If you wish it," she said in her silvery voice, "I will come."

Léonie was so astonished that she flung her arms around Isolde, startling her. She could feel how thin Isolde was beneath her clothes and corset, but she put it out of her mind. She had never expected Isolde to acquiesce and so was delighted. Perhaps it was a sign that her aunt was, at last, ready to look to the future. That she would start to get to know her beautiful son.

IT WAS A SMALL PARTY that set out by train to Carcassonne.

Marieta was watchful of her mistress. It fell to Pascal to occupy Louis-Anatole with military tales, the current exploits of the French army in western Africa, Dahomey and the Côte d'Ivoire. Pascal talked with such relish of the deserts and the roaring waterfalls and a lost world hidden on a secret plateau that Léonie suspected he had borrowed his descriptions from the writings of Monsieur Jules Verne rather than from the pages of the newspapers. Louis-Anatole, for his part, entertained the carriage with Monsieur Baillard's tales of the medieval knights of old. A thoroughly satisfying and bloodthirsty journey was passed by both.

They arrived at lunchtime of the morning of fourteenth July and found themselves in lodgings in the lower Bastide, hard by the cathédrale Saint-Michel, far distant from the hotel where Isolde, Léonie and Anatole had stayed six years previously. Léonie passed the remainder of the afternoon sightseeing with her excited, wide-eyed nephew and permitted him to eat too much ice cream.

They returned to their rooms at five o'clock to rest. Léonie found Isolde lying on a couch at the window, looking out over the gardens of the Boulevard Barbès. With a sinking feeling in the pit of her stomach, she immediately realized that Isolde did not intend to come with them to view the fireworks.

Léonie said nothing, hoping she was wrong, but when the time came to venture out for the evening *spectacle,* Isolde claimed she did not feel equal to the crowds. Louis-Anatole was not disappointed, for, in truth, he had not expected his mother's company. But Léonie allowed herself an uncharacteristic stab of irritation that even on this one special occasion, Isolde could not rouse herself for her son.

Leaving Marieta to tend to her mistress's needs, Léonie and Louis-Anatole set out with Pascal. The *spectacle* had been planned and paid for by a local industrialist, Monsieur Sabatier, the inventor of L'Or-Kina aperitif and the Micheline liqueur known as "La Reine des Liqueurs." The display was as an experiment but with the promise that the event would be bigger and better the following year should it be deemed a success. Sabatier's presence was everywhere, in the promotional leaflets that Louis-Anatole collected in his small fists, souvenirs of their outing, and on posters affixed to the walls of buildings.

As daylight started to retreat, crowds began to mass on the right bank of the Aude in the quartier Trivalle, gazing up at the restored ramparts of the Cité. Children, gardeners and maids from the big houses, shopgirls and boot boys all swarmed to the church of Saint-Gimer, where once Léonie had sheltered with Victor Constant. She pushed the memory from her mind.

On the left bank, they gathered outside the Hôpital des Malades, every handhold and foothold occupied. Children balanced on the wall beside the chapelle de Saint-Vincent-de-Paul. In the Bastide, they gathered at the Porte des Jacobins and along the riverbank. No one knew quite what to expect.

"Up you come, *pichon,*" said Pascal, swinging the boy onto his shoulders.

Léonie, Pascal and Louis-Anatole took a position on the Pont Vieux, squeezing into one of the pointed *becs*—the alcoves—that overlooked the water. Léonie whispered loudly up into Louis-Anatole's ear, as if confiding a great secret, that it was even said that the Bishop of Carcassonne had ventured from his palace to witness this great celebration of Republicanism.

As darkness fell, diners from the nearby restaurants swelled the numbers on the old bridge. The crowd became a crush. Léonie glanced up at her nephew, worrying that perhaps it was too late for him to be out and that the noise and the smell of gunpowder would be alarming, but she was delighted to see the same look of intense concentration on Louis-Anatole's face that she remembered seeing on Achille's on those occasions he sat at his piano composing.

Léonie smiled. And realized she was increasingly able to enjoy her memories, without being overtaken by the sense of loss.

At that moment, the *embrassement de la Cité* began. The medieval walls were enveloped in a fury of orange and red flames, sparks and smoke of all colors. Rockets shot up into the night sky and exploded.

Clouds of acrid vapors rolled down from the hill and over the river, stinging the watchers' eyes, but the magnificence of the spectacle more than compensated for the discomfort. The blue sky was purple now, glowing with green and white and red fireworks as the citadel was enveloped in flame and fury and brilliant light.

Léonie felt Louis-Anatole's small, hot hand creep onto her shoulder. She covered it with her own. Perhaps this would be a new beginning? Perhaps the grief that had dominated her life for so long now, for too long, would loosen its grip and allow thoughts of a brighter future.

"*A l'avenir,*" she said under her breath, remembering Anatole.

His son heard her. "*A l'avenir,* Tante Léonie," he said, returning the toast. He paused, then added, "If I am good, may we come again next year?"

WHEN THE DISPLAY was over and the crowds dispersed, Pascal carried the sleepy boy back to their boardinghouse.

Léonie put him to bed. Promising they would have such an adventure again, she kissed him good night and retired, leaving a candle burning, as always, to keep away the ghosts and evil spirits and monsters of the night. She was bone tired, exhausted by the excitements of the day and her emotions. Thoughts of her brother—and her guilt at the part she had played in leading Victor Constant to him—had plucked at her all day.

Wishing to be certain of rest, Léonie mixed herself a sleeping draft, watching while the white powder dissolved in a glass of hot brandy. She drank it slowly, then slipped between the sheets and fell into a deep and dreamless sleep.

A MISTY DAWN crept over the waters of the Aude as the pale morning light gave shape back to the world.

The banks of the river and the pavements and cobbles of the Bastide were littered with pamphlets and paper. The broken tip of a boxwood walking cane, a few sheets of music trampled underfoot by the crowds, a cap detached from its owner. And everywhere Monsieur Sabatier's leaflets.

The waters of the Aude were as flat as a looking glass, barely moving in the quiet of the dawn. The old boatman, Baptistin Cros—known to all of Carcassonne as Tistou—was steering his heavy, flat barge across the still river toward the Païchérou weir. This far upriver there was little evidence of the celebrations for the *fête nationale*. No spent cases, no streamers or advertisements, no lingering smell of gunpowder or singed paper. His steady gaze took in the purple light that shimmered over the Montagne Noire to the north, as the sky turned from black to blue to the white of morning.

Tistou's barge pole caught on something in the water. He turned to see what it could be, adjusting his balance with practiced ease.

It was a corpse.

Slowly, the old riverman turned his barge. The water lapped close to the wooden rim of the boat but did not spill over. He stopped momentarily. The overhead wires that linked one side of his river crossing to the other seemed to sing in the soft morning air, even though there was not a whisper of wind.

Anchoring the craft by plunging his wooden pole deep into the mud, Tistou knelt down and peered into the water. Beneath the green surface, he could just make out the shape of a woman. She was half floating, facedown. Tistou was glad. The glazed dead eyes of the drowned were hard to forget, the blue-rimmed lips and the look of surprise etched on skin as yellow as tallow. *Not long in the water,* Tistou thought. Her body had not yet had time to change.

The woman looked strangely peaceful, her long blond hair swaying back and forth, back and forth, like weeds. Tistou's slow thoughts were mesmerized by the motion. Her back was arched, her arms and legs trailing gracefully down beneath her skirts, as if she was somehow attached to the riverbed.

Another suicide, he thought.

Tistou braced his legs and leaned forward, locking his bent knees against the thwarts. He stretched over and grabbed a fistful of the woman's gray morning dress. Even sodden and made slimy by the river, he could feel the quality of the cloth. He pulled. The barge rocked dangerously, but Tistou had done this countless times and knew where the tipping point lay. He took a deep breath, then pulled again, clutching at the collar of the woman's dress to get better purchase.

"*Un, deux, trois, allez,*" he said aloud, as the body slithered over the side and flopped, like a netted fish, into the damp hull of the boat.

Tistou wiped his forehead with his neckerchief, then rearranged his trademark cap on the back of his head. Unthinking, his hands drifted to his chest and he crossed himself. It was an act of instinct, not belief.

He turned the body over. A woman, no longer in the first flush of youth but beautiful still. Her gray eyes were open, and her hair had come loose in the water, but she was clearly a gentlewoman. Her white hands were soft, not those of one who worked for her living.

The son of a draper and a seamstress, Tistou knew good Egyptian cotton when he saw it. He found the tailor's mark—Parisian—still legible on the collar. She was wearing a silver locket around her neck—solid, not plate—with two miniatures inside, of the lady herself and a young, dark-haired man. Tistou left it be. He was an honest man—not like the scavengers who worked the weirs in the center of town, and who would strip a corpse before turning it in to the authorities—but he liked to know the identity of those he reclaimed from the water.

ISOLDE WAS quickly identified. Léonie had reported her missing at first light, the moment Marieta had woken and found her mistress gone.

They were obliged to remain for a couple of days while the formalities were observed and the paperwork signed, but there was little doubt as to the verdict: suicide while the balance of the mind was disturbed.

It was a dull, overcast and soundless July day when Léonie brought Isolde back to the Domaine de la Cade for the last time. Guilty of the cardinal sin of taking her own life, Isolde would not be allowed by the Church to rest within hallowed ground. Besides, Léonie could not bear the thought of her being buried in the Lascombe family vault.

Instead, she secured the services of Curé Gélis from Coustaussa, the village with a ruined chateau midway between Couiza and Rennes-les-Bains, to conduct a private memorial within the grounds of the Domaine de la Cade. She would have approached the Abbé Saunière, but she did not think, under the circumstances—he was still suffering at the hands of his critics—that it was fair to taint him with the scandal.

At dusk on July 20, 1897, they buried Isolde beside Anatole in the same peaceful patch of ground on the promontory overlooking the lake. A new, modest headstone set flat into the grass recorded their names and dates.

As Léonie listened to the murmured prayers, holding tight to Louis-Anatole's hand, she remembered how she had already paid her respects to Isolde in a graveyard in Paris six years ago. The memory swooped down upon her, so sharp and vicious that she caught her breath. Herself standing in their old drawing room in the rue de Berlin, hands clasped before a closed casket, a single palm leaf floating in the glass bowl on the sideboard. The sickly aroma of ritual and death that had insinuated itself into every corner of the apartment, the burning of incense and candles to mask the cloying sweetness of the corpse. Except, of course, there had been no corpse. And on the floor below, Achille hammering endlessly on the piano, black notes and white seeping up through the floorboards until Léonie thought she would be driven mad with his playing.

Now, as she heard the thud of earth on the wooden lid of the coffin, her only consolation was that Anatole had been spared this day.

As if sensing her mood, Louis-Anatole reached up and curled his little arm around her waist.

"Don't worry, Tante Léonie. I will look after you."

91

The private drawing room on the first floor of a hotel on the Spanish side of the Pyrenees was full of acrid smoke from the Turkish cigarettes the resident guest had smoked since his arrival some weeks before.

It was a warm day in August, yet he was dressed as for midwinter in a thick, gray greatcoat and soft calfskin gloves. His frame was emaciated and his head shook slightly in perpetual motion, as if disagreeing with a question no one else could hear asked. With a hand that shook, he raised a glass of licorice beer to his lips. He drank carefully through a mouth scabbed in the corners with pustules. But despite his haggard appearance, his eyes held the power to command, drilling into the souls of those observed like the sharpest jab of a stiletto.

He held up his glass.

His man stepped forward with the bottle of porter and filled his master's glass. For a moment they made a grotesque tableau, the disfigured invalid and his grizzled servant, his scalp blistered and raw from scratching.

"What news?"

"They say she is drowned. By her own hand," the servant replied.

"And the other?"

"She cares for the child."

Constant made no answer. The years of exile, the remorseless progress of the disease, had left him weak. His body was failing. He could no longer walk easily. But if anything, it seemed to have sharpened his mind. Six years ago, he had been forced to act faster than he had wished. It had deprived him of the pleasure of enjoying his revenge. His interest in ruining the sister had been only for the purpose of torturing Vernier himself with the knowledge, so that mattered little to him. But the quick and clean death meted out to Vernier disappointed him still, and now it seemed he had been cheated of Isolde as well.

His precipitate flight over the border to Spain meant that Constant had not learned for some twelve months after the events of Halloween 1891 that the whore had not only survived his bullet but had lived to give birth to a son. The fact that she had escaped him again had played obsessively on his mind.

It was the desire to complete his revenge that had kept him patient these past six years. The attempts to seize his assets had almost ruined him. It had taken all the skill and immorality of his lawyers to protect his wealth and his whereabouts.

Constant had been forced to be cautious and circumspect, staying in exile on the far side of the border until all interest in him had died down. Finally, last winter, Inspector Thouron had been promoted and assigned to the investigation into the conduct of the army officer Dreyfus, which was so occupying the Parisian gendarmerie. More relevant to Constant's all-consuming desire to take revenge against Isolde, word had reached him that Inspector Bouchou of the Carcassonne gendarmerie had retired four weeks past.

At last, the way was clear for Constant to return quietly to France.

He had sent his man ahead to prepare the ground in the spring. With anonymous letters to the town hall and the Church authorities, it had been easy to fan the flames of a whispering campaign against the Abbé Saunière, a priest associated particularly with the Domaine de la Cade and the events Constant knew had taken place in Jules Lascombe's day. Constant had heard the rumors of a devil, a demon, released in the past to terrorize the countryside.

It was his paid associates who spread new rumors of a beast stalking the mountain valleys and attacking livestock. His servant traveled from village to village, rousing the crowds and spreading rumors that the sepulchre in the grounds of the Domaine de la Cade was once again the center of occult activity. He began with the vulnerable and the unprotected, the barefoot beggars who slept out of doors or found shelter beneath the drayman's cart, the winter shepherds in their isolation on the mountains, those who followed the assizes from town to town. He dripped Constant's poison into the ears of drapers and glaziers, boot boys from the big houses, cleaners and pantry maids.

The villagers were superstitious and gullible. Tradition, myth and history confirmed his calumnies. A whisper here and there that the marks were not those of an animal's claws. That strange wailings were heard in the night. That there was a putrid stench. All evidence that some supernatural demon was come to demand retribution for the unnatural state of affairs at the Domaine de la Cade—an aunt taken in marriage by her husband's nephew.

All three were now dead.

With invisible threads, he drew his net around the Domaine de la Cade.

And if it was true that there were attacks for which his man did not claim credit, Constant assumed these were no more than the usual litany of the savagery of mountain cats, or wolves, stalking the higher pastures and peaks.

Now, with Bouchou's retirement, the time was right to act. He had waited too long already, and because he had done so, he had lost his chance to punish Isolde appropriately. Besides, despite the endless remedies and treatments, the mercury, the waters, the laudanum, Constant was dying. He knew he did not have long before his mind, too, would fail. He recognized the signs, could diagnose himself now as accurately as any quack. The only thing he now feared was the brief, final flare of lucidity before the shadows descended for good.

Constant planned to cross the border at the beginning of September and return to Rennes-les-Bains. Vernier was dead. Isolde was dead. But there was still the boy.

From the pocket of his waistcoat, he pulled the timepiece stolen from Vernier in the Passage des Panoramas nearly six years ago. As the Spanish shadows lengthened, he turned it over in his decaying, syphilitic hands, thinking of his Isolde.

92

On September 20, the anniversary of Marguerite Vernier's murder, another child went missing. It was the first for more than a month, taken from the bank of the river downstream of Sougraigne. The girl's body was found close to the Fontaine des Amoureux, her face badly disfigured by claw marks, red slashes across her cheeks and forehead. Unlike the forgotten children, the dispossessed, she was the beloved youngest child of a large family with relations in many of the villages of the Aude and the Salz.

Two days later, two boys vanished from the woods not far from the Lac de Barrenc, the mountain lake supposedly inhabited by a devil. Their bodies were discovered after a week but in such poor condition that it was not observed until sometime later that they, too, had been savaged by an animal, their skin ripped raw.

Léonie tried not to pay attention to the coincidence of the dates. While there was still hope the children might be found unharmed, she offered the assistance of both inside and outside staff to participate in the search parties. It was refused. For Louis-Anatole's sake, she maintained a veneer of calm, but for the first time she began to accept that they might have to leave the Domaine de la Cade until the storm had blown over.

Maître Fromilhague and Madame Bousquet maintained it was obviously the work of wild dogs or wolves come down from the mountains. During the hours of daylight, Léonie could dismiss the rumors of a demon or supernatural creature. But as dusk fell, her knowledge of the history of the sepulchre and the presence of the cards within the grounds made her less assured.

The mood of the town grew increasingly ugly, turning ever more against them. The Domaine became the target for petty acts of vandalism.

Léonie returned from walking in the woods one afternoon to see a cluster of servants standing around the door to one of the outbuildings.

Intrigued, she quickened her pace.

"What is it?" she asked.

Pascal spun round, a look of horror in his eyes, blocking her view with his wide, solid frame.

"Nothing, Madama."

Léonie looked at his face, then to the gardener and his son, Emile. She took a step closer.

"Pascal?"

"Please, Madama, it's not for your eyes."

Léonie's gaze sharpened. "Come now," she said lightly. "I am not a child. I am certain whatever you are concealing cannot be so bad."

Still, Pascal did not move. Torn between irritation at his overprotective manner and curiosity, Léonie reached out her gloved hand and touched him on the arm.

"If you please."

All eyes were on Pascal, who, for a moment, remained steadfast, then slowly stepped aside to allow Léonie sight of what he so keenly wished to hide.

The skinned corpse of a rabbit, some days old, had been impaled to the door with a heavy furrier's nail. A swarm of flies buzzed furiously around a crude cross daubed on the wood in blood and, beneath it, words printed in black tar: PAR CE SIGNE TU LE VAINCRAS.

Léonie's hand flew to her mouth, the stench and the violence of it making her nauseous. But she kept her composure.

"See it is disposed of, Pascal," she said. "And I would be grateful for your discretion." She looked at the assembled company, seeing her own fear reflected in their superstitious eyes. "All of you."

Still, Léonie's resolve did not waiver. She was determined not to be driven from the Domaine de la Cade, certainly not before Monsieur Baillard returned. He had said he would be back by the feast day of Saint Martin. She had sent letters via his old lodgings in the rue de l'Hermite, increasingly frequently of late, but had no way of knowing if any had found him on his travels.

The situation worsened. Another child disappeared. On October 22, a date Léonie recognized as the anniversary of Anatole and Isolde's clandestine marriage, the daughter of a lawyer and his wife, pretty in white ribbons and ruched skirts, was taken from the Place du Pérou. The outcry was immediate.

By ill chance, Léonie was in Rennes-les-Bains when the child's torn and ripped body was recovered. The corpse had been left beside the Fauteuil du Diable, the Devil's Armchair, on the hills not far from the Domaine de la Cade. A sprig of wild juniper had been pushed between the bloodied fingers of the child's hand.

Léonie turned cold when she heard, understanding how the message was left for her. The wooden cart rumbled along the Gran'Rue, followed by a ragtag cortège of villagers. Grown men, toughened by the hardship of their daily lives, wept openly.

No one spoke. Then a red-faced woman, her mouth bitter and angry, caught sight of her and pointed. Léonie felt a frisson of fear as the accusing eyes of the town turned upon her, looking for someone to blame.

"We should go, Madama," whispered Marieta, hurrying her away.

Determined not to show how frightened she was, Léonie held her head up as she turned and made her way to where the carriage stood waiting. The murmuring was getting louder. Words shouted, abusive, ugly insults that fell upon her like blows.

"Pas luènh," Marieta urged, taking her arm.

Two days later, a burning rag soaked in oil and goose fat was pushed through one of the library windows that had been left partially open. It was discovered before any serious damage was done, but the household became even more timid, more watchful, unhappy.

Léonie's friends and allies in the town—and Pascal and Marieta, too—all tried their best to persuade her accusers that they were mistaken in believing that there was any such beast quartered within the estate, but the town had made up its narrow mind. They believed it was incontrovertible that the old devil of the mountain had returned to claim his own, as he had in Jules Lascombe's time.

No smoke without fire.

Léonie tried not to see Victor Constant's ever-present hand in the persecution of the Domaine but all the same was convinced he was preparing to strike. She attempted to persuade the gendarmerie of this, she begged the mairie, pleaded with Maître Fromilhague to intercede on her behalf, but to no avail. The Domaine stood alone.

After three days of rain, the outdoor staff put out several fires set on the estate. Arson attacks. The disemboweled corpse of a dog was left on the front steps under cover of darkness, causing one of the youngest parlor maids to faint. Anonymous letters were delivered, obscene and explicit in their descriptions of how Anatole and Isolde's incestuous relations had brought such terror down upon the valley.

Isolated with her fears and suspicions, Léonie understood this to have been Constant's purpose all along, to stir the town into a frenzy of hate against them. And she understood, too, although she did not speak the words aloud, even to herself in the darkness of night, that it would never end. Such was Victor Constant's obsession. If he was in the vicinity of Rennes-les-Bains—and she feared he was—then he could not fail to know that Isolde herself was dead. The fact that the persecution continued made it clear to Léonie that she had to get Louis-Anatole to safety. She would take what she could with her, in the hope that they would return to the Domaine de la Cade before too long. It was Louis-Anatole's home. She would not allow Constant to deprive him of his birthright.

It was a plan easier to execute in thought than in deed.

The truth was that Léonie had nowhere to go. The apartment in Paris had long since been let go, once General Du Pont had stopped paying the bills. Other than Audric Baillard, Madame Bousquet and Maître Fromilhague, her confined existence in the Domaine de la Cade meant she had few friends. Achille was too far away and, besides, occupied with his own concerns. Because of Victor Constant, Léonie had no immediate family.

But there was no other choice.

Confiding in no one but Pascal and Marieta, she prepared for departure. She felt certain that Constant would make his final move against them on Halloween. It was not only the anniversary of Anatole's death—and Constant's attention to dates suggested he would wish to observe this—but as Isolde had once let slip in a moment of clarity, October 31 of 1890 was the day on which she had informed Constant that their short-lived affair must end. From that, all things had followed.

Léonie resolved that if he came on the Veille de Toussaint, he would find them gone.

ON THE CRISP AND COLD afternoon of October 31, Léonie put on her hat and coat, intending to return to the clearing where the juniper grew wild. She did not wish to leave the tarot cards for Constant to find, however unlikely it was that he should stumble upon them in such an expanse of woodland. For the time being, until she and Louis-Anatole could safely return—and in Monsieur Baillard's continuing absence—she had in mind that she would give them into the safekeeping of Madame Bousquet.

She was on the point of exiting through the doors onto the terrace when she heard Marieta calling her name. With a start, she turned back to the hall.

"I am here. What is it?"

"A letter, Madama," Marieta said, holding out an envelope.

Léonie frowned. After the events of the past months, anything out of the ordinary she treated with caution. She glanced down and did not recognize the hand.

"From whom?"

"The boy said from Coustaussa."

Frowning, Léonie opened it. The letter was from the elderly priest of the parish, Antoine Gélis, inviting her to call on him this afternoon on a matter of some urgency. Since he was known to be something of a recluse—and Léonie had met him only twice in six years, in the company of Henri Boudet in Rennes-les-Bains on the occasion of Louis-Anatole's baptism, and at Isolde's burial—she was puzzled to receive such a summons.

"Is there any reply, Madama?" Marieta inquired.

Léonie looked up. "Is the messenger still here?"

"He is."

"Bring him in, will you?"

A small, thin child, dressed in nut-brown trousers, open-necked shirt and red neckerchief, holding his cap in clenched hands, was ushered into the hall. He looked dumbstruck with terror.

"There is no need to be frightened," Léonie said, hoping to put him at ease. "You have done nothing wrong. I only wish to ask if Curé Gélis himself gave you this letter?"

He shook his head.

Léonie smiled. "Well, then, can you tell me who did give you the letter?"

Marieta pushed the boy forward. "The mistress asked you a question."

Little by little, hindered rather than helped by Marieta's sharp-tongued interventions, Léonie managed to tease out the bare bones of the matter. Alfred was staying with his *grandmère* in the village of Coustaussa. He had been playing in the ruins of the *château-fort* when a man came out of the front door of the presbytery and offered him a sou to deliver an urgent letter to the Domaine de la Cade.

"Curé Gélis has a niece who does for him, Madama Léonie," Marieta said. "Prepares his meals. Sees to his laundry."

"Was the man a servant?"

Alfred shrugged.

Satisfied that she would learn nothing more from the boy, Léonie dismissed him.

"Will you go, Madama?" asked Marieta.

Léonie considered. There was a great deal she had to accomplish before their departure. Conversely, she could not believe that Curé Gélis would have sent such a communication without good reason. It was a unique situation.

"I shall," she said, after a moment's hesitation. "Ask Pascal to meet me at the front of the house with the gig immediately."

THEY LEFT the Domaine de la Cade at nigh on half past three.

The air was heavy with the scent of autumn fires. Sprigs of boxwood and rosemary were tied on the door frames of the houses and farms they passed on the way. At the crossroads, impromptu roadside shrines had sprung up for

Halloween. Ancient prayers and invocations scribbled on scraps of paper and cloth were laid as offerings.

Léonie knew that already in the graveyards of Rennes-les-Bains and Rennes-le-Château, indeed, in every mountain parish—widows draped in black crêpe and veils would be kneeling on the damp earth before ancient tombs, praying for deliverance of those they had loved. More so this year, with the blight that had fallen over the region.

Pascal drove the horses hard, until sweat steamed up from their backs and their nostrils flared wide in the chill air. Even so, it was almost dark by the time they had covered the distance from Rennes-les-Bains to Coustaussa and negotiated the very steep track leading up from the main road to the village.

Léonie heard the four o'clock bells ringing down the valley. Leaving Pascal with the carriage and horses, she walked through the deserted village. Coustaussa was tiny, no more than a handful of houses. No *boulangerie,* no café.

Léonie found the presbytery, which adjoined the church, with little difficulty. There appeared to be no signs of life inside. No lights were burning in the house that she could see.

With a growing sense of unease, she knocked on the heavy door. No one came. No one answered. She rapped again, a little louder.

"Curé Gélis?"

After a few moments, Léonie determined to try the church instead. She followed the darkening line of the stone building around to the back. All the doors, to front and side, were locked. A guttering, dim oil lamp hung miserably from a bent iron hook.

Increasingly impatient, Léonie made for the dwelling on the opposite side of the street and knocked. After a shuffling of feet from within, an elderly woman slid back the metal grille set within a hatch in the door.

"Who is it?"

"Good evening," Léonie said. "I have a rendezvous with Curé Gélis, but there is no answer."

The owner of the house looked at Léonie with sullen and distrustful eyes, saying nothing. Léonie dug into her pocket and produced a sou, which the woman grabbed.

"*Ritou* is not there," she said in the end.

"*Ritou?*"

"The priest. Gone to Couiza."

Léonie stared. "That cannot be. I received a letter from him not two hours past, inviting me to call upon him."

"Saw him leave," the woman said, with evident pleasure. "You're the second to come calling."

Léonie threw out her hand and stopped the woman from closing the grille, leaving no more than a fraction of light dripping from inside out onto the street.

"What manner of person?" she demanded. "A man?"

Silence. Léonie produced a second coin.

"French," the old woman said, spitting out the word like the insult it was intended to be.

"When was this?"

"Before dusk. Still light."

Puzzled, Léonie withdrew her fingers. The grille slammed immediately shut.

She turned away, pulling her cloak tight about herself against the onset of the night. She could only assume that in the time it had taken the boy to make the journey on foot from Coustaussa to the Domaine de la Cade, Curé Gélis had given up waiting and had been unable to delay his departure longer. Perhaps he had been obliged to attend to some other urgent errand?

Increasingly anxious to return home after her wasted journey, Léonie took paper and pencil from the pocket of her cloak and scribbled a note saying how sorry she was to have missed him. She pushed it through the narrow letterbox on the presbytery wall and then hurried back to where Pascal was waiting.

Pascal drove the horses even faster on the return journey, but every minute seemed to stretch, and Léonie almost cried out with relief when the lights of the Domaine de la Cade came into view. He slowed on the drive, slippery with ice, and Léonie felt like jumping down and running ahead.

When at last they stopped, she leapt out of the gig and ran up the front steps, possessed by a nameless, faceless dread that something, anything, might have happened in her absence. She pushed open the door and rushed inside.

Louis-Anatole came running toward her. "He's here," he cried.

Léonie's blood turned to ice in her veins.

Please, God, no. Not Victor Constant.

The door slammed shut behind her.

93

B*onjorn*, Madomaisèla," came a voice from the shadows.

At first Léonie thought her ears were deceiving her.

He stepped out of the gloom to greet her. "I have been absent for too long."

She leapt forward, her hands outstretched. "Monsieur Baillard," she cried. "You are most welcome, most welcome!"

He smiled down at Louis-Anatole, hopping from foot to foot beside him.

"This young man has looked after me very well," he said. "He has been amusing me by playing the piano."

Without waiting for further invitation, Louis-Anatole ran back across the black and red tiles and threw himself upon the stool.

"Listen to me, Tante Léonie," he called out. "I found this in the piano stool. I have been learning it on my own."

It was a haunting melody in the key of A minor, lilting and gentle; his small hands struggled not to split the chords. Music, at last, heard, played beautifully—by Anatole's son.

Sepulchre 1891.

Léonie felt tears brim in her eyes. She felt Audric Baillard's hand take hers, his skin so dry. They stood listening, until the last chord faded away.

Louis-Anatole dropped his hands into his lap, took a deep breath, as if listening to the reverberations in the almost silence, then turned to face them with a look of pride on his face.

"There," he said. "I have practiced. For you, Tante Léonie."

"You have a great talent, Sénher," said Monsieur Baillard, applauding.

Louis-Anatole beamed with pleasure. "If I cannot be a soldier when I am a man, then I shall travel to America and be a famous pianist."

"Noble occupations, both." Baillard laughed. Then the smile slipped from his face. "But now, my accomplished young friend, there are matters your *tante* and I must discuss. If you will excuse us?"

"But I—"

"It will not be for long, *petit*," Léonie said firmly. "We will be sure to call for you when we are finished."

Louis-Anatole sighed, then shrugged and, with a grin, ran off toward the kitchens, calling for Marieta.

As soon as he had gone, Monsieur Baillard and Léonie went quickly into the drawing room. Under his precise and careful questioning, Léonie explained everything that had happened since he had quit Rennes-les-Bains in January, the tragic, the surreal, the mystifying, including her suspicions that Victor Constant might have returned.

"I did write of our troubles," she said, unable to keep the reproach from her voice, "but I had no way of knowing if you had received any of my communications."

"Some I did, others I suspect went astray," he said in a somber tone. "The tragic news of Madama Isolde's death I learned only when I returned this afternoon. I was sorry to hear it."

Léonie looked at him, seeing how tired and frail he was. "It was a release. She had been unhappy for some time," she said quietly. She clasped her hands. "Tell me, where have you been? I have missed your company greatly."

He pressed the tips of his long, slim fingers together, as if in prayer.

"If it had not been a matter of great personal importance to me," he said softly, "I would not have left you. But I had received word that a person . . . a person for whom I have been waiting for many, many years, had returned. But . . ." He paused, and in the silence, Léonie heard the raw pain behind the simple words. "But it was not she."

Léonie was momentarily diverted. She had heard him talk only once before with such affection but had received the impression that the girl of whom he spoke with such tenderness was some years dead.

"I am not certain I understand you, Monsieur Baillard," she said carefully.

"No," he said softly. Then a look of determination came over his features. "Had I known, I would not have left Rennes-les-Bains." He sighed. "But I took advantage of my journey to prepare some refuge for you and Louis-Anatole."

Léonie's green eyes flared wide in surprise.

"But I came to that decision only a week ago," she objected. "Less. You have been gone for ten months. How could you have . . ."

He gave a slow smile. "I feared, long ago, that it would be necessary."

"But how—"

He raised his hand. "Your suspicions are correct, Madomaisèla Léonie. Victor Constant is indeed in the vicinity of the Domaine de la Cade."

Léonie fell still. "If you have evidence, we must inform the authorities. They have refused to take my concerns seriously thus far."

"I have no evidence, only assured suspicions. But I have no doubt Constant is here for a purpose. You must leave tonight. My house in the mountains is prepared and waiting for you. I will give directions to Pascal." He paused. "He and Marieta—his wife now, I believe—will travel with you?"

Léonie nodded. "I have confided my intentions to them."

"You may remain in Los Seres for as long as you wish. Certainly until it is safe to return."

"Thank you, thank you."

With tears in her eyes, Léonie looked around the room. "I shall be sorry to leave this house," she said softly. "For my mother and for Isolde, it was an unhappy place. But for me, despite the sorrows that have been contained here, it has been a home."

She stopped. "There is one thing I must confess to you, Monsieur Baillard."

His gaze sharpened.

"Six years ago, I gave you my word that I would not return to the sepulchre," she said quietly. "And I kept my promise. But as for the cards, I must tell you that after I took my leave of you that day in Rennes-les-Bains . . . before the duel and Anatole . . ."

"I remember," he said softly.

"I took it upon myself to take the path home through the woods to see if I might find the *cachette* for myself. I wanted only to see if I might find the tarot cards."

She looked at Monsieur Baillard, expecting to see disappointment, even reproof, on his face. To her astonishment, he was smiling.

"And you came upon the place."

It was a statement, not a question.

"I did. But I give you my word," Léonie said, rushing on, "that although I looked upon the cards, I returned them to their hiding place." She paused. "But I would not now leave them here, within the grounds. He might discover them, and then . . ."

As she was speaking, Audric Baillard reached into the large white pocket of his suit. He took out a square of black silk, a familiar parcel of material, and opened it. The image of La Force was visible on the top.

"You have them!" Léonie exclaimed, taking a step toward him. Then she stopped. "You knew I had been there?"

"Obligingly, you left your gloves as a memento. Do you not remember?"

Léonie flushed to the roots of her copper hair.

He folded the black silk. "I went because, like you, I do not believe these cards should be in the possession of such a man as Victor Constant. And . . ." He paused. "I believe we might have need of them."

"You warned me against using the power of the cards," she objected.

"Unless or until there was no other choice," he said quietly. "I fear that hour is at hand."

Léonie felt her heart start to race. "Let us leave now, right away." She was suddenly horribly aware of her heavy winter petticoats and her stockings scratching against her skin. The mother-of-pearl combs in her hair, a gift from Isolde, seemed to dig into her scalp like sharp teeth. "Let us go. Now."

Without warning, she found herself remembering their happy first weeks at the Domaine de la Cade—she and Anatole and Isolde—before tragedy struck. How in that long-ago autumn of 1891 it was the darkness she had feared most, impenetrable and absolute, after the bright lights of Paris.

Il était une fois. Once upon a time.

She was another girl then, innocent, untouched by darkness or grief. Tears blurred her vision, and she shut her eyes.

The sound of running feet across the hall set her memories to flight. She leapt up and turned in the direction of the noise, at the precise moment the drawing-room door burst open and Pascal stumbled into the room.

"Madama Léonie, Sénher Baillard," he shouted. "There are . . . men. They have already forced their way through the gates!"

Léonie ran to the window. On the distant horizon, she could see a line of flaming torches, gold and ocher against the black night sky.

Then, closer at hand, she heard the sound of glass breaking.

94

Louis-Anatole ran into the room, breaking free of Marieta, and threw himself into Léonie's arms. He was pale and his bottom lip was quivering, but he tried to smile.

"Who are they?" he said in a small voice.

Léonie squeezed him tightly. "They are bad men, *petit*."

She turned back to the window, shading her eyes against the glass. Still some way off, the mob was advancing on the house. Every invader held a burning torch in one hand, a weapon in the other. It looked like an army on the eve of battle. Léonie assumed they were only waiting for Constant's signal to attack.

"There are so many of them," she murmured. "How has he turned the whole town against us?"

"He played upon their natural superstitions," Baillard replied. "Republican or Royalist, they have grown up hearing stories of the demon that stalks the land."

"Asmodeus."

"Different names for different times but always the same face. And if the good people of the town profess not to believe such stories during the hours of daylight, at night their deeper, older souls whisper to them in the dark. Of supernatural beings that rip and tear and cannot be killed, of somber and forbidden places where spiders spin their webs."

Léonie knew he was right. A memory flashed into her mind of the night of the riot at the Palais Garnier in Paris. Then last week, the hatred on the faces of people she knew in Rennes-les-Bains. She knew how quickly, how easily, bloodlust could sweep through a crowd.

"Madama?" Pascal said urgently.

Léonie could see the flames darting and licking the black air, reflecting off the damp leaves of the tall sweet chestnut trees that lined the driveway. She dragged the curtain across and stepped back from the window.

"To hound my brother and Isolde into their graves, even that seems not enough," she murmured. She glanced down at Louis-Anatole's black, curly head nestled against her and hoped he had not heard.

"Can we not talk to them?" he said. "Tell them to leave us alone?"

"The time for talking has passed, my friend," Baillard replied. "There comes always a moment when the desire to act, however ill the cause, is stronger than the wish to listen."

"Are we going to have to fight?" he said.

Baillard smiled. "A good soldier knows when to stand and face his enemies, and when to withdraw. Tonight we will not fight."

Louis-Anatole nodded.

"Is there any hope?" Léonie whispered.

"There is always hope," he said softly. Then his expression hardened. He turned to Pascal. "Is the gig ready?"

He nodded. "Ready and waiting in the clearing by the sepulchre. It should be far enough away to evade the attention of the mob. I have hopes I can get us out from there without being observed."

"*Ben, ben.* Good. We will go from the back, cutting across the path and into the woods, praying their target is the house itself in the first instance."

"What of the servants?" Léonie asked. "They must leave too."

A deep flush spread over Pascal's broad, honest face. "They will not," he said. "They wish to defend the house."

"I do not want anyone to come to harm on our account, Pascal," Léonie said immediately.

"I will tell them, Madama, but I do not think it will alter their resolve."

Léonie could see that his eyes were wet.

"Thank you," she said quietly.

"Pascal, we will take care of your Marieta until we join you."

Pascal nodded. "*Oc,* Sénher Baillard."

He paused to kiss his wife, then left the room.

For an instant, no one spoke. Then the urgency of the situation pressed down on them once more, and everyone was jolted into action.

"Léonie, bring only what is absolutely essential. Marieta, fetch Madama Léonie's valise and furs. It will be a long and cold journey."

Marieta swallowed a sob.

"In my traveling valise, Marieta, already packed, there is a small wallet of paper, inside my workbox. Paintings, about so big." Léonie made the shape of a missal with her hands. "Take the workbox with you. Keep it safe. But bring me the wallet, will you?"

Marieta nodded and rushed into the hall.

Léonie waited until she had gone, then turned back to Monsieur Baillard.

"This is not your battle, either, Audric," she said.

"Sajhë," he said softly. "My friends call me Sajhë."

She smiled, honored by the unexpected confidence. "Very well, Sajhë. You told me once, many years ago now, that it was the living, not the dead, who would be most in need of my services. Do you remember?" She glanced down at the little boy. "He is all that matters now. If you take him, then I will know at least that I have not failed in my duty."

He smiled. "Love—true love—endures, Léonie. Your brother, Isolde, your mother, they knew this. They are not lost to you."

Léonie remembered Isolde's words to her as they sat on the stone bench on the promontory the day after the very first supper party at the Domaine de la Cade. She had been speaking of her love for Anatole, although Léonie had not known it at that time. A love so strong that without it Isolde's life had been intolerable. She would have wished for such a love for herself.

"I want you to give me your word that you will take Louis-Anatole to Los Seres." She paused. "Besides, I would not forgive myself if harm came to you."

He shook his head. "It is not yet my time, Léonie. There is much I must do before I will be allowed to make that journey."

She darted a glance at the familiar yellow handkerchief, a silken square of color just visible in the pocket of his jacket.

Marieta reappeared in the doorway, holding Louis-Anatole's outdoor clothes.

"Here," she said. "Quick, now."

The little boy obediently went to her and allowed himself to be dressed. Then, suddenly, he darted away from her and into the hall.

"Louis-Anatole!" Léonie called after him.

"There is something I must fetch," he cried, appearing moments later with the piece of piano music in his hand. "We will not wish to be without music where we are going," he said, looking round at the grim faces of the adults. "Well, we would not!"

Léonie crouched down. "You are quite right, *petit*."

"Although," he faltered, "I do not know where it is we are going."

Outside the house, a shout erupted. A cry to battle.

Léonie quickly stood up, feeling her nephew's little hand slide into hers.

Fueled by fear and the darkness and the terror of all things that were abroad in these hours of the Eve of All Saints, the men armed with fire and clubs and hunting rifles began their advance on the house.

"And so it begins," Baillard said. *"Corage,* Léonie."

Their eyes locked. Slowly, as if even now reluctant, he passed her the deck of tarot cards.

"You remember your uncle's writings?"

"Perfectly."

He gave a slight smile. "Even though you returned the book to the library and led me to believe you never revisited it?" he chided gently.

Léonie blushed. "I may, once or twice, have reacquainted myself with its contents."

"It is fortunate, perhaps. The old are not always wise." He paused. "But you understand that your fate is tied up with this? If you choose to breathe life into the paintings you have done, if you call forth the demon, you know he will take you, too?"

Fear glittered in her green eyes. "I do."

"Very well."

"What I do not understand is why the demon, Asmodeus, did not take my uncle."

Baillard shrugged. "Evil attracts evil," he said. "Your uncle did not wish to forfeit his life and fought the demon. But he was marked forever afterward."

"But what if I cannot—"

"Enough now," he said firmly. "It will become clear, I believe, in the moment."

Léonie took the black silk package and buried it in the capacious pocket of her cloak, then rushed to the mantelshelf above the fire and took a box of matches balanced on the corner of the marble surround.

On her tiptoes, she placed a kiss upon his forehead. "Thank you, Sajhë," she whispered. "For the cards. For everything."

. . .

THE HALL WAS DARK as Léonie, Audric Baillard, Louis-Anatole and Marieta emerged from the drawing room.

In every corner, every nook, Léonie could hear or see signs of activity. The gardener's son, Emile, now a strong and tall man, was organizing the indoor staff with any weapons he could lay his hands on. An old musket, a cutlass taken from the display case, sticks. The outdoor servants were armed with hunting rifles, rakes, spades and hoes.

Léonie felt Louis-Anatole's shock at the familiar faces of his day-to-day life transformed. His hand tightened in hers.

She stopped and set her voice high and clear.

"I do not wish you to risk your lives," she said. "You are loyal and brave—I know my late brother and Madama Isolde would feel the same, were they here to witness this—but this is not a fight we can win." She looked around the hall, taking in the familiar and less familiar faces. "Please, I beg you, leave now while you have the chance. Go back to your families and your children."

No one moved. The glass of the black-and-white framed portrait hanging above the piano glinted, catching her eye. Léonie hesitated. The souvenir of a sunny afternoon in the Place du Pérou, so long ago: Anatole seated, Isolde and herself standing behind, all three of them content in one another's company. For a moment, she was tempted to take the photograph with her. But mindful of the instruction to take only what was essential, she stayed her hand. The portrait remained where it had always been, as if keeping watch over the house and those in it.

Seeing there was nothing to be done, Léonie and Louis-Anatole slipped out through the glazed metal doors and onto the terrace. Baillard and Marieta followed. Then, from the assembled crowd behind her, a voice rang out.

"Good luck, Madomaisèla Léonie. And to you, *pichon*. We will be here when you return."

"*Et à vous aussi,*" the little boy replied in his sweet voice.

It was cold outside. The frost nipped at their cheeks and made their ears hurt. Léonie pulled her hood up over her head. They could hear the mob on the far side of the house, still some way off, but the sound struck fear into them all.

"Where are we going, Tante Léonie?" Louis-Anatole whispered.

Léonie heard the fear in his voice. "We are going through the woods to where Pascal is waiting with the gig," she said.

"Why is he waiting there?"

"Because we do not want anyone to see us or hear us," she said quickly. "Then, still very quiet, mind, we will ride to Monsieur Baillard's house in the mountains."

"Is it a long way?"

"It is."

The boy was quiet for a moment. "When will we be coming back?" he asked.

Léonie bit her lip. "Think of it as a game of *cache-cache*. Just a game." She put her finger to her lips. "But we must hurry now, Louis-Anatole. And be very quiet, very, very quiet."

"And very brave."

Léonie's fingers went round the deck of cards in her pocket. "Oh, yes," she murmured. "And brave."

95

"M*ettez le feu!*"
Down by the lake, on Constant's order, the mob now at the rear of the grounds plunged their torches into the woody base of the box hedge. Minutes passed, then the hedge began to burn, first the network of branches, then the trunks, crackling and spitting like the fireworks on the walls of La Cité. The fire rose and swayed and took hold.

Then the cold voice came again. "*A l'attaque!*"

The men came swarming across the lawns, around the water, trampling the borders. They leapt up the steps to the terrace, pushing over the ornamental planters.

Constant followed, limping, at a distance, a cigarette in his hand and leaning heavily on his stick, as if following a parade on the Champs-Elysées.

At four o'clock that afternoon—when he was certain that Léonie Vernier was already on her way to Coustaussa—Constant had had yet another slaughtered child brought home to torment its parents. His man had carried the slashed corpse on an ox cart to the Place du Pérou to where he sat waiting. It had taken little skill, even with his depleted energies, to catch the attention of the crowd. Such terrible injuries could not be inflicted by an animal but only by something unnatural. A creature being concealed at the Domaine de la Cade. A devil, a demon.

A groom from the Domaine had been in Rennes-les-Bains at the time. The small crowd had turned on the boy, demanding to know how the creature was controlled, where it was kept. Though nothing could make him admit to the absurd tales of sorcery, this only inflamed the crowd.

It was Constant himself who suggested they storm the house to see for themselves. Within moments, the idea had taken hold and become their own. A little later, he allowed them to persuade him to organize the assault on the Domaine de la Cade.

Constant paused at the foot of the terrace, exhausted by the effort of walking. He watched the mob divide into two columns, spreading out to front and side, swarming up the stone stairs and onto the terrace at the back of the house.

The striped awning that ran the length of the terrace went up first, sparked by a boy climbing up the ivy and wedging his flaming torch into the folds of material at the end. Although damp from the October air, the material caught and ignited in seconds, and the torch fell through onto the terrace. The smell of oil and canvas and fire filled the night in a cloud of choking black smoke.

Someone called out above the chaos: *"Les diaboliques!"*

The sight of the fire seemed to inflame the passions of the villagers. The first window was broken, the glass shattering at the end of a steel-tipped boot. A shard became wedged in the man's thick winter trousers, and he picked it out. More windows followed. One by one the elegant rooms were breached by the violence of the crowd, jabbing their torches in to ignite the curtains.

Three others picked up a stone urn and used it as a battering ram on the door. Glass and metal buckled and shattered as the frame gave way. The trio dropped the urn, and the mob flooded into the hall and the library. With rags soaked in oil and tar, they set fire to the mahogany shelves. One by one the books ignited, the dry paper and antique leather bindings catching as easily as straw. Crackling and spitting, the flames leapt from one shelf to the next.

The invaders ripped down the curtains. More windows were shattered, from the mounting heat and twisted metal, or smashed by the legs of chairs. With faces distorted by rage and envy, they upturned the table where Léonie had sat and first read *Les Tarots*, and ripped the stepladder from the wall, struggling with the brass fittings. Flames licked around the edges of the rugs, then flared into full-scale fire.

The mob exploded into the checkerboard hallway. Walking slowing, throwing his legs awkwardly out before him, Constant followed them in.

The invaders met the defenders of the house at the foot of the main staircase.

The servants were heavily outnumbered, but they fought bravely. They too had suffered from the calumnies, the rumors, the gossipmongering, and were defending their honor as well as the reputation of the Domaine de la Cade.

A young footman delivered a sharp and glancing blow to a man coming toward him. Taken by surprise, the villager stumbled back, blood pouring from his head.

They all knew one another, had grown up together, were cousins, friends, neighbors, yet they fought as enemies. Emile was brought down by a vicious kick with a steel-tipped boot from a man who once had carried him on his shoulders to school.

The shouting grew louder.

The gardeners and groundsmen, armed with hunting rifles, shot into the mob, hitting one man in the arm, another in the leg. Blood burst through split skin, arms raised to ward off the blows. But by the sheer force of numbers, the house was overwhelmed. The old gardener fell first, hearing the bone in his leg snap as a foot came down on it. Emile lasted a little longer, until he was seized by two men and a third drove his fist time and time again into his face, until he collapsed. Men with whose sons Emile had once played. They picked him up and hurled him over the banisters. He seemed to hang in the air for a fraction of a second, then fell, head over heels, to the bottom of the stairs. He landed with his arms and legs splayed at unnatural angles. Only a single trickle of blood dribbled from the corner of his mouth, but his eyes were dead.

Marieta's cousin Antoine, a simple boy but clear enough in his mind to know right from wrong, saw a man he recognized, a belt in his hand. He was the father of one of the children who had been taken. His face was twisted in bitterness and grief.

Without understanding or stopping to think, Antoine threw himself forward, hurling his arms around the man's neck, trying to wrestle him to the ground. Antoine was heavy and he was strong, but he did not know how to fight. Within seconds he found himself on his back. He threw up his hands, but he was too slow.

The belt struck him across the face, the metal clasp of the buckle driving into his open eye. Antoine's world turned red.

CONSTANT STOOD at the foot of the stairs, holding his hand up to shield his face against the heat and soot, waiting as his man ran across the hall to report.

"They are not here," he panted. "I have searched everywhere. It seems they left with an old man and the housekeeper some quarter of an hour ago."

"On foot?"

He nodded. "I found this, Monsieur. In the drawing room."

Victor Constant took it in his trembling hand. It was a tarot card, an image of a grotesque devil with two lovers chained at its feet. He tried to focus, the smoke taking his vision from him. As he looked, it seemed that the demon was moving, twisting as if under a burden. The lovers came to resemble Vernier and Isolde.

He rubbed his painful eyes with his gloved fingers, then an idea came to him.

"When you have settled Gélis, leave this tarot card with the body. It will confuse matters, if nothing else. The whole of Coustaussa knows the girl was there."

The manservant nodded. "And you, Monsieur?"

"Help me to the carriage. A child, a woman and an old man? I do not believe they can have gone far. In point of fact, I think it is more likely they will be hiding somewhere within the grounds. The estate is steeply wooded. There is only one place they are likely to be."

"And them?" The servant jerked his head in the direction of the mob.

The sounds of screaming were rising in crescendo as the battle reached its zenith. Soon the looting would begin. Even if the boy did escape tonight, there would be nothing for him to come back to. He would be destitute.

"Leave them to it," he said.

96

It was hard going in the dark once they got to the woods. Louis-Anatole was a strong boy and Monsieur Baillard, despite his age, was surprisingly fast on his feet, but all the same they made slow progress. They had brought a lamp, but it was unlit for fear of drawing the mob's attention.

Léonie found that her feet knew the path she had so long avoided to the sepulchre. As she walked, climbing uphill, her long, black cape stirred up the fallen autumn leaves, damp underfoot. She thought of all the journeys she had made around the estate—the glade with the wild juniper, the clearing where Anatole had fallen; the tombs of her brother and Isolde, side by side on the promontory on the far shore of the lake—and her heart wept at the thought that she might never see any of it again. Having so long felt confined by her narrow existence, now that the time had come to leave, she did not wish to go. The rocks, the hills, the copses, the wooded pathways, she felt as if each was seamed into the structure of the person she had become.

"Are we nearly there, Tante Léonie?" said Louis-Anatole in a small voice, after they had been traveling some quarter of an hour. "My boots are pinching me."

"Almost," she said, squeezing his hand. "Be careful not to slip."

"Do you know," he said, in a voice that gave the lie to his words, "I am not in the least afraid of spiders."

They arrived at the clearing and slowed their pace. The avenue of yews

Léonie remembered from her first visit seemed more knotted by time and the canopy less penetrable than before.

Pascal was waiting. Two weak lamps on the sides of the gig spluttered in the cold air, and the horses stamped their metal hooves on the hard ground.

"What place is this, Tante Léonie?" said Louis-Anatole, curiosity for the moment driving away his fear. "Are we still within our grounds?"

"We are. This is the old mausoleum."

"Where they bury people?"

"Sometimes."

"Why are Papa and M'man not buried here?"

She hesitated. "Because they prefer to be outside, among the trees and the flowers. They lie together by the lake, remember?"

Louis-Anatole frowned. "So they can hear the birds?"

Léonie smiled. "That is right."

"Is that why you have never brought me here?" he said, stepping forward to approach the door. "Because there are ghosts here?"

Léonie threw out her hand and grabbed him. "There is no time, Louis-Anatole."

His face fell. "Can I not go inside?"

"Not now."

"Are there spiders?"

"There might be, but since you are not afraid of spiders, you would not mind."

He nodded, but he had turned quite pale. "We'll come back another day. When it is light."

"That is an excellent idea," she said.

She felt Monsieur Baillard's hand on her arm.

"We cannot delay any longer," said Pascal. "We must cover as much distance as we can before Constant realizes we are not within the house." He bent down and swung Louis-Anatole into the gig. "So, *pichon,* you are ready for a midnight adventure?"

Louis-Anatole nodded.

"It's a long way."

"Farther than the Lac de Barrenc?"

"Even farther than that," replied Pascal.

"I shall not mind," Louis-Anatole said. "Marieta will play with me?"

"She will."

"Tante Léonie will tell me stories."

The adults cast stricken glances at one another. In silence, Monsieur Baillard and Marieta climbed into the carriage, with Pascal settled on the driver's seat.

"Come on, Tante Léonie," Louis-Anatole said.

Léonie closed the carriage door with a sharp snap. "Keep him safe."

"You do not have to do this," Baillard said quickly. "Constant is a sick man. It is possible that time and the natural run of things will bring this vendetta to an end, and soon. If you wait, it might be all this will pass of its own volition."

"It is possible, yes," she replied fiercely. "But I cannot take that risk. It might be three years, five, even ten. I cannot allow Louis-Anatole to grow up under such a shadow, always wondering, always looking out into the darkness. Thinking there is someone out there, waiting, to cause him harm."

A memory of Anatole looking down at the street from their old apartment in the rue de Berlin. Another, of Isolde's haunted face gazing ever out at the horizon, seeing danger in the smallest thing.

"No," she said, more firmly. "I will not have Louis-Anatole live such a life." She smiled. "It has to end. Now, tonight, here." She took a deep breath. "You believe this too, Sajhë."

For a moment, in the flickering light of the lamp, their eyes met. Then he nodded.

"I will return the cards to their ancient place," he said quietly, "when the boy is safe and there are no eyes to see me. You may trust me with that."

"Tante Léonie?" said Louis-Anatole again, a little more anxiously.

"*Petit,* there is something I must do," she said, keeping her voice level, "which means I cannot come with you at this moment. You will be quite safe with Pascal and Marieta and Monsieur Baillard."

His face crumpled as he reached out his arms to her, instinctively understanding this was more than a temporary separation.

"No!" he cried. "I don't want to leave you, Tante. I won't leave you."

He hurled himself across the seat and threw his arms around Léonie's neck. She kissed him and stroked his hair, then firmly detached herself from him.

"No!" the little boy shouted, struggling.

"Be good for Marieta," she said, the words catching in her throat. "And look after Monsieur Baillard and Pascal."

Stepping back, she slapped her hand on the side of the carriage. "Go," she cried. "Go."

Pascal cracked the whip, and the gig jerked forward. Léonie tried to close her ears to the sound of Louis-Anatole's voice calling out for her, crying, getting fainter as he was carried away.

When she could no longer hear the rattle of the wheels over the hard, frosty ground, she turned and walked up to the door of the ancient stone chapel. Blinded by tears, she grasped the metal handle. She hesitated, half turning and looking back over her shoulder. In the distance was an intense orange glow, filled with sparks and clouds of smoke, gray against the black night sky.

The house was burning.

She hardened her resolve. She turned the handle, pushed open the door and stepped over the threshold into the sepulchre.

97

The chill, heavy air rushed to meet her.

Slowly, Léonie let her eyes become accustomed to the gloom. She pulled the box of matches from her pocket, opened the glass door of the lamp and held a flame to the wick until it caught.

The blue eyes of Asmodeus fixed themselves on her. Léonie stepped farther into the nave. The paintings on the wall seemed to pulsate and sway and move toward her as she walked slowly up toward the altar. The dust and grit on the flagstones scratched beneath the soles of her boots, loud in the silence of the tomb.

She was unsure what she should do first. Her hand stole to the cards in her pocket. In the other was the leather wallet containing the pieces of folded paper, the paintings she had attempted—of herself, of Anatole, of Isolde—from which she had not wished to be parted.

She had, at last, admitted to Monsieur Baillard that after seeing the cards with her own eyes, she had returned to her uncle's volume on several occasions, poring over the handwritten text until she was word perfect. But still, despite this, a doubt remained over Monsieur Baillard's explanation of how the vivid life contained within the cards, and the music carried on the wind, might work one upon the other to summon the ghosts who inhabited these ancient places.

Could it be so?

Léonie understood that it was not the cards alone, not the music, nor only the place, but the combination of all three within the boundaries of the sepulchre.

And if the myths were the literal truth, then she knew, even in the midst of her doubts, that there would be no way back. The spirits would claim her. They had tried once before—and failed—but tonight she would willingly let them take her if they would take Constant, too.

And Louis-Anatole will be safe.

Suddenly a scratching sound, a tapping, made her jump. She cast her eyes round, looking for the source of the noise, then with a sigh of relief realized it was only the bare branches of a tree outside knocking against the window.

Putting the lamp on the ground, Léonie struck a second match, then several more, lighting the old tallow candles set in metal sconces on the wall. Drops of grease began to slide down the dead wicks, solidifying on the cold metal, but gradually each took, and the sepulchre was filled with yellow, flickering light.

Léonie moved forward, feeling as if the eight tableaux within the apse were watching her every move. She found the space before the altar where, a generation and more before, Jules Lascombe had spelled out the name of the Domaine in letters upon the stone floor. C-A-D-E.

Without knowing if she was doing the right thing or the wrong, she took the tarot cards from her pocket, unwrapped them and placed the whole deck in the center of the square, her late uncle's words reverberating in her head.

Her leather wallet she placed beside the deck, undoing the ties but not taking the paintings out.

Through the power of which I would walk in another dimension.

Léonie raised her head. There was a moment of stillness then. Outside the chamber, she heard the wind moving through the trees. She listened harder. The smoke still rose undisturbed from the candles, but she thought she could almost discern the sound of music, thin notes, a high-pitched whistling as the wind threaded itself through the branches of beech woods and the avenue of yew trees. Then it came, slippery, in under the door, through the gaps between the lead and the glass of the windows.

There was a rushing of air and the sensation that I was not alone.

Léonie smiled, remembering the words on the page. She was not frightened now, she was curious. And for a fleeting moment, as she looked up to the octagonal apse, she thought that perhaps she saw the face of La Force move. The faintest smile had come across the painted face. And for an instant, the girl looked precisely like her—like her own face, which she had painted into her copies of the tarot images. The same copper hair, the same green eyes, the same direct gaze.

My self and my other selves, both past and yet to come, were equally present.

Around her now, Léonie was aware of movement. Spirits, or the cards come to life, she could not say. The Lovers, to her hopeful and willing eyes, so clearly taking on the beloved features of Anatole and Isolde. For a fleeting moment, Léonie thought she could recognize the features of Louis-Anatole shimmering behind the image of La Justice, sitting with her scales and a run of notes around the rim of her long skirts, the boy she knew contained within the outline of the woman on the card. Then out of the corner of her eye, only for a second, the features of Audric Baillard—Sajhë—seemed to imprint themselves upon the young face of Le Pagad.

Léonie stood completely still, letting the music wash over her. The faces and the costumes and the landscapes seemed to move, to shift and shimmer like stars, revolving in the silver air as if held by the invisible current of music. She lost any sense of herself. Dimension, space, time, mass, all vanished now to insignificance.

The vibrations, the rustling of the air, the ghosts, she supposed, brushed against her shoulders and neck, skimmed her forehead, surrounded her, gentle, kind, but without ever really touching. A silent chaos was growing, a cacophony of noiseless whispering and sighing.

Léonie reached her arms out in front of her. She felt herself weightless, transparent, as if floating in the water, although her dress still hung red round her, the cloak black on her shoulders. They were waiting for her to join them. She turned over her outstretched hands and saw, quite clearly, the infinity symbol appear on the pale skin of her palms. Like a figure eight.

"Aïci lo tems s'en, va res l'Eternitat."

The words fell silver from her lips. Now, after waiting so long, there was no mistaking their meaning.

Here, in this place, time moves away toward eternity.

Léonie smiled and—with the thought of Louis-Anatole behind her, her mother and brother and aunt before her—she stepped forward into the light.

THE JOLTING over the rough ground had caused him great discomfort, opening several of the sores on his hands and on his back. He could feel the pus seeping through the bandages.

Constant descended from the carriage.

He poked the ground with his walking stick. Two horses had stood here—and recently. The wheel ruts suggested only one carriage and appeared to lead away, rather than toward, the sepulchre.

"Wait here," he instructed.

Constant felt the curious force of the wind insinuating itself between the tightly knit trunks of the avenue of yews that led to the door of the tomb. With his free hand, he held his greatcoat tight around his throat against the strengthening currents of air. He sniffed. His sense of smell was almost gone, but he could just pick out an unpleasant odor, a peculiar mixture of incense and the malodorous scent of rotting seaweed on the shore.

Though his eyes were watering with the cold, he could see there were lights burning inside. The thought that the boy might be hiding there powered him forward. He strode ahead, paying no attention to the rushing sound, almost like water, nor to the whistling, like wind chasing down the telegraph wires or the vibrating of the metal track as a train approaches.

It was almost like music.

He refused to be diverted by whatever tricks Léonie Vernier might or might not be attempting, with the light or smoke or sound.

Constant approached the heavy door, turned the handle. At first, it did not shift. Assuming it was bolted or furniture had been piled up as a barricade, he nonetheless tried again. This time, all at once, it opened. Constant almost lost his balance and half stepped, half fell into the sepulchre.

Straightaway he saw her, standing with her back to him in front of a small altar set within an eight-sided apse. Indeed, she was making no attempt to conceal herself. Of the boy, there was no sign.

His chin jutting forward, his eyes darting left and right, Constant proceeded up the nave, his stick tapping on the flagstones as his feet fell awkwardly from step to step. There was an empty plinth just inside the door, jagged on the top, as if the statue had been torn from it. Familiar plaster saints, set around the walls behind the modest rows of empty pews, marked his passing as he drew nearer to the altar.

"Mademoiselle Vernier," he said sharply, irritated by her inattention.

Still, she did not move. Indeed, she seemed unaware of his presence.

Constant stopped and looked down at the pile of cards strewn on the stone floor before the altar. "What absurdity is this?" he said, and stepped into the square.

Now Léonie turned to face him. The hood fell from her face. Constant threw up his diseased hands to shield his eyes from the light. The smile slipped from his lips. He did not understand. He could see the girl's features, the same direct gaze, the hair now tumbling loose, as it had been in the portrait he had stolen from the rue de Berlin, but she was transformed into something other.

As he stood there, captivated and blinded, she began to change. The bones, the sinews, the skull beneath the skin started to push through.

Constant screamed.

Something swooped down on him, and the silence he had not recognized as silence was broken in a cacophony of shrieking and howling. He clamped his hands over his ears to stop the creatures from entering his head, but his fingers were pulled away by talons and claws, even though not a mark was laid on him.

It seemed as if the painted figures had stepped down from the wall, each now transformed into a dark version of their fairer selves. Nails turned to talons, fingers to claws, eyes to fire and ice. Constant buried his head in his chest, dropping his stick as he curled his arms over his face to protect himself. He fell to his knees, gasped for breath as his heart began to lose its rhythm. He tried to move forward, out of the square on the ground, but an invisible force, like an overwhelming wind, kept pushing him back. The howling, the vibrating of the music was getting louder. It seemed to come from outside as well as in, echoing inside his head. Splitting open his mind.

"No!" he shouted.

But the voices were increasing in volume and intensity. Uncomprehending, he looked for Léonie. He could no longer see her at all. The light was too bright, the air around shimmering with incandescent smoke.

Then, behind him, or rather from beneath the very surface of his skin, came a different noise. A scraping, like the claws of a wild animal, grating along the surface of his bones. He flinched and jerked, crying out in agony, then fell to the floor in a rushing of air.

And suddenly, crouched on his chest, with a reek of fish and pitch, was a demon, gaunt and twisted, with red, leathery skin, a horned brow and strange, penetrating blue eyes. The demon that he knew could not exist. Did not exist. Yet the face of Asmodeus was looking down on him.

"No!" His mouth opened in one final howl before the devil took him.

Instantly, the air in the sepulchre was still. The whisperings and sighings of the spirits grew fainter until at last neither could be heard. The cards lay scattered on the ground. The faces on the wall became flat and two-dimensional once more, but their expressions and attitudes had shifted subtly. Each bore an unmistakable resemblance to those who had lived—and died—in the Domaine de la Cade. Like Léonie's paintings.

OUTSIDE IN THE CLEARING, Constant's manservant cowered from the wind, the smoke and the light. He heard his master scream, once, then again. The inhuman sound kept him too petrified to move.

Only now, when all had fallen quiet and the lights within the sepulchre had steadied, did he summon the courage to come out of his hiding place. Slowly, he approached the heavy door and found it slightly ajar. His tentative hand encountered no resistance.

"Monsieur?"

He stepped inside. "Monsieur?" he called again.

A draft, like an exhalation, emptied the sepulchre of smoke in a single, cool breath, leaving the place lit by the lamp on the wall.

He saw the body of his master immediately. He was lying facedown on the ground, in front of the altar, a deck of playing cards scattered all about him. The servant rushed forward and rolled his master's emaciated form onto its back, then recoiled. Across Constant's face were three deep and red gashes, like the savage marks of a wild animal.

Like claws. Like the marks he had carved on the children they had killed.

The man crossed himself mechanically and leaned forward to close his master's wide, horrified eyes. Then his hand stopped as he noticed the rectangular card lying across Constant's chest, over his heart. Le Diable.

Had it been there all along?

Uncomprehending, the servant's hand went to his pocket, where he could swear he had placed the tarot card his master had instructed him to leave with the body of Curé Gélis in Coustaussa. The pocket was empty.

Had he dropped it? What other explanation could there be?

There was a moment of recognition, then the manservant staggered back from his master's body and started to run down the nave, past the unseeing eyes of the statues, out of the sepulchre, away from the grimacing face on the card.

In the valley below, the midnight bell began to toll.

Part XII

The Ruins
October 2007

98

Domaine de la Cade
Wednesday, October 31, 2007

D r. O'Donnell," Hal shouted again.

It was ten past twelve. For more than fifteen minutes he'd been waiting outside Shelagh O'Donnell's house. He'd tried knocking. Neither of her neighbors was in, so he'd gone for a walk and come back, started knocking again. Still, nothing.

Hal was certain he was in the right place—he'd checked the address several times—and he didn't think she could have forgotten. He was trying to keep positive, but it was becoming more of a challenge with every second that passed. Where was she? The traffic was bad this morning, so maybe she'd gotten held up? Maybe she was in the shower and hadn't heard him?

The worst-case scenario—and he had to admit, the most likely—was that Shelagh had thought better of going with him to the police. Her dislike of authority was clear, and Hal could easily see her losing what little nerve she had without him and Meredith there to back her up.

He took a step back and looked up at the shuttered windows. The house stood in the middle of a pretty row of homes overlooking the River Aude, overlooking the water, shielded on one side from the walkway by a fence of green angle iron and split bamboo canes. It occurred to him that he might be able to see into the garden from the back. He followed the line of the buildings, then doubled back on himself. It was hard to tell which house was which from the back, but he matched the color wash of the walls—one house was painted pale blue, another a thin yellow—until he was confident he knew which was Shelagh O'Donnell's property.

There was a low wall at right angles to the hedge. Hal walked closer to get a glimpse of the terrace. Hope sparked in his chest. It looked as if there was someone there.

"Dr. O'Donnell? It's me, Hal Lawrence."

There was no answer.

"Dr. O'Donnell? It's a quarter past twelve."

She appeared to be lying facedown on the small terrace next to the house. It was a sheltered spot, and the sun was surprisingly warm for the tail end of October, but it was hardly sunbathing weather. Perhaps she was reading a book; he couldn't see. But whatever she was doing, he thought with irritation, she had clearly decided to ignore him—to pretend she wasn't there. His view was obscured by a pair of unkempt planters.

"Dr. O'Donnell?"

His phone vibrated in his pocket. With his mind only half on it, he pulled it out and read the message.

"Found them. Sepulchre now. xx."

Hal stared blankly at the words on the screen, then his brain flipped into gear and he started to smile, understanding Meredith's message.

"At least someone's having a productive morning," he muttered, then went back to the matter at hand. He wasn't going to let it drop. After all the effort he'd put into persuading the commissaire to see them this morning, he wasn't going to let Shelagh duck out.

"Dr. O'Donnell!" he called out again. "I know you're there."

He started to wonder. Even if she had changed her mind, it was odd that she was taking no notice at all. He was making enough noise. Hal hesitated, then pulled himself up and climbed over the wall. There was a heavy stick lying on the terrace, half pushed under the hedge. He picked it up, then noticed there were marks at the top.

Blood, he realized.

He ran across the terrace to where Shelagh O'Donnell was lying motionless. One look was enough to see she'd been hit and more than once. He checked her pulse. She was still breathing, although she didn't look great.

Hal pulled the phone from his pocket and dialed for an ambulance with shaking fingers.

"Maintenant!" he shouted, after he'd given the address three times. *"Oui, elle souffle! Mais vite, alors!"*

Hal disconnected. He rushed into the house, found a blanket draped over the back of the sofa and ran back outside. He laid it carefully over Shelagh to keep her warm, knowing he shouldn't attempt to move her, then went back into the house and out the front door into the street. He felt guilty about what he was about to do, but he couldn't wait around in Rennes-les-Bains for the paramedics. He had to get back.

He hammered on the neighbor's door. When she answered, he told the startled woman what had happened, asked her to stay with Dr. O'Donnell until the ambulance arrived, then bolted to his car before she had a chance to object.

He fired up the engine and put his foot on the accelerator. There was only one person who could be responsible. He had to get back to the Domaine de la Cade. And find Meredith.

JULIAN LAWRENCE slammed the car door and charged up the front steps of the hotel.

He shouldn't have panicked.

There were beads of sweat running down his face and soaking into the collar of his shirt. He stumbled into reception. He needed to get to his study and calm down. Then work out what to do.

"Monsieur? Monsieur Lawrence?"

He swung round, his vision a little blurred, to see the receptionist waving at him.

"Monsieur Lawrence," Eloise started, then broke off. "Are you all right?"

"I'm fine," he snapped. "What is it?"

She recoiled. "Your nephew asked me to give you this."

Julian covered the space in three strides and snatched the paper from Eloise's outstretched hand. The note was from Hal, curt and to the point, wanting to set up a meeting between them at two o'clock.

Julian screwed the paper in his fist. "What time did he leave this?" he demanded.

"About ten-thirty, Monsieur, just after you went out."

"Is my nephew in the hotel now?"

"I believe he went to Rennes-les-Bains just before midday to collect the visitor who was with him earlier. To my knowledge, he hasn't yet come back."

"Was the American girl with him?"

"No. She went out into the gardens," she replied, glancing at the doors to the terrace.

"How long ago was this?"

"At least one hour, Monsieur."

"Did she say what she was doing? Where she was going? Did you hear anything between her and my nephew, Eloise? Anything?"

Her growing alarm at his manner showed in her eyes, but she answered calmly.

"No, Monsieur, although . . ."

"What?"

"Before she went out to the gardens she asked if she might borrow a—I don't know the English word—*une pelle.*"

Julian started. "A spade?"

Eloise leapt back in alarm as Julian smacked his hands down on the desk, leaving two damp palm prints on the counter. Ms. Martin would hardly ask for a spade if she didn't intend to dig. And she had waited until she knew he had left the hotel.

"The cards," he muttered. "She knows where they are."

"Qu'est-ce qu'il y a, monsieur?" said Eloise nervously. *"Vous semblez—"*

Julian didn't answer, just turned on his heel, strode across the hall and threw open the door to the terrace, sending it slamming back against the wall.

"What shall I say when your nephew comes back?" Eloise called after him.

From the small window at the back of reception, she watched him stride away. Not down to the lake, as Madame Martin had done earlier, but in the direction of the woods.

99

There was an avenue of yew trees straight ahead and the echo of an old path. It seemed to lead nowhere, but as Meredith looked closer, she could see the outline of foundations and a few broken stones on the ground. There was once a building here.

This is the place.

Holding the box containing the deck of cards, she walked slowly toward where the sepulchre had once stood. The grass was damp under her feet, as if it had recently rained. She could feel the abandonment and isolation of the place through the soles of her muddy boots.

Meredith bit back her disappointment. A few blocks, the remains of an outer wall, otherwise just empty space. Grass as far as the eye could see.

Look closer.

Meredith looked into the space. Now she saw that the surface was not entirely flat. With a little imagination, she realized she could just about work out the footprint of the sepulchre. A patch of ground, maybe twenty feet long by ten feet wide, like a sunken garden. Clutching the handles of the box a little tighter, she stepped forward.

As if stepping over a threshold.

Straightaway, the light seemed to change, to grow denser, more opaque. The roaring of the wind in her ears was louder, like a high repeated note or the buzz along telephone wires in the breeze. And she could detect the slightest scent of incense, the heady smell of damp stone and ancient worship hanging in the air.

She put the box down, then straightened up and looked around. Some trick of the air made a soft mist rise from the damp soil. Then pinpricks of light began to appear, one by one, hanging suspended around the periphery of the ruin, as if some invisible hand was lighting a set of tiny candles. As each halo of light connected to the rest, they gave shape to the vanished walls of the sepulchre. Through the veil of a thin cloud, Meredith thought she saw the outline of letters on the ground: C-A-D-E. As she stepped forward, the surface beneath her boots felt different, too. No longer earth and grass but hard, cold flagstones.

Meredith knelt down, oblivious to the wet seeping through the knees of her jeans. She took out the deck and shut the box's lid. Not wishing to spoil the cards, she took off her jacket and laid it, inside out, across the workbox. She shuffled the cards, as Laura had showed her in Paris, then cut the deck into three separate piles with her left hand. She put them back together—middle, top, bottom—and placed the entire deck facedown on her makeshift table.

I cannot sleep.

Meredith could not possibly attempt a reading for herself. Every time she read the notes she'd made, she was more confused by the meanings than before. She just intended to turn the cards—perhaps eight, respecting the relationship of the music with the place—until some pattern emerged.

Until, as Léonie promised, the cards told the story.

She drew the first card and smiled to see the familiar features of La Justice. Despite the shuffling and cutting of the cards, it was the same card that had been on the top when she found the deck in the *cachette* in the dry riverbed.

The second card was La Tour, a card of conflict and threat. She placed it beside the first, then drew again. The clear blue eyes of Le Pagad looked up at her, one hand pointing to heaven and one to earth, the infinity symbol above his head. It was a slightly menacing figure, neither clearly good nor clearly bad. As she stared, Meredith started to think she knew his face, although she could not yet recognize him.

Card four made her smile again: Le Mat. Anatole Vernier, in his white suit, boater and walking stick in hand, as painted by his sister. La Prêtresse followed him, Isolde Lascombe, beautiful and elegant and sophisticated. Then Les Amoureux, Isolde and Anatole together.

Card seven was Le Diable. Her hand hovered over the card a moment, watching while the malevolent features of Asmodeus took shape before her eyes. The demon, the personification of the terrors and mountain hauntings related by Audric S. Baillard in his book. Stories of evil, past and present.

Meredith knew now, from the sequence she had drawn, what the last card would be. Each of the dramatis personae was here, portrayed in the cards

Léonie had painted yet modified or somehow transformed to tell a specific story.

With the smell of the incense in her nose and the colors of the past fixed in her imagination, Meredith felt time slipping away. A continuous present, everything that had come before and everything that was yet to come, joined in this act of the laying out of the cards.

Things slipping between past and present.

She touched the final card with the tips of her fingers and, without even turning it over, Meredith felt Léonie step out of the shadows.

Card VIII: La Force.

Leaving it still unturned, she sat back on the ground, not feeling the cold or the wet, and looked at the octave of cards laid out on the box. Then she realized the images were starting to shift. She found her eye drawn to Le Mat. At first it was just a spot of color that had not been there before. A speck of blood, almost too small to see, growing larger, blossoming, red against the white of Anatole's suit. Covering his heart. For a moment, the painted eyes seemed to hold her in his gaze.

Meredith caught her breath, appalled yet unable to tear herself away, as she realized she was watching Anatole Vernier die. The figure slipped slowly to the bottom of the painted ground, revealing the mountains of Soularac and Bézu visible in the background.

Desperate not to see more, yet at the same time feeling she had no choice, a movement on the adjacent card drew her. Meredith turned to La Prêtresse. To start, the beautiful face of Isolde Vernier looked calmly up at her from card II, serene in a long blue dress and white gloves that emphasized her long, elegant fingers, her slim arms. Then her features started to change, the color shifting from pink to blue. Her eyes widened, her arms seemed to glide above her head, as if she was swimming, floating.

Drowning.

The echo of Meredith's own mother's death.

The card seemed to become darker, as Isolde's skirts billowed in the water around stockinged legs, shimmering silk in the opaque green underwater world, slimy fingers slipping the ivory shoes from her feet.

Isolde's eyes fell shut, but as they did, Meredith saw that the expression shining out of them was release, not fear, not the horror of drowning. How could that be? Had her life become such a burden to her that she wanted to die?

She glanced to the end of the row, at Le Diable, and smiled. The two figures imprisoned at the feet of the demon were no longer there. The chains hung empty around the base of the plinth. Asmodeus was alone.

Meredith took a deep breath. If the cards could speak the story of what had happened, what of Léonie? She reached out but still could not bring herself to turn the last card. She was desperate to know the truth. At the same time, she feared the story she might see in the shifting images.

She tucked her nail under the corner of the card, closed her eyes and counted to three. Then she looked.

The face of the card was blank.

Meredith rose up on her knees, not trusting the evidence of her own eyes. She picked it up and turned it over, then back again.

The card was still blank, completely white; not even the greens and blues of the Midi landscape remained.

At that moment, a sound broke into her reflections. A broken twig, the crunch of stones knocked out of place on the path, the sudden beating of a bird on the wing as it flew up out of the tree.

Meredith stood up, half glancing behind her, but could see nothing.

"Hal?"

A hundred thoughts flashed into her mind, none of them reassuring. She pushed them out. It had to be Hal. She'd told him where she was going. No one else knew she was here.

"Hal? Is that you?"

The footsteps were getting nearer. Someone walking fast through the woods, the swish of displaced leaves, the crack of twigs underfoot.

If it was him, why wasn't he answering? "Hal? This isn't funny."

Meredith didn't know what to do. The smart thing would be to run, not stick about waiting to figure out what the person wanted.

No, the smart thing is not to overreact.

She tried to tell herself it was just another guest out for a walk in the woods, like her. All the same, she moved quickly to pack away the cards. Now she noticed that several others were blank. The second card she'd drawn, La Tour, and Le Pagad was empty, too.

With fingers made clumsy by nerves and the cold, she snatched at the cards to pick them up. She had the sensation of a spider running over her bare skin. She flicked at her wrist to get it off, but there was nothing there, although she could still feel it.

There was a different smell now, too. No longer the scent of fallen leaves and damp stone or the incense she'd imagined a few minutes earlier but the stink of rotten fish or the sea on some stagnant estuary. And the smell of fire: not the familiar autumn bonfires down in the valley but hot ash and acrid smoke and burning stone.

The moment passed. Meredith blinked, suddenly pulled herself back. Then, out of the corner of her eye, she noticed a movement. There was some kind of animal, its fur black and matted, moving low through the undergrowth. Circling the glade. Meredith froze. It looked to be the size of a wolf or a wild boar, even though she didn't know if they still even had wolves in France. It seemed to spring from leg to leg. Meredith clutched the box tighter. Now she could make out obscenely misshapen front legs and leathery, blistered skin. For a second, the creature turned its piercing blue gaze on her. She felt a sharp pain in her chest, as if the point of a knife had been jabbed into her, then the creature turned away and the pressure on her heart was released.

Meredith heard a loud noise. She looked down and saw the scales of justice slip from the hand of the figure on card XI. She heard the clatter as the brass dishes and iron weights fell to the stone floor of the painting and scattered.

Coming to get you.

The two stories had merged, as Laura had predicted they would. The past and the present, brought together by the cards.

Meredith felt the short hairs on the back of her neck stand on end, and realized that while she had been staring into the woods, trying to see what was out there in the gloom of the forest, she had forgotten the threat from the opposite direction.

It was too late to run.

Someone—something—was already behind her.

100

"Give me the cards," he said.

Meredith's heart leapt into her mouth at the sound of his voice.

She spun round, clutching the cards tightly, then instantly recoiled. Always immaculate whenever she had seen him before, in Rennes-les-Bains and in the hotel, now Julian Lawrence looked wrecked. His shirt was open at the neck, and he was sweating heavily. There was the sour smell of brandy on his breath.

"There's something out there," she said, the words bursting out of her mouth before she had a chance to think. "A wolf or something, I'm telling you. I saw it. Outside the walls."

He stopped, confusion clouding his desperate eyes. "Walls? What walls? What are you talking about?"

Meredith glanced to the side. The candles were still flickering, sending shadows outlining the shape of the Visigoth tomb.

"Can't you see them?" she asked. "It's so clear. The lights shining where the sepulchre used to be?"

A sly smile moved across his lips. "Ah, I see what you're doing," he said, "but it won't work. Wolves, animals, ghosts, all highly diverting but you're not going to divert me from getting what I want." He took another step closer. "Give me the cards."

Meredith stumbled back a pace. For a moment, though, she was tempted. She was on his property, she was digging up his grounds without permission. She was the one in the wrong, not him. But the look on his face turned her blood cold. Piercing blue eyes, his pupils dilated. Fear trickled down her spine when she thought of how isolated they were, miles from anywhere, in the woods.

She needed to keep some kind of leverage. She watched cautiously as he glanced around the clearing.

"Did you find the deck here?" he said. "No, I dug here. It wasn't here."

Until now, Meredith hadn't bought into Hal's theories about his uncle. Even if Dr. O'Donnell was right, and it had been Julian Lawrence's blue car on the road just after the accident, she could just about believe he might not have stopped to help. But now none of that seemed so crazy.

Meredith took a step back. "Hal will be here any moment," she said.

"And what difference does that make?"

She glanced round, trying to figure out if she could run. She was much younger, much fitter than he. But she didn't want to abandon Léonie's work-box on the ground. And even if Julian Lawrence thought she was just trying to scare him with talk of wolves, she knew she had seen something, some predator, skulking around the edges of the clearing just before he had arrived.

"Give me the cards and I won't hurt you," he said.

Meredith took another step back. "I don't believe you."

"I don't think it matters whether you believe me or not," he said, then, like a light being switched, he suddenly lost his temper and roared, "Give them to me!"

Meredith stumbled farther back, clutching the cards to her. Then she smelled it again. Stronger than before, a stomach-churning stench of rotting fish and an even more pervasive smell of fire.

But Julian was completely oblivious to everything but the cards she was holding. He just kept walking toward her, getting closer and closer, holding out his hand.

"Get away from her!"

Both Meredith and Julian spun round in the direction of the voice, as Hal came running out of the woods, shouting, heading straight for his uncle.

Julian twisted round and charged to meet him, drew back his arm and caught him under the jaw with his right fist. Taken by surprise, Hal went down, blood exploding from his mouth and nose.

"Hal!"

He kicked out at his uncle, striking him on the side of the knee. Julian stumbled, but he didn't go down. Hal struggled to get up, but although Julian was older and much heavier, he knew how to fight and had used his fists more often than Hal. His reactions were quicker. He gripped his hands together and brought them with combined force down on the back of Hal's neck.

Meredith ran to the workbox, threw the cards inside, slammed the lid, then ran back to where Hal lay unconscious on the ground.

Julian has nothing to lose.

"Pass me the cards, Ms. Martin."

There was another gust of wind, carrying the smell of burning. This time, Lawrence smelled it too. Confusion flared briefly in his eyes.

"I'll kill you if I have to," he said, in so casual a tone that it made the threat all the more believable. Meredith didn't reply. Now the flickering candle-light she had imagined on the walls of the sepulchre was turning to leaping orange and gold and black flames. The sepulchre was starting to burn. Black smoke was enveloping the clearing, licking over the stones. Meredith imagined she could hear the crackle and spit of the paint on the plaster saints as they started to scorch. The glass in the windows exploded outward as the metal frames buckled.

"Can't you see it?" she shouted. "Can't you see what's happening?"

She saw alarm flood across Julian's face, then a look of pure horror leap into his eyes. Meredith turned round, but she was too slow to see it clearly. Something rushed past her, some kind of animal with black, matted fur, a strange jerking movement, and leapt.

Julian screamed.

Meredith watched in horror as he fell, trying to propel himself backward on the ground, and then arching his back like a grotesque crab. He threw up his arms, as if wrestling with some invisible creature, striking out at the empty air, screaming that there was something ripping at his face, his eyes, his mouth. His hands were clawing at his own throat, tearing at the skin, as if trying to free himself from the grasp of a hand.

And Meredith heard the whispering, a different voice, deeper and louder than Léonie's, reverberating inside her head. She didn't recognize the words, but she understood the meaning.

Fujhi, poudes; Escapa, non. Flee you may, escape you cannot.

She saw the fight go out of Julian, and he fell back to the ground.

Silence immediately descended on the glade. She looked round. She was standing on a bare patch of grass. No flames, no walls, no smell of the grave.

Hal was stirring, raising himself up on one elbow. He put his hand to his face, then held out his palm, sticky with blood.

"What the hell happened?"

Meredith ran over and put her arms around him. "He hit you. Put you out for a while."

Hal blinked, then turned his head to where his uncle lay on the ground. His eyes widened. "Did you . . . ?"

"No," she said quickly. "I didn't touch him. I don't know what happened. One minute he was . . ." She stopped, not knowing how she could possibly describe to Hal what she'd seen.

"Heart attack?"

Meredith bent down beside Julian. His face was chalk-white, tinged with blue around his lips and nose.

"He's still alive," she said, pulling her cell from her pocket and tossing it to Hal. "Call. If the paramedics are fast."

He caught it but made no move to dial. She saw the look in his eye and knew what he was thinking.

"No," she said softly. "Not like this."

He held her gaze for a moment, his blue eyes flickering with hurt and the possibility of paying his uncle back for what he'd done. A magician, with power over life and death.

"Make the call, Hal."

For a moment more, the decision hung in the balance. Then she saw his eyes cloud over and he came back to himself. Justice, not revenge. He began to punch in the number.

Meredith crouched down beside Julian, no longer terrifying but now pathetic. His palms lay exposed to the air. There was a strange red mark on each, much like a figure eight. She put her hand on his chest, then realized he was no longer breathing.

Slowly, she straightened up. "Hal."

He glanced over at her. Meredith just shook her head. "It's too late."

101

Sunday, November 11

Eleven days later, Meredith stood on the promontory overlooking the lake, watching as a small wooden casket was lowered into the ground.

It was a small party. Herself and Hal, now the legal owner of the Domaine de la Cade, together with Shelagh O'Donnell, still bearing the evidence of Julian's attack on her. There was also the priest, and a representative from the mairie. After some persuasion, the town hall had given permission for the service to go ahead on the grounds that the site could be identified as the place where Anatole and Isolde Vernier were buried. Julian Lawrence had plundered the graves but not disturbed the bones.

Now, after more than a hundred years, Léonie could finally be laid to rest beside the bodies of her beloved brother and his wife.

Emotion caught in Meredith's throat.

In the hours after Julian's death, Léonie's remains had been unearthed in a shallow grave beneath the ruins of the sepulchre. It looked, almost, as if she had simply laid down on the ground to rest. No one could account for the fact that she had not been found before, given the extensive excavations that had been carried out on the site. Nor why her bones had not been scattered by wild animals in all that time.

But Meredith had stood at the foot of the grave and seen how the colors of the earth beneath Léonie's sleeping body, the copper hues of the leaves above her and the faded fragments of material that still clothed her body and kept her warm, matched the illustration on one of the tarot cards. Not the replica deck but the original. Card VIII: La Force. And for an instant, Meredith imagined she saw the echo of tears on her cold cheek.

Earth, air, fire, water.

Caught up in the formalities and endless French red tape, it had so far been impossible to find out precisely what had happened to Léonie on the night of

October 31, 1897. There had been a fire at the Domaine de la Cade, that much was on record. It had broken out around dusk and, in the course of a few hours, destroyed part of the main house. The library and the study were the worst damaged. There was also evidence that the fire had been started deliberately.

The following morning, All Saint's Day, several bodies were recovered from the smoldering ruins, servants who—it was presumed—had found themselves trapped by the flames. And there were other victims, men who didn't work on the estate, from Rennes-les-Bains itself.

It was not clear why Léonie Vernier had chosen—or been forced—to remain behind when other inhabitants of the Domaine de la Cade, her nephew Louis-Anatole among them, fled. There was also no explanation as to why the fire had spread so far, so fast, and destroyed the sepulchre, too. The *Courrier d'Aude* and other local newspapers of the time made mention of the high winds that night, but could they have bridged the gap between the house and the Visigoth tomb in the woods?

Meredith knew she would figure it out. In time, she'd fit all the pieces together.

The rising light glanced off the surface of the water, the trees and the landscape that had held its secrets for so long. A breath of wind whispered across the grounds, through the valley. The priest's voice, clear and timeless, called Meredith back to the present.

"*In nomine Patri, et Filii, et Spiritus Sancti.* In the name of the Father, the Son, and the Holy Ghost."

She felt Hal take her hand.

Amen. So be it.

The curé, tall in his heavy black felt cloak, smiled at her. The tip of his nose was red, she noticed, and his kind brown eyes glittered in the chill air.

"Mademoiselle Martin, *c'est à vous, alors.*"

She took a deep breath. Now that the moment had come, she was suddenly shy. Reluctant. She felt Hal squeeze her fingers, then gently let her go.

Struggling to keep her emotions in check, Meredith stepped forward to the edge of the grave. From her pocket, she took two items recovered from Julian Lawrence's study, a silver locket and a gentleman's fob watch. Both were simply inscribed with initials and a date: 22 OCTOBRE 1891, commemorating the marriage of Anatole Vernier to Isolde Lascombe. Meredith hesitated, then crouched down and dropped them gently into the ground where they belonged.

She glanced up at Hal, who smiled and gave the slightest nod of his head. She took another deep breath, then pulled out a white envelope: the piece of music, Meredith's treasured heirloom, carried by Louis-Anatole across the water from France to America, and down the generations to her.

It was hard to let it go, but Meredith knew it belonged with Léonie.

She looked down at the small slate plaque set into the ground, gray against the grass.

LÉONIE VERNIER

22 AOUT 1874–31 OCTOBRE 1897

REQUIESCAT IN PACEM

Meredith let go of the envelope. It twisted, then spiraled down, down through the still air, a flash of white slowly falling from her black-gloved fingers.

Let the dead rest. Let the dead sleep.

She stepped back, hands clasped in front of her, her head bowed. For a moment, the small group stood in silence, paying their final respects. Then Meredith nodded to the priest.

"*Merci, Monsieur le Curé.*"

"*Je vous en prie.*"

With a timeless gesture, he seemed to draw in all those gathered on the promontory, then turned and led the small party back down the hill and round the lake. As they struck out across the lawns, glinting with early-morning dew, the rising sun was reflected like flames in the windows of the house.

Meredith suddenly stopped.

"Can you give me a minute?"

Hal nodded. "I'll just see them settled inside, then come back for you."

She watched as he walked away, onto the terrace, then she turned back to look across the lake. She wanted to linger awhile longer.

Meredith pulled her coat tight around her. Her toes and fingers were numb and her eyes were stinging. The formalities were over. She didn't want to leave the Domaine de la Cade, but she knew it was time. This time tomorrow, she'd be on her way back to Paris. The day after, Tuesday, November 13, she'd be on a plane above the Atlantic on her way home. Then she'd have to figure out where the hell to go from there.

Work out if she and Hal had a future.

Meredith looked across the sleeping waters, flat as a mirror, to the promontory. Then, beside the old stone seat, Meredith thought she saw a figure, a shimmering, insubstantial outline in a white-and-green dress, tapered at the waist, full at the hem and arms. Her hair hung loose around her, shining copper in the sun's cold rays. The trees behind her, silver with hoar frost, glinted like metal.

Meredith thought she heard the music once more, although she wasn't sure if it was inside her mind or from deep within the earth. Like notes on manuscript paper but written on the air.

She stood in silence, waiting, watching, knowing it would be the last time. There was a sudden sparkle on the water, a refraction of the light, perhaps, and Meredith saw Léonie raise her hand. A slim arm silhouetted against the white sky. Long fingers encased in black gloves.

She thought of the tarot cards. Léonie's cards, painted by her more than a hundred years ago to tell her story and that of the people she had loved. In the confusion and chaos of the hours immediately after Julian's death on Halloween—while Hal had been at the commissariat and calls were going backward and forward between the hospital, where Shelagh was being treated, and the morgue where Julian's body had been taken—Meredith had quietly, and without any fuss, replaced the cards in Léonie's sewing box and returned it to the ancient hiding place in the woods.

Like the piece of piano music, *Sepulchre 1891,* they belonged in the ground.

Her eyes stayed fixed on the middle distance, but the image was fading.

She's leaving.

It was the desire for justice that had kept Léonie here until the full story was told. Now she could rest in peace in the quiet ground she had loved so well.

She felt Hal come up and stand beside her. "How's it going?" he said softly.

Let the dead rest. Let the dead sleep.

Meredith knew he was struggling to make sense of things. For the past eleven days they had talked and talked. She had told him everything that had happened, leading up to the moment when he burst into the clearing, minutes behind his uncle—about Léonie, about her tarot reading in Paris, about the obsession stretching back more than a hundred years that had taken so many lives, about the stories of the demon and the music of the place, about how she felt she had somehow been drawn to the Domaine de la Cade. Myths, legends, facts, history, all jumbled together.

"And you're okay?" he asked.

"I'm good. Just a little cold."

Meredith kept her eyes fixed on the middle distance. The light was changing. Even the birds had stopped singing.

"What I still don't understand," Hal said, pushing his hands deep into his pockets, "is why you? I mean, obviously there's the family connection with the Verniers, but even so . . ."

He trailed off, not sure where he was going.

"Maybe," she said quietly, "because I don't believe in ghosts."

Now she was no longer aware of Hal, of the cold, pale purple light spreading through the valley of the Aude. Only of the face of the young girl on the other side of the water. Her spirit was fading into the backdrop of the trees, the frost, slipping away. Meredith kept her eyes centered on the one spot. Léonie was almost gone now. Her outline was shifting, sliding, slipping away, like the echo of a note.

Gray, to white, to nothing.

Meredith raised her hand, as if to wave, as the shimmering outline faded finally to absence. Slowly, she lowered her arm.

Requiescat in pacem.

Until, finally, all was silence. All was space.

"Are you sure you're okay?" Hal said again. He sounded worried.

She nodded slowly.

For a few minutes more, Meredith stood staring into the empty space, unwilling to break the connection with the place. Then she took a deep breath and reached for Hal. He felt warm, solid flesh and blood.

"Let's head back," she said.

Hand in hand, they turned and walked across the lawns toward the terrace at the back of the hotel. Their thoughts were running down very different paths. Hal was thinking of coffee. Meredith was thinking of Léonie. And how much she was going to miss her.

Coda

Three Years Later

Sunday, October 31, 2010

L adies and gentlemen, good evening. My name is Mark, and it's my great
honor to welcome Ms. Meredith Martin to our bookstore tonight."

There was a burst of enthusiastic, if sparse, applause, then a hush descended
on the tiny independent bookstore. Hal, sitting in the front row, smiled encouragement at her. Her publisher was standing at the back, her arms folded.
She gave the thumbs-up sign.

"As many of you know," the manager continued, "Ms. Martin is the author
of the acclaimed biography of the French composer Claude Debussy, which
came out last year to rave reviews. However, what you may not know . . ."

Mark was an old friend, and Meredith had a horrible feeling he was going
to start way back, taking the audience all the way from elementary school
through high school to university, before he even got onto the subject of the
book.

She let her mind wander, run down familiar paths. She thought about
everything that had happened to bring her to this point. Three years of research, evidence, checking and double-checking, trying to fit together the
pieces of Léonie's history at the same time she was struggling to finish and
deliver her biography of Debussy on time.

Meredith never did figure out if Lilly Debussy had visited Rennes-les-Bains,
but the two stories collided pretty early on in a more exciting way. She discovered that the Verniers and the Debussys had been neighbors in the rue de
Berlin in Paris. And when Meredith visited Debussy's grave in the cimetière
de Passy in the sixteenth arrondissement, where Manet and Morisot, Fauré
and André Messager were also buried, she had found, hidden in a corner of
the cemetery beneath the trees, the tomb of Marguerite Vernier.

The following year, back in Paris with Hal, Meredith paid a visit to lay flowers on the grave.

As soon as she'd delivered the biography in the spring of 2008, Meredith had been free to concentrate full time on researching the Domaine de la Cade and how her family had emigrated from France to America.

She started with Léonie. The more Meredith read about Rennes-les-Bains and the theories surrounding Abbé Saunière and Rennes-le-Château, the more convinced she was that Hal's opinion that it was all part of a smoke-screen to draw attention away from what had happened at the Domaine de la Cade was right. She was inclined to think that the three corpses discovered in the 1950s in the garden of Abbé Saunière's home in Rennes-le-Château were connected to the events of October 31, 1897, in the Domaine de la Cade.

Meredith suspected that one of the bodies was that of Victor Constant, the man who murdered Anatole and Marguerite Vernier. Records showed Constant had fled to Spain and had been treated in several clinics for third-stage syphilis, but that he had returned to France in the fall of 1897. The second could have been Constant's manservant, who was known to have been among the mob that attacked the house. His body had never been found. The third was harder to account for. A twisted spine, abnormally long arms, a person of no more than four feet in height.

The other event that caught Meredith's attention was the murder of Curé Antoine Gélis of Coustaussa, sometime during the same night in October 1897. Gélis was a recluse. On the surface, his death seemed unconnected with the events at the Domaine de la Cade, apart from the coincidence of the date. He had been attacked first with his own fire tongs, then an ax lying in the grate of the old presbytery. The *Courrier d'Aude* reported that there were fourteen wounds to his head and multiple skull fractures.

It was a particularly savage and apparently motiveless murder. The killers were never found. All the local newspapers of the time carried the story, and the details were much the same. Having killed the old man, the murderers laid out the body, crossing the old man's hands on his chest. The house had been searched and a strongbox forced open, but it was said by a niece who looked after him to be empty anyway. Nothing appeared to have been taken.

When Meredith researched a little deeper, she discovered two details buried deep in one of the newspaper reports. First, that on the afternoon of Halloween, a girl matching the description of Léonie Vernier visited the presbytery in Coustaussa. A handwritten note was recovered. Second, that a tarot card had been left pushed between the fingers of the dead man's left hand.

Card XV: Le Diable.

When Meredith had read that, recalling what had happened in the ruins of the sepulchre, she thought she understood. The Devil, through his servant Asmodeus, had taken his own.

As for who had placed Léonie's sewing box and the original cards in their hiding place beneath the winterbourne, that remained unresolved. Meredith's heart imagined Louis-Anatole creeping back into the Domaine de la Cade under cover of night and replacing the cards where they belonged in memory of his aunt. Her head told her it was more likely to have been Audric Baillard, whose role in the story even now she'd not yet figured out to her own satisfaction.

The genealogical information was more straightforward. With the assistance of the same lady in the town hall in Rennes-les-Bains, who turned out to be both resourceful and extremely efficient, during the summer and early fall of 2008, Meredith had put together Louis-Anatole's history. The son of Anatole and Isolde, he had grown up in the care of Audric Baillard in a small village in the Sabarthès Mountains called Los Seres. After Léonie's death, Louis-Anatole had never returned to the Domaine de la Cade, and the estate had been allowed to go to ruin. Meredith assumed Louis-Anatole's guardian was the father, maybe even grandfather, of the Audric S. Baillard who had written *Diables et esprits maléfiques et phantômes de la montagne.*

Louis-Anatole Vernier, together with a family servant, Pascal Barthes, had enlisted in the French army in 1914 and seen active service. Pascal was much decorated but did not survive the war. Louis-Anatole did and, when peace was declared in 1918, he made his way to America, officially signing over the abandoned Domaine de la Cade to his Bousquet relations. To start with, he paid his way playing piano on the steamboats and in vaudeville. Although Meredith couldn't prove it, she liked to think he might have at least crossed paths with another vaudeville performer, Paul Foster Case.

Louis-Anatole settled outside Milwaukee, in what was now Mitchell Park. It had been pretty easy to uncover the next chapter of the story. He fell in love with a married woman, a Lillian Matthews, who became pregnant and had a daughter, Louisa. Soon after, the affair ended and Lillian and Louis-Anatole appeared to have lost touch. There was no evidence of contact between father and daughter that Meredith could find, although she hoped Louis-Anatole might have followed his daughter's progress from a distance.

Louisa inherited her father's musical talent. She became a professional pianist, in the concert halls of 1930s America rather than on the steamboats of the Mississippi. After her debut concert, at a small venue in Milwaukee, she found a package waiting for her at the stage door. It contained a single photograph of a young man in uniform and a piece of piano music: *Sepulchre 1891*.

On the eve of World War II, Louisa became engaged to a fellow musician, a violinist whom she'd met on the concert circuit. Jack Martin was highstrung and volatile, even before his experiences in a Burmese prisoner-of-war camp ruined him. He returned to America, addicted to drugs, suffering hallucinations and nightmares. He and Louisa had a daughter, Jeanette, but it was clearly tough, and when Jack disappeared from the scene in the 1950s, Meredith imagined Louisa had not been sorry.

Three years of painstaking research, and she'd made it right up to date. Jeanette had inherited the beauty, the talent and the character of her grandfather, Louis-Anatole, and her mother, Louisa, but also the fragility, the vulnerability of her French great-grandmother Isolde and her father, Jack.

Meredith looked down at the back cover of the book, resting in her lap. A reproduction of the photograph of Léonie, Anatole and Isolde, taken in the square in Rennes-les-Bains in 1891. Her family.

Mark, the store manager, was still talking. Hal caught her eye and mimed zipping his mouth shut.

Meredith grinned. Hal had moved to America in October 2008, the best birthday present Meredith could have had. The legal side of things down in Rennes-les-Bains had been complicated. Probate had taken a while and there had been problems with ascertaining exactly why Julian Lawrence had died. Not a stroke, not a heart attack. There were no visible signs of any trauma whatsoever, apart from some unexplained scarring on the palms of his hands. His heart had just stopped beating.

Had he survived, it was unlikely he would have faced charges for either the murder of his brother or the attempted murder of Shelagh O'Donnell. The circumstantial evidence in both cases was persuasive, but the police were reluctant to reopen the inquest into Seymour's death under the circumstances. Shelagh had not seen her attacker, and there were no witnesses.

There was, however, clear evidence of fraud and that Julian Lawrence had been skimming the profits and borrowing against the Domaine de la Cade for years to fund his obsession. Several valuable Visigoth artifacts, all illegally obtained, were recovered. In his safe were charts showing his detailed excavations of the grounds and notebook after notebook of scribblings about a particular deck of tarot cards. When Meredith was questioned, in November 2007, she admitted she had a replica copy of the same deck, but that the originals were believed to have been destroyed in the fire of 1897.

Hal had sold the Domaine de la Cade in March 2008. There was no money in the business, only debts. He had settled his ghosts. He was ready to leave France, although he had stayed in touch with Shelagh O'Donnell, who now lived in Quillan. She told them that an English couple with two teenage children had taken over and had successfully transformed the business into one of the leading family hotels in the Midi.

"So, ladies and gentlemen, please put your hands together for Ms. Meredith Martin."

There was an explosion of riotous clapping, not least, Meredith suspected, because Mark had finished talking.

She took a deep breath, composed herself and stood up.

"Thank you for that generous introduction, Mark," she said, "and it's great to be here. The genesis of this book, as some of you know, comes from a trip I made while I was working on my biography of Debussy. My research took me to a delightful town in the Pyrenees called Rennes-les-Bains, and, from there, into an investigation of my own family background. This memoir is my attempt to lay the ghosts of the past to rest." She paused. "The heroine of the book, if you like, is a woman called Léonie Vernier. Without her, I wouldn't be here today." She smiled. "But the book is dedicated to Mary, my mother. Like Léonie, she's one amazing lady."

Meredith saw Hal hand Mary, who was sitting between him and Bill in the front row, a tissue.

"It was Mary who introduced music into my life. It was she who encouraged me to keep asking questions and to never close my mind to any possibility. It was she who taught me to always stick with it, however hard things got. Most important"—she grinned, lightening the tone a little—"and especially appropriate tonight, I guess, it was Mary who showed me how to make the best Halloween pumpkin lanterns ever!"

The gathering of family and friends laughed.

Meredith waited, now excited as well as nervous, until silence fell over the room once more. She lifted the book and began to read.

This story begins in a city of bones. In the alleyways of the dead. In the silent boulevards and promenades and impasses of the cimetière de Montmartre in Paris, a place inhabited by tombs and stone angels and the loitering ghosts of those forgotten before they are even cold in their graves.

As her words floated out over the audience, becoming part of the mass of stories to be told that Halloween night, the comfortable sounds of the old building were Meredith's accompaniment. Chairs creaking on the wooden floorboards, the spluttering of the old water pipes in the roof, the blare of horns from cars in the street outside, the coffee percolator wheezing in the corner. From the bar next door, the strains of a piano coming through the walls. Black and white notes winding through the skirting, the floorboards, the hidden spaces between floor and ceiling.

Meredith slowed down as she came to the end of her reading.

For in truth, this story begins not with the absence of bones in a Parisian grave-yard, but with the deck of cards.

With the Vernier Tarot.

There was a moment of silence, and then the applause began.

Meredith realized she'd been half holding her breath, and exhaled with relief. As she looked out at her friends, her family, her colleagues, for a fraction of a second, there in the shifting of the light, she imagined she saw a girl with long copper hair and bright green eyes standing at the back of the room, smiling.

Meredith smiled back. But when she looked again, there was no one there. She thought of all the ghosts that touched her life. Marguerite Vernier in the cimetière de Passy. Of the cemetery in Milwaukee, close to the point where the three rivers met, where her great-grandfather Louis-Anatole Vernier—soldier of France, citizen of America—had been laid to rest. Of Louisa Martin, pianist, her ashes scattered to the winds. Meredith's birth mother, buried on the shores where the sun set over Lake Michigan. But most of all, she thought of Léonie, sleeping peacefully in the ground of the Domaine de la Cade.

Air, water, fire, earth.

"Thank you," Meredith said, as the applause died down. "And thank you all very much for coming."

Sepulchre 1891

Author's Note on the Vernier Tarot

The Vernier Tarot is an imaginary deck, designed for *Sepulchre,* painted by artist Finn Campbell-Notman and based on the classic Rider-Waite deck (1910).

Experts cannot agree on the antique origins of the tarot—Persia, China, ancient Egypt, Turkey, India—all have claims. But the format of the cards we associate now with tarot is usually accepted to date from mid-fifteenth-century Italy. There are hundreds of decks—and more come into the market every year. The most popular continue to be the Marseille Tarot, with its distinctive bright yellow, blue and red illustrations, and the narrative Universal Waite deck, devised in 1916 by the English occultist Arthur Edward Waite and with illustrations by the American artist Pamela Colman Smith. The deck used by Solitaire in the James Bond film *Live and Let Die,* the Tarot of the Witches, painted by the artist Fergus Hall, drew strongly from the Universal Waite Tarot.

For those wishing to find out more about tarot, there are plenty of books and websites. The best all-round guide is Rachel Pollack's *The Complete Illustrated Guide to Tarot,* published by Random House (2004).

Acknowledgments

I have been extremely fortunate to have the support, advice and practical help of so many people during the course of writing *Sepulchre*. It goes without saying that any mistakes, in fact or interpretation, are mine.

My agent Mark Lucas continues to be not only a superb editor and a good friend but also the purveyor of multicolored Post-it notes—this time red! Thanks, too, to everyone at LAW for their hard work and support, especially Alice Saunders, Lucinda Bettridge and Petra Lewis. Also, Nicki Kennedy for her enthusiasm, Sam Edenborough and the team at ILA, and Catherine Eccles, friend and fellow Carcassonnais, at Anne Louise Fisher.

In the UK, I'm lucky to be published by Orion. It all started with Malcolm Edwards and the incomparable Susan Lamb. With *Sepulchre*, publisher Jon Wood (super-energetic), editor Genevieve Pegg (super-efficient and calm) and copy editor Jane Selley have worked tirelessly and made the whole process, from start to finish, huge fun! Also, thank you to the often unsung heroes and heroines in production, sales, marketing and publicity—in particular Gaby Young, Mark Rusher, Dallas Manderson and Jo Carpenter.

In the United States, I'd like to thank George Lucas and my wonderful editor at Putnam, Rachel Kahan, as well as Rachel Holtzman and everyone in sales, publicity and marketing.

A special thank-you to author and composer Greg Nunes, who helped with the Fibonacci passages and who composed the beautiful piece of music *Sepulchre 1891*, which appears in the book. I'm also very grateful to Finn Campbell-Notman in the art department at Orion for painting the eight Vernier tarot cards.

My gratitude goes to tarot readers and enthusiasts on both sides of the Atlantic, who were generous with their advice, suggestions and experiences. I would especially like to thank Sue, Louise, Estelle and Paul; *Mysteries* in Covent Garden;

Ruby (aka the novelist Jill Dawson) for doing a reading for Meredith; as well as those who prefer to remain anonymous.

In France, thanks to Martine Rouche and Claudine l'Hôte-Azema in Mirepoix, to Régine Foucher in Rennes-les-Bains, to Michelle and Roland Hill for giving me sight of the diary, to Madame Breithaupt and her team in Carcassonne, and to Pierre Sanchez and Chantal Billautou for all the practical help over the past eighteen years.

A huge thank-you to friends, especially Robert Dye, Lucinda Montefiore, Kate and Bob Hingston, Peter Clayton, Sarah Mansell, Tim Bouquet, Cath and Pat O'Hanlon, Bob and Maria Pulley, Paul Arnott, Lydia Conway, Amanda Ross, Tessa Ross, Kamila Shamsie and Rachel Holmes. Special mention must go to the Rennes-les-Bains research gang of Maria Rejt, Jon Evans and Richard Bridges, all of whom have spent more time than they might have wanted at that pizzeria!

Most of all, my love and gratitude to my family, most particularly my fabulous parents, Richard and Barbara Mosse, and my wonderful mother-in-law, Rosie Turner, who keeps everything on track. Our daughter, Martha, was always happy and enthusiastic, upbeat and supportive, never doubting the book would get finished. Felix spent months and months walking the Sussex Downs, brainstorming ideas, making plot suggestions, offering editorial insights and ideas—without his input, *Sepulchre* would be a very different book.

Finally, as always, Greg. His love and faith, providing everything from editorial and practical advice to all that backing up of files and food night after night, make all the difference to everything. As they always have.

Pas a pas . . . every step of the way.